THE D'ARC GATE

DAVID REMER

DEDICATED TO TEDDI FOR FANTASTIC SUPPORT AND BEGGING FOR NEW CHAPTERS

TABLE OF CONTENTS

CHAPTER 1

Nathan sat at the counter of the bar and grill sipping his beer from a glass while munching on a greasy bacon cheddar burger. Pretending to watch the football game on the TV directly in front of him gave him the added ability to avoid any other human interaction. Several long-haired young girls to his immediate left were having a boisterously loud conversation but were thankfully making no attempt to talk with him.

Nathan would have called it a "foul" mood, but that was almost a permanent condition these days. To his right was a balding older man quietly whispering to himself while eating and watching another TV. He had some food stuck in his beard. Nathan paid him little mind.

The bartender Nick seemed to be in his early twenties. He had tried multiple times to do more than take Nathan's order, all to no avail. From Nathan's vantage point – if Nick wasn't gay, it was probably unfortunate for him, as he had to be driving off every straight woman for miles around between that haircut and his lilting laugh.

"How about that freaking game?" he asked in an overexcited tone. "Can you believe the damn Patriots are winning again…?" Apparently, there was an important football game in progress, at least to New Yorkers. Nathan could not have cared less. But he just kept staring at the one screen with the game going on right in front of him as if his life depended on it.

Nathan was doing what he often did: avoid conversation without being overtly rude. Ordering another beer at one point just so he could be left alone for a while longer, he glanced at the time on his phone. Pretending not to hear Nick's follow up question in the noisy room he gazed, as if in rapture, at the TV screen. He simply hoped to just zone out in peace. Watching the game with any brainpower at all was torture, anyway, as this game was now a complete blowout.

The burger was quite good, despite dripping grease as if it had been dunked in it. And, as he had noted to himself before, the fries at this bar were outstanding. It also wasn't far from where he both worked and lived, so it was convenient stopping here either going in late for an 'IT emergency' or coming back home from one.

Nathan sat upright as his friend Gary came into view in the bar mirror. With him was Jennifer, a pretty, young coed who was doing her internship at the firm. Nathan wasn't unattractive to women. He was told he was quite handsome, in fact. But his rather peculiar features, even for someone in New York, tended to be noticeable in bothersome ways. That, plus his natural inclination for solitude didn't allow for much long-term companionship. At least…not anymore.

Jennifer was different, though. She didn't seem at all put off by Nathan's white, blond hair that stood stick straight, nor his peculiar purple tinted eye coloring. Gary was laughing with her about something as they came up. Nathan resisted the urge to think they were amused at something about himself. He tried to put on his best smile as they approached from behind him.

"What's up, guys?" he inquired, turning around. Gary just looked at him as he often did – an amused twitch of a smile. Gary was very tall, and at least 250 pounds, which was mostly muscle. His curly brown hair, smiling brown eyes, and that infectious smirk made him an easy mark for conversation with strangers without impedance.

"It's Thursday, Nathan," he answered. "You remember what Thursday is, right?"

"The day before Friday…?"

Jennifer giggled again as he turned to her. Apparently, the laughing had indeed been about him. She dropped her eyes, but that sweet smile never left her face. At least she wasn't trying to be mean. Nathan held back his irritation as he searched his brain for what in heaven's name was so important about Thursday.

Nope. Nothing surfaced.

Gary burst out laughing. "I told you!" he declared loudly to Jennifer as she looked up at him again, before reaching over and squeezing Nathan's arm consolingly. Then she smiled again, reaching over, and touching Nathan's face with her palm as well, looking him squarely in the eyes. She was clearly not being unkind, just enjoying the moment. She even looked a bit sorrowful for him. Jennifer was quite pretty.

"We had a bet you wouldn't remember, Nathan," she said, dropping her hand. Her green eyes danced as they stared into his own, winsome smile returning to her face. "I lost."

One of the girls on the other side got up to leave, swinging her purse onto her shoulder as she strutted off in her high heels. Nick pointed Jennifer to the open seat, so Jennifer went behind him, sat down, then turned around fully to order a martini from Nick, who had showed up promptly to take her order.

Maybe not so gay after all.

Jennifer was shorter than average (maybe 5'3 or 5'4), extremely fit, tan, and got glances wherever she went, no matter how dressed up she was. Tonight, she was in a tight miniskirt and a halter top too cold for this time of year. At least she had her black leather coat over it all. Nathan appreciated just sitting next to her. Very pretty.

Gary remained standing as there wasn't room for a third at the bar yet, so he ordered a beer for himself from behind them. A sudden cheer from the crowd at the football game drowned out what Jennifer tried to say to him, so he just stared at her and pointed to his ear.

She looked around a bit in bewilderment, then tried again as the crowd went back to its normal level of clamor. Then, "It's Thursday, Nathan… my birthday? You and Gary promised to take me to the New York Hall of Science in Queens tomorrow over lunch. There's that new Egyptian exhibit that has all the scientists and archeologists in a tizzy! Remember now?"

His eyes suddenly widened as a look of understanding hit his face, followed by a grimace of remorse. It really was a fascinating story. And he had completely forgotten it was her birthday. He was surprised he had forgotten about that, but even more so the Egyptian artifact. After all, stuff like that had been his life.

Once upon a time.

Maybe he had wanted to forget. A long article had showed up on his phone app not two weeks ago. Fact always did seem stranger than fiction. Once, Nathan would likely have been on the cutting edge of something like this. Back before…before this void in which he found himself. This had been his wheelhouse. He really was shocked that he had forgotten. Depression. He nodded to her as he thought about it. Nathan didn't forget much about physics or history.

This was both.

"The Egyptian monolith…The one found in the old tomb near the lost pyramids near Giza. I remember," Nathan said after a moment. "Oh yes. And happy birthday!"

Jennifer kissed him on the cheek, and then leaned back, smiling at him in a way that made his heart skip. He was nearly ten years older than she, but at that moment neither of them seemed to mind. He smiled back at her. Gary cleared his throat. Loudly.

As they looked up at him, Gary and his smirk were in full bloom. In that beard, it was almost menacing. "You two are so cute. Listen. I'm the one who's from Queens. The museum is easy to get into on a weekday, but it's always somewhat crowded over there. This exhibit just got here, so it'll be a bit busier than usual. Not to mention the geek squads from Columbia and St. John's are supposed to be out in force. The *Times* did a piece on it; so, the nerd packs, plus lots of locals, will be all over it. Hey! Maybe your old professors will be there, Nathan!"

He said this like it was a good thing. He, at least, should know better.

This was what Nathan had secretly dreaded about this trip before he had simply forgotten about it entirely. Freudian slip of some kind, he decided. Almost certainly the real reason he had shelved it in the back of his mind and completely blocked it out. At one time, he was considered a candidate to join those 'geek squad' professors' elite little club. At one time, nothing would have pleased him more.

"I doubt it. That was years ago," was what he said back as blandly as he could, turning towards his beer. He took a long pull. Jennifer had no knowledge of his past. He glared a quick look at Gary behind her back just to be sure he got the message. Gary's smile returned to fullness as he looked towards the football game with feigned interest. The Jets were getting pummeled but had managed a touchdown somehow. Nathan turned back and glanced at the screen – he could relate to the Jets' players. "Pathetic losers" should be the club's name. He could wear that jersey with pride.

Returning to his plate, he purposefully took the last bite of his cheeseburger, stuffing in a few straggler fries before continuing. "They likely won't even remember I went to school there. They have thousands of faces walk through those doors." And his face hadn't been at Columbia or his alma mater since he had left. Not once.

Gary shrugged and matched him drink for drink. He had been told the whole story. He knew better but also could take a hint. Jennifer's cocktail arrived and she raised a toast. "To tomorrow!" she said and sipped delicately from her fruity concoction. Gary and Nathan raised their beers a bit towards her and drank enthusiastically.

Nathan felt the dark in his soul recede just a little. Jennifer had a way of doing that to people.

New York subways aren't the most pleasant way to get around, but they are the most common way for New Yorkers. Other than straight walking or taking the inevitable cab when you have to get somewhere specific in a hurry.

And they are remarkably efficient. It wasn't an hour after boarding the downtown subway that they emerged off the 111th Street in Queens, close to both the tennis center where they held the U.S. Open and the New York Museum of Science. All had taken a "long lunch" before and had told their boss of their upcoming excursion. IT set their own hours and were worth their weight in gold. The rest of the day was theirs. Nathan had gone to the tennis center annually during the Open for years back in the day. It seemed like a ghost of itself as he looked at it from afar.

The museum loomed in the other direction, and they all sauntered off towards it. It was November, when the cold and the wet just sticks to you like glue before tunneling into your bones. The sky was one giant gray wall of cloud and, despite the lack of bustle of the inner city, it was busy. But then again, it was always busy in New York. Even in the boroughs during the daytime. Traffic and people wandered to and fro, cars honking and people yelling.

Jennifer suggested they stop at a Starbuck's for a coffee before proceeding to the museum itself. Gary thought it a great idea, so Nathan had to quell his rapidly growing interest and subsequent irritation at being delayed. He ordered his standard Americana and was appreciatively sipping some as they walked back out into what was now a light November rain. The rain was heavy enough to patter on the ground and they all pulled up hoods to avoid getting soaked.

The coffee turned into a fantastic idea, as the lines to get in to see the Egyptian monolith that somehow qualified as "science" were longer than expected. The heat from the coffee was welcome as they shivered outside, waiting to get in. By the time they did, Nathan tossed his empty cup into a trash receptacle. Gary followed, chucking his shoulder as Jennifer walked in front of them.

Nathan had dressed up a bit for the occasion, actually taking a shower and putting on one of his better shirts with a matching sweater. He wore his best long coat, with buttons and leather gloves. Jennifer looked cute as always, hair pulled back into a ponytail, just the right amount of makeup, and dressed in a skirt with leggings to stay warm. Her coat – leather and white – was immaculate and fit tightly about her form. Nathan was stunned at how beautiful she could look in something so ordinary. Gary looked as he always did – dressed in a coat that looked like it came right off the rack at "Hunters R Us". Puffy camo all the way. Somehow it suited him even in the Big Apple. He reminded Nathan of a grizzly bear turned human.

"Well…. let's go!" Jennifer said, looking back at them, light dancing in her eyes. So, they did.

The reasons for the archeological find to be here in the science museum made sense. According to the *Times*, a heretofore buried early dynasty pyramid had been unearthed. It was smaller than the later giants, but sitting right next to another buried sphinx that was being uncovered, as well. Within it, artifacts pre-dating anything found heretofore had been uncovered. Untouched and unseen for millennia.

Also, something extremely odd had been found along with all the usual ancient things one found in pharaoh's tombs. A large metal and stone monolith resembling a huge arch.

Early tablets and walls dating from at least the 38th century BC were on display. A statue of a dark dog god with a long staff standing only 4 feet high was next to a small sarcophagus worked with black paints, blue and gold foil. A wrapped mummy of a slender Egyptian – "probably a young female" from the x-rays, according to the little sign – was still inside. The coffin was almost crib sized. They had scans for viewing next to the exhibit. Apparently, the mummy still had a nearly full head of hair – but it was completely white, so had to have been a very old woman, not young. And she was unusually short – even for the time. At least it seemed so to Nathan.

Everywhere there were artifacts, including some of the earliest "ankh" symbols made of painted wood, ivory, and gold known to exist. A rope holding two strange items of desiccated wood was in a glass box near another tablet with an early ancient form of hieroglyphic writing on it. Multiple vases, casks, and jars painted in fanciful Egyptian art were everywhere. A vase painted in gold leaf and black and blue paints that stood nearly six feet high dominated another room. The pattern was still amazingly bright and stunning.

Another anomaly was that the writing (hieratics) was of a unique form that was still being deciphered by all the right experts. It contained interesting departures from known forms. Apparently enough to be viewed as a true precursor to the currently known ones.

"Fascinating…" Nathan heard himself mumbling.

Jennifer grabbed his hand and nodded, taking Gary's in her other as they walked about. Nathan was both distracted by her soft, warm hand in his as well as miffed he had to share her with Gary. Gary was the athlete and the man to whom women were attracted to so easily. Couldn't he let him have just this one to himself? He fought down his irritation. Not his fault. If Jennifer truly were into him, he wasn't sure what he would do, anyway. Probably scare her off like the others. And they were all just friends here. Still, just touching her made his heart race a little faster. It had been far too long since he'd felt that way.

Instead of the grimace he originally intended to give Gary behind Jennifer's back, he gave him a smile. People you can trust were hard to find. Friends who have your back, even harder. Gary was as true a friend as anyone could want. Gary smiled back not knowing anything of Nathan's rapidly vanishing irritation.

They'd been through a lot together. And when his former college roommate had found Nathan was without a job or a place to live, he had taken him in immediately. He also had recommended him for his current role – IT specialist at HDS Security systems, a company that did monitoring for dozens of downtown office buildings in New York. It wasn't his dream job, by any means. But it paid the bills and had allowed him to forget his former life. A life he was all too aware might come walking into this museum at any moment.

The central focus for that would be coming in the following room. The Monolith.

Somehow in this small, previously hidden tomb this massive black monstrosity of dark balefulness had stood for millenia. A huge, mostly obsidian and metal oval that had minute points of reflecting crystals imbedded in it, along with certain other very strange and unique properties. Those properties were what had placed this exhibit in the science museum first and foremost. It was also what had scientists all over the world coming to study it in force. St. John's and Columbia professors, amongst many other onlookers and scientists, filled the room along with casual observers.

The monolith had, according to the article, very unusual properties making it unlike anything yet found on earth, let alone amongst other Egyptian ruins. For one thing, it was massively dense, and was made up partially of stabilized Technetium 98 and 99, along with a bizarre concoction of other heavy metals. And neither of those isotopes could be found anywhere on earth. More importantly, the sun couldn't even manufacture them. It wasn't big enough.

Also, it seemed some of the radioactive portions of the rare metal created a macroscopic version of a long chain aromatic ring not dissimilar to a benzene ring – allowing electrons to move freely back and forth endlessly about the oval. There was also some liquid metal, probably mercury, inside it forming its core. The entire structure was extremely chemically complex and seemed completely out of place in any ancient civilization, let alone the early Egyptian period.

And then there were the hieratics all over it. Bizarre and unique forms and pictograms that seemed to indicate – well – a godlike race taking care of their flock of common Egyptians. But those "common" Egyptians included a pharaoh bowing before these other gods.

Nathan being a physicist by training knew little of Egyptian writing. But he did know something about heavy metals, conductivity, and radioactivity - something Gary and Jennifer probably did not: not only does Technetium not occur naturally on earth. Technetium is also slightly radioactive in virtually all forms, hence the large leaded glass around it, warning signs labeling it "radioactive" and the massive distance between the object and the walkways. The signs probably gave them a hint of the danger, though. People didn't lean in much, including his friends.

Plus, Nathan had read that the monolith also emitted multiple magnetic fields of its own, creating a barely audible hum. Like a machine. That was what made this exhibit so dynamic. As soon as it was discovered, scientists from all over the world had traveled to see it. For its first three years of being found, Egypt wouldn't even let it out of the country. But as time had waned and nothing new was discovered, the dangers associated with keeping it in one place eventually had allowed it to travel around the world, going from museum to museum, country to country,

University to University to be studied. Sampled, probed, photographed, and x-rayed.

Now the relic simply stood next to twin obelisks that named it: "Star's Echo Monolith". Some scientists had theorized the oval monolith even had pieces of dark matter in it, based on the unique magnetic fields it created. Whether that was true or not, it was denser than it should have been, and no one seemed to be able to figure out any other reason why. Containing dark matter would make it far beyond the scope of even modern science to be able to create it. So, who…or *what*…could have done it? And why?

Nathan was so mesmerized at finally seeing the famed black monolith in person, that it took him a moment to realize someone outside his little trio was calling his name.

"Nathan! *NATHAN!*" That someone was waving from inside the glass containment behind the far side of the obelisk.

His stomach went Tilt-a-Whirl. It was Ellie. Surrounded by several older men wearing glasses, Ellie seemed an unlikely member of the group. She wore the same white lab coat, and was wearing glasses making her appear more cerebral, but that was the only thing marking her as one of them. The entire group of scientists were somehow inside the glass enclosure, which would explain why her yelling had gone unnoticed. The thing stood at least 40 feet high, barely fitting in the largest chamber in the museum. Dwarfed by its size, somehow Ellie being there made it all fade into the background.

Jennifer looked at Nathan quizzically as he pulled his hand free to wave back at her. His expression must have been horrible, as Jennifer quickly looked down. Gary's face was granite. He wasn't waving. His face had grown dark without the slightest trace of a smirk.

Ellie left her group, showing in the process the glass door through which the scientists must have entered. There was another lead glass room inside the larger one, mostly hidden from sight behind the massive thing. No one from her group seemed to notice her leaving. Her dark hair bouncing, Ellie came running up to them. Almond brown eyes made Nathan's heart skip a beat.

As she approached, Gary said to Jennifer, "Let's go back and check out the statuettes. I think we should leave Nathan to his old home week for a minute." Jennifer looked back at Nathan, who glanced over at her for a moment. Her eyes showed hurt. Whether it was for him or herself, Nathan had no idea. She turned and they left for the other room. Ellie ignored Gary completely. They had never liked each other. Nothing that happened afterwards had done anything to discourage that.

Ellie ran into his arms, giving him a long hug. Nathan barely returned it. Ellie pulled back, lifting her glasses to the top of her head. She pulled her blue gloves off and then dropped her head towards her chest. "I'm sorry, Nathan. I was hoping we could at least still be friends. It's been long enough, don't you think?" She looked up underneath her glasses, hopefully. She still looked so damn good.

Nathan said nothing. He just stood there staring down at the face of the woman whom he thought he would marry. Have nerdy kids with. Grow old with. Apparently, her career had kept right on going up after he'd left. She raised her deep brown eyes fully up to his, pulling away.

"Nathan, I know you're never going to forgive me. But…just for a minute, forget about us! You've really *got* to see this thing!" She was literally bubbling with excitement.

Just for a minute, forget about us.

There was no "us". He nodded to her, trancelike, as if in a dream. He'd dreamt about this meeting often enough, to be sure. He let her grab his hand and started walking with her toward the monolith. Following almost unwillingly.

"You're supposed to get special permission to get in. But I think that no one will notice one more. Anyway, as a decorated physicist now, I have clout!" she giggled at the thought, pulling her former beau by the hand. "Come *feel* it!"

Nathan had read that the actual radiation was extremely low. It hardly was radiation in the truest sense at all. Few alpha or beta emissions. Mostly just low-level gamma radiation and some other "noise" from the electrical distortions emanating from the multiple magnetic fields. Somehow those same fields also scattered the radiation away into the air.

He also knew that almost everyone in that room would know him, despite his protestations to the contrary the evening before. He drew in a deep breath, looking up at this glittering black monstrosity. It was beautiful and frightening all at the same time. He swallowed the last of his pride and nodded.

Then he followed her into the chamber. Inside the six-inch thick glass fortress, the Monolith did hum…and it seemed to pulse somehow. It was like a living thing. Rumors about it being the mythical endless energy source had gone rampant a couple of years ago.

Not just in the *Times* article, but in popular magazines, and even the tabloids and the internet. After all, this thing had pulsed in a dead room buried in the sand for almost 6000 years. Possibly much longer. Deciphering the makeup of the monolith could be more than just another intriguing archeological find. It could potentially aid in the global energy crisis and perhaps do far more things, as yet unknown. As he approached, a few of the other professors noticed him. Looking a bit shocked, they offered him tentative greetings. His former mentor, Professor Reschevsky wasn't one of them. He just stood apart a bit, his face growing increasingly red. Nathan didn't even bother to look at him.

He had to admit it - Ellie knew him well. Better than anyone. She knew how this thing would draw him in. Moth to a flame.

She simply held out a pair of blue gloves, grabbed a white coat someone had laid aside, and stood back. At one point, he had been the "next Einstein". *Scientific American* had done a piece on him, pointing to his early papers in the field of physics and dark matter as "ground-breaking" and "strikingly insightful". Once he had been far more than a simple IT desk jockey fixing motherboards. He had been a renowned genius in physics, math, and science at one of the most prestigious universities on the planet. And these people had considered him their equal. Or more than their equal.

Nathan's hands reached out and gently touched it. He felt the obelisk pulsing beneath his palm. He heard the faint *thrum thrum thrum* of the harmonics to his bones. It did feel alive. He closed his eyes and just listened and felt it for several seconds.

Ellie was watching him, he knew. Probably with a look of pain on her face. By the time he opened his eyes and turned towards her, though, the look was gone – if it had been there at all.

Nathan forgot everything in the excitement of the moment. "I can't believe it. It really is *full* of power! Have you read all the magnetic fields around it? What do they signify? Has anyone been able to sample it to truly diagnose what all it's made up of? How in God's name did ancient Egyptians discover something of this magnitude? Or make it up? And why put it in a tomb and bury it? Do you know *anything* more than the papers say about it?"

The room was alive with movement, and one could almost feel the electricity both inherent and emotional coming from the group. Ellie laughed at him. "Well, a little bit. For one thing, it has a good amount of gold and platinum in its core, like a kind of tubing. Then there's the mercury inside. All of it pure – like purer than anything we've found in ancient coins or treasures. It seems they somehow conduct small electrical charges throughout the circle. Like a wave. That's the hum you feel and hear. The magnetic fields also have perpendicular electrical pulses that coincide with, and somehow complement the pattern. Whether they support it, or are part of it, or even a counterpoint to hold it all in – that we don't know yet. It's amazingly intricate inside, chemically. Parts of it are lead, too. So, with all those heavy metals…"

"…it's impossible to see inside. Radio-opaque." Nathan finished for her, fully looking at her for maybe the first time. Ellie nodded. Grant, Nathan's former lab partner and friend, rushed up to them, sporting a new, finely trimmed beard. Very professorial. Ellie stepped back a pace to make room for him. Grant was dark haired, handsome, and tall. Utterly Nathan's opposite. Nathan looked up at his former colleague and friend as he approached. No expression readable on his face.

"What do you think, Nathan? Isn't it amazing? You were one of the foremost researchers on dark matter. Any thoughts as to whether this thing could truly contain any?"

He clearly had no clue that Nathan despised him now. Nor did he even note the slight – referring to him in the past tense on dark matter research. Nathan wanted him to feel the loathing he felt – and to know why.

He was with Ellie.

Nathan managed to replace his grimace with a smirk before answering. "Yes. It's amazing, Grant. No, I don't have any thoughts, as I just walked in here and really wasn't planning on more than taking a look. I came with friends…" he vaguely pointed in the direction Gary and Jennifer had vanished what seemed like hours ago.

"So…you're not doing research again? When I saw you, I hoped…" his voice trailed off, looking over at Ellie. He dropped his head and mumbled something, then turned and walked away, not looking

Nathan in the eye again. He'd noticed the grimace. Ellie stepped into the void quickly, trying to put some lightness in her voice.

"Why don't you come down to the University? Let's all go out to eat together! You, me, Grant…we could talk…about the monolith! You could help us investigate it…!" Nathan just stared at her dumbfounded. She was serious. He was supposed to just come back and act like no time had passed, and nothing had changed. Like the last three and a half years of his life hadn't happened…?

He simply shook his head. "I've got to be in for work tomorrow morning, Ell. Computers and software tend to die during off hours. Just to piss us off. All that type of stuff. I'm an IT guy now, didn't you hear?"

Ellie pulled her glasses down below her eyes and studied him. No smile now. Anger. He also saw a pained expression this time, although it was different. Softer. Like his mother used to look when he took sick, as he often did as a child.

All she said was, "You look thin, Nathan. Are you eating? You can't be happy fixing monitors and cleaning up the poop of the computer illiterate! Why don't you come back? It can't be because of me. If so, I'll stay away from you! You're brilliant, Nathan! The world needs you… it…it…" Her voice trailed off. Nathan didn't move; didn't say a word. He just eventually dropped his gaze as her voice trailed off.

"You're a gifted physicist, Nathan! *Damn* it, you're the best one we've had at Columbia since Novick!" Nathan snapped his head up, looked her straight in the eyes, and started to laugh. Ellie dropped her head with a little smirk. So damned sexy. He wished he could hate her. But he just still loved her.

"Ok, so I'm overdoing it a little. But damn it, Nathan! You're amazing…! So what that we're not sleeping together anymore. Big deal!" She was almost yelling now. "Find some coed and bang the shit out of her,

Nathan! Get over it! We didn't work out. It's life. Move on! You've got so much to give back! Hell, go to another university. Just bring that damned magazine for a resume. You'll get hired in a second!" People in the area had stopped what they had been doing and were staring. They had become the focal point of the room now. Not the obelisk.

Usually, that would have made Nathan withdraw into himself. Instead, it somehow empowered him. He just drank it all in, saying nothing.

Nathan watched his former lover grow red-faced herself as she realized nearly all the scientists in the room had stopped talking as her voice had grown louder and louder and were instead looking at her in open amusement. A moment later, after a few chuckles, they were getting back to their conversations and their computers. But a few raised their thumbs up in appreciation to Nathan before doing so. One or two, including Reschevsky, even nodded to him affirmatively. He did, after all, have his doctorate. He had been in the elite. For a time, at least.

He had been doing his post-doc work with Reschevsky when the nuclear warhead had hurtled into his life. Before he ran away to be anywhere but near her. What Ellie said made sense, though.

Nathan turned back towards the huge dark oval of the monolith. It was the most fascinating thing he had ever seen in his life. "I'll think about it," was all he said. And he found he actually meant it. He then took out his phone and took a quick picture of the thing. Just in case he didn't come back. Just in case he didn't want to rejoin the land of the living. Staying dead and hiding alone in his self-appointed prison.

He wanted to remember this moment better than even his memory would allow for. Ellie tried to stop him once she saw him doing it but was too late. There was a brief flash from the phone just as her hand reached out. Nathan hoped it wouldn't mar the image.

"Don't…!" was all she could get out. But it was already done. The flash left a blind spot on his eyes for a moment. The look on her face was truly horrified. He vaguely felt like asking her why but decided against further conversation.

"No one died," was all he said as he turned to go. Then, stopping, he smiled at her and gave her a slight bow, before turning back and walking out of the enclosure without saying another word.

Ellie just stood watching him leave. The glass room holding the monolith had a greenhouse like ceiling that was able to be opened, as the object was too large for any other room, and people probably wanted air to breathe or something. It likely was how they'd gotten it in here in the first place. Nathan walked out one of the two glass doors and slipped out of the exhibit room altogether a moment later.

Nathan found his friends near the sarcophagus of the old woman, and said as he approached, "Let's get out of here." Jennifer gave him a long look before she nodded. The hurt expression was altered, softened, but still apparent. Gary had filled her in during his absence, clearly.

Well, she deserved an explanation after that, so he was glad it was done so he wouldn't have to do it. And Nathan had never told Gary explicitly not to tell her. He sighed and turned to walk out the door, buttoning up his coat as he walked.

The subway trip back to the city went without ten words between them. They played games or checked email on their phones to fill the void. Nathan got in a good twelve rounds of his favorite game in. As Jennifer got off at her stop, she just hugged him wordlessly with one arm, kissing him on the cheek. Gary patted him on the back as they got off at their stop and headed to their shared apartment. Nothing more really needed to be said, anyway.

Ellie had been there, after all. He should have known.

Nathan pulled the door open to his bathroom and stared at himself in the mirror. His dour expression and sunken eyes told the tale of a sleepless night before he cracked his jaws in yet another yawn. Wearily, he stepped to the sink and began to brush his teeth with little enthusiasm. Eyeing his own gaunt form as he brushed, one that used to be fairly filled out, he sighed inwardly before spitting. The growing bristle of white-blond beard seemed appropriate, inordinately aging him in the mirror.

He had to catch the 6:27 train if he was going to make it to work on time. He found he scarcely cared. Pulling on a thermal over his dark gray T-shirt, he mussed his hair in the mirror, and decided shaving was not in his immediate future. He liked looking disheveled. It fit, somehow.

Sighing again, he headed for the door. Gary was sipping a coffee from his *Iron Man* mug in the tiny kitchen area. He gave Nathan one long glance before simply nodding. Setting it down and wiping his mouth as they both headed out wordlessly to catch the train.

Minutes later, at the station, Gary broke the silence. "Ellie looked good. She's still a complete bitch, of course, but she ages well."

Nathan chuckled despite himself but said nothing.

"You know, of everything you told me, I think one thing she said last night is right though: 'You shouldn't let one little bitch ruin an incredible academic career. Fuck her.'"

"I'm…pretty sure she didn't word it that way." Nathan grinned up at Gary, though, and his eyes sparkled for a moment. Gary was a true friend. If he ever had to bury a body, he knew who to call.

"Well, I did. You should go back. You're wasting your life fixing hard drives and resetting passwords, Nathan. Maybe just wait for the little cunt to leave for lunch or something and talk with your former colleagues. Ask around about a fellowship. You know they'd leap at the chance. Get back on the horse."

The train arrived by the time Nathan answered. He looked over at Gary and admired his ability to be the focal point of any room or space, just by his sheer presence and personality. It was comforting somehow, knowing he had a friend with that level of magnetism and energy. "Honestly, I've thought about it quite a bit. I didn't sleep much, as you doubtless know."

"Yeah, I gathered that from the black holes where your eyes used to be." At least he smiled as he said it.

"I guess it can't hurt to go back and talk to Reschevsky. Or Blythe. Or Qweng Zhu. I'll see if anyone has a Post-Doc research slot. Maybe… maybe…"

"Maybe not be just the IT guy known for spilling coffee in the break room, but maybe something a little more profound than that?"

Nathan laughed. "Yeah…that."

So, it wasn't quite twenty-four hours later that he found himself back outside the museum, staring at the front entrance and holding another nearly empty Starbuck's coffee. He tossed it idly into a round trash receptacle and strode in. He had decided on a plan that wouldn't involve waiting to see when Ellie left. That was a coward's way, anyway. He paid for another admission ticket and walked in, barely noticing items that had fascinated him just the day before.

It was another cloudy November day about an hour past lunchtime, but as he approached the monolith room upstairs, there were few lights on and a big thick rope across the entrance. He could still see into the room, but some track lighting above the glass case showed that the room was completely devoid of any people.

The monolith gleamed in the dim light eerily. All the activity from the day prior had vanished. No people swirling about with their mouths and eyes wide open. Not a single white coat or computer showed in the nearly impossible to see glass room behind it. Yet Nathan could still feel the thing thrumming even from where he stood.

It was majestic. Powerful. Like a dark god fallen from heaven.

An overweight security guard ambled over after he noticed Nathan lingering by the entrance. "Room's shut down today, sir. Power issues of some sort. Drove the researchers back to their rabbit holes, too it seems! And it is the weekend…" The portly, middle-aged man seemed amused. He scratched his straw-colored beard looking into the dark room, stopping him short as he did so.

"Ah. When do they expect power to be restored?" Nathan replied cautiously.

"Not sure. A day or two. It seems sometime late yesterday, not my day, mind you – but I heard – late yesterday, they attached some gizmo to the thing and it shorted out pretty much everything they had in there. Including the main lighting and fried half our board downstairs, to boot. They called somebody, and patched the breakers as best they could, but no one from the power company can be here until tomorrow. So, I'm guessing next week at the earliest."

Nathan nodded thoughtfully, starting to turn away. "Hey wait a minute. You don't happen to be a…" he looked at something on his hand "a… 'Nathan', do you? Some researcher girl left a note for a guy named Nathan matching your description – white hair, dark coat, and all – in case he showed up."

Nathan raised an eyebrow, nodding in the affirmative.

The guard waddled back over a few steps to his stand near the corner, pulling out a folded piece of yellow tablet paper with some handwriting on it. "Here you go. Glad I remembered! Shift lady from yesterday told me to watch out for you. This researcher lady told her it was very important."

"You know…I didn't know you were one of the research team. Thought I knew 'em all! Must've been off yesterday, huh? If you want, you can go in. You'll need to use your own lighting though. That track lighting is all that's working in there now. Emergency systems. Don't knock anything over in the dark!" he chuckled as he turned to waddle away down another hall. Apparently, he amused himself quite often.

Shaking his head and dismissing the guard mentally, Nathan turned toward the roped off entryway. Most people were avoiding the area, as the rope and sign were clearly visible from quite a long way back. Some came closer to peek in at the Monolith. But it was so dark and difficult to see inside the room, with only the top part of it visible, it failed to hold anyone's interest for long. All the while, Nathan just stood there, feeling the thing pulsing – and pondering. The pulsing was comforting somehow. Like sleeping in a bed at sea. It was like a rocking chair, or a faraway thunderstorm. Nathan had gone on a short cruise once. With Ellie. It seemed a lifetime ago.

He opened the note. *"Nathan, I don't know if you'll come back. But I'm betting on you. So, if you're reading this, it's a good thing. The obelisk is amazing, isn't it?!!! It just draws you in, doesn't it? But you shouldn't go near it right now. It literally arced electricity when we simply tried to put probe wires on it in various areas to read the pulses and fields more accurately. We didn't even have it all hooked up and suddenly several arcs of current came from nowhere and blasted three or four of our most expensive pieces of equipment. The power it drew or threw (?) – we don't know which – knocked out the power box for the display room, too. Ouch!"*

The note went on: "*…Fortunately, it's all wired separately, or the entire museum would've fried. Anyway, come see me. I'm finishing a paper at the nearby coffee shop around the corner all day. It's called "Mozinga's". We need to talk. I've got some leads for you, if you've decided to get back into research…and none of them are near me. – Ellie*"

A little drawn heart and the word "HUGS" was scrawled below her name.

Nathan crumpled the note and tossed it towards the nearby canister. It hit the rim and bounced infuriatingly behind it, out of sight. Nathan fought with his conscience about going to pick it up just long enough for a young boy and his mother to come up to the obelisk room rope behind him.

"Oh," the boy said, sounding disappointed, "Momma, I really wanted to see it! They only had drawings of it in the paper, but they were *amazing!* They say it has magnetic fields, and emits energy, and all sorts of cool stuff!" The boy could barely hold his excitement in, despite his obvious disappointment. He could only have been 8 or 9 years old. The mother nodded her head, distractedly, typing a text on her phone. The boy looked up at Nathan. "Do you work here? Can you let us see it better?"

Nathan laughed as he looked down at the eager little boy. The boy reminded him of himself at that age. Dark hair (ok that was different), glasses. Minus the hair and dark complexion, it could have been him. "No. But I DO have a picture from when I was here yesterday. I have a few friends who are researching it, and I sneaked a picture! Don't tell anyone. I wasn't supposed to do it."

The boy nodded conspiratorially, and the mother looked up from her phone, smiling and nodding that it was ok for Nathan to do so. So as Nathan unlocked his iPhone and opened his photo library, the mother added, "Thank you," in a New Jersey accent, and then went back to her texting.

She added, without looking up again, "He's been talking about visiting this thing all week. I came all the way over here just so we could see it and, of course the exhibit is closed." She was clearly not happy and was showing it in a way only Jersey people could manage without screaming out loud.

Nathan chuckled. "Not a problem." He squatted down, showing the boy the photo and the little man gasped in delight. In it, one could see a few of the monitors behind it and the magnetic rings it was giving off graphically depicted on a computer nearby. The obelisk also showed up very well with the little glowing flecks buried in the ominous blackness of it all. Even photographed, it loomed.

"So…cool…!" After thanking him again, the mother and her boy went on their way. It seemed the little boy was just as satisfied to have gotten a private picture showing as he would have been from seeing it person.

Then Nathan remembered the guard had said he could go in. Making a quick decision, he ducked under the rope and hurried into the enclosed area. He had to open the door to the glass room behind the obelisk by pulling on it hard. It was extremely dark, but he found the opening without needing extra light. However, after banging into a piece of standing equipment, Nathan muttered angrily to himself and pulled his phone back out, turning on the flashlight.

When he minimized it, the picture of the obelisk that he'd shown the boy was still there. As Nathan swung the light around to view the objects near the base of the thing, something…odd… happened. As Nathan lined the light up directly with the base, the picture of the monolith and the monolith itself "flashed" on his screen, superimposing themselves upon one another on the screen and a bright light like the flash from his camera phone turned back on him blasting him directly into his eyes.

For a moment, the light parts were dark and the dark parts light, blinding him. The whole room seemed to whirl into whiteness and a sudden dizziness hit him. Nathan yelled out, dropping his phone and covering his eyes. He heard the phone bounce onto the tile flooring.

Still blinded, Nathan staggered backing away, feeling around himself so he wouldn't stumble into another piece of equipment. He tripped over something behind him, falling into…grass??? As he stood blinking trying to regain his vision, he realized that somehow, he had gotten outside, and sunlight was streaming down on him. Outside…he whirled his head around in an arc…not on the lawn of the museum…but…*in a field….* with trees all around?

"What… the… *hell…?*" Rubbing his eyes again, he searched around trying to orient himself and found he could not. He stood up, gazing in disbelief, rubbing his eyes again even as his vision cleared, not quite grasping what he was seeing.

Wildly looking around him, Nathan wasn't sure he hadn't been unconscious or shocked enough to have gotten out of the city somehow. It was the only thing that made sense. But where was he…? Upstate New York…? He didn't recognize the area, nor did he see a road, any vehicles…even a house. He was standing somewhere on a hill, surrounded by trees at various distances, on a hill, looking straight at a tall blue mountain range…there was not a soul in sight.

Looking around some more, he spotted his iPhone lying in the grass nearby.

The area was completely foreign and unrecognizable to him…and… he suddenly realized: It had been another cloudy, cold fall day in New York. Here, wherever "here" was…was sunny without a cloud in the sky and the air was becoming swelteringly hot. Especially in his dark black coat. Far warmer than it should be this time of year. Despite all his pride in his usual level of self-control, Nathan was suddenly feeling scared…and inexplicably dizzy. Staggering, Nathan passed out. He barely realized he was falling before all went totally black.

CHAPTER 4

Morgaine sat on her reading couch, sipping a hot cacao more to busy herself and distract her mind from recent events than anything. The fire lay banked in bright red embers with the occasional spark still sputtering out here or there. Outside of that, the room was pitch black. Her curly white locks were down, hanging below her shoulders, and her sparkling eyes watched for any signs of movement.

She was perfectly safe here in her keep, and she knew it. But old habits die hard. And after over 1000 years of accumulated experience, she knew this all too well. Dressed only in a long robe open to the belly, she was proud of how fit she had kept herself. Despite her unnaturally long life – even for one of pure blood like herself – she still looked to be barely over 250. Smiling her secret smile, she quaffed the hot drink until it burnt her tongue completely. She hardly noticed. Her mind was racing.

Somehow. Somehow, the Arc Gate had reactivated. And again… somehow…her accursed brother had found out she was still alive. *But how?* In frustration, she got up and stalked around the very large room, hands holding the opposite arm against the cold.

Three times she had assaulted him and his "brethren" over the course of the centuries. Three times she had failed. At least in part. The last time, he had thrown her bleeding from the top of a cliff into the ocean far below.

The first time had been an unmitigated disaster, as well. Thinking she was coming to wipe out the cornered last remnant of the Dark Brethren, her team had found themselves surrounded by seven full Dark Lords and a legion of heavily armed *Siday* – the most elite warriors of the Kuthra Kai. The "Dark Men" as mortals liked to call them.

Even then they had known she was coming. Again…*somehow.*

Still, she prided herself on her artful escape, utilizing every trick she knew and making up a few in that very moment. Even then it had taken a lucky turn – one of her pursuers guessing wrong and following a random hologram she had created, to escape.

A very narrow escape, indeed.

The second time, she had returned after decades of battling the effects of the Dark on mankind at the periphery of the outer rim of the galaxy with all that remained of the Elder Race. She had brought a small army that time. The result was the same, although four of the seven Dark Brethren remaining were ultimately annihilated in the war. Again, she escaped with her life and a bare handful of her strike team. None of the Elder Race had survived past that battle.

Except Morgaine herself. But at least the Gates had been closed by then.

Her half-brother and two of the strongest of his lieutenants had survived without a scratch, however. In the end, it seemed she had only increased the power of those who did survive, not weakened the standing of the Dark Lords themselves, nor destroyed them utterly, as she had vainly hoped.

The third and final time, she had brought Luan and his band of barbarians. Multiple tribes from the Hinterlands. Luan had become her lover, and he had convinced her to try again to break the *"Triumvirate"*, as they had become known by then. Nearly a century since her previous attempt, she hoped at least to catch them unawares.

But multitudes of people in multiple lands by this time worshiped her brother and his twisted Brethen as gods. They were cruel gods to be sure, as all mortals are when given such undeserved adoration. Evil had proliferated to such an extent, that most of the remaining common people on this planet had become completely warped – and those amongst the Elder Race had interbred enough to become almost… human. None of the bloodline, nor the powers and technology of the Elder Race were visible amongst humankind any longer.

The humans that worshiped the Dark Lords were even worse. Becoming like the evil gods they adored so well, with darkened eyes to match their darker souls.

By the time of her assault, almost all of mankind on this world had been brought under the Dark Brethren's direct or indirect subjugation. Only the barbarians of the Hinterlands were exempt. That is where Morgaine had fled after her second defeat. She had spent years in the caves of the Ember Forest lands trying to figure out how to get back to the Arc Gate.

Ultimately, all those decades later, her desire for companionship had driven her to a wandering tribe and Luan's people. An unfortunate thing indeed. Meeting her had led to his death and the death of every member of his tribe, eventually leading to the extermination of 11 of the 13 warrior tribes in total.

One could say that Morgaine and her quest to satisfy her own longing for companionship had caused more destruction and death than anything her brother had ever done on purpose. But Morgaine and Luan had had many months together before his death.

At least she had that.

Only the Corillion tech of her necklace had saved her that last time – and in so doing it made certain her brother would think her dead. Such brilliant power her father had sown into it, likely with prodigious help from Tabor, her elder brother and an Arc Tech genius. Even she had never known to what extent the necklace could work the interface with the Gates until that moment when she had needed it most.

Her corrupted half-brother's last words to her rang in her ears, even now. *"Why do you care for these lesser beings, sister? They live brief, miserable existences. Their grandchildren's grandchildren were dead before you even reached adulthood. They were made for us to be our servants — our cattle. Yet you fight for them as if they were of the Bright Race. Their dogs barely outlive them!"*

It hadn't been the first time he had questioned her motives in trying to save the remaining "lesser" races from his tyranny. Just the last.

And the Corillion medallion had been her deliverance. It had been only by chance Morgaine had even been able to save the Pendant and her Black Sword on that Day way back when. The very day when the sickness of The Dark had become fully known.

She had been training with them both, per her father's instruction like every other day. Morgaine remembered with a shudder every time how she had almost skipped it to go riding instead on that particular sunny afternoon. What a tremendous disaster that choice would have become!

Only shutting down the Gates decades later had averted complete destruction of the outer worlds; and that had only been possible with the Sword and the Pendant combined. Morgaine had managed all that in the end by herself. The last of the Elder Race not infected somehow by the Darkness. But now, today, as she stood huddled with her hot drink near a dying fire, nearly six hundred years later, she once again knew fear.

Morgaine shuddered despite herself.

Fighting back the Dark effects of the Arc Gates in mankind and their progeny had kept her more than busy in the ensuing centuries, but it had had the redeeming effect of keeping her relatively safe from their "gods". Her half-brother Jezerah and the other two, K'Thul and Emorion, had proven to be dark gods, indeed. Even Morgaine's peripheral battle had turned into a losing fight in the end. Smaller and smaller remnants of men resisted the urge to plunge into the lustful power and extended life offered by the Dark "Magic" her brother and his kind proffered….

A knock at the heavy wooden door of her study jerked Morgaine out of her reverie and her purple eyes snapped towards the crack under the door where light leaked through, her muscles immediately taut and ready for action. Without waiting for an answer, her servant Maitan slipped silently into the room. He noticed her still awake and started, eyes widening before bowing deeply. His slight but muscular form noticeable beneath his servant attire.

"Mistress, shall I rekindle the fire for you? Winter is still cold here in the hill country. It will be freezing tonight; and your fondness for this particular room and its heights doesn't protect it from the aggressive mountain winds, as you well know.

She looked at him. A descendent of the *Biaki Mor* – the "Shining Warriors" – his people had fallen far from their great height nearly five hundred years hence. She simply nodded at Maitan and turned back towards the fire.

There would be no sleep for her this night.

Meditation and prayer perhaps. The Great Deity still had purpose for her. Excitement ran through her thousand-year-old veins. Clearly her destiny wasn't to kill her half-brother and his ilk, as she had originally hoped, perhaps even assumed. To cleanse the galaxy of the blight of the Dark Void had always seemed to be her calling. Grimacing, she knew this was not ever to be. She had, in fact, given up on that idea long ago. But something had changed today. Somewhere.

Somehow.

The Arc Gate in Arth had reopened. She knew it. She felt it through her Corillion medallion. *But how…?* Morgaine currently had no idea how that was even possible. But it did mean she wasn't done yet with this life. The Almighty still had more for his White Falcon to do.

Morgaine took another pull from her cacao, then set it down on the corner table nearby. "Maitan, ready the Guard, my cruiser, and my horse for tomorrow. I'm going to travel to Rondor and seek audience with the king. There are some still who are willing to fight against the Dark. And I must seek some allies before investigating this new disturbance."

Maitan's eyes widened slightly, but only nodded his mostly bald head before bowing himself out of the room. Of course. What she had known for hours now, she had just spoken aloud without thinking. Even with his training, she was impressed he didn't shout aloud in horror.

"Disturbance" could only refer to the Arc Gate itself. The formerly 'dead' Arc Gate. Well, dead no more. Morgaine would spend the night praying. Hoping that something would change for the better.

And soon.

CHAPTER 5

It was nearly dawn, and the crisp air of early autumn in the northern Hinterlands felt oddly comforting as Brianna made her way down the hill towards the river. Being a young widow living alone was considered foolishness by the townspeople. But the village was only a few miles down the road, and there hadn't been threats in the hill country for decades.

There were only a few trees in the area near her cozy stone farmhouse. The clear pre-dawn morning caused her to notice once again that many of the leaves had fallen and made their way downstream already. Some were still hanging on near the top branches, for some reason. But they were still mostly brown and wrinkled. Winter was coming. It was likely still very warm everywhere further down south. The change of the seasons never lost their charm for Brianna. It made her remain young at heart. It was strange to consider herself "old".

Her twenty-seven summers could hardly qualify her as an old woman. But having lived in the country of the Hinterlands all her life, she did feel a bit isolated at the best of times.

Other times she felt starkly alone out here by herself. Especially in winter. And winters were long in the north. She knew of the other lands: like the Kingdom of Rondor, who had rebelled sometime before she was born and single-handedly disemboweled the previously unchallenged Empire of Nelrae and its spiral into the Dark. There were also the Petty Kingdoms to the southeast, and the mysterious Eastern Empire far, far to the east beyond them.

The Hinterlands where Brianna lived was simply an area no longer claimed by any king, duke, or country. It was too far north for most, and cold much of the year. But the people lived free here. Made up of mostly farmers, herders, and shepherds. Others were woodsmen or furriers who shipped their pine wood and furs downstream to the kingdoms and countries far to the south for their gold, silver, and wine.

Brianna stopped by the barn to check on her two milk cows. They lowed at seeing her but didn't seem in any real distress yet this morning. Making a quick decision, she decided to head down to the nearby south branch of the White River by the edge of her property to gather some water for washing before milking the cows and making breakfast. This would save her at least half an hour in the long run.

Grabbing a large wooden bucket and a pitcher from the wall in the barn, she noted with a small sadness all the spots she and Sirles had worked to set the barn up for their future together. The workbench with tools had some small rust stains and the iron hammer sat by itself on the rack covered in dust.

The remembrance of her husband's eyes and his smile made her pause in her walk and brush some straw from the one calf of her older milk cow, Heather. The calf was strong and already ran in the fields like the young bull he would become. She smiled, "You will be a strong one," as the little calf licked her hand with its rough tongue, then lowed at her.

Sighing, she returned to the task at hand and picked the pitcher back up where she had set it down to brush the straw from the calf's face. Closing the barn door behind her, one of the cows sounded a bit more distressed than before, seeing her leave. "I'm sorry, Idina, you will have to wait. I have water to fetch."

The dawn was appearing over the horizon as she hustled down the well-worn path towards the stream shivering a bit in the morning air. This time of year was usually still warm enough that getting up before dawn should be easier. Yet it became harder and harder as the air in her homeland chilled after the fire was banked for the evening. The wind howled often at night, bringing storms and rain. Summers were short in the north.

A loud *CRACK* of a branch from across the quiet hillside startled Brianna, and her head whipped towards where the sound had come from. Then she gasped in horror. Two Dark Marauders dressed in full leathers, black cloaks, and wearing black masks over their nose and mouth were moving directly towards her from across the far hillside and were closing fast. There was little doubt who their target was.

Whirling and wasting no time on a scream, she pitched her bucket back at the men in a vain attempt to slow at least one of them, and then ran with all the speed her lithe form could muster towards the churning river at the bottom of the hill.

There was some distance yet between them – maybe a hundred yards. Brianna had a good head start, but the speed at which the "Dark Men" moved was legendary. It was said they could catch a horse not at a full gallop and hardly break a sweat.

Knowing from an early age what the Dark Men did to young women alone gave Brianna's heart spasms as she raced towards the edge of the water. Her heart pounded as her mind grasped wildly for rational thought.

The Dark Men hadn't crossed the Grey Mountain borders in a decade or more….! It had been literally centuries since they had been this far north. Hundreds of miles from their home. She herself had only seen one Dark Man ever. And he had been in a cage as he was paraded through town by the North Guard at Summerfest over 8 years ago.

No one had said where that man had been found, but the Guard patrolled the southwestern border where they were most likely to cross into the Hinterlands. That certainly wasn't anywhere close to the town of Anders.

Shaking off her reverie as she approached the river, Brianna sucked in a fast gulp of air as she hurled her body headlong into the icy water. There had been not a split second of decision here. She had only one possibility of escape.

Since she had become a widow, she had always known in her mind if anything ever befell her out here in the wilds, she had only avenue of escape – the White River. With a shock of fear, she felt fingers grasp at her ankles and the back of her blouse as she dove.

How did they move that fast and get so close?

The shock of the freezing cold water made her surface in the middle of the river with a gasp. Risking the freezing temperatures of the water from the higher mountains was simply what had to be done. Dying in the water was a much more pleasant way to go than what would happen at the hands of those men. Or whatever they really were. No one had ever seen their faces. Even the one in the cage had still worn a black mask over his mouth and nose. It was like even the Guard that had caught him feared to look at what was underneath that scarf.

And…those *eyes*…

It was said that the Dark Marauders raped women repeatedly before they killed them. Those who screamed excruciatingly were rumored to be taken back to their camps, forcing the women to scream until they eventually died from the grisly usage of their bodies simply because the Dark Men enjoyed the screaming ones more.

According to everything she had ever heard, they were simply not human. The dark gods they served didn't allow them to have a soul. Let alone a conscience. All Brianna knew was that no one thus captured had ever come back. These stories had been told to her by the men who had fought in the wars over two decades ago. They also hinted about the things that they hadn't told her about. Brianna remembered staring at those men in horror as a little girl.

As she began floating downstream, Brianna was half expecting the ravenous and crazy Dark Men to leap after her. So, she ducked her head back under the surface in the frigid waters as long as she could, listening for the large splash that never came, while swimming furiously to stay in the middle where the current was fastest. Suddenly aware of her desperate need for air, she came to the surface of the ever-widening river and literally cried aloud despite herself.

Fool!

Even though Brianna realized it had simply been an instinct, she also knew that sound could draw the Dark Men back. After all, she had been underwater for at least a minute, perhaps more.

Brianna hastily wiped the water from her eyes while still swiftly moving downstream. She looked wildly behind her for signs of pursuit either on the banks or in the water itself. No one was there.

Like the shadows the Dark Men were rumored to spawn from, they had simply vanished. However, Brianna continually scanned the hills behind her as she continued floating downstream with the rapid current. Shivering from the cold, she knew she couldn't last long even in the late summer water. The White River never ran warm, coming out of the mountains as it did.

Watching both banks just to be certain, she kept her vigil up as the land slowly revealed itself in the morning light. The farmstead she had lived in alone since Sirles had died of the Black Fever four years ago was long lost behind her already, thanks to the White River's strong current.

Brianna gritted her chattering teeth, took another deep breath, and quickly submerged again just to be sure. Not taking any chances, she swam underwater with only occasional breaks for air for what felt like an eternity but was likely only ten or twelve minutes. When she began to feel somewhat safe, she pushed through and swam for the opposite shore, climbing up the sharp bank with an effort. Her limbs were like stones, and Brianna knew she was still in danger.

Shivering uncontrollably, hands wrapped around herself in a futile attempt to stay warm, Brianna walked slowly away along the riverbank. Water dripping from her as she unsteadily trudged towards the nearest farm. She knew she might freeze to death in the cool morning air, now made far worse with her sopping clothes and sodden hair. The river had moved her rapidly around to the eastern side of the village, but no closer to the town itself.

Heart still pounding, Brianna willed herself with the last of her energy, and pulled herself up onto the high riverbank above the river, using tree roots and grass clumps to get up the last bit of the way. She then walked up the next hill towards the familiar homestead of her friend's farm.

Where had the Dark Men come from? Why had they been on her property? How had they come so far north and east with no detection from the North Guard, or the nearby constabulary? Perhaps the rumors that the local patrols had grown lax were true. Questions that needed answers.

But no one was going to answer her questions now, and there were other things she required. What she needed now was warmth. And fast. Her hands and arms were blue, and she was so cold now she wasn't shivering at all. She was almost in a trance. Her body felt like lead.

She climbed the opposite hillside slowly, pulling herself into the morning sunlight quicker by angling a bit around toward the back of the house. Since it was at least still early autumn, the sun's light immediately added some warmth to her bones, even as the mild breeze made her skin get bumps from the cold. Overall, though…the sun warmed her enough to at least get the shivering going again.

Brianna, now shaking uncontrollably and her teeth chattering, staggered towards Carlina's farmhouse. Her normally long and wavy brown hair now dripped water and hung heavily down her back, she felt like an icicle wrapped in a farm dress. But Brianna then began to laugh with the laugh one could only find when one has just escaped a fate worse than death, even as she slogged over the final hill towards the Dunnau farm and her friend's kitchen.

Her mirth at her own survival interfered with her noticing no one was moving about the property, despite the late hour of the morning. Farm work started early everywhere. It was the singular rule of farm life. As sunlight fell on the doorway, Brianna saw the front door standing strangely ajar as she approached. The laughter and the smile on her face fell away as quickly as it had come.

No one was home. At least no one she could see. And someone should be here.

"Hellfire!" she muttered, immediately and instinctively crouching low, she scuttled over to a nearby oak and peered towards the house. Not a sound came. Not a thing moved. She could hear the cattle lowing in the barn, seeking relief from their over-full udders, just as she presumed Indira would be by doing by now. The horses were nickering to each other nervously in the barn at the excited state of the other animals, but no one in the farmstead moved.

Shivering as she crouched behind the tree, Brianna felt a tightness in her stomach. She simply did not know what to do. If she went back to the river without drying off, she would most assuredly die soon from exposure to the cold. The water was frigid even in the warmest summer months, coming directly down from the mountains. Year round, it was barely above freezing. Even in mid-summer, it was barely tolerable. Brianna herself knew of two people who had died swimming in its icy waters simply by not being careful enough.

The White River was used for drinking and washing. Almost never for bathing or swimming. The town of Anders was at least six more clicks downstream and then almost another from the river's edge. The road to Anders from the Dunnau farm would normally be the choice here. But simply walking down the road dripping wet and hoping to remain unnoticed, let alone alive, was clearly questionable strategy at this point.

Brianna realized she was faced with either going into that house and not finding it empty, or the barn. The house seemed more dangerous. She had already seen in her mind what the Dark Marauders would do to her if she were caught a scant thirty minutes ago. Not particularly proud, Brianna knew she was a pretty woman. There was little doubt that such men would take their time with one such as her.

The quaking in her body reminded her that there really seemed to be no other option. The animals were upset, but not showing fear. It would be easy enough to slide around the back hill and slip into the rear of the barn completely unnoticed from anyone in the house. If those inside had not seen her – assuming anyone was there – they wouldn't see her now. Also, she reasoned if anyone had seen her already, they would have come for her.

Risking a glance around the base of the large tree, Brianna peered up towards the farmstead and the wide-open door, swinging softly in the wind. It was beyond quiet inside. She only prayed it was because Carlina and the Dunnau family had gotten away from whatever had caused them to leave their home in such a hurry.

Clearly there were more than two of the Dark Men beyond the border, if this was the situation just outside the township. Slipping away as only a country girl could do, Brianna made her way quickly to the far side of the hill. Working her way up on her hands and knees, she pushed along to the far corner of the wooden barn.

Inside, the animals were still impatiently lowing and neighing. The back latch to the barn would likely be unlocked, as there simply were no cattle thieves out this far from White Rock, the only city in the Hinterlands of any size. Yet when Brianna tried the latch, she still almost cried in relief when it gave.

Slipping inside, she noticed a lantern had been lit and left in the barn some time ago. It was sputtering from lack of oil and the wick was nearly out. But it was there. This was a very bad sign – no one leaves a lit flame of any type near animals and hay.

First things first!

Clenching her jaws to keep her teeth from chattering, Brianna's shivers returned in force as she looked around for the inevitable birthing blankets. She found some and quickly stripped to her underclothes. Drying off as the cows increased their noise (and her anxiety over the attention this might raise), she made another scan and found Carlina's gardening clothes hanging on a hook. It included a bonnet and a long, sharp hoe. There was also a long knife for emergencies and a scythe for the fields. Birthing was often a brutal choice between mother and calf. The knife would be for that. She quickly put on the dry clothes. Far too big for her frame and dirty besides.

"So be it…" she breathed.

Proud people didn't survive long in the Hinterlands. And dirty and too big was better than naked and freezing any day. Realizing she had just spoken out loud and wincing at the timing of it, she mentally clamped down on her jaws again, and put her hair into the loose ties of the hair bonnet. She let it slip over the back of her neck to prevent her from losing peripheral vision, however. She felt her thick hair soak the bonnet instantly, but it held.

Brianna felt half-warm again.

Grabbing the long knife, she finally saw in the dim light of the barn that one of the horses was out of her stall and over by the front near the barn doors. She had been making noises with the other animals, but not noticeably more and it was a much larger barn than her own. Glancing quickly into the open stall as she passed by, Brianna stopped cold.

"No!"

Inside lay the still, naked, and bloody remains of her friend. Carlina wouldn't be needing her gardening clothes back. She had been stabbed multiple times and left for dead. The hay had soaked up a good deal of the blood. Plus, this had not happened long ago. Perhaps an hour, or two at most. The blood was dark and drying, but not completely dried yet. Her friend's eyes were still wide-eyed in terror. Despite her rising concern for her own safety, Brianna knelt down and closed them.

Tears suddenly wet her face. And, in bitter anger and fear, Brianna fought down the urge to panic. Biting back wails fearing she'd be heard, Brianna struck herself on her left arm to gain control.

She leaped back onto her feet, racing towards the freed mare. Her thoughts chaotic, panic turning her stomach upside down. The horse offered her a chance. Maybe those damned Dark Men could outrun a horse before it hit a dead run. But this horse sure as hell wouldn't be going that slowly soon!

She threw a saddle onto the mare's broad back and slowly kicked the barn door open from the side, preparing to make a break for it. If there were Marauders in or near the house, she would have a head start to the road. It was said Dark Men were averse to riding horses themselves. No one knew why. Although this did not guarantee success due to their legendary speed, she liked her chances aboard Carlina's prized mare much better than afoot and alone.

Brianna knew the mare's name.

"Star" had been named for the white mark on her otherwise black head and body. Her fetlocks were also white, and Star's hooves were stomping a bit, back and forth in her anxiety. Brianna grabbed bridle and reins, putting them over Star's nose, quickly cinching the saddle tight. And, before mounting, she pulled the already slightly open barn doors open a bit further. Brianna could feel Star's readiness to move. Brianna was glad to have her under her. The horse, clearly excited to be free of the barn and the dead body of her mistress, bolted out the doors into a full gallop as Brianna dug into her sides with both heels.

Brianna looked back and gasped in relief. No one was following her.

What is going on? What is happening?

It was all Brianna could think to herself over and over as she raced down the road toward the town of Anders. Not slowing down until she'd gone at least four hills beyond the farm, she rode the horse at as fast a speed as she could maintain, looking back every few seconds.

Hopefully someone older and wiser than she would be able to figure it out and make sense of all of this. She considered the possibility that there might be more Marauders between her and the town, but she really had no choice.

At this time of day, there should be other travelers, and if there were that many of the Dark Men abroad in the area, she was dead already.

And if she tried to go a back way through the fields, she might run right into the very people she was trying to avoid. Especially if they were avoiding roads to hide their presence, she was only increasing the odds of being caught. Not to mention, she was still only partially dry, and her hair was sopping wet and felt like a frozen crown on her head in Carlina's bonnet.

Two sets of dark eyes watched Brianna's horse race down the road towards the village on her stolen steed. Instead of chasing her, however, the Dark Men merely saluted the young woman for her guile and bravery with a hand closed into a fist slapping their chest, before slipping back into the forest and loping back towards the group encampment.

The Dark Men had always admired those with the strength and will to elude their grasp. Stories were told of the brave ones who had found a way to beat them in some way. Always with great admiration. Dark Men knew those types of people were few and far between. These two would report everything to the Master. He would know what to do. And they had, after all, been ordered to make sure at least one escaped.

The woman had earned that right.

CHAPTER 6

Nathan awoke with a start, sitting bolt upright. He was lying in a field of high sawgrass, with a swelteringly hot sun shining almost directly overhead.

Blinking his eyes to get the sun bleaching effect to dampen, he realized he was both severely burnt on the entire right side of his face and desperately thirsty simultaneously. Not worrying about where he was at that moment, he stood up and swept his eyes around him, looking anywhere for a sign of some fresh water.

Stunned, he realized he was somewhere in a hilly region by himself. The faraway mountains he had noticed before were still there, but somehow seemed quite a bit closer in the full daylight. Between the hill he stood on was a rocky plateau and a valley filled with trees. He also noticed a repeated, flashing glint of sunlight sparkling through the leaves. Noting how the trees were wandering in a crooked line nearby, he surmised that that must be a small river or stream, and those trees were thriving due to the nearby source of water.

It didn't seem very far away, so he licked his parched lips, tried to swallow some spit he managed to force into his mouth, and began walking. About five or so minutes later, he reached what was indeed the edge of a stream. It flowed from somewhere up towards the mountains and ran over this flattened valley before vanishing in the tree line towards the tilting sun.

Kneeling down, he began washing his face, then drank deeply of the cold, clear water. Throwing some onto his head and hot face again, he sat back in the shade of one of the larger trees to think.

Where the hell am I? And how did I get here? Asking himself this was all he could immediately manage. Shaking his head, he was simply at a loss.

Suddenly, a grunting sound following by some leaves and twigs snapping and a general crashing sound moving towards him made Nathan stand up and peer closely into the trees in the direction of the noises. Without warning, a wild boar shot out from the underbrush, heading directly towards him.

Nathan leaped to the side, clearing a small side stream of the river as the dangerous animal raced by him, pursued almost immediately by a pair of large foxlike dogs.

"What is going on?" Nathan asked aloud, slumping to the ground beneath yet another tree, his heart pounding in his chest. "Where in New York state are there wild boars and foxes? Not anywhere close to the city, that's for sure. I must be near the Adirondacks. I've never been…" he looked about himself doubtfully, "…here."

"And maybe it's an Indian…summer…today…?" *In November?* His inner voice trailed off even in his head, incredulity at his situation stopping suddenly as he searched for his iPhone. He touched all his pockets… rapidly growing in panic as he remembered dropping the phone at some point in the series of events that had transpired. Determined to find it, he took another long drink from the stream before standing up and looking back the way he had come.

He had to find that phone or he would be lost out here without any help – possibly for days. And warm weather or not, it was going to get cold again – probably as soon as sundown. He looked up at the sun, which hadn't moved much, but had clearly moved substantially further up into the sky since passing out. Middle of the day for sure, then. Plenty of time. He began hiking back towards the hill he had left searching for a drink.

Fortunately, the distance wasn't far and the hill he had been on stood out amongst its otherwise flat-topped sisters. He found the bent grass where he had fallen even, then as he surveyed the area further into the hills, he jumped as he noticed something back in the trees less than fifty yards away.

The Monolith…!

Somehow…it had come here, too. Standing sheltered by enormous trees not 100 feet from where he had fallen. It was standing near the mouth of an enormous cave set into a higher hill. How he hadn't noticed it before, he had no idea. Perhaps because as he had surveyed his situation upon awakening, his sole goal had been to find water. And the hills behind him were dark and likely were darker when the sun had been further down towards the horizon.

Either way, how and why was the monolith standing in on a hill with him?

Nathan shook his head looking at it. He found himself sitting on the grass several minutes later, just staring at the monolith in wonder, trying to grasp what the hell had happened.

The monstrous thing was still in the shadow of all those trees – and, strangely, it looked to have been there for decades, at least with those trees towering over it, with the dirt and vines that vainly tried to wrap around its base. Even here, it sparkled in the half light of a sunny day in the forest. Despite the chirping of birds, and the distance it was from him, he thought he could even hear it hum.

He got up and started walking towards the thing. As he approached, the trees in the canopy above it were lit up by a luminescence that made it seem like the sunlight had suddenly burst through, ignoring the trefoil leaves. Except the light was almost pure white. Then it went out as quickly as it had arrived.

Nathan stopped his advance when the light had appeared, but now that it was gone, he slowly began moving towards it once again. As he got within about 20 feet of it, he stepped on something. Looking down, he saw his iPhone peeking beneath his sneaker. None the worse for wear, still in its plastic case. Overjoyed, he picked it up and put his finger on the button. The phone lit up, but when he looked for a satellite signal, there was none. The phone even said, "Power Save" on it. "SOS" in the upper righthand corner.

A cold feeling washed over him and his eyes shot up at the monolith. "Where are we? Where have you taken me?"

His only answer was the quiet of the hillside and the chirping of birds in the trees. Eventually, Nathan picked a direction, deciding to follow the river. Then he just started walking.

Hours passed. Literally no one came. From anywhere. There was no road. There were no people. There were only rolling hills, the stream to which he had returned to walk along as a guide, and the birds endlessly chirping. Nathan checked his phone for the twentieth time.

Apparently, it was only about 2:30 in the afternoon. Power was still being saved. Yet the sun told a different tale. By that reckoning, assuming it was truly late fall, it was at least three hours past that. Maybe later. Another thing Nathan noticed when he opened his phone was that the charge still read: *100%.*

Odd. Nathan hadn't charged it since leaving home, and even though his case was a backup charger, it still didn't account for the charging, as it was turned off. Nathan checked that, too.

Again.

Since he had bigger problems – which included a rumbling belly and a half-burnt face, he began following the stream down from the hills. Stopping occasionally to drink, he just hoped to find someone before sunset.

Just as the sun was setting and he was about to give up hope of finding anyone, he spied some smoke lazily rising from a chimney, apparently from a nearby farmhouse. In fact, all he could see was a bit of the roof and a chimney belching smoke. If it was a farmhouse, it was an old one. And, Nathan realized, it was still several hills away – maybe over two miles. It would take the remaining light to get there if he hurried.

But at least it was a sign, the first sign he had seen of anyone living anywhere nearby. He didn't even check his phone again for a signal. It literally hadn't changed in hours. But with darkness approaching, and the possibility of being alone in the dark at night, he marked in his mind clearly the direction of the farmhouse and set off at a brisk pace.

His feet hurt, but fortunately his shoes were designed specifically for long walks and running. Excellent padding had kept his feet from getting blisters, and he was grateful once again for buying the "expensive" pair of Adidas not two months prior.

Coming up on each crest, he checked his direction and corrected it, as needed. He was surprised and pleased how little off course he was each time. By the time he crested the third hill, he could see the ground lying between himself and his target. The sun had set, but there was just enough light on the hillside to make out the house and the tops of the trees near it. Only one large field lay between him and his destination.

And it apparently had been planted recently, as rows of some kind of plant were peeking above the topsoil. Smoke still rose continually from the chimney, but he had set eyes on no one.

Brushing himself off a bit, he raced for the house. It was an odd design. It looked Dutch or German or something. Mostly wooden slats on a stone base wall with some glassless windows hung with small curtains and wooden shades. It definitely did not fit the type of farmhouses he had seen in pictures or on any drives to upstate New York. Those were made mostly of brick and stone. Painted red wood was the other option. And still no sign of any roads or cars.

Another oddity.

Yet, it was civilization of sorts. And he was ravenous at this point. That alone was enough to make even Nathan bold and willing to talk to anyone. "Hello?!" he yelled as he approached the house. He didn't want to alarm anyone. That certainly wouldn't get him fed. He called out again, "Hello…?"

The door opened slowly, and two of the oddest men Nathan had ever seen stepped out. Living in New York, that said a lot. He had more than half expected an older gentleman in overalls. Or a farm wife in an apron bearing a towel or an oven mitt.

But these two men were dressed in dark leathers and wore dark scarves over their faces. One had his high enough that it almost masked his eyes. They wore dark round hats and clearly had very long knives strapped to each thigh and behind their backs. What Nathan could see of their skin color from their hands and faces was that it was much darker than his could ever be.

One of them slowly drew one of his knives and held it up in a way that made Nathan stop moving in an instant. He held it between Nathan and himself, pointing it as if to say, "keep away".

"Hold on!" Nathan said in as calm a voice as he could muster, raising his hands wide and smiling in what he hoped was received as a friendly manner. I'm just looking for a place to sleep and maybe a little food. I'm… lost…and I just need a phone or internet…is there any signal out here?"

The men narrowed their eyebrows and looked at each other quizzically, clearly not understanding him. Nathan kept talking, trying to keep his voice smooth.

"You know…uh…food…?" he said again as he raised his left hand slowly to his mouth and pretended to eat. He was beginning to get irritated.

How do they not speak English?

The men eyed him suspiciously, and seemed to visibly check him up and down, one pointing right at Nathan's face. He said something Nathan could not understand.

"I've…got nothing…no weapons!" his voice got high and almost squeaky with anxiety. "Just me…" he said and kept both hands raised.

The men then nodded to each other, rushing straight at him.

CHAPTER 7

540 years ago…

Morgaine slammed down atop the ledge, ducking quickly to avoid being seen.

That beast of a man is everywhere!

Quickly wiping the smear of the wet grass from her fingers upon her leggings, she spun her head around in all directions, scanning below and above for signs of her opponent.

Feeling along her customary 'war gear' of dark metal and plastic armor for holes while she was scanning, she found neither a sign of her foe, nor of any breach in her armor, although her black leather boots were nearly shredded. It was said that the tech of that armor was impossible to tear. But after the beating she had just taken, she had to be sure.

Gripping her photon blaster with her right hand, she pulled herself up with her left; pointing the weapon towards the ledge she had just vacated.

A metal floating eye the size of two hands cautiously drifted over the edge. Immediately, Morgaine fired the blaster, catching the pupil of the Drone Eye, bursting it into flames as the power that held it was sundered by the might of her own specially crafted weaponry.

Leaping up, she swung her legs around and quickly raced to the other side of the promontory, jumping, then catching herself on the limbs of the gigantic pine trees of the battleground. Even as she did so, the crest where she had just blasted the eye from burned into flames, followed quickly by multiple blasts of electric bolts from the clear blue sky.

She had done this type of thing since she was young, literally leaping from branch to branch, ending up on the ground now almost one hundred feet from where she had been. Morgaine rubbed her eyes and looked around again, even onto the area she had just landed, to be sure that the man who was hunting her had not anticipated this maneuver.

Assured her target was still unaware of her true location, Morgaine touched one of the two battle rings on her right hand, and it began to spin, turning from brassy gold to green. The green appeared to Morgaine to rapidly stretch from her finger to her hand and spread over her entire body.

To any casual observer, it would appear as if the woman known as Morgaine had literally been eaten up by the air around her, vanishing from sight. Of course, Oligarchs or Techs who were watching this sham of a fight could likely still see her, had any of them survived the cataclysm.

That bastard cousin of hers would likely figure it out soon enough.

But all Morgaine needed was a few precious minutes. She had measured him as an opponent. She was certain of her tech. At least as sure as one could be. Covered now in her cloaking device she was likely far safer than her armor itself could ever make her. So Morgaine raced back up the path of the hill with the cliff on the back side of the ridge directly behind the area she believed her enemy had just vacated. As she ran, she almost subconsciously pulled her hair, wound into a tight ponytail, to secure its snugness. No sense letting hair get in the way of a clean shot at a crucial time.

What in blazes was I thinking when I agreed to this madness? What could have possessed me…to try to fight them again?

Then she remembered. Her sister-in-law Terrace and Terrace's mother Jaecis weeping uncontrollably over the dead form of Terrace's husband, her only full brother Tabor. He had been the last, besides herself.

Morgaine just standing there in shocked disbelief. The Patron of the Hinterlands, an Arc tech genius in his day – slain by that twisted shell of their distant cousin Markam; the man whom she battled even now.

Such an act of evil demanded retribution.

The Battle of Megiddo provided that for her, though she worried about the fate of the lesser races, she could not think on that at the moment. The battle was lost regardless, and Morgaine herself was on her last legs. Still, she had killed or critically wounded five of these so-called "Dark Brethren" in their previous encounters. Chances like these did not *come around very often. One had to make the most of one's opportunities.*

Focus.

Cautiously, Morgaine slipped off the path and up the hill, having learned from watching her foe defeat others, how his mind worked. He would blast an area with his weaponry, then slip in behind and look for the next trail. Ever aggressive, ever attacking. The relentless butchery of it was almost admirable in its sheer ferocity.

It also had worked four times against three of the best members of her strike team. This Darkened version of her cousin was not used to even being staggered, let alone harried or mastered. Wherever the Dark from within the Gates had taken him, he was more than a lethal killer now. He was a war machine.

There!

A black and blue robed figure with no visible tech armor and a single blaster strapped to his side, floating in a magnetic field barrier. But clearly that blaster was also no ordinary weapon, glowing luminously between sickly green and light blue, even when holstered. Although Markam was nowhere near the fighter Morgaine was before his... *change...* he had been an accomplished warrior, not to mention a gifted tech master and wielder of certain other powers, as well. Now…he was deadly enough completely unarmed, Morgaine was quite certain.

But now, he's facing me. And I'm no ordinary fighter myself.

Morgaine was also fairly sure her former cousin looked at it the other way around. She was counting on it, in fact. Picking two trees separated by her own arms width stretched out, Morgaine hung a small crystal box of sky-blue color from a small twine rope she wound around a high branch.

Of course, she knew as soon as she let it go, it would become visible, but at this distance and with his back turned, she hoped Markam (and his roving drone eyes) would not be able to notice without full monitoring scans amid the natural camouflage the surrounding area gave it.

Her opponent was still in plain sight, standing arrogantly in those blue-black robes while scanning the tree line below. Clearly believing in his ultimate superiority, he felt no counterattack would even be attempted, let alone succeed.

"Pride cometh before the fall," she whispered.

Markam had watched Morgaine run, dodge, and hide during the first ten minutes of this fight – cutting through lesser opponents when they got in the way – but always avoiding direct confrontation with him and he was obviously assuming that the fight would go no differently now.

Without a doubt, he also wouldn't be without some level of protection. Morgaine was certain there were powerful force shields around the "mage", so anyone approaching him would be suddenly and most powerfully stopped. Permanently.

Morgaine simply wasn't going to fall into that trap. The only reason Markam would allow himself to be seen like this was to draw his opponents in. After all, it had worked on all the others. The reason it kept working is that, it seemed, only Morgaine had spent time in scouting the battle tactics of her enemies, noting to herself which ones they leaned upon during a fight.

Perhaps the other warriors from the Elder Race that had once fought at Morgaine's side had assumed they were good enough to beat anyone under any conditions, and perhaps others fought simply to survive. Morgaine knew better on both counts. More importantly she knew her limits. It was simply a matter of maturity. After so many hundreds of years, one grew wise, or one grew cold and dead. Unfortunately, the latter had happened to far too many of her kin. All of them, in fact.

Morgaine chuckled to herself, though, as she ran. Knowing she was an underdog often was what kept her alive. Gently opening the crystal box, Morgaine took the black metal ball inside and attached it to the trigger of a large throwing weapon attached to her back. Designed for use in close combat fighting and hunting, she was very familiar with the weapon – called the '*Djune*' by both the lesser races and the Elder Race, as well.

The lower races considered such a blade sacred and used it only to "cut the Darkness" out of dead people before burying them, in hopes of eternal resurrection. Well, before the rise of the Dark Men, anyway.

This *Djune,* although not holy in any way, was a very fine weapon, regardless. It had a particularly wide tip with short handles so it could be thrown long distances. Morgaine had trained with this exact weapon for years, hitting targets fifty to even a hundred feet away with deadly accuracy.

She had attached it yesterday to her back armor in the unlikely event she was able to close with any of the other Dark Lords. She hadn't. The metal ball of the box still had a touch of the blue liquid, which, when it touched the trip of her *Djune,* caused it to shine brightly, binding the tip to the liquid in the box.

Morgaine immediately jerked the tip towards the ground as low as she could without it actually touching anything and raced back around to the other side of the hill. Once she got there, she pulled one white-blonde hair from her head and touched it to the blue spot on the *Djune's tip.* The brightness immediately faded, and the hair vanished with it. Morgaine never understood exactly what that did – but she suspected it had something to do with the genetic code her hair contained. This way, she would be protected from what came next. Hopefully.

Now to do the unexpected thing.

Markam had been busy blasting the area below the hill now, and many of the trees were ablaze. Trying to smoke Morgaine out from her former hiding spots. So, he had been watching.

Perfect.

He was so sure she was still in the main part of the battlefield, and he knew someone ascending from there would be easily seen. The smoke and fire and noise from the constant explosions and the rest of the battle were providing the perfect cover for her now. Another trick the Dark Lord had used to smoke out his last opponent that Morgaine had carefully planned for by coming up invisibly.

Scrambling up the far slope was easier than climbing that sheer cliff on the opposite side would have been, but it was still far from easy. Invisible as she was, she was afraid of dislodging too many rocks and dust, giving her position away. The only easy way up this hill – the highest in the area – was the trail. Still, for one of the Elder Race with her small stature and athletic physique, this was more than feasible and not something the fool would likely consider himself.

Raising her head up just enough, she peered around the grass and tree lined plateau of the hill. There were enough trees…there! Markam should be right there…! Oh, there he was again…what?! Now there were five of them?!

Damn!

Crouching down while gripping her *Djune,* tip pointed carefully up in the air now, she watched, eyes peeking over the hilltop. All the forms were moving in complete tandem. Some sort of mirroring hologram. And there was no real guarantee any of those was the actual man himself. All of them seemed to be creating more explosions below – firing them from some mini-blaster cannon held with both hands. He and his images were now spreading destruction around the entire far side where she had climbed up from, and occasionally striking the path up the road, as well. Black scorches and fires raged seemingly everywhere in the valley below now. The screams and cries of men fighting and dying were everywhere.

Think, damn it!

Morgaine suddenly realized that for her plan to work, all she needed was the real Markam. The images wouldn't have to matter. They were irrelevant. It did hinge on one of those images actually being Markam, however. Moving with the stealth only those of her training and lineage could manage, Morgaine slowly worked her way around to where she was close enough to almost touch the first of the five "Markam" figures.

Lining up the five forms as best he could, with the trees and the blue box somewhere behind, she raised the *Djune* up…and threw. The balance of the weapon and her skill, plus the liquid on the tip made it unerringly strike the box hanging from the black cord hanging slightly behind and away from the line of images.

An explosion, followed immediately by a sudden rent in the earth ripped the ground rapidly away from the box, rumbling its way towards the line of figures at least appearing to blast the battlefield far below. It tore right beneath the line of images quickly, tearing a deep furrow into the earth from the trees all the way up towards Morgaine herself. Not until the fourth image (second closest to herself) faltered, did any of the images stumble, cry out, or change movements.

Her second *Djune* was already in her hand. Morgaine knew it was a perfect throw before it even struck the falling Markam in the back. The knife struck right through his armor, spurting blood, and causing him to cry out while falling, cursing…just as Morgaine herself was hit by the ground's destruction, causing her to tumble also.

Not knowing exactly where the weapon had come from that struck him, and despite sliding and falling down the hillside, the wounded Dark Lord turned his body so he slid headfirst downhill while lying on his side, blade still protruding from his back, firing a series of blasts from his weapon behind him dangerously close to Morgaine's position.

Morgaine managed to grasp an edge of hillside to break her fall some ten or twelve feet from the ledge, but Markam followed with another volley of blasts from his weapon, managing to fling a metal disc that suddenly brought a bolt of electricity down not five feet from her. The resulting thunderclap was so loud, it nearly knocked Morgaine unconscious, causing her to lose her grip and begin sliding rapidly downhill again herself.

Knowing she was still cloaked gave her little consolation, as her fall accelerated with sickening speed. Her head hit something very hard, and all went dark. A short time later she awoke, lying within ten feet of the now deceased Markam, blaster still clenched in both hands, Djune now wedged deep into his skewered back.

Apparently, she had gotten him with the well-timed throw. The fall had apparently finished the job, pushing the blade right into his heart. What there was of one, anyway.

Even as she stood, his body exploded into flames, throwing Morgaine back and slamming her body hard into a tree. Nearly losing consciousness again, another raft of lightning strikes pounded the valley and the trees all around her, stunning Morgaine and causing her to fall to the ground. Getting up, ducking, and rolling again, Morgaine fled quickly away from the blast radius.

Android Simulacrum! Damnation! How do I beat this bastard if I can't find him? All of them were fakes – the images just added the twist!

Admiration and respect were hard things for Morgaine to dole out, but she was mentally handing out buckets full of both right now. Had she not remained cloaked…and just pulled her blade out…the result would have been fatal. The android had simply done what they were designed to do – explode within five minutes of their "demise". This simply to draw in would-be attackers first.

Shaking her head, Morgaine looked about herself, still groggy. The man had to be out of subterfuge now. A gleam of metal showed that Markam himself was indeed coming to the spot. Shining shock-lance out, face enraged. None of his previous foes had lasted half as long as Morgaine had. The remaining members of her strike team and the other humans were in full retreat now. She could hear the horns and could see the signs of it from where she sat on the high hill.

Smiling and chuckling darkly to herself, Morgaine gripped her side tightly – she obviously had broken some ribs when she had crashed into that tree. The pain was sharp, but bearable.

Suddenly, the Dark Lord named Markam whipped his head almost completely around, looking in Morgaine's direction and walking right towards her. Apparently, the cloaking device had run out of energy. Morgaine was visible again.

She sighed. That hurt too.

Tossing her blaster to the ground as she stood and drawing the last *Djune* from her back – her father's special one – Morgaine readied herself. Her weapon's imbedded crystals glowed darkly – crystals from the gates merged with the metal of the weapon blade, reflecting the sunlight darkly with perhaps a touch of light inside of their own.

Another sudden sharp pain in her side made Morgaine clench her teeth. She made every effort not to groan as she waited out his approach. She wasn't sure how long she would be able to hold up her weapon, let alone fight.

Markam seemed to be in no hurry. Sensing he had finally cornered his opponent – and on top of that, a wounded one – he was taking the opportunity to gloat as he sauntered forward, shock-lance firing bursts of electricity and making crackling sounds.

Morgaine took the extra seconds she was being afforded to reach into her pouch and quaff a dose of Vitalis. The payback, should she live, for using such would be dreadful. Morgaine hoped she would have the opportunity to regret that decision.

But the pain in her side and her head eased immediately, and the fog cleared. She felt a sudden renewed energy – coupled with the constant loathing she had for all the Dark Lords. She had enough energy to at least stand straight and hold her weapon in a proper and ready position. Her father would have been proud.

Running was simply not an option in any event.

"Morgaine…'the Destroyer'. Or perhaps 'The White Falcon', as the humans call you," Markam announced quietly, stopping ten or so feet from the wounded woman. "We call you 'the White Witch', by the way. You have proven a very difficult opponent indeed, cousin. Running you to ground has taken more time than all the rest of your kin and 'Strike Force' combined! That trick with the Box of Discordance - impressive."

He studied her.

"Concede and I won't kill you," Markam declared, "I will take your … Dark Blade … and throw you through the Gate. But you will be alive. I sense we are more alike than not." The curve of his lips did nothing to enhance her confidence in his word, had she been tempted for a second to take his offer.

She was not. He also didn't know yet that the Gates would never operate again.

"We are nothing alike," Morgaine spat back. "You're the scion of your self-proclaimed 'Lord of the Void. Terror, control, and power are all you understand. The Blackness of the Void is all you know now. Yours is but a perverse desire to live forever – as if we were not meant to live long enough! The Creator's gift, yet you and your kind pervert even that! At the cost of the souls of millions."

Shaking his head and lowering his lance a bit, Markam chuckles softly, "That is simply not true; you must know that! The Gates are Power itself. They are the source of eternal life! Your…older brother refused to accept that. And he paid the price. I'd offer you the same, but I think we both know your answer."

Markam paused. "We all dominate those weaker than ourselves, Morgaine. You simply do it more charitably, but control is control. We both despise the old Order of the Oligarchs – the very group from which all this new technology emerged. Perhaps for different reasons… we both use others. But we use them, nonetheless. How many died for you…today…to put you in front of me? Here. Now….?" He gestured below them to the battlefield.

Every feature on Markam was dark. Eyes, face, skin…. only his hair remained white. It was sickening to even look at him. He looked more like a demon than a member of the Elder Race. More frightening that he could even speak, glowing with the Dark Power that colored his very skin.

But his eyes glittered the darkest, staring at her in the sunlight.

"Don't make me kill you," Markam said quietly, looking at her directly for perhaps the first time. "You can live a very long life far from here. Your former sister-in-law Terrace is Empress now, so I have been told, with her sister married off to the current king in Talim. Leave this world, marry a lesser race mortal…have children if you wish…I'm told you're nearly immortal still. Leave here and I will never hunt you down, nor let others do so from amongst the Brethren. Even Jezerah. I swear it on the Void itself."

The source of their power. And the reason the Darkness had been released upon the galaxy. But Markam worshiped it. He might even mean what he was saying. Despite this, Morgaine clenched her jaw tight to keep from howling obscenities back at him.

The former Emperor of Nelrae had died at Markam's own hand. Her brother. Her real brother.

Her sister-in-law Terrace was a widow now because of this man before her. The moment Morgaine thought of Terrace again, weeping over her brother's body, her eyes went stone cold. She took a deep, calming breath, lowered them a moment, and then raised them up again.

She was ready.

The whole time, Markam had been studying her face.

Sensing her thoughts, he said, "I know…you wish to avenge your friends and family. Your brother Tabor. But I sincerely doubt an alliance between the Hinterlands and Nelrae would have lasted beyond one generation, regardless.

Despite Terrace's sister's reputation as the "most beautiful woman in the world". I think it would be a shame for the world's most beautiful woman to remain un-bedded by that paltry little freak of a man. He prefers men, as you doubtless know. Wouldn't you agree?"

Markam leaned forward, his black eyes looking up from under his white eyebrows. Tousled white hair fell over one eye as he did so. He knew he had her. She couldn't win at her best. He just wanted to hear it from her.

"I'm offering clemency. You're beaten, Morgaine. I do this out of respect for you and those you fought for. No one gave you a chance to emerge even from that first battle decades ago. Yet here you are, having beaten creatures of legend and children of the gods! You are a woman deserving of a statue. A happy ending. Don't ruin it by trying to defeat me now. You can barely hold your Djune upright."

Just a little closer, you bastard.

Markam's lance rose suddenly. It flashed a dark red instead of its normal white electric crackle for a second, and then turned a whitish blue. "You cannot win." His voice had gone cold.

"If you're so certain, why not come a little closer?" Morgaine retorted.

Suddenly, Morgaine leaped forward, her own weapon flashing black circles in the sunlight. Their diverse weapons met with a shock of electricity, coupled with amazement on the face of Markam.

That alone was priceless.

Morgaine's weapon felt as light as a feather. Her intense training with these weapons over the decades made holding the blade almost as easy as standing upright, or walking. And the Adreno-elixir she had drunk was more than mere healing. It was a mixture of her own design, increasing strength, fortitude, focus, and constitution.

This was before the augmentation of her strength she had carefully added in with her own gear. Blow after blow and defense after defense pushed Markam to the edge of the cliff. Winding the Clock became Shadow Biter. Horse's teeth became Sand Blaster. No one beat Morgaine in a duel. No one in over five hundred years.

Clearly, Markam was an excellent fighter, and knew his weapon well. Morgaine might not be able to land a truly fatal blow. Hurt him, yes. But to win, she knew she didn't need to. She just couldn't give him time to concentrate enough to bring the power of the Dark into play.

Two more blows, barely parried. Then Morgaine's foot suddenly planted in Markam's midriff, sending him staggering to the edge of the cliff, then he fell out of sight. Knowing she only had a second, she dropped to her knees, flinging the Djune with all her might…right…THERE…!

Just as if it seemed the weapon would fly off harmlessly into the cavern, Markam flew up exactly where he had been kicked off the cliff, staff aglow with a power charge. Of course he had anti-gravity boots.

Morgaine had counted on it.

The Djune flew right by his outstretched shock-lance, striking him straight in the chest, causing his head to rock back and his arms flew aside, dropped the lance, blasting sparks all over the ground. The lance suddenly glowed white and a massive ball of white without a target literally blew up right in Markam's face.

The result was deafening, as well as blinding. Even Morgaine, nearly fifteen feet from the blast, was blown back, momentarily blinded, and deafened by the explosion.

Morgaine skidded across the dirt ground, averting her eyes. When she could see again, she looked back, and the only thing she saw was a remnant of blue-black cloak fluttering down in the breeze, burning. A thin suit of body armor lay in puddles of wrecked bone, tissue, and a huge circle of dark red blood. Almost instantly, the remains began to fade away into tiny pieces of black ash.

Rising unsteadily to her feet, Morgaine nodded to herself, hand once again to her aching side. Oh yes, she was going to pay for this day.

But the being known as Markam was no more. And another of the Dark Lords was destroyed.

She had won.

CHAPTER 8

Nathan woke to find himself bound to a wooden chair, gagged, but not overly harshly. He could move a bit and his circulation wasn't impaired. He hastily scanned the room. It appeared to be an old stone and wood cabin, probably the very place he had approached when the two men jumped him. He remembered getting struck, and his head still throbbed at the base of his skull.

I hope I don't have a concussion.

The inside of the cabin was not much different than the outside. Plain. Still no glass or framing in the windows, just some flat wooden slats which were closed, with no curtains to keep out the sunlight. It was very hot and stiflingly humid inside. A bench stood nearby. Nathan could only assume that it was a place to prepare meals; holding a few bowls, plates, silverware, and an iron kettle with a large stirring spoon sticking out on the side.

There was a fireplace directly in front of him and it was dark, being a warm summer day…apparently…which make the hackles on Nathan's neck raise.

What the hell actually happened? Where am I? How is it so warm? Did I end up in…South America? Was that why these men look and dress so oddly, not understanding English and living in a wooden cabin in the hills? How the hell did I get here?

Sitting there and trying to piece it together just made his head hurt worse. It seemed — assuming he wasn't dead, or this wasn't a very disturbing dream — that the monolith had somehow been involved. It had been — for all intents and purposes — with him when he passed out and with him when he woke up. Transporting itself and him…wherever this was.

He gave up. He needed more data. More facts. More information.

No one was in the room; he was by himself. He had to get free somehow. Clearly his captors didn't think much of him as a threat. Perhaps they had just grabbed him until they could find the local authorities.

Looking around the room again, he spotted another two chairs like his from the table placed near the fireplace. And a couple bedrolls or sleeping bags of some kind were stretched out behind them next to the darkened fireplace. Perhaps it got cold at night, and this was how these dark-clothed men stayed warm.

A sound outside and the door jerking open caused Nathan's head to turn, seeing one of the men as he entered. He had lowered his scarf and his full face was showing. Nathan tried not to scream. The man…wasn't…human. He resembled one, to be sure. But his face was dark complected and pock marked. It seemed he was missing…flesh in places, also. His eyes were a bit too large and…without white in them at all! And he seemed to move without making much of a sound. His hair was also pitch black and there was just something odd about the way he walked. His hands were also very long fingered and had nasty claw like talons instead of regular fingernails.

Nathan felt fear rise in him like a tide. Whatever his captors were, they were not human, or not normal ones, at the very least. The dark-skinned man stopped when he saw Nathan was awake, bowing slightly in acknowledgement…it appeared…or deference? Then he promptly ignored him and went over to the long counter with the plates and then began sweeping everything off rapidly, causing everything in his way to crash to the floor.

The noise was deafening.

Just then, Nathan saw why the man was clearing off the counter. Behind him, the other dark man was backing in (apparently still cowled), dragging a small deer by its ankles, two arrows sticking from its neck. They'd been out hunting evidently.

As Nathan watched (this hurt his neck a bit, as he had to crane it backwards somewhat to see properly), they gutted the animal, severed its head, and threw the entrails and inedible parts outside. Blood poured down from the counters. Hacking the deer into thin slices of meat, they piled those into two wooden bins in the corner.

When finished, they then proceeded to grab two wooden buckets Nathan hadn't noticed from behind the door and take them outside. They returned, pouring water out from the leaky buckets, washing the blood from the counters to the floor. The watery blood seeped down and mostly disappeared below the wooden slats. One of them grabbed a large cloth from a drawer and proceeded to mop up the area until one could barely tell anything had happened there.

They left with the buckets again, this time returning to put one into the kettle and using the other to refill leather water skins they had secreted within their garb. Taking the rest, they put some into nearby porcelain cups, taking drinks.

All this water had made Nathan realize he was quite thirsty himself. He didn't have to wait too long, however, as the unmasked one refilled his cup and walked quickly over to Nathan. He stopped and used his open hand to pat Nathan's mouth, shaking his head vigorously in the negative.

Got it. Nathan nodded. No talking.

The man then removed the dark scarf covering Nathan's mouth and gave him a long drink. He pulled back and kindly offered it again, slowly raising his black eyebrows away from his coal black eyes. If the being weren't being so kind, it would have scared the shit out of him.

Nathan just nodded "yes" and the man gave him another drink. This happened a couple more times, and then Nathan shook his head negatively, having had enough.

The man gingerly replaced the scarf, went behind him to check Nathan's bonds, then went to help the other man with the business of making supper. They cut strips from the meat, chopped up some vegetables they had brought from somewhere outside, and proceeded to add spices from packets within their backpacks, making some sort of stew. While one was preparing the pot, the other went to the bins of meat and started putting large amounts of salt on the meat on both sides.

Together, they then lit a small fire in the fireplace, and by the angle of the sunlight, coupled with the air coming in from the now open doorway… it was clearly near sunset and getting a bit chilly…the fire idea felt a lot different than it would have not too much earlier. That was probably because they were higher up in the hills than Nathan had realized. Maybe they were in the Andes? But…then what were these… "men" that looked like no human Nathan had ever seen?

Nathan began to hope it was just the Andes Mountains and not somewhere where these men were common and people with white eyes and untorn flesh like him were not.

The fire was going quickly, as these men clearly knew how to start one. Soon the stew was hanging from a metal hook over the flames, and savory smells began to fill the room. As the sun set, the men went outside and blew smoke out of some sort of pipe in large rings. They then returned, shut and latched the door, and pulled the slats down over the windows.

Outside, the wind began to blow and by nightfall it was howling. A storm was coming.

CHAPTER 9

The two *Kuthra Kai kept mostly to themselves. Often looking nervously at one another without speaking, they really had no idea what to do with this conundrum. Having faced many battles in their lives, they had both worked hard to achieve the status of "Runner" with the Black Horde. A scout often had to be the deadliest of killers, assassin quality, with dozens – if not hundreds – of enemies all about them.*

They were used in stealth, quick butchery, and sometimes to capture an enjoyable woman to use. Or two. But this day…presented a puzzle. This was simply not in their wheelhouse. It was not part of the training for the Runners, or even that of the Hands.

One of them, Kilmarin, looked back stealthily out of the corner of his eye as he helped prepare the evening meal. Deer stew – his favorite. He turned back to the work at hand. His mind wandered. On the one hand, their captive was clearly a member of the Mishraille – the Elder Race. White hair, purple eyes, white skin. These men had lived their whole lives worshiping and serving such beings. They had also gone their whole lives without ever seeing one up close.

Especially the White Ones. The "Lost Ones" as their leaders called them. Kilmarin had seen a picture of one once. They were supposed to all be dead. Even the Lost One named Morgaine – the half-sister of the greatest of all the god kings, Jezerah. Their Master.

These beings were to be honored, each one of them, even when one was opposed to the Dark Ones, or their way. Kilmarin was confused if they had simply not ever found the Dark or lost it. It was a bit confusing. They were, after all — from the Elder Race, the Builders — but this one. He just wasn't… what? Anything, really. He seemed like a normal man.

He and his partner had fortified their outpost position these past few days, as they had been ordered. Taking over some farmhouses in the northern Hinterlands of the Land of Men. Living as quietly in the outback of what the white skins called "civilization". They had shed as little blood as possible. Wiping out just a few farmhouses and one small village.

Of course, word would spread. People traveled out here occasionally. But the Kuthra Kai would be long gone by then.

Then, seemingly out of nowhere, this strangely garbed Mishraille had appeared, trying to communicate. He wore none of the Dark Armor of their god kings. Nor did he bear any weapon to speak of, let alone any artifact of legendary power, as one would expect. He and Ne'Ash had gone through his belongings three times but had only found the small box with the Voice.

The man spoke none of the Common, nor the Elder Tongue. He seemed confused, even a bit fearful, his face badly sunburnt on the right half. After tracking his path to the cabin, they found he'd been wandering at least a day. Lost, most assuredly.

He had come from beyond the White River, where they had lost his tracks in the rocks on the far side. No entourage of warriors, no weapons, speaking no known tongue. Yet he bore all the marks of the Lost Ones in his flesh.

It was beyond understanding.

Kilmarin cut some vegetables on the fine wooden countertops, then moved the large pot to the floor, finally sweeping them all into the soup with satisfying plops. He pulled some packets from his vestments and poured them carefully into the mixture. He searched the cupboards of the former owners and found a bag of salt. He added a generous helping, then walked it over to the fireplace where Ne'Ash helped him start a fire.

Kilmarin walked by the white god, staring as he did so. He shook his head as he looked away, shutting the door most of the way, shuttering the windows against the inevitable winds. Soon the god of the night sent his answer, and the cold wind of the mountains blew harder, shaking the shutters. Sitting down behind their captive, Kilmarin returned to his mind's meanderings.

Every story he had been told said that this Mishraille, once awake, should be able to shred his bonds, likely killing Kilmarin and his partner in seconds simply by wishing it so. Or simply vanishing in a flash, as the god kings were said to do.

Kilmarin had shaken for almost an hour contemplating whether there would be anything left of him to bury while backtracking the stranger's path, then again while helping Ne'Ash hunt. Ne'Ash was the more skillful hunter by far. Silent like death himself. Such skill was highly honored amongst the Kuthra Kai.

Yet…when they had returned, nothing had happened. The man-god had apparently slept like the dead for at least 10 hours, even while they had been gone. When he finally awoke in his bonds, he seemed content simply watching them ready the cabin and cook dinner. His eyes flashed in anger once, though. Kilmarin had seen it.

But when he had offered him water, he made signs to the Lost One not to speak, lest he simply speak a Word of Power and end Kilmarin's sad, insignificant little life. And yet again, the stranger had only nodded and drunk some water, clearly thankful. He was probably quite dehydrated. He had yet to piss since being captured, despite having followed a river for at least an hour, by his reckoning.

He would take him outside after dinner, before it got too cold to do so, he decided. But still…nothing. No flashes of power or even a normal attempt to escape. These Lost Ones were said to be killing machines. Lethal. Thankfully, only a handful of the Lost Ones had ever lived long enough to reach his world, to nip at the heels of his great masters.

But this one was almost…gentle. Willing to wait patiently as a captive. For something. What that might be made Kilmarin shudder at the mere thought of it. He couldn't stop tapping his left foot nervously as it was. Ne'Ash frowned at him again until he stopped.

Finally, in confusion and frustration, he and Ne'Ash had argued their way to a conclusion. Risking disobeying their very explicit and exact orders against communication – a disobedience that could result in fierce punishment… even death. They had left a note for those that followed at the furthest point back they dared: The Eye of the Dead God.

They killed a boar they'd spotted near there, then left the carcass with a knife stuck in its right eye and a note with a string tied to the hilt. Anyone from the Black Horde would recognize this for what it was: A distress call.

Kilmarin hoped that would be enough.

Ne'Ash didn't agree, but this had been their compromise. Hold the Great One until someone came who knew what to do with him. They could justify killing him, of course. But what if this honor was beyond ones of their station?

What if one of the god kings, especially their own Master, wanted to question him, or perhaps make him a slave – to build weaponry or force him to the Crystal of Knowledge? These things were not for scouts, nor anyone amongst the fighting forces of the Dark Horde. He and his companion's service would be forgotten. They would be shredded by the gods. Jezerah would eat their souls, most assuredly.

Kilmarin nodded to himself. It would have to be enough. It was right. They'd left their message.

They would wait.

CHAPTER 10

Ellie was surrounded by people. And every single one of them was focused on her. Somehow, she had become the spokesperson for this disaster. This secondary room was now considered "minimum safe distance" from the monolith – something Ellie had serious doubts about – and the more she thought about it, the more worried she became.

The room itself stood in the foyer outside the monolith room and was literally full of people, mostly press with some police and security. Ropes and tough looking cops were at all corners and entrances. Standing room only. Many people were shouting, and cameras were clicking endlessly.

Behind her, Ellie could still feel the monolith pulsing…sometimes she could even hear it crackling with energy. The barely audible hum from before had been replaced with dancing lights on the crystals imbedded within it, and a very audible thrumming. For at least the fourteenth time, Ellie took a deep breath and answered another inane question.

"No, we do not know exactly what happened or what activated it. We are pretty sure it wasn't an alien signal. Yes?" she said, pointing to another person.

This was endless. And pointless. She couldn't wait to get back behind her computer and find out what *had happened. Why had she been appointed to be the spokesperson? She didn't remember losing any bets.*

Forty minutes later, the media mass exodus was over. The museum was shut down once again, and the team of researchers – now triple the original number coupled with police and beefed-up security – was all that was left in the building. Ellie wandered back to the back corner where her computer slept next to a cold coffee mug she had never even had a chance to get a single drink from.

The others left her alone, but several glanced her way for more than a moment, trying to gauge her emotional state. She was doing the same herself. Ellie didn't know how to feel exactly. There wasn't much information. But what there was – was simply frightening.

At approximately 2:08 PM yesterday, the cameras caught Nathan – her former lover – ducking under a containment rope and hustling into the monolith room. He then entered the doorway to the glassed-in research zone, bumping into a desk near the door. Almost immediately, he pulled out what turned out to be his phone and turned on its flashlight. He swung his phone around, seemingly to get his bearings…ended up pointing it directly at the monolith…and then a monstrous flash. Then nothing.

At that exact time, the instruments recorded a massive power surge, followed by magnetic pulses off the charts of their instruments. This was all exactly one minute and thirty-eight seconds past when Nathan had entered the room.

By the time the video cameras picture could be seen again…there simply was no Nathan in the room. Or anywhere else. Not a shred of his clothing remained. Not even his phone had survived.

The implications fell somewhere between striking and horrifying. Ellie and the team with her in that little room were 99% sure Nathan had activated the artifact causing it to give off a massive power surge. Whatever it had been designed to do…it had done. Something any or all of them would have deemed impossible, had they even conceived of the idea in the first place. The power surge had been extreme, blowing out power lines and transformers yet again, frying hard drives, and even causing a small fire in the research area.

But the big question was: what happened to Nathan? Had he been vaporized, as most theorized, by the surge? Or was he instead…transported, teleported…as Ellie and a few others surmised…which would mean the monolith was in fact a warp gate of some kind. Bending time and/or space and sending him…somewhere. Or even somewhen. The frightening thing was Ellie wasn't sure which fate was worse.

Where would a gate built at least 10,000 years ago send you, exactly? That might depend upon who built it in the first place. Perhaps it went to another gate buried over a hundred feet underground…? That might be a bit unpleasant. Maybe to the spot it had been excavated from? The bottom of the ocean…? How would they ever find out in that event?

And…if it were an alien artifact, as many believed it had to be…would he still even be on earth at this point? Perhaps it had taken him to some other hidden gateway near Egypt. 'Just' across the world…or…maybe it took him somewhere…beyond.

Ellie shook her head. Too many possibilities and nowhere near enough data. She clicked for her screen to come on and entered her elaborate password by rote. Nothing happened. The password page didn't even appear. Swearing in frustration, she realized she hadn't even had time to check her computer for effects from the surge. As everyone else had by now.

"Someone get me the IT guys in here, now! I need a new power supply for my computer and probably a new mother board, too!" A few of the grad students raced to comply. She felt bad for yelling. It wasn't their fault. Ellie just hoped her hard drive wasn't destroyed, as several in the room had been. Most of those were in the front of the office, closest to the thing.

Ellie had to hope her desk in the far back had given it enough shielding to survive. Or they'd be in worse shape, if that were possible, than they were in right now. She had some information none of the others had, she was quite sure. She didn't even want to think about what would happen if the thing pulsed again. She couldn't escape the feeling that they were all in very real danger even now.

Damn you, Nathan! What the hell were you thinking? And what the fuck did you do?

Jezerah, Morgaine's half-brother, seethed where he sat. For centuries now, he had been slowly consolidating his power. He and his "brethren" stayed far from each other, lest the old animosities spark out of control. Each held roughly a third of this pathetic little world. Each was worshiped as a god, and in complete control of the region in which they lived.

Both of the other two recognized Jezerah as their de facto "leader". Slightly more powerful than either of them. But not nearly enough to defeat the two of them together.

His spies told him his former allies were as luckless in bearing children with their concubines as he. Not a single member of the Dark had ever borne a child, or had a child borne to them. Somehow that ability was lost when they'd turned from the Light.

But this was not why Jezerah burned with anger, not today.

Morgaine was alive!

His hatred for his half-sister had been there long before he took his oaths at the Crystal. When his skin had turned as black as his soul. She had always been father's favorite. She was the one who received his eternal and constant affection. The gifts, the artifacts… One would think…but no. It was simply his disdain for Jezerah – calling him "weak" to his face – that made her his favorite. Tabor had been borne to him centuries before. He had always been more like an uncle than a brother to them both.

Well…what would father think if he saw him now? Certainly, he wouldn't see all he'd accomplished. He would only spit from his pathetic holy seat and judge him for how he'd done it. Not see what he'd truly achieved.

Jezerah had always been simply the "other" child. Born later, a mix with one of the lesser races from one of his father's concubines, he had hoped at least that curse could have turned into a boon. After all, he was half human. So why could he not impregnate even ONE human woman after all these centuries? The answer was as clear as it was simple: it simply could not be done.

That didn't keep him or the other Dark Lords from continuing to try, however. The power that coursed through what remained of his veins was pure energy. The consummation of their bond with the Void and the power of the Dark provided them with endless life, boundless energy, and immense power.

The price of all that power and eternal life — apparently — was to be separated from any of the original life given them by the Creator. And now, after all his successes, somehow that bitch of a sister still survived!

He had thought her dead multiple times, the last over a century ago. In her last, rather well thought out attack with the barbarian tribes of the north back in the day. He was sure the fall she'd taken that night would kill anyone. Even her.

Perhaps…even himself, he admitted.

And now news that simply defied reason: The Arc Gate…the last one…the one from which he and his brethren had run through to escape and plan over six hundred years ago — had reopened! The last time anyone had come through it, Morgaine led over a thousand of their kind — those his brothers had deemed "the Lost" to their followers — in an attack to eradicate the Dark Brethren. These were the very last of the Elder Race and when they came, they were all ambushed and many killed. Slaughtered really. The first time he had thought his foul sister dead. But some had survived. Those that did began a war that lasted for centuries. Until only one of the pathetic Lost Ones survived — Morgaine. Always…Morgaine. And now she somehow lived again!

It was simply beyond him.

Growling and shaking his head in anger, he rose to pour himself a drink. The bourbon from these local distilleries – after centuries of his prodding and teaching – was finally worthy of him actually tasting it before swallowing it. He poured himself a tall one and enjoyed the pure burn down his throat, even as the taste lingered in his mouth.

What could cause an Arc Gate to reopen? And where had it opened from…?

These were answers he knew he needed. And fast. Likely that wench Morgaine was behind it all. Another scheme to destroy him, surely.

Jezerah threw the clear crystal glass directly into the fireplace that burned in his central office. Somehow it felt good to smash something. The fire wasn't necessary, of course. His central air heated and cooled the entire complex with power gathered from the nearby star. But it also felt good to watch things burn. He touched the communicator located behind his ear.

"Yes Master!" came the instantaneous answer on the other end.

"Gather the Hounds. Get my cruiser prepared. We have some hunting to do."

"Right away, Master. Should…I inform…?"

"No!" Jezerah cut him off. "Tell them nothing. I'm sure they all felt something – even as I did. But, like me, they will need confirmation. Their peoples and power bases lie far from here. I need any extra time my spies can buy me."

Jezerah sensed the fear on the other end. Curtaise had been a faithful dog for many years. Too bad humans lived such short lives. This one deserved to live at least a couple centuries. It was so hard to train good slaves. It was time, perhaps, to give him some of the Dark Elixir men so craved.

"You are right to ask, Curtaise," he paused, "After all, your team brought us upsetting news. But we mustn't let our rationality fail us. I will investigate this myself. If I need their help, I'll reach out."

"Yes, Master. Seyrea is waiting by your cruiser now. She anticipated your response."

Seyrea.

The woman had been an especially fun toy at one time. Now, although still attractive, she lacked the proper…hormones…to be bred. But she did still have a very sharp mind. And she could kill with the best of them. Had she been of the Elder Race, she would have gone far. She'd gone quite far as a member of the Dark Horde, even so. Far indeed.

"Good. Tell her to bring another of the Hand and another Quartermaster. We may have need of their special…skills."

"Right away." The comm closed.

Jezerah stood, grabbing another of the crystal glasses and poured himself a final drink. It would be a long night. It would be good to warm the tongue a bit first.

CHAPTER 12

Brianna awoke from a nightmare and nearly jumped out of her blankets. The images faded quickly, but the face of her dead friend lingered. Carlina had been screaming at her to run, blood running out of her nose, mouth, and eyes.

Great.

Brianna hoped it was just a dream. Not some portent or warning. At the mouth of the cave in which she had slept, the light of a new dawn had appeared, making the valley below seem like a vision of warmth and happiness. She was quite some distance further down the mountain now. Star was busily chewing some tall grass nearby where she had tethered her.

Brianna knew better than to trust the apparent peacefulness of the scenery, however. Heart still racing a bit and remembering Carlina's face in her dream, she looked around carefully for anyone; any sign of movement, scanning with special scrutiny any nearby trees before moving.

There were many more trees and vegetation this far down the mountain. And she needed to be sure. After satisfying herself that no one was about, Brianna hiked up Carlina's borrowed oversized skirt and walked towards the freezing cold water of the waterfall pool just up beyond the cave entrance.

She washed her face, drank some water, and scrubbed some soda onto her gums. Carlina had always been good about keeping supplies in the barn as well as the house. Along with the knife and blankets, a small bag of feed for her mare, water bags, and a small bag of beans had been in Star's saddle bags. Good fortune. Brianna wasn't sure of the original intent of the beans, but she was more than happy to have them. Finding berries this time of year wasn't easy.

And Brianna could eat beans all day, every day if she had to. She had grown up in these hills and no one was too good not to eat what they had in front of them.

Beans did give her gas, though. They upset her stomach, but they were a small price to pay to be alive. Already feeling the heat of the day, Brianna pulled her long, curly brown hair from her bonnet, allowing it to fall into the river. Holding her breath, she dipped her whole head into the water and scrubbed at it with the remainder of the soda in her hands. This would both make her feel better and look better. In the event she found help, she didn't want to look like a crazy woman.

Plus, her hair often took almost a day to dry, so the dampness would help keep her cool while riding her mare during the heat of the day. Fear gripped her insides again for a moment. The entire village when she had gotten there…. The images were going to be with Brianna a long time. At least she hoped so. They deserved that much, at last. That would require surviving in the present, however. Something she was determined to do.

Scrubbing at her eyes, refusing to feel the hopelessness of her situation, Brianna pulled her hair back meticulously, pinning it into the bonnet with two hair pins she had found with the provisions. She relieved herself by the pool, and then returned to her cave to eat some of the remaining beans. Grasses in this valley were lush, and Star had indulged quite a bit already – likely before she had even awakened. So, when she was finally astride the horse again, the mare was ready to move. Even excited. She probably hadn't been ridden this much in years.

Brianna let Star drink her fill up by the pool, drank one more time herself, then carefully filled and closed her water bags. They were small and only two were in the bags. So, she cherished every lukewarm drink by the end of the day. She'd been on the run for almost four days now. She didn't even know for sure where she was going. Just away from Anders and down the mountain towards the cities of Nelrae and Rondor. Somewhere she was bound to find a trail or even a road. At minimum another human being without dark skin wielding large knives.

At least when she passed gas, the gentle breeze and the mare's trotting pace would keep her from having to sit in it. Brianna chuckled despite herself. Worrying about passing gas when someone had tried to kill her – or worse – mere days ago. The mare caught the lighter mood and nickered, picking up the pace a bit.

All in all, it was a fine day for a ride. Sunlight streaming down the valley through which she rode. Rocks made them sidestep or cause them to have to jog to the side far too often. But overall, it became just a pleasant consistently downhill ride in high grass.

Hours later, stopping for water and shade at a nearby stream, Brianna noticed some smoke rising towards the southwest. Refilling her water bags, Brianna gave the mare her head to drink once again, then started off towards the smoke at a crisp gallop.

Within the hour, she was approaching a town of some size. It was a walled city, in fact, with a small keep built into the hills behind it. Elaborate tower defenses showed it to likely be those of the rebel kingdom of Rondor – hostile to the empire of Nelrae since its inception. Although Brianna herself was of neither country, she identified much more strongly with the rebel king and his men – who had denounced the corruption of the emperor and his empire over fifty years before. The most recent conflict had been about twenty-five years ago. Roughly two years after Brianna's birth.

Brianna realized she must have ridden over a hundred clicks to be this far south. Smiling to herself now that she was at least near people and hope, she began to relax just a smidgen. The sounds of hammers hitting anvils, horses trotting and people talking as she approached the gates were welcome beyond thought to her ears. Then she noticed men practicing fighting just within the gates, and the scurrying people reeked of tension.

The guardsmen paid her no notice, probably assuming she was a local country girl come into town to market, but a younger officer stepped out of the gatehouse and raised his hand to stop her. He had a small metal cap on his head with the emblem of a white horse rearing on its hind legs stamped upon it. He was tall and handsome, with dark black hair and a dark mustache.

"Woman! What is your name? Where do you come from?" He was speaking the Common tongue, which Brianna knew well enough. The hill country had its own dialect, but no one here would speak that. Sirles, her sweet husband, had taught it to her since he'd served in the guardsmen.

Brianna sat up straight in her saddle, telling the young officer with the fine dark mustache her name. She then said she had come from the Hinterlands, and his eyes, squinting in the sunlight went wide with shock.

"You…traveled all the way here…? Did you…meet with any…trouble?" he asked, eyes again narrowing.

"If, by 'trouble' you mean Dark Men chasing after me to rape and then kill me…" Brianna said blithely, "…then, yes. I had 'trouble'. This is my friend's horse, my friend's clothes, and frankly, my friend's food, blankets, and everything else. My friend didn't fare so well. She and her family were dead when I got to her farm."

"I fled to our village, but it had also already been attacked. No one survived. At that point, I just tried to elude any pursuers and found my way here. Where…is…'here', by the way?" Brianna looked around at all the people in the courtyard. The men training, the women hustling about with loads of laundry, water buckets, and grasping little children tightly to them as they moved.

The young officer stood there in shock for a several seconds, then said hastily, "Hold one moment!" almost running inside. Brianna could hear excited talk within, even with all the clanging of weapons and orders being shouted outside in the courtyard. About a minute or two later, an elderly gentleman, dressed in a much higher ranking officer's uniform and with several bars and medals attached to his person, came out, followed by the handsome lieutenant.

The man was a bit short, stocky, and had almost all white hair with a white mustache as part of a small goatee; but he carried himself with a great deal of authority, and as he approached, everyone else veered to stay out of his way.

He stopped at the watchtower landing, slightly above where Brianna sat on her mare, and fixed his gaze upon her. His light blue eyes were as sharp as nails.

"My lady…Brianna is it…? Lieutenant Delaney here tells quite an interesting tale of you. You say you were attacked by Dark Men and escaped all the way here? Yes? What town do you hail from?"

"Anders, sir," Brianna answered, being more formal as the elderly man was being. "And yes, they attacked my village. I wasn't there. I did see one or two of the Dark Men…trying to capture me near my home. I was in my farmhouse about seven clicks away from town. And…I'm a widow. I was going to fetch water that morning, but they chased me from my house as soon as I went outside. I barely escaped by jumping into the river. When I made my way to the village by floating downriver…well…everyone was already dead or gone. I had stopped at my friend's farmhouse nearby first…" her voice trailed off and her head dipped, starting to cry.

Then she suddenly looked back up into the older man's face. "She was dead, too." Tears started streaming down her face, but in the moment, Brianna didn't care much.

"I took her clothes, as mine were soaking wet from the river. I took her mare and rode the rest of the way into town, as I said. When that was clearly not going to help me, I fled for the southern hills and crossed the mountain trails to get here. I assume I'm in Rondor now…? Somewhere? I ask again, as your young officer declined to respond: Where am I?"

Looking a bit discomfited, the older man cleared his throat, "Bistern. Lady Brianna. Northernmost keep in the Kingdom of Rondor. Yes. And…my apologies. You have had a rough go. But congratulations on surviving and making it all the way here! I am Captain Brondt. This is Lieutenant Delaney, as I mentioned."

The young man with the dark eyes and mustache gave a short bow. Brianna nodded and looked back at the captain.

"It is quite…amazing that one such as yourself – please don't take this the wrong way – a young woman by herself…managed to escape the Dark Men! We had heard rumors of them having crossed the mountains, of course. Reports of traders finding villages burned. People fleeing every which way. But we hadn't seen anyone ourselves until you arrived. From the way you describe it, your home is about as far from here as any we've heard about."

"Unfortunately," the captain said, turning his head towards the men practicing with their weapons, "these men aren't preparing to fight Dark Men. Nelrae has declared war on Rondor once again. But if what you and these others are saying is happening, we have quite the dilemma on our hands. With war to the south and invaders from the north, we won't have a backside should both attack at the same time." Brondt looked distantly beyond or through her for a second before recovering himself.

Brianna sagged. Not much hope of refuge here. A fortress town near the border already preparing for war with another country. And not just any other country. The Empire.

"Come now," the captain said. "Climb down and go get a room at the inn just around the corner and get some rest. Calls itself 'the Cat's Tale'. Tell that old hag Emily that Brondt sent you, and to give you an upstairs room with a good meal. Tell her I'm paying for it! Ask for a stall for your horse, too. I will," he added, "be wanting to talk with you in the morning, however." He waved his goodbyes and turned without another word.

Brianna just nodded. Whispering a thank you that she hoped he heard, then gently booting Star into motion. At least she was safe for the time being. And a bath and a real bed sounded like a dream right now.

The Cat's Tale turned out to be a little further than "just around the corner" but Brianna found it easily enough and did as she had been instructed. Emily turned out to be a sweet woman of middling years, red hair tinged with gray, wearing a long dress worn to strict Rondorian standards (no cleavage, barely a neckline), and having a sweet, warm smile. Not anywhere close to the "hag" Brondt had indicated.

Soon, Brianna was in an upstairs room with buckets of hot water being brought by a young blond girl for her bath. Improvement and another day breathing. A groomsman had come for her horse before she'd even left the main hall.

Brianna tried to feel true relief as she slipped off her clothing and into the hot water. It didn't come. A warm meal with steaming piles of roast beef and bread with butter was waiting outside her door when she finally emerged. And a bottle of wine, opened, with a large mug next to it. A note simply read, "Sounds like you deserve this. Enjoy. – Emily".

Brianna snatched her treasure up, shut and bolted the door, and returned to the bed to eat her meal. The meat was spiced strangely but tasted wonderful and was still steaming hot. The bread was just out of the oven, too, and was her favorite: sourdough. The hard butter melted into it with ease.

And the wine…the wine was simply perfect. Brianna felt herself truly unwind for the first time since that morning nearly a week ago. Locked into her tiny room, eating the last of her bread and sipping her wine, she finally felt…safe.

For now, that would have to do.

CHAPTER 13

Morgaine knew not to ride on her tech vehicles near human villages. When her kind had started closing the Arc Gates, they had reached the conclusion that mankind should not be given any technology they didn't already possess on any world. When there had still been a 'Council', they'd decided to blend in as much as possible. Once the final gate was closed, and Morgaine and the rest were all trapped here with their Dark cousins, they'd stuck to it. As much as the war allowed, at least.

Unfortunately, after the war came, and all fell to chaos…only the inner worlds had retained any semblance of true civilization. At least from the last contact they'd had with them. With the Arc Gates down, eventually all communication went cold. No one outside this little world remembered the Elder Race any longer.

And some of these outer planets became truly…barbaric near the end. Those in this world hadn't gotten better under the thumb of their Dark Lords, either. With all their technology freely used, they appeared as gods to them. The other races on other planets had treated the Elder Race the same at one time, of course.

Morgaine still remembered the day she had ridden her black land racer through what she thought was the last Arc Gate, searching in vain up to that point for the place where the Dark Brethren had run to. The shock of finding yet another world not on any Galactic Map had been followed almost immediately with wonder at its stark beauty.

Arth was a true gem of a world. Situated so near a lazily burning yellow sun. Strong magnetic poles from the iron core capturing 98% of the harmful radiation…and the vegetation and wildlife thrived on it. How it had become erased from all galactic maps was simple enough to deduce. Jezerah and his brethren had planned their attack and subsequent escape for years on the Orbital Platform back home. They had always planned on hiding on this distant star's world. Then emerging when they were ready as if from nowhere, Dark Horde behind them.

Seeing as how it was extremely likely to have been a modified star system – erasing all but the basic records and leaving it in the database as what it was before terraforming – would have been simple. Of course, they hadn't counted on Morgaine, nor of the unifying force their attack had been to those who survived amongst the Elder Race. They'd all come. They had come once Morgaine found this world to rid the galaxy of those infected by the Dark. How little they had known then.

Arth had clouds scudding across skies with weather milder than any other planet she'd ever visited. Seasons were short and peaceful. Hot was just warm to her here. Cold was a good day on other planets she'd been on. Just as it was today.

Pulling her round, black-brimmed hat off her head and shaking her hair out, Morgaine signaled her entourage to stop. The land cruiser itself had been creeping along slowly for several clicks now.

"We will rest here. Make camp, as we're near the human city. Cloak the tech and unload the animals for riding. Captain, I'll need half of you to accompany me to the town. Edged weapons only. Hide your blasters. Ride single file. If we're attacked, follow me out. No matter where we are."

They all nodded. Her troops were elite. They already knew what she'd say and what her orders would be. There were over a dozen of them coming with her, though. And of course, her medic, butler, and erstwhile "mother hen" – Maitan.

The *Biaki* Mor were no longer, of course. What remained of their race had become meek, humble servants, until only Maitan himself remained. Morgaine casually wondered if Maitan's ancestors would kill him simply for being what he was, rather than what they had been. Probably. They had been the best warriors ever genetically engineered by her people. Relentless, yet always guided by the higher principles of the Creator.

Her Elite Corps were not the *Biaki Mor,* to be sure. But they were twenty-four of the best fighting men she could find on the planet. Honorable, sworn to protect her, and deadly killers. She'd only requested half of the team to accompany her. After all, this was a peaceful mission.

For now.

Maitan was fussing over her steed's saddle. An elaborate, silver lined black monstrosity that alone said, "I am your better." It was all part of the show, of course. Morgaine herself was quite petite. Almost diminutive. The muscles rippling from her arms and legs told a tale of hard exercise and fitness training. Her beauty was simply unavoidably good genetics.

Her long black sword – made of the same foreign metal as the Gates, and with the same dark crystals embedded in it, was buried to the hilt in a sheath set parallel to the ground to avoid injuring the horse while moving. Morgaine's "armor" was a formulation of plastics, tungsten, and steel. Weighing less than eight pounds, it could take a direct hit from a blaster, a shock lance, or a blade.

One could do little for one's neck and face, but her armor did go almost all the way from her backside to the middle of her neck. When she turned, she was able to without interference. Well. It had been made for her, after all. Lined with the same silver trimmings as her saddle, she appeared as a queen on her black horse.

Or a goddess.

She knew otherwise, and silently prayed for forgiveness from the Almighty for her arrogance. But she did need to put on the show. Her small mercenary band was fast and unbelievably tough. Especially with her weaponry added to the mix. But they were no match for a true army. Or even a full Cadre of the Dark Men.

If what Morgaine suspected was true, an ally of her brother's must have found a way to open the Gate. Or her brother himself. Either from this side or…she shuddered…another. Perhaps one of the ones she thought she'd already killed had opened it from another world. After all, Morgaine had survived despite the long odds. She had always feared they'd closed the Gates too late.

If so, that one would be bringing his armies through, as well. The final Eclipse whispered of by the Council and harboring all the Dark Prophecies would then be at hand.

Creator, help us all in that event!

Morgaine and her partial team of Elite Guards ambled their way down the mountains towards the Northern Keep of Rondor. Captain Brondt was likely still in charge there. He'd been a younger man when Morgaine had first met him. Capable, intelligent, but too eager to please and too easily settled into the safest fort in the kingdom. He could have been far more.

Still, he was a capable leader. It would take convincing him first before he'd send word to the king. Morgaine had little fear that she would fail to do that much, at least. She sighed and adjusted her leather riding pants in her saddle. It was getting hot. Staring up at the yellow sun, she found it interesting that most humans couldn't see the variances in color, nor the flares of this rather cold, dark star.

They considered it abnormally bright and had often commented in her presence how they'd go blind staring right at it too long. She had always found that amusing. Having grown up on a planet with a blue-white star – well, really a moon of a planet – it had been so much brighter looking up at that sky in her youth despite the distance variance of that star, than the brightness of this star from Arth.

Looking away, she sighed again. She was alone now. Yes, she had her guard. She had Maitan, although he was staying behind with the encampment today. But there were none like her now. All the Elder Race – the pure Elder Race, unmarred by the Dark or mixing of blood with the lesser races – all gone except her.

For the millionth time, Morgaine felt the creeping loneliness tear at her heart. Her father, her mother...her real brother Tabor here on Arth... her uncle Santone during the war...so long ago. When was the last time...But she already knew.

The last time she'd been with Santone. That day in the Council meeting. The day she'd volunteered to shut the Arc Gates. Close the doorway home for all of them. Even as the meeting place itself was being bombarded. Trap all the Dark Lords on one planet. Isolate. Destroy. Even as they were being shelled by the Dark Hordes on that world.

It had been their only hope. Shut down the gates and the Dark Power that emanated from them into their vassals. They barely knew of it, let alone understood it. But it was very, very real. Cut off their armies from their Dark Lords and they would perish. Or at least lose their connection to its power. It seemed that part had worked, at least.

"Morgaine!" Santone yelled above the shelling. "Take this," handing her back for the first time the sword-like weapon father had designed for this tragedy. The one he'd had her practice with as a young girl. Santone had carried it once the war had started. Somehow, father had known. Over a two hundred years before anything had happened.

Perhaps even longer…

"Ignite the crystals before you go through with the Corillion," he continued at a yell, "hold it high over your head and its field should extinguish the Arc Gate – overwhelming it. I'll follow you if I can. It will take some time for the Gates to close fully."

Looking up at her uncle for what turned out to be the last time, her then young eyes wide with fear. "But what…?" she began.

"We will hold the line here for as long as we can. I'll send those that remain. Our hope is that once you quell this world's Gate, their ammunition and blasters will eventually falter. Hopefully…" his voice dropped off, looking back at the screens showing the Black armada of flying fortresses firing at their very doors.

He had been about to say, "Hopefully before we are destroyed." Morgaine knew the chances of that hope. As dark as the hearts of their enemies.

A hope beyond reason.

Morgaine took the weapon. Knowing fully what it was now was terrifying. Her father had made it an exquisite work of art, even so. He'd always done things masterfully. Everything was art to father. Dark crystals gleamed with ever so dim a light. Horrifying and yet beautiful. Of the same mysterious metal that they'd found all those centuries ago.

Dark Metal from a darker master. But back then, no one had known. How could they have?

"I need you to follow me. I need more than me to go through!" Morgaine yelled.

Santone looked at her and nodded. "I'll take those of us who are left if I can. We'll go back to their home world together. Catch them by surprise."

Of course, Santone himself never made it. But he was as good as his word. Many had fled through with her.

Only to meet with another ambush.

Taking the blade and then setting it gently on the floor, Morgaine rushed to hug her uncle. He hugged her back warmly, kissing the top of her head. Another round of shelling hit the area, making talking impossible for a moment. The ceiling was beginning to crack above their heads.

"Young one, you go where no one else dares. My heart will go with you… always. Remember us."

* * *

Morgaine slipped out of her reverie as they approached the fortress town. Activity was swirling. The sounds of men training with metal weapons rang from the courtyard long before they reached Bistern's iron gates.

The watch was calling for more men before they opened those gates. Morgaine allowed a little smile to herself as she waited. Hastily having closed them at their approach, Morgaine could hear Captain Brondt's voice calling for them to be reopened. He did know her, after all. Although by now it had been a dozen or more years.

Morgaine was shocked at how much older Captain Brondt looked, although one would think she should be prepared after all her years of experiencing such things. It still amazed her how quickly these mortals…*aged.* Such a brief time to live! What was that he had he said to her…?

"Thank you for your welcome, Captain," she responded after a moment. "We are here on business, but nothing to concern your solid little fortress town. May we have leave to enter…?"

She looked him squarely in the eyes now, and she could see it all too well. Most men, well…all men…found her irresistibly attractive. When Brondt had been younger, he probably had fancied, as many had – finding her a willing subject of his affections. At least for a night.

All those years ago, she might have allowed that. Once. He had been a rather attractive and confident man, back then. But he'd unfortunately married some young porcelain doll from the south by the time she had met him. And Morgaine strictly did not disobey the Law or her own personal codes. Not ever.

Even after all these years.

Under her full scrutiny, Captain Brondt swallowed hard. "Er…yes! Of course…!" Nodding and throwing his arm towards the gate, Morgaine simply nodded. She was aware of the audience. Dozens of women inside the courtyard, clucking about Morgaine's manly outfit or the captain's behavior, most likely. At least none were openly calling her 'the White Witch'. They clearly didn't like Morgaine's effect on their men. Morgaine smiled despite herself. Her amazement at the pettiness of mortals was about all that seemed to exceed her amazement at their aging.

Riding past several such women openly staring at her, Morgaine simply tapped the top of her brimmed hat cordially. It's not their fault. Their beauty – what there was of it – would be gone in decades. When you have so little, she imagined you hung on with both hands. And your teeth if need be.

Morgaine's men surrounded her black stallion Steel as if they were in hostile territory, if not an open fight. Hands on weapons, they looked in all directions, seeking threats. Morgaine was quite sure they'd find none. But she appreciated their zeal, nonetheless.

Captain Brondt and a particularly handsome younger officer followed her inside. Walking as close as they dared to her horse, Captain Brondt tried to speak with her. She liked it this way. She wasn't about to beg to speak to the king. But if she acted like she needed nothing, the man would be much more likely to give her all she wanted.

"What…may I ask…is the occasion for your visit, Lady Morgaine?" He looked up at her as best he could, with the sun behind her had to be difficult for him.

"I have a favor to ask…and I'll of course be happy to do whatever is required to follow your laws and protocols. I know you all are such sticklers about them. I need to speak with the King." There she said it. Ask like it was just as simple as visiting a tavern or asking to go for a long walk.

She decided to look down at him then. So…*much*…older. A pity, too. He'd let himself go a bit. Large barrel belly and pants that were too tight for him. Clearly not comfortable walking. Her men nearest him eyed him as if he were a panther.

His moustache was still beautiful though. She smirked at him.

"What…? Is your king too busy for the 'Great Lady' who helped his grandfather win this kingdom's freedom from Nelrae in the first place?" she asked casually. "I would suppose such a man would eagerly welcome a guest from the Golden Age of Rondor! With a celebration, perhaps!"

"It…isn't *that* milady," Brondt began. She knew what he was about to say…'blah blah' this and 'protocol' that.

Not bothering to listen, she cut him off and snapped, "Do you – or would he – *dare* to think I would come just for a casual visit? It's an emergency, Captain! Things are happening in the world that need his direct attention. It's not up for debate. Get me that meeting! I'll be at one of the inns. Let me know when you hear something."

There went her whole plan of acting casual. Up in smoke. Her temper had not improved with the years. If anything, she supposed it had gotten worse. But it did have the desired effect.

Brondt mustered a simple, "Yes, M'Lady Morgaine! Of…*course*! Right away. It cannot hurt to ask if such a *dire* need is presented…I'll get the message sent off today." He bustled off with his lieutenant in tow as fast as they could scurry towards the guardhouse and its barracks.

Watching them go, Morgaine idly wondered if a visit from the lieutenant might ease her mind for a few hours…Hmm? One of her Guard had asked her a question. It took her a moment for it register. Ah. Of course.

"I don't care! Find the nearest inn. Get us rooms. I'll take whatever 'suite' said inn can muster. And get me that lieutenant's name. The one that was with the captain. I have a question or two for him."

Smiling the slightest of smiles, Morgaine made her way with her entourage towards the first inn she saw at the crossing street. It was always fun to play with the mortals. Of course, every game had the highest of stakes.

'Cat's Tale'. Hmph. Well. So be it.

CHAPTER 14

Brianna was sitting in the main hall having porridge with butter, honey and with some sort of smaller kind of raspberries when the hall doors burst open and in walked the strangest group of individuals she had ever seen. At least a half dozen of the most lethal men in strange black armor strode in, bristling with weapons and walking like panthers in human form. Each, in turn scanned the room like they were walking into a den of lions.

Behind these fascinating warriors came...well...the most beautiful woman Brianna had ever seen, or perhaps could even imagine. Just looking at her made Brianna feel inadequate.

Diminutive, also dressed in that same non-reflective black armor, but set off with glistening silver workings, and black leggings, the woman seemed like a queen amongst her subjects. At her back was strapped a sword, of which she could only see the hilt. The sheath and the hilt of the weapon, though, were worked with similar accents of silver, along with some sort of glistening dark crystals.

Her hair was white – pure white – curly, though, and clearly not the hair of an older woman. This goddess had perfect features, perfect body, and some sort of eye mascara that both accentuated and hinted that her purple-blue eyes knew more than any other woman. Brianna guessed she could not be much older than herself, perhaps thirty-five or so. And those *eyes! That color was surreal.*

As this mysterious woman scanned the room before entering further, another four or five of those graceful warriors – who were apparently her own personal bodyguards – came in around her, hands on weapons and eyeing everyone in the room, as the first group had. The two women's eyes met, briefly, as the white-haired woman looked over everyone already in the room. In that instant, Brianna felt both stunned at the presence of this woman, and immediately dismissed simultaneously.

Trying to quell her instant response of anger and resentment, Brianna simply dropped her own gaze and returned to eating her porridge. Whatever the woman wanted, or who she was, had nothing to do with her, anyway. And staring at her wasn't going to help her feel better in her dirty, oversized clothing, to boot.

Brianna half-listened as Emily came out herself to speak with the woman. There were a few moments of talking, a couple moments of raised voices, which didn't help Brianna understand enough to care. Moments later, some coins were changing hands from one of the woman's subordinates, and then they all proceeded upstairs. As soon as they vanished, Emily came over to her and sat down.

Brianna looked up at her, wondering why the woman had stopped her busy schedule to sit down and speak with her. She had been very kind these last two days since her own arrival. But every other time, she had simply stopped by while still standing – drying her perpetually wet hands with a towel. Keeping an inn of this size clean was a non-stop affair, Brianna had no doubt.

"Yes," began Brianna, setting her spoon down beside her bowl, "to what do I owe the pleasure? How are you today, Emily?" Emily smiled her genuinely warm smile. A wide mouth and large lips made her far more attractive than she actually was when she smiled so.

"Well, dear…. I was wondering if I might ask…a small favor?" Emily squirmed, seeming a bit nervous.

"Of course! What is it?"

"Well," Emily stopped, and her smile faded a bit, licking her lips, "I'm sure you saw our new visitors? It seems…uhm…. they need…uh…your room."

"My…room?" Brianna's heart jumped. *What could they possibly want with…?*

"Yes…It's just that uh…I'll move you to another room, of course! A room down the back hall near my own rooms. It's quite nice and even has a couch. It's just that…well…"

"It's fine, Emily. Whatever you need. You've been more than gracious to me."

"Thank you dear. It's just that this…Morgaine woman…she asserted she needs the entire floor so she can have her men around her. She's taking the back suite and her men are taking the rest of the floor, including the attic room! Which is literally the one we save for emergencies. It's got narrow ceilings and is always too hot in summer and too cold in winter. But she insisted!"

Morgaine… where have I heard that name before…? Brianna honestly couldn't remember.

"I was hoping you'd not be upset, but she made me give her your room for one of her men. But she did say she's pay for whatever room you had to be placed in instead. So…. I figured it was the least I could do to give you the largest room downstairs." Emily got up to leave.

Brianna looked up at her. "So, who is she, Emily? Who can just come into town and take over its largest inn?"

"Honestly, child. I have no idea. At least not one that makes any sense! But I think you'll feel safer down near me now, anyway. I've never seen such men in my life, either! But if Captain Brondt let her into town, I suppose that is good enough for me. But I will be asking, to be sure." With this she turned and walked off, towel back in hand, "To be *sure.*"

Emily continued muttering to herself as she walked away, drying her already dry hands on her towel as she stalked off.

So it was that Brianna, about a half an hour later, plus the few remaining belongings in her possession, including her precious saddle bags, were sitting in a new room that was indeed much larger than her previous room. A small couch sat next to the fireplace. A sink that drained out somewhere to the back and a bowl of water with a cloth sat next to her double sized bed. A small sofa table nestled next to the wall with flowers in a vase and a pitcher of water with a cup sat next to it. A beautiful quilt sat on top of the bed, and the pillows were newer, bigger, and softer.

Brianna decided she should thank the white-haired woman for moving her out of her room upstairs to this comparatively palatial room downstairs. Of course, upstairs rooms *were* safer. Anyone could just break into the one window in her room from the courtyard beyond. At one point in her life, Brianna wouldn't have cared or even had a second thought about such a thing.

Now, after the Dark Men…she couldn't help feeling quite differently about it. Staring out the window towards the barn where her mare Star still was being kept, she thought briefly of just leaving. Then, with a shock, she realized running away from this town was simple stupidity. Rubbing her arms and standing up, Brianna purposefully opened the glassed-in window. It opened at an angle, pushing the bottom out and towards the top a bit.

This was, Brianna assumed, a way to keep rain from coming in. The breeze felt wonderful and afternoon air brought calm into the room with it. She was safe. She was in a fortress town. No one was after her any more…all was good. This city had at least one hundred armed men around its walls. Surely everything would be just *fine*.

* * *

Meanwhile, upstairs, Morgaine was busily checking off her list of things she wanted to bring up to the king. It would take at least two days for actual word to reach him. Another for the response. Assuming it was a positive one, several more days to reach the capital of Rondor. Then the customary one to two days before being brought before the king himself.

Shaking her head, Morgaine knew time was of the essence. And such bureaucratic checkpoints coupled with the natural time loss these humans experienced due to their simple lack of technology was beyond irritating.

She also knew it was simply impossible to speed things up. She could not just *fly* in on her sky cruiser and land in the courtyard. Well…. she *could*…but that would be against every principle the Council had once stood for. Plus, it would simply frighten the king and likely not make for a faster audience. More likely, it would lead to a necessarily hasty exit. When was the last time she'd even flown it…?

Sighing for at least the hundredth time since arriving in this rural shack of a town, Morgaine made her decision. These humans were always wanting something for something else. She would give it to them. Smile returning to her face, Morgaine set up her mirror and began painting cosmetics on. A woman had to look her best for a king, after all.

CHAPTER 15

Treyborne was getting uncomfortable. Laying atop a peaked roof at night wasn't the best way to get comfortable, to be sure. And lying under a patch of tar and thatch was somewhere approaching intolerable.

The smaller moon Sanshe was nearly full and quite beautiful. Her older, larger sister Alonna lay mostly dark on the opposite horizon. Staring at Sanshe's brightness, he wondered how such spheres existed in the space above the sky.

Treyborne had been in Morgaine's guard for nearly a decade now. And besides the ongoing training in lethal hand-to-hand and weaponry combat, he had been educated beyond what he presumed most of the scholars of his age were, at this point. Understanding the basics of physics, astronomy, electronics, and math were not requirements of Morgaine's guard. Being a deadly fighter who excelled in physical attributes and loyalty were.

But Morgaine had seen something in him all those years ago. She had spent a great deal of her own personal time, and that of her manservant's, on one thing: developing his mind. This is what led her to discovering he had as sharp a mind as anything in his hand-to-hand arsenal. As quickly as they taught him, he picked it up. That was why, at 29, he was commander of her Elite Guard. It was also why he was stuck up here, hiding in the roof, in the unlikely event someone came to…

What was that?

A movement that partially blocked Sanshe's light caught his eye. A big owl swooping? Something large had partially blocked the light but moved in near complete silence towards the back end of the rooftop.

Moving quietly to his feet, Treyborne loosed his *Djune* from its sheath, easing it out and rolling from underneath the roofing tiles. There it was again! Crouching now on the lower side where he had hidden above Morgaine's window, he saw two men clearly slipping across the back side of the rooftop.

Thieves or burglars from a town this small might be able to move that quietly. But Treyborne supposed they would not move in pairs as these two were. Observing them as his eyes squinted against the light of the younger moon, they didn't appear to be thieves.

For one thing, they were moving like a military tandem. For another… they wore some type of cloth covering most of their faces. Only the Dark Men did so, to his knowledge. Burglars were expecting not to be seen, slipping in and stealing what they wanted, then slipping out. Treyborne could also see that one of the men, at least, had a large weapon strapped to his back. Burglars would carry a small knife, at most. Not a blade visible even in shadow strapped to his back.

Instantly on full alert, Treyborne tossed the red stick to his contingent behind him by the front door. No comms on this one. The men in the courtyard near the horses would be somewhere directly in front of him, beyond the Dark Men. No way to warn them without alerting the enemy to his presence.

He felt for his blaster, slipping the *Djune* back into the sheath at his right thigh. Stealing across the back side of the roof towards the peak, Trey made sure to keep the greater moon's dim light away from any angle which would allow the Dark Men to see him. He heard the agitated sounds of his men alerted below. They would know better than to make vocal sounds, but he heard them on the move.

Good.

Now…if they weren't trying to get directly into his Mistress' chambers… where were they going? Stealthily, Treyborne eased out his blaster and pulled the shock-lance from his back, putting one into each hand. He could still see one form on the far edge of the roof. The other Dark Man must have already slipped into a roof window on the other side or dropped into the courtyard below. The shadows were perfect to hide them on that side of the building.

Not even a torch or lantern was lit in the courtyard, except at the far side stable area. And the bonfire of the men staying outside by the horses had become embers. As he watched, the second man dropped straight down.

So. The courtyard then. Perhaps they were here simply on reconnaissance. But he considered that highly unlikely. If they knew Morgaine was here, they were after her. If not, this was beyond odd they were on this roof on this night simply to check out the fortress town.

They had a target.

Shaking his head, he made his way over to the point where they had slipped down. He could hear one of them trying to scrape his knife into a window lock to open it. The noise was unmistakable, even though he could see nothing of the men below from his vantage point. Sighing a bit, he made his decision.

Leaping down and landing like a cat, he immediately aimed his blaster and fired "one-two" as he had been trained at the dark area beneath the small window. The sharp bolt of the blaster was followed by the whip-like crack of the lance lit up and then struck home.

A cry from one and a slight movement in the dark from the electricity on the lance was all he could see. Then the closer Dark Man was upon him, striking his hand and knocking his blaster away. Rolling and pulling his *Djune*, Treyborne barely avoided the swift downward strike of the man, parrying but falling backwards onto the ground to avoid the second thrust towards his mid-section. The shock-lance was too long except to use as a parrying weapon this close, but he needed both. The Dark Man was moving like a whirlwind. And in the shadows… Treyborne did not like his chances.

He'd fought these treacherous creatures many times in his life – each one a true test. These Dark Men were both incredibly fast and incredibly deadly. He had known two of them together would likely be too much for him under these shadowy conditions.

Near completely darkness was no hindrance to a Dark Man. Whatever "the Void" did to them, it granted them abilities regular humans simply did not have. Here and now, he had put himself at a severe disadvantage.

Treyborne's plan had been simple: One, stop the Dark Men before they got into the building. Inside, many more would die, whether their goal was achieved or not. Two, take down at least one of them, and pray the sounds of fighting would draw the alerted men to the back and the guards at the stable quickly enough he wouldn't be killed.

The whirring blade and his parrying attempts while still attempting to roll away on the ground was, in a word, *difficult*. As his blade clashed and clanged against the Dark Man's thrusts and swings, he heard shouts and the sounds of rushing feet from the far side of the inn, where he'd dropped the red warning baton.

Good. He had a chance. The sound was also not lost on the Dark Man. Still pushing his blade in and around Trey's defenses, he half-turned his head. Apparently, his companion was up, but was not joining the fray.

In a moment, the Dark Man closest to him whirled and leaped impossibly far, hitting the rooftop and ran quickly out of sight. Leaping up himself and keeping his guard up, he saw no one. It seemed both assailants had taken the better part of valor and retreated. Men rushed to him from two directions. The gate burst open from the front while the barn door crashed open and men ran towards him, weapons brandished, even though some of them were nearly naked.

Smiling while retrieving his blaster and returning his weapons to their respective holsters, Treyborne raised his hands letting his team know the danger had passed. In a few minutes, he had several of them racing to the rooftops to make sure they were gone for sure and for good. Following them would be pointless. Discretion was always preferred by the Mistress.

Another minute passed, and one of his shift commanders, a tall, strapping blond from these very lands named Cam, raced inside to inform their mistress of the incident. He was one of those barely clothed. Trey chuckled to himself at the 'dressing down' he would get for that infraction.

The danger past, Trey looked up at the moons. Barely five minutes had gone by since he had noticed the men. A pretty, dark-haired young woman had lit a lamp and was cautiously peering out from the very window that the Dark Men had been trying to break into.

Curious.

He considered it doubtful in the extreme that they were after her. So… what had they been after? Surely a shot at 'the White Witch'. A way to move up in their evil ranks for harming or perhaps fatally wounding the scab on the face of their leaders. As long as she lived, their control and power were not absolute.

And countries like Rondor would still be able to thwart the tide of the Dark.

His mistress summoned him with a clearly chastened Cam returning moments later. Sighing deeply, he went to speak with her. Treyborne did still feel love for Morgaine. Lust was a thing from a time that seemed a distant life, long ago. She was the very essence of beauty. But it was her soul he loved. And the cause she fought for, his own. He would gladly die for her at any given moment.

But to visit her in her chambers in the middle of the night and likely be cut by her sharp tongue for breaking protocols; this Treyborne did not relish. Brushing the remaining thatch and tar from his dark uniform, straightening his weapons in their respective sheaths and holsters, he then quickly brushed his brown mustache with his fingers to make sure it didn't contain any foreign objects as he began to amble slowly towards the back door of the inn.

CHAPTER 16

As he entered the common room and began walking up the steps, one harried and bleary-eyed Lieutenant Delaney was quick stepping his way down. Treyborne spared a glance for the man as they passed. Lieutenant Delaney kept his own eyes down and kept walking.

Trey couldn't help but chuckle a bit and twirl his brown mustache with his right finger as he did so. Poor man.

He's going to regret this night before too long. As Treyborne himself knew all too well.

Mortal men were simply not designed to be so thoroughly and savagely pleasured, as only the fantastically beautiful Morgaine – his former lover – could accomplish. With the knowledge of a hundred whores and literally hundreds of years of practice, it must have become child's play to scorch the earth with her lovemaking.

That's what she had done to him, anyway.

Treyborne himself ruefully remembered the last time he had had the pleasure of "not sleeping" with Morgaine. Once she had lost her fancy for him…he himself had lost his fancy for all other women. How did one come down from the mountaintop to the rest of the herd? It had been nearly six years since he'd last bedded the woman. Or any other woman, for that matter.

From that time on, all other women seemed so…*ordinary*. Even the most beautiful ones.

It was like being approached in your thirties by an eighteen-year-old doe-eyed girl. She couldn't possibly be worth the time. And quite possibly might cause other long-term problems a man like himself could ill afford. Even a practiced courtesan would only be a trifle. A small candy after having eaten at the banquet table. No, he was doomed to never be with another woman.

Ah well.

Treyborne came out of his reverie standing stock still in front of Morgaine's slightly open door. Apparently Master Delaney had left in quite the hurry after being discovered by Cam not five minutes before.

Uncovered?

A soft chuckle once again escaped his throat. Life had a way of becoming more amusing these days. He pushed the door open to find his mistress already fully dressed and wrapped in a blue shawl sitting by a freshly lit fire in the fireplace.

The suite in this inn was rather nice, with deep plush red carpeting, a bench with two chairs and a tea table by the fireplace, a bedroom with a door to it, and two washstands. Not to mention an indoor outhouse. Quite modern actually. Unless one lived at one of Morgaine's compounds, that is.

As he entered, Morgaine turned her attention towards him. Her direct looks when he was her full focus could still cause his heart to move a bit. He swallowed, cleared his throat, and said, "Mistress Morgaine…"

"Oh, stop with the courtesies if you please, Trey! We've been together for nearly a decade. You know better after all these years!"

"Yes, M'…yes, Morgaine."

She narrowed her eyes. "You can't be jealous after all this time…? And," she said, turning her eyes back towards the fireplace, "he's not nearly as skilled as you were, anyway. Sit down next to me. It cranes my neck to look at you that way."

Treyborne took a seat, and as she used to do back in the day, Morgaine got up herself to pour him a drink of wine from her bottle, before refilling her own.

"What do you think of the sudden appearance of Dark Men here, Trey…?" she asked, handing him his glass as she sat down, fixing her gaze upon him before leaning back. Then her eyes glazed over a bit in thought.

Even for her, Morgaine appeared in a strange mood, and more than a little preoccupied – perhaps even troubled – by the evening's turn of events. Her hair was still frazzled from having been recently in bed. But she was still, and would always be, the most stunning creature he'd ever met. It was often hard to focus looking at her directly as he was, especially when her gaze was on him, which it was again now.

Treyborne turned to take in the fire, which was in full swing at this point.

"I'm not certain, Morgaine. It appears they were trying to break into a downstairs window for some reason. They didn't even head to your side of the building. I honestly doubt they knew you were even here…"

"Yes. Curious. Isn't it? So, what do you suppose they were after?" she asked. Morgaine's eyes were not glazed even a bit now. She was in active search mode. Another look Trey knew all too well.

Sighing, he replied, "I have no idea. There is a young woman I saw peeking out the window they were trying to enter. Perhaps…". Not finishing the sentence, as it seemed beyond trivial.

But Morgaine took up the thread immediately, for once not picking up on his hesitancy. "Yes…! Let's get the girl. Find her in the morning and bring her to me. I'll breakfast with her and find out if she knows anything. Perhaps she can at least give us a clue as to what might be going on. And ask the innkeeper – what's her name? – see if anything unusual is stored or kept anywhere near that area of the inn. They had to have had a purpose. Too much risk for anything trivial."

Treyborne noted the dismissal in her last directive, standing up and saluting before turning and exiting. Morgaine's eyes watched him go.

He had always been one of her best men. Balding a touch now, but still all muscle and quite attractive. That mustache…Morgaine remembered times where that alone had gotten her a bit…randy. It was a shame she'd grown tired of him. But it was also for the best. Continuing to sleep with the man would have ruined him for any other service to her. Experience over many lifetimes with humans had taught her that much, at least.

And she needed him to stay sharp. He was perhaps the best Elite Guard Commander she'd had in a century or more. Possibly longer.

CHAPTER 17

Several hours later Brianna was sitting at a table, staring at what could only be described as an inhuman goddess. The woman introduced to her as "Morgaine" was exquisite, with long white hair curled around her perfect face and eyes. This was the woman she'd seen coming in the day before, but the woman was still shocking. Wearing a beautiful set of clothing with silver inlays on black and gold, she appeared to be a noblewoman of great wealth. On top of that, she was wearing some type of cosmetics and eye paints that made Brianna feel extremely ordinary sitting in her presence.

"What is your business here?" The woman asked her. "Why is it you feel the need to not speak to me?"

Brianna realized she had been so mesmerized by the woman's appearance she had been talking to her for several seconds prior to her acknowledging it.

"I'm…sorry!" Brianna said. "It's just…" shaking her head, she decided to focus on the array of foods spread out before her. Boiled eggs, fattened hog bacon, several breads and cheeses covered the small round table between the women in her guest room. "It's just…overwhelming!" she finally finished. "And…I'm afraid if you're looking for a reason they were coming here, you need look no further."

This got Morgaine's attention. Cut off in the middle of buttering a flaky breakfast roll, her head cocked sideways as she asked, "And…why is that? What do the Dark Men have to do with you?"

Brianna took a deep breath, then told her story for at least the third time since entering the city. The first time was to Captain Brondt the morning following her arrival. The second was to the innkeeper, Emily at lunch yesterday. She'd made a delicious brisket, given her a special dessert, and another bottle of wine that night afterwards. "…to help you sleep," she'd said. Brianna hadn't awakened until mid-morning.

But this retelling…she somehow felt she was being dissected, each morsel or kernel of every word was being finely scrutinized before being packed carefully away. Trying not to look into Morgaine's eyes helped. They were razors.

The woman looked like a purple-eyed, white-haired eagle…dressed in black as she was, and with the way she stared at her through half-lidded, skeptical eyes.

When Brianna had finished her tale of escape and flight to the town, Morgaine resumed buttering her roll, and took a bite or two before saying another word. She seemed to be chewing her thoughts as much as the bread.

"But why track you all the way here and…try to enter your room? What could you possibly have of theirs to warrant such direct action?"

Brianna had not the slightest idea. Then, suddenly remembering something, she said, "I think I might know!"

Racing out of the room and down the stairs, one of Morgaine's eyebrows shot up in irritation. She took a few calming breaths, and grabbed one of the boiled eggs out of the green bowl in which they were set, and heavily salted one before stuffing it into her mouth.

Before she was done chewing, the girl Brianna was clomping back up the stairs at what must be nearly full speed, carrying something large in her arms. Saddlebags…? She tossed them onto the floor near her chair and got down on her knees, digging into the pouches and larger bags, apparently searching for something specific.

"Aha!" she cried, holding up the curious round, black object she'd found that first night in the caves; and then had simply forgotten about, as she still had no idea what it was, or what it could possibly be used for.

The object glowed in the firelight as she held it up in her hand. The round part was about the size of her thumb. And the clip, or whatever it was, stuck out between her fingers. It looked like a miniature black button of some kind, made of a black metal much like the armor she'd seen the Lady Morgaine wearing the day before when she'd come in. It had tiny black crystals in it, as well.

For the second time in a span of minutes, one of Morgaine's eyebrows raised up in surprise. She held out her hand to the young brown-haired woman. Brianna handed it to her without preamble.

So. She truly has no idea what it is.

The first bit of good news all morning. Morgaine would have hated to have to kill the girl. Quite beautiful, really. And young. So...*so....* young. Perhaps Treyborne...no. He was another of her victims. Sighing, Morgaine, took the *archim* from her, lightly touching the top, making sure it was switched off. Looking up at Brianna, she let out a small breath of relief.

Noticing this, Brianna asked her quietly, "What is it?"

"It's called an *archim*," Morgaine began, "and it's attuned to the Void." Morgaine stared at Brianna frankly, setting the tiny artifact on the table in front of her. "It is most often used as a short-range communicator but can also be used as a small explosive. Your would-be captors must have put it into the saddlebags thinking they were going to use it in some way. Or they were going to take the bags and you simply got to them first. Or perhaps they simply left it in the place it was stored to explode it to divert enemies...or kill them...in the event of an ambush."

"Losing it..." Morgaine finished, leaning back and looking up at her, "...would mean the offender loses his life. I have no doubt when they discovered it was missing, they redoubled their efforts to find you. Based on what you told me, you are quite lucky...or stronger than you look...to be alive."

Brianna didn't know whether to be offended or pleased with that comment. She decided to choose the latter. "Thank…thank you…?"

Morgaine nodded as if that had been her meaning all along. Perhaps it was.

"I'm afraid I must ask you to remain in our company awhile longer. Should those Dark Men – or worse, others of the Dark, return – we may need to flee and leave them to Captain Brondt and his militia. I have no desire to lose even one of my men fighting for ground I do not intend to keep. Nor to be dissuaded from my own plans."

"Why…do I have to stay with you…? You can keep the thing! I certainly don't want it."

"Because little lamb, they aren't tracking *it* now– somehow you turned it off. I can only assume when you found it the first time. Or they moved slower due to other factors. Either way, I think they were tracking *you*!" Morgaine let this sink in for a moment.

"And I hate to see the Dark Men win at anything. Especially when it comes to pretty, young girls capable of escaping their clutches in the first place. Perhaps we both can make use of this chance encounter – are you, perhaps, open to employment? It sounds like your life is basically taken from you out in the Hinterlands as it stands, regardless."

Morgaine tried to soften her tone when she saw Brianna's face fall and her eyes drop down towards her lap.

"I mean…no hurt to you in saying this plainly. You yourself told me your husband has been dead several years. The land is swarming with Dark Men, by all reports. And that leaves your farm several dozen clicks behind enemy lines. Now and likely for the foreseeable future."

Brianna looked up, her eyes becoming hard despite the tears welling up them. "What…what did you have in mind?"

CHAPTER 18

Nathan found himself alone again.

Several hours had passed and still…no one. It must be nearly noon by now. The "men in black" as he referred to them in his mind now, had not returned since leaving last night shortly after dark. They had left him locked in the back barn. The structure was sturdy and had literally zero windows. It must be vented up high above the hayloft.

It was better than being tied to a chair, but certainly not ideal. They had also left him some supplies, making sure he saw them. Dried jerky and drinking water were all he had – but again better than nothing. And eating it gave him something to do.

That, and wonder at how his iPhone had, as yet, all its power. "Power Save" was all it said on the face of it now.

And damn it if he couldn't find a way out! The barn doors were being held with something from outside. He and the animals were being treated equally. Plenty of food, water, and areas to relieve oneself. As a result, the entire barn had the faint smell of piss and the sour odor of dried dung. The horses moving about, and cows lowing was so constant, Nathan didn't even hear it anymore. The result of all this was simple to assess, however: Nathan was trapped like all the other farm animals.

So, nothing new.

Nathan winced at his predicament. He was God-knew-where in some other country (or worse) with strangely garbed black-eyed men keeping him prisoner. It was so unreal – yet he had accepted it as his reality. He could hardly do otherwise.

Nathan also was still at a complete loss as to how he had gotten here. Or even where "here" was. The one thing he *was* certain of: the Egyptian artifact – the black monolith – was a gateway or portal of some kind. And Nathan had accidentally activated it. After millennia of lying dormant hundreds of feet below ground.

Nathan entertained himself, imagining the scurrying of the researchers that must be going on in New York City right about now. He chuckled despite himself. He would give a lot of money to watch some of his former colleagues all agog trying to figure out what had happened to him.

Put Ellie at the top of that list. Serves her right. Still, she had left him that note. She wasn't pure evil, after all. And Nathan had to admit…at least he was still alive. He had that.

Plus, I have some tasty beef jerky! At least…I hope it's beef.

Chuckling again, Nathan took some out from the leathery pouches they were in, as his stomach was rumbling, tore off a piece of the dark, dried meat, bit off a piece, chewed carefully. It was so hard, he had to take his time. It was well-spiced at least. Strange spices he was unsure of. But delicious. Maybe that deer meat the other day was being prepped to become this. Well, venison is good, too. Finishing his small meal, Nathan carefully took a swig of water from one of the two small water jugs his captors had left him. He had to ration it in the event they did not return by evening.

The *men in black* had not mistreated him in any way, up to this point. They even seemed…unsure of what to do with him. They were also obviously truly baffled that he did not speak their language. Nathan idly wondered if they had mistaken him for someone else. Or simply had captured him since he had happened upon them at the wrong moment. He had to treat this like he was in danger, however. One could never be too cautious. Especially when you were already being held prisoner.

Trying to get away also ensured his living in the event they never returned. Which he deemed at least semi-likely. They clearly had not been the original owners of this farm. Where they were, Nathan did not wish to contemplate. The 'Men in Black' completely ignored the cattle in the stalls, including milking the cows, and had hunted for all their meals. It was likely good for the cows that their calves were still not weaned.

For at least the tenth time this morning, Nathan searched for a weak board or a hole where he could possibly pry an opening. And for at least the tenth time, he found nothing. This barn had been built of stone and large, thick planks.

Shaking his head, he laid back down on the haystack he had piled for himself, with a blanket beneath it. He was beginning to stink, as he'd not showered in days. But it wasn't much worse than the overall smell of the entire barn, anyway.

In a few minutes, he was fast asleep.

A sharp sound startled Nathan from his slumber, and he jolted upright, sitting up on his hay bed. It was getting dark out…or very cloudy…?

Either way, I've been asleep for quite a while.

Shaking himself, he stood up and stretched. There were sounds of activity outside. Apparently, his captors had finally returned. The rolling sound of thunder outside resolved one question at least. The darkness outside was an impending storm.

It was a relief, in a way, to know he hadn't slept on a haystack for six to seven hours, despite not sleeping well the night before. It was, after all, rather stuffy in the barn. Clanging sounds outside the barn doors indicated some chains were being removed.

The barn doors opened and one of his captors entered…no! It wasn't one of them. It was another man in black, to be sure. But this one was unusually tall, and wielding a dark scimitar-like weapon, approaching Nathan like he was a tiger, or something else incredibly dangerous. His scarf was covering a black mustache, and this one's eyes were beyond totally black. They glowed in the dark barn. His eyes alone were unnerving, nasty black weapon notwithstanding.

Immediately raising his hands, Nathan said, "I'm unarmed! It's just me…my…name is Nathan!" He backed off a few steps as the new man in black started shouting at him and waving his weapon.

This could be bad.

Nathan looked for options. A few years of karate wouldn't help him much against such a long, edged weapon. Sighing, he kept his hands up and got onto his knees. "I'm…unarmed…. like I said." Lowering his head – hoping this wasn't a fatal mistake – he raised his eyes at the man.

His eyes literally had no white in them at all and seemed to suck light into them, causing an inverse glow.

Approaching Nathan like a cat, crouching and waving his weapon, suddenly a swift crack against his skull and the lights went out.

* * *

Pain struck Nathan like a knife in his temple as he awoke. Reaching for his head, he realized his hands were tied behind his back again. This time, however, his hands were bound to his legs, and he was still on his knees.

He couldn't feel his feet very well.

This is not good.

The pain was strong enough that Nathan became nauseous and almost vomited.

That's not good, either. I've got to get out to this!

Opening his eyes without raising his head, he realized he was outside near the large tree stump he'd seen upon his arrival at this place. The sun had returned, clearly after some amount of rain, as the ground was still wet and the humidity was becoming oppressive.

Hearing no noises, Nathan carefully raised up his head. His captor, along with several other men in black like him – maybe eight of them – all rose from beneath the shade of a nearby tree as he did so. His assailant, a foot or more taller than the rest, stood out easily as they all rose as one. Unlike the others, he ran ahead of them and began shouting again in that strange language. Nathan started to shake his head negatively and the nausea immediately returned.

Concussion. Definitely not good. What was this one so angry about?

Scanning the others quickly, Nathan quickly realized none were the original two who had treated him with such reverence and respect. This was another band entirely. It was likely they had come from some sort of message and were perhaps simply wondering where his original captors were.

Becoming increasingly angry, the tall, glowing black-eyed one pulled a medium-sized metal rod from within his cloak somewhere. Suddenly crackling with energy, the top looked very dangerous. Pressing some sort of switch on the handle, the blue-white dancing of crackling energy rose to a thick, moving arc of electricity.

Waving the rod directly underneath Nathan's face, causing him to pull back as far as he could, the man continued his shouting tirade. The lance moved. A sudden jolt of fire and pain hit his side and Nathan cried out. The pain in his head went up by a magnitude of four and he nearly passed out again.

A few moments later the pain had reduced to just a massive throbbing pain still exponentially more than what he'd awakened with. It seemed the tall, dark man had not ceased shouting at him. Another jolt of electric heat in his other side forced Nathan to cry out and squeeze his eyes shut, trying to manage the pain. He vomited.

Starting to feel real fear for his life, Nathan shouted through pain and in frustration, "I…. don't…know *anything*! I don't know where the other men are! I don't know…who you are…! Just *stop*…! Let me go!"

Another shock to his midsection sent him to the ground…Not feeling pain any more…yet still unable to open his eyes, Nathan began to despair of living.

Shock. Pain. Jolt. Dull pain. Shouting…shock. Jolt…more shouting. Jolt. Jolt. Jolt. The pain and the cloudiness of his mind was all he could feel. His eyes still squeezed shut, Nathan began blacking out again.

Then something…*shifted*. Perhaps it was delirium brought on by all the shocks, but it seemed… in the darkness and agony and near unconsciousness…that he'd felt the same as when he'd been transported here. He also felt a surge of energy and not a single bit of pain. In fact, it was like the jolts were energizing him now…not hurting him. Revitalizing him.

Nathan opened his eyes…and saw something he didn't expect to see.

These "men in black" were not good-looking men. Not at all. Likely the need for scarves wasn't because they were merely bad men. They didn't want their features seen. Now Nathan could see why. By this time, the tall one's scarf had fallen around his neck.

The fury with which he had beaten Nathan half to death, then shocking him non-stop must have caused the scarf to drop. In the sunlight, Nathan could see missing teeth, a half-torn lip just hanging there, and a nearly black tongue; along with dark features showing deep scars and wounds on a face that made it seem unlikely that this man should still even be counted amongst the living. His glowing black eyes and half-destroyed lower face seemed more in place on a zombie than on a living man. Nathan's floating mind wondered briefly if that wasn't closer to the truth.

At this moment however, the "zombie man" was backing away in sheer terror.

From Nathan. Nathan, who was still tied like a pig about to be barbequed.

Somehow, though, Nathan wasn't feeling pain anymore. And…he suddenly realized he could stand. His bonds, apparently charred or burnt from the jolts of electricity, fell off him like no more than tattered ribbons. Feeling his hands were free, he raised them up.

"You see…? I'm…"

The hideous black man's eyes widened in terror, but he suddenly leapt at Nathan once again, attempting to shock him directly in his face. Instinctively, Nathan jerked his head back and reached out without thinking, grasping the weapon right on its business end, keeping it from hitting his face.

Voltage coursed through his right arm. The electricity should have been painful. Like before. But all Nathan felt was invigorated. Power. Nathan eyed the man intensely from around the glare from the arcing light. The horror in the eyes of the "man in black" became even greater.

The man let go of the weapon as if shocked, backing away. And Nathan suddenly found himself holding the thing all by himself. It was time to act. Flipping it around, he pressed the button, sending a jolt of light and electricity to again form on the top. The second time, the electricity shot a jolt straight out at the man, who fell backwards, hands up…then scrambled quickly back to his feet.

Nathan thrust the weapon menacingly at his former captor. And then the leader, along with the rest of them, did something totally unexpected: They ran.

Literally without a sound or sign from any of them ordering a retreat that Nathan could hear or see, the entire group just turned and ran in the opposite direction. Down the hill and towards the river. They ran… fast, too. Like *unreal* fast. They didn't stop or even look back. Not one of them. They just ran right out of sight. Like deer bolting from a gunshot or an approaching car. An eerie cry rang out from the forest though. Like a wail from a lost animal.

Bewildered, Nathan just stood there. Looking down at the weapon in his hand, in what must be an endorphin-induced floating reality…this seemed almost too good to be true.

Nope. There it is…shock lance. Wait a minute… "shock lance"? Where did that come from?

It seemed appropriate though, somehow…so Nathan just shook his head and looked one more time in the direction those Dark Men had run.

Wait… Dark Men? No, "men in black". Yes… Nathan liked the sound of his original moniker better…where those "men in black" had run.

Gone. Didn't look like they were coming back, either.

The birds were chirping and the sun angling across the fields showed no one within sight. The humidity and sun suddenly felt like a hammer blow, however. Nathan staggered where he stood, knees buckling. He barely held himself from falling to the ground, using the shock-lance as a crutch.

Feeling his head and his side, Nathan groped felt wildly about his temple, sides, and stomach. Throwing the weapon away, he felt all around, even where the ropes had chafed him the first time he had been bound.

Not a scratch, bruise, or burn! Not even any rawness. Even my sunburn feels better. What the…?

No…headache either. Nathan realized in an instant his concussion was gone, as well. Or at least it seemed like it was. Shaking his head in confusion brought back the dizziness a little. But just a little.

Well. At least the pain is gone, if not the concussion.

Stumbling towards the house and the open front door, Nathan reached forward with his hands trying to balance himself. More dizziness. And sudden aching fatigue. Not caring much at the moment whether his captors returned or not, Nathan stumbled forward, trying to get into the house to lie down. Now. Before he fell down. He made it almost inside the doorway. before he did just that.

Blackness returned for a third time.

CHAPTER 19

Jezerah's cruiser landed back at his loading bay mid-morning that same hour. He had been flying everywhere he could think of, checking on every single clue. Now, as he returned, Curtaise stood alone, dressed in his customary black leathers, touched with gray and two silver bars, showing his rank as Jezerah's compound commander.

Curtaise had reached his forties still in fine physical shape. At well over six feet tall, he stood quite a bit closer to his master's height than that of other humans of his kind. Dark brown hair had become flecked with silver, making him the very image of the compound leader and spy marshal that he was.

Apparently, he had news.

It took years and many – *lessons* – to train most humans in what was to be shared via comms that anyone could overhear, and what must be kept to direct communication.

Curtaise had sent a signal yesterday – and one the day before – but Jezerah had chosen to wait on whatever news his spy master had considered too important to send over comms. Jezerah had wanted to make sure there was no way to use the Arc Gate from this side first and foremost. He considered nothing more important than that.

Had that been the case, he would immediately fortify the position, and begin sending scouts to see what worlds had been reopened to him. Perhaps the power of the Void itself had been the reason it had opened, had that been the case.

Jezerah's lean black face twisted in a grimace. It had not been the case.

The Arc Gate had, in fact, been used recently. Once. But now it was as dead as he'd found it since his accursed sister had closed it nearly 600 years ago. Frankly, it was baffling. Also, from early findings…Jezerah had determined that his sister, for all her failings, had not caused this event to happen. Whatever it was, *however* it was that it had happened, it wasn't because of anything she could have done of this side of the Arc Gate. Jezerah had spent almost two full days trying to determine what that event had been, and if he could somehow repeat it. But there had been no sign of Morgaine. Had she used it, she'd have done something else. Perhaps try to move the Arc Gate itself. Someone came through, though.

From somewhere else.

Again, every answer turned into a "no". No idea what had sparked the event – but no idea on how it was that this particular Arc Gate had suddenly been brought back to life whatsoever. Even for a moment. Morgaine's closing of it seemed to take hold again immediately thereafter.

Whatever Gate had been the *origin* point – that Gate, Jezerah knew, likely was still ablaze with power. Biting his lip in frustration, he willed himself to outward calm, walking out serenely where his spy master awaited him. The engineers would continue to monitor the Arc Gate and report their findings soon enough. The Black Guard hustled to stay around him, as they always did. He barely noticed them.

Curtaise bowed low, waiting for consent to rise and speak to his master.

"Yes, yes, what news do you have that couldn't go over comms this time?"

The human may have learned the lesson well. But the reason Jezerah hadn't rushed back while doing his investigative work at the Gate was simply because the man had learned the lesson a bit too well. Some news could have been shared without compromise or hurting his position with the others. One never knew for sure on each man in his employ. But some news simply wasn't worthy of that level of protection.

Rising, and completely unruffled at the slight, Curtaise said, "I believe two of our scouts have found an anomaly, Master. A white-haired, white-skinned stranger was captured by them while on their scouting mission in the Hinterlands. This stranger…according to the scouts… resembles one of the Elder Race. They…"

Jezerah held up his hand, causing Curtaise to pause.

What? Could it be…? Well, at least this news had been worthy of keeping it off comms. His brethren could not be aware, at least not yet. Unless they had spies in his midst. If so, Curtaise was certainly not one of them.

Hiding the rising excitement in his voice, he asked, "Where are they exactly? How did you find out? Did they reach out over comms themselves?"

"No, Master. They followed protocols. Their comms are still dark, in fact. They left a signal for their quartermaster at the Eye, at great personal risk to themselves. They apparently realized the significance of their find. When I didn't hear from you the first day, I sent the QM out himself to retrieve the captive and return him here. Although he also is observing scout runner protocols, I expect him back here before tomorrow."

Nodding in approval, Jezerah turned to walk back towards the entrance to his keep. "Keep me advised. As soon as they arrive, bring them to me. I want to see this 'Elder Race' anachronism, should that truly be the case, immediately upon arrival."

Curtaise sensed the dismissal and stayed where he was, bowing. "Yes Master." Only the Black Guard followed at Jezerah's heels until he had walked through the portal and was well on his way to his chambers.

An Elder Race man…though. It reeked of a trap. It would explain the portal opening, however. Well, we shall see…

Morgaine had inadvertently told him herself when they'd fought in the Barbarian Wars – that she had witnessed the death of every single one of her other kin in the second war – this was also in line with everything his spies had ever heard her speak to anyone. Plus, all the empirical evidence. No purebred Elder Race remained here; none were fighting them any longer. If they were anywhere else, they'd likely done as they had here and intermarried with the humans.

Arc Gates had been closed for hundreds of years. Long-range communications across the stars gone with the Platform. Even before the war, the Elder Race had struggled for centuries to reproduce amongst themselves.

Everything Morgaine had ever done through her actions indicated the end of the Elder Race, as well. She herself, even in utter defeat, had never even attempted to leave this world. She also was exiled here. Trapped in the outer rim, without the ships and technology to travel the former way – via warp gates in space or utilizing warp drives. Not for the first time, Jezerah wished for just one of those interstellar ships. But even he wouldn't be able to pilot one. No one had for millennia. They likely didn't even exist any longer.

Their father had died while still on the orbiting platform upon which the original Arc Gate had been built. Jezerah should know. That had been the beginning of it. The rest of the Elder Race had already fled or were living amongst the other races back then; or so he had heard. And the Elder Race army had rushed here to Arth right to their doom; following Morgaine into the waiting ambush the Dark Brethren had prepared for them. Most of those were slaughtered that day. The others died in the ensuing years of the war.

Somehow, though, amid all the losses, Morgaine had brought with her the tools to shut down the other Arc Gates. Something previously thought to be impossible.

Set up on every colonized planet and given to the ruling nation on every inhabited world, she'd taken the time to travel through them all before arriving here to fight the "last battle". Neither Jezerah nor the others of the Dark Lords had ever been able to open the Arc Gates again. With the time lag between the worlds, some of them had likely been shut down for millennia on the far side of the galaxy, by their timeline. Perhaps not even a remnant of their former status as gods on those planets even had survived.

Such a pity.

Exiled to this last lonely world as they were, the Dark Brethren had made the best of it that they could – eventually ruling nearly every inhabited area on the planet. Their destiny had been to rule them all. Over 120 worlds.

Even in defeat, his pathetic sister had managed to lock them into this prison. Living forever to rule less than one third of one percent of what he knew was his Void-given right. In effect, she had won even though she had lost every major battle they had ever fought. Morgaine deserved every misery she ever experienced. But he had to hand it to her. She had prepared for defeat before ever attempting victory.

The result: This accursed exile.

Here he was – the Darkest of the dark gods…banished to this backwater planet like a common criminal. With his *sister*. One would think that whore had sold *her* soul, as hard as she was to kill. Morgaine simply refused to die. It defied description, how infuriating that truly was.

Jezerah would wait for this quartermaster to return with his prize. Jezerah had reason again to hope to fulfill his destiny. He would check into the validity of it and then he would resume the hunt to kill his sister. Perhaps information from this 'Elder Race' being would prove fruitful. This time, he would dissect Morgaine himself, burning the pieces of her to ash. But not before he ascertained for certain she had had nothing to do with the Gate opening.

That above all else was what mattered.

CHAPTER 20

Gary sat with Jennifer at the *Chai House*. It was about half past noon, and both had left early for a lunch neither felt like eating. It had been over a week since Nathan had vanished. Ten days since that Friday afternoon.

Life sure can change in an instant.

Sitting together seemed enough. Jennifer scowled into her chai latte. Greg sat, endlessly stirring his coffee, even though he'd added cream almost ten minutes ago.

A steady rain fell outside, and it was starting to turn to snow. The door clanged open, and an older woman hustled in, clutching a small purse in one hand and her gloves in another. Gary barely noticed, even when she bumped into his chair and said, "Excuse me!" before hustling to the counter to order. Jennifer looked up at him…eyes dark.

"What do you think happened to him, Gary?" came out, almost a whisper.

Taking a deep breath, he just kept looking her back straight in the eyes, sighed deeply and shrugged. Sipping his coffee seemed appropriate to break eye contact, so he did. When he looked up again from his coffee, she was back to staring, this time out the window, presumably at the falling snow. Gary cleared his throat, causing her to turn back to him.

"We've done all we can, Jenn. Ellie and her team are working on it. They think they know what happened. They just don't know how or why. But you already know all that because you were there. What can I tell you? Nathan got zapped by that…*thing*…and…maybe is…"

"…not coming back." Jennifer said quietly.

Gary just nodded. Looking down, he said, "Look. Ellie. She's a bitch, but she's really, really, smart. If anyone can figure it out and get Nathan home – it's her. And I got to admit – Nathan – he's smarter than that little *cu*…that little girl ever was."

Jennifer smirked a bit and looked up at Gary's near faux pax.

He went on, "I wouldn't put it past Nathan to bring himself back on his own. If you can go one way through a doorway…" Now he was quoting Ellie verbatim, so he stopped himself. It was hard enough having gone to her for information in the first place.

But it was all he had.

Jennifer's tears were a daily thing these days. She'd come over to his and Nathan's apartment two of the last three nights, saying she "…just didn't want to be alone."

Gary didn't mind. Even though she just slept on the couch and was mostly as morose and silent as she was right now.

Suddenly, she sat up bolt upright, squealing something he couldn't understand. She was holding up her phone, pointing to a picture on it. Tears still streaming down her face, but now she was smiling, even starting to laugh.

"Look!!! Gary…look at this! Nathan texted this to me the day we went and saw the… thing! It's the picture he took of the monolith. *Look at it*! Remember, Ellie and her team…they couldn't figure out what Nathan's phone had to do with it. What if…? No…they would have checked that."

"If…they'd known he'd broken the rules about taking pictures. All those signs about how it interfered with their magnetic field readings…" Gary suggested.

Jennifer's enthusiasm returned, "So…it's possible…it's a shot…that somehow a lighted picture of the thing somehow pissed it off!? *Turned it on…??* What if…?"

"What if Nathan happened to have had that pic up on his phone, and somehow that alone was the trigger," Gary finished her sentence for her. It made a weird sort of sense. As much as any of this could make sense. He opened his mouth to speak, but Jenn was faster.

"We have to take this to Ellie! What if she can duplicate it? What if she can send someone or…something to find him…? What if we can help get him back?!" Even with her hair tied back and red eyes, she was something to look at. Gary tried not to get distracted.

But he shook his head.

"Hold on, Jenn! First…we don't know for sure that had anything to do with it. And…second…frankly I still don't want to trust Ellie more than I have to, period. She stabbed Nathan in the back and left him for dead, as far as I'm concerned. So, I for damned certain am not giving her *shit*. Not without checking it myself, first, at least. So, let's hash this out a bit on our own, ok? Maybe…just *maybe*…if we figure anything out, we tell her. After all, let's face it: it's a long shot."

Jennifer's smile faded. She lowered her phone and nodded. But he could tell, she was listening. He went on.

"Let's say for argument's sake, you're right. Nathan had a picture of the monolith on his phone. Unlikely…as he was staring right at the bloody thing. But ok. He's got the pic there because it just happened to be left there…and he's looking around, using his phone for a light but the pic on his phone somehow activates the real monolith to vault him somewhere else." *And not just vaporize him.*

Jennifer spoke again, quietly, "But what if it sent him underground or like…underwater…or to the moon? Or somewhere else…not safe…"

"Jenn, we have to look at this like a computer program. Possibilities are nearly infinite. Maybe…that's the activation. Maybe. And…also maybe…it does the same thing every time. Pretty big stretches already, Jenn. Sorry, but logic and linear progression are my forte. What if… Nathan was sent to the tomb that thing came from, but the next time, it takes us to the museum it was in last year in Brazil? Or just blasts us to coordinates behind the moon. Except…it was an alien spaceship that took off 10,000 years ago? What then?"

Jennifer's face fell. She hung her head. "I don't know. I just…I just…" She was crying again. Gary sighed and went over to hug her. She didn't let him go for several minutes. Finally, she did.

Gary, still on his knees at her chair spoke into the silence. "I understand, Jenn. I truly do. He's my *best friend*. I know you…like him. And it's cool. Really. But…why don't we just try a little experiment first ok? Let's see if…"

He paused.

"Hey I got it! I've got an older phone at home in a drawer. Let's put the picture on it…roll it out into that room. On a skateboard or a cart of something…assuming we can even get near it…and see what happens?! I mean…it's worth a shot, right? And if we're not touching it, and we're in the other room, it shouldn't do anything to us. Right…?"

He tried to sound convincing enough to at least convince her, if not himself. He wasn't doing a very good job on himself, he had to admit. She looked up at him. Eyes sharp, despite the puffiness. Wow, she was beautiful. Nathan was a lucky son of a bitch. Assuming he was still…no!

He was alive somewhere. He had to be! And Gary was going to punch Nathan out the minute they got him out of whatever deep shithole he'd fallen into. Maybe twice.

Jennifer sat up. "Let's do it," was all said.

Captain Brondt arrived in the morning, interrupting a perfectly peaceful breakfast, knocking loudly enough to wake the dead. Morgaine had Brianna admit him, as they'd just begun her training on being Morgaine's lady-in-waiting and maid. The girl was bright, so this was not going to be the chore it could have been.

Brondt huffed into the room, bowing briefly to Morgaine, before walking over and handing her a small curly note, about the size of a leaf on a tree.

Unrolling it, Morgaine read, *"His Majesty, the King of Rondor, will gladly welcome the Lady Morgaine and her company to court three days hence. Please advise the Court Regulator should any delays be required."* No signature.

None was necessary.

Letting it roll back up by itself, she tossed it onto the table. "Thank you, Captain. I assume with the potential hostilities; you won't be accompanying us…?" She didn't want him to, but the formality had to be offered. She knew his answer, anyway.

"No, milady. We have Dark Men in the Hinterlands and the forces of Nelrae forming at our southern border. A separate note was sent to the Duke of Mantessa warning him of the potential pincer effect on our forces and supplies. I did," his eyes lowered for a moment, "hear there was a bit of excitement here at the inn last night."

Morgaine brushed it off, "Nothing we couldn't handle, Captain. I'm not sure what the Dark Men were after, but my men chased them off. If they were after me, they sent about one thousandth of the right number of men."

Captain Brondt's eyebrows hit his forehead on that one.

Smiling, Morgaine paused, pulling a piece of meat from her tray, and adding some cheese. She took a bite first before continuing, ignoring his incredulity. "Two Dark Men might scare the locals, Captain. But each of my men have killed at least a dozen such." The captain nearly swallowed his tongue at that one.

Let him believe what he wanted.

"Nevertheless, madam…" he interrupted.

"Nevertheless, none of us knows what they were after, as my men sent them packing, Captain. Had they not had to defend civilians in the inn…including the Lady Brianna," Morgaine inclined her head slightly to her new maid.

Brondt swung his head towards the girl, a curious look in his eye. "Surely…there is something you…"

Morgaine cut him off. "I've told you all we know for certain. Which is about as much nothing as my empty glass of grape juice. If you'd prefer, I could make something up. But I'm telling you that what you likely heard is more than we know about it: Two Dark Men were found prowling on the rooftop of the inn. One tried to get into a ground floor window that just happened to be Lady Brianna's. My men showed them their teeth and their numbers likely made them scramble in retreat. The end."

She looked at him with her most practiced stare. She added an arced eyebrow after a moment. Grimacing and nodding, he bowed his way out. Brianna shut the door behind him. Giggling a bit.

Morgaine cracked a smile. "You're a sharp girl, Brianna. I like that."

"Why did you…?"

"Dismiss him so quickly? Because I simply have no time or care for his troubles. We have plenty of our own, as you shall no doubt see." Morgaine stopped for a moment, eyeing Brianna's clothing for the first time. She cared little for such things in most cases.

She clucked her tongue.

"Now, we're suddenly in a hurry, Brianna. To get there in three days, we'll have to move. Sit down with me, finish your breakfast, then go find Treyborne, immediately. Get him to take you shopping. Tell him I said to buy you whatever you need. Whatever you need, mind! I want a lady-in-waiting for the King's Court. Not a mere maid. I think you'll find working for me will require you to take on several roles."

Brianna nodded, but she was already moving to sit down and began scarfing up whatever food she could. She was still quite hungry. And shopping could be exhausting. But this sounded fun.

Morgaine took another bite, watching her before continuing, "I mean it. Buy whatever you see that you like. Get more than you need, as likely most of what you'll find in the nicest shop in this backwater town wouldn't be worn by a scullery maid in Rondor's Castle. And find someone to do your hair. We'll touch it up once we arrive. How are you with hair…?"

"I'm all right…" Brianna answered slowly, looking up from her food.

Morgaine eyed her appraisingly. "We shall see."

CHAPTER 22

The activity around the Arc Gate was impressive. Nearly seventy Dark Men and a full cadre of the Dark Knights were standing guard. If anything or anyone else came through it now, they would be ready.

Smyslin checked his readings again. Nothing.

If he hadn't been told by the Great Master himself, he'd say this gate had been dormant since its last use: the infamous attack on the High Lords centuries earlier. Which they had repelled at great loss of life amongst the Dark Race and even amongst the High Lords themselves. It was well-known that on that day, and in the battles that ensued, the High Lords had lost four of their beloved brethren.

Defending the Dark Men and their world from the Lost Ones had come at great cost. Somehow, the treacherous ones had also – he'd been taught since he was young – broken the great Arc Gates and shut the universe off from their world.

Now, it was perhaps possible they could spread the truth of their religion to the cosmos. What a glorious prospect! Smyslin looked at the scanner again and his heart sank. Surely it was a mistake. The Gate readings were the same as those recorded by Breyonis over four hundred years ago. Yet…it was impossible for the Great Master to err!

Smyslin shook his head.

How had one lone Lost One fallen through the Arc Gate, well over 500 years after the others had come, and then shut it down again? If the rumors were true, then this incredible straggler had also escaped capture, and was on the loose in the hill country. Possibly not far from this very location even now.

Shuddering, the engineer uttered a short prayer to his Master's ear. Perhaps he'd be heard. He wasn't very important, like the Warrior Class was. Until something like this came up. Then they were all wide eyes and open hands. Adjusting the red scarf about his face to cover his cheeks more properly, Smyslin looked up at the sun. It was so hot this time of year. He couldn't wait for evening, with its wind and rain.

The instrument in his hand pinged. Looking down at it, Smyslin raised a dark eyebrow. He was smaller than the warriors, with lighter skin and lighter eyes. His red scarf showed he'd been purposefully bred and taught to maintain and improve equipment and gear.

Smyslin had never even seen any fighting. Perhaps this year, he would. After all, he was well over thirty years in field service at this point, and nearly a hundred total. His son had seen fighting…he sighed again, trying to focus on his work.

The *ping* had just been a data quorum reached, apparently. Almost no change to the activity of the Arc Gate itself. Why couldn't he have been amongst the healing class? They got to see fighting all the time. Why were engineers so different?

Because I work on ships, cruisers, weapons, and armament. Any injuries we would get would be from incidental or accidental things, a sign of failure.

Failure was not taken well by the masters. The scope suddenly winked out completely, then clicked on again.

Odd.

Smyslin made a mental note to check its wiring, power source, and calibration before going to sleep. One of the Dark Knights turned and walked straight towards him. Bowing low, Smyslin awaited instruction.

"What have you found, Lead Engineer? The master wishes a report." The voice was a rasp, barely audible.

"Nothing yet, Lord K'Rinn. The scope has only begun taking any readings at all. When we first got here, the Gate showed nothing. Now, at least, I am getting some readings. Though none make sense. Please remind the Master the last time this portal was used, my grandfather's grandfather was not yet born. All I have is theoretical knowledge…"

"That is your problem! Get me information I can relay to the Master!"

Whirling, the lethal Headmaster left him. Smyslin let out an audible sigh.

Loathsome creature! How he even still walks is a mystery to me.…

Well, the Dark Knights were very good at what they did. It was said this one was cut down by Morgaine herself in the Barbarian Wars of the last century. It was also said he even wounded her before falling himself.

Her powers and abilities were fabled. The only Lost One to still survive. A black mark on the world, although she'd been defeated multiple times. She was either very tricky or not worth the effort to finish off – although news of her survival was still quite new. Of course, the Masters had known all along. She must be incredibly impotent by now, anyway…

Perhaps that was why the Great Master kept K'Rinn around. It certainly couldn't be because he could still fight like a true Dark Knight, let alone defeat anyone in his unit – as was customary. But a field general with experience was hard to come by. And this one had seen over a century of hand-to-hand combat, including multiple wars and skirmishes.

Smyslin was certain K'Rinn was the oldest living amongst the Death Watch clan. He watched him cross the open area of the camp, skirt the gate, and walk into the dark cave behind it. Those of his ilk craved the darkness. This sunlight must be horrible for him especially.

At least Smyslin didn't mind being in the outdoors. It was rather pleasant – if not a bit too hot outside this shade. A breeze blowing made the day even tolerable. Smyslin bent down and focused again on his work.

One had to be productive in society, after all.

CHAPTER 23

Treyborne was not built for this type of duty. But when the mistress calls you out – you do it. No matter no inane or how dangerous. Standing in shops for countless minutes and hours was worse by far than any torture a Dark Man could ever invent. He idly wondered if they ever caught him, if they'd just make him follow their little girls around like a dog, watching them try on clothing and buying little or nothing– endlessly.

Shaking his head, his companion coughed a bit too loudly. "Eh?"

"Sir, the Lady Brianna is leaving."

Jerking his head up, Treyborne caught just a glimpse of the girl putting on her hat as she walked out the door. He grabbed his cap off the nearby chair and hustled out of the boutique. Or whatever it was. It had a strange name and had strange items for sale. Not just clothing. But purses, ribbons…ah who really cared?

Reylarin was openly laughing as they chugged out of the store, always making sure to keep at least ten paces behind Morgaine's newest hire. He had to admit, she was quite a bit more attractive and vastly more mature than her last one.

That girl hadn't lasted a week as Morgaine's maid. She had been this little wisp of a girl, barely seventeen. The daughter of someone from some line that had served her decades ago. His mistress had tried to use her – for their sake. In the end, she simply sent her home with a note and a small bag of gold.

It was worth it to her to save face without having to live endlessly with a servant clearly not cut out for the work. Brianna seemed different though.

More…*mature.* Her eyes held mysteries. Treyborne had to admit it: she was pretty enough for even someone as jaded as he to notice.

And for him…post-Morgaine…that was saying quite a lot. He shrugged to himself as he trudged along. The girl did have a nice form. Suddenly stopping, she turned around and asked, "Would you boys like a drink? I've forgotten completely about the time! You must be thirsty!"

Treyborne didn't even bother to use words. He just pointed to his water bottles, pointedly taking one out and drinking from it. The girl had been served all sorts of treats and small glasses of this and that at the various shops. The city guard Captain had recommended several to Brianna, as Mistress Morgaine had sent her to him to ask where his wife shopped before this ever started.

The list has been very long.

Surely, they must be nearly done! Brianna, noting Treyborne's silent response, simply smiled and walked towards the storefront nearest to her. Shoes. Hadn't the woman tried on every pair in the city already?

"Ok then! According to the city clocktower, I've got another hour, then we are to leave. Why don't you rest out here on this bench…?"

Trey shook his head. "Mistress Morgaine specifically told me to keep my eyes on you. If you're changing, I'm watching the changing room. If you're in the shop, I'm in the shop. Those are my orders."

Brianna just shot her eyes up towards her eyebrows a moment, then continued into the store. "I doubt anyone is going to gut me while I'm trying on shoes in the middle of the day!" she muttered loudly enough for the deaf beggar down the block to hear.

Sighing, Treyborne opened the door and followed her in. Reylarin took the liberty of staying on the bench outside. He had no specific orders. Trey grimaced out the window at him. Reylarin doffed his cap from his pile of curly dark hair, then mock saluted. These were his men. All of them. Including Rey. But damn, that boy could be insolent! Trey smiled a fake smile at him. Turning his head, the smile fell off his face.

There would be hell to pay some day for that boy. He just had to think of something truly special first.

Inside, Brianna was being offered candies and some sort of sweet cakes. What that had to do with shoes, he had no idea. He sighed audibly. This brought a look from the shopkeeper and Brianna herself.

"It seems my escort is tiring of the day's events," she said simply, cutting the shopkeeper off in the middle of some sort of trivial story about the making of said cakes. "Perhaps we could get the shoes…?"

At least the girl had some sense of decency.

At this particular store, Brianna ended up buying three pairs of shoes; doing as she had with all the other items: sending a random shop girl to the inn with the purchase and instructions to take them to Lady Morgaine's quarters. Treyborne pulled out the money bag to pay for the shoes and the service.

Some poor fool – probably Maitan – would be having to find places on the horses for the trip back to the cruiser. No tech in front of the locals. But he always managed to squeeze his way in where he was needed. He'd been ordered to stay in camp with the rest of the Guard, of course. But he would never allow his Lady to pack her own clothing and gear.

Let alone her cosmetics.

Maitan would have his hands full. They'd be adding at least fifteen pairs of shoes, fourteen dresses, riding pants, hats, and countless other knick-knacks and items – including face paints and lip coloring – to the horse packs for half a day before they reached their actual transportation.

It was why they were able to take this long and still make the King's deadline. The King was counting on them riding the entire way on horseback or by carriage. They'd be outside the city in some remote hiding place by nightfall in the land cruiser.

Brianna squeezed Trey's arm and said, "Thank you!" as she turned to slowly walk out the door. She also listened to instruction then. Good. He didn't want to have to rush to keep up with her. Reylarin was already standing and waiting to walk behind the woman by the time he left the shop.

Pointing, he said, "I think she's heading back, sir. She said something about getting some 'real food' and being a little tipsy with all the wine."

Trey turned to look at the girl, a bit further ahead than he would like, but again not rushing as requested. But he just nodded and trotted to catch up. She could also not be so selfish as to make over a dozen people, including their mistress, wait for no apparent reason. It seemed they'd be leaving on time after all.

As they walked, Brianna was swaying a bit. The rotation of her hips in puffy women's pants and the blouse only accentuated her curves. Her long, slightly curly dark brown hair blowing in the wind only added to the woman's effusive sexuality. It came naturally to her, not forced.

Both men scanned the crowd for threats, but all Trey could see were men stopping to stare and several wives slapping their man's arm in protest. The ones that were walking alone often stood for several moments as Brianna walked by, blissfully unaware of the swirls of activity she was causing.

This time, Treyborne followed her at no more than five paces, leaving Reylarin to hold the up the rear guard. Watching Brianna walk, Trey thought he might enjoy 'holding up the rear' a bit himself. It was shocking really. Realizing one could still find any other woman attractive after Morgaine.

Maybe there was hope for him yet.

CHAPTER 24

The ambush came about four hours before reaching the intended campsite outside Rondor proper.

The land cruiser, huge and armored as it was, could still carry up to a dozen or so horses and twice that many men. Adding Brianna, Maitan, and all the extra gear, it was a little cramped. Therefore, on their final rest stop before heading to the last campsite, five of the Elite Guard took their gear and five of the horse and headed off at a gallop ahead of the cruiser leaving again.

The cruiser would catch up to them easily over time and then the men would be bringing up the rear. The route they traveled was meant to avoid as many locals as possible. Showing tech wasn't the same as sharing it, but they still didn't want to broadcast their superiority more than was necessary.

So it was that about two hours before sunset, an attack hit the land cruiser from all sides. Dark Men poured out from the forest, the banks below the river, and the hills to the northwest. They themselves had two smaller four-wheeled vehicles with blaster cannons in the back.

The cruiser had two forward cannon, one rear, and a rotating gun like those on the assault vehicles. The first blasts rocked the cruiser and adding to that, the roar of the Dark Men screaming as though they were out of their minds was a bit unnerving.

Of course, Morgaine and Trey had planned for such an event. Contingencies must be considered on any such trip into the wilds. Morgaine's cousins and half-brother had to know she'd be heading for Rondor at some point – to the one possible ally she could possibly find once the Dark Men showed their scarved faces this side of the Brightshard Mountains.

Aiming carefully from the rear gun bunker, he and Messau were firing almost as quickly as they'd been struck. Morgaine's Elite Guard were, well…*elite.*

Dark Men started dying all over the field, yet still they came. It was strange, as when one fought with them on the field normally, the twisted Dark Men rarely made a sound except those of their weapons. Today they were acting like they were facing Death himself.

It was only in the presence of Morgaine did the Dark Men cry out like this. Assaulting a god must take on some special fear or significance. Trey knew Morgaine would likely be calming Brianna about now. He'd heard Morgaine coaching her on this very possibility at the last stop.

"Damn! There's a lot of them!" Trey shouted to Messau over the roar of the guns and the blasts rocking their cruiser. The thing was a tank. Dark green and black, it was ballasted on the bottom and literally floated above the ground about two feet. No terrain stopped it. Water, like lakes and rivers, only slowed its progress.

Hills required more energy, shortening the distances one could cross if there were many of them. But they presented no real challenge. Mountains were too much for it. But those were far to the north and west. Nowhere near here.

Blasting two Dark Men's heads off just for sport, Messau yelled as a blast struck just above his head, showering him with fire and sparks.

Both men redoubled their efforts. At least a thousand of the Void scum had been sent. Whichever of the 'god-kings' had sent this cadre, he meant business. Dark Men may be very tough to kill – and easily revived – but they were not easily made. From what Treyborne had gathered, anyway.

Certain rituals and many "treatments" of the dark force elixir that turned human beings into… these *things*. Screaming as they ran, only quieting when they died, the fierce roar of the battle raged on.

A Dark Man leapt from somewhere above the vehicle and landed on the top, quickly swinging into the back gunner's trough – blade whirling and shock-lance fired up. Cursing, Trey slipped just under the swinging blade, bringing his blaster out from his hip simultaneously.

Messau was reeling backwards from his cannon himself, left hand grasping for his *Djune*. Firing several quick blasts, Trey took two direct hits on his body armor from the Dark Man's shock-lance, knocking him off his feet. And damn, it still hurt!

As their assailant crumpled, two more climbed into the back right behind him, followed by a third. The guns going offline had been their sign to push. Messau and Trey blasted, knowing that only Morgaine herself and Brianna were behind them. One was completely helpless. The other would be furious if she had to fight in this skirmish herself.

Blaster empty, Trey rolled himself back up even while parrying blades. Messau had taken one of the men out and had begun firing again to dissuade further influx of the Dark Men. He was bleeding badly from his shoulder and was firing with one hand. Trey redoubled his efforts and cut both men down – one at the leg and then a quick slash at the throat. The other he finished with a thrust through his midsection followed by decapitation.

Behind him, he heard Brianna cry out in horror or relief at that. Trey really couldn't tell and didn't much care. Grabbing a med pack off the nearby wall, he immediately opened a large bandage and put a hasty patch on Messau's shoulder, then another on his leg, which was also bleeding from a blaster hole below his armor. The man didn't even flinch, continuing to fire the cannon.

Morgaine was moving now.

Another Dark Man had slipped in quietly behind them but was dead from one of her blades before he'd even noticed. Throwing his body backwards with a small leap, he jumped back into the blaster chair and immediately rejoined the fray outside the cruiser.

Morgaine began administering to his wounds. Unaware of being injured, he spared a glance down and realized his own right leg was slashed deeply, and something was marring the vision in his right eye. Problems for later.

Two more Dark Men made it past the cannons outside the craft, but his *Djune* made short work of them. He'd kept it in his lap for just such an occasion. Morgaine's hair and scent backed away from him both times, letting him finish them before completing her own work.

The nearness of her brought back the fire within him. Rather than fighting the sensation, as he had to when at rest in her presence, he let it burn brighter – adding the testosterone to his arsenal and increasing his fury.

The shouts were lessening outside. Apparently, the five riders had reached the battle scene. They had probably raced their horses once they heard the battle and their sudden flanking maneuver had flipped the battle focus away from the cruiser somewhat. The ability of Morgaine's Elite Guard meant that a thousand of them were not enough. At least with them in the land cruiser with its tank-like armor and weaponry.

Suddenly, as one, the cries of whatever it was they did when in Morgaine's presence ceased. The remaining Dark Men on the field fled the way they'd come. Some to the hills, some down the riverbank towards the river, others to the forest. His men knew not to follow. Such retreats were almost always traps.

Scanning the horsemen to the northwest, he noted that at least one horse and one horseman were down. Another horse was off by itself, limping badly. It was bleeding from its flank and was favoring another leg on the opposite side.

Trey glanced back at his mistress, who had rejoined Brianna after administering First Aid to him.

"They're retreating, Morgaine. I need to assess the damage and losses. But we dare not do it here. I'm going to jump out and grab the men and whatever horses we can salvage and return to the cruiser. Slow it down so we can reach it without putting any more strain on the horses, please."

She merely nodded to him. Her eyes were ablaze, but she said nothing. Brianna was openly weeping. Trey noted the gory mess as he stepped over bodies to hit the hatch button.

"Keep firing as needed, Messau. If you see one Dark Man's head, I want it to be exploding before it can even scream." The man barely nodded, already sagging way back in his gunnery seat. He was in bad shape. But there was nothing for it.

Maitan finally appeared from the bottom area where they kept the horses and supplies. Looking around as he climbed up into the rear chamber, his eyebrows popped.

"Captain! You're in no condition to go out there. If I heard correctly, you'll simply fall off the cruiser and hit your head on a rock. I'll go."

"Not a chance..." Treyborne said, objecting with his hand as well. "I'm..."

"About to fall over..." Morgaine finished for him. "Go, Maitan. You know how to protect yourself. Gather the survivors from our riders. They likely took heavy casualties attacking unprotected as they did. It also saved us further losses."

She pointedly glanced over at Messau, who was clearly struggling to stay conscious, let alone man the blaster cannon.

"Go quickly!"

Nodding, the man literally leaped down the open hatchway, vanishing in an instant. Brianna gasped, startled at the sudden injection of speed and agility from the older man. Morgaine just patted her hand, knowing all too well the trauma such violence did to the soul. Especially the first time one saw it.

Within minutes, the cruiser was stopping and the entire cargo bay door below the gunnery bay and rear transport chamber was filling with the survivors. Three horses and all five men, although one was being aided in walking by two men on either side and another was being carried over the shoulder of the other man.

Two lone blaster shots outside told the tale of the other two horses. Maitan followed the last man in, blaster still glowing and smoking.

Brianna watched as Treyborne came up to them, the lone man carrying the other simply shaking his head. At least one of the Elite Guard was no more.

Treyborne shouted a curse. He then pointed out Messau to the other man. "Messau…go below decks with Mikell and let Maitan fix you up. Get some food. Drink something. I'll man these guns myself for now." Messau merely nodded and staggered to his feet. Half-walking, half-limping, he held the still bleeding patch on his thigh as he worked his way down the hatch from which Maitan had first appeared. Without a word, Maitan followed him down the hatch stairs.

In all, three men were gravely wounded, two dead. Several others nursing injuries as bad or worse than Trey's own. The other man to die had been the top gunner. An exposed position that all the men begged for the privilege of manning.

It had been Reylarin's turn today. It turned out to be his last. There would be no special prank for him, after all. Death had played it for him. Trey reported the attack results to his mistress a mere hour after the battle had started. Then he withdrew to go below decks and wait his turn for further medical assessment and aid.

Maitan was, after all, an accomplished surgeon. No one on Morgaine's staff had only one job or ability.

As Treyborne left, he spoke last to Brianna. "I'm sorry you had to witness that. At least being so new to the team. It doesn't happen every day. Just so you know. It's a rare thing that the Dark Brethren dare attack us. Usually, it's us attacking them. And we never leave any alive. But, as you can see, we're still human. At least most of us." This, with a smirk, he directed at Morgaine. It wasn't intended as rudeness and her small twitch of a smile back to him said she wasn't offended.

It was more than he'd thought he'd get. He read her mood well enough.

Brianna mumbled a thank you. Then she added, "And thank you also for fighting so hard and so bravely. You kept those men from breaking through in here...I'm sure of it."

This stopped him in his tracks, and he looked back at her, narrowing his eyes and assessing her again in full measure. This woman was harder than she looked. He merely nodded, and then turned away, taking his leave.

Brianna watched him go. That man was lethal. And he had the walk to match it. More like a lion than a man. He also was quite attractive when he wasn't killing something. Sandy brown hair and bright blue eyes. Strong build. Cute mustache.

Brianna realized she was still holding Morgaine's hand in her own, which had been offered her as soon as her new mistress had sat back down again.

Withdrawing it, she leaned back, looking directly into Morgaine's eyes. The woman was looking back towards her but wasn't seeing her. Her mind was clearly elsewhere. Morgaine was still stunning, however, even unkempt as she was from the turmoil. Sweat and someone's blood smeared on her cheeks and forehead.

She was magnificent even with rage boiling out of her every pore.

As she was even now.

CHAPTER 25

Nathan was walking by himself in the country again. It was different this time, though. The sun and humidity didn't bother him at all. He stopped to wash himself in the river, finding some sort of leaves to help scrape the mud off.

Which was a slight miscalculation, as those areas were now itching a bit. He had to chuckle at that one. He was allergic to several plants back home after all. This may not be home, but plants were plants.

Nathan had awakened hours earlier, face down in a puddle of his own spit. He had no idea how long he'd been there. But none of the men in black had returned, thankfully. It was now evening, as the sun had wheeled around the sky in the interim and was already setting.

Apparently…there was a small moon rising on the other horizon. Not the moon he was used to, either. And another one was rising behind it!

That…was news.

Not knowing how to take it, Nathan simply shelved it, as the implications were beyond any simple solution. Just no way to figure all that out right now. Find somebody normal. Find civilization. Not "men in black" marauders or their cities, if they had any. Something. Anything.

Nathan was still in wonder about what had happened with the men in black. And how. However it had happened, the sheer horror on their faces – what he could see of that, especially the zombie-like leader— made him smile, remembering it. Hopefully, whoever they were, they would stay away from him for good.

A fox ran right in front of him, startling him as it scurried through the high grass after something.

It was bigger than any fox he'd ever seen. But it was a fox. Looking up at the rising moons…Nathan shook his head. Briefly, he wondered if he were really in a coma in a hospital somewhere. If so, he decided he'd rather not know. This adventure, at least, was better than laying in a burn ward in a forced coma. And burn ward it would be – based on the electrical energy that monolith put out. If it ever focused on anything or anyone in particular…Nathan remembered there had been a bright flash before everything inverted.

Who knows?

Nathan began to whistle. Just the visceral feel of the wind, the whistling, the sunlight shining as it set. It all seemed real. Shrugging, he continued to whistle while he walked. A trail near the river. He learned as a young boy not to stray too far from water. Towns and even cities did the same.

Some activity at the corner of his eye caught Nathan's attention. Cocking his head to the side, he could make out something. A noise and some lights flashing up in the hills. Ducking low, Nathan scurried towards the nearest tree.

It was some sort of fir tree, barely large enough at this juncture to cover him. Looking back up into the hills, more flashes of light and small sounds. At this distance, it was impossible to make out, even with his vision.

At that moment, a man in black burst from the bottom of said hill, looking more like an ant than a man, but running fast in Nathan's general direction. Ducking even lower, keeping his eyes just above the grass level. This one, like all of them, was moving fast.

Looking back repeatedly, this one seemed a bit different than others he'd seen. For one thing, he wasn't bristling with weapons. For another, he wasn't completely decked in black; he wore a dark red mask instead of the usual black one and he was noticeably smaller. Finally, this one was alone. They had always come in pairs, or more, in Nathan's limited experience.

If there was anything else that seemed different – it was that this one showed an emotion outside anger. Fear, in this case. Nathan almost felt sorry for him. After all, those first two hadn't hurt him at all. After his second encounter, that seemed a little more than odd, in retrospect.

The runner in question stopped, scanning the area ahead of him for the first time. Nathan ducked below the weeds, hoping any movement caught peripherally would be presumed as wildlife.

Slowly raising his eyes again, Nathan caught the red-scarved man again in motion, racing towards the trees that proliferated by the river not two hundred yards behind him. The man was running at an angle, however, that would bring him nearly across Nathan's path.

"Shit!" Nathan ducked low again and tried to crab run towards the river, which was almost level with the field he was in currently. There was a bit of decline, however, and Nathan was going to utilize all of it. Reaching the river, he saw that it wasn't deep at all, with a natural fjord not fifty yards back up the river. Making a quick decision, he raced for the narrows, where the river turned naturally and had a lot of rock lying flat.

He hadn't gotten even to the crossing point, however, when he heard scrambling sounds behind him. Whirling, he saw the red-scarved man in black leap down into the lowered area and stop dead still when he saw Nathan.

He didn't move for a good five or ten seconds, so Nathan turned slowly, keeping his eyes firmly on the man, but moved to cross the river where he'd planned. The man made only one move: to cross his arms, while slightly tilting his head.

Just as he reached the far side, the man began to move again, carefully watching Nathan, but also looking back once or twice. Then the man bolted down the far side riverbank, moving as fast as a horse. Even on the sandy soil.

Nathan shook his head and climbed the far bank, muddying his hands and knees in doing so. Climbing up, he scrubbed the worst of it off in the grasses on top and looked back across the river. Several other black-clothed men emerged now from the bottom of the far hills. Nathan ducked down into the weeds and shimmied his way towards the taller grasses and trees. He kept his head down and kept moving.

About twenty minutes later, completely exhausted, he collapsed in the shade of what appeared to be a looming forest at the base of some much larger hills or even mountains. There was a small stream nearby, winding its way towards the larger river. Nathan washed his face, took several long drinks, and laid back down in the shade of a large maple tree.

How are there trees I recognize on a planet with two moons?

Feeling hungry, he shelved that for later, as well. Nathan searched for any of the remaining food scraps he'd been left two days ago. Nothing remained, and his stomach complained in protest.

A voice emerged from the trees. "Lost One is hungry, yes?"

Nathan leaped to his feet, hands up. He felt at his back for the electric rod and whipped it into his hands. The red-scarved man emerged, hands up, pulling his scarf down. Nathan could understand him somehow. Even though he recognized simultaneously that the man wasn't speaking English, either. His face also wasn't all scarred and nasty.

"I have food. I will share with you," he said, reaching into his side pack slowly and pulling out some of the same dried meat Nathan had just been searching for. "You…I think…you are the reason for all the commotion? I think, yes. You are the reason the Great Lords are fighting with each other. Why I am running for my life."

Nodding to himself, the man sat down where he was, both hands up as if in worship, offering the meat up in one of them. Sitting cross-legged as he was had to be uncomfortable, especially for a middle-aged man of his years. Yet this seemed easy for him. Also…he didn't have any visible weapons, nor did he have any facial damage. Except for the irrationally black skin, and mostly black eyes, he appeared almost normal.

Nathan just stood where he was. *If I can understand him…can…he understand me?*

"What's your name? How did you track me? Why did you follow me?"

The man didn't move, but he did respond, head still down, "I followed the Lost One as I was curious. I almost died just going about my business at the slumbering Gate. One moment I was reading my instruments. The next, I was being shot at with blasters, and my lord's entire cadre of Dark Knights and Dark Men were scattering – being attacked by our supposed brethren."

At this point, he looked up, eyes growing wide, then down again. "The Great Masters seem to be angry with each other. My Master took the position of guarding the Arc Gate and analyzing its recent reawakening. Apparently one of the others took offense at this. We are but pawns in the Great Game. But I will not so easily give my life. Especially when I do not know the reason."

Nathan stared at him. He walked over and snatched the meat from the man's proffered hands, quickly grabbing it and taking a bite.

He had no time to poison it, so it clearly was for his use, he reasoned. *At least we can understand each other now, although I have no idea how or why.*

Chewing around his words, Nathan asked another question, noticing the man had lowered his arms after Nathan had taken the food. "Ok. So, your name. And how did you follow me? I got the 'why' of it, at least."

"I hesitate to give the Lost One my name…but I suppose if you curse me and burn me where I sit, then that is that." The man audibly sighed and looked up. His eyes at least were closer to normal, with some white at the edges of his eyes. "My name is Smyslin. It is an old name. It means 'Trickster', but I wish to assure you I am merely an engineer who works with equipment. As you can see, I am not honored enough to wear the Black Scarf of the Warrior Class."

"I can see that, yes," Nathan scrambled with all the new information. *People are fighting over the monolith… 'recently reawakened'?*

"Why do you refer to me as 'Lost One'? Most assuredly, I am lost in this world…but you are putting particular emphasis into it."

This brought Smyslin's head up in a snap. "You are of the White Race. The Elder Race who lost their color because they betrayed the Void. The ones who betrayed and murdered several of the Great Masters. Surely, you know we refer to all of you as 'the Lost Ones'…?" The man's look of utter bewilderment said it all. He meant every word.

"I'm…fair-skinned and white-haired to be sure. Almost albino. I know it's *odd*. But…you think I'm from some race of…albinos called 'the Lost Ones'? I can assure you…"

"You are the White Clan of the Elder Race! You are Lost Ones!!" the man demanded. "We thought all but the Witch Queen were dead!! Your coming has brought great grief to the Masters! Most assuredly, if even your mere arrival has them fighting each other. You bring misery and ruin, just like the Witch! Why did you return? Did you come to torture and kill us? Those who have remained loyal to the Dark since our birth?"

This was starting to sound more like religion than objective viewpoint. For an engineer, Smyslin was clearly a true believer in whatever nonsense these 'Dark Men' operated under. And apparently, they had worker classes and warrior classes. Like the Aztecs, Mongols, or Samurai had hundreds or even thousands of years ago...*fascinating*!

If not entirely helpful.

"OK. You're right...I'm...a Lost One! You got me...but I'm not here to...*torture* you or even hurt you. If your lords are fighting because I arrived, that's their problem. You can't blame that one on me! But... uh...you said there's another one like me? A 'witch queen'...?"

The man stayed sitting in that uncomfortable way, but he responded emphatically, nodding his head up and down, "Oh yes! The dreaded *Morgaine*! Surely *you* have heard of her, my lord! Slayer of the Great Lords and thorn in their side for centuries. They have allowed her to live to test and torture the virtuous, it seems. But her very existence is a bane on all mankind! Someday, they have prophesied that she will die. The lesser lords were the only ones to die, of course. The weaker ones, as is fit and proper."

Smyslin looked up, eyes wide, "The Triumvirate defeated her. But each time they've killed her, she has reappeared somewhere else! Even recently, I'd been told my whole life she was dead until a few weeks ago. She is like a cancer or a swarm of locusts. Kill them, wipe them out wherever you find them...and then years or decades later, the bane emerges again!"

Nathan had to take that all in. "So...she's *evil*? Bad? Someone you don't want to meet?"

Smyslin nodded. "Oh yes! And so are you! You are acting kind right now, but I know. You can just think it, and I'll vanish into dust, or you'll burn me where I sit. The powers of the Lost Ones are legendary.

Equal almost to the Great Lords themselves! They stamped out your kind all over the universe. But in the last battles here on Arth...well... the witch somehow put the Arc Gates to sleep. It was assumed she had poisoned them somehow. It is said she thought she'd win, and destroy all the Dark Brethren, but they defeated her and her armies. Many, many times she came at them."

Smyslin nodded to himself, looking down once again. "But she has never won. The Lost can never win. The Dark and the Void are too powerful for them. For you," he said, raising his eyes again, defiant.

"Hey, I'm not taking sides in all this. I'm just a hapless visitor. Sent here by your...'Arc Gate'...? Or so it seems. By accident! You pronounced the world 'earth' kind of funny, too. I'll get back to that. You said something curious. She's apparently been your enemy for...hundreds of years...?"

"Oh yes."

"And...she keeps getting...*killed*...but then comes back to cause problems for your overlords?"

Smyslin nodded again, looking at him strangely.

"Hmm...so...you don't happen to know where she supposedly *lives*, now...do you?"

If ever such a person existed, she's long since fallen to dust by now. They're using her as some sort of hobgoblin or scare tactic to keep their people in line. How original.

Horror leapt onto Smyslin's face, dropping his head again. "Oh please, Great One!! I know you have not a shred of the Void left in your veins but have mercy on me! I'd rather you burned me here and now to ashes than try to find the hiding place of that horrible, cursed, foul, wretched woman!"

Then the man literally started to cry.

"OMG…man! Come on!" It was at this point Nathan decided the man truly was an engineer and not a threat. He put his lance away and walked over to him. "Stand up, at least."

Smyslin, looked up underneath his eyebrows, tears streaming down his face. The man was completely wrecked at the thought of this Morgaine.

This is almost as unreal as two moons!

Taking the man's hand, he hauled him to his feet. "I'm not going to burn you to ash – not if you do as I say, got it?" Smyslin nodded his head, blubbering a bit at this.

Nathan continued, "But I order you to take me at least to the vicinity of where you think this Morgaine lives – or lived. Help me find someone besides those of your kind…they do exist, don't they?" Smyslin could only nod, he was crying so hard. "Good. Take me somewhere close and to people who aren't all black and have pieces missing from their faces, and I'll let you go. I swear it on…"

What would an evil 'lost race' of destroyers swear on? "I swear it on my mother!" Everybody loved their mother. Even gangsters. "If I do not do as I say, she will rise and rejoin the…Void…on the side of your masters! Deal?"

The man named 'Smyslin' nodded again.

It appeared they had a deal, then. "Give me some more of your rations, too! Then you eat, we get a drink and we set off." This was going to be interesting.

CHAPTER 26

Fury bubbled like lava from Jezerah's eyes.

Mount Hyperion, with all its steam vents and lava bubbling over its open maw, could not compete today. He smashed his fists into his oak and black metal desk so hard that a monitor and some cups jumped into the air before tumbling back and falling over onto the floor.

Morgaine and her small contingent of soldiers, had actually beaten back over 1000 of his best men! Unfathomable…and now…yet another disaster was walking into his war chamber office.

Stopping and standing before him was the formerly useful K'Rinn – Head of the Dark Knights and an entire cadre of the Dark Men. Or he was. What was left of that cadre and its contingent of Knights were lying dead halfway between Rondor and the Hinterlands.

Two disasters in one day. Jezerah's eyes were glowing lava bubbling and oozing fury. K'Rinn's own black eyes showed the slightest hint of real fear. The first Jezerah had ever seen in them.

K'Rinn himself was missing his right arm below the elbow, and even his face scarf couldn't hide the fact that his lower jaw was hanging down to his throat. Jezerah swallowed, closing his eyes deliberately and lowering his head, taking deep breaths for several moments.

Must. Keep. Calm.

When he raised them again, K'Rinn hadn't moved a muscle, left hand resting on his blaster as if he expected a fight. He just might be right.

The lava bubbled over once again. Jezerah stormed around the right edge of the desk to get within an inch of K'Rinn's ruined face. The stink of blaster residue and oily blood was all over him. Having just arrived, he had done what he should – report immediately.

But what he had reported was yet another unmitigated disaster.

"Tell me again, K'Rinn…how a full cadre of *your* best men, along with my own elite fighting forces were 'surprised' by Emorion and his men…?" K'Rinn moved to speak, but Jezerah raised his hand forbidding it. "I wasn't really asking. Tell me, instead, how you managed to survive to return with barely a handful of our troops?"

This time K'Rinn stood in stony silence, not moving a muscle.

The volcano erupted. Jezerah reached for the power of the Void – the power of dark matter from a thousand million black holes –feeling its massive pull on his very being. The incredible blackness of it all threatened to overwhelm him, as it always did. Mastering it and holding its power firmly in his mind…he envisioned his fist gripping it and holding its seething mass of power like it was his own. For now, it was.

Instantly both calm as the Void itself and still bubbling with unleashed fury, Jezerah grabbed the Knight Commander's face around both ears and whispered in his ear, "You were sent to defend the Arc Gate and gather information! How dare you fail me?! Emorion could have barely learned of the Gate's reactivation…! He couldn't have sent half that many men to investigate!"

K'Rinn tried to step back, but Jezerah gripped him tightly…squeezing his head with ever increasing force. "Great Master…we…"

"…were *surprised!*" he shouted. "Yes, I know! How is it that the Dark Men of *my forces* can be 'surprised' in the first place?! By anyone…! Let alone my weaker cousin's lesser forces…? It defies logic! You were in command,

K'Rinn! I told you…to be ready for *anything*. 'Anything' would include an assault from one of my brother's forces…would it not?"

K'Rinn tried to nod but was held too tightly…he let out a tiny squeal. Barely audible. Suddenly, Jezerah felt more than heard something snap, and K'Rinn crumpled to the ground, skull askew.

Pausing a moment, he added, "I'm done with you…and you're fired," Jezerah said, letting go and just staring at his former Commander's lifeless husk. Sighing, he let go of the Void's power along with his anger. He pressed one of the many lit buttons on his desk near one of the fallen drinking cups.

"Get the cleaning crews in here, Curtaise. I've got another one for you. Bring one of the maintenance crew, also. I have some repairs on my desk that need to be made."

The leader of the assault on Morgaine had had an equally grisly exit not an hour earlier. Good leaders were so hard to find these days.

Morgaine seemed to be managing it. Perhaps he should just visit her and have some tea to discuss her methods. He chuckled darkly. The next time he had tea with his half-sister would be standing over her corpse and the tea would be mixed with her blood for good measure. Throwing himself back and slouching into his chair, Jezerah felt the anger building again. This time, however, it came more slowly…. more controlled.

Turning, he looked out the windows to the fields of troops training below. Morgaine and her little band of pets would have to wait. Rondor couldn't really help but be crushed in the campaign he'd devised with his cousins before all this had suddenly happened. The Empire of Nelrae had been goaded into war with Rondor by Emorion and his own people, and the bulk of Jezerah's men had already crossed the mountains and worked their way down the Hinterlands towards the north side of Rondor. Crushing them had seemed so easy at the time.

Since then, the Arc Gate had reawakened, and Morgaine had come back from the grave. Pushing her back in had proven as hard as it had in the past. Her reemergence only meant one thing – she at the very least knew about the portal opening as well, and that was why she had suddenly come back and was inadvertently interfering with his long-term plans.

His desire to eviscerate Morgaine would have to wait for now, though. Emorion had to be dealt with. This attack had to have been from him. K'Thul was halfway around the world, settled as he was in the Eastern lands. Order must be reestablished. Full chaos would erupt if he decided it was time to play "Eldest" again, on top of everything else.

Fools!

He didn't have to explain his actions to anyone. He would have told his 'brothers' in his own good time. At least he wanted them to think that. He was, of course, planning to try to use the Arc Gate first...see if their exile was truly over. Doubtless, Emorion would be trying the same now that he had control of it.

He would find it just as dead as it has been the last five hundred plus years. That's what his engineers had said once they had gotten to the site, at least. Jezerah had to hope his "brother" did not figure out how to reignite its fires for a few days, at least.

Either way - this attack was unwarranted – even rebellious. There had to be an answer. A quick, strong answer. Emorion's forces may be less in numbers, but they were still formidable. Most of his energy was spent influencing and controlling the Petty Kingdoms and the areas beyond the trader city of Talim. That and creating his pets. The lands had largely been divided between himself and K'Thul.

Exercising control on this planet and recruiting to the Forces of the Night were two different things. Emorion was perhaps best at the latter...if least effective at the former. One should not underestimate the gamesmanship of Emorion, however. If Emorion had felt an outright attack for control of the Arc Gate was the right move, Jezerah would have to be cautious in his response. Quick and painful, to be sure – but *careful*. Measured. Like a strong glass of whiskey.

He had much planning to do.

CHAPTER 27

The capital city of Rondor was busy. Men were marching everywhere in the courtyards and fields in and around the capital. War camps were being erected inside and outside the city gates, and siege preparations were very much underway.

Morgaine eyed all these things from her stallion's back. Steel's black coat shining in the sunny skies of mid-summer. It was hot, riding on his back as she was – with her black leather saddle and saddlebags. They'd left the cruiser with just enough guards to man the blaster cannons before riding the quarter of a day it required to reach the city proper.

From far off, across the southern plains, Morgaine could see the farmers in the fields – hastily working and likely praying for a delay in this war. So that at least some of their earlier crops could be taken in. Peasants working with hand and animal-driven tools. It still seemed unreal to her, having come from a world where machines had planted and harvested crops – and drones and other robotics had watered and protected the seeds from pests.

Inside the city, men made way for Morgaine and her nearly two dozen men with her this time. Brianna rode beside her, on a mare much smaller and easier to control than the black stallion Morgaine sat upon. She looked down at the girl, staring in awe at the city as if it were a modern wonder.

It's all about perspective, I suppose.

Out loud, Morgaine said, "It's a beautiful city, isn't it? Nestled as it is, protected on three sides. Rivers to the east and west, mountains behind and beyond the western river to the north. Doubly protected from there.

It's probably why the Dark Men are coming through the Hinterlands and crossed the western mountains so far north. Crossing here would be suicide."

Brianna looked up at her, tearing her gaze away from the white castle in the center of the city. "Oh yes! It's marvelous! Look at how the stone streets and the aqueducts from the mountains wrap the city and castle! It's truly beautiful."

Morgaine smiled down at her, nodding before turning her head forward again. It truly was a beautiful city. Just about ten thousand years of technology behind what she'd left oh so many centuries ago. "We'll find an inn and freshen up before sending notice to the court. I want you in that blue dress I saw you bought. Wear that and the white hat and gloves."

Brianna nodded, then remembered to add, "Yes, Mistress!"

Had she giggled a bit?

Well, she would take her role seriously soon enough. Despite the battle and the blood that had stained the flooring of the cruiser earlier, Brianna had brightened at the idea of visiting the "fabled city of Rondor". Morgaine was certain she was even more mesmerized at the idea of meeting the king and being in the castle itself.

Treyborne led the troupe around a corner past the city well, heading towards a familiar sign: The White Castle Inn. Mistress Armenia likely was still in charge. The woman simply didn't die. She had been old the last time Morgaine had led an entirely different cast of characters into this city. That had been nearly two decades ago. Perhaps the woman's daughter was running it now, at least.

Stopping at the front, Morgaine dismounted, allowing Treyborne to help her and Brianna towards the open doorway. People were stopping and staring now. Their entrance into the city had been muted by all the war preparation. But here, amongst the general populace, Morgaine's raven black steed, white-blond hair and small army of strangely armored men caused an understandable commotion.

One child pointed and said, "Look mama! It's the Witch Queen!"

Morgaine smirked as his mother chastened him and scurried away, looking back fearfully to see if retribution was coming for the remark. It seemed the influence of her brother and his followers was already at work once again. Even here, in the rebel kingdom. Brianna looked questioningly at her.

"It's the stories, my dear. Remember, I've lived ten of your lifetimes in this world alone. I'm the 'White Witch', the 'Witch Queen', and a host of other nefarious characters. I'm the one who steals children's souls and otherwise causes mayhem if you're a bad child!" She laughed as she walked towards the doorway.

"Now, their worst fears have arrived in the flesh. I'm sure it's at least mildly disconcerting. My brother and his 'brethren' told those stories to these people's grandfathers' grandfathers' grandfathers. The work of their Dark Cult is everywhere in the culture now. It seems to have stuck – even after I was presumed dead. Possibly ramped up a bit after that, I suspect."

Brianna nodded thoughtfully, following her in. Four of Morgaine's Elite Guard had preceded them into the inn. And sure enough, they were negotiating with Mistress Armenia herself. She must be nearly eighty by now. Shorter perhaps a bit. But still tough as nails.

"…I'm not taking only twenty silvers for an army to take over my inn!" Armenia bellowed in her cracked old woman's voice. "I won't…" she stopped, noticing Morgaine's entrance. "Ah, my Lady! Looking as beautiful as ever! Can you tell your men that this just won't do…?"

Morgaine assented to this with a nod. "Of course, you can't take so little for so much, Mistress Armenia. It seems you are as long-lived as the 'White Witch' herself! I wish to congratulate you, as well, as it appears you are as beautiful as ever."

The old woman blushed at this, and actually giggled.

"How much for our twenty men with horse, plus my maid and myself to stay here would you feel is appropriate? I also would ask for a local doctor or alchemist you recommend, as we have need of some salves. We had some…trouble…on the road in."

Armenia cleared her throat, then put her head up a little and said, "Four gold Rondorian, or five Empire. Per day." Morgaine's eyebrows rose for a moment. Then after a moment, she merely nodded pulling out her coin purse.

"Fair enough. After all, no one in the city will want to stay now that we've arrived. I'm assuming…"

"Yes, my lady. The king sent word you might be coming. I have prepared suites for you and your men. All three floors and all your men are in the same wing. As before. And I'll fetch Doctor Amakin. He's the best."

Morgaine nodded again, smiling at the woman. "Ever masterful, Mistress Armenia. Your memory serves you well. Pay the woman, Trey." She handed the entire purse over to her Captain. Nodding again, she looked to Brianna, who took her cue and went to get a key before leading Morgaine upstairs to open the door, per her instructions given on the ride into the city. Morgaine must be seen as a high lady, doing nothing for herself.

The suites had been remodeled and updated in the intervening years. Now two water closets adorned the dark wood-floored suite. Huge bay windows gave magnificent views of the city. Taking the top room on the top floor meant that two of her men would be sleeping on the roof.

But appearances must be kept.

The rest of the suite showed a maid's quarters with a bed and a washstand in a room not bigger than the smaller water closet. The larger one was the size of a large bedroom and included a bathtub. The main room took up half the upper floor, with a large fireplace, a full dining table and chairs, a small bar with wine and glasses ready. Along with a reclining couch near the fireplace and three chairs, all of which looked like they had been stolen from the palace itself.

Brianna closed the door quietly behind her mistress, turned the key in the lock, and immediately asked, "Should I change now, Mor... Mistress?"

Morgaine noted the catch and smirked at her. "You can call me by name in our chambers. Just remember if anyone can hear, it's 'M'Lady' or 'Mistress'. Yes. Change now. I'll change after you request a hot bath for me. It would seem strange to Mistress Armenia if I didn't act like the king should be waiting on me, rather than the other way around. If you wish to bathe, note that to her that you will do so after you've finished with me."

Brianna nodded, but just stood there. "What child? What is it?"

"It's just that...I have no idea what I'm doing, Morgaine! I can look and act the part with coaching. But what happens when I'm in the palace and you're somewhere else? Or worse, what if we're together and I forget something in front of others?"

"It's a concern, to be sure. But the weight and portent of the war coming and my coming to court will cover many small discrepancies. Everyone will be on edge. They're going to be a bit more antsy, I presume, at my arrival. No matter what, the best of them must wonder at all the stories of me. King Rondor himself, Creator rest his soul, had his doubts. But these descendants of his...I've never met. At least not as adults. So, they're going to be a bit afraid of me and won't be watching you much, I assure you!"

Morgaine laughed as she took off her riding clothes, stopping a moment to ask, "Now, are you going to get my bath water, or should I ask Mistress Armenia myself?"

Brianna gulped and reopened the door, racing down the hall without properly shutting it. Morgaine sighed and went to close it herself. As she did so, she saw two of her men standing in the hallway outside their respective doors guarding the hallway. They both nodded to her and resumed their statue-like poses before the door fully closed.

Top notch. Treyborne has truly made them the best of the best.

With that, Morgaine proceeded to remove all but her undergarments and walked to her personal chambers, closing the doors behind her. Brianna would let her know when the bath was ready. She needed time alone to think and pray. It was important she get some aid before attempting to reach the Arc Gate.

One or more of her brother's armies would be stationed there, picking, and prodding by now. Whoever and whatever had opened it would also be under scrutiny.

I must reach that Gate!

It was the only way to be sure it was still closed on this side, at least. For at least the hundredth time, she tried to figure out how…How had it reopened?!

Did I miss one? Did we, somehow, forget a world or a people we'd given them to? We were in such a rush to close them all. To seal the galaxy off from the danger my brother and his warped allies had become. We were so sure we'd gotten them all! Yet…we didn't even have this world on our maps anymore. There could have been another…

Shaking her head, Morgaine laid down luxuriously onto the feather bed and didn't move. Staring at the wooden beam ceiling and the light playing through the windows on the crystal candelabra hanging from it.

Prayer time would come. The Creator still lived. He who made the Light and the Dark. He was still in control. Morgaine had to believe that. After all, even 'The Void' had exploded into creation all those millennia ago. The black hole at the center of the universe had been manipulated and conquered by the Light.

It would happen again.

Not for the first time, Morgaine wished she could have seen it. As her grandfather and his generation had. The creation of all the stars and the planets…all coming into being at once! She imagined it in her mind's eye. Nebula, and galaxies…star clusters…livable planets.

Closing her eyes, trying to capture it in her mind somehow, she found herself to be more tired than she had expected from such a light ride.

A little nap is in order, perhaps. With that, Morgaine fell asleep.

CHAPTER 28

The corridors were dark — as if the power were out of the fluorescent Ca-cells and the backup coils, but there was some light leaking out a partially open doorway down the hall.

The temporal lab entrance door pushed open with a metallic squeal. Some damage had been done to it, knocking it partially off its two huge steel hinges. Morgaine lowered herself to a crouch, seeing some movement in a back office.

Drawing the Djune from her back, she scrambled behind a fallen desk and peered over the side. Her half-brother Jezerah…standing over her father! There was a dark blade in his hand…

Morgaine screamed as Jezerah stabbed their father through the chest. Even as he did so, the scream caused him to whirl, drawing a second blade from his back.

"Morgaine…? Sister…? Is that you…?" He snarled a laugh.

"What have you done??? What are you doing? The lab, the Platform…! It's collapsing. Why did you kill our father? Was this all your doing…?"

"I've become something…else, sister. You and your kind are a thing of the past. Father had to die. All of the Elder Race must die…". His voice trailed off. It sounded raspy and hollow. Like something was missing. As if a part of his soul simply had gone…cold.

Suddenly he was in front of her, lunging with his blade; and Morgaine was twisting away from his Djune while whirling hers to fend off secondary attacks. Leaping back, she…

Waking up, Morgaine heard a knock at the door. It wasn't the first one, either. "Mistress? Are you alright? You were sleeping, so I told Mistress Armenia to…".

Brianna.

"Come. I…it's all right. I did fall asleep, but I'm awake now. Is my bath ready?"

Brianna's face appeared in a crack in the door as she opened it. "It's… been ready, Morgaine. You've been asleep for over an hour. I came up and you were passed out. So, I asked Mistress Armenia to hold off on the rest of the hot water until you were ready. I didn't tell her you'd fallen asleep…just in case you didn't want that known for some reason."

So. The girl has a mind on top of her looks. She will make an excellent maid, I think.

"Have her bring the hot water now." Arching an eyebrow, she added. "It appears you've already taken advantage of the hot water yourself."

Brianna blushed. "Well…er…Mistress…I could tell from the way I couldn't awaken you that you needed the rest, so I figured…and I've already dried and cleaned the tub out again. Brand new towels, as well. It's all ready for you."

"Yes well, it's fine," Morgaine looked away to hide her irritation. "I'm sure you can come up with a good explanation as to why you bathed before your own Mistress did. You could start by telling her I fell asleep now. In this case, it won't make her wonder. As much."

Brianna nodded quickly. Ok, I will. I'll send up the girls with more hot water right away. Oh, and Morgaine…?" Morgaine looked up at this.

"There's an elderly gentleman downstairs. He appears to be quite old. But he asked for you by name and knew you were here. I told him I'd tell you and let him know your answer once you were not indisposed."

Who could that be…?

"Well, whoever he is, he'll have to wait until I'm ready. Tell him that, and if he's still here by the time I come down for dinner – we're eating with the men today in the main hall – we will all find out together why he's here. If not, it must not be that important."

Brianna nodded, closing the door behind her.

The bath was simply marvelous. Hot steamy bath water, with extra buckets heated up in the fires of the kitchens, coupled with bubbly soap and soft brushes. Dismissing Brianna, Morgaine bathed herself, taking care to wash her face twice and remove all possible layers of dust and dirt from her travels.

Sighing, she dunked her head under and washed her hair with the remaining liquid soap she had brought in her packs with her. It would likely be centuries before anything more than the occasional indoor toilet was going to exist with these people. Let alone showers and soft scented soaps.

Stepping out and toweling off, Morgaine noticed the window was cracked to let the cool evening air in. Brianna had thought ahead. She knew that some of the Elite Guard would be on the roof, and the window was small enough in this room that any invader would have to be a midget or less than nine years old. Morgaine laughed aloud at the idea.

"Is everything all right?" Brianna asked from the outer room.

"Yes, dear. Get my black and white gown and my hair pins. I'm going to put hair up wet and let it dry in this heat. Yours looks good with its curls, mine will need to dry a bit before we go down."

"Okay," came the answer from behind the door.

So it was that nearly two hours after waking from her nap, Morgaine and Brianna strolled carefully down the main stairwell. The men in the upper hallways had changed guard, as now a new set stood at attention as they walked by. The others – including Maitan and the rest of Treyborne's crew, were already downstairs and being entertained by a dancing girl and an older man playing the flute.

Quite the flirtatious tune. Morgaine was a bit surprised they were allowed to sing it – or have a girl dance quite that lustily in conservative Rondor. As she entered, the dancing girl's face fell noticeably. Suddenly her smile returned, and she whirled away from the outstretched arms of the nearest of her Guard. Mikell. He was quite the ladies' man. She had already probably given him her room number. Or vice versa.

It seemed the men needed a diversion after the recent events. Morgaine would not begrudge them that. Sitting down at the far corner booth from the door, fairly near the stage, Treyborne and another man, Jairus – a man in his early thirties and head of night command, approached and saluted. All business in front of the locals.

Morgaine nodded her assent to be spoken to.

"Mistress, apologies for the men…" he began.

"No need, Captain. Men must be men. Especially after fighting for their lives. And mine. I'm sure proper courtesans can be found, even in Rondor. If not brothels, which I know they made illegal. Keep the men in the building though. And…Treyborne?"

"Yes, Ma'am?"

Nodding to Jairus, she said, "Leave him in charge. You need a night off, too. I don't care with whom…". At this she stared fiercely at him. "…but I will survive without your direct protection for one night. Especially in this city, I likely would be fine just with Brianna at my side."

Treyborne opened his mouth to protest, but Morgaine stopped it with an eyebrow. Sighing, he said, "Of course, Mistress." He saluted, as did Jairus – hand to chest – and stalked off. Jairus stopped near the stage with the other remaining men and began boisterously singing the bawdy tune being played. Treyborne kept walking.

Brianna looked wide-eyed at Morgaine, not saying a word. Two plates of covered beef strips arrived, followed by bowls of mashed potatoes, carrots, peas, and bread with butter. The slip of a girl from the kitchens nearly ran away as soon as she brought them out on the huge tray bigger than she. Wide-eyed and staring at Morgaine the entire time.

Morgaine took several bites, waiting for the inevitable questions.

Brianna finally half-whispered, "What…?"

"…was that all about?" finished Morgaine, chewing a bite of bread. Brianna nodded, ducking her head, and spooning herself another portion of the carrots and peas.

Brianna was a beautiful girl, and bright. She hadn't been married long before becoming a widow, though, to be sure. Morgaine's eyes missed nothing. The girl found Treyborne attractive.

"He and I have a bit of…a history." Brianna's eyes shot up at this.

Morgaine feigned any level of caring, "It was quite a while ago. Years, in fact. But the man hasn't had another woman since. I have…weaknesses. As all living creatures do." Saying this, Morgaine again looked directly into Brianna's eyes, turning her own head a bit. She reached across the table, taking Brianna's face gently into her left hand.

"You are a pretty woman, Brianna," she said, studying her, "But we should do something about that tan. And…maybe a better haircut, now that we're in Rondor, let the curls move more." Brianna flushed but didn't say anything. "And some makeup around the eyes…yes. You've got beautiful brown eyes. Let's find something for that while we're in the city."

The attempt at changing the subject didn't work as well as Morgaine hoped. She could see Brianna's mind spinning, even as she sat there, head literally in Morgaine's hand. Sighing, Morgaine released her and resumed her eating. It had been a long week, and traveling food was never as good as this was. The White Castle Inn was legendary for its food.

"Treyborne is a fantastic leader and captain, Brianna. But my former weakness has caused him what I hope is not irreparable harm. 'Scorched earth', I believe he calls it. So, when presented with the opportunity…I try to…*gently*…encourage him to seek another woman's arms. Mine are not for him any longer. Mine are not for any man any longer."

Brianna nodded slowly. "I understand," was all she said. "Though, if that's gentle, maybe you should try being…*more*…gentle?" Brianna then dropped her eyes, clearly embarrassed at her own boldness, and continued eating in silence.

Perhaps the girl was right.

Someone cleared his throat at a nearby table. Turning to look, the women saw a balding, older gentleman sporting a goatee sitting alone, with a bottle of wine and half empty wine glass in front of him. Nodding to them, he spoke up, "Mistress Morgaine, I am sorry to bother you…".

Suddenly Morgaine leapt up from her chair and ran over to him, giving the man a huge hug, saying just one word, "Bantor!" The man laughed, hugging her back from his chair, neither noting the wine glass that had fallen over, nor the wine rapidly heading towards the floor.

Leaning back, Morgaine sat down in front of the man. He was still laughing a bit, wiping a tear from his eye. "I was afraid you wouldn't recognize me…" he began.

Laughing, Morgaine stood and hugged him again. Brianna leaned back, watching the two with puzzled amusement on her face.

Morgaine turned to her while sitting back down and said, "Bantor was a little boy the last time I saw him! His father and mother used to work at our…compound…and he used to entertain us with his impromptu songs and multiple attempts at juggling…"

Brianna looked at the older man and suddenly grasped how old Morgaine must be, and how odd her life was compared to her own.

"Yes…I remember those days," Bantor said. "When poppa died… momma decided moving back to the Rondorian kingdom you and poppa helped fight for seemed a better place for me than…"

Morgaine's smile faded a bit, but she nodded, "Your mother was right to do so. I hid my direct intervention so as not to draw undue attention from…those we didn't want it from. I was thought to be long dead. Keeping it that way made sense. But helping Rondor fight for and establish a kingdom untouched by the Dark was worth the risk. And… afterwards…an attack on the compound was still a very real threat back then. You needed children your own age to play with, too. It seems you did well for yourself. Is Nyella still…?"

This time, Bantor's smile faded. "No, Mistress. She died about six years ago when the black lung returned to the northern kingdom. But don't worry, momma always said she lived a good life, and she died seeing four grandchildren. She always spoke of her time with you and poppa at your compound as the best time of her life. She wanted me to live my life after that – and maybe not end up being a fighting man like poppa was. So," he said, "I became a merchant, then a banker, and finally a City Councilman!"

"Good for you, Bantor!" Morgaine said. "I'm happy you've done so well for yourself! So, did you come by just to visit, or…" she was speaking casually, but her eyes were sharp.

He shook his head. "No, Mistress. I made it clear to the King that I had known you when I was younger. There was a question as to your authenticity in the Court. And since Rondor III ascended the throne, no one in the Court is left who could recognize you. Twenty years is a long time, and most who knew you, knew you from the war over fifty years ago. It's not like you visited often. They wanted me to make sure it was really you, and not some trick from the Emperor. After all, only those within the court itself knew you were involved at all in the war. You kept yourself hidden and didn't partake in any of the fighting. But now…"

"Now," Morgaine continued for him, "…the word is out that I live. Yes, I know. And my involvement in the rebellion also has become known. Or at least suspected. This was very intelligent of them. Don't feel badly, Bantor. I'm glad to see you. I hadn't even visited the northern part of the realm in over a dozen years, let alone the capital. And you know: Legends of the White Witch have been around for centuries. People dress up as me at costume parties…"

Bantor shook his head disapprovingly.

"Oh, don't worry, my little man!" Morgaine said laughingly, using her old affectionate term for him, "It doesn't affect me in the slightest! It's a privilege to have a reputation. Sometimes, it helps when negotiating. "And" she added, "there won't be too many trying to dress like 'The White Witch' for decades if this doesn't go the way it needs to. The way I must have it!"

Morgaine's eyes flashed.

There she is! Brianna marveled that someone who had lived as long or seen as much as she had could still show such passion.

Bantor cleared his throat. "You know I'll stand for you, Mistress. But what is it you want? No one even knows why you have come, to be honest."

"I've come," Morgaine began, "to start another war."

CHAPTER 29

Brianna walked as casually as she could, approaching the palace of the great city of Rondor. It was made up of beautiful, shining white stone painted with multiple colors and framed between the city's two aqueducts from the adjacent mountains on either side. The White river's east and west streams flowed around the city, but these aqueducts assured its citizens no siege would ever prevail here.

The castle itself had multiple courtyards surrounding it, with grounds dedicated to crops, animals, and other ways of protecting food sources. Military flags and men were everywhere.

Walking behind her, Treyborne and another man she didn't know were watching for signs of trouble, pacing behind her like feral dogs. When they came near to any Rondorian city guards or military men, they would nod casually, always keeping their hands ready. Brianna saw none of this, of course.

She herself was dressed in the blue dress Morgaine had prescribed for her, with white gloves, a white shawl, a white hat with a blue sash, and a white pearl-inlaid clutch, patterned with blue. The ornate shoes she wore were not meant for long walks and were already hurting her feet considerably. But they were gorgeous.

Morgaine had been insistent upon this one point: Act like a young high lady herself. Morgaine must be seen as more than this kingdom, or her plans might fail. Second, but just as important: Find whatever information she could prior to Morgaine's arrival. Get some dirt, drink with the other serving girls. Ply them with questions.

The background story was that Brianna had been sent to surveil the rooms for her mistress and make sure they were "adequate" for her lady's needs. As if anything they'd give her in that castle would be less than adequate! Nonetheless this was to be her cover, to give Brianna hours to wander around, gather what gossip she could, pry open mouths with questions. Giggle behind gloves at silly aristocrats.

Bribe as necessary.

Brianna was armed with small bottles of alcohol, a veritable fortune in gold and silver Rondorian coin, and some sweet candies purchased that morning across the street from the inn at a local shop. Brianna had tried one herself. Simply delightful! Humming as she went along, she began the slow walk up the winding stone staircases on the right side of the great entryway. Even this was preplanned. She was to be seen lollygagging only a bit but humming and acting whimsical. Just in case anyone happened to be watching.

Flags upon pillars and statues adorned the entire area. Wishing she had more time to look at everything, Brianna picked up the ends of her dress and began the hike up the lengthy staircase, hoping she didn't fall over from exhaustion before reaching the top.

CHAPTER 30

"You want me to do…*what*?!?"

The third King Rondor was clearly not amused. Barely into his twenties, he still held all the regal poise of a monarch of the rebel northern kingdom. Standing slouched a bit as he was, he appeared almost to be sulking.

Morgaine simply waited, as more would surely follow.

The wood-paneled meeting room was filled with important people of the Kingdom. She'd been introduced at the reception less than an hour ago: The Queen, Peniella, formerly of the Petty Kingdom of Daystrom in the East, Duke Mantessa – General of the Rondorian Armies, Duke Iranias, Lord of the Western Realms, and three of the seven City Council members including Morgaine's former "little man", along with the Contessa Ryalla – aunt to the current king and sister to the former, as well as sister to the Duke of Mantessa – she herself would have met Morgaine only once, had she been in Rondor at the time. Mantessa himself had been an infant the first time, and in the field commanding the armies the second.

Morgaine's last visit had been at the dedication of the current monarch, King Rondor III, shortly after his birth. But the Contessa herself had not attended either, having been married to a count in Nelrae, and living in the Empire. Her marriage had sealed the peace over forty years ago. At the time, she had been barely ten years of age. Now she was well over fifty, her husband long dead. Apparently, she now lived in Rondor again full time. Although her estates were surely still in the northwestern part of Nelrae's vast empire. A few other dignitaries were there in the background, standing by the tiers of bookshelves. Rondor had always loved his library. This was but the first floor of it.

Morgaine returned her attention back fully to the king.

He was still reeling, sipping from his drink, and staring daggers across the table at Morgaine. Dressed in royal robes and wearing a small crown, his dark hair and brown eyes were offset by a hooked nose that reminded Morgaine more of his grandfather than his father. His father had been quite the handsome man.

Pity.

The king looked back up, finally continuing, "We are about to engage in war with the Empire of Nelrae at our southern borders, as you are well aware! A war we did not initiate, I might add. The Captain of the Northern Keep – whom I believe you know – tells me of Dark Men gathering in the northern lands close to our borders. Now I have word our border patrols have had several skirmishes with them. And you…". His voice faded off again, still in stunned disbelief.

"I request you to declare war upon the Eastern Empire," Morgaine continued for him. "And the three Petty Kingdoms that are loosely allied with them," Morgaine paused in her highly artificial casual tone to look over at the Queen. "This does not include Daystrom, of course."

"It's outrageous!" the king bellowed again. "Why would we, or should we, declare war on an Empire located halfway across the globe from us? Why invoke their wrath? And…who cares…pardon, my Queen…about the Petty Kingdoms? They have virtually no standing armies themselves. They are mostly trading states that sell their precious metals, wool, and other goods through the trade routes! Why even bother declaring war on *them* at all?"

Morgaine sighed, sitting down for the first time, at the table spread out with the map of the known world. She hadn't bothered adding her own knowledge to it. It was enough. The Eastern Empire wasn't even on this one. This map only showed Nelrae's empire to the south, the much smaller kingdom of Rondor to the north, and a few of the Petty Kingdoms east of the Gloom Wood to the East, past the Alisandre River.

Sipping her wine, Morgaine sat down, motioning for the others to sit down, as well. Despite this being Rondor's castle and the monarch himself standing there, they all complied.

"I do not ask this lightly. Nor have I done so without measuring the cost with proper forethought. The truth is, Your Excellency…I believe that they are about to go to war with you. Over me. I know this, because, I too have informants all over these lands."

"My 'resurrection' has caused quite a stir. As you well know, the Eastern Empire is saturated with the Cult of the Dark. Their so-called mages and priests from their evil religion are the only accepted one in the entire eastern lands. K'Thul himself rules as emperor. Add that to the fact that the Arc Gate has somehow reactivated…"

The few people in the room who had not heard of this already gasped in horror. Morgaine nodded to them and continued. "Yes. It is true."

"But why declare war on them, Morgaine? You've been a supporter of Rondor since before its inception. Surely you can see this would end us!" This from the Duke Mantessa, general of the armies. "If what you say is true, should they all bear down upon Rondor at once, their sheer numbers would be overwhelming!"

Morgaine studied the king and his advisors a moment, then continued, "The Dark Brethren and their Cult, who control most of the central and eastern lands, will be storming this way soon either way. They all must assume my sudden reappearance is connected to the Arc Gate's reawakening. Or that I am responsible for it in some way."

"I can assure you," she added, "that I am not! My suspicion was that one of the Dark Lords had done it – and not told the others – or that it was truly a random event. I would have destroyed the thing hundreds of years ago, instead of simply shutting it down, had I had the ability. But that was and is simply beyond my power and skills. If the Cult and the Dark Lords were to gain control of an active Arc Gate…"

"The world would perish," the king concluded darkly. "I think we all understand the severity of those consequences, Lady Morgaine. All of those here realize that your Race and your forebears had awesome powers and weaponry at your disposal. A mere fraction of which has proven enough to dominate our own world. But what advantage is there for us in declaring war first? How can you know they will all come here to Rondor? And why would they come here seeking you in the first place?"

"First," Morgaine began, "more than this world stands to lose if the Arc Gate is theirs to control. And I believe they will come for Rondor… because my brother and cousins will not take well to being fooled. They thought your kingdom's rebellion and unlikely success at staying a separate entity a glitch…an anomaly. One they doubtless felt would self-correct on its own given time, but will wish to correct immediately, with the new information they now possess. You are no longer merely some locals fighting the Dark on your own. You have allied with the White Queen. By their own religion, you must be stamped from Arth itself! I'm sure their original plan was to wait a few generations, allow time for a few of the Black Cult to secretly move in…"

"My Lady!" Rondor interrupted, "You know full well my grandfather banned that religion here. The Creator is worshipped here only. And… members of that sect are put to death upon discovery! It has ever been so!"

"And yet…" Morgaine countered, "the Black Cult is here even now!"

Shock showed on everyone's faces. The mere thought had shut the conversation down like a lightning strike interrupting power at her compound. King Rondor's face grew redder and redder, but he said nothing. Finally, he blurted, "That is simply impossible! Those Dark practices are forbidden here!"

Morgaine watched him, then glanced at every other person in the room. Measured. Carefully. Shock showed on each face perfectly.

Time to play her card. Morgaine snapped her eyes back towards the king, "If that were so…how is it that the Empire recently learned of my survival and continued existence in the first place, Your Majesty? How…" she added darkly, looking back at the king, "and why did the Empire suddenly turn hostile and declare war on you? Within weeks of the news coming out! Do you know? Have you even thought about it…?"

Looking angrily back at her, the young monarch grudgingly shook his head. "We do not have any idea. Until you brought it up, we hadn't even connected those two dots. We thought their hostility was due to the last Emperor's demise almost eight years ago. They have always tried to blame his death on us."

"Let me advise you, then, King Rondor! You see, my maid came by earlier to review and set up my quarters a few hours prior to my arrival. Upon my instructions, I asked her specifically to ask about the health of your close family members. Any unusual characteristics or interesting tidbits. In short, to glean as much casual court gossip as she could. It seems," Morgaine said, pausing to glance sideways as she spoke, "that the Contessa Ryalla is…*remarkably* well-preserved for her age! It seems she's taken on a much younger lover, recently, as well. Perhaps we should ask her how the Empire found out about my survival…?"

Gasps at the not-so-subtle insinuation burst forth all over the room.

Morgaine had her audience right where she wanted them now. "After all, The Dark Brethren offer their followers much longer life. Eternal life for the 'Chosen,' in fact. The pull of the Dark religion is a powerful one to those seeking to extend their short, miserable lives just a little while longer! Or their very fancy, cushy ones, equally I suppose." Then Morgaine sat back and watched the room.

Morgaine's brother and his proteges parceled out power to those who served them directly. More to their inner circles. Leaders were said to live centuries.

Rondor himself erupted, "How dare you insult my personal court in my own keep! Not one of us has lived beyond sixty years in this room, apart from one or two esteemed Council members! More than half of us here are well under forty! And you, who've lived a reported five hundred years in our world alone…dare to *insinuate* that my aunt is…a…*what?* Member of *the Dark Horde?* How do we know you aren't just another arm of the Dark, yourself?"

Morgaine continued, completely unruffled. "I'm more than insinuating, Your Majesty. And you know I'm not of the Dark. Or your grandfather would never have survived. You yourself would never have been born. Surely, they told you enough to know that the idea itself is preposterous. I nearly died many times defending your family. But…I'm *curious…* who put that thought into your head? Surely it didn't just pop out at this very moment…?"

The king glanced at his ministers on that note. Morgaine's eyes caught to whom he glanced in case further investigation was going to be necessary.

"And not the 'Dark Horde' for goodness' sake! She'd have to be clothed in a black mask and riddled with weapons for that 'honor'. But a member of their *religion…?* Someone who has partaken in their rituals to extend life, health…and *beauty?* How old are you, Contessa? You must be nearing fifty! Yet you appear as though you're barely over thirty!"

The Contessa screamed, taking several steps forward, enraged, "How *dare* you indeed!? I married into that accursed Empire's elite to end the war as a child! I've given my entire life, sacrificed everything for this kingdom! Even my former husband wasn't a member of their Cult. My father refused to marry me to anyone who was…I…"

"…protest far too much." Morgaine said calmly just looking back at her. Touching her pendant, cold touching her voice for the first time, "You see, my dear…what is whispered at in the courts is simply gossip. My maid…" she began.

"Your spy!" The Contessa countered bitterly.

Morgaine acceded to the amendment. Rising and turning fully towards the Contessa for the first time, she continued, "My maid…acting as a spy upon my orders…simply gathered what she could. But my pendant… it can *sense* the Void. Its connection to the Gates and the power behind them makes it a sort of sounding board for it. The corrupting power that our engineers knew nothing about until too late…the Void behind the power…it can sense. Your power, Contessa…your beauty…now comes from *the Dark*."

Before the woman or anyone else could even react, Morgaine touched something on the pendant, and the central clear gem flared to life, shimmering, shining radiantly in the room. Suddenly, the Contessa gasped, then stumbled, falling to her knees, grasping at her throat as if choking.

The king leaped to his feet, as did the two Dukes, and several guards leaped forward to stand at either side of the king, from their former positions by the entryway. They placed their hands on their weapons menacingly.

The king shouted, "Morgaine! Release her at once! Your magics have no place here!!"

"It isn't 'magic', Your Highness. It is science. And this is simply a siren's call. The power that closed the Gates, let alone that of the Gates themselves, was designed specifically to focus the power that is within this pendant. If I deactivate it now, all power from the Dark is cut off. Forever. Whatever or whomever is connected to that power – that connection ends once I turn off its light. It also," she added, "takes a great deal from me personally to do such a thing. I do not do it lightly. I risk my own life. I did this every time I passed through a Gate. And not one time since has the gem been reignited this brightly until now. But to show you the infiltrating ability of the forces we hope to combat…"

Morgaine twisted her finger around the gem again. The Contessa fell on the floor, writhing in pain.

The King looked down at his aunt, shock, and horror on his face. Looking up, he asked, "How do we know this isn't just some trick of yours, Morgaine? My grandfather knew you well. My father knew you. I do not. I have no reason to trust you. You yourself could have finally fallen to the Dark. This could be just some trick conjured up to confuse us."

Morgaine looked straight at him, standing up to her full height, cocking her chin in defiance.

Staring him down, she declared, "I am the Lady Morgaine, the White Falcon herself! I was named by the Creator at birth! I fought against the Dark long before this Kingdom ever existed! And I worked to establish this kingdom with your grandfather and his men long before you were ever born! How dare you accuse *me* of siding with the *Dark*? I swore an oath to your grandfather to defend Rondor to my dying breath, as this is the only place in the world that has lived to defy the Dark's evil spread!"

Morgaine continued, "Rondor is where the Dark is *shunned*, and its adherents *slain* –not idolized or worshipped as gods like everywhere else in this evil world! If even now you doubt me, you will have plenty of time to search the Contessa's quarters for further proof! If nothing appears, I will submit to any punishment you require of me. Should I awaken from the backlash myself!" Morgaine took a step back, planting her feet.

Rondor III, staring down for a moment at his father's sister still moaning and gasping in pain on the floor tiles, nodded his assent without looking up.

Morgaine braced herself, touching the stone a second time with two fingers, holding them there. The pendant flashed white hot heat. The shock was almost unbearable. The blast knocked Morgaine off her feet, fortunately landing her in the chair behind her rather than the floor.

The Contessa fared far worse. Screaming in agony, she suddenly wrinkled and aged, her hair turning white…and her eyes turned partially black. The entire room erupted in horror. Then the Contessa coughed a few times, contorting her body like an insect in the flame before what was left of the light in her eyes winked out.

Morgaine herself saw none of this. Unconsciousness had come like a mountain falling upon her mere moments after her fingers released the gem.

CHAPTER 31

The Triumvirate didn't meet often together. Not at all, in fact, for decades. Messages had sufficed. Why risk violating the tentative peace the intervening years had wrought?

Still, it was past time for such a meeting. Jezerah tried to quash the inner feeling that he should have called one before all the infighting and turmoil had begun. But that would have been giving away his advantage.

An advantage he no longer enjoyed, to be sure. But by calling the meeting, it should serve to do the same to Emorion. After all his scheming and carefully plotted moves, this would surely ruffle his feathers. For that reason alone, it was worth doing. The Dark "brothers" were hardly on warm terms with each other. All blaming each other for the failings of the group, the lack of total victory even over this one little planet. Let alone the ultimate demise of their dream.

But now…that dream had come alive again! Surely that was a reason to call a meeting. K'Thul would have, by now, received word of all the doings west of the Eastern Empire. His input and resolve to fix all details could prove useful. But ultimately, it was about winning. If he must include his "brothers" to win, he would. He had just hoped…

Shrugging, Jezerah pressed "Enter" on the holographic display before him. Cloaked as the room was in darkness, the sharpness of the lights struck his eyes harshly. The room around him faded further.

His brothers had "arrived" ahead of him.

This digital forum was their way of communicating. In the early days of their labor, the Council – as it had been then – was eleven. Backstabbing and advantage-taking caused that number to dwindle to seven. By the time Morgaine and her crew came flying through the Arc Gate, the Dark Brethren were a mostly stable team. The weak had been culled from the herd. What remained was iron.

Existing for the pure power of the Dark and ultimately, an endless rule of the galaxy. It all had seemed within their grasp back then. Then, one by one, they had fallen. Battle after battle was won, yes. But always at a cost. Shaking his head, Jezerah closed his eyes, focusing on the moment.

"Brothers…" he began, nodding to each of their images on either side of his own. Both Emorion and K'Thul nodded in silence. "I have come… to tell you what you already know. And perhaps…something you do not." This sparked their curiosity. Neither said a word, of course.

But they both had twitched at that. "As you are both well aware – and as Emorion now knows for certain," this with a glance to the shorter of the two on his left, "the Arc Gate has reawakened. The how and the why of that…though…I think I now know."

The information from Curtaise needed to finally reach their ears. The story he'd tell should interest these two greatly. Emorion turned his head completely at this, revealing the black eyes they all shared, sitting on his gaunt elongated cheekbones. His hair remained white, as it did for all of them. Yet somehow, on Emorion, it was even more starkly juxtaposing.

"Yes, I found out the Gate had opened without telling either of you for several days. Of course, you had to sense it, even as I did. Yes, I sent a team to investigate. But tell me," he asked carefully, "What would you have said to me had I told you all before investigating? 'Go find out what occurred and tell us what you find.'? Of course. So, I simply did that. Before my investigation at the site was complete – and as I'm sure Emorion has already found out, now that he controls the site – the Gate is not awakened on our side. At least not…fully. It is not operational, but it is not completely dormant either."

Emorion finally spoke, "I know all of this, Jezerah! You always act superior to us because you were the first to discover the Void! But you are no more powerful or important than either of us! We are all together Lords of the Dark. You always seek advantage! This time was no different. Don't try to deny it! I simply took what should have been shared in the first place! And yes, it's dormant! Yes, it's in a strange state of "near death" – if it were a living being, it would be comatose. What news do you have that we do not?"

Jezerah waited, smiling. K'Thul finally spoke in his booming deep bass voice, "Speak Jezerah! I have heard Emorion's complaints about you long enough!"

Jezerah's smile waned, just a little. They still needed to fear him. He was still the most powerful of this Triumvirate. After the pause, he nodded. "At least one of the Elder Race triggered the Gate, brothers. He – and it is a 'he' – came through and was briefly detained by two of my Dark Men, before they lost him. A Quartermaster and his team were sent, and he defeated them. So now, we have proof that at least one more of the Elder Race has arrived on Arth. I do not know my sister's level of involvement, yet. But I feel somehow this had to have been her doing, even though no evidence ties her to it. Her arrogance and desire to destroy us will prove her undoing! If she has reactivated the Gate somehow…brought whoever still was alive after all these years through for aid…! Well then, we will crush them both! Either way, we then we will take from them the key, and begin what should have been ours all along: ruling the entire galaxy of inhabited worlds!"

There had to be a key. The Gates always worked so. Whatever Morgaine had done to close this Gate – now it was somehow simply no longer completely closed. A crack existed. And, after all this time, if a crack was there…that crack could and would be widened.

Even K'Thul was nodding now. Emorion was positively gleeful. He was grinning ear to ear, and practically dancing at the news, hopping from foot to foot.

Emorion said, "So, it wasn't some random event! A true Elder Race being has survived and come through?! What a fool! Coming alone?! Perhaps that is truly the last of them all then! Morgaine must have lied like a snake to him to get that fool to come here! And now…We may be freed from this prison planet once and for all!"

Jezerah smiled his deepest smile, nodding to his smaller Dark Brother.

Oh no, cur! Once we pry open that Gateway, there shall be only one of us going through it. Two, perhaps. If K'Thul bows and acknowledges my superiority for all time. But not you, dog! I've been stabbed in the back by you for the last time!

Outwardly he said, "We shall all drink the wine of our mother planet again together someday soon! This was why I waited to share the news! I wanted to be sure before wasting all our collective time. If it had been just an anomaly…or worse, nothing had actually happened…would that have been worthy of calling a meeting? Would that have been worthy of fighting over? Don't we all have better things to do? Would you have done differently, had the Arc Gate been closer to either of you…?"

Grudgingly, the other two Dark Lords nodded this did make sense.

Jezerah just kept right on smiling.

CHAPTER 32

Jennifer sat alone in her apartment. The lights were off, and sunset had come an hour or more ago. The sounds and lights from the city leaked through the windows. Peace and quiet were foreign to her, anyway. None of Jennifer's roommates were home tonight, at least. All were out either working or hitting the bars.

Nathan had been gone over two weeks now. Jennifer's "great idea" had failed. Miserably. The cell phone tied to a skateboard just rolled right into the room. Zero happened. Nothing changed. Explaining a phone tied to a skateboard rolling into the restricted area while retrieving it to the two older professors and scientists or whatever that were still in the monolith room at the time had been more than a little tricky.

Ellie and her crew had left before they had even attempted it. She and Gary had stayed outside on the grounds, keeping an eye on the door for hours waiting for their opportunity. They'd even played cards until it had gotten too windy, and then they just sat telling each other stories. Mostly of Nathan.

Jennifer pulled her legs up, hugging them to her chest. Laying her head down onto her knees, she just closed them and felt her hot breath hit her knees. Tears were a thing that mostly didn't come any more. Maybe she was cried out.

Some days she wished she simply had just taken another intern assignment all those months ago. CTI had needed her. They'd even said if she came, she'd likely land a full-time position with them up front. Something had led to her to HDS and Nathan. Now, with Nathan gone, she had been offered his position. Gary had eventually had to tell the managers that his (former) roommate had gone missing, that he wasn't just sick…and that Gary had no idea where he was. "Last seen" at a museum in Queens.

Not much to go on.

Jennifer felt guilty about taking Nathan's job. But it also kept her close to him. Left her something of him for her to remember. And the hope of his return could eventually bring him back to work and Gary. So, staying close meant having a chance – however slight – of seeing him again. She sat at his desk during the day. He had had no pictures of family there, though. Just one of himself, Gary, and her that night on Broadway.

Nathan had been so…different and kind and…and funny and wonderful! Intelligent, even a little distracted, sometimes – but in a good way. All she had wanted in a man. And those beautiful eyes! Sighing, Jennifer realized she was thinking of Nathan in the past tense. Gary had said to her – gently, just this morning – that they had to come to some sort of realization that maybe he wasn't ever coming back. It didn't mean he was dead, or even hurt. Just…not able to return.

Jennifer's eyes raised and she heard Ellie saying, for the millionth time,

"…It's like he walked through a computer monitor or television screen. On the video replay – which is admittedly as high def as it could be – it shows Nathan there, and then simply not there after the flash. But the light seems to come outwards from the center of the monolith and then retreat. It's as if it encoded him digitally and that was it. Taking him wherever the monolith was programmed to go last."

"So where in the blasted hell is that?!" Gary had shouted at her.

To that, Ellie could only shrug and look away. It was clear no one had any clue what the monolith truly was, who built it, or where a portal like that could have taken him. Or even when. And that was the "good news" version.

The *bad news* one: the monolith had just vaporized him. One of those older scientists had said that to the three of them while they had talked about it. He thought the monolith had been one giant disposal unit. A galactic trash remover or enemy disintegrator.

Ellie had said she doubted that. "Why spend so much energy for something like that?" She was convinced it was a spatial transporter. But she likely had no more idea how it worked than the ancient Egyptians who had buried it in their tombs. Clearly the usefulness of it had been lost by then. The fact that it still operated whispered…maybe even *screamed*…of alien intelligence. Something Jennifer had thought preposterous before recent events.

Jennifer remembered one more thing: Ellie's back. A lab coat, slowly walking away from them, and towards the enclosed computer area. The hum of the monolith in the background was the only thing breaking the silence.

Gary just watching her go.

Ok, she was wrong again. She still had tears. Lots of them. Sobbing, she just held her knees and rocked herself as the honking and yelling of the New York City streets throbbed and pulsed twelve stories below her feet.

CHAPTER 33

Nathan himself at that very moment was crossing a sweeping valley, trudging behind the steps of Smyslin as he had done for the last four days. The grasses were very tall here, and there were times he even lost him in the high grass for a moment. But apparently, Smyslin's fear of Nathan's "powers" were enough to keep him in line.

Nathan couldn't help but shake his head in amusement. The best control techniques anyone in power had was to use the fears of the oppressed against them. Fear and terror. They worked all too well. Whoever these "Great Lords" that Smyslin talked incessantly about were, Nathan was beginning to feel they had a lot in common with the Nazis.

They stopped to eat their midday meal beneath a huge oak-like tree with a wide bowl of shade. The breeze blowing on the hilltop was glorious and the sun was bright. It was, after all, a beautiful world. This time, however, as they sat down, Nathan caught sight of a walled town just down the valley lying on the other side of the river they'd been following.

"We are approaching the human border. This is the only human town I saw on the maps of this area prior to leaving. I was not in charge, not part of the military, so I only casually observed. But the rumor is, the Lost One Morgaine had something to do with this kingdom."

Nathan looked back from the town, still chewing. He nodded in thanks. He and Smyslin had seen no other Dark Men for days. Those they had seen, Smyslin had amazingly gone over to speak with, and they all had left saluting hand to chest and then waving. Once he had promised to help Nathan, Smyslin was as good as his word. Beyond anything anyone Nathan had ever known would have done. If someone had been forced to do such things in New York, they'd have run screaming to the nearest police officer they saw. Or just pulled the cop's gun and shot you themselves!

When asked what he had said to the other Dark Men (the correct term, as he had also learned), Smyslin simply said, "I told them you were our Great Master's high servant, disguised to look like one of the hated Lost Ones. I said I was taking you near to the human lands to set you up as bait for the dreaded Morgaine. Once we were near, you had been implanted with explosives, so that if she came out to meet you, you both would die together in a glorious conflagration!"

Clever. The explosives would explain why an engineer was taking him and not someone else.

"Why not just run away, or have them fight me?" Nathan asked, not for the first time.

"Why should my brothers die for my mistake? I should never have tracked you. Your powers are too great for them. It would take an army of the Dark Men to kill one such as you. Better to save our armies for a fight they can win."

Nathan nodded, trying not to openly grin. "Ever the practical one, Smyslin!"

Smyslin smiled, as if that were the highest compliment he had ever been paid. He had a nice smile. It…also seemed like his skin had gotten lighter in the sunlight, rather than darker. And his smile showed extremely white teeth. It had to be some sort of reverse tanning. The whole effect was quite startling to see against the general blackness of the man's formerly darker skin and clothing.

Nathan was about to look back at the slowly rolling clouds above the town again when he jerked his eyes back to study Smyslin. His mask was still down, but it was Smyslin's eyes he noticed first. The eyes were normal white for the first time, with a green-colored iris and simple black pupil. His eyes had…changed in the last few days completely.

Noticing the sudden scrutiny, Smyslin asked, fear coming into his voice, "Have I done something to offend you, Master? If so, please forgive Smyslin, as he is very ignorant of the ways of the Lost Ones!"

Seeing Smyslin shaking and about to cry, he quickly said, "No! No! It's fine…! You said just the right thing! Like I said, you are practical and what you said was perfect. I was just noticing…do you go out into the sunlight a lot in your lands, Smyslin? You appear to be…changing color a bit."

Smyslin gasped in horror, jumping, and running to his pack lying a few feet away under the tree. Jerking out his shaving blade and small mirror, he looked over his entire face. Noticing his eye color, Smyslin began making a sound Nathan had never quite heard before. Rapidly checking his teeth, underneath his face scarf, everywhere…the sound slowly rose in pitch.

Nathan finally recognized it. It was wailing. Smyslin was in major emotional distress at finding what Nathan had said to be true. He was blanching…or getting sun-bleached…*or who knows with these people…?*

Smyslin fainted.

Nathan just stared at him. *What do I do now…? Maybe I should just head to the city from here. He can go back to his people and hide in the darkness until he gets darker again, I guess. Might be best for him.*

Nathan grabbed the small pack Smyslin had made up for him to carry, complete with small brush, a packet of that tasty, dried meat, a half loaf of dried bread, a small knife, and a water bottle. They had gotten the last from the most recent Dark Men they had seen. It appeared that most of them did, in fact, travel in twos.

"Thank you, Smyslin," he said to his unconscious guide. "You are an interesting man. I have obviously inflicted some serious psychological pain upon you, and for that I am sorry. But perhaps it's best if we part ways. You to your people and me to anyone else but your people! Cheers, brother!"

"So, you would just leave me like this, lying like a dead man on the ground?" came Smyslin's voice. His eyes were still closed.

Nathan jerked around in shock, having already turned and taken several steps toward the riverbank far below them. "Why did you fake passing out, then? What was I supposed to do? And you said yourself if the men in that town saw you, they'd arrest you immediately. You also said the entire kingdom which this village belongs to is a 'rebel state' against your lords. I thought I was doing you a favor!"

Smyslin opened his eyes but did not raise his head up. "I did not fake passing out. I did pass out. I just woke up quickly, and I have kept my eyes closed and been praying for forgiveness in shame ever since. If the Great Lords saw me now, they would know I had become tainted. Just being close to you, I think the color has been slowly fading from my body. It seems you Lost Ones not only have lost all connection to the Dark, but you are able to suck it like lifeblood from those around you! I believe I am dying because I have dared to aid a Lost One and the Darkness no longer wants me…!"

The man sounded truly miserable. He also hadn't moved anything but his jaw in speaking. Nathan walked over to where his lone eye could see him without difficulty.

"If that is so, I am truly sorry. But I can tell you honestly, I do not think that is the case. Head back to your people. I'm sure the Darkness will return once my… 'taint' or whatever is further away from you. I release you! Go in peace! I'll head to that town and hope they don't lock me up for being a 'Lost One' also!"

"Oh, those poisonous snakes wouldn't do that! They allied themselves with Morgaine. The truth has all come out these last few weeks and months. All our news bulletins are full of it! The White Witch has been behind the rebel state since its inception over fifty years ago! She had been thought dead, so she stayed hidden. But now that it is openly known about her, the Empire of Nelrae to the south and the Dark Men from the north are going to crush that little kingdom to bits and scatter its bones into the sea!"

Wonderful. And I'm heading right for it!

"You go for it, Smyslin! Best of luck. But I'm going to find either this 'horrible Witch Queen' or possibly someone else who can help me. All you Dark Men have done – with you being the notable exception – is tie me up or try to beat me to death! And let's face it – you were coerced. I'll try my luck with some people with lighter skin. I'm not racist – don't give me that face! I'm just saying you just don't have the best track record. Also: your 'Great Masters' sound like jackasses and seem to try to keep you all afraid one hundred percent of the time. Not cool. If I were you, I'd look for new employment elsewhere. But hey! That's just me. Take care, Smyslin. I like you, and that's a fact."

Nathan turned to walk down the hill again, and Smyslin didn't stop him. Nathan was almost down the hill when he heard running behind him. Whirling, he saw Smyslin half jumping, half running down the steep hill to catch up to him. Raising his eyebrows in puzzlement, he stopped and waited for him.

"Master Lost One," Smyslin still refused to call him 'Nathan', "There are likely dozens of Dark Men surrounding that village now. It was to be encircled on the northern border on this side of the river by at least one hundred of the Dark Horde. You will never get past them without me!"

Nathan's eyebrows stayed up at this. He turned to scan ahead of him. The city lay no more than a mile or two down the valley slope and across the river. There was a large field on the northern side, as well. He saw no one.

"It doesn't appear…"

Smyslin interrupted him, "The Dark Men are as hard to see as a shadow in the back of a cave, Master. I promised to take you safely to the city of the white men. Somewhere the hated witch might be. With the rebels. I will do as I have said." He picked up the pack he'd laid down while speaking and strode ahead of Nathan, continuing his hopping and jumping down the steep slope.

Nathan shrugged and followed.

CHAPTER 34

Morgaine awoke to dim lights, quiet talking in the outer rooms, a gentle breeze blowing, and an incredible headache. Putting fingers to her head, she kept her eyes slitted, looking about her slowly. Palace rooms, clearly.

So. Not a jail cell, at least.

Sitting up, she saw Brianna reading a book quietly at the far side of the room. Hearing her stir, Brianna looked up, closing her book and setting it aside on a small round marble tabletop. An oil lamp was wicked down to a low glow, making Brianna's face dark enough Morgaine couldn't see her eyes.

"How are you feeling?" she asked quietly.

"Like the land cruiser ran me over, then backed up and parked on my skull." Brianna giggled, making Morgaine break into a wry grin. "What happened after I passed out?"

Brianna sobered up quickly at that, saying gravely, "They…took out the Contessa's body and guards were sent to search her quarters and that of her maids and retainers. Apparently, in the last hour, all her guards and maids have been arrested until they can be questioned further… It sounds like they found some evidence of the Contessa linking her to the Dark Cult. Just as you surmised. Or did you know?"

Morgaine again had to be impressed with the girl's wit. Beauty and brains were a powerful combination. Their coincidental meeting had turned into quite a windfall. "It was…a calculated guess. Most of their adherents must be near sources of the Void's power, or vials of their dark liquid. I'm honestly not even close to knowing why. It is just a fact

I have found to be true. I wasn't sure of the woman's involvement until she spoke. Her voice triggered the stone…".

Morgaine reached up to fondle her pendant but found it missing. Sitting bolt upright, she exclaimed, "Where is it?" Looking around her, Brianna simply stood up and walked over, handing it to her. Snatching it back and unclasping the back, she put it back around her neck.

"Why did you remove it?" she snapped.

"I hope you can forgive me, Mistress…but it appeared it was causing you further pain while you slept. The gem would…*pulse*…and you groaned. After the tenth time, I took it off you and you were quiet."

Morgaine looked up at her, and then nodded slowly. "Thank you. I'm not sure what that means…I haven't used it like that before. I will say," she said, tapping the gemstone that was now lit only by the small light of the gas lamp in the room, "that by taking it while it was alight means something for you that you likely did not intend. But we will talk more on that later. Right now," she said, rising, "it appears I must dress myself again and see what our team has been discussing without me. Without us," she amended, touching Brianna's arm to let her know all was well.

Brianna smiled. "I'll let them know you're awake. It's the middle of the night, but they refused to leave. They were all very worried about you." Morgaine nodded and Brianna turned and left the room.

She's a good girl. I hope she can stick around awhile.

It wasn't uncommon for Morgaine to immediately dread the regret she would feel in the future when someone of great value to her died or became too old for service. It had happened far too often to count. Brianna would one day be added to that very long list.

Assuming, of course, Morgaine lived that long herself. Feeling the ache in her head still, she slowly put on her outer garments, checked herself in the large oval mirror on the nightstand, and went out to her team.

Brianna had told them she was coming, so they were all seated – as many as could be – with Treyborne and Messau standing at the doorway, but clearly watching her as she approached. The cushioned couch nearest the fireplace was clearly the "throne" of the room, and they had all vacated it before she had entered the room. She knew someone had sat there recently, because as she sat down, it was still warm, and the cushions were not quite fully pushed back out.

It was an ornate piece, with beautiful artisan level woodcarvings, plus cushions and high arm rests. No one spoke, waiting for her to speak to them.

Nodding to them all, she said, "I am fine. I would apologize for taking unnecessary risks, but this was a most necessary one. The King must have confidence in me, as I am going to put his entire kingdom in mortal danger." She stopped, waiting for comments. None came.

She continued, "The King will doubtless call for me in the morning to tell me of his findings. Apparently, all of you kept your heads about you, and did nothing to further irritate him. Now that he's found out that I was correct about the Contessa, it should aid us in our attempt to get to the Gate. Not that I had any doubts about the Contessa, but he must have had some."

More silence.

"What we do not know, is if the King will accede to my request to engage in a war he cannot win without our help. I must convince him, and perhaps others of his court, that what we have to offer him is worth the risk. After all, it is not his kingdom, ultimately, that is in peril. Yes, Nelrae has renewed hostilities, and yes, the Dark Men from the

Triumvirate are everywhere in the northlands. But what I'm proposing is suicide if he's left alone. He must understand the true nature of the Dark and the danger it represents to the cosmos, should it get through the Gate once again. Everything depends on me making sure that Gate remains closed. And if it is not, then closing it again. This time, forever. If we fail, his kingdom is doomed, either way. He must see it that way."

"What is the… 'true nature of the Dark'…?" this from Brianna.

"The Dark is the Essence of the Void itself. Dark matter from wherever it is that matter and life go once sucked into the Black Hole at the center of the galaxy. It captures all matter, all light. It is the destroyer of worlds. Of stars. Of galaxies…of life itself."

Brianna's blank stare could not have been plainer.

"I'm sorry, dear. It is a power so grave, that even light cannot escape it. The Creator, in His great wisdom, created the universe from the matter within it. But the Dark is ever greedy, seeking to suck all life, light, and color from the universe back into itself once again. To pull everything into its Dark core again forever."

"And…we're trying to stop this?" Brianna's eyes were wide, her mouth open.

Morgaine could see Brianna was beginning to grasp the magnitude of what this small band was trying to accomplish. "To put it simply: yes. The Elder Race found the power of the Void and dark matter could bend time and space and pull matter through to wherever we wanted. We freely gave this technology to the greatest peoples of each planet we were sent to, in order to bring their cultures along. We even helped them with their progeny and…made adjustments to their genetic code. So, they could be smarter, live longer, fight better. Even have children with us."

Brianna stared at her.

Morgaine continued, "What our scientists didn't know was that the Dark was sentient or at least has some form of consciousness. And it is evil. Its hunger cannot be sated. Its thirst for vengeance against the Creator is never ending. It reached out to those who traveled through these Gates the most, my brother Jezerah among them. And if my brother, or one of his proteges get through an open Arc Gate…then not just this world, but all worlds could fall under the shadow of the Dark once again. Back in the day, they fled here and then were cornered by the Elder Race. We were trying to exterminate them. We shut the Gates down – I – shut the Gates down before we lost control of them."

"So, what would you have *us* do, Morgaine?" Treyborne asked. We are your men. We will die for you if need be. But what can we do?"

"I'm not sure, Trey…" Morgaine responded carefully. "It will all depend upon the King. If he won't put his troops out into the field to distract the Dark Men from the Gate, we will never reach it. And if we don't reach it, and any of the Dark Brethren go through, it's over."

One of the newer men, a lithe little fighter from the East named Dax just whistled. No one else spoke.

"I've always placed us in fights I thought we could win, running when we could. I tried always to keep us from battles, and to defend our territories. Staying out of sight of the Dark Brethren used to be our mantra. Not letting them know I still existed was the goal. But now, today…I'm telling you: if you see a Dark Man, kill him! And if we must fight the Dark Brethren themselves, then we must. But I will fail and die before I let even one of them walk through that Gate without at least trying to stop them!"

For a great long time, no one else said another word.

CHAPTER 35

Ellie was staring at her computer screen, desperately fighting against sleep. Coffee had lost its potency. Energy drinks were like drinking a glass of sweetened water. Removing her glasses and rubbing her eyes, Ellie went back to studying the varying gravimetric and magnetic fields that intertwined in moving arcs on her screen.

These moving arcs of power, of course, showed nowhere when she looked over at the monolith itself. But on the screens, it literally pulsed and churned with waves of power and movement. All of this was radically different from when they had first discovered it.

But ever since Nathan had made his magnificent disappearance, it had all changed. The monolith pulsed with life. Several researchers had noted that it seemed to fluctuate day-to-day. And even the dark crystals imbedded in the thing pulsed with power and a dark light.

It was as if the monolith itself was alive.

Shaking her head, Ellie stood up. All the other researchers had gone home for the evening. Looking at the time on her computer in the upper right-hand corner, she saw that it was approaching 1 am. On a Saturday.

Ellie sighed. Grant was going to be so pissed. *Again.* They were supposed to go out tonight. Grant himself had gone home around seven himself to get ready. At the time, Ellie had promised profusely that she would be right behind him.

"I'll be back! I'll be ready. We'll get it on later, too!" Well, *that* didn't happen! Grant likely went out by himself or with a few of his friends. Again.

She could hear the argument as if she were there right at that moment: *"Why is the disappearance of your ex-boyfriend so important? Is the bloody black monolith going to vanish tomorrow, too? Clearly, not!! Then why the fuck can we not go out on a date? Everyone needs a life, Ellie! It is going to take years to figure this out! Oh and, by the way, your EX-boyfriend is probably dead! The end!!"*

She could hear it because that is exactly what he had said last weekend. Sighing again, she studied the fluctuations some more. *Wait a minute! What was that?* The core of the thing seemed to be pulsing. Almost like a heartbeat. That was different.

Suddenly, the magnetic power within the chamber grew so powerful, that Ellie could feel the pull within her very being. It took everything in her to grab ahold of the desk nearby and hold on, as even it started dragging itself towards the monolith! And it didn't have a shred of iron in it! It was all aluminum. So…not just magnetic field pull…it was gravimetric too…..!

Ellie's brown eyes grew large studying the sudden output of energy. It was off the charts! Her fascination with what was happening dampening, however improperly, any sense of fear.

Holding on to the desk with one hand, the pulsing waves began to move ever faster and faster. The dark light from the crystals grew bright enough to light up the entire room.

Then suddenly, there was a bright flash of light.

Ellie's glasses dropped to the desk, and then the floor.

The waves and fields of energy slowly subsided…and the pulses returned to the normal hum and throb they'd been at since the beginning. Since the day it had been brought out of its tomb those many months ago.

The only difference today…in this room…was that Ellie was no longer there to see it.

CHAPTER 36

Emorion slipped into his hidden sanctum in the trader city of Talim as he always did – through the dark alleys that his guards quietly watched and protected just so he could come and go completely without notice. If any poor sap, drunkard, or orphan wandered into this dark alley and happened to be thinking he would be able to set up camp here…that poor human would be disposed of.

Of course, Emorion could not care less about such things. He had ordered such a complete lack of mercy on anyone coming into this area on purpose. The word on the street would eventually get around – don't find yourself anywhere near the Peach Street Inn. And for the Creator's sake, do not go into the Black Alley.

No one comes out again.

And word apparently was getting around. Not enough for anyone outside the city to care. Neither of Emorion's "brothers" would ever hear of such things. Why would they care if an orphan or some miserable drunk disappeared in some alley halfway around the world from them?

Answer: they wouldn't. Emorion smiled without showing teeth. He hated such things. But a nice smirk, that was perfect. These pathetic mortals. Useful, to be sure. But pathetic. Perfect for slaves. And for lifeblood. Not much more.

Shrugging off his outer armor, Emorion slipped by the two women guarding his rooms. Emorion had always preferred women warriors. Completely ruthless and always with a chip on their shoulder. Something to prove. That they were just as good as men for starters. Emorion was quite convinced that in some ways they were better.

The women nodded. Scarves hiding their faces, Emorion knew they would not be anything he would want to see, anyway. Quite rotten or beaten up if they were part of his guard.

But the one waiting in his bed. That one might be worth looking at. Oh yes, indeed she was. As he entered, the girl shot up to a sitting position in the bed, pulling at the chains holding her in place in the middle. She had the rather unoriginal idea to scream.

How *delightful.*

Slowly disrobing, Emorion made sure his manhood was clearly visible in the dim light. He wanted her to know he was quite motivated and interested in her.

Hmm…this girl was from somewhere far away from Talim. He vaguely wondered where his men had found her. Up north perhaps. Where did blonds come from? He didn't really care. He knew it wasn't close to this city or even this region. As he headed towards the huge four-poster bed, he crawled in and pushed the girl down onto the sheets. Her screaming was as high-pitched as he had perhaps ever heard. Absolutely marvelous. It was beautiful, really. It was like an orchestra playing a classical song. He smiled down at her to show his appreciation for her efforts in all of this.

His mind wandered.

Soon. Soon, I will have that Gateway open. How Jezerah had been inept enough to leave it so poorly guarded was beyond him. And that fool and his ridiculous excuses would be shoved sideways up his asshole very, very soon. Hmm…speaking of that…

Emorion became engrossed in his work of trying to produce an heir. Oh yes, Jezerah had told him of his conclusions that somehow the Dark blocked their ability to produce offspring. What a pity, and a waste, if true. But Emorion was quite sure Jezerah lied as a matter of course. That would make this a lie, as well.

Or not.

Oh well. The screaming alone was worth it. It seemed this one had stopped for some reason. Looking down at her for the second time, he realized she had passed out. Fainted perhaps. Emorion frowned his disapproval but did not slow his motion.

But this was a bit disappointing. He vaguely hoped he hadn't killed her. He wasn't going to be able to impregnate the slave girl for sure if she died, now, was he? He decided to focus on his work. The Dark must have progeny. Without one, everything they'd been promised would never be able to come true. And it must. It had to.

And that damnable Gate had to be reopened.

He was close now. He felt it.

CHAPTER 37

Nathan stood on the riverbank, standing next to Smyslin. He stopped and nervously pointed towards a copse of trees.

"What? I don't see anything."

"Members of the Dark Horde are there, Master."

Nathan squinted his eyes. About a dozen trees, some branches…leaves… shade…grasses in patches underneath. Sunlight shining through in places.

"Nope. I got nothin'."

Smyslin turned to stare in amazement at him. Shaking his head, he said, "How is a Lost One so blind? I am beginning to think all the stories are not true."

Nathan just shrugged. "Are we crossing here, or not?" he asked, beginning to survey up and down the riverbank for other areas where they might cross. The shallows here were perfect, and the riverbank on the other side, while steep, was eminently climbable. The channel cut by the river rose towards the east, but stayed low and even declined towards the west before it turned north away from the city. The flatlands to the south of the river there created quite the fallow fields. An abundant wheat field was waving in the breeze under beautiful yellow sunlight off in the distance.

"It appears we will not have a choice."

Nathan snapped his attention back, as a dozen Dark Men approached from out of the shade of the trees across the river. Turning to go back, another four were approaching from their backside, loping down the riverbank on the near side about thirty yards from them.

Smyslin stole a glance at Nathan and adjusted his scarf before stepping forward, towards the nearest of his kin.

"Brothers! How goes the hunt today for the rebel souls? Surely word has reached you now from the scouts we encountered over the last few days…? Before you, I hold the Master's High Servant: Nat'an. His black soul has been entrusted with the gravest of endeavors…"

"Hold your tongue, equipment manager!" shot a raspy voice from the leader of the four approaching Dark Men. "We have heard something, yes. But word has also reached us from the Great Lord that no such mission has been launched. In fact, the Great Master is searching for one such as he…! It appears you are either a complicit traitor to this Lost One or are enslaved to his power! Either way, we will…"

"Hold on!" Nathan said, raising up his hands. "Which of the 'Great Lords' do you serve?"

This brought a sharp pause to the conversation. The leader looked back at his companions. One shrugged slightly. The leader turned and answered, "We serve Master Jezerah, as does he," he said, pointing directly at Smyslin. "Or at least…he used to." He said this with dire implications and disgust in his voice.

"Well…I don't serve him," Nathan said truthfully. "In fact, I serve another…" and he turned to casually begin crossing the river. Smyslin had given him more information on the attack at the monolith over time. It appeared that the 'Dark Brethren' weren't unlike real brothers and fought like hell with each other. "Go ahead. Halt my mission. Bring me back to your Master. But when my Master learns of this…well…" he shrugged casually, "…someone's head will have to roll. Come along,

Smyslin. You still serve the Dark as a whole, do you not? Let him come with me, or I will make sure you personally burn…!"

Nathan said, staring as hard as he could back at the leader.

The Dark Men stared at one another in confusion. Clearly, they were not used to being thwarted. And this situation was beyond unusual for them, as well. Smyslin raised his head and acted haughty. Then he simply began to follow Nathan across the water.

The four Dark Men on their side simply watched them go. The ones on the far side had stopped once they saw Nathan and Smyslin detained on the other side. Now, they watched in amazement as they simply crossed the river and walked right by them. Arguments began amongst the two groups.

Nathan spoke as loudly as he dared, "Once we get over that riverbank, we run for it."

"I think that would be best."

Just as they crested the hill, an angry roar was heard behind them. The eight on the near side apparently weren't worried about burning. They were charging straight up the muddy bank right at them.

"Run!" he said, and they did.

One never knows how far something is away from oneself until he has to run full speed trying to get there. Burning in his lungs and running in jeans through high grasses Nathan found to be more than difficult. Once they reached the edge of the wheatfield, they plunged into it, with the Dark Warriors nipping at their heels.

Man! They are fast!

The sense of urgency to stop became overwhelming just as Smyslin caught up with him. Nathan pulled out his stolen shock-lance and flipped the trigger. Immediately, he was surrounded in the high grass by all eight of the others. Smyslin crouched down and covered his head.

Multiple long black knives and shorter shock lances appeared, crackling with energy at their tips. Nathan had to hope he was still somehow immune to the shock lances and kept a wary eye on the waving knives.

It appeared these Dark Men had heard the stories of the Lost Ones, as well. None was in a hurry to be the first to die. It appeared they were attempting with their waves and lunges to get him to more open ground where they could wield the knives without catching them on forty or fifty wheat stalks. Nathan decided it was time to take his chance.

He lunged forward at one of the knife-bearing men and managed to hit him with a shock. The force threw him backwards into the field. As he did so, however, two of the those with similar weapons to his own lunged almost immediately, hitting both flanks right about at kidney level. But, as before, instead of feeling pain any longer – Nathan felt a flood of power and energy.

Whirling with that energy, he crouched and wheeled, using every bit of his several years of karate training to avoid a couple knife stabs and deflect a third. While doing so, he spun his shock lance in a circle, catching two more. One got it right in the face, burning his face scarf and sending him flying into the air.

These things packed a punch! A glancing slice from a knife slid by his attempt to block it and sliced his forearm and side. Pain flared bright and blood poured out. Nathan pulled back and swung around in a small circle again, sweeping with the opposite leg for balance and to keep attacks off his rear.

But there were too many of them. Two of those he'd lanced returned and they all closed with him simultaneously. Four shocks hit him from head to toe, while at least two more knife cuts went deep into his flesh.

But by now, power from the lances was flowing fully in him. However, or whatever shock-lances did to him, Nathan leaped straight up into the air, surprising himself with how high he jumped. Leaping so high, it seemed he floated for a second, toes completely above the wheat tips and the Dark Men's heads. The Dark Men's eyes grew large as he did so, staring in stunned amazement as he landed.

When his feet touched the ground, a blast of power went out in a circle all around him, blowing back the Dark Men and causing the crouching Smyslin to roll like a ball several feet away. The force knocked down wheat in all directions. He clicked the "full burn" mode on the shock lance, something he'd figured out while messing with the switches days earlier while sitting with Smyslin under the twin moons.

He lowered his eyes below his eyebrows, playing it as best he could. "I won't ask again – leave or I will burn you all!" And they ran. Once again, Dark Men fled from Nathan. And once again, the bizarre wail came after.

Smyslin was looking at him like he'd grown horns and was wielding a pitchfork.

"What's that sound, Smyslin? Why do they make that wail when they run?" eyes lingering on the Dark Men as they vanished into the hills.

"It is the 'Hymn of the Lost'. The Dark Warriors mourn for those who should be great masters but have lost the fullness of the Void. It is the deep regret of failing the High Lords. We all learn the old songs. They also know they will soon die. But they cannot stand in the face of the power of the Lost."

Nathan whipped his head to look at the still-crouching Smyslin. He appeared be more afraid of Nathan than he had been of his brothers. His eyes, now with all white around his irises, were as wide as he'd ever seen them. Or maybe it was just the added effect with the white added in.

"Will they be punished?"

"Most assuredly, Master. Their leaders, at least, will likely be put to death."

Nathan switched off the power to his lance, no longer caring to look for them to return. "You live in a harsh reality, Smyslin. Failure resulting in death means that everyone in your entire culture should perish. How do you survive?" He began walking towards the city walls, which were within sight over the tops of the wheatfield that had survived the blast.

"The Masters show us great mercy, Lost One. Surely you would kill for such failure as well…?"

"Not on your life. No…pun intended, Smyslin. Failure is only the opportunity to learn and do better next time. Maybe your 'Great Lords' are hoping the lesson is not lost on the survivors. But…" he just stopped talking and shook his head. "Just go, Smyslin. You're free to leave. Go home to your people and tell them I altered your mind or something. Surely you won't be hurt, as I have such 'great power' and all…!"

Smyslin stood up, but lowered his head, shaking it. Removing his red scarf, Smyslin showed a deeply tanned skin tone, but no blackness any longer. Rolling back his sleeves to show the same skin colorings. His gloves came off and they were even lighter. He then pointed to his eyes.

"I am no longer a Dark Man. They would surely execute me out of pity. If you no longer wish me with you, I understand Master. But I will die alone then. The rebels will surely kill me for the clothing I wear. Perhaps with you, I have a chance at protection. Should I wander the world alone, I will be killed by anyone who meets me. You have cursed my existence. But it is I who is at fault. My curiosity about you was my undoing…".

He sounded as lost as his words.

Nathan closed his eyes, raising his head and sighing in exasperation. "Look. I need a helper full time, anyway. I don't know this world. I swear to try to protect you from the rebels, as you did me from the Dark Men. Remain loyal, do as I say, and I will spare you and you can be my servant. For as long as I remain in this world. Once I leave – and I will leave – again, I can no longer help you. But, for now, you will live a little longer and we can both benefit from the other's company and aid. I may not be able to pay you, but what I can provide, I will. Deal?"

Smyslin nodded miserably. "I am a little Lost One myself now, it appears. The Dark has abandoned me. I would rather be lost with you than lost and alone by myself. A target for every Dark Man I meet and for every rebel in this pathetic little kingdom!"

"Great…that's just great. Come on then!" And they walked side-by-side towards the high gates of a town whose name Smyslin did not know.

Nathan heard him mutter, "It seems not all the legends are untrue." He was staring at the places where the wounds on Nathan's body had been. Now completely healed. Only the rents in his shirt and the blood stains marked that they'd ever been there at all.

CHAPTER 38

The King received Morgaine in his Assembly Hall where he greeted foreign dignitaries and held court for the people. It was a massive, tiled stone hall, with huge high pillars, paintings on the ceiling, chandeliers, stained glass windows, and a marble platform with stairs cut into it all the way to the gold-inlaid throne.

King Rondor III of the Kingdom of Rondor was a powerful appearing man, with a bold nose and sharp cheeks. He was not handsome, per se. But he certainly had charisma, and the presence of a true high king.

A half a dozen or so advisors – men and women of nobility – stood on either side of the throne, with the Queen nowhere to be seen. The nobility around him were dressed in their finest – with jewelry and coloring appropriate to their family crests. The common people had been let in on the balcony and the one side wooden bleachers, so that they could see the White Queen herself.

Or so Morgaine had been told. Morgaine approached the throne with an immaculately dressed Brianna to her right, Treyborne in full uniform on the left, and Maitan bringing up the rear, holding important documents and other writing utensils, should they become necessary.

Morgaine herself was dressed all in black and silver, a form-fitting, full length "dress" in outward appearance. Underneath, though, she had thin sheath-like body armor leggings, riding boots. The large, hooped dress also concealed a wicked looking blaster with a long barrel. Brianna had helped put all this together and, although she had seen it, made no comment. Morgaine had said this formal greeting could all be just an elaborate tribute – or a trap. They were to be ready. She had even hidden her strange, black sword between the mattresses of her bed before leaving the room. "Just as a precaution," she said.

Stopping before the throne, Morgaine bowed. Her entourage did the same. Morgaine held the bow for a long moment, then rose. The others remained bowing as she had instructed.

King Rondor nodded, looking at them. "Rise Morgaine, and all with you!" he said, clearly ignoring her doing so earlier. "Welcome to the Assembly Hall of the House of Rondor! We receive you in the presence of the people. This is also called 'The People's Court', where I sit and judge between their issues once every month."

"Thank you for the formal welcome, Your Majesty. May I ask why we are doing this now, after I've been in the castle for two days?"

"Because today is a special day, Lady Morgaine. Since my grandfather and father's wisdom is failing me, I seek the court of public opinion today. I wish the people to see the hero that helped create this kingdom. And I wish them to see the one who would throw us into a world war, as well. I hope that makes it clear to you."

Morgaine looked at the crowded bleachers on the side. They seethed with people staring wide-eyed and slack-jawed at a legend coming to life before them. Brianna stole a glance at the mezzanine balcony behind them. It was equally full.

"I see them," Morgaine responded, "Welcome, people of Rondor! May the peace of the Creator rest upon you. Nowhere else in the world may you worship him freely other than right here! Cherish that privilege! And never take it for granted."

Turning back towards the King, she gave a slight nod, indicating he could proceed with whatever was going on this day. He smiled a small smile at the irony of being allowed to continue in his own court and in front of his own people.

"Lady Morgaine, the Court, and the Throne recognize you and your contributions to the creation of this kingdom. Your aid to my grandfather, King Rondor I – may the Creator shelter him forever in his wings – has been added to our official history and public records as of this morning."

Turning to his people, he added, "Her help was not widely known for decades, as the leaders of the Dark Horde had thought her dead. She wished to keep it that way. Now that it is known far and wide that the mighty Morgaine yet lives…we wish to honor her, as is proper, for what she helped our forefathers accomplish over fifty years ago. Would you not agree that this is right?" he asked the crowd. Murmurs of approval and even a little applause and a few small cheers came from both areas.

Morgaine nodded as if this were all very acceptable. Brianna felt her tension, though. On her other side, Treyborne looked like he was about to chew rocks. She leaned backward a tad and saw his jaw muscles clench and unclench repeatedly.

"Now, there is one more matter. A grave one. Lady Morgaine, you know our laws. Some would call them 'strict', even 'oppressive'. In some cases, I have been led to agree in this very court. I have repealed some archaic and outdated rules so that my people may live in harmony and peace."

A cheer rose from the crowd. It might even have been spontaneous. King Rondor III acknowledged this with a small motion of his hand. Or perhaps it was to end it. Brianna was not sure.

"It has been brought to my attention by several members of my Court that the death of the Contessa of Burleyne – my aunt – could very well be attributed directly to your actions. The King and the Court are aware of what you were trying to accomplish, Lady Morgaine. But…the law *is* the law. So now…a hearing has been called and you must answer. As complete as you can, by the Will of the Creator. Do you swear to do so…?"

Morgaine stared for a moment, lifting her head slightly and to the side. She nodded her assent.

The Court Vizier, a stout man with a monocle, stated loudly, "Answers must be given verbally, My Lady."

Sharp eyes directed at the man for a moment, then back at the King. "I so swear," Morgaine said. Her words were cold as ice.

Brianna gulped.

"Lady Morgaine, you asserted that my aunt, the former Contessa and married to the Count of Burleyne, in Nelrae, was a member of the Dark Cult." The crowd reacted to this in gasps and amazement. Rondor ignored them.

"Yes, it is as you say," she responded.

"I want this Court and the people to know…that evidence of this was found after my aunt, the Contessa, died. It shows she had been, in fact, involved with the Dark Cult." More gasps and people shouting, "No! I can't be!" amid gasps and murmuring. Rondor held his hand up.

Brianna noted he held his royal scepter in the other, resting it on the floor. *Has that been there the whole time?*

"The Lady Morgaine did reveal this to the Court and a spy in my own house was uncovered. It is with deep sorrow I must admit these things. My father's sibling and only sister, at some point fell to the lust of the flesh that is the Dark Cult. We have only the Lady Morgaine herself to thank for revealing this to us. It is not a pleasurable thing to find out. But it was both necessary and worthy of note. The issue before us now is that the law states that if someone – whether through forethought, intention, or accident, causes the death of another – that someone must be held over for trial. If convicted, the person must serve a sentence, or even face death if the ruling is that the death was intentional and had been planned beforehand. Lady Morgaine, with your actions, did the Contessa die by your hand? Did you cause her death in any way?"

"Yes. I did." More ice.

Brianna wanted to take her hand and squeeze it, but she dared not do it.

"Did you, in any way, enter that chamber where we met with the intention of doing said act, knowing it would or could cause the death of my aunt, the Contessa?"

"I knew it was a strong possibility, at the very least. 'The Dark must be exposed to the Light.' I knew that the consequences of shining the Light of the Creator on that much Darkness could possibly kill her." Several people drew in shocked breaths at this.

Rondor nodded, having noted the quote from the holy scriptures with an additional nod. "And…Lady Morgaine…could you have held your hand? Allowed us to search the premises and chambers of my aunt without, in fact, killing her first?"

Morgaine glared at the man. King or not, Brianna feared the sudden ripping off of the hoop skirt, and a quick reach for the blaster. Morgaine's hand nearest the thing twitched.

The court administrator spoke up, "The Court requires an answer."

"You know that I could have. I addressed the room with the accusation and the room erupted. The woman, Contessa Burleyne…was angry and shouting. You, yourself, King Rondor, were quite angry and the room was devolving into chaos. You also nodded your own assent to the action. But in truth, I could wait no longer…I was afraid my accusations would not be taken seriously…"

"Enough!" the king roared. "What you are speaking of now must come during a trial. If what you say proves true…"

"If what I say proves *true*? You were there! No one was listening! No one was going to search her rooms unless I did something! She would be alive to this day, to be sure. But she also would not have been exposed as an Agent of the Dark! I would already be…"

"Guards. Take Lady Morgaine to her chambers. This hearing is over. Put her under round the clock surveillance. As a courtesy and in acknowledgement of her former service to the throne, she will simply be held in her chambers, and not put into the prisons. However, *no one* comes or goes but by my orders." Rondor tapped his scepter on the floor three times.

The room erupted into shouts. Some were cheering for Morgaine for exposing the Contessa's evil intentions. Others were yelling just as loudly she needed to be hanged. Brianna looked over at Morgaine, who was calmly looking back at her.

"Peace, child. This is not over yet. And whether these laws are being thrown upon me by Dark agents or simply misguided legalism, we will not be detained. We must and will get to that Gate."

Guards from all sides, dressed in full armor, were approaching Morgaine and her three retainers. Treyborne flinched, moving to drawing his weapon before Morgaine laid her hand upon his.

"This is not a fight we want. These people are our only allies."

"Allies, my Queen? With allies like this, who needs enemies…?"

Looking at her, he didn't move a muscle again, even as a guard pulled his bladed weapon out of its sheath before handing it to another and grabbing one of Morgaine's arms. Amid the shouts and chaos of the room, Morgaine said, "Keep Brianna and the others safe. Make a second barrier around their guards with our own. If they resist, cite the First Citation of Freedom!"

With that, Morgaine was out the door, half-carried by much larger men in bright armor and followed by dozens of the King's Guards.

Brianna just stood in the middle of the vast cathedral-like courtroom, confused, and shaking. Tears were streaming down her face. It took Treyborne and Maitan each taking one of her arms to lead her from the room before she knew what was happening.

How had it all gone so wrong?

CHAPTER 39

The gates of the hill town opened as Nathan approached. Several guards, dressed like they were in a Renaissance fair, whipped nasty looking crossbows and held spears in a circle just inside the inner courtyard behind the massive wooden doors.

Nathan held up his hands…stopped, and said, "My name is…Nathan. Have we done something to offend…?"

A short older man, sporting a curled mustache barked, "Sir, you have as a traveling companion a Dark Man! And you yourself seem to have had your issues yourself. Your clothes are all torn. But this Dark Man with you, he must be…" Stopping to look carefully at Smyslin, the older man started to chuckle and held his hand to his mouth.

"Lower your weapons, men. Guards, I agree these men appear to be strange. A man with hair like the Lady Morgaine traveling with a Dark Man. But which of you has ever seen or heard of a Dark Man with a *red* scarf?" He started laughing, and all the men slowly did, as well.

Scrutinizing Smyslin some more, the man came closer as the gates opened and pulled the scarf down from his face, causing Smyslin no end of consternation. Nathan just stood there, watching, and waiting.

Turning to Nathan, he said, "If you're going to have one of you pretend to be a Dark Man, you might want to use a black scarf next time…". He shook his head. Had you run into any, you'd have noticed the difference immediately. So too, would they!" he added with a stern look.

Nathan started to object but thought better of it. Instead, he nodded as if the information was well-received.

The commander added, "And this one's paint is coming off or something. He might pass for a Dark Man at a distance. But up close…". He just kept shaking his head. "Either way, congratulations on making it to the town alive. Clearly, you have heard of the Dark Men sweeping into the northern hill country. Where are you coming from? And why…" he asked, "do you appear to be as white-haired and strange eyed as the White Queen herself? Not to mention wearing clothes that look like they have been sliced to pieces and have blood all over them. Not yours, apparently. You don't have a scratch on you! If you don't mind me asking."

Nathan thought it was about time to say something, "My name is Nathan…this is…Smythe," he said, just in case 'Smyslin' meant something horrible to these people or was a name known to be from the Dark Men. Naming someone 'Trickster' didn't seem like a good idea for ordinary people.

"I'm traveling from a distant city called "New York" and wanted to find people of like minds. I was scratched by something on the way here, but I'm all healed now. Just didn't have any other clothing." He paused, "You spoke of Morgaine as if you'd seen her yourself at some point. Is that true? Do you know her and have you met her? Perhaps she's…from where I come from."

"Indeed, I have seen her! And recently! But I doubt she's from anywhere you hail from," the commander said.

Smyslin let out a little whimper, which Nathan quashed quickly with a sideways glare.

The commander seemed to not notice and kept on talking, looking out over the courtyard for no reason Nathan could see. The other guards seemed not to notice either, as they were intent upon keeping their eyes on Smyslin even though their commander assured them he couldn't be a Dark Man. "Not too long ago, in fact! We hadn't seen her around these parts in ten or twelve years. But she rode into this very city just over a week ago!"

"Is she still here?" Nathan asked excitedly.

Wow…so the legend lives. Or maybe it's just an heir and a carefully constructed ruse. Honestly, who would know the difference?

"Oh no. She left several days ago for the capital. King Rondor sent word to send her down. She left in a hurry, in fact. She's likely there by now. If you mean to catch up to her, you'd better hurry yourself. I doubt she'll stay in the capital city too long. She's a strange one," he added as an afterthought.

One of the other officers standing behind the guards nodded especially long on that last part. Nathan had no doubt a woman who lived hundreds or thousands of years would be somewhat of an oddity. She sure sounded inhuman.

"Can you perhaps point me in the right direction? Is it safe to travel to 'the capital'? Or are Dark Men everywhere on the way there, too?"

"Oh no, no, no, no!" the commander laughed. Dark Men wouldn't dare come within our borders. They would be executed on sight. He sniffed, redirecting his gaze to Smyslin. "As well they should be. Your friend may not have the best disguise in the world. But I'd get some other clothes on him now, just in case. You don't want him mistaken for a real Dark Man."

Smyslin's head dropped.

The commander misread this, of course, "Oh don't worry man! It was apparently good enough for those heathens at a distance out there! You did well! Even if your darkening stain – or whatever you used to make your skin black – seems to be wearing off! But if some housewife or farmer sees you and mistakes you here in town or out in the countryside, you'll be mobbed! Do either of you have any coin?"

Nathan started to say no, but Smyslin interrupted, "I have some…M… Nathan." It was the first time Smyslin had ever used his real name. He seemed like he was about to drop himself off a bridge. Let's get some rebel…uh…real clothing. Is there an inn here we can stay at?"

"Of course! My men will escort you, so there's no trouble. You two might attract it. No offense, I hope! I strongly recommend you stay one night and head out in the morning. I'll make sure you get protected going and coming one night. After that you're on your own, and that's my word! No matter what, you two are highly irregular. *Highly* irregular!"

He surveyed the men and shouted, "Lieutenant Delaney! Escort these two gentlemen to the Cat's Tale. That's where *she* stayed. They might as well go there, too. Keep a guard there to avoid any trouble. Have them escorted out the southern gates in the morning. Good day, gentlemen." And the short man strode off.

The Lieutenant who had nodded emphatically earlier spoke up, "Well, let's get this over with! I've got rounds to make yet today." Two of the guards turned to follow him with a flick of the Lieutenant's wrist.

With that, Nathan and "Smythe" were walked a few blocks around the courtyard, past a well, several horses, and what appeared to be a butcher shop. Around the next corner, they came to a sign that read, "The Cat's Tale".

Nathan just shook his head. This was becoming all too real.

CHAPTER 40

Treyborne stormed down the hallway, set to meet with his team outside Morgaine's chambers. He was in full view of four armed guards standing outside her suite. At seeing Treyborne's face, one of them reached for his weapon, pulling at it before another man said something to him.

The hallway was huge and ornate; the area was reserved for high-ranking officials from within Rondor and without. Marble floors spotless and shining, marble pillars, huge walnut doors, ornate tables set with crystals and high burning lamps, sunlight spilling through huge double-glassed windows framed with lace and colorful curtains.

None of this did Treyborne notice one bit. His jaw hurt from clenching it shut to not scream at everyone and everything. Stalking down the hall, he walked around the corner and down the hall towards his own rooms where his team had congregated per his orders. Two of the men lingered in the hallway, also according to his orders, to keep an eye on those keeping their eye on his mistress.

Trust no one.

That mantra had served him all too well. This day had certainly proven no different. As he burst in through the double doors of his chambers, every man who had been sitting jumped to attention. Waving them to sit, he moved to take a chair behind the large desk that was situated in the middle of the room.

Someone at some point had needed a desk in these chambers, and he had moved it from the back room to this one. Sitting down, he studied the crew. Maitan fidgeted nervously in the corner. Several others were fondling their weapons. This was a group ready to explode. He needed to restore calm first.

It would be nice to have some to share with them. I need to find a little myself.

"Ok. We all know this has not gone the way the Mistress had hoped or planned. But we always have contingencies. We had a plan for the possibility of being utterly rejected and possibly having to fight our way out of the city."

Some of the men sat forward on their chairs at this. All three of the younger men squeezed onto the smaller couch leaned forward almost on their toes.

"However, we are not doing that." Those same men reclined back to slouching with disappointment clear on their faces. "Not yet anyway. We're still beat up from just getting here. Ramus is still recovering back at the cruiser with the horses. "How is he doing, by the way, Maitan?"

"He's better, Captain. He lost a lot of blood. But he will live. I wouldn't count on him for more than manning a blaster from his cot for quite a while, however." Maitan leaned back against the wall as he finished speaking.

Nodding, Treyborne returned to the matter at hand. "I have not been allowed to speak with Morgaine directly, but our new girl…"

Brianna entered through one of the doors and smiled an apology as she did so. Someone had shut the double doors as Trey had sat down. Brianna slipped in and shut the door quietly behind herself.

"Well, speak of the Dark! I was about to say you have been our communication channel. What news do you have for us?"

Brianna looked at the roomful of men and cleared her throat. "Morgaine is fine, if spouting off curses and throwing things at the guards in her inner chambers can be labeled as such. Rondor has even put two female guards to stand in her bedchamber and bath. She told me to tell you she's planning on taking a bath in an hour and will attempt to bully the guard in that room out so she can use communicators and speak with you directly."

Brianna paused and looked right at Treyborne, "She also said no fighting or causing any trouble. If we must break her out, we will do so if she cannot be freed by legal means. As she tried to point out earlier – these are our only allies. Without them, we are just a 'ragtag little band of well-armed fools.' Her words, of course."

A man in the middle chair next to the couch muttered something. Brianna ignored him, continuing with Morgaine's instructions, "She did say that we cannot wait forever. If they delay this trial at all, we will attempt to slip out in the night. The Gate must be the goal. She said to give it a week. If the King attempts to drag things out any longer than that, we move."

Treyborne nodded. "It's about as I thought. A week then. Messau… Jairus, take three of the men and go check on our equipment with Maitan the next time he goes out to the cruiser. Bring in any and every blaster we can hide in our leggings or shorts. They likely won't recognize them for what they are but might figure out they're dangerous. And bring some cy-packs just in case something needs blown up. And Messau," he said pointedly, "be discreet."

Messau saluted from his seat, never even raising his eyes.

Treyborne sighed but let it go. "Anything else? I want everyone traveling in twos. No one goes anywhere alone. That includes you," he said, looking at Brianna. If you're with Morgaine, fine. If you're going anywhere else, one of us goes with you. Clear?"

Brianna nodded, eyes wide.

"We have each other's backs. If anything happens, or anything unusual is noticed, you bring it to my attention. I don't care if it's the middle of the night. Dismissed."

The group began to get up to depart. The door opened and the men left, two-by-two. Brianna lingered, as did Maitan. Treyborne lifted an eyebrow. "Maitan, you have something for me?"

"Yes commander. Since I am also unable to see the Mistress, I need confirmation on something. Before we entered the city, she had me put her cloaking ring into her saddle bags. Should I retrieve it? And, if so, where should I take it?"

"The Ring! Yes! Go get it and bring it to me. I'll give it to Brianna, and she can get it to Morgaine. It might be just the ticket!" Maitan nodded and rushed out of the room, shutting the door behind him.

Brianna waited expectantly.

Treyborne looked at her a moment, nodding. "You're probably wondering what we just talked about. You'll learn soon enough." My, but she was *outstanding*! Not Morgaine's pure beauty…Brianna's was more subtle. The dark skin and hair made a nice counterpoint, as well. Her allure was somehow…almost as powerful? Amazing.

"What is it you wanted to say to me?" he added.

"Morgaine has one more instruction just for you," she said closing the other door. "She said to apologize in advance, but when she goes into her bath – if she successfully chases out her female guard, she wants you and I to meet her in there and discuss her plans. Her *real* ones." Brianna took a deep breath.

"How in…she wants me to climb on the stones over to her bathroom…?" Treyborne said incredulously. "I mean…sure…but…that won't be easy. And I could be spotted…"

"Unless you use the Ring. She specifically said to remind Maitan of it. It was fortunate he remembered on his own, but otherwise I would have by now. Morgaine told me all about it. She called it a 'Light Shield'. It sounds quite handy. I'm surprised she doesn't keep it on her."

"Apparently all that old battle gear she used to wear takes a certain level of energy. It all needs to be charged up. That's why she doesn't wear her armor all the time – it's amazing stuff, but she also said the green and black mix doesn't match her eyes." He chuckled. "Anyway, the ring also needs to be charged. There is a small black box it's kept in that keeps the power up in it. Kind of like keeping enough oil in the gas lamps."

Brianna just nodded. "I'll tell *Mistress* Morgaine you will be arriving within the hour." She emphasized the title, probably to keep in practice of doing it correctly. "And I'll tell her to leave the window cracked."

She giggled and turned to go.

Treyborne watched her for a moment. Then added, "Tell her I might be a little late. Maitan is fast, but he just left to retrieve the Ring and the stable is outside the city. I'm thinking two hours, minimum. Tell her to be clothed, too. I'm still a man, after all."

Brianna looked back, eyes bright and laughed. "I'll tell her. But I think she knows." And she slipped out of the room.

CHAPTER 41

The next morning, Nathan and Smyslin, dressed in new clothes, both with backpacks full of two water bottles, cherries, bread, cheese, and some dried beef, walked out through the southern gates of Bistern, escorted by the city watch.

The inn had been delightful, with good food, fun music, and blissfully comfortable beds. Nathan had almost forgotten what sleeping in a bed was like. He'd slept on the ground for weeks now. Fully rested, he watched Smyslin try to adjust to walking around in unfamiliar clothes and not wearing what he referred to as "appropriate face covering".

Nathan himself was trying to get used to baggier leggings and a much looser shirt, but it was quite comfortable and kept him cooler. Although his jeans had survived and been hand-washed by a girl for one of Smyslin's smallest coins, they were packed away in Smyslin's pack for the time being. His old shirt had been cut and torn into tatters, so he'd thrown it into the corner in the room and left it. His socks and underwear had also been washed and were back on.

Smyslin had bought several shirts for each of them, a pair of leggings, boots which fit wonderfully, and several pairs of socks and underclothing. Smyslin insisted on carrying all the extra clothes himself. He felt he "... had to be worth something to someone...". Nathan was more than a little worried about him.

Nathan's iPhone was also still fully charged, showed no signal and was resting in a pouch of his new backpack, as well. He'd checked it in the room before going to bed, just to see. No change meant it was of no help.

As they trudged by the farmer's carts, horses, and other people coming into the city as they left, it began to mist and then rain. Nathan stopped and pulled out a cap they'd bought, but Smyslin just let the rain fall on him, looked up, opened his mouth, and drank some as it came down. He did it repeatedly, so Nathan just ignored him. It was a cool rain, and after the heat of the previous few days, it felt good. They'd both gotten baths the previous night, so Nathan felt almost human. He couldn't even imagine what he'd smelled like by the time they had reached Bistern.

It seemed there were "regular people" in this world, after all. At least not everyone was trying to capture or kill him. That made them "regular" in his book. And now all he had to do was find this Morgaine and see if, by some miracle, she could return him to his own world. It wasn't much of a plan. But it was his only plan. It seemed the Gate and she were linked somehow in this world, from what little he had gathered from Smyslin. She had used it centuries ago, anyway. And that was enough to know more about it than he did.

As the morning wore on, the rain stopped and the clouds slowly blew away, leaving the sun to dry and warm them. Looking up and studying it, it appeared very much like his own sun: yellow, warming, and bright. Occasionally as they walked along what appeared to be a highway road paved in stones, several more carts, a carriage and a pair of horsemen who looked like military passed them going the other way.

Other than nodding or waving, no other interaction came of any of it. At one point, they came to a fork in the road and a guidepost was there, like the ones Nathan had seen in pictures of rural Scotland.

"Which way, Smyslin?"

"I have no idea, Master. But the name of this country is the same as the name of its capital. That is the custom amongst these lesser humans. Nelrae is the capital of the Empire of Nelrae…"

"…and Rondor is the capital of Rondor," Nathan finished for him. *Makes thing simple.*

"Ok…so where's the sign for Rondor?"

"I don't see one, Master. But the man in charge in Bistern said 'south'. Therefore, I would say we go left, as it clearly is heading southwards. The other road is turning more westerly." He shrugged. "Perhaps we can ask the next traveler we meet on the road…?"

"That might evoke some suspicion. We're trying to blend in. Everyone from this country knows darn well where the city of Rondor is." He sighed, then added, "But we can ask at some point or try to figure it out discreetly. The next town we stop at, we'll figure it out before leaving."

Smyslin just nodded, not looking at him. Nathan peered over at him. It did appear that whatever was causing it – sun bleaching, not drinking calf's blood, or whatever Dark Men did at home – that Smyslin's skin was lightening. Rapidly. It was weird and a bit concerning. But Nathan was afraid to bring it up and cause the man to burst into tears again.

So, Nathan just turned and kept walking. By the time the sun was low in the sky to the southwest, the stone road had become wider, and a town appeared in the valley below them. It seemed appropriate to try to stop there, so Nathan asked, "How much coin do we have left, Smyslin?"

"Oh, enough, Master. Engineers are paid well, and although I didn't think I'd need it, I packed quite a bit of my gold and silver. I was hoping we would conquer a city and I could buy some souvenirs."

Nathan snorted, and Smyslin laughed. "It appears I have picked up a truly unique souvenir. But now it owns me!" At least Smyslin said it like a joke. Nathan was pretty sure it wasn't very funny to him. Not at all, in fact.

CHAPTER 42

Treyborne stood on the rounded stone balcony, the breeze blowing back his hair. Sighing deeply, he purposefully walked back inside so if anyone happened to be watching, he would be seen going back into his quarters. Morgaine's balcony was nearby on the same level, of course. But he had made sure not to look at it before withdrawing. He kept the doors open. For the breeze.

Or so anyone watching should believe.

The sun was about halfway down towards the horizon. As a matter of extra precaution, he went into his bedroom and then carefully twisted the green and gold ring on his finger.

Instantly, the green took over, and the field warping technology was released. Treyborne grinned at himself as he vanished in the oval inset mirror on the wall.

It was astonishing every time. He'd done this countless times on surveillance missions or when he simply did not want to be seen. The ring had a limited time that it could function. So, it was very important to stay within that window.

Moving back out from his inner rooms to the balcony, he now looked around to see if anyone was watching. Sure enough, there were two of them. One man was casually sitting on his balcony one floor up across the courtyard, where he had a bird's eye view of both his and Morgaine's balconies. Another, a woman, was boldly looking through a nautical spyglass – pointing it directly their way from the balcony diagonally left and below where the man was sitting.

He waved, knowing they could not see him. Turning, he made a mental note to be careful not to disturb the vines that grew around some of the stones and balconies, if possible. The grounds crew kept them cut back some, so it shouldn't be too much trouble. But he noted where they were before grabbing hold.

Looking down, he of course did not see his own hands, either, cloaked as they were. But he felt the tough leather gloves on his hands and the spiked boots on his feet. Swinging his legs out over the edge closest to Morgaine's larger veranda, Trey stood where he could find purchase for his feet and then reached over, grabbed two deeply inset stones and began to shimmy over towards Morgaine's rooms.

Rock climbing – often without guides or ropes – was part of their routine training. But these stones were cut and fitted, so finger depth was hard to find, and twice a foot slipped despite the cut steel pinions screwed onto his boots. Grunting quietly, he made his way to where he could reach the wide stone railing and utilized a small leap. Grabbing hold with both hands, he then simply climbed in.

At that moment, one of the female guards came out, perhaps thinking she'd heard a sound. She might have, as the rings did not make one inaudible, just invisible. Holding his breath and his body still, Treyborne waited.

The woman was dark-haired, short, and very muscular. She carried some sort of thrusting weapon, like a halberd, but cut to her size. Scanning the entire perimeter, the woman just nodded to herself and went back inside.

Trey took a moment, relaxed, then stood up onto the stone railing and began climbing over to the bathroom window. It was a little higher than the balcony and had the same limited rock handles. After another five or so minutes, he managed to grab the windowsill and gradually pulled his body with his aching arms up to where he could see into the room.

Sitting in her bathrobe was Morgaine, with Brianna standing beside her. Neither of them was looking his way, which was good should anyone burst in. Unlikely, to be sure. But a good precaution.

As he was about to speak and pull himself fully into the room, Morgaine spoke up, "I will continue to sit here, Jaca, until you leave! I deserve my privacy and the King's orders be damned! What? Do you think I'm going to climb out that window naked and leap three stories to the courtyard?"

"I have my orders, Lady Morgaine," came the buttery smooth reply.

"I believe I have said 'I do not care!' enough, don't you?" Morgaine shouted. "Go and ask the King. If he wants me watched while I bathe, which I only allow my maid to do because she helps me – I might as well have him watch as well! Go! Go get him and bring him in here! Oh, and be *sure* to tell the Queen he's coming. I'm sure she won't mind."

The woman guard appeared from behind the dressing area, where she had been hidden from Treyborne's view with a dark look on her face. This girl was also dark-haired, but noticeably taller and thinner than the other guard. She had the grace of a deer, and she carried knives at her side and a bow at her back. A few arrows peeked above the small light brown leather quiver at her back. "I will tell the King. And if I get into trouble, you will have me sleeping in your bed with you, too!" The girl stormed out, slamming the door. A second slam was heard not three seconds later.

Brianna let out a sigh of relief.

But Morgaine spoke up right afterwards, "You can turn visible now, Captain. She has gone. But be quiet, as we have neither much time, nor do I know if the other girl will dare to come in here or not. Plus, a man's voice in here will alert her."

Brianna whirled, looking for him before he turned the ring back to neutral, appearing right next to her, making her jump.

Morgaine didn't even turn her head, knowing where he was somehow. "Was that necessary? Startling Brianna? Or simply for fun?" was all she said.

"*No* to necessary and *yes* to fun," he replied, grinning at Brianna before walking quietly over to Morgaine. He knelt in front of her so their faces could be nearer to each other before speaking further. "What is the plan?"

"The plan is to leave tonight. Damn these fools, but we won't be getting any help from them! Rondor certainly won't be willing to declare war to draw more of the Triumvirate forces to his border for me if he's willing to engage in this mockery of a trial. I wanted them to 'hear' I was angry, but willing to be patient. I am angry, to be sure. But I am also not going to wait to see if I need to escape their dungeons, rather than their luxury suites."

"What are we to do?" Treyborne asked in a tight whisper, all business.

"Brianna is to accompany Maitan to 'see about our supplies' and getting me more of my facial paints and clothing to prepare for the trial. At least that is what you're going to tell everybody to get her out of the city. You are to ride Steel, as you're the only one who can, and the others are to ride any of the horses they can to accompany her. About half the men is all they won't be suspicious of. Once outside the city, Maitan doubles up on his horse with Brianna, and they ride to the transport to get it ready and to keep her safe. That will free up a horse for you for later when you double back for me."

Treyborne nodded that he understood before she continued.

"The rest of the team will be laying around the hallway, until all but the two outside guards go to eat dinner. By then, I'll have my weapons and armor on. Brianna will bring me the ring before she leaves, and I'll put it on. When the girls go about their rounds, I'll retire to my room – telling them I'm going to bed early. I've got my comm still, so when I leave my room – sliding out a window or walking by the girls as they change shifts. I'll just have to let you know when it happens… and you meet me outside the city gates with my horse. We'll ride, just you and I, straight to the cruiser, which will be coming to get us. The others will slip out whatever way they can. Even the two watchers in the hallway should leave once I send the signal. You can send them a silent alert, letting them know to bolt after I'm gone. The likelihood of them getting out is the worst, so leave two of your best at stealth. Once they see my guard is missing, they'll soon try to see if I'm in still in my bedroom. All hell will break loose at some point. Hopefully, after all of us are outside the city and long gone."

Treyborne let out a low whistle. "All right," he said, "We will do as you have instructed. Just know that if you don't get to me, I'm carving my way back in to get you!" With that, he dematerialized, and Brianna heard some small grunts as he lifted himself out through the window.

Morgaine began disrobing for her bath. "Get me that ring, dear. Leave in about ten minutes or so, to give me time to be done with this bath and get my hair washed. I want to look good for my escape!" She smiled and slid her naked body into the still-steaming bath water. Sighing and closing her eyes, she said, "I've changed my mind. Go get the ring and its charger box now. I just want to soak a bit. It will need to recharge some, anyway, and I need to relax."

Brianna tried not to look shocked. Seeing another woman naked was one thing. This wasn't the first time for her. But none of those other women were Morgaine or had a body like hers. Not even close. It was a fascinating mix of feminine curves and muscular fitness. Shaking her head as she left, Brianna suddenly felt very flabby and soft.

CHAPTER 43

The Inn at the town of Nestor – and there was exactly one inn – was quaint, but adequate. Even for the level of technology in this world, it seemed a bit rustic to Nathan. The furniture had clearly seen decades of use. The tables and chairs were a bit worn, but sturdy. And probably because it was literally the only game in town, full to the brim.

The dining hall and entertainment stage were rowdy. The food was good, served on cracked plates while the mugs of ale were served with whatever cups they had. The singer was a busty young woman who told bawdy jokes, showed a little skin, then went back to dancing. Her hair was bright orange-red, and her eyes were a brilliant blue.

Her partner was an older man who was quite skilled at the bent lute… or was it a guitar? It was hard to tell from where Nathan was sitting. He just sat on a stool near her and followed whatever she seemed to do or wherever she took him in song or verse.

"She really is quite good!" Nathan yelled at Smyslin over the din.

Smyslin nodded, not taking his eyes off the girl. In fact, he didn't take his eyes off her for a second, even while eating or drinking. He seemed mesmerized by her. When she finally left the stage to take a break, his eyes followed her even then. Only when she went behind his back to the bar did he stop staring at her.

"You're going to spook the girl!" Nathan said, finally drawing Smyslin's eyes. "It's like you've never seen a woman before."

"Well, to be sure I haven't. Not like her. Not all white skinned and… that hair…those…eyes…" he swallowed. "I was married for a time. It is for the service of the Master to bear children. 'Produce productive individuals'… having girls meant they would be child-bearers themselves. Men would become workers, engineers, warriors, and farmers. All people have a place. Our women also work. When not pregnant, they must do something." He stopped, looking longingly at something else instead of the singer. It was the inn door.

"No one just sings," he finished, looking back at Nathan again. "And no one is simply allowed to sit and just be pretty. Telling jokes and making people laugh. That would be unproductive."

Nathan just stared at him. Raising an eyebrow, he began to speak, but Smyslin stopped him, "I know what you'll say. 'The Masters are harsh; the Masters are cruel'…"

"I was going to say that that is simply sad. In my world…things are different. Women…and some men…are paid to just wear clothes and have pictures taken of them."

Smyslin frowned at this but said nothing.

Nathan continued, "Others are paid to review our taxes, work in banks, and still others are paid just to play a game. Or perform like these people, but for millions of people in film or on TV…It's kind of crazy. I know it's not perfect, but it's better than what you had apparently."

Smyslin stared back at him, eyes wide. "What are 'pictures', 'film and TV'? I understood most of your words, but those did not create in me any image or knowledge."

"Well…a picture is like what I took that night of the sunset. When you asked about it, I offered to show you and you declined."

Smyslin made a strange face.

"And film…is moving pictures that tell a story. I have some short videos on my phone. When we get to our room, I'll show you." Soon they were headed to their room, up two flights of stairs, and all the way to the back of the hall. They entered the room one at a time. It was a tiny one with a lamp and a nightstand and with two small beds against opposite walls. No fireplace, just blankets, and a small window for fresh air. It made even the smallest of New York City apartments look massive.

"Home sweet home!" Nathan said, getting a strange look from Smyslin. "I'm kidding, Smyslin." He just turned and nodded, making up first Nathan's bed and then his own for the evening. The puzzled expression didn't leave his face for quite some time.

Digging in his backpack, Nathan pulled out his iPhone and started scrolling through his pictures. He started showing some of the pictures of himself and Gary and Jennifer – the most recent ones he had – and Smyslin was enthralled.

"We do not have such things. I have heard the Master can see into any room in the complex where he lives. Pictures are joyous. Take one of me. He tried to pose and smile. It was kind of hideous. Nathan hit the button, though, if for no other reason than to just appease him.

"Show it to me!" Smyslin said eagerly. Nathan obliged, showing him the new picture added to his library. "Fascinating!" he said. "When I return…if I return…I will build such a thing and we can all take… pictures!"

Nathan just smiled and nodded. "Great idea. Now let's get some sleep."

He was about to put the phone away when Smyslin asked quietly, "You have a picture of the Arc Gate in your world. I saw it there. Can you show me that one…?"

Nathan hesitated, then pulled the phone back out, and opening it, selected the monolith. Blowing it up as much as he could and showing it to him. Smyslin studied it for a few seconds, then concluded, "That is a different Gate than the one that is here on this world. It is bent slightly differently, and there are more of the dark crystals." Nodding to himself, he said, "Thank you. I was again curious, and you did not chastise me. Thank you for that, also." Disrobing down to his underwear, he trimmed the lamp to a dim glow, climbed into bed and turned towards the wall.

"Good night, Master. You may be right. The Dark Masters are cruel."

"I never actually said that Smyslin."

Smyslin said not another word. A slight snore came not long afterwards. Nathan was still very much awake. So, he just laid on his back, arms behind his head, trying to get a little drowsier.

It didn't help him that the inn was still rocking, either. Even two stories up and down a long hallway, the sounds of singing, music, and laughter carried to their room. The air grew cooler here at night. Or a cold front had moved in. Either way, he listened to some of the sounds coming through the window as they mixed with those coming from down the hall.

Eventually, sleep came to him as well.

CHAPTER 44

It was about 1:30 in the afternoon. Just about that time you wanted to take a nap but couldn't – because you are at work and that is generally frowned upon.

So, Julie did what most people do. She got up, walked around, got some coffee from the break room, and talked to people until she felt guilty enough – and awake enough – to continue working. Sometimes that lasted the rest of the day. Today, it was already twenty minutes or so into her afternoon stroll, when her mostly inane conversation with the new girl Jennifer was suddenly and rudely interrupted by Gary bursting into the break room yelling, "Jenn!!" at the top of his lungs.

Now, this was not completely out of the norm for Gary, but he'd been especially subdued since his friend and roommate Nathan had vanished suddenly several weeks ago.

Julie was so *over...* hearing about it! *But whatever.*

Julie had known Nathan, too, of course. Morose, kind of boring. Didn't talk much. Julie just raised an eyebrow and gave Gary a cool stare. Which he had the gall to totally ignore. Grabbing Jennifer by the arm, he said, "Come see this! I don't know if it's good news...but it's news!"

Julie just rolled her eyes and made the perfunctory decision to head back to her desk a little earlier than normal today.

Jennifer was being half-dragged away by Gary anyway. "Look at this!" Gary said, pointing to his video monitor. A YouTube video was frozen on his screen, and it was a bit blurry, having been stopped at a bad time. "Read the headline...!"

"Another disappearance at the Egyptian exhibition in Queens.'" Jennifer's eyes nearly popped out of their sockets. "What happened?"

"I'm not sure yet. But it appears that one or more of the researchers is gone this time. I know that isn't great…but…"

"It means that at least the doorway that took Nathan away from us is still active. There's a chance," she finished. Less enthusiasm than at first.

Gary noted it and looked at her. "I've tried calling Ellie. No answer, of course. But I'll keep trying! I just wanted you to know. I just saw it when I was browsing for more information on my, er…break."

Jennifer looked up at him and her smirk turned into a small smile. She shook her head and said, "Thank you. But let me know when you hear more. Somebody has to come back for us to get super excited. At least… that's what it will take for me. I'm sad if someone else was snatched away suddenly and unwillingly. The 'disappearance' portion of that indicates it wasn't entirely on purpose. Thank you again, though! It does make me a bit happier. A little hope never hurt anybody!"

She squeezed his arm and headed towards her own desk just opposite his own. The picture of Nathan, himself, and Jennifer all together still sat right there in front of him.

Gary sighed and turned it face down as he'd done many times before. Just to pick it back up again and place it where he could see it. Putting on his headphones, he listened to the news broadcast.

It was from two days ago. Gary didn't read the newspaper anymore. No one did. Back in the day, this would have made the headlines. Of course, this had made the local news, and he hadn't seen that, either.

"…still searching for clues as the lead researcher, Doctor Eleanor Cooper, was declared missing after never having left the museum's research facility Tuesday night. Co-worker and fiancé Grant Grothen was contacted, but

had no comment… other witnesses say the video footage revealed a bright flash around 1:02 am Sunday morning…"

Gary's heart sank.

Oh no. Ellie…is now out there with Nathan. This can't turn out well.

Even if they were both dead, those two would find a way to fight. Gary took a deep breath and looked up at Jennifer. He watched as her face fell, clearly hearing the same news feed he just did. She pulled the wireless headpieces from her ears slowly, got up, and walked out of the office.

CHAPTER 45

Morgaine took a deep, calming breath and walked right past her guards while they sat in the outer room. They were separated by no more than four feet, and the possibility of feeling the air move was a real one. But Morgaine had thought of this, as well, leaving the balcony doors wide open for the "fresh air" before she'd "retired for the evening."

The women didn't move. They were in a discussion about the value of sharpening their weapons versus the balancing factor, then fixing flaws in the aerodynamics of shot and thrown weapons. In a normal circumstance, she would have put her own two coppers into the mix.

Not today.

The women had already opened the hallway doors in anticipation of the changing of the guard. As Morgaine entered the hallway, she saw her two men, Cam and Jessin, lounging in the hallway. Both had their eyes fixed on the open doors, just as they and their compatriots had been doing for the last two days. Realizing she could just tap their heads as she passed, she did just that. The men were seasoned enough to know exactly what had happened. Even as she did so, two women guards turned into the hallway and began heading their way.

The sharp one, Cam, buckled on his sword belt and approached the two new guards, "What are you bitches coming for anyway…? Why don't you tell your King to let our Mistress go, and we'll be gone!"

Apparently, he meant to have words with them. Morgaine smirked and nodded in admiration as she slipped by the group, heading down the stairs. Cam was going to start something, and then both could storm off in a huff, supposedly to find Treyborne or something similar. The noise would also cover her escape in the event she made an inadvertent noise.

Excellent. I'm going to give that young man a bonus. Assuming we live.

Morgaine hurried down the stairs as quietly as she could, even as the shouting at the top of the stairs escalated. Hurrying by a maid scurrying upstairs, she passed her on the next landing, the woman's eyes looking worried. By the time Morgaine reached the ground level, she heard boots stomping down the stairs. Those would hopefully be her men running off to "find Trey". In reality, they hopefully would be on her heels, flanking her, as she topped Steel and rode off into the hills to meet the land cruiser.

The main floor was crowded with people. Some guards, and a few of the lesser nobles walking out in front of her, staff scurrying about their jobs. Not to mention a handful of guards at the doorway to the Assembly Hall.

But these halls were massive enough to drive a land cruiser through them. Morgaine walked right out the front doors. Before she reached the stairway going down to the streets below, her men were stomping out the doorway, as well. Avoiding and eluding running into people who could not see her was taking up most of Morgaine's focus. But she had to get outside those gates before they shut for the night. Treyborne would be waiting outside the northern gates somewhere nearby. As soon as she was in the clear and away from ears that could hear, she would signal him.

Cam and Jessin ran right by her as she continued her wandering walking, trying to avoid people. Jumping in behind her men, she sped up, grabbing Cam's belt.

"Good evening, soldier. Well done!"

Both men heard her, but neither moved their heads an inch. Still half-running, half jogging, they were already nearing the gates. "Well met, Lady. We'll be outside in a few minutes. They won't…"

A blasting horn rang from the castle. Then another. Morgaine cursed. At least two dozen guards at the city gates ran out from the barracks, drawing weapons. Morgaine herself was still invisible. But her men were not.

"It's time for blasters, men. Cut them down! We're not losing a man tonight. But by the Creator, that traitor Rondor will!"

CHAPTER 46

Nathan and Smyslin had been traveling for over four days on what the locals called "the Rondorian highway". Nathan thought the name a bit embellished, since although most of it was paved (in stones), much of it was no more than a glorified trail. On the other hand, there were always people on it, and the road was undeniably safe.

No marauders or bandits. Certainly, no Dark Men. Smyslin's mood even seemed to brighten. Most days, the weather had been mostly sunny. And the one day it had been cloudy and rainy, it remained warm, and they were never quite drenched. If the rain came down too hard, they just pulled themselves off the "highway" and took a break and ate some of their bread or rations under some trees.

The road followed, for the most part, right along with the river – still the White River, according to Smyslin. It was very much like the rivers he and Ellie had hiked along a few years back in Colorado. Memories of happier days and bright sunlight had apparently helped Nathan, as well. He didn't feel so tired and morose all the time. In fact, he felt better than he had in years.

Smyslin pulled off the road to relieve himself, so Nathan waited patiently, scanning the countryside. He pulled his hat off, holding it to better shade his eyes from the lowering glare of the sun. Off to the southwest, he saw a massive city. Not New York City massive, but massive compared to anything he'd seen in this world. It was getting towards sundown, and the first moon had already risen.

"That must be the capital city there, Smyslin."

Smyslin collected himself and came to look, as they'd just reached this hilltop moments before. He nodded. "Doubtless, Master."

He sighed heavily, so Nathan turned from gazing at the beautiful white city with the castle situated on the highest hill. "What's the trouble, Smyslin?"

He sighed again before answering, "It seems that there is indeed a good chance of finding the White…*Morgaine.*"

He paused.

"And…?" Nathan asked, motioning with his hand to continue.

"And she may well realize that I am…or *was*…a Dark Man. I am simply preparing myself for possible execution. Or annihilation. But it is my fate. I will be your humble servant until that time." His tone indicated he thought that wouldn't be much longer.

"How do you know she will just outright kill you on the spot? I mean, like it or not, you don't even look the same as when I met you. That, at the very least, should give her pause. If she is the murdering butcher 'Lost One' you are still so sure she is. Me, I'm not convinced. You've been told a lot of things and lived a certain way your whole life. Much of what you were told is skewed, if not just outright lies. There are places in my world – some would argue my own country included – with people like you. They grow up being told something and it's the exact opposite of the truth. Or they simply have no other point of reference, so they just swallow whole what the rest of their society accepts as 'normal'."

Smyslin eyed him but said nothing.

Nathan shook his head and continued. "Anyway, I'm not buying. I want proof of just about everything I'm told by anyone or any organization. And the governments in our world – are out for themselves. They're not looking out for the people, especially when they tell us all they are.

It's complete bullshit. So just believe that almost nothing is absolute, Smyslin. If your leaders tell you something is that way and your society has just accepted it themselves, take it with a whole bag of salt. From what I can see – your masters aren't to be trusted on a whole other level maybe even than the ones from my world. And that's saying quite a lot!"

Smyslin's head was down, but Nathan knew he was listening. "Maybe this Morgaine is just as bad. I don't know. They're from the same species, according to you. But stop accepting what you've 'known all your life' as purely factual. Investigate it on your own. Maybe this Morgaine isn't so bad. But, either way, judge for yourself. Don't listen to what others say about her."

Smyslin nodded thoughtfully. "If we ever actually find her."

"Exactly!" Nathan picked up his bag again and started off down the trail, which started to curve towards the city. They'd reach the gates within a couple of hours if they hurried. And Nathan meant to hurry. As they began to walk down the next hill, a group of about a dozen riders moving very fast coming the opposite way topped the next ridge. Although the riders apparently noticed them, they didn't slow down even a little.

Nathan eyed Smyslin and raised an eyebrow.

Smyslin shrugged and they moved off to the side of the road, to better allow the galloping horsemen to pass. As they rode by, it was apparent to Nathan that they wore very different armor than the other military-types that had been on this road every other day. They were escorting a brunette woman in very fine clothes, and it seemed they were carrying weapons on their hips resembling...*pistols*?

Snatching off his hat again to block the sun's glare, he put it in front of his eyes and squinted to try to get a better look. There were at least a dozen of them...and yes! For sure...! High tech looking weaponry at that! If those were pistols, they looked like military grade from his world and his time – not theirs.

One of the last of the riders looked back and saw him staring back at them. He slowed his horse immediately, reining it in savagely. The horse obeyed well and turned to the side. The rider was looking back at the two of them…intently.

Nathan took that as his cue to stop being so curious, turn around, and leave. Placing his hat back on his head, he and Smyslin just began walking the other way. Nathan was going to act…*very*…casual.

That man's stare had been unnerving. Just as he was sure they were in the clear, he heard horse hoofs returning down the road behind them.

"Damn!"

Smyslin looked at him sideways but said nothing. Until the man said something…

"Hold! A word, traveler."

Nathan turned and placed his hands on his chest, fingers spread, "Me?"

The man nodded from his horse. He had long dark, hair, wore that strange armor, and was decked in weapons. He had stopped about twenty paces back. His companions were nowhere to be seen, although the galloping hooves were somewhere off in the distance over the next ridge. Nathan started mentally calculating his options. The shock-lance still hung strapped to his side. He touched the handle with his hand.

At that moment, the man's eyes flicked down, seeing it. Then they snapped up again like a hawk. Whipping his weapon out, he leaped from his horse, rolling off to the side.

"Don't move! I don't know who, or what you are…"

Nathan pulled the shock-lance out but didn't fire it up. "We want no trouble from you! We didn't do or say anything to warrant this…"

"Shut up! Shut up, I have to think! You…look like someone. And…that weapon…" he shook his head negatively. "The only people I've seen with those before wore black scarves and were trying to kill me."

Nathan wasn't certain, but he was pretty sure any gun-type weapon was going to be more than a match for his would-be Taser pole. Negotiating seemed like the better choice. He slowly placed it back in its holder on his leggings. Putting his hands up, he said, "My friend and I…ran into some trouble before entering Rondor. As you can see, we handled it. But we want no trouble with you. I'm sorry for staring. But your weaponry is…unique, and that caught my eye."

"I believe you're telling the truth. But you talk funny…and like I said, you remind me of someone. Someone dangerous. And that guy with you…he looks a bit off, too. Now, we've got some urgent business. That's for damn sure. But I also can't leave a very strange loose end like you hanging out here tonight, of all nights. You'd best come with me. I promise, we won't hurt you. But…I have learned to listen to my gut. And my gut is screaming that leaving you on this road when we have need of it tonight…" he just shook his head.

He waved it one more time, before adding, "Don't make me use this. Trust me. It won't end well for you."

Smyslin whispered, "We should do as he says, Master. I've seen those before on other…people."

Nathan just kept looking the man in his eyes, before nodding his assent. As they approached, the man snatched the shock-lance from Nathan's side. Putting it into his saddle strap, he remounted one-handed, never taking his aim off Nathan's head.

Two of the other riders had backtracked by now, as well. Noticing their comrade was missing, they had apparently turned around. He waved that he was all right, but to come to him, anyway.

Within minutes, Nathan and Smyslin were walking at a brisk pace back up the same road they had just come down. The other riders had stopped not much further than where Smyslin had taken his short "break" awhile back.

Their captor went over and talked to someone while the other two kept watch. Probably the commander of this little party. Pointing the man's eyes back towards his captives, the man just nodded quickly and then began leading the team away from the highway opposite the river.

Nathan began to wonder if they meant to just kill them somewhere quiet and leave their bodies for the wild animals. When they stopped, however, they came to a massive tank-like vehicle with multiple short cannon and a huge hatch in the back like some sort of military transport from the Army. Dark green, gray metal and all. "Sit over there, shut up and wait. The captain will know what to do with you!"

This got Nathan's attention. "And who would that be?"

But the man said not another word. One of the other men, a slightly taller man of smaller build came over, offering them each a water canteen. When they both refused, he said, "I'm sorry, but I'm going to have to bind you. No one is sure what to do with you…but this was suggested as a necessary precaution."

Nathan just raised an eyebrow before nodding. Smyslin's head dropped, but he proffered his arms, wrists together, for binding. After he was done, Nathan did the same. No sense making it any worse. He'd gotten out of a similar situation with the Dark Men. He'd figure something out.

We must have interrupted some sort of raid, or something! They're like thieves or pirates…or… But their weaponry is far more advanced! What is going on here…?

About seven men and the woman were stationed in the rear area with Nathan and Smyslin. There weren't seats for more. The horses and the rest of the men had walked down a long hatchway to the bowels of the "transport", which had lifted and closed once they were all in. It apparently could hold quite a bit. The woman, Nathan noticed, was a beautiful brunette and was still in a riding dress. She seemed completely out of place with these men. Perhaps she was the one they were guarding. But her eyes were hard as she watched them. Then Nathan heard something. Placing his ear closer to the rear, he clearly heard electronic communication coming from the forward chamber.

"…Check that, Captain! We've run into an issue, but nothing we couldn't handle. Will explain when you're aboard. How's the package? Is the cat out of the bag?"

"Check that, Messau. But have Maitan ready! We've got casualties. It appears the Mistress and the last two men got pinched before they could get out. There was a horn blown, then we heard blaster shots and fighting. But they came out the gates before we could even get there. We are en route now. Should rendezvous within half an hour. Make all speed. We are being pursued, but we have discouraged it as best we can. You know the drill."

"Check, Captain! We left about seven minutes ago. Glad to hear we won't have to sit around on our hands. Mine want the neck of that scrawny little bitch of a king. Messau out."

Well. This should be interesting. Nathan hoped it just didn't end with him dead.

CHAPTER 47

Morgaine's side hurt. Badly.

At some point in the melee at the city gates, someone had slid a blade about four or five inches into her left side. No arteries were sliced, but the kidney and perhaps other areas had been affected. Blood was still oozing from the wound, even after Treyborne had utilized the field med kit on it. She was probably also bleeding internally. The whole area felt like it was on fire.

Steel was racing at nearly full speed, and the bounces and jarring did nothing to help with the agony, either. Each landing brought sharp, fiery stabs, never dulling. Morgaine clenched her teeth and rode high in the stirrups, keeping her knees bent to absorb some of the shocks.

Both guards who had been with her in the fight were also wounded, but they were riding just as hard as she. Their mounts were smaller than Steel, so her black stallion had outraced them easily, even though they had gotten a head start. Trey had patched their wounds while the men kept firing their weapons – weapons Morgaine had never before used in the presence of any but Dark Men prior to today.

That bastard Rondor! He deserved it!

Once they had been patched up, they'd bolted. It didn't take long for the pursuit to follow, either. Treyborne reached the cruiser on comms around then, but Morgaine only had the energy to listen and ride.

They were on the way. That was all she needed to know.

Treyborne himself was riding behind the other two, keeping an eye out for any further hostilities and dealing with them. One of the last of their pursuers had had his horse shot out from underneath him by Treyborne's blaster. Several others had been dealt with the same. When two more appeared after them, Treyborne showed no mercy. Dropping one of the precious little charges and pressing the helix button on his wristband once the targets were in range.

The blast could probably be seen all the way from the castle. No one else followed them after that.

It had been at least thirty minutes since getting on her horse, and even Steel was getting tired. Morgaine felt light-headed and was starting to lose focus. The light was still good, as the sunset was lighting up the clouds to the west back towards the city, and both moons had risen and were bright and nearly full. Even so, it was hard to make out faces or details even up close.

Reining in Steel, Morgaine felt the relief in his flanks. Patting him gently, she touched his head, saying, "You ran well, my brave warrior! Treats will abound once we reach the transport."

His snort and stamped hooves meant he found that acceptable. Smiling, she began to gingerly slide off his side. Hitting the ground, even that carefully, she winced and cried out, gripping her side.

Cam and Jessin arrived a moment or two later and leaped from their horses. Both men regretted that decision; Jessin literally crumpling to the ground. Cam staggered but caught himself and looked back as if he expected the entire Rondorian army to descend upon them in moments. Drawing his weapon, he held it in one hand while the other one leaned on his horse, which was wheezing loudly.

Morgaine put her hand on his, "We won't be needing those, I don't think, Cam. Well done." Going over to Jessin, she checked his pulse and looked for new wounds.

"What about you, Jessin? I see you're still wincing and groaning. You must be alive. How are you feeling?"

"Like someone stabbed me in my ass, Mistress. And then I rode for near half an hour to make sure it stung just perfect right!"

Laughing despite herself, Morgaine rose and said, "You'll live. And that ass of yours will be no worse for wear, I assure you! I'll pay the best courtesans in Nelrae to say so, if not." She knew he had other wounds, as well. But apparently, none were truly serious.

"Thank you M'Lady," he said as if she's offered him knighthood.

Treyborne reined in a moment later. "Why are we stopping, Mistress? We could still have some on our tails."

"If so, we will execute them, Trey. I'm not having a single witness of our escape or of our land cruiser survive this night. But I'm quite certain that last 'discouragement' you doled out was enough. Any military or city guardsman worth his salt would be smart enough to face his king's wrath at our eluding him in the dark of night versus sleeping open-eyed in a burial chamber."

Treyborne nodded curtly, but he looked back anyway. *"Trey to Messau. We are stopped on the road approximately ten clicks east and north of the city on the highway. How far out are you?"*

"Another five to ten minutes, Captain. Had to evade some local militia, per prior orders. Slid the cruiser into a forest and then resumed two minutes later. How's our Lady?"

"Alive, but bleeding. Haul ass. I don't care who else is on that road! New orders are to eliminate anyone in our way – minus the usual wandering orphan."

"Check that. Burying the hammer."

Not five minutes later, the cruiser came over the ridge, reflective lights on only. It pulled to a stop with a screech of gears. The anti-gravity pods, whirring into silence moments later.

The hatch popped and out boiled six men. Two of them were hauling out a gurney, which had fluids and other med injectors at the ready in case anyone was critical. Messau stepped out the front hatch behind the front cannon seconds later. Saluting hand to chest, he asked, "Anyone in dire need, Captain? Mistress, great to see you! What're our next steps?"

Treyborne skipped the return salute. "Get these men down below to Maitan. I know you've got him waiting. But put the Mistress in there first. She's got a nasty cut in her side and honestly, she might be the worst of all of us."

Messau saluted, handing the hatch opener to Treyborne, and gently put his arm around Morgaine, helping her walk by holding her on one side. He was so much bigger and stronger than she, she was nearly being carried, which seemed to suit her just fine.

Corianis, a veteran of the team, saluted as the others made their way to the land cruiser.

"Yes, Cor? What's the story?"

"Well sir, it's an odd one. On the way back to the cruiser, we ran into these two strange fellows. One I'd swear is a Dark Man who lost his shade…".

Treyborne raised both eyebrows at that one.

"But it gets better, sir. He's not even the weird one. The other guy… he carried a shock lance and, well…" he looked back at the retreating Morgaine. "he looks like her!"

CHAPTER 48

Morgaine's eyes were bleary. Touching her side, she felt the blood that had oozed into her clothes. It was mostly dried and caked, but she still felt like she'd been kicked in the side by a mule. Or three.

Messau helped her down into the lower bunker, where Maitan laid her on a bunk, pricked her veins with an IV feed, and began giving her some of her saved blood. He also pressed a button, and a plethora of medicinal feeds began in her feet. At some point, there was a syringe put in that gave her a boost of energy for a split second, then she passed out. Upon awakening, Treyborne, Brianna, and Maitan were all there, talking in low murmurs, but heatedly.

"What are you arguing about…?" Morgaine managed. They all looked over at her at once, Maitan leaping to his feet to check her various signals and inputs. The IV was gone, but the sensors were all making various pings, squeaks, and squawks.

Treyborne spoke from his chair, having leaned back away from Brianna and Maitan's empty seat in the middle. "We have…an issue, Lady Morgaine. Our team encountered a couple rather unusual individuals right before arriving at the cruiser. Corianis decided to detain both, pending your release or whatever interrogation you might want to perform. Are you sure you're ready for this…?"

Morgaine nodded sleepily from her half-lidded eyes, lying on the bunk. The cruiser was clearly running at full speed. At this rate, they'd be at her main bunker by midday tomorrow. No more hiding her superiority in technology from the Rondorian people. They'd burned their bridges with her. Treyborne still delayed, looking to Brianna for support. She made a non-committal gesture with her head.

"Out with it, Captain!" she snapped. I saw my father die right in front of me. My mother died when I was very young. Every single person I've ever known or cared about has died; present company excluded. My half-brother turned to the Dark and started this entire shitstorm of a situation centuries ago. What could you possibly think is going to affect me, especially in this drugged and extremely beaten down condition?"

Treyborne let out a little sigh, "It's just that…well…we think we've found another of the Elder Race. Not corrupted with the Dark. Just…" he shrugged. "He looks like he's of the First Race."

Morgaine's eyes barely moved. "So…you're telling me that after hundreds and hundreds of years, another of the Elder Race has suddenly just popped up. On the road. To Rondor."

Treyborne just nodded.

Morgaine began to laugh. A few muffled chuckles at first. Then openly shaking her head and laughing. Finally, she was laughing uncontrollably. "I'm sorry…!" she choked out after a moment, still laughing. So hard, her side hurt again, despite the surgery and obvious medications she was still affected by.

Maitan spoke up, "My Lady! You must settle down! You might tear open your wounds. I sealed and laser-seared them, but you still might tear something. Please *stop laughing!*"

That did not help.

Morgaine found the idea of someone from the extinct Elder Race – her race – just wandering along the road to be beyond hilarious. She simply couldn't help it. She knew the drugs were likely exacerbating this response. But it was still so far beyond preposterous, that she laughed until she cried. The pain in her side increased and suddenly a very large pain hit her. Maitan hit two buttons and suddenly the world went very blurry and very dark once again.

CHAPTER 49

At some point, Nathan had fallen asleep in the hold. So it was with some surprise that upon awakening, he saw that the transport he had been traveling in had stopped. The back hatch was open, and he was all alone. Sitting up in confusion, he checked his bonds. They were loosed, lying next to him. Smyslin was nowhere to be found, but Nathan's backpack and even his shock-lance were lying next to him.

Furrowing his brows, Nathan looked around for literally anyone. *Nope. I'm here by myself!*

Sunlight was streaming into the cabin from the open hatch in the back, and birds were singing and chirping noisily outside. Nathan had slept the night in here. He must have been sound asleep, as one would think a small army parking, disembarking, and leaving this shuttle would make a little noise. Especially if you included the horses!

Standing up, Nathan felt the stiffness of a nightlong lack of movement. Stretching, perhaps a bit too much, pulled a muscle in his leg. Grabbing at his calf, he realized he had to get moving before the cramp got any worse.

Picking up his backpack, Nathan put his shock lance into the holster at his side, then started to limp down the hatchway, grabbing his calf as he did so to minimize the cramping, leaning heavily to the one side.

One of the men he'd seen the night before was sitting lazily in a wooden reclining chair outside, staring at nothing. Seeing Nathan emerge, he jumped up, grabbing his weapon. He didn't point it at Nathan, at least. But he did say, "About time!"

Pointing his weapon towards the largest building, he sat back down. "The captain is inside that building in the main chamber. He's been waiting for you."

Nathan studied the man oddly for a moment, then raised an eyebrow, shrugged, and started off towards the building indicated. It was the largest on the compound, which had several in a circle. As he approached, he saw it had multiple doors, some man-sized and some for larger things (horses or transports, probably).

Everything in the compound was painted light tan mottled with dark green. Some things had netting over them. It made Nathan feel like he was on some hidden military base in south central Europe. Lush forests surrounded the whole area, mostly shading the grounds, with little patches of sunlight showing through here and there.

Paths toward the various buildings were packed dirt only. But near each building was what appeared to be a generator or shed that emitted a low hum.

Nathan walked as slowly as he dared, trying to plan for any and every eventuality that might get him shot or killed. But far too many presented themselves in his brief time walking towards the main building. Sighing, he resigned himself to whatever fate had in mind for him.

Entering the building he felt the wonderful feeling of conditioned air immediately. The humidity went way down, as did the overall temperature. It was close to ninety outside. In here, it was mid-seventies. Even though the door remained open, there seemed to be some sort of barrier at the doorway keeping it all in, as well.

Inside, several of the men were sitting around one of three tables, finishing up a meal of some sort. Nathan's stomach growled in protest seeing the food. It had been quite a while since he'd eaten anything. One of the men noticed him and nodded to a larger man on the left.

They all looked, but the man indicated stood up, walking over to where Nathan had stopped.

The others just kept their heads turned towards him, neither moving nor talking. Some were still chewing, however.

The room or hangar was huge, with high ceilings and phosphorescent light coming from everywhere. It had a bit of a homey feel, though, as there were furnishings that looked to be quite comfortable, some various stretching and lifting areas, and some sort of game table set up.

The larger man stopped about five feet away, placing his hands in his belt and his feet spread far apart. He was in whatever gear the others had worn when he'd met them, minus the armor – light and dark tan clothing with a gun holster, a couple knives at his back with hilts sticking up, and several other strangely shaped things attached to his belt. The man himself was very rugged and probably quite attractive to the opposite sex, maybe thirty years in age, with tanned skin and brown hair.

"Sir," he said, "apologies for detaining you and your…man. But you caught us in the middle of a very important maneuver…and it seemed wise to my men to bring you both on board so that you did not inadvertently interfere. Or advertently," he added.

Nathan nodded. "Is that all? If so, can we go now?"

The man nodded a small negative, "I'm sorry. It's not personal. But it seemed to my men – and to me after arriving last night – that perhaps some talking first might be appropriate. My Mistress…needs to know more about you."

Nathan's head shot up at that. "Would your 'Mistress' happen to be the legendary Morgaine? Better known perhaps as the 'White Queen' or… White…whatever?"

The man paused, no expression on his face. "What makes you say that…?"

"Well, let's just say it makes sense, based on what little I've heard of her. I've just got to say, if it is true, you might as well tell me, as I'm sure I'll find out soon enough. I understand. Most people hate her. Ever since I've come here everyone either hates this woman or fears her. Or both. But she also is, from my perspective, my only hope. I've been trying to catch up with her for weeks now. And frankly, if your mistress isn't this 'Morgaine', then I'm not sure what you or she could possibly need or want from me. We were simply traveling to her last known location: the capital city of Rondor."

The man nodded slowly. "I guess that would make sense. One of…*your* kind…would probably want to find Morgaine, if possible. But that's not my real concern. My main goal is to make certain you're not a threat to *my* Mistress in any way. Your man has already been questioned by me and my men, but my *Mistress*," he said stressing the word to let him know he wasn't going to reveal anything about her himself, "insisted she wanted to talk with you first. Then your manservant. Or whatever he is. If my mistress decides to tell you her name, that is her choice. I will not do it, nor will any of my men."

Nathan took all this in, nodding his head back and forth a bit. Shrugging, he said, "OK. Well…. let's get this over with, then. I'm assuming if you meant to kill us, we'd be dead by now, anyway."

The man seemed about to agree on the point but said nothing. Instead, he turned on his heel and started walking towards one of two staircases built into the back wall of the building's interior. From what he could see outside, Nathan was sure this part of the building must be built into the hill behind this 'hangar', or whatever they called it.

Walking up the stairs, they went up two flights, entering the top doorway. The door opened on its own, sliding to the right into the doorframe with the sound of a small hiss.

As Nathan walked in, it became evident this was the men's dormitory. Small bedrooms, mostly with doors open, showed beds and nightstands. Luminescent light panels in the ceiling, although several rooms were dark. A few of the rooms clearly had men in them, some sleeping, others doing various activities. They passed a shower room, a toilet area – but very odd looking, with seats all built side-by-side like an outhouse – and then a small staircase up again to another doorway.

Another 'hiss' and they were walking down a long corridor that led by a monstrous kitchen, with several people scurrying around cleaning up after the recent meal. Nathan's stomach growled loudly enough that the man ahead of him heard it over the clanking of pots and pans.

Stopping and turning, he asked, "Are you hungry? That sounded bad."

Nathan nodded.

The man hesitated for a split second, then walked back toward the kitchens. Nathan followed. "Alise! What are the chances we have some leftover breakfast and juice for my friend here?"

One of the three women in the kitchen (there were two men there also) looked up for a second then dropped back to her drying of pans, nodding. She set it down, pointing, "Over there! We just put them in the coolers. I've got two plates for our guests. There are glasses with juice already poured in there, also. Mistress told me to have them ready less than an hour ago. She sent that new girl down to do it!"

This was apparently news to the Commander, or Captain, or whatever. He went to a large metal box with a lid like a small freezer, opened it up, reached in and brought out two very large plates full of meats, cheeses, and fruit. He gave one to the smaller man nearby and told him to take it back down to his men to give to the other 'guest'. He grabbed out the juices, as well. Holding one for Nathan and sending the other with the smaller man.

Grabbing a small table in the back, he found some two-pronged forks and a wide-mouthed spoon, giving them to Nathan with a small cloth. "Eat. A few more minutes won't matter. We were waiting for you to wake up, as it is. No rush."

The man then muttered something under his breath that Nathan didn't catch. At that moment, he didn't care, either. Trying not to smack his lips or drool, he pounced on the food, eating every morsel. Sucking down the strange juice right behind the food.

The man raised an eyebrow. "Might want to slow down a bit; you might choke."

Motioning for Nathan to follow him, he stood up and began walking out the way they'd come. They passed through several other living quarters, recreation rooms, and even a large living room that overlooked a huge valley, and then finally up another flight of stairs made of glass or crystal.

Walking into a large room there were two women there with an older man, partially balding. But it was one of the women that caught his eye immediately.

Morgaine. It had to be. The woman had medium-long curly white hair, and was sitting in black and silver leggings, wearing a black shirt that was hiked up strangely on one side with a bandage wrapping her midsection. She was also literally and simply the most exquisitely beautiful woman he had ever seen. She was jaw-dropping. And Nathan could tell the woman was wearing little to no makeup and was quite possibly ill, as well as wounded.

She was in obvious discomfort, leaning back in a very soft well-cushioned chair with a pillow propping her up and another being held in her lap, partially covering her bandages.

Tearing his eyes away from Morgaine for a moment, he noticed the other woman was the woman he'd seen yesterday in the transport. She was quite beautiful, but with dark curly hair and looking quite…plain next to Morgaine. Had Morgaine not been in the room, he would have noticed this girl out of a hundred in a second. But next to *her*…

Nathan stopped walking when the 'Captain' did, nodding to the woman Nathan had identified as Morgaine. She nodded back, her eyes wide studying Nathan. She motioned to the couch opposite her with some space between them to sit. Nathan sensed this distance had been prearranged to give extra distance between them, in the event he truly was a threat.

"Mistress Morgaine, I presume?" Nathan said, sitting.

After a moment, she nodded. "And what is your name? I find myself at a loss and a disadvantage."

"Nathan Arvad is my full name," Nathan answered. "I'm…not from here, as you may have guessed."

She nodded again, this time waving away the captain, "Go back to your men, Trey. But have someone bring me this man's servant. Or friend." Looking up at him, she added, "Did he eat, or do I have to send for the food, as well?"

"He ate, Mistress. Just a few minutes ago."

"Good. Then that will be all. I don't think we're in any danger here." He clearly hesitated, bringing a sharp look from Morgaine. Saluting hand to chest, he turned and stalked out of the room.

Morgaine looked back at him. "Where...*are* you from, then, may I ask? Am I to assume you are the missing piece to this whole puzzle?"

"I'm not sure what 'puzzle' you are referring to. But I'm from Earth. A city called New York City in the United States of America." He paused to see if that rang any bells with her. It did not.

"I see...." She said finally. "Tell me: How did you get here? And who told you of me that made you seek me out?"

So, Nathan began telling her the entire story, starting with his friends at the museum exhibition, the monolith, the whole thing. The smallish man went to fetch him a glass of water at one point, and Nathan kept talking.

Morgaine, for her part, didn't interrupt much, not until... "Wait a minute! You were getting hit with multiple shock-lances and *Djune*... er...knives...? And then you suddenly just stood up, grabbing a Quartermaster's shock-lance and...chased them all off?"

Her beautiful face was a mixture of shock, awe, and disbelief. Her pretty companion's eyes were bulging, and the man who'd brought the water looked about to swallow his tongue.

"Yeah well...like I said, some of this I don't understand, either. I'm just telling you what happened."

Nodding, Morgaine motioned for him to continue, not interrupting him again until he was finished. About midway to the end, Smyslin was brought in, carrying both of their packs and a large canteen. Smyslin sipped nervously every few minutes after he arrived but added nothing to the story. His eyes were huge, staring at Morgaine as if she were a huge spider about to eat him.

Nathan finally concluded his tale with, "...and that is how we finally got here!"

Morgaine took a deep breath in through her nose. The two men who had escorted Smyslin had never left, standing at attention by the doorway at the opposite side of the room.

Morgaine spoke, "I find it…very odd." She stood, walking a bit stiffly over to her men, shooing them out and closing the door. Smyslin tracked her, watching her every movement.

"Which part?" Nathan asked nervously. "It's all the truth, I swear it."

Morgaine looked at him sharply, but her eyes seemed to tell another story. They seemed almost…haunted. Maybe even a bit afraid. It was strange – seeing someone with eyes the same color as his own. That had certainly never happened before.

"Honestly, I have little doubt of the veracity of your tale, Nathan. It is, from all accounts, quite beyond anything someone would likely be able to make up. It seems this world you come from…what was it called…?"

"Earth."

"Earth. Yes. I don't remember it. But there were many worlds the Elder Race traveled to over the course of our history. Genetic modifications enhancing intelligence, followed by teaching various civilizations agriculture, architecture, art, science, and so on. I was barely around for any of that. I am from the third generation. The…last generation of my people."

She looked at him, leaning back, "Either way, it appears, we have left an Arc Gate open somewhere out there in the galaxy. My major focus cannot be to get you home, though, Nathan. I'm sorry. But that is the cold, hard truth. I cannot say I even want to try."

Nathan's heart sank. "Why not? I don't belong here and…I want to go *home*!"

Morgaine stood and poured herself some dark liquid from a large bottle. Perhaps some sort of wine, it glistened a deep reddish blue in the crystal-like glass she held it in. Taking a long drink, she poured another, bringing it, and offering it to him.

He took it, and she sat down again. Morgaine reclined back in her chair, propping her side with the pillow again. Nathan saw a bit of what appeared to be a stain, possibly blood, on the pillow as she did so.

"Because," she answered, "your being here is a world-changing event for our planet. And not a good one, I'm afraid. If you can go back to your home, others can leave this world, as well. Perhaps going to all the inhabited planets in the galaxy. I spent my life, lost my entire family – my very race – to close those portals and keep that from happening. My half-brother and cousins, poisoned by the Dark, cannot ever get off this world. Not *ever*!"

There was a long pause. "And there is one other small thing."

Looking up, he saw she was staring Nathan squarely in the eye. "You appear to be a being of my race, Nathan Arvad. You're *not* human. You are one of the *Elder Race*. Like me. There is a very large set of questions that come from that alone. It also explains how the Arc Gate was activated in the first place."

Nathan started to protest, "I told you…"

"Yes, I know what you *told* me. You speak of being raised in a human world by humans in a relatively technologically advanced civilization. You've allowed me to study your communication device during our conversation. Yours may be a very advanced society. But it is hardly at a level capable of energy or matter transportation. Let alone able to utilize anti-matter, pulsar gravity, wormholes, or any advanced propulsion to achieve interstellar travel. And yet, as far as you know, no one on your entire planet looks like you."

She motioned with her hand as she said this.

"I ask you: How is that possible? How did one…*straggler* from the Elder Race grow up as a human hundreds of years removed from our timeline and just stumble through an Arc Gate? From the sounds of it, the people who raised you weren't even your real parents! Equally problematic is what you've told me about these 'Egyptians'! The very civilization that was gifted the Arc Gate in your world has been insignificant or even virtually extinct for thousands of your years! No one even remembers the great civilizations the Elder Race built there! How did you come to be on your planet at all?"

"But how does my genealogy or Earth's technology level matter here?"

"They don't. It's just another rather huge mystery. The danger factor here is if my cousins or my brother – what your friend here would call 'the Great Lords' – figure out how to use the Gate you came through before I'm able to even reach it. There is no doubt they would use an active Arc Gate and pass through it, taking their poisonous Void with them. Straight to your planet first, I might add. It has always been their plan to dominate every known world. Not just this one."

Shaking her head and looking at Smyslin, Morgaine's eyes narrowed further. He gulped visibly.

"And yet another issue is *him*! My pendant pulses whenever I even look at him! Not all the Dark is gone from him, yet he is clearly a Dark Man."

Smyslin smiled a bit, hearing that.

Morgaine continued, returning her attention to Nathan. "Or at least he *was* one. So, yet another question pops up: how did any of the Void power leave him, at all? What has happened to him, being with you? I can't even conceive of believing the Darkness of the Void can be reversed, if he were not sitting here in my very presence!"

Smyslin said very quietly, "Forgive the interruption, Mistress. But I did not ask for this. I simply did as I had to. I have learned that…perhaps… there is more to the world than what we as Dark Men are told. As for the Dark, I was always taught…please forgive…that you were the 'Lost Ones'. I have come to think that it is we as Dark Men who may be the true 'Lost Ones'." He dropped his eyes, quivering in fear.

Morgaine's mouth opened and closed, looking at Smyslin. "You see, Nathan…?!" she said pointing at Smyslin. "The implications for my world are clear, at least to me: can we 'drain' the rest of these people trapped by the Dark of the Void? Or can only you do it…somehow? Did your servant do it himself…? Is it possible my brother and cousins can have it removed from them, as well? Perhaps I've missed something seminal here that might allow us to recover those who have fallen victim to the Dark, rather than just trying to defeat and kill them all. Your arrival here has literally turned my world upside down."

Nathan tried to get his head around all of this, but he just couldn't. So, he interjected, "Morgaine, I assure you I cannot do anything close to what you're saying. I'm also not of your 'Elder Race'. Sorry, I'm human. Adopted, sure. But a lot of albinos and near albino kids are given up for adoption. At birth, I probably looked like one. I've come to accept that. Fortunately, I can tan and I'm not an albino. But I am very light skinned. I may resemble your Elder Race in some ways, but there's just no way I'm more than that. As for the Dark: Maybe you just didn't know you could do it by being yourself? Maybe Smyslin did it for himself by opening his eyes to his own reality. Me, I just want to go home – like I said. Why not just let me through and shut the Gate down again behind me forever? It sounds like your enemies haven't found a way to open it again…and you've used them before, getting here. You must have some idea of what to do…"

"Yes, I know how to use an active Arc Gate. But so does my brother. Currently, ours isn't one. It does appear that the Dark Lords also have not yet reopened the Arc Gate in our world, despite your arrival through it; meaning it is still closed. At least somewhat."

Morgaine took a long drink, then looked back at him, "If they had opened it, Nathan, their forces would not be congregating around Rondor, but likely leaving this world far behind. Just know that if those 'cousins' of mine – or my brother – do open that Gate before I can get there, not only will you never get home – you won't even want to!"

She set her cup down on the table, looking at him with her amazing purplish blue eyes.

"As for your being human…you see that drink you've been drinking: the blue-red wine I gave you? It's called 'Eel Fin wine'. It's from the original home planet of the Elder Race. A world that functionally no longer exists. No human can drink that wine. In fact, they will pass out or have strong hallucinations if they get even a strong whiff of it. That's why I served you myself and just had Maitan bring the bottle into the room before you arrived. You're of my blood, Nathan Arvad. I think it's time you began to deal with it."

CHAPTER 50

Brianna walked slowly from her Mistress' bedchambers. Morgaine had gone to bed exhausted, using up the last of her energy in the hours of conversation before and during her meeting with this newest anomaly. Her injuries were still seeping blood, and Maitan had not been pleased with Morgaine's insistence that she meet the man immediately upon his awakening.

Brianna didn't know what to think about this Nathan, or the Dark Man with him… turned 'not' Dark Man! What an odd thought. It was like learning the moons were made of cheese, or that she had borne a child without being aware of it.

Walking the halls, Brianna realized it was nearly dinnertime. She herself was new to the compound and had gotten lost twice trying to find her own chambers not far from Morgaine's wing. Soon, Brianna was told, she would be sleeping in a room in the same area once one was prepared for her.

Since literally everyone but the cooks and maids had been in their expedition, no one was at the compound with comms on any longer.

There was an emergency one in the "bunker", wherever that was. But Brianna had been instructed by Maitan never to use it unless in dire need during her orientation earlier that day. He had said many things would be shown to her in the coming days and weeks. But for today, she needed to know where to eat, sleep, bathe, and other basic need fulfillment.

As she turned the door on her room, Treyborne entered the hallway. He stopped still a second before proceeding. He *was* a handsome man. But something in Brianna gave her a bit of a warning. Maybe it was just the way he walked, like a lion or a leopard in a cage. Brianna had seen one once, as a child visiting a traveling menagerie.

He walked past Brianna as she entered her room. He nodded but said nothing. He seemed to be heading towards Morgaine's quarters. Curious. She was asleep and Maitan had given orders for her not to be disturbed.

Brianna stopped to watch him go up the stairway towards Morgaine's chambers. Shaking her head, she entered her own rooms. It wasn't the palace suite Morgaine had enjoyed in Rondor. But these were Brianna's own rooms! And it was larger than her home had been on the farm.

There was a private toilet, a large stone tub with running water, a luxurious reading room with several books, and a huge bedroom with a closet and a wardrobe. Her new clothes had been brought into the outer rooms, so Brianna set about putting them all away.

The drawers in her vanity were perfect for the powders, paints, and brushes she's bought in Bistern. She'd had no time to supplement in Rondor, as originally planned. But there was more than enough. More than she'd ever owned previously.

She undressed from her clothes, lying in her underclothes on the bed. Closing her eyes, she fell asleep. Some amount of time later, there came a loud knock on her door. Sitting up, Brianna realized the sun had gone down and a cool breeze was blowing in through her open windows. She'd opened them earlier to freshen the rooms, as they hadn't been used in some time.

Throwing on her dress, she said, "Just a moment!"

Going to the door, she opened it. Captain Treyborne stood there with a puzzled look on his face, about one foot back from the door. Brianna looked up at him.

"Yes, Captain? Does the Mistress need something?"

"No. I'm afraid I do. May I come in?"

Brianna hesitated a moment, then opened the door wide so that he could enter. Shutting the door behind her, she said, "I apologize, Captain. I've not put all my things away yet. There's a seat over at the reading desk."

Instead of sitting in a chair, he leaned against the desk mentioned, crossing his arms.

"I need a favor, Brianna. I know you're new. And I know it's been a lot these last few days. But there are moments…even hours…where I cannot defend our Mistress as she needs to be. I'm not a trusting man. It's not in my nature. But I feel you've passed the test. I'm not so sure about our new 'guests', and frankly, I'm just generally concerned now that it's out in the open that Morgaine is alive."

"Thank you for your trust, Captain. But what can I do…? I'm just the Lady's maid, after all. If she calls, I come. That's my job in a nutshell. At least according to Maitan."

Treyborne nodded. "Yes, but your quarters will soon be upstairs, and you'll have a bed near hers. You will still be a good deal closer to her where you sleep than I am. Think of the dangers: unknown people in our own compound, Dark Men all over the northern hill country, and an organized front either coming or driven here as we speak by the Dark Lords themselves! Not to mention the possibility of the Hollow Men."

"Hollow…Men…?"

Treyborne looked at her sharply. "You've never heard of the Hollow Men?"

Brianna just stared at him. "I…thought they were a myth. I guess I can say I've 'heard' of them, yes. But the idea of servants of the Dark who can literally move through shadows…murdering people in their sleep without opening a door or a window…it sounds a bit fanciful. Or just plain awful."

"Not fanciful, Miss Brianna. Fact. Absolutely awful. According to Morgaine, they have rules they must follow. They must know at least somewhat where they're going and who they're going to by name. There are several others, and I don't remember them all. But the fact that all her enemies now know she's alive isn't good. How long will it take for them to discover this compound? Or the others?"

"There are … others?"

Treyborne nodded distractedly. "We have three. One on each sub-continent. The Mistress has stayed at this one the most in my experience – nearest the dormant Arc Gate. Formerly dormant, I guess I should say. I always thought her hawklike watch over that thing and staying in proximity to it was a complete waste of time."

"Apparently not." Brianna said, wide-eyed.

Treyborne looked up, really seeing her for the first time. Her hair was a bit unkempt, and her dress was a bit off, like she'd put it on quickly. She was…very alluring looking all ruffled as she was. He cleared his throat.

"Apparently not," he agreed.

Brianna's breath had caught for a moment as their eyes locked. He stood up, taking his leave. She also stood up, going to the door to open it for him again, taking the opportunity to break eye contact.

He stopped, inches from her right at the door. Staring right at her, he said, "Just keep an eye on her. She's hurt pretty badly. Her wound from earlier isn't healing right, either. I know her pendant has some sort of 'Dark sensor' and warns her somehow. But that only works if she's awake. I want eyes on her – you, me, Maitan – all hours of the day. If you must sleep in bed with her somehow, make the excuse. *Please*. For me."

Brianna's heart was racing. This close, inches from her, she felt something she hadn't felt since Sirles had died. Longing. Afraid to talk, she just looked up into his eyes and nodded.

Then he was gone. Shutting the door, she let out a long breath, holding hand to chest.

What have I signed up for? And what am I going to do with that man!

Brianna plopped herself down right on top of a couple blouses she hadn't put away yet that were still lying on her couch. At that moment, she didn't care if she wrinkled them. It took her heart minutes to calm down.

CHAPTER 51

Jezerah was tired of failures. He'd had an entire compound full of them these past two weeks. Lost mystery man. Failed attempt on Morgaine's crew headed to Rondor. Lost control of the Arc Gate. Now this. Curtaise stood at attention in his office. The flooring had been replaced and his desk repaired since the last execution.

So many recently. Jezerah sighed. "What have you done to remediate the situation?"

"Master, the other key placements around the King of Rondor have been heavily chastised. One has been given a…*permanent*…reminder where no one can see it. You had been explicit that no one who'd gotten the King's ear was to be…removed."

The man stood stiffly at attention, clearly expecting anger and punishment. But he'd done exactly as instructed. He always did. Even when he knew it was risky for his own personal health. Disobeying and thinking for himself were not Curtaise's strong suits.

Jezerah appreciated him for that. So, instead, he only nodded thoughtfully. Curtaise was efficient, as well. Not a grain more than needed. But always enough. That was why he had been elevated to his position in the first place. The man was downright extraordinary.

"As for the other matter…?" Jezerah spread his hands as if in supplication.

"Dispatched. Of course, as you yourself noted, Master. Success is unlikely. We must catch our target in a distracted or meditative state. Failure will lead to further complications. I still advise against this course of action, as it could compromise your own personal protection."

Jezerah laughed out loud at that. "No one can touch *me*! Oh, they can take ground, kill, or disperse some of my men. But nothing and no one can penetrate my defenses here. And I'm always prepared for the worst. That's why I'm the highest of the Dark Lords. It isn't coincidence, Curtaise. It's continual planning in action. I lose battles. Not wars."

A stiff nod was all he received in reply.

"Get out! Send me anything you deem newsworthy. I trust your competence in all things, as you know. I must rest and meditate. My power is waning, and I must reattune to the Void."

Another nod, a stiff turn, and Curtaise was gone. The thing that irked Jezerah was that the advice he'd just been given was most likely correct. Open war within the Triumvirate would likely result from either success *or* failure. But Jezerah was beyond caring at this point. It was clear that the Arc Gate awakening had reopened old wounds and jealousies. No sense whining about it.

Power grabbing was bound to result. It was their nature. And there was only really the need for one Dark Lord. It was time to pare down. Again. Most of all, the Arc Gate and control of its portal must be his.

And his *alone*.

CHAPTER 52

Nathan was a bit tipsy. One might even say "drunk".

Apparently 'Eel Fin' wine has quite a bit of 'kick' to it. Or should that be 'bite'?

Laughing at his own mental joke, Nathan bumped into the wall before finally getting his shirt off and sliding into bed. It was at least an hour since his meeting with Morgaine, and he'd been given some quarters across the compound from the main building. He and Smyslin were literally the only two souls staying there.

The building was smaller, of course, but could house up to forty men. Nathan was in the "Captain's Suite", while Smyslin was next door in one of the three officer's quarters.

They'd had to turn on a few pieces of equipment first, he was told as they had walked – or staggered – across the compound's crisscrossing trails.

Their guide was a younger man by the name of Mikell. He had long, curly dark hair, was tall, tough-looking, muscular, and had a goatee so sharply defined one would think he meant to cut someone with it. But he also had a great, boisterous laugh and enjoyed joking and talking as he showed them around their temporary home.

This was a rarely used building called 'the Guest House' for obvious reasons. At one time, they were told, it had been used by a larger unit that had served under Morgaine in her 'previous endeavors'. It was constructed of different material than the other buildings – largely stone and cement – and had a cool feeling to it inside. The windows were smaller, as well. Looking outside had been less cared about back then, perhaps. Or they had made it as a war bunker in the event they were attacked.

"We have just turned on the air units, so it will smell a bit stale and musty, for a day or two. Nothing you cannot handle, I'm sure! There is a sparring room inside, including a ring for one-on-one battle. Pads and gloves to avoid injury. So, maybe fight and see who wins?! I have my money on the not-Dark Man! But who knows?"

He'd smiled at that, prodding Nathan with his finger. "You maybe are too drunk right now to win. But maybe tomorrow you prove me wrong!"

The building had all sorts of hallways and other rooms that he'd kept closed off. "Don't go in those. Bad things could happen, and you'll get lost. This building was designed to allow for time to escape and has confusing passages and dead ends exactly for that purpose. Tunnels underground are a way out. But finding them is tricky. Stay in the areas I showed you, and don't wander!" He waggled a thick finger in Nathan's face. Then he pointed to Smyslin, "You make sure tomorrow he remembers! He may be too drunk tonight and will be stupid."

Smyslin nodded gravely. Mikell left shortly afterwards.

After Smyslin made sure Nathan was heading to bed, he went down the hall to his room. The light went out minutes later.

Nathan just laid in his bed staring at the dark of the ceiling, his brain reeling from the drugged effect of the foreign wine and the events of the last twenty-four hours.

Focus, Nathan!

But in his condition, all Nathan could do was remember how stunningly beautiful Morgaine was. Surreal, like a photo of a super-model on her best day. And he'd spent hours with her. They'd gotten to talking about many things. He had shown her pictures of his home, his friends, along with the storytelling.

She, in turn, had told him that she would share her history with him tomorrow at lunchtime. He was fascinated at the prospect of getting to know her. She was captivatingly beautiful, sexy beyond mortal understanding, and incredibly intelligent. And...*alien.*

So weird.

The swirling of the ceiling made him feel dizzier. Getting up, he went into the next room and relieved himself for a full minute. He'd tried drinking some water before leaving the main compound when the effects had begun to hit him. But, if anything, it seemed to make them worse. Now he had to pee two gallons.

Sighing, he slapped the flushing mechanism button and stumbled back into bed.

As he laid back, there were suddenly two hands at his throat, so strong and hard Nathan couldn't breathe. The force of his assailant's weight pressed down and the vice-like grip around his neck immediately brought spots to his eyes. Grasping at the hands holding his neck, he tried pushing them away. They didn't move an inch.

Knowing he was seconds away from passing out, he flailed for the shock-lance. He'd just lazily dropped it on the floor by the bed after his nearly failed attempt at removing his shirt.

It has to be right there!

Training took over. Kicking with his knees, as he'd been taught in Shotokan all those years and scrunching his neck down, he managed to both land a blow to the midsection of his assailant, bringing a grunt, and a blessed lessening on his throat enough to gasp and gather a short breath.

Rolling to one side, he managed to leverage his body again and land a solid blow with his right fist while reaching for the lance with his left. Those hands were still pressing hard into his throat, and he could again no longer breathe. Feeling the cold steel of the lance on his fingertips, he leaned into the death grip around his neck, bringing more pain to the throat, but allowing him the necessary inches to grasp the shock lance with his left hand.

Swinging it around, and letting it slide a bit so he could grasp the hilt, he activated the shock button simultaneously with where he guessed the business end would be hitting the back of the man's head or neck. A violent jolt and an inhuman scream erupted right by his ear, jarring Nathan's eardrum with its intensity.

The hands came free, though, and whoever the man was, he'd jumped up and away from Nathan and the lance. The sizzling blue electricity was the only light in the room. Nathan was still in bed, but he quickly leaped up himself, swinging the lance back and forth to hopefully divert a charge from the man. In the darkness, he could still see nothing of him, though.

It was just too dark!

Hearing the commotion, Smyslin's light came on and Nathan could hear him racing down the hallway.

"Stay back, Smyslin! Someone's in here and tried to strangle me! I got him off me, but I can't see him! Run! Go get help! I'll hold him off!"

Running footsteps went the other way and seconds later the door outside crashed open. Nathan reached for the bed lamp, still swinging the lance back and forth.

"Come get it, you bastard! Attacking a sleeping man is one thing. Let's see how you do against me armed and standing!"

Nothing. No breathing. No response. Not even a sound.

Did he run away?

Suddenly, a flash of hot searing pain hit Nathan in his abdomen, causing him to crumple to the ground. Nathan knew in an instant, he'd been stabbed - and it was deep!

"I wasn't trying to kill you," came a ghostly, whispering voice, *"or you'd be dead already. This is a message from my Master. We know your name now…Nathan…we have your…friend. Get away from the White Witch, or we'll kill Ellie! Return to the Gate, alone. And we will give the woman back to you as payment. Along with thanks, and honor worthy of a hero. All my Master wants is the key to unlock the Arc Gate. Then you both can leave together. You can go home…with your friend! He gives his word on it. But…you must…come…alone…".*

The voice seemed to fade even as he spoke. Nathan's hand pressed into his lower right side.

Blood was gushing out…*So fast…still so… drunk…dizzy…*

Blackness.

CHAPTER 53

Smyslin raced towards the main compound building as fast as he could! "Help! Attack! Help!!!"

A couple of the guards on duty ran towards him, "What's happening?" one of them asked.

"My Master! Someone has attacked him in his rooms. He sent me for help!"

Without a word, one man raced towards the other building, while the other one ran the opposite way. Smyslin followed the former, catching up to him, but not as easily as he would have before. It always amazed him how slowly these humans ran.

Panic gripped Smyslin's gut as he followed the man into the compound building. Slapping a switch near the wall, every light in the entire hallway lit up at once. Not slowing, the guard lifted his left hand to his mouth and spoke to it, "Approaching guest's room. Please advise." He stopped just outside Nathan's doorway, leaning tight against the wall.

"Secure the area. Make sure he's not in danger. Kill or capture any assailants."

"Check that," and the man pulled a blaster from his holster with his right hand, keeping the other hand up by his mouth.

Making a sudden turning move, he bolted into Nathan's chamber and yelled, "Don't move! I've...*Shit!* White hot, white hot! Guest is wounded, down, and bleeding badly. No sign of assailants. Will administer aid. Kolvin out!"

Smyslin, hearing this ran into the room. Nathan was lying on the floor, between his bed and the wall, shock lance still emitting arcs of blue power as it lay near his hand. A horrific slash in his stomach had created a huge pool of blood all around him. His eyes were closed. He was either unconscious…or dead.

The *Wail of Mourning* erupted from Smyslin's insides without conscious thought. Rushing to get hand towels from the toilet room, he pressed them into Nathan's wound to help keep the blood in while the guard checked for signs of life: pulse, breathing. Smyslin's eyes weren't working. They were leaking fluid, causing him to not be able to see clearly.

"Get me more towels!" barked the guard. Smyslin jumped to obey, as the man took over holding the ones already completely soaked in red. Within another minute, three more men were in the room, one carrying syringes and large bandages. These men were well-trained.

Smyslin backed off when the others arrived, since they'd pushed him out of the way twice when he tried to help.

There was a lot more shouting, barking of orders, and talking to their left wrists. Smyslin's head was swirling, and his eyes were still leaking. He sat down against the far wall like a limp rag, staring at the men working to save his…Master's life. That was how Smyslin had come to think of Nathan. Nathan was no longer just a Lost One that he called "Master". And Smyslin was no longer a Dark One. He was a Lost One, too. If not of the original race. And Nathan was his Master.

They had stopped the bleeding, it appeared, and were now readying to carry him on a stretcher.

My eyes will not work right. He tried blinking fast in rapid succession to no avail. *What is wrong with me?*

Openly sobbing now, Smyslin remembered reading about this. Humans had this pathetic weakness called "crying". Their eyes would leak when they were sad and pathetic and weak. They would often shake and curl up like piglets.

Nodding to himself, Smyslin said, "I am pathetic and weak." One of the guards standing aside and watching looked at him oddly. Smyslin looked up at him, eyes all leaky and said, "He's not going to die, is he?"

"I don't know," said the commander as he walked in, "but put that thing under arrest and get him out of here! Put him in the dungeon. I'll interrogate him in the morning. Or maybe I'll just fry him if his 'Master' dies tonight."

CHAPTER 54

Ellie woke up in a dark room. There was a stench about the place, and the only light was from a tiny window with iron bars in it. There was a bucket of something she could only assume they meant for her to eat.

It looked like regurgitated oatmeal in the dim light and smelled awful. God only knew what it looked like in daylight and with her prescription lenses or contacts in. Even the thought of eating it made her wretch, and she was hungry. Not to mention there was no spoon or fork. She'd been made to pee near the hole by the back wall twice. She'd quickly pulled her pants and panties down, let it out and pulled them up so fast, they'd gotten a little wet in the process.

Her captors hadn't violated her – yet. But she had no doubt they wanted to. Her guards had made that clear. Something…or someone was holding them back. For now. But that wouldn't last. Ellie grew up in New York City. You either accept life as it is, or you fade away. Those that had taken her were scary, masked, black-eyed men with a strange way of talking and with obviously violent natures. They bristled with weapons and everything they did with their body language was threatening.

Wherever she was, Ellie knew she was far from home. Not for the first time, she shivered in fear.

It was clear to her she'd gone through the portal like Nathan had. And all she could think was that if he had been found by these masked men, he was probably already dead. Being here frightened her beyond words. But somehow being truly alone in this world felt even worse.

But, for good or for ill, they clearly wanted *something* from her. Or they were holding her for something big. Sighing, she hoped it was for more than to sacrifice her in some ritual or be horrifically raped by the king badass while the crowd cheered.

Don't think like that! There's always a way out! You're a smart woman from New York-fucking-City! Get it together! Figure it out!

The positive self-talk worked for the time being. But the truth was, she was in a dark cell in an unknown world with a window that spiders had to duck to crawl through, and she was surrounded by natives that were clearly hostile.

Maybe it's more like New York than I give it credit for!

Laughing at her own feeble attempts to stay upbeat, Ellie went about the process of feeling every square inch around the floor of her cell with her hands. Her eyesight wasn't good without glasses in the best of circumstances. And this was not ideal lighting, to say the least.

There were several inconsistencies with the stone flooring. It seemed to be very old, and the grout or cement or whatever had long since departed or worn away. Some of the stones were even a little loose. But the stones beneath the window were either newer, had been repaired, or both. No cracks, seams, or weaknesses of any kind.

So, what good does that do if I can only dig myself into another cell?? No! I can get out through this wall under the window! Stay positive. That cell might also have no one in it and is therefore not locked, too. There are always options!

A guard walked by, looking into her cell cage as he did so. The door was made of hardened metal casings around foot thick wooden beams. The cage surrounding it was either iron bar or these small brick-like stones. Ellie would have called it a "dungeon" rather than a jail. It was positively primeval.

Shaking her head after the jailer passed her, she again felt around underneath the door and around it, looking for weaknesses. Finding none, she sighed heavily and returned to her four-foot cot. It had an old foamy mattress of some type that smelled vaguely of urine. But it was decently comfortable enough to curl up and fall asleep on.

She'd already had to do that last night. She was determined not to have to do it again, however. The next chance she got…

Around the corner came a wash of light and a group of men carrying fluorescent hand torches and all wearing black – did they have any other clothing color here? – they marched right up to her door. One of the men produced an old-fashioned key of some type and inserted it into the locking mechanism.

With a sharp crack, the lock released, and the door was opened towards the outer hallway. One of the five men carried no light. He was taller and thinner than the others, but Ellie couldn't make out any key facial or other differences in the poor light.

The man without the light spoke. He sounded like a man who needed some water, his voice was so dry. "We have sent a message to your *friend*…Nathan. We expect an answer shortly…

"Nathan…? What…? How did you…do you know *him*?? Did you two meet when he…"

"Human female…I do not remember your name…"

"Ellie."

"I didn't ask, and I don't care. I simply didn't know it…"

This guy is an asshole.

"…we probed your mind with neuro-link drugs and questioned you. You told us all about him two days ago."

"Two days ago! You just grabbed me last night! What kind of bullsh…"

"Enough! I'm not here to debate you. If I have need of you, you will know it." That sounded ominous, so Ellie went quiet.

"Wait a minute!" she burst out. "How can I understand you suddenly. You jack-holes were talking gibberish not two hours ago…!"

The four men around the leader moved nervously and the man himself seemed to be visibly restraining himself. "We…placed a neuro-link on your temple next to your ear. It translates for you. Now be quiet!"

He paused waiting to see if there were further outbursts. Remembering his previous statement, Ellie decided to be prudent.

"Good…as I said. I have sent a…message of sorts to your precious boyfriend…"

Ellie started to open her mouth, then thought better of it. Details regarding their relationship were not relevant in the here and now. And it might be helpful if they thought they were still together.

Waiting to see if she spoke, he nodded when she did not. "If he values you, he will come. He has something…I need. And I have something of his. A fair exchange. As long as you cooperate…and keep your mouth *shut*…we will not harm you. Try to escape…or…fight…or anything to anger me…"

He didn't even finish the sentence. He didn't really need to. He just slowly looked her up and down…. then turned and walked out.

A girl grew up knowing that for her whole life she could suddenly and horrifically become a victim, all because she had a vagina. These creatures apparently knew that, as well. And they were more than willing to leverage it.

CHAPTER 55

It was morning, and Morgaine had awakened to the news that during the night, Nathan had been stabbed and almost died. His Dark Man servant was being held pending questioning. Morgaine had to consider all options.

On the one hand, the man was literally of the Dark Race. Filled with the power of the Void and the Dark, they were capable of extraordinary things. Usually extraordinarily evil things. On the other hand, he could have tried to run into the forest surrounding the compound if he were truly guilty. Instead, he had run to get help, saying Nathan was being attacked. Not to mention the fact, that he'd traveled alone with one of the Elder Race for an indeterminable amount of time prior to coming here. Why not just kill him along the way?

There was sign of a struggle, to be sure. But no evidence of anyone being in that room except Nathan and this "Smythe", or Smyslin character. Whichever name he was using now. Morgaine grimaced. She had planned on sharing some history of the Elder Race, to see if something would catch with Nathan this very afternoon. Instead, Nathan was in intensive care and not completely out of the pit. Sighing, she took a piece of toasted bread, added some of the avocado slices on it, and took a bite. Brianna was sitting opposite her, watching, but saying nothing.

"Thoughts, Brianna? You're unusually quiet this morning."

"You seemed…distracted by the night's events, Morgaine. And frankly, so am I. I don't know what to think. I heard about it when you did. But I can see Treyborne's all but made up his mind that the manservant is guilty." She shrugged. "On the evidence, I would have to agree, if

I were completely honest about it. There's no evidence of anyone else even being there!"

Morgaine nodded, looking at her and chewing thoughtfully. But she said nothing.

"What's more, the knife that stabbed him was lying in the hallway and it clearly was from the kitchens down the hall. It seems the only thing left is to wait for Nathan to recover enough to verify that's what happened."

Morgaine took in a breath, then spoke. "I suppose I could agree… except that I slipped into the cell block not half an hour ago while you were washing up." Brianna dropped her jaw in shock, starting to say something.

Morgaine held up her hand, wiping her mouth with the napkin in her other. "I don't need a lecture. I can still walk. Albeit slowly. I looked in on the man. He's wretched. I've never even seen a Dark Man crying before. It seems to be all he's doing. Now, he could be crying because he is in prison. But the only other Dark Men I've ever seen in captivity were defiant to the end. Meanwhile, this 'Dark Man', had been reportedly crying *before* we ever arrested him! On top of that, my pendant… the Medallion gem…detects no more of the Dark in him, anymore, Brianna. None!"

Brianna gave her a blank stare.

"He's not being influenced by the Void…the 'Dark' has no hold on him. He's no more a Dark Man now than you or I are! I'm telling you, he's innocent. I'm sure of it. I have agreed to wait until Nathan recovers… or not…before we act, however. That seems wisest."

Brianna nodded, grabbing a piece of a citrus fruit native to the southlands called "granite fruit". It was particularly tart and sour, but tasted good despite that, somehow. She'd tried it for the first time the other day and was becoming addicted to its flavor.

She still didn't like the seeds, though.

"What if Nathan does die? What then? Not about Smyslin…it's clear you think he's innocent. I assume you'll just let him go or whatever. But I mean…about the Gate. About…the rest of it."

Morgaine, not for the first time, appreciated Brianna's intellect. The girl simply was sharp.

"I wish I had a great answer for you, Bri. Likely, I'll take his corpse if he's dead and preserve it the best I can. Perhaps his genetic code is the key. His hair, his…eyes…I'll try the picture-carrier…I cannot remember what he called it. Oh yes, 'Eyephone'. I remember he opened it with his face, so it should still work if he's dead."

"That's…incredibly morbid, Morgaine. Is that really necessary?"

"Quite. Alive or dead, I will exhaust every resource to figure out what opened that Gate. Because if I can turn it on again, I can shut it down forever. If I cannot, then it remains a threat to be opened again from the other Arc Gate. Perhaps there are even more than one out there still active. Nathan shouldn't exist either, Brianna. Not according to what I know. But somehow…somewhere…there must be more of the Elder Race. On his planet, or somewhere else. If so, I also must warn them before I close the portal: never use the existing Gates or create any new ones. If they do, they will unleash hell on the universe! Just as my father's generation did."

CHAPTER 56

Gary and Jenn took the subway ride to the museum. Again. They were getting used to this ride, and for all the wrong reasons. Since Nathan's disappearance, they'd go as often as they could, snatching time with Ellie and the latest they'd found out or studied in hopes of getting him back. Now that she was gone, there was no one who really knew them.

They were left to stand outside with the protesters claiming the monolith was the beginning of the end of the world. They had no access and couldn't even get past the security outside the building. Still, they were going just to be close. Hoping against hope that something would have changed. When they arrived, the area was still cordoned off. The tired-looking and patently patient faces on the police were no different than the last time they'd come. Gary again was trying to get someone's attention inside the doors when a movement behind Jenn caught her attention.

There was a little boy carrying a little brown bear and holding his mother's hand. He was crying and looking around. Jenn looked at the mother. "What's wrong with him? Did he lose something?"

The mom stopped in her attempts at hushing the boy to look up at her. "He met the first person who went missing right before he vanished. The man was so nice to him, and my son feels badly for him. I can't console him, so I let him come here occasionally. I don't know what to do. He can't let it go…!"

Jenn just stooped down to the boy's level and rubbed his head. Seeing Jenn and how pretty she was, he dropped his head, blushed, and smiled. "It's ok, little man! I'm missing Nathan, too! He was our friend," she said, pointing behind her to Gary. "And we just keep hoping they can reverse whatever happened in there. You just keep praying and keep believing. But don't let it own your life! I can tell you – that's a dark place you don't want to go!"

The boy looked at her, wide-eyed. Gary had turned around at the exchange. No one had responded to him yet, anyway.

"You knew him?" the boy asked incredulously.

"Yes, honey…I know him! He's not gone. He's coming back!" She nodded affirmatively to him, standing up and straightening her hair with one hand. "Now go home and play with your bear! It's not your fault. Yes, Nathan is a good person. I'm glad you got to meet him. When he comes back, you come back with your mom, and I'll make sure you get to see him. I'll look for you. But don't make her come back until then, ok? You just play, go to school, and be a good boy."

The mother said, "Thank you!" while the boy nodded and said, "OK!"

And then they were off.

Jenn sighed. Looking over at the "It's the End of the World" signs, she sighed again before taking Gary's hand for the long walk back to the subway station. They would keep trying. Eventually, the crowds would go down, the ruckus should settle, and they'd get in to talk to someone again.

Unless someone else got sucked in, too.

Then maybe she'd start carrying a sign herself.

CHAPTER 57

Emorion walked back up from the halls of his prison block in the city of what was called "the Free State of Mystrom". It was a sham, of course. He was in complete control. He controlled the entire lands west of the Petty Kingdoms all the way to the Desert beyond the city of Talim. With the notable exception of the northern state of Daystrom.

Irritating little shithole.

It was such a simple thing to let the people think they were "free". It was the best type of control. Give them a semblance of power and a 'voice'. Let them do what they want – within reason – while taxing them into a state of near complete poverty, then lavishly bestow a portion of their wealth back to them as a benefactor. The people in these little dung heap countries ate it up like it was candy.

Fools.

But they were "free" and "happy". Just the way he liked them. Of course, the ones who thought for themselves and talked openly about it were kept here. In the Prison Keep of Swadesh north of the city. It was where he was currently holding his prize prisoner.

The girl…whatever her name was. He'd just heard it. It didn't matter. The friend of the Lost One. Incredibly, more had survived than just Morgaine, apparently. She'd probably always known it. Her damnable brother had to have known. He always kept the real knowledge to himself.

Only tell us about it when you're forced to Jezerah! Damn him to the Abyss of Darkness at the bottom of the Void!

But not this time! This time, Emorion held all the cards. He was the one in possession of the Arc Gate. He was one with the prize jewel it had spit out at him a few days ago. He was the one playing the high games now.

Jezerah must be seething over all this. His pious show at our Triumvirate meeting proves that. He thinks we're fools like this degenerate populace of Mystrom! He will learn otherwise.

Emorion smiled as he walked, not noticing the people in the cells cringing in horror. He wore no mask like his warriors. His old self would have looked at his face in horror, too. But Emorion had long since passed caring what he looked like. He was going to live forever! And he alone would sit atop the Triumvirate – if there still was one – ruling the eight quadrants of the galaxy as befit his greatness. The Void had spoken. He was the chosen one. Soon all Dark Men would bow only to him. As he entered his personal chambers, one of the Elevated *Siday* was there. He must have been the one that was sent. He was standing by the doorway, but light bent around him like the event horizon of a black hole. It bent in such a way even Emorion had to feel rather than see exactly where he stood.

"What news, Hollow One? Blessed to be devoid of anything but the Void itself."

The voice was like someone trying to whisper, but it came out like whirling leaves in a windstorm. Emorion was used to it, of course. He'd made these beings himself. One of his finest achievements.

"The message…has been sent."

"When should we expect an answer?"

"The Lost One…angered me. I may have struck a bit deeper than I intended."

This drew an immediate glare from Emorion. He may not be able to see the Hollow Man's exact shape, nor see into its eyes, but it would know that this wasn't a look it should want.

The quick response indicated it did, in fact, not wish to anger Emorion, *"The fool will live! But it may take a few more…days…for him to recover than planned."*

"Get out! Before I tear you apart! I made you; I can *unmake* you! Defy my exact orders again and see where you end up. Go!" Emorion grasped for the Void…already considering punishing the creature. The being fled the way they always did, sliding into the shadows and vanishing. It was hard to tell even when they were gone, exactly. The light bent so much when they were there.

Well, they had their uses. Would that such a creature would have a chance against the White Witch, Morgaine. But that had been tried more than once. It was simply a waste of resources. And there were only a handful that could survive the process. Emorion had lost count of how many had died making the transition. Only the most dedicated to the Dark were able to withstand the transformation.

Whatever the exact number, it was well over a thousand warriors each time, and only seven had ever made it through. He'd given one to Jezerah in exchange for some of his creations ages ago. Two of his others had died in separate attempts on Morgaine centuries before that. That left this one, and three others as his only Hollow Ones left. Precious commodities in times like these.

Sighing and openly moaning at the failures of these lesser beings, Emorion thumbed a button on the panel by his door.

"High Lord?" came the immediate response.

"Bring the human girl out of the prisons. Give her a room with a guard, clean her up, get her some clothes from your women, and some food she will eat. I can't have her starving herself in the prisons as it appears she will be our guest a bit longer than I had planned."

"As you command, Master."

Nodding, Emorion shut off the comm and began the long walk towards his bed chambers. He idly wondered what little snack his servants had prepared for him tonight.

Delicious little things recently. Soft and supple. Northern girls with strong limbs but everything else was so curvy. The hair was beautiful and their screams were positively delightful!

It was going to be a glorious evening.

CHAPTER 58

K'Thul waited at the head of the massive army streaming over the Great Central Mountains. More than half his troops were still crossing the upper trails, they were so narrow.

Even with the several mechanized transports they'd salvaged from the old wars, they had over fifty thousand human warriors on horseback, plus another ten thousand of the Dark Men running ahead, parallel to, and behind the main army. Scouting in all directions.

K'Thul himself kept an eye on the sky for any aerial attack. Although the number or surviving flying vehicles were probably less than the number of digits on either hand, they still had to be accounted for.

The transports weren't even carrying men, but supplies. Scouts among the Dark Men had already traveled as far as the northern wilderness and the Western forestlands.

Soon. My time is coming soon.

Emorion and Jezerah were playing their typical games. Ignoring K'Thul because he was the one always slowest to act. K'Thul had known what the other two never seemed to learn: it takes wisdom to wait for the right action.

This was the right action.

My armies will sweep into the west before they even have word of it! The petty little war Jezerah's Empire has sparked with the rebel king will keep them occupied. That, coupled with the Dark Men Emorion has scattered all over Arth, scouring the hills of the Hinterland trying to anticipate some quiet countermeasure of Jezerah's. Meanwhile, the hammer from the East will drive right up their collective asses.

K'Thul chuckled.

They forget I was their field general. I was the one they leaned upon to thwart the attacks and the countermeasures the Lost Ones sent at us! They attacked with all they had. And they lost. Not because of the hordes of Dark Men – although they were a part of it, to be sure – but because I was leading them. I put them in the right places with the right amount of attack and defense to flex and flush them into the killing fields of the Megiddo. I am the reason we won. And I will be the reason again.

K'Thul looked back at the hordes of riders pouring through the Gap. Everywhere beyond them Dark Men were running as fast as the horses. Silent. Deadly. This was going to be the biggest army Arth had ever seen! The tides of this army would surge and smash everything before them.

Including Emorion and Jezerah.

Then who would rule the galaxy? The Arc Gate would simply be amongst the spoils. It was a simple matter, really. K'Thul had cultivated the warriors of the Eastern Empire for generations. He'd sharpened this weapon against his own Dark Men at times, pitting them against each other as he saw fit.

When the time came, more than half the Petty Kingdoms were just snatched up from his brother's lands. A happy "accident" of his lack of control over the area and the merciless armies at K'Thul's command. Oh, he had made it look like it had all been local politics.

Emorion's biggest fault was that he never thought anyone could be as clever as he. That made him the perfect sucker. Now, he was going to get a taste of that same punch again. The kick from this one would unseat him and his obnoxious scheming for all time.

CHAPTER 59

Clarion alarms began to sound everywhere at once.

'Please proceed to nearest drop pods. Solar Platform is destabilizing. Orbital decay is in progress. Please proceed to nearest drop pods. Solar Platform is destabilizing. Orbital decay is in progress. Please proceed to nearest…'

Morgaine was not listening. She could not hear. Her father, bleeding from multiple wounds, was gasping for breath, lying on the floor. Morgaine ran to him, grabbing his hands. "Get up! I can get you to the drop pods, but I can't carry you!!"

Looking up, seeing her, Urion smiled his little smile.

Willing, rather than pulling himself up onto his elbows, he said, "Ah my sweet little Morgaine. Would that my visions and dreams had no basis in reality. That they had not come true. I would have chosen otherwise for you. Yours is a burden that was not meant for you to bear. But as the Creator wills, so be it. For the next six hundred years, you must carry this burden, even as I have carried it for a thousand before you".

"What are you talking about? Get up! The Platform…it's falling! We have to get you out of here! Can you walk?" So much blood! It was pouring out of her father's chest. What did one do for that? Why was this happening?

A memory of helplessness.

The gem in the middle of the pendant her father had worn since she was a little girl suddenly lit up with a bright white light.

"I pray that the Light of the Creator shine not only on my daughter Morgaine now, but that it shine through her and upon others. This remnant from the creation is no longer mine. I give it up freely. The Corillion Medallion is now the property of Morgaine…my beautiful White Falcon".

Coughing, blood started to pour from his mouth. He laid his head back… looking at her.

"I love you, little one. Now take the pendant and go! Is the weapon I made for you with you?" All Morgaine could do was nod, tears streaming down her face. "Good. I told you to always keep it with you. You will need it and the pendant. There is a great work ahead of you. And it will not be complete for many, many years…"

Closing his eyes, he breathed his last.

"Nooooooooo!" Morgaine screamed. This couldn't be happening. It can't be real.

The Platform lurched and Morgaine barely kept from collapsing onto her father's still form.

Snatching off the pendant, the glow slowly lessened as she put it around her own neck. She felt, rather than saw, the crystals within the metal of her sword snap to life.

"…Platform is destabilizing. Orbital decay is in progress. Please proceed to nearest…"

Racing for the pods, she found there were none left at Bay 4. Things began tilting wildly and screeches of metal and things falling and breaking were everywhere now. "Warning: Life support is now offline. Please proceed to nearest drop pods. Solar Platform has destabilized. It will reach solar corona in six point five minutes."

Another major lurch and Morgaine suddenly felt the pull of the sun's gravity on the base. It was starting to get very hot in here, as well. Racing, she almost ran by Bay 5. Bay 5 had two pods left. There had never been enough. How many people were going to die today?

She leaped into the nearest one, hit the "EMERGENCY RELEASE" button and the "GO" backup switch.

The pod flew out into space as Morgaine woke up.

CHAPTER 60

Bantor walked nervously down the halls of the palace. King Rondor III had been in a horrible mood ever since Morgaine had slipped through his fingers. It had not been overlooked either, that Bantor had stood for her and vouched that she was, indeed, his mother's former employer. The Court Officer had all but accused Bantor of aiding in her escape! Preposterous! And yet, here he was, being called in once again for further questioning.

What more can I tell these people?

Out of one side of their mouths, they still gave lip service to Morgaine for uncovering the rat in the pantry. Out of the other…they accused her of fomenting rebellion amongst the people by not adhering to the legal procedures and laws that are '…set in place for the good of all…'

Bantor harrumphed as he walked. "The good of all, my fat ass!"

Turning, he came upon the Assembly Hall doors. They were open. Taking a deep breath, Bantor adjusted his hat, smoothed his mustaches, and straightened up. Then he strode in like he was the king himself.

The Court Officer, Vizier, and several other officials were all talking casually amongst themselves. Most seated in their various judges' seats. Of the seven seats, two were empty: the king's seat and one other – Count Mykor's seat…? Bantor couldn't remember. It hardly mattered. Upon seeing him, all the judges took their chairs, and the other officials took benches in the gallery area to the left side reserved for nobles and high officials.

The Vizier spoke first, from his seat just to the left of the king's, "Councilman Bantor. Welcome. Thank you for coming in such haste! We have a few more questions for you…"

Bantor's patience was at an end with this nonsense. "With all due respect, Honorable Vizier, there is nothing else I can tell you. I've told you what I know already. I left the house of Morgaine as a *child*. My mother moved to Rondor, and I've been here ever since. I am a loyal citizen and do not have any inside information about the woman."

"I beg to differ, Councilman! You know where she *lives*. We have not asked this of you before, have we?"

A cold stone dropped into Bantor's stomach. "No…sir. But again…I was but a child! I don't know…"

"We have an answer for that, Councilman! Our esteemed Court Officer said he has found a Mesmer able to hypnotize almost anyone. He has wisely suggested that perhaps you know more than you think. We know you want to cooperate with the Court of our Righteous King in any way possible, therefore…"

"I will not be Mesmerized, Vizier! The practice is *evil*…I…I'm shocked it's being suggested in the King's Court! By the Creator, I…"

"You will do as you are *told*! We are not going to allow anyone – even the White Witch – to subvert our laws and disrespect our King this way! The process is painless, Councilman, and…"

"It's been linked to the power of the Dark, Honorable Vizier! Surely you know that. How can you recommend that I…"

"Guards! Take Councilman Bantor to Morgaine's former suites on the third floor. Hold him there until the Mesmer comes. Again, Councilman, this will not hurt you at all and I assure you…"

Guards pressed in from the corners to encircle Bantor as he spoke. Looking at them, Bantor did something he'd never done since he was a child. He grabbed the green and gold ring on his pinky finger and twisted.

And he vanished.

Moving faster than one would think an overweight older man of his age could, he bolted for the doors, before they realized he was still here, merely invisible.

All those years ago, his mother had found one of the precious rings in an unoccupied room and realized it was a copy of the one that Morgaine kept in her own chamber. When they'd left, the ring had come along for the ride.

He had no way of charging it, and he knew it wouldn't last long. He'd played with it as a boy while living with Morgaine until his mother told him of its weakness: it didn't last and there was no way for it to work ever again once it lost all power. Coveting the ability to leave suddenly at any given time, no such time had ever presented itself. Until now.

Shouts and general confusion hit the room about the same time Bantor started to move.

"I knew it!" shouted the Court Officer. "He's been her spy all along!"

Another few called for the room to be secured, but Bantor was already out the door and heading for the stairs. Before the general alarm could even sound in the palace, Bantor was on the street heading towards the northern stables.

He had hoped for the best but had prepared for the worst the last two times he'd been called in for "further questioning". This time was no different. His best horse was packed and saddled in the northern stables on the opposite side of his estates. He'd packed plenty of food, gold, and a bedroll. There was nothing left for it. He had to flee to Morgaine's closest compound. Of *course* he still knew where it was. The worst thing was, he would need to use the ring until he was out of the city. It might not last that long. If it did, and he needed it again – would there be enough charge left? All he could was pray.

Morgaine wouldn't be happy knowing he'd kept this ring to himself all this time. But he was not going to apologize for that now. The Dark had corrupted more than the Contessa, it seemed. Rondor had fallen already. It was just a matter of time before the armies and the people knew it, as well.

It was several days later when Nathan woke up. His side was still painfully sore, and he felt incredibly weak. Even though he woke up to sunlight streaming into the room from an open window, he still struggled to keep his eyes open, he felt so drowsy. He leaned back against his pillows and half-closed them again, just breathing.

One thing was sure: this was not any hospital back home. He was somewhere on the compound still. The window in his room was wide open, and birds and other sounds were flowing in with the warm air.

No such thing as fresh air in New York City! And leaving a window open might let an allergen or a germ into the room! Oh my!

Laughing brought instant pain, and a young woman came running from around the corner to bring him some water in a glass. She couldn't be more than thirteen or fourteen, and yet they'd apparently left her to tend him. It seemed he wasn't supposed to be awake yet.

What happened? Oh yeah. I was attacked in the dark. Choked, then stabbed. This place is full of fun. What's next? Maybe sensory deprivation! Torture and death? Can't wait!

Soberly, he realized that was a possible future event. At least if Morgaine's "cousins" ever showed up unannounced like his attacker had. The girl bowed and ran out of the room as fast as she had run in. A few minutes later, a whole mass of people came in. The captain – Treyborne, Morgaine, still holding her side and walking gingerly. Her maid – Brianna. A few others of the militia armed and bristling with weapons if none out at that moment.

"I see you're awake as well as alive today!" Morgaine said as she walked over to feel his head. Lord, she was beautiful! All the sultry fire you'd feel from Ana de Armas, coupled with the perfection of Margot Robbie. It was unreal. Just having her this close…she was dressed in a simple black dress that covered her wounds but fit her form wonderfully. It was amazing how such simple clothing that showed absolutely nothing made her look ravishing.

"I felt it was time to stop laying around just bleeding and sleeping today!" he responded after she pulled back. With her so close, it had been hard to focus on anything but her.

Morgaine, nodding as if he'd said something incredibly wise, pulling back and looking at him.

He added, "Where's Smyslin? He didn't get hurt, did he?" A look passed from Morgaine to Treyborne that worried him. "He *is* ok, right? The attacker didn't get him when he came back or something, did he?"

Treyborne walked out of the room, heading somewhere towards the men's quarters. Nathan's head hurt and he still felt very light-headed. *I wonder what pissed him off so much.*

Morgaine answered him, "Treyborne will get him for you. He's fine. Trey hates it when I'm right. And I usually am. Tell me, Nathan: do you remember your attacker then? What did he look like? Was he a Dark Man, or…?"

"I didn't see him at all! It was pitch black, and suddenly he was on top of me in my bed, strangling me. I fought him, got ahold of my shock-lance from the floor and got him off me. I managed to stand up, then he stabbed me, and…delivered his '*message*'."

Morgaine's eyes snapped up at that, "What message?"

So, Nathan told her what he remembered from the attack in more detail, ending in the "...*come alone...*" part. "And then I passed out."

Morgaine sat down in the lone chair in the room by his bed at that last bit. She swallowed and kept her head down several moments. Looking up, she said, "It is as I feared. You have reopened the portal, Nathan. Now others can come and go. Soon, it may be all the way reopened. That *cannot* happen. If your friend is through, then others can come, also. This has the mark of Jezerah all over it...but...*Emorion* supposedly took the hill. And he's the one with the Hollow Men. Perhaps they've combined forces again. Or this is all Emorion's play. I guess we will find out."

She put her head into her hands and just rubbed her temples for a minute. Treyborne returned with Smyslin, who – upon seeing Nathan – ran over and hugged him. Treyborne just watched them dispassionately, but the exchange caught Morgaine's full attention.

Smiling, she stood up. "You two talk for a bit. Nathan, get some sleep. I'll have the cooks bring in a meal for you and Smyslin first. I have some thinking to do. And some praying. This is all bad and I need...I need to think of a strategy here."

"I have an idea, Morgaine."

Stopping and turning, she said, "Oh? What is that?"

"An idea is a sudden helpful thought or plan, but that's not important right now." The old joke fell on deaf ears. "OK...here it is, but you might not like it."

Not fifteen minutes later, after quite a bit of pushing, cajoling and outright begging, Nathan was in the sparring room where the regular troops worked out and obviously did most of their battle training. Weights, wooden "swords", a target range, and even a circular track were all in this enclosed area.

They'd had to carry Nathan down on a stretcher, as he could not begin to consider walking down all those stairs by himself. Walking to one of the open areas very slowly, Nathan was quickly surrounded by six men carrying shock-lances. As he had proposed.

They snapped them on, and, again at his urging, put them at maximum. The crackling and snapping filled the room, echoes reverberating about.

"Are you sure about this, Nathan?" Morgaine asked over the din, trepidation clear on her face. "This could set you back days, or even kill you if you're wrong!"

Nathan took a breath, putting hands in the ready position as if he were going to spar with the men, instead of simply getting electrocuted willingly. He turned his head sideways to look at her. "I'm sure. Keep shocking me until I either pass out, or what happened before happens again."

She gave a loud sigh, then nodded. "Go ahead men. At the first sign of him being out, you back off! The first one to hit him when he's unconscious gets a *personal* reprimand from me!"

The men looked at each other with raised eyebrows and grimaces. Apparently, those had happened before.

"Come on, boys! Let's get this over with," one of them said.

And they closed with him. A shock in the side opposite his wound and one in his back sent ripples of pain into him, and he cried out. Two more on each arm, and one on his leg knocked him to his knees. Again, he couldn't help a cry of pain.

"Keep doing it! Don't let up!"

Then the shocks came even faster, hitting him everywhere but his face and neck. As he fell onto his knees and then his stomach, suddenly the pain ceased as it had before. It simply flowed out of him like water down a sinkhole. The ripples of shocks were no longer painful, but like doses of pure energy. They kept coming, and he slowly rose back onto his knees and elbows.

The pain in his side was gone. The dizziness and tiredness were gone, as well. He felt like he'd slept a month and had several energy drinks in him already. Standing up, even as the men kept shocking him, he straightened all the way up and looked right at Morgaine. Her eyes were as wide as saucers. Motioning with his hand, he indicated for the men to cease. They stepped back, looking at each other in amazement.

But Nathan's gaze was for Morgaine alone. Walking slowly over to her, he lifted his shirt and tore the bandage from it. Soaked in dried blood, it came off with difficulty. But below it, there was barely even a sign he'd been stabbed. Except for a thin white line. He reached her, and her hand, trembling, stretched out and touched where his stab wound had been.

She looked up at him, eyes still wide like a little girl with a pony.

God, she is so damned beautiful!

His blood racing from all that energy must have lit a fire in them, but she did not withdraw her hand when she noticed it. They were very close. Close enough that Nathan could feel his blood stirring with fire for her. Passion poured from his eyes into hers.

"Be careful of that flame, Nathan Arvad," she said very softly, raising her chin. "Your eyes are willing to pay a price that your soul may not. To drink from this cup is likely to sour all others after it."

Her eyes lowered for a moment, then looked up into his again. "I say this not out of pride, but out of experience. The sweetest of wines can only be savored once before becoming less sweet itself. Others, even if only slightly less sweet, may seem bitter indeed." She lowered her hand

and stepped away, dropping her eyes once again, then looking back at Treyborne for a moment before returning them to his own.

"I think this has proven successful," she said loud enough for all to hear. "Treyborne, Brianna, Nathan…follow me! We have some planning to do."

Turning briskly, she strode away like the White Queen that she was.

CHAPTER 62

Nathan and Smyslin arrived at Morgaine's chambers about an hour and a half later, having eaten and cleaned up a bit. Nathan's body was aching to sleep. But at least he didn't pass out unwillingly as he had before. Guards were also now posted outside the building they occupied and in the hallways.

"Not to watch you," Treyborne had assured Nathan while he ate, "Just to be sure you don't have any further…issues."

It made sense.

Dinner had been fried bird of some kind – Nathan couldn't remember the name – along with carrots, peas, and bread smeared with honey butter. Some cow's milk and slices of cheese were added in case they needed more. Nathan did. He felt he could eat the entire cow, hooves, and all! Finally, after having sated his voracious appetite, he and Smyslin headed towards the other building and climbed the stairs to Morgaine's suites on the far west wing. They passed several guards stationed throughout the halls. Apparently, the attack on Nathan had caused the compound to beef up security everywhere.

Morgaine and Brianna were in the main meeting room with the view, sitting on couches opposite each other. When they arrived, Brianna spoke into the comm at her ear, and Treyborne appeared minutes later. They all sat down, were given a glass of whatever they wished from Maitan – Nathan only wanted water – and then they got down to business.

"Nathan, first I must say, that what you did in the training hall was extraordinary. To my knowledge, the only one of the Elder Race who was able to even withstand the power of the shock-lances was my older brother Tabor. And he helped develop them. He told me he had attuned the harmonics of the electrical current to his own biometrics, thereby making him effectively immune to their power. But…to take in the power and use it for self-healing…!"

Morgaine just shook her head. "I wish I had time to just stay here and analyze that for a few months! It must be fascinating just watching how that even occurs!"

She shook her head again. "Unfortunately, we have more pressing business. As we always seem to these days…" she said this while looking at Treyborne, who merely shook his head negatively at the truth of it. "Now on to the business at hand. Nathan, I think we may be able to push this situation into an advantage in our favor. I need to get to the Arc Gate. It's being defended by Creator knows how many Dark Men and their superiors. But you have an open invitation to the place itself. You can literally walk right up to it! How about we just play a little game of our own…and accomplish both our goals?"

Nathan looked at her skeptically. "What type of 'game', Morgaine? I mean, Ellie dumped me like a bag of trash by the side of the road a few years ago. I'm not all madly in love and about to go risking my life to save her immediately…but she doesn't deserve to be incarcerated and enslaved by the Dark Lords forever, either. She's not a bad person or anything. Just a bitch. Sorry. I mean, I still *care* about her. I loved the girl, for God's sake! But, as much as I'm loathe to admit it: if we have to take some risks to try to save her and get control of the Arc Gate back for you, I'm willing to listen to the plan. She frankly doesn't deserve me rushing in blind and alone because I'm so crazy about her. Three years ago, maybe. Probably, even. Now…*eh*…she can wait."

Morgaine seemed to follow this and nodded gravely, even appreciatively. Brianna most certainly understood, hiding a smile by ducking her head and then taking a drink before raising her face again. Nathan noticed and winked knowingly to her when she did so.

Brianna blushed.

Treyborne seemed almost to not be listening. He was leaning back, sitting in the couch next to Brianna, but as far from her as he could possibly be, leaning his arm on the outer armrest. Brianna was on Morgaine's side nearest her. Morgaine sat on her own at the head of the table, and Nathan and Smyslin were sitting next to each other in single chairs on Morgaine's left, across from the others on the couches.

Morgaine continued, "So…you're ok with us bringing in others despite the 'come alone' warning?"

Nathan just nodded.

"Fine. So, let's discuss another issue: do you think you can even open the Arc Gate in the first place? I mean…what happens if you arrive and they just say, 'Here it is,' and put a knife to her throat?"

"I've thought about that. Honestly, I'm not sure what I'd do then. Truth be told, I woke up next to the Gate however long that was ago – three or four weeks now, maybe a month? If I could have opened the Gate, I'd have done it then! Maybe I've learned some things. Whatever it is that helped me suddenly speak the language…heal from shock-lances and make Dark Men run…maybe it's changed me…". He shook his head. "But it's a longshot if they think I can open the Arc Gate just by showing up and wishing it so."

"The language is a mystery. But perhaps…I don't know…" Morgaine's voice trailed off. "I've thought perhaps you're Tabor reincarnated. Or…a child left behind on some other world who had visited or lived here in the first years when we were thinking we were winning and going to be able to eradicate the Dark Lords and their Darkspawn and go home…"

Morgaine shook her head. "I wish I knew. But it's not relevant to the here and now. Here's what I propose we do…"

As she laid out her plan, Treyborne's eyes went from mildly surprised to shock. By the time she was done, Brianna was sitting back, staring blankly and Treyborne was on his feet, angrily strutting back and forth.

When she finally finished, Treyborne shouted, "That's simply not going to happen, Morgaine! If we fail in this. If *you* fail in this, you die! The Lords will almost surely open the Gate and we will have lost. You're literally gambling everything on this play – and it's 100% likely that they know you're going to come anyway. Even if Nathan himself didn't know it!"

Morgaine leaned back, smiled, and nodded at Nathan. "I'm counting on it! What they don't know is his ability to withstand shock-lances. His healing…his…rather limited but interesting side effects from absorbing excess energy! We…"

"You don't know either! You're risking everything – now – just because you both feel you need to save his former girlfriend! Let her die! Let us plan…we can hit the Gate later!" Treyborne's face was flushed with anger. Nathan, sitting close to where he stood, saw Brianna's face looking up at him. She was wide-eyed and her face was flush, too. Like she also was angry.

Weird.

What Nathan said, though, was, "I think it's a good plan! I can do whatever I want to get there, they'll let me. Whoever and whichever of you comes with the ring comes right along with or behind me. And then we hit Morgaine's brother, or whichever Dark Lord it is in the gut, grab Ellie, and at least ascertain that the Gate is still closed before running out! Your airship, which is apparently one of only a few in the world, will at least be able to cover us and at worst can just airlift us out…at least I'll have tried to save Ellie! If I try, I'll feel like I did what I could do. If it doesn't work, at least I'll know that. And so will she. They won't want to kill me, in the event I'm the only person who can even open the bloody thing. I hope."

Apparently, he still did have some small amount of feeling for his old girlfriend. He'd have to watch her suffer in that event. Or even die.

Ugh. How annoying. Nathan tried to ignore the inner gyrations of his stomach. He wanted to be through caring about Ellie.

Treyborne looked at Nathan darkly. "I cannot defend Morgaine against thousands of Dark Men and dozens of Dark Knights. Let alone against one of the Dark Lords! I'm human, for crying out loud! I have limits! And so do you!" he said, whirling back on Morgaine. "Especially right now. You aren't gifted with instantaneous healing. And no! I won't let you take a bunch of shock-lance hits to find out for sure!"

Morgaine smirked at him. "I…see…" she paused. "And what else will you not *let me* do?" She said and he almost winced, realizing how over the line he'd been. She was all White Queen again, staring up at him, but it seemed she was ten feet tall even sitting, and he was about three.

He bowed his head, nodding. "I will do as you command, of course, Mistress. But know that I do not agree with the idea and am not happy about it."

"Noted. I'll add that to the long list of things you don't agree with that I've done or will do." She stood up slowly looking at them all, "We're done here. Nathan, stay with me a moment longer."

Turning to Brianna and Treyborne, she said, "I have some…personal questions for Nathan. I'd like to figure out his past, how he's gotten some of his 'gifts', perhaps even dive into the question of the language just 'coming to him' out in the wild with the Dark Men. We won't be long. Maybe an hour. But I'm going to ask him about his parents, his childhood, and what he remembers about various things. A bit more about this 'Ellie' possibly, as well. I'd rather he didn't have to share all that with everyone."

Morgaine paused here, looking over at Brianna, "Get us some tea, and then withdraw to your own quarters. We will be up awhile longer, as I mentioned. You needn't be. Trey, the guards are posted. Get some sleep. It's been days since you've gotten a real night's rest." He started to protest, and she stamped her foot, "That's an order! I need you in top shape, because you are leading the rescue team on the sky cruiser. Our lives will depend upon *you*. So, *sleep* damn it! And stop being a little child!"

Chastened, Treyborne stormed out without another word, but he did shut the double doors with a bit of extra force than was necessary. Brianna raised her eyebrow at Morgaine, saying nothing. She left, as well, but returned minutes later with some tea and two cups. Apparently, it had been brewing beforehand. Bowing, she murmured, "Mistress Morgaine," and left again, shutting the door quietly.

In the intervening few minutes, Morgaine had slipped into her back chambers, exchanging her day dress for a very long white robe and some matching slippers.

Nathan spent the time growing nervous and wondering where this was going. He also wasn't sure how much he really wanted to share about Ellie…or what he could recall from his childhood that could be of any real relevance to the here and now.

Morgaine came back with the robe on while tying her hair back into a ponytail. Brianna had poured tea when she'd come back, leaving one each for Morgaine and Nathan before withdrawing.

Morgaine sipped her tea quietly for several minutes.

Nathan just decided to wait her out. This woman…*wow*. Just wow. It was just enough to watch her sipping tea. Somehow that seemed more sensual than a naked woman dancing on a stage, or a strip tease from a normal woman.

Nathan had to start thinking about other things…soon he was remembering a beach in New Jersey with his grandfather and his mother…

"Nathan, I want to tell you something. This is going to be me sharing, as well. I had hoped a couple days ago – before you were stabbed – to get some of this out with the goal of getting to know each other better. After all, we are literally the last of our race. It seemed…*appropriate*… to me to do so. Now that we have some time, and it may be relevant to our newest crisis. Well. It's just time we got more acquainted with each other." She looked over at him, eyes mysterious.

"What do you want to tell me Morgaine? I get that you feel that way: 'last race' and all. But honestly, I still feel that I'm quite human. And… well… whatever. What is it you want to say, and what can I tell you to help us out in our rescue plans for Ellie?"

Nathan sipped his tea for the first time. It was a black tea. Very hot, tasty, but rather bitter. He leaned over and grabbed the sugar lumps and put one in, grabbing the smallish spoon, and stirring. He even added a little cream.

"My father was a prophet of sorts, Nathan. He was able to see the future…at times in his dreams. He was never wrong in my experience. But…he told me three things that have never occurred. Three things I thought were never going to happen because they never could. But one – now – has seemed to be fulfilled. Therefore, I have renewed hope for the other two."

"What were the three things," Nathan asked.

Morgaine eyed him curiously, then smiled slightly. Her eyes were bright. "I will you tell you the one – and only one – as the other two haven't happened yet. One is about to, though. And I must say, it is…a tremendous relief to know father was not blinded by optimism or false visions in his last years. The last thing, well, one of the last things he said to me was that this pendant of mine would be my 'burden' for six hundred years. It has been less than that here. But time moves differently in different zones of the galaxy. Hours around a sun here are different than others. Time warps every time one walks through a quantum field…It's possible it's been well over six hundred years on our home world. I wouldn't know. But I suspect it has been."

Nathan just looked at her, "I have…*no idea*…what you're talking about."

Morgaine stood then, and the robe slipped a bit from around her chest, showing her cleavage down to her navel. Her nipples weren't showing, but a very large amount of skin did. Nathan's mouth went dry. Her body was amazing. All he could see on her was the black pendant made of the same dark metal as the monolith hanging between her breasts.

The 'Arc Gate' pendant… was set with a white gemstone the size of a small egg. As she walked over to him, she took off the pendant from her neck, leaning down to do it.

Every move she made had the grace of a ballerina. He couldn't help himself. It was erotic and he became extremely aroused. She came and stood just within the area between his knees, looking him squarely in the eyes. "Lean over," she commanded, and he did so, ending up just an inch from between her naked breasts.

Nathan could see quite a bit more now, and the view was magnificent. He could even see the bandage on her left side, still gauzed up and with tape around it. After a moment, he closed his eyes, in the event she'd drunk a bit too much or something and didn't realize she was exposing herself as much as she was.

Sometime in those few seconds, she had reached around his neck and placed the pendant on him, clasping it behind his neck to keep it in place. But she neither withdrew, nor moved. Opening his eyes, she touched his chin and raised his head to look at hers. She was mesmerizing. Beautiful beyond description, with amazing eyes, perfect lips, and her body was oh…so…very…close…

Their lips were a scant inch or two apart. Make that half an inch. He could smell her sweet breath and the faint smell of some flowery perfume that made his head swim.

"My father," she whispered, "told me the pendant was a 'burden I was not intended to carry', in fact. But after the betrayal by my brother and his fiendish friends, it apparently became something I had to do for six hundred years….as my father had for over a thousand before me. Or so he said. He also plainly said…this pendant had been intended for someone else."

Nathan swallowed. He couldn't think. Her words didn't make sense, but he was beginning not to care. The most beautiful woman in this world…and perhaps any other was half-naked, in a robe, only inches from him. She was a bit intoxicated from the smell of her breath. And he could sense she was more than a little horny.

Holy shit! How do I handle this?

Morgaine sat down slowly into his lap. Her panties were lace, and he could feel her perfect ass as it sat neatly on one of his legs. Her arm was still around his neck. She was breathing heavily, above his face by a few inches. Her breasts were now very much exposed.

Oh yeah. She knew.

Nathan couldn't take it anymore; he reached up and started kissing her. She not only didn't resist; she engaged. Enthusiastically.

Kissing her was like soft, sweet strokes and caresses from her lips. Nathan had never been kissed like this before. And he realized, he might not ever again. Her tongue was darting everywhere, always in the perfect place and with the perfect touch! Just kissing her was incredible. This beautiful, exquisite creature was in his arms, and he knew right then that nothing was ever going to compare to this.

The kissing became so incredible, time seemed to stop and go sideways. At some point, and Nathan was unsure when, they had gotten onto the couch. She was taking his shirt off, her robe no longer visible, laying in a crumpled heap on the floor somewhere. Her bandage and her underwear were all she was left wearing.

The kissing paused, but never stopped completely. Even as she pulled him up and drew him towards her bedroom, they never quite stopped. Nathan had never experienced true ecstasy in kissing until here, in this moment, with Morgaine. The wicked smile she gave him when they did part for a moment as she took off the rest of his and her clothing was more than he could take.

"I warn you, Nathan," she said, "I'm going to make love to you like no one else ever has, or even can. I hope you can take it like one of our Race. Because I'm going to give it to you like one, I assure you!"

CHAPTER 63

Nathan woke from their lovemaking, hearing Morgaine whispering words in his ear, "…I freely give this remnant of Creation…"

What?!

To say he felt groggy would be an understatement. There had been more wine in the bedroom. The red-blue stuff. Nathan could hear Morgaine speaking, but she wasn't making any sense. Or the wine was still overpowering him. Whatever that stuff was, it was crazy strong.

Some fishy name…

The pendant flashed white from where it rested on his chest. His eyes popped open, and he immediately regretted it. The room was spinning, and although the curtains were still closed, it was clearly morning.

Morgaine was laying with her head on his chest, just looking at the pendant. The light died down slowly, allowing him to crack one eye open. "What was that all about…?" he asked slowly, trying not to slur his words.

"You are now the bearer of the Corillion Medallion, Nathan. That's all. It will warn you of the Dark being near, even protect you, if it can. Preserve you and take you home if it cannot. It is no longer mine. It is yours. For as long as you can bear it. And…it is a burden."

She kissed his lips, and he hungrily reciprocated. But this was no longer the playful Morgaine.

She let him kiss her a moment longer, then pulled back. "You need to dress and leave before Brianna wakes and comes in. We always have breakfast together, and then you need to come meet me for lunch. We do need to talk. About the attack on the Gate. And other things."

With that, she was up, and nearly dressed before he could even raise his head. "Up! You have about ten minutes and it looks like you need thirty! Move!"

Groaning, his head now pounding, Nathan got up slowly, looking for his clothes. Then he remembered. Most of them, except his underpants, were in the other room. He hopped into those and opened the doors to her outer chambers.

Scrambling over to them, he threw them on hastily, while Morgaine put her hair in a ponytail again. At some point last night, that had come off, too. He remembered her on top of him, brushing her hair on his chest…! It was quite the memory.

More spinning!

She stopped him and looked him dead in the eyes for a moment, "This didn't happen. You weren't in here. I'm sure the guards know, but they have strict standing orders from years back not to report any such things to Trey. Understood?"

Nodding dumbly, and not really understanding anything, Nathan just said, "Uh…huh?"

Morgaine shook her head. "No time to talk. Lunch. Don't be late!" and she shooed him out of her bedchambers. In the hallway, the guards stationed down the hall didn't move an inch. So, Nathan just straightened his shoulders, and walked with as much dignity as he could muster down the hall, down the stairwell, and made his way out of the building, ignoring them.

Outside, several men and one of the women cooks were walking around the grounds, but no one seemed to pay him any mind. When he got to the other building, Smyslin was waiting on the stairway up to their bed chamber hallway. He apparently had been there for some time.

"Smyslin! Did you…get any sleep at all? What are you doing? You look *exhausted*." He stopped on the landing and didn't stagger a bit. Well, not *much*.

"I was…worried, Master! I've learned that perhaps not all of what I've heard about…*her*…may be true! But some things…that are said…are too vile to speak of. And frightening!"

"Such as…?" Nathan said, crossing his arms and spreading his feet. It wasn't because he was wobbly. Of course not.

This should be good.

Smyslin looked uncomfortable, looking down at Nathan under his eyebrows, somehow. Despite the angle. "It is said…she…*eats* her lovers after they are done!" he blurted.

Nathan burst out laughing, making his way up the stairs and right past Smyslin as he responded, "That is not funny, Master! It is also said that she can turn into a snake person and then poisons her lovers, so that they cannot see or hear any other woman after being with her! They become her slaves!"

Another chuckle. Shaking his head, Nathan kept walking. Guards were still in the upper hallway, keeping watch. Not a word from either of them. He walked by them, as well.

"And…and…she is said to…" Nathan shut the door behind him. The room was very dark, and for a moment, he got spooked, remembering the last time he'd slept in this room. He hit the button turning the light on above the bed near the wall. Breathing rapidly for several seconds, he went about investigating the entire room. Twice. But the darkness called to him. He was tired. There had not been much sleeping last night. Drinking yes. Lovemaking, most assuredly. But sleeping? That had been intermittent, at best.

He hit the switch, turning the room to pitch black once again. An inner room with no windows and only vents. This room was ideal for major 'sleepage'. Not one minute later, Nathan was snoring, laying on top of his bed covers.

Memories of having sex with Morgaine filling every dream.

CHAPTER 64

A knock at Brianna's door as she was brushing her hair startled her. It was only about the third hour! Clearing her throat, she asked, "Who is it?"

"Open the door! It's me – Trey!"

Hurriedly, she set her beautiful silver-backed brush down on her vanity, and rushed over, holding her skirts up as she made her way to the door.

Unlatching it, Trey burst in without waiting for her to open it herself. He blew right by her and sat down on the receiving couch, near the tea table. Blinking in surprise, she turned and watched him go and settle in.

Closing the door, she asked, "What…may I thank for the *pleasure* of your visit…?" she said with as little acid as she could.

Trey caught it, though. Turning, he wilted a fraction under her sharp look, and said, "I'm…*sorry*! But I'm pretty sure Nathan spent the night in Morgaine's chambers. No one will tell me anything, and that tells me enough! This is no time for her to be taking on new lovers! Especially when we've got work to do!" He huffed. "For the Creator's sake, we've got an attack to plan!"

"Is that…the *only* reason you care?"

He glared at her. "Of course it is! I'm in charge of Morgaine's safety and captain of her militia. Meanwhile, we've got 'the regenerating magic man from another planet' in there with her, alone! And he's about to go… wherever…trying to save his former lover from Morgaine's brother! And she *knows* that! It's just too messy! She always has to complicate things…"

Brianna came over and took his hand, looking him in the eye. "I'm not supposed to tell you this. I'm not even supposed to *know*! But I know about you and her. It's ok! I get it! It's got to be hard to see someone you admire…and who…at one time…was more to you…with other men! I cannot even imagine! If Sirles had lived and left me for another *woman* instead of dying…and I'd have to pretend to *like* her and be nice to her and that I didn't have feelings for my man…? Ugh!"

Treyborne looked positively lost. He was such a little puppy at that moment, that she couldn't help it. Brianna sat down next to him, and despite the differences in their height, she just took his head and laid it on her shoulder, pulling him down.

"She's fine. You know it. I know it. I think she can take care of herself if there really was any danger…! She has…*needs*, apparently. She told me about that when I first met her. And I think there was someone in that town…the Lieutenant…?"

Trey just nodded without taking his head off her shoulder and sighed. "She does that fairly frequently. Sometimes it's other men in the corps for a night. But most times, she tries not to…ruin anyone she has to work with, because most of those leave soon after. I'm the exception. Yea, me!"

Rubbing his hair, Brianna realized her heartbeat was elevating. Shaking herself, she thought, *Foul woman! He's mourning a loss and you're getting all riled up! If it's going to happen, it will happen. But not today. He just needs a friend today!*

Brianna nodded, not remembering what he'd said, but remembering she had agreed with it, at least in part.

"Ahhh!" Trey nearly shouted, "It's pointless. I need to get up to the sky cruiser dock and check on it. Make sure it's ready for flying!" He moved to sit up, but she held his head like a vice grip.

"Not yet, you aren't! You always run from the room whenever feelings come up! I've seen it several times and I just got here! Just sit for a minute. You promise to sit…?"

He nodded glumly.

Brianna gently eased his head off her shoulder and went to warm some tea. There was a small electric heating element in the room for just such a purpose. This place was so full of wonderful inventions! After setting the pot down full of water, she came back, being careful to sit across from him.

Trey looked over at her, sitting up. "I'm a mess. I guess this one is a bit different. I mean… Nathan appears to be from her race. I guess, being here…I'd always held out a little hope. It's my own fault. We haven't been more than respectful workmates for years. *Years*!" He stood up. "OK. I'm done sulking. Thanks for being there. I won't embarrass myself further…"

Brianna stood up too, taking his hands in hers again.

Heart racing again, damn it!

She looked as casually as she could into his eyes. "When you're done mourning her, you can come visit me and we will have dinner together. I'll make you something myself down in the kitchens. It's probably time you gave that up that ghost, don't you think? Perhaps someone…*else* will come along. But that won't happen if you keep pining after that lost goat. As far as Morgaine is concerned, it's over. It needs to be that way for you now, too. Life has a way of … well, you know! Life is never dull, is it?"

He laughed a little and shook his head. "No. Never dull. Especially around *her*! I need to start a new hobby. Maybe wood carving, or drawing…Take my mind off things, and accomplish something besides guarding and fighting and shooting…"

Brianna raised an eyebrow but said nothing. She swung his hands together once, letting go. "Get over her, Trey. Get to living again. The Creator always has a plan. When you're ready, let me know, and I'll make us a nice meat pie!"

Treyborne's eyebrows raised, then nodded appreciatively. "Thanks Brianna! You're good for her! And for me, apparently. Morgaine needs another strong woman around. The servant girls – well, the other servants – they just bow and curtsy and run. You talk to her like a person." He nodded to himself. "It's good."

Tilting his head in farewell, he turned and, opening the door, he left, closing it behind himself.

The tea pot behind Brianna started to wail.

CHAPTER 65

Jezerah stood in the Triumvirate meeting room. Alone. Well, it was his hologram. But he was there, standing in the room. He'd called a meeting to get some sort of pulse on the status of their 'brotherhood'. Well, he had his answer now. Even K'Thul defied him! Emorion was consolidating his forces around the Arc Gate, setting up bunkers and fortresses. More troops poured in by the day.

While Jezerah had been trifling with Rondor and inspiring Nelrae to war – as they had all agreed upon – Emorion had gathered his forces into a tight bundle. When the Arc Gate opened, Jezerah had known his forces were scattered, and that he had little time to secure the area.

But not in his wildest dreams did he think Emorion would attack him outright. Nor that he would bring as much force as he apparently had. K'Rinn *perhaps*…shouldn't have been blamed for the loss entirely. No matter, strength and success were all that mattered. Jezerah idly wondered if he would have been executed by a superior – if such a creature existed – with his recent setbacks.

There is a first time for everything. If I don't resecure that Gate and reestablish dominance over my 'brothers' soon, I will have effectively executed myself as surely as if I'd squeezed my own skull until it crumpled…

Jezerah laughed out loud at the image of squeezing his own skull until it turned to jelly. Realizing his staff was still in the hologram room, Jezerah clicked the button, ending the meeting that never was.

As the image faded, and his staff room came into view again, Jezerah barked, "Curtaise! Assemble the generals, the Knights, and the Quartermasters! I want every one of them in this room in fifteen minutes!"

Curtaise didn't even bother to bow. He was gone. Two of his female staff members, attractive and lean noticed his glance and bowed deeply. Each had serviced him as he had need. The taller one, Trixa, she was always a special one. Energetic. Better than average and when not around his slave girls, she filled in nicely.

Curtaise returned and reported, "Leaders are assembling and will arrive shortly, Master."

Jezerah nodded absentmindedly. Within minutes, the generals, Dark Knights of the *Siday*, and the Quartermasters of the Dark Men were assembled, about forty in all.

"It has become apparent to me that the other Dark Lords have their own agendas that do not coincide with our own. From now on, if they do not bear my Mark and are not Dark Men of our clan, they must be considered the enemy until further notice. The times have changed."

"Morgaine has reappeared like the foul phoenix that she is. The Arc Gate has opened. And from what my long-range sensors can detect, it may have opened briefly yet again. I certainly felt something…but we cannot be sure until we resecure that area. My former brother Emorion, although a revered Dark Lord himself, is working against us to hold that area for himself. I'm open to plans and suggestions at recovering it."

Omrion, the new leader of the *Siday* spoke up through his mask, curiously marked with a red skull over the front. That was new. "Master… Emorion's clan is weak! We were surprised due to K'Rinn's carelessness. But if we can approach from here, here, and here," he said, pointing to the digital map above the holo-table, "…they simply do not have the manpower to keep us out! We will crush them, and their middle will collapse. It will entail reasonably heavy losses but ensure success."

Jezerah nodded. "Anyone else?"

Curiously, Curtaise spoke up, "Surprising Emorion is impossible. They will be expecting an attack. And the easiest access is clearly from the riverbanks on the north, east, and southeastern sides, as General Omrion so wisely pointed out. But Emorion knows he's weaker and must prepare with cunning. He will likely expect the full assault from those areas, and will have fortified them doubly, including mining the area on the opposite sides of the riverbank."

"But this type of maneuver also will leave his backside weak. Yes, there are hills that one could even call 'mountains' on that side. But he's likely to have them sparsely protected, gambling because he must in his efforts to retain the area. Why not send a visible force he can see coming from miles away exactly where he expects it to come, but hold up on the opposite shore just long enough for him to buy in completely. Then send the real attack in a pincer move around the hills from the north," he pointed, "and the southern forest," pointing again. "The result will be that he will think he's outwitted you – again – Master. But you will instead blow through his paper-thin reserves at the flanking positions and pin his men against the riverbanks. Their only escape would be through their own mine fields and into our waiting reserves!"

Jezerah looked amazed. He had no idea Curtaise was this capable. The other generals were nodding, including Omrion, who voiced approval by saying, "I can lead the forces of the reserves into the viewing zone, adding credence to the illusion of direct attack. When the time is right, I will split off with my Dark Knights and join the northern flank troops, redoubling their efforts, leaving a battalion of Dark Men led by their Quartermasters above the river. We must assume that the Dark Lord Emorion himself will be there, as well. I will deal with the traitor, personally."

"Do not engage Emorion alone, *Siday* Commander Omrion," Jezerah commanded. "You are full to the brim with the power of the Dark, to be sure. But Emorion is a vessel of the Void itself! Do not underestimate him! Take four of your best men and attack him together, at a minimum. Otherwise, you will never succeed."

Even then, it will be nearly impossible.

Omrion bowed without saying another word.

"We have a plan then! Go and execute it with all haste. Prepare the field support crew and the engineers to maintain and haul the larger blaster cannons. Curtaise, suit up. You are my lead general now. I'll get you the Field General ring I took off K'Rinn. Get down there. But before you go, send me your assistant Blage to take over your duties here in the command center."

Curtaise bowed deeply, turned, and left. He seemed to walk taller out of Jezerah's staff room. Jezerah nodded thoughtfully. He had always been capable at everything. Perhaps he'd been under-utilized, even so.

CHAPTER 66

As Nathan walked in with Smyslin, he saw that Morgaine's lunch table was set with enough food to feed a dozen people. But only Treyborne, Brianna, Nathan, and perhaps Smyslin were going to eat any of it. Two of Morgaine's Elite Guards were stationed just inside the room.

That was new.

Seating himself, still staring at the guards, Treyborne said, "New days, new rules. We have to expect that our situation here is compromised. Until we can move, guards are going to be stationed around all high-level personnel."

He continued, "Non-essential personnel are being reassigned to our compound in the southern Petty Kingdoms sanctuary. Kind of a hybrid keep and secure compound. Much larger and much safer. The rest are going to check out the one in the Eastern Empire. All comms are to be set to "Mute" unless an emergency is in progress. Once they all reach their destinations, we will reassess. Assuming we're still alive."

Saying that, he looked straight at Morgaine, who didn't even flinch.

"Good afternoon, Nathan. Welcome to the party! Just this morning, word reached me that Rondor is not merely a questionable ally, they have also apparently succumbed to the Dark Cult! It is worse than I had feared after our encounter there. With all these groups actively seeking information on our whereabouts, coupled with the attack on your person not three days ago – we have concluded we all need to leave. And as soon as possible. This will make preparation for our maneuver to the Arc Gate possibly a little slower than we would like. But they didn't set a deadline, so we must hope we have the time. Comments?"

Treyborne spoke up first. "We have one more little problem that I just found out about before arriving: the sky cruiser won't start. The power cells are completely drained, and we cannot charge them. So, we may have another problem getting into and, more importantly, out of the Arc Gate area."

Morgaine looked at him like he'd just said he'd joined the Dark Cult. She started shaking her head, "I'm not sure we can safely even consider an assault on the Arc Gate without air superiority. Or at least equality."

She sighed heavily.

In the silence, Smyslin, standing behind Nathan spoke up, almost too quietly to hear, "I…can fix it." Everyone looked at him. Cowering under the scrutiny, he lowered his eyes, "Forgive my intrusion, great ones. I am but a lowly engineer. But I have worked on the Master's…er…Dark Lord Jezerah's personal craft for decades. I know it inside and out. If they are similar, I am quite certain I can make it function. The Na-cells and Ca-cells often interact, draining both if not properly wired. This is a common mistake of junior techs. My guess is, I can fix it in less than five minutes."

Treyborne looked at him like he'd never seen him before.

Morgaine spoke up, "Guards, one of you take Smyslin to the Sky Hangar! Get him everything he needs. *Everything!*"

One of the guards walked up and nodded to the former Dark Man. It seemed odd, Nathan realized, to see him like this. He looked…healthier than he had before. More muscular and his skin was a nice even light brown. His eyes were brown with green circles in them, and there was a new light in his eyes.

"I'll be delighted to help!" he said as he left.

Morgaine shared a look with Treyborne, who just shrugged.

Nathan finally spoke up, "It seems you're wanted all over the planet, Morgaine. It must feel like old times!" She spared him a dour look before taking a bite of her food.

"I'm sorry our discussion cannot be continued from last night, Nathan. But we're at war now. Officially or unofficially. Anyway, eat! It may be our last real meal for some time. I had the kitchen staff cook up anything that couldn't be brought with us. We have to assume we won't be returning here any time soon."

She paused and said under her breath, *"If ever."*

She shared a quick look with Nathan, and her eyes were full of pain.

CHAPTER 67

Bantor had reached the compound right before noon. At first the guards flew at him from everywhere. Falling to his knees and putting his hands in the air, he yelled, "I'm Bantor! I used to live here! I have a message for Morgaine!"

Soon after some degrading searches and a runner being sent for their Mistress, Bantor was on his feet and relaying his message to the Lady herself. She looked tired, and he noticed her wincing as she walked down the trail from the main building to where he was being held and watched by no less than six of her Elite Guard with blasters in hand.

He'd easily remembered the codes and the underground tunnel to reach this hidden grove. But apparently most if not all the cameras and relays were down, as no one had noticed his approach until he'd literally walked onto the compound grounds. That had been odd.

Mentioning that to Morgaine before she left brought a raised eyebrow and a jerk of her head to one of her men. Bantor didn't recognize him. But then, he didn't recognize any of them. Any of those who had served with his father would be long retired…or more likely dead, by now.

Kissing him on the cheek, Morgaine left and said, "You will always be my 'little man'! When we go, you go! Get some food, find some extra clothing, bedrolls, a blanket, and a razor. You need a shave!"

He always loved Morgaine. He loved her more now.

Several hours later, Bantor was fed, and lying in a room located at the far end of the compound. He was told this was their "special guest" quarters now, and they had two others who would be sleeping in the same hallway. "Maybe only for one night," the housekeeper had said. "We're leaving in the morning, if I don't miss my guess."

Bantor had no idea, but he had to agree. If people were looking for you and had an idea where you were – you didn't stay put. You moved. Curling up, he fell asleep immediately.

Waking up, he realized it was dark outside. But a light had come on in the hallway. His door had been shut, but he was wide awake and hungry again. Opening his door, the sound surprised someone in the hallway, causing him to jump to his feet, whirling and pulling out what appeared to be a Dark Man's shock-lance. He'd seen those when he was little and remembered them well.

The man was odd, too…appearing to be…Morgaine's brother or something. Cousin? Shaking his head, Bantor said, "Pardon my manners, son! I'm Bantor! The Queen's former friend from Rondor. I just arrived. Didn't mean to startle you!"

The man relaxed, snapping off the electric shock coil on the top with a flick of his hand. Sheathing it, he reached out his other hand for some reason saying, "I'm Nathan of Earth." Seeing Bantor looking at his hand like a viper, he said, "Sorry! Old habit. How do people great each other in Rondor? I made it to the country, but not the capital, sadly…"

"Typically, we nod. If we're friends, we hug, or place a kiss on the cheek. Are you…related…to Morgaine? You seem…similar. Pardon my asking."

The man who called himself 'Nathan of Earth' laughed and said, "Ask her and she'd say yes. Ask me and I'd say no!" As he laughed, a medallion identical to the one Morgaine always wore popped out from his shirt, swinging back and forth. Bantor's eyes locked on it and looked up at Nathan in shock.

Noticing his reaction, Nathan put it back under his open-necked shirt and said, "Oh that! Yeah, this is Morgaine's. She…gave it to me last night. I'm not sure why yet. I haven't had the chance to ask her about it."

Raising a skeptical eyebrow, Bantor said, "If…you *say* so, Nathan of Earth. Perhaps we can discuss it over a drink…? Or some dinner? What time is it? I seem to have slept through the regular mealtime."

"It's late…maybe what you call 13th hour or so…? I was told there was someone here with us, but you came out right behind me, and it startled me. I had an…incident here a few nights ago. I'll walk you over to the kitchens. I could use a snack myself. And there's simply nothing but water to drink in this building. They have some excellent beer they're trying to get rid of. Let's go help them…!"

With that, Nathan of Earth turned and starting walking back down the hallway to the stairwell, "Come on! I'm buying."

Whatever that meant, it must have been funny, because the man chuckled loudly as he hit the stairs. Bantor just shook his head and walked. His stomach rumbling all the way there.

CHAPTER 68

Smyslin reached into the back panel as far as he could, pulling the wiring out completely. The under panel for the Na- and Ca-cells was, in fact, completely fused. Pulling it all out took about two minutes. But rebuilding the under panel took almost two hours. Smyslin had never seen anything this bad. It seemed no one had really known how to maintain this vehicle in over a century. Grabbing some new wiring and carefully tying the lines off separately, grounding them to the sideboards on the opposite walls of the confinement zone for the power cells took another almost thirty minutes.

He was disappointed.

It had been a while since had had to do so the same for his former Master's sky cruiser, granted the damage here was far more extensive; so, it had taken far longer than his prescribed five minutes, just for the wiring. Feeling defeated, he rose and walked slowly down the stairwell from the underbelly of the cruiser.

But it was not fifteen minutes after Smyslin was done that Treyborne was firing up the power cells and the sky cruiser lifted off. Treyborne took it up and out over the perimeter for a quick two click run before landing it back on the hangar pad.

Leaping out of the pilot's seat, he ran over to Smyslin and gave him a huge hug. Smyslin just stiffened up, not knowing how to respond. But Treyborne then slammed him on the back a couple times, apparently in a friendly gesture, and thanked him profusely.

"You don't know how much this means, Smyslin! I just wanted to thank you and Nathan for doing this! Now we have a chance and can also get some of the women and children out of this compound today. I'll take them to our bunker in the Petty Kingdoms as soon as I can get the cells charged and be back by tomorrow. Thank you again. I want you on our crew as long as you can stay…!"

He then ran off, right out of the hangar for some reason.

Smyslin, rubbing his back, wondered if all things human were going to be this strange. When he reached his quarters, he realized that the Master's door was open, and he was not in his rooms. He frowned. Searching the area of the compound they were to stay in, he was not to be found there, either. He was sure that his Master had specifically said he was heading to his room hours ago…!

Looking down the back stairwell, he saw a small light coming from one of the windows behind one of the locked doors in the back of the building. He moved his head sideways. Would the Master have gone into the back rooms, which were forbidden?

Perhaps he is searching for something that might be inadvertently left. That is wise. I will help him!

Going to the door, he found it unlocked. "Master…?" he called, opening the door. Light flooded in from the back hallway, but the little light far off winked out. "Master…? Is that you? We are not to be back here, Master! Come back and Smyslin will make you some tea! Or tell me what you are looking for, and I will help you…!"

Looking down the dark hall, Smyslin fumbled for a light button or an emergency light pad. Nothing. Strange. But these compounds were not what he was used to, either.

Something made the hackles go up on Smyslin's neck and he realized he had felt such a presence before. Slamming the door behind him, he ran screaming from the back door into the dormitory hallway where his and the Master's rooms were. The door from the prohibited area opened and Smyslin turned his head, still running.

"You! I knew it was you! Stay away from me! I have left the Master! I have a new Master now... He will protect me from you! He is a brother to the gods!"

Several blaster shots flashed in the hallway and Smyslin's still body skidded down the hall and thudded down the stairwell all the way to the landing.

CHAPTER 69

As Nathan was walking back with Bantor – who was really quite a funny guy – the pendant around his neck flared bright white.

It was lit enough that even through his shirt, it made the central compound seem like twilight and not after midnight, which is what it really was. Maybe they'd stayed a bit too long in the kitchens drinking beer from the open keg and eating sandwiches.

Maybe.

What was this light about…?

Suddenly blades were everywhere, and Nathan had to literally dive backwards to avoid getting his throat cut. Bantor exploded with expletives, pulling a sword from his walking cane and slashing left and right, trying to avoid getting gutted himself. Flood lights blasted on from everywhere and the compound alarms went wild.

Nathan and Bantor found themselves facing a half dozen armed Dark Men. Most with only blades, but a few wielding shock lances. Standing so he could partially guard Bantor, Nathan flipped out his own shock lance and purposefully turned sideways from those of his enemies with lances.

It had the desired effect. The blades whirled, but clearly these Dark Men had fought together before and did as they should – take the opening given to them. While Nathan was parrying the blades, the shock lances shot in, hitting him on both sides. Pretending to take painful hits from them without dropping his guard, he suddenly slammed one of the Dark Men with a shock-lance full in his face, grabbed the weapon that flew up into the air – somehow with minimal effort – and gutted another.

Bantor was parrying, crouching, and ducking as much as he could. Nathan began to whirl his lance at a speed he'd never conceived of before. It became a whirlwind, slamming into heads, knocking aside blades, and shocking Dark Men all over exposed areas with ease.

About thirty seconds into the fight, all six Dark Men were on the ground and Nathan did not hesitate to stab those that still moved. Shouts all over the compound said that this was not the only attack. That, and the lack of men rushing to their aid.

Nathan yelled at Bantor over the alarms, "Get back to your rooms! Lock the door! Only let someone in if you know them!" Turning, he ran back up towards the main building, where screams and cries were coming over the din.

Reaching the guard dorms, he saw almost a dozen Dark Men battling three or four of the guards. Having to guard all the hallways and rooms upstairs had depleted the dormitory of its usual contingent. These men were hard pressed and defending with all their might halfway up the stairwell on the landing. It was the best place they could have gone.

The medallion around Nathan's neck blasted pure white again, and Nathan leaped an impossible leap, landing in the midst of the attackers at the base of the stairwell. Whirling his weapon, he spun, shocked, grabbed weapons, stabbed, and leaped until only two of the Dark Men still stood, a little ways off.

Seeing him pause and stare at them, breathing heavily, they turned and ran. Leaping again, he came down with the lance into the back of one and spun, slamming the back of the lance into the skull of the other. A sickening sound followed, and the man skidded across the floor, the base of his skull crumpled, blood and brains oozing out.

The men on the stairs literally cheered, then turned and raced upstairs themselves. Nathan turned from the grisly scene in front of him and followed them.

Another battle was happening in the hallway. This time it was Treyborne and one of the Dark Men that looked like the one who had originally shocked Nathan out in the forest that day. Taller, leaner, and somehow…Darker…this one moved like Death himself. Twisting, whirling his blades, Treyborne, a master of just about everything from what Nathan had seen – was struggling to survive.

Nathan yelled at the being, who turned to look as Nathan approached, "Why don't you take on someone your own size, you bastard!" Somehow, Nathan knew…he was just better. Treyborne leaped back and sagged against the railing behind him, bleeding from at least a half dozen wounds.

Nathan didn't hesitate. The 'whirling dervish of death' came at him, but Nathan parried everything with the shock-lance, twirling it easily and almost lazily as the tall, thin Dark Man slowed his advance. Then started to back away. *Clang!* Click. Clang! The being's dark eyes widened in amazement.

Nathan stared at his opponent, the white fire of the pendant blazing brightly. Barely noticing, Nathan suddenly swept under his opponent's legs, spun the lance, and shocked him twice in the stomach as his weapon went up and then backwards. It fell beyond his grasp and Nathan kept shocking him until he stopped moving. Then one more time for good measure.

Treyborne staggered to his feet, wide-eyed. "I've…never seen anyone move like that. Except the Mistress…!" Nathan just nodded and jerked his head upwards.

"We need to see about the others."

Treyborne gripped his mid-section like he was holding it together but nodded adamantly. "Let's go." His expression was iron.

By the time they got upstairs, they found Morgaine, naked above the waist, standing with her sword over at least a dozen of the Dark Men's unmoving bodies. Brianna was there, shoving her back into their rooms as Nathan and Treyborne approached. Morgaine's eyes looked up at Nathan.

They were fire. Her wound, still wrapped on her left side, was oozing blood again. She also had cuts on her left leg, right arm, and across her cheek. It made her more beautiful somehow. Then she was gone. Brianna was clearly about to see to her wounds, but Nathan and Treyborne both ran down the hall towards where she had disappeared into her quarters.

"Are you all right?" Nathan yelled.

"Are there any others?" Treyborne shouted right afterwards.

Brianna answered, "The Mistress has dealt with her assailants. Thanks for the late arrival, boys! She will be fine. I'll see to her wounds. She says to search the entire compound and check the perimeter for more. She also says we have to leave – now!"

Nathan and Treyborne – now bonded by the tides of war – nodded to each other and raced back down the stairwells and hallways outside to see if anyone outside still needed any help.

CHAPTER 70

Emorion was beaming. How much more fortune could the Void bestow upon him? He was overwhelmed with gratitude. His lone spy in the city of Rondor had just so happened to be attached to the Court Vizier of Rondor not two months ago. The man, a native to the land, had simply wanted for his lover to live after becoming severely ill.

What a pity. Now she was well, and the man himself was bound to the Dark.

And fortune upon fortune! He had been the Court Stenographer the day that some former brat that had lived with the White Witch at one of her compounds was brought in for questioning. From what Emorion understood, the man had owned a Light Shield. Wonderful inventions that somehow no one amongst the Dark Brethren had managed to retain. At least, that he was aware of. And here this man was, trying to escape using one of the ancient green-gold rings from his youth! Ah, the memories! Stealing pies and mutilating his sister's kittens!

Happy days.

His man had even managed to notate the escape before running off out of the Courtroom himself. From his own report, he had known that anyone associated with the White Witch would be cunning. He had asked himself: what would he have done? Well, run to the stables furthest from his home, stolen a horse, and raced out of the city.

Apparently, the only variance here was that the brat turned fat, old man had actually kept his own horse there for just such a purpose. Emorion's charge had tracked the man all the way to the tunnels that led right to the compound.

Once he reported to his handler, the news reached Emorion within minutes. Emorion had known just want to do.

Jezerah could never resist his inner need to purge the universe of his one and only sister. He'd simply sent a note – and a map with some digital images – of the compound to Jezerah. He'd even signed it. "*Your brother, Emorion.*"

Giggles and laughter burst forth from Emorion for several minutes just thinking of it again. After he'd regained control of himself, he once again patted himself on the back.

Another dilution of Jezerah's forces. He will come for me eventually. His ego will not allow anything less. But, yet again, I'll have whittled his stock without any losses to myself! Kill the bitch or not, Jezerah, I win!

Imagining the chaos and bloodshed at Morgaine's heretofore hidden compound made Emorion laugh. And then laugh some more. Emorion's maniacal laughter filled his chambers as he readied himself to ride towards the Arc Gate. The slave girl tied to his bed huddled in fear as far from him as she could, completely forgotten in his own orgy of mental masturbation.

It is time to open the Portal to my Destined Kingdom! It is time to ascend to the greatness I have always known is mine! And mine alone.

"Bring the prisoner!" Emorion yelled into his comm. "The heretic will come soon. And we will be ready."

Turning his attention to the slave girl…Emorion smiled his best smile.

CHAPTER 71

Nathan just stared as they hauled away Smyslin on a stretcher. Someone had shot him in the back with a blaster. Three times.

He was breathing. For now. There were casualties all over the compound. Two of the housekeeping staff had died. Four of the Elite Guard. Another seventeen were injured, including Morgaine.

Again.

Thankfully, Maitan and the compound "doctor" who was more like a nurse, were ok. They began on the worst of the injured and worked their way down.

As soon as Smyslin was in the makeshift medical tent outside, Maitan ran from the woman he was treating for a shattered shoulder and knife wound to him. He barked an order to sear the wound and then set the shoulder back in place to his assistant, and then ran to get some wound sealant for Smyslin.

The skin on his back was burnt and his shirt was destroyed. Blood was oozing past the scorch marks as big as softballs on his back, and his breathing was ragged. It appeared he'd bloodied his nose and had a black eye. Probably from falling down the stairs.

Treyborne had left the morning after the attack with the sky cruiser. The plan yesterday was to drop off some of the kitchen staff, wait staff, and housekeeping at what he termed "the upper compound". From there, they were to then go immediately into the city for supplies and to stay overnight until that compound's safety could be verified. He was to return with another set to go into the base proper on the next run with only a handful of guards.

Much of that had changed.

By the time he'd returned several hours later, those remaining who could walk were loading into the land cruiser with a guard contingent. Those who couldn't walk were to be carried into the med station below decks on the land cruiser before it left. Some horses were going to have to be left behind. Food stores also. They were cramming everyone into those two vessels.

Morgaine was out seeing to the wounded personally, and consoling those who had lost a loved one. When she came to Nathan, she just stepped up and leaned onto his shoulder, gripping his hand as they watched Maitan work on Smyslin.

Treyborne joined them, looking at Nathan a long moment before saying, "He's the reason we can fly the sky cruiser at all. I had just told him…". He looked over at the now very pale face of the former Dark Man engineer. "that he had a place here as long as he wanted it."

Maitan shouted at them without looking back, "Get out of the way and give him some air! He'll be fine, or I'll die trying. But all of you crowding me is infuriating!"

Apparently, when being the doctor, he had the right to command anyone, even Morgaine. Because everyone, including Morgaine, turned to leave the crowded tent. Nathan went with them.

Morgaine dropped Nathan's hand as they walked. "We need to get as many people out of here as possible, Trey. But we need to be smart about it. I'll go in the Land Cruiser with the wounded. You and Nathan should take the Sky Cruiser yourselves and verify the new site is safe. Then come back for me and the Land Cruiser. We're going to be more vulnerable, obviously. But that's why I'm going with them. You two need to make sure we've got a safe place to go. All the Guard will be with me, too. We will be fine."

Trey grimaced but nodded. Nathan didn't like it much, either. It meant leaving Smyslin and Morgaine to whatever Dark Men were out in the wilds between wherever "Nyx" was and this compound. They exchanged glances.

Nathan started to speak, but Morgaine cut him off, "I've survived centuries without you two watching over me like mother hens. Go! Come get me once the central compound is secured and deemed safe. That is an order, Treyborne."

Sighing as loudly as a human possibly could, he turned, taking his blaster rifle, and turned back towards the hangar. "Come on, Nathan. She's not going to budge on this. We might as well get it over with. I could use your help, anyway. If that place has been compromised, I want you to kick their asses with me."

CHAPTER 72

Ellie was frightened now.

She had been taken…somewhere. Blindfolded. For a few days, they'd fed her and kept her in a nice room. Sparse, even Spartan. But nice. A bed, a pillow, a blanket. A toilet and sink. Some soap. Food that didn't stink or look like it had been regurgitated.

But that was all over.

One day, they'd come in, thrown a hood over her head and then carried her off to something that ended up feeling like a truck bed or rail car. She'd been told to lie there and stay still, as the neuro-link in her temple still worked even when slammed up against walls, apparently. How long the trip was, she wasn't sure, because she'd fallen asleep in the dark, stifling mask at some point.

Awakening to her ankles and arms being grabbed and hauled bodily out of said "truck bed", they'd literally tossed her into some grass. Itchy grass, too. But then, for some reason, they had left her alone after that.

Her hands were not tied any longer, so she took off her hood and found herself in a treed grassy hillside. Warriors dressed in all black with black scarves and looking like the horrific killers they appeared to be, were running everywhere. Others in red and yellow scarves seemed to be working amongst them without being the same as them. "Workers" of some type, most likely. Then she saw it.

Ah. That explains it. The Monolith.

The Monolith from her museum – or more likely its twin – was towering over the entire area. It was literally in front of some cave entrance, and there were large trees all around it. Despite her blurred vision, she could tell this monolith had vegetative growth surrounding it. Not on it. Maybe it discouraged that somehow. Probably the magnetic fields.

But this one had clearly been here a long time. A receiver port, then. Or maybe it worked both ways. Hopefully it did. What Ellie wouldn't have given right then for a laptop and some field probes!

A shove in the back reminded her of where she was. "Move, female! You are to be up underneath the Arc Gate. There you will sleep, and eat, and piss until your Lost One comes for you, or not. If not, then you die. But not before you are punished." This all from a hissing, nasty-sounding voice behind a black mask that clearly hid a face that needed to stay there.

Ellie did her utmost best not to retch or start to cry.

Her tormentor kept shoving at her back until she yelled, "Stop it! I'm moving!" For some reason, that had an effect. Stopping in the shadow of the Monolith, she looked up and saw the light of the "sun" for this planet. For the first time, she realized it was maybe a little more orange than her own. And a bit closer or larger.

A bedroll was thrown down at her feet, along with a water jug, some dried meet in a cloth wrap, and some rags. "Eat, sleep, but stay. Try to run, I kill you. Try to cry out or make me angry, I kill you. Do as you are told – you may live."

"Gee…thanks for the motivational speech, Tony Robbins! Maybe you can go rally the troops now." She sat down, glaring as the scarved black man simply turned and walked away, completely unruffled.

My Lost One?

She knew they thought Nathan was somehow important. More important than she, for some reason. Maybe because he was the first one through. Who knows? It was good to know he was alive, at least. He certainly wasn't going to save her against this army himself. Ellie would have to save herself if she wanted to live. Sighing deeply, she surveyed the entire area. Lots of these black dressed men and their entourage. Lots of metal boxes set into the ground. Tents? Bunkers?

No one was paying attention to her. What was to keep her from walking away…?

A sound next to her made her jump…the sound of a voice behind her made her jump again. It sounded like dry leaves burning, rather than a real voice. Looking around, she could still see no one.

"The…female…will not resist…the…female…will not run…or the female…will be torn apart by the Hollow Man…."

Feeling but still not seeing who…or *what* was talking to her struck horror into her bones. It seemed the voice was coming from everywhere. Ellie couldn't help it, she started to tremble. Then cry. Nothing else was heard. She wouldn't be going anywhere. She just hoped Nathan was bringing an army with him.

If he came at all.

CHAPTER 73

Flying in the Sky Cruiser was amazing. It didn't make a lot of noise, using some sort of electrical anti-gravity technology and air thrusters that were far quieter than any jet he'd ever experienced.

It also moved fast! The day was breaking as they flew over a large field about an hour from the compound. Nathan had gone in to see Smyslin before he left, but he was still unconscious. Maitan could not give a prognosis on survival yet. He had been burned badly, and it was fortunate he'd made it this far.

Flying over a grain field just south of what Treyborne called the 'Gloom Wood' and a wide, slow-moving portion of the river, Nathan thought he heard something fall over in the hold behind them. Looking back was difficult, as the pilot seat restraints were no joke. Criss-crossing belts with pads to minimize scuffing or bruising. It was more like a harness, really.

Another sound of something crashing.

"You hear that?" he asked Treyborne, who nodded negatively. They weren't using comms, as the sound of flight wasn't overly loud. But it wasn't silent, either. Especially in what Treyborne had called the 'pilot crib'. When Nathan had referred to it as a 'cockpit', Trey had raised an eyebrow, but said nothing.

"I'll go back and check it out," Nathan said. "I think I heard something crash and I want to make sure whatever is back there is secured properly. Treyborne nodded.

Unstrapping and unbuckling took almost a full minute. Standing up, he stepped up onto the platform behind the pilot seats, which were lower toward the middle of the ship. Their seats were literally surrounded by some sort of plexiglass, allowing them to see below, above, and anywhere in between while flying. A third crash back in the cruiser confines got Nathan to start to jog back towards the origin of the sound.

"I heard that!" came Treyborne's voice from behind him. It was probably nothing, but whatever it was, they didn't want some boxes or equipment to come rolling up and hitting them in the backs of their heads, either.

The sky cruiser was big. Not as big as the land cruiser, by any means. But it could easily fly with probably fifteen to twenty individuals and whatever gear they might be bringing. In a pinch, it looked like it could fit double that. But they'd be tight and not everyone would have a seat or a harness.

The rear of the cruiser was filled with locked cabinets, strange symbols, and even had a sort of cooler in the back filled with medium-sized water containers. As Nathan approached the cooler, suddenly a Dark Man of some sort stepped out from where he'd been crouching and lifted a blaster.

Nathan, startled, had already been a little off-balance from a sudden wind gust, so instead of stabilizing, he just let the movement push him over and he rolled away from any potential first shot, reaching for his shock-lance, and flipping it into his hand as he leaped back up behind a seat for some cover.

The Dark Man didn't fire, however. Instead, he casually walked forward, waving the blaster idly.

"Trey! Trouble in the hold! Stowaway Dark Man!"

"Can't hear you! Come up front!"

Shit!

"I wouldn't come any closer. I've already killed over a dozen of your kind earlier today."

"I'm aware," came the raspy response. This Dark Man was stockier, more muscular. Maybe even a tad shorter than others he had seen. His armor was striped with dark red marks like claws. And his face covering was almost like a piece of armor itself, connected to a helmet or hard hat cap on his head. It bore a small red skull painted on one side.

"What are you doing here? Do you want to surrender? I accept."

A dry laugh came from the other. "I'm not here to surrender. Nor, I assume, are you. I was hoping to hide my presence here and discover your retreat location before exiting. However, the food packs in the back weren't tied down, as they are in our airships. A shame. When one hasn't eaten for days, one takes risks."

He paused, so Nathan chimed in again, "What do you hope to accomplish now? You can't take me alone, and I've got help if I need it. Once we set down, there's nowhere for you to run."

"Yet, I have my blaster," was the response. He sat down, holding it in Nathan's general direction, but not pointing it directly at his position behind one of the seats.

"You're the one who shot Smyslin! None of the Dark Men we captured or killed even had one. They're rare, from what I understand. Why do you have one? And why did you shoot him?"

"Shoot him? I meant to kill him. He's a traitor and a heretic, just like you. Forsaking his oaths. Letting the Dark no longer fill him with the power of the Void. I do special work for my Master. When something needs found, or a job really needs done – I do it. I was merely finishing this task, before heading to the next. I haven't been sent to kill you. Not yet anyway. Apparently, you are wanted very much alive. Therefore, I have no issue with you."

"Well, I have an issue with you," came the cold response.

"I understand. If I had friends or a family, perhaps I could even say I would feel the same. But I don't, and I don't care. Come find me if you think you can." He shrugged.

"And how do you propose to get off the ship?"

"Like this." Hitting a wall panel that had been pulled open, the stocky Dark Man hit a switch. Suddenly a hatch near the back directly behind him opened and he simply hopped backwards.

Nathan ran to look but couldn't see him out the small port windows. The hatch automatically closed two seconds later.

Treyborne yelled, "Nathan! Are you ok? The rear drop hatch light just clicked on and off! You still there? Nathan!!"

"I'm still here," Nathan said as he ran up. "We need to practice using comms on this thing too." Looking down and behind them from the pilot's wide-angle view, he could see the man floating downwards and guiding himself with some sort of jetpack attached to his armor. Perhaps that is why he had appeared so stocky.

Nonetheless, he was moving fast. Nathan pointed back. "We had a stowaway! A Dark Man. He's the one who shot Smyslin."

Treyborne looked over to where Nathan was pointing, and immediately pulled the sky cruiser into an arc, decelerating, but turning around at a high speed. "I've got eyes on him."

As they got him in their forward view, Treyborne leveled the cruiser, then hit the accelerator. But by that time, the Dark Man had landed and hit the ground running, dropping from his arms whatever had been propelling him through the air on his armor.

He was headed straight for the trees. Trey hit a button on the panel and a red target light appeared as a hologram in front of his viewscreen. Another panel box opened, which Treyborne slipped his left hand onto and pulled it into line to aim at his target. It used some sort of ball mechanism to refine the target and calculate range, apparently.

Almost to the tree line, the target acquired him, beeping a signal, and Treyborne fired off some blaster cannon shots from somewhere below the ship. The trees around him got hit, and one grazed the top of his armor, but the Dark Man kept running and was gone into the woods.

"Damn!" Treyborne said, "I didn't get a clear shot on him. But even a glancing blow should have torn his shoulder off! That armor he has must be rock solid. I've never seen any Dark Man with that level of protection!"

Nathan could only nod. "What are our chances of finding him in that forest?"

"Almost zero. And there are other dangers in there that have nothing to do with Dark Men or forces tied to the Dark. I'm sorry we lost him. But I'm also glad he's off our ship! Go make sure there aren't any more of them if you haven't already. I'll keep her steady and get us back on course. That one will just have to wait until later. Pretty smart, though. Hide out in one of our cruisers. Attack us or find our other hideout. It's also a way for him to escape. But he almost had to have had to plan on them losing…unless he always had another agenda." He paused. "I hope the land cruiser didn't have any stowaways, too."

CHAPTER 74

Forest green was not a color that Brianna particularly liked to wear. It was just so...*green*! But everyone on the land cruiser was to wear something green for their breaks and stops as they skirted the forests to the southeast and made their way through and around the uncivilized lands between the Empire of Nelrae and the Petty Kingdoms, where the town of Nyx was located.

The land cruiser was crowded with people. Children were lying on bedrolls when they weren't running around playing and screaming everywhere. Sleeping bays were on rotations, and food stores and water containers were all kept close to hand.

Morgaine had relented, and all but three of the horses were in the stalls in the lower levels, but crammed in so they could barely move. They were out on breaks with the people as well, grazing amongst humans like this was normal for them.

Every stop, all water resources were refilled, in the event they ran into areas less verdant or without as abundant a rainfall as the area they'd left. Brianna felt quite hot in her green travel cloak. It was itchy, too, so she only wore it when they went outside. The idea was to blend into their surroundings as much as possible, and not raise alarms or make it so any word spread of a large group migrating and moving in a magical device without horses pulling it.

If possible.

They avoided towns, villages, or anything resembling a farmhouse. It was quite a ride, however, as there were no roads or even trails. This was "undiscovered country", as Sirles had liked to call it. Places no human had gone before. Or at least lived to tell of it. Grimacing remembering his warm smile and big hands, Brianna suddenly felt very alone in the world. Morgaine was up and about constantly, buoying people's attitudes, checking on the injured, and making sure everyone got fed. Brianna probably should have been shadowing her more. But what was she supposed to do for her, hold her hair back as she kissed one of the scared little ones, or help her thank her guards for their bravery?

It wasn't like there was food to order, dishes to move, a bath to draw, or meetings to arrange. Hugging her knees to her chest, Brianna did feel alone. But it was honestly far less than those four years she'd lived alone in the farmhouse before that fateful morning that now seemed like a century ago.

Now, Brianna had a purpose…she also lived better than most people on the planet. They had fantastic machines that did amazing things, guards, food prepared every day, and the best medical staff she'd ever known. Better than a king's staff. Or even the Emperor's! All in all, she'd made some good friends here. That included Morgaine. She was her boss, to be sure. But they were also becoming friends.

And then there was that man.

Shaking her head, Brianna tried not to think of Captain Treyborne. He was off on the sky cruiser with Nathan, scouting ahead to make sure they had a safe compound to retreat to. Halfway around the world, it seemed, from the one she'd just gotten comfortable at and had accepted as home.

"A silver mark for your thoughts…" came a voice from behind her.

Brianna turned her head. "Bantor! I'm sorry, I was just thinking of home…and having just left my new home…and heading further and further away from everything I've ever known. How did you handle it when you were only a boy at the time? I have come to understand these 'migrations' do occur at times."

"Oh, it was all an adventure when I was a boy! I was utterly fearless, of course. My father would ride with the guards. Back then, we went a lot slower. No one to run from, I suppose. So, the guards would ride horses and escort the cruisers, which were full of non-military. We had two then. I'm not sure what happened to the other. Maybe it's at one of the other compounds. It's possible that as her staff has dwindled – and it clearly has – that they didn't need the central one. Or it isn't functional any longer. It is very large."

Bantor fiddled with his mustache as he spoke. His eyes were somewhere else. "Dad used to come into the cruiser on his off shifts and rest. We'd eat together at stops. There was always something cool to see. When I got older, I'd get to ride with him, if there was clearly no imminent danger. One time, I had to jump down and run toward the cruiser in a big hurry. I never did see the reason why."

Brianna watched him. He seemed sad for some reason. "What happened to your dad, Bantor?"

"He died. That day he had me jump down and run...something happened. An attack of some sort. Wild animals, wandering bandits, Dark Men...?" He shrugged. "I don't know. Mother would never tell me. I'm not sure she even knew. But she never brought it up, and wouldn't answer questions about it, not to her dying day. It all came back to me just now. Me running through grasses and weeds so high, they were over my head. I heard some banging and blaster fire behind me. Nothing I'd not heard before, but that time was different. There were shouts and more firing. I reached the cruiser and just ran in. The bay doors were open, and more guards rode out from their ready positions. Everyone came back, except dad. Him, they brought in on a stretcher. He never woke up. Lasted for days, though. Mom and I got to say our goodbyes." A tear rolled down his round, wrinkled face.

"I'm sorry," Brianna said.

"It was a long time ago. This trip and me trying to remember the traveling days as adventures. Well, they were that. But some days were… better than others, obviously. Today, I couldn't even tell you where we were going, or where from. That was almost fifty years ago. We won't have any trouble going this speed. It's maybe a better way. I'd like to think that maybe my dad's death helped bring about a change that made it all safer for everyone."

Neither of them talked after that. Brianna glanced at Bantor out of the corner of her eye a minute or two later. His head was down, and tears were rolling down his cheeks.

CHAPTER 75

The Central Compound, situated in the hill country above the city of Nyx, was located in the middle of a massive olive grove. The buildings were almost entirely underground, and the upper areas were housed by permanent residents, who worked the orchard, and harvested the olives.

There were even olive presses on site, where they pressed out the oil and filtered it for cooking and as a base for ointments and tinctures. The average height of these trees was at least thirty feet, and the hills around the grove made a natural bowl shape. As the moons were rising and the sun was far to the other horizon, an open area with what appeared to be a tool shed on it in the middle of the grove simply opened up into a deep hangar after Treyborne hit a button above his head.

Sliding the sky cruiser into landing mode, they eased their way onto the exposed landing dock, which then lowered with some kind of hydraulics, shutting the "shed door" above them. It was quite impressive.

"This place is…way more hidden and higher tech than the one we just left. I'm curious…"

Trey looked over before responding, "Like I said, Morgaine tended to favor staying near the Arc Gate, even before it reopened. This base was built during the war years by the Elder Race. Or so I'm told. When they'd come through with an army full of technology, engineers, and technicians, along with the time and mind to build a fortress to defend families, equipment, and such. At one point, it was the central base for the entire planet's operations."

"So, what happened?" Nathan asked as they disembarked into a multi-story, fluorescently lit chamber. It looked to be designed for more ships than just this one.

"They got older. The Elder Race brought everyone. Morgaine was the highest-ranking person left almost immediately. She said she'd been ordered to close all the Gates. It was either bring your family or live out your life separated from them. Over time, everyone joined the war effort. About sixty years in, the Battle of Megiddo – the one where they risked all to win all – every one of the Elder Race died but her. They'd been cut down to less than eighty by then, as it was. She and her team took down over half the Dark Brethren, mowing down tens of thousands of Dark Men to get to them. If you count numbers, it sounds like they won. But Morgaine called it the battle that ended the war."

"So, this compound…" Nathan began.

"…became a dungeon for her. I'm sure that's her main reason for not coming back here much. It has too many ghosts for her. This was the place she lived when she became not only the last in her family, but the last of her race." Trey paused, looking sideways at him, "At least, until now."

The hallways below ground were silent. No one came here, clearly. The lights all worked; the power was on everywhere. But it wasn't until they walked up a regular concrete staircase to emerge into the strange hut that covered the aerial entrance did Nathan see any people. A whole cast of over twenty locals had gathered. They clearly lived and worked here and were of all ages and types.

Seeing Treyborne, they all cheered. But when Nathan emerged behind him, they became strangely quiet. Nathan did a quick and friendly wave, coupled with a smile to them.

It didn't seem to make a difference. For a long moment, there was only the wind in the trees.

Treyborne said, "Come on, guys…! I know the staff I dropped off earlier must have told you about Nathan. This is him! Nathan Arvad. He came to us from another world. He's already saved my life. You'll like him."

They all came up to greet Nathan formally, hugging him like family. Some even gave him the formal kiss on the cheek. It was like meeting a new family in France or Italy. Totally foreign, but cool. The children were very reserved, staring at him. One little girl was staring at him from between her mother's legs. Nathan just smiled and waved at her. The girl retreated where he couldn't see her behind her mother's leg. Eventually, it was over, and most of the people vanished into the night.

"Have there been any unusual events lately, Malvern? We didn't want to ask over comms, and I didn't want to scare the staff – since they were told to go into the city to get provisions. Plus… 'unusual' can mean a lot of things. Right now, it could be just about anything from something seemingly inconsequential to a cadre of Dark Men."

Treyborne looked up at the huge man with a large wild beard and curly round mop of hair. Nathan had to look up just to see his beard. The man had to be almost seven feet tall!

"No, Cap'n. We've been largely forgotten out here except during harvest season. We keep a steady supply o' olives and oil going to Nyx and the smaller villages, and the locals leave us alone. We haven't even seen a civilian patrol come by in weeks. I know they patrol all the roads out of a matter of course. Few get out this far, though. Nothing strange. No visitors. Nothing."

Treyborne nodded, "Good." Looking back at Nathan, he said, "I know you've heard we had our share of trouble in the western base. We didn't want to go into any detail but imagine the worst and triple it. Lady Morgaine wanted to make sure this compound was untouched before taking everyone downstairs. It would be a major undertaking to take the entire crew to the far eastern base. And it's small enough, it might not be easy to even house everyone. But we know that one is untouched. Even by us, for over a decade. All its monitors are still working, as well."

Malvern had nodded through most of this. But he stopped when he mentioned the monitors. "Our monitors are working, too, are they not?"

"Yes, didn't mean to imply otherwise, but most of those are in the actual base, below ground and at the rim bunkers. Not the farm. That's your realm, and we only have grounds cameras, to keep the privacy of your family."

"No worries, then Captain! We'd love to see the Lady. It's been over six years since she's been here, herself. Preparations are already underway, truth be told. Food stores have been purchased and placed in the upper bays. Air systems have been turned on. Power generators checked and logged."

"You move fast. Efficient as always. Well, I've got to turn right around and get the Lady Morgaine and her senior staff here with the air cruiser. We just wanted to make sure all was well before moving forward."

"Understood." Turning to look at Nathan, who was listening but staying some distance back, Malvern asked, "So what's he here for then?"

"He's here to watch my back. Like I said, he's already saved my life a couple times. He may not be much to look at, but he fights like her."

That brought the bushy eyebrows all the way up to Malvern's hairline.

"Well, it's full dark now, you can't be flying in the pitch black of night! Come on in, eat, rest, and leave in the morning. Lydiya will have all sorts of good food made up for you by now!"

"That was the plan. We'll scout out the hallways tomorrow before we go back. Call the staff back from the city, too. They have work to do." Malvern just gave him a look, nodded, and turned, waving for them to follow.

CHAPTER 76

Morgaine's "crew" stopped again for dinner, before resuming the trek for the evening. The night team would slow the pace down, using the ground lights, but they kept moving. Avoiding towns was still easy, as civilization usually involves fires, guard posts, and other things like fences and roads to warn of its proximity. The random farmhouse was a potential problem, especially if it was one that put out no sources of light at night, had no fenceposts, and the like.

But Morgaine was willing to take the risk to eat as a family.

Even if someone was out in the fields with their cattle for some reason and saw the lights moving, they likely wouldn't be able to, nor want to, investigate if they kept moving as fast as they did.

The dinner was quite nice, having all those extra food stores that needed eaten. Some roasted lamb, curried potatoes, beans, and, of course, vast quantities of the bread they'd brought. Ale, wine, beer, and water were available, and even goat's milk for the little ones.

Brianna sat next to Morgaine, lost deep in thought. They were eating with Maitan serving, as he always ate last. Bantor was eating elsewhere for some reason tonight, and even the guards on duty were just eating while standing. They were camped under some trees near a stream and an open field of grasses. The air was filled with bugs, but the breeze kept them off and the field wrens were having a great day catching them by the score.

Morgaine spoke up, "Where's Bantor? Have you seen him? I was going to ask him about his estates. The King may confiscate them to the crown, if he doesn't go back soon and defend himself."

"We talked earlier. He told me about his father…do you know what happened to him, Morgaine? He said he didn't. His mother didn't, or didn't tell him, at least. It went from a happy conversation about his memories on trips like these to that in a hurry. That's probably why he isn't dining with us tonight."

Morgaine's mouth stopped mid-chew. Looking sideways at Brianna, she nodded. Resuming her eating, she said nothing. Brianna finished several more mouthfuls before finally asking, "Can you tell me about it? Is it that bad? I mean, the man only wants to know how his father died. In your service."

Morgaine set her plate down, and said to those close by, "Leave us for a moment, please. We need some space." The few people nearby scattered to other campfires, lit to fight back against the chill of the evening, not to mention seeing. The two guards on duty stepped back at least ten paces, well out of earshot in this wind.

Brianna stopped chewing, watching all of this. Taking a drink of her wine, she swallowed. "You're acting very strangely, Lady Morgaine. Have I offended you, or asked something I shouldn't have? If so, I apologize. I just wanted to help out Bantor. He was so despondent over it all this afternoon."

Morgaine nodded negatively, leaning over to touch Brianna's arm with her fingers. "You can always ask me anything you want. That is your prerogative as my assistant and personal maid. There are times I will tell you I cannot or will not tell you something. That is my prerogative that you also must respect. As for Bantor, the reason he does not know, and must never know, is that his father's death was likely caused by himself."

Brianna's hand went to her mouth, "No!"

Ignoring her, Morgaine continued, "I say 'likely' because to this day I'm not certain. His former Captain, a man by the name of Kovan, was a very thorough and decent man in all respects. He was a man nearly the equal of Treyborne in many ways. But back then we had more military gear on our persons, and we had to expect anything and everything. Bandits raided constantly on the roads. The Triumvirate had won, and the world was in chaos. They also thought me dead, and we wished to keep it that way. So, we often had to avoid anything resembling settled lands when we moved about. If we ran into Dark Men, we hunted them down and killed them if they ran."

"On the day in question, young Bantor was riding along with his father. It was unsettled lands with no dangerous wildlife to speak of, and he was making quite a bit of noise, riding with his father on perimeter patrol while we traveled. This was commonplace then, and other young men patrolled with their fathers often. I've had three or even four generations of guards come from one family before. According to the other men on patrol that day, Bantor suddenly pointed into the forest, telling his father he'd seen several men run off to his left into a copse of trees, really a small thicket. Bantor's father, whose nickname was 'Chase' by the way – I cannot recall his real one, we used it so seldom – well Bantor's father brought this up on the comms. Protocol required letting the cruiser crew know and investigating it immediately. Calling for backup if need be. Bantor was told to run back to the cruiser, whose back hatch was open in case there was a need for the reserve patrolmen to rush out and aid them. Which they ended up doing because of the commotion that followed."

Morgaine stopped to take a drink of her own wine, "Eat dear. This story is long, and we need to leave soon."

Brianna picked up her fork but paused mid-bite as Morgaine continued.

"Suddenly blaster fire rang out, and one of our mini explosives was thrown. We're not sure if it was Chase who threw first, because several others followed suit. From the angles we were able to reconstruct, it appears that one of the rear patrolmen had come around the thicket far enough to be in the line of fire. Obviously too far, as seeing through that dense patch of trees proved impossible."

"When blaster fire started hitting near him, the rear patrolman fired back. From what we could gather, as Chase was about to throw his second explosive "chip" as we call them, to flush out his "attackers" – the rear patrolman's blaster shot hit his hand and the explosive blew up in his face. He died days later, but never woke up."

"The saddest part, Brianna, is we investigated the entire area. No bandits, no signs of Dark Men, not even a deer could be found. It seems he saw a shadow, or was simply being a child, making something up and not knowing the possible consequences."

Morgaine looked up, eyes wide and glistening, "It was 'friendly fire', Brianna. That's why no one ever told Bantor. Because his father likely died only because he was with him; and he died for nothing."

Morgaine picked up her plate and finished eating in silence. Brianna did the same. But her throat hurt from trying not to cry for the boy that had been poor little Bantor. And, after all these years, he still didn't know his father had died because of him.

And Brianna was certainly not going to be the one to tell him.

CHAPTER 77

Jennifer was walking the busy night streets of Manhattan. Sipping a coffee against the cold, she hurried along, trying to catch a cab. It was busy, and it wasn't going well. The wind howled around the buildings, whipping her. Finally, a cab stopped, dropping off another passenger. Grabbing it immediately, she hopped in, slamming the door against the cold.

"Where to?" came the foreign accented voice. A young Indian man with a nice smile.

"East 10th and 5th Avenue." Jennifer sipped her coffee and leaned back as the cabbie headed off around the corner. Snow had turned to rain hours ago. Slush and puddles were everywhere. The last week had been a rough one.

Ellie was still gone, and no one was around the museum any longer. The monolith had been moved off site to an undisclosed location. The news coverage and the headlines in the paper were starting to put up false flags, saying it had all just been a hoax. They were saying that 'the two former lovers had concocted the entire thing' and had run off to the Caribbean with the money they made from all the videos they posted online that were now conveniently all taken down. Jenn just put her head into her hand for a minute. Then she sat up resolutely, took a sip of her coffee, and began to hum a song she'd heard earlier that day.

Something uplifting.

When she got out of the cab, she paid the fee, threw on a generous tip, and walked across the street to Gary's apartment. Formerly Nathan and Gary's apartment. They had gotten a steal on the lower east side years before she'd ever met them. Her apartment was shared with four other girls. Jenn was pretty sure two of them were escorts. Sighing, she rang the buzzer. Gary was waiting and buzzed her in immediately. She ran over to the elevators, heading up to the 11th floor. By the time she got there, Gary was waiting for her outside his apartment.

"You want to come in first? It's super nasty outside." She just nodded, walking past him, coffee still in hand.

Almost an hour later, they were both walking out and heading towards the subway station. One of Ellie's former co-workers had said "the suits" had come in the middle of the night two weeks after Ellie's disappearance. Rumors had already started of it being a "hoax", and days later, the monolith was quietly seized by the government. This worker said that he'd placed an Apple tag on the monolith as soon as the hoax rumors had started. It seems he trusted the government about as much as Gary did.

The monolith was in a warehouse by the harbor. Apparently, someone wanted it shipped somewhere. Jenn and Gary were determined not to let the last link to their friend vanish into thin air. They just had to break a few laws to do it. Gary was given the tag code, and while Jenn was heading over, he had put them into his phone.

A short subway ride later, they were walking off the rail stairs into an area that one does not want to go after dark. Jenn huddled close to Gary, who put his arm around her as they walked. Hats on, gloves on, they were still cold. The wind just was horrible tonight.

"Are you getting anything?" Jenn asked as he looked at his phone for the twelfth time in a minute.

"Not a thing. It shows the arrow location, but when I try to get directions, it just keeps spinning...".

Jenn looked at his phone as he held it down for her to see. "It's that way, I think," she said, pointing down a narrow road with no one on it. One streetlight was working on the whole lane as far as they could see.

"Great," Gary said as they started walking. "What could go wrong?"

CHAPTER 78

Morgaine woke up on the cruiser, her "commander's cabin" had its own toilet area, and a bed no larger than what her guards slept on at the compound. But it was more spacious than anything else on the entire ship.

The sky was still dark, but the vehicle had stopped. Perhaps they were waiting for direction from her, or perhaps the sky cruiser had returned with Trey and Nathan. Her heart skipped a beat in excitement over that last bit.

Careful, Morgaine! Don't develop feelings again. It's too painful, in the end.

Yet the excitement of the possibility of their return would not allow her to return to sleep. She'd retired early to maximize healing, as the cruiser was set to cross into the badlands north of the major forests. It would make for speedier movement and reduce the possibility of humanity seeing them to zero.

Getting up, she hurriedly put on her green and light gold shirt and trousers. Even dressing in camouflage, she had to wear something that didn't diminish who she was to her people. She brushed her teeth with the small water jet and anti-bacterial scrub. Brianna loved this versus her old soda wash. Then she brushed and pulled her hair back into a soft band to hold it near her right collarbone. Looking in the small mirror on the wall, she nodded in satisfaction.

No need to do more today.

As she walked out the back hatchway, she saw that indeed the sky cruiser had returned. Nathan was eating breakfast with Treyborne, Bantor, and Brianna. They had all apparently decided to let her sleep. They turned as she came down the gangway, guards beginning to salute all over the campsite.

Standing, they awaited her slow stroll to their seating area. Nodding, she sat down.

"What were we discussing before I arrived? Please don't let me interfere." A bowl of oatmeal, kanan fruit, and cinnamon arrived with a steaming cup of slightly sweetened tea at the hands of Maitan.

The man never sleeps.

"We were talking," Trey began, "about how we're going to avoid the sweeping horde of an army coming from the Eastern Empire."

"What?!" Morgaine leaped to her feet, spilling her oatmeal onto the ground. "Why didn't you awaken me immediately?" In her anger, she stomped her foot, splattering a little oatmeal on Nathan's face.

Instead of responding, Trey started laughing. Then they all chimed in, even Maitan started chuckling, even as he walked over to the pot of oatmeal near the cooks to get another bowl. Meanwhile, Morgaine was very much trying to stay angry. But their laughter took hold. She grimaced a smile, shaking her head.

"Apparently," she said as Maitan returned, handing her another bowl, "the rule of the White Queen has ended." She then sat down and began eating her oatmeal, waiting for them to catch her up, holding impatience with both hands on the inside. Or so she hoped.

Maitan began cleaning up the mess as Nathan spoke up, setting his own cloth down from the oatmeal he'd removed from his face, "We discovered them accidentally, Morgaine. We had a…stowaway on the air ship. Sky cruiser. Whatever. He…". Morgaine moved to interrupt, and he gently held up his hand. "In due course, please Morgaine."

She sighed and took another bite. She tried not to grind her teeth as she was chewing. "He was the one I believe that shot Smyslin. It seems he was sent by his former master, as Smyslin was now a 'heretic'. They want me alive for obvious reasons. But when he jumped from the ship, we tried following him. He had some sort of jetpack on his armor. The chase took us slightly north of where we were originally heading. That's when we saw them."

Treyborne chimed in, "It's amazing, Morgaine. I think K'Thul must be taking every armed horseman and every Dark Man from the 'shrines' in the western provinces. There are over 60,000 of them at least. We couldn't see the end of them. And they're all headed this way. The stowaway had a blaster, so we know he was no ordinary Dark Man. That and the jet pack. Nathan is convinced he not only shot Smyslin, but that he's the one who found us and our base."

Morgaine looked at the two of them, "Since when did the two of you become friends?" she asked sipping her tea. Her eyes watching carefully.

Nathan looked over at Trey, who just smiled and grinned, "I guess I'm fond of my ass, and he saved it a couple times, my Queen!" he said, bowing from his sitting position. They laughed.

Nightmare.

Nodding, she said, "Tell me more about the Eastern Empire's forces. What could he be doing? He wouldn't bring that much force to bear to go after little old me. What does it mean?"

"It means," Brianna spoke up, "that their Triumvirate is in ruins. It's all it can mean. Everyone here thinks I'm just the new girl and should be quiet. I can't know anything…right?" She asked looking around. No one spoke up, so she continued, "It's clear to me that such a trek with an army that size means he doesn't trust going with less. The Arc Gate seems to have created a division. Maybe the other two are trying to keep it from him now. Maybe they're all three bickering, as Nathan believes. But, to me, he's taking that force for one reason only: to take control of the Arc Gate himself. Remember, Smyslin told us that his group, belonging to your brother Jezerah, was attacked by other forces that took control of the Gate for Emorion. Now it seems K'Thul is playing his hand."

Morgaine nodded at her. *I need to stop calling her my maid. She needs a better title.*

"You're quite possibly right, of course. I'd be curious what other reasons you all came up with."

Treyborne said, "With all due apologies, Morgaine. But the Gate could be open. They could be marching his forces to move into another realm." Morgaine glanced sideways at Nathan's chest for a moment. The *Corillion* was hidden, but no light showed from within his shirt.

"I hate to ask, Nathan," she said turning to him, "but the medallion I gave you. Does it throb or pulse? Do you feel it at all right now?" Trey's eyes widened in shock. As did Maitan's. Neither of them had known, of course.

Nathan unconsciously felt with his hand for the pendant. "Yeah...I mean...it's pulsing a bit. But it's...odd. I could give it back to you. Maybe you can tell me what you think...?"

Morgaine held her hands up. Then she addressed them all, "I want you all to know. I gave the *Corillion* to Nathan based on a prophecy of my father's. I thought he simply had to have been wrong all these centuries. Even though he was never wrong up to that point, *ever*. He said three things to me that hadn't come true in over 500 years. Now that number is reduced by one. My father told me as he died that the medallion was 'not supposed to be my burden' to carry, but that I was then to carry it for six hundred years."

Lowering her head, she shook it. "He personally knew and met the Creator. He often got spoken to in dreams and visions. I wish I had that blessing. Now, I can have hope for the other two prophecies again." She set her bowl down and held both hands across her chest, hugging herself for a moment. Looking up, she added, "Nathan, this is your burden now, as I told you. I believe it was always intended for you. That's what my father must have meant. How he knew, or why it's yours are not for me to know. At least not yet. But whatever it teaches you, and however long it takes…that is between it and you. But perhaps I can help today. Tell me what the pulses feel like."

Nathan just looked at her. What an amazing, complex creature she was. "It feels…like a weight pulsing. Pulling me down a little. Like an anchor tugging at a boat mooring."

Nodding, she walked over, placing her hand onto his chest over the medallion. No perfume. No makeup. She closed her eyes and felt it with him.

God, she's beautiful! No one should look that perfect.

Dropping her hand, she walked back to her seat on the grass. Looking up, she said, "It's the army you're feeling. That much of the Dark in one place. Moving. It's powerful. Draw closer to them, the feeling will intensify."

Treyborne piped up, "If that's the army, what does it mean?"

"I honestly have no idea," Morgaine replied. "It's going to have to remain a mystery. But I believe your two theories should be combined. The Triumvirate is clearly battling over the Arc Gate. And K'Thul, perhaps the most powerful of them in terms of armed forces – and certainly the best general – is taking a big stick to the conversation. Or into the next realm, Creator forbid. The question now is: can we skirt them and get these people to the base and still make it to the Arc Gate before the hammer reaches the anvil?"

"I think so," Nathan said, "but only if we split up. I think we take as many as can go in the Sky Cruiser and head back to the compound we just left, as it's far closer than the one in the olive grove. For one thing, who would expect that? For another, we can recharge the cells and resupply with what's left there. Then we fly in, go with a modified version of our original plan, and get the hell out of there!"

Treyborne nodded. "I agree. In fact, we were just waiting for you to get up to tell you."

Morgaine nodded, looking at them both. "I hope you realize this is still my team and my decision. Nathan, I know it's your friend. And I know you're not a member of my team. But I'm risking the lives of myself and everyone who comes on this mission. Therefore, it must be my determination. I just hope that is clear. Our goal is the Arc Gate, and not your friend. That also must be clear."

He nodded at her, ruining it with a small smile. *It would help if that didn't make him more attractive.*

Looking away to calm her anger, she added, "But I agree with the plan. Trey, get Messau and gather a dozen of your best men. It's all we can bring in the sky cruiser. Brianna and Maitan, you're going to come along, but you're going to stay in one of the bunkers at the compound when we leave. We can't have you around amid that level of danger. But our former compound is compromised. I want it defended. If we're going back, we might as well handle that, too. Maitan, I'll have you show Brianna how to set charges, since we only buttoned down what we had before leaving. You're going to make it a veritable mine field if anyone else tries to get in there. Which base we run to after the mission will depend upon many factors, but this way both bases will be open and hopefully somewhat protected. Is this all understood?"

Everyone nodded. "Good. Get after it. Trey, appoint someone in charge to lead the land cruiser team. Jairus would be a good choice. Maybe the two that helped me ride out of Rondor, as well. They showed what they were made of. Let them lead these people to Nyx."

"Check, my Lady!" Treyborne said, getting up, "Team, we have our mission. Let's get on with it!"

CHAPTER 79

Bantor watched as Morgaine and her retainers broke up and scattered to the four winds. Brianna and Morgaine remained a moment, talking quietly between themselves. Bantor was close enough to hear if he tried, even in this wind. But he knew when to have discretion. All things can come with age – even wisdom to a spritely youth. He was neither of those things now.

As Brianna rushed off, Morgaine turned to him and asked, "Are you willing to head towards the central compound, Bantor? We could use your help there. Most of these people haven't been there before."

"Of course, my Lady Morgaine, of course! But…uh…I have something…I think I'd like to discuss with you." His tone got her attention. About to leave, she instead sat down on the tree trunk next to him.

"What is it, Bantor? Have you need of something?"

"Er…no, Lady Morgaine. I have something…I need to return to you." With that, he produced the green and gold ring he'd worn only a few nights before to escape Rondor. It had run out of power before he'd quite made it to the northern stables. But it had been enough.

Morgaine's eyes shot up, then she slowly reached for the ring and held it up into the sunlight. "Oh, dear Creator!" she said, almost whispering. "Where did you find this…?" she looked at him as if he were a hero. Not the thieving little wretch he'd been so many years ago.

"I…uhm…I've had it all along, Lady Morgaine. I'm afraid that when my father died, I'd found one of these just uh…lying around. I decided to take it when we left. I honestly thought you must have dozens of them. And it was so fun to go invisible…!" Bantor hung his head, huddling like the boy he used to be. "I'm sorry. I never should have taken it. But when I saw you again…I felt I should get it to you. I was going to take it to you the day the Contessa…er…the day the Contessa…"

"The day the Contessa was revealed as an agent of the Dark? Yes, that would have been a good day for it, up until then! Look, I can see this is eating you up. Don't let it!" Morgaine said firmly.

Taking the ring and gingerly putting it into a small pocket in her trousers, she added, "All is forgiven! We'd lost this decades ago and I'd given up looking for it. I used to have three of these things. One was lost in the barbarian wars a century ago. This one…well, this one just simply vanished. I thought perhaps it had turned itself on somehow, or someone had misplaced it into our storage room with the advanced weaponry. I tore that room apart looking for it more than once!"

She laughed.

Seeing Bantor's expression still so mortified, she said, "This is a good thing, Bantor! What's lost has been found! I forgive that little boy who didn't know what he was taking. And I realize it probably got forgotten for quite some time. We hadn't seen each other in forever. I'm just glad we both found each other, and that you had the courage to give it back to me!" With this, Morgaine kissed his cheek, bringing a huge blush that made his mostly white mustaches stand out.

He smiled. "I'm so glad you're not angry. It will…need a charge. The little boy that took it was wise enough, at least, to not use it all up stealing meat pies, or looking into girl's changing rooms!" he laughed. "And one day, I did need it, indeed."

Briefly recounting his exit, adding in the ring's assistance brought a nod or respect from Morgaine. "You risked much in being my friend,

Bantor. I will make sure you are handsomely rewarded for it. If we cannot recover your estates, you will have something of your own whenever this disaster can be overcome." She paused, lowering her head. "If it can be overcome."

Bantor jerked his head up, then stood straight, taking Morgaine by the shoulders. "You…Lady Morgaine…you are a legend! You're a thousand years old, and every woman on the planet wants to be like you! Not only will you get that Arc Gate rescue executed flawlessly…you will look good doing it!" He nodded like he'd just said the sun was yellow, turned and walked back towards the hatchway.

Morgaine just stood there…too stunned to speak. Amazed at Bantor's belief in her.

Perhaps he's not the only one who thinks of me as a legend. Maybe we can use that.

CHAPTER 80

Emorion checked his body armor, gauged the energy on his defensive shielding, and felt at his sides for the blaster and shock-lance he carried more for show than need. Attaching the comm and checking his visor, he walked out to his troops surrounding the Arc Gate. It was only a few weeks ago that he'd sent his shock troops in to take the Gate from Jezerah and his unsuspecting band of incompetents.

The forward bunkers were all doubly reinforced along the riverbank to the north, the northeast, and the southeastern banks. The only advantage Jezerah's troops truly had was in sheer numbers. Like K'Thul, Jezerah had cultivated and developed an Empire of humankind dedicated to his ideals, without being completely part of the "Dark Brethren". They felt they had independence, autonomy, and even had a large percentage of their citizens that despised the "Cult of the Dark" and it's 'dark magic'.

Yet when Jezerah called, the Empire of Nelrae answered.

K'Thul's hold was even stronger in the East. But his lack of imagination made him positively boring. It felt like outwitting a child or a simpleton.

Jezerah was hardly that. He was a rival that Emorion respected, even admired. But he also knew that he himself was the one destined for the highest rung on the ladder of the Dark. But Jezerah's Empire and its numbers had to be considered. From what he'd gotten from his scouts and spies, so far, however, he had not rallied them all.

He had left some Dark Men in the northern hill country, continuing their outdated plan to devour the Kingdom of Rondor as if nothing had happened. As if the Arc Gate hadn't happened. As if Jezerah had not attempted to secure it and hide it from his "brothers". As if Emorion hadn't snatched it from him like he was a petulant child caught with a stolen sweet.

Laughing, Emorion stood looking at his defenses. They were flawless. Even if Jezerah's Dark Men pressed from all three riverbanks, they'd never be able to withstand his blaster cannon, carefully placed pits, explosive mines, and trigger bombs. He had two complete regiments watching either flank, plus his best Knights were to be held in reserve for whichever area was hardest pressed. Jezerah was going to give his all to get through. And Emorion was determined that was never going to happen. Once the girl's boyfriend came – the Gate would be open and Emorion would pour through the opening like water through a sieve.

Sidling down to the campsite, he stopped to check on the girl and her guard. He'd placed one of his prize concubines with her to try to make the girl more comfortable. She barely ate, and he couldn't have her dying before he used her connection to the Gateway opener.

Not for the first time, Emorion questioned his methodology in sending his "message". But Hollow Men were devoted to the Dark. And Emorion was devoted to being the Master of the Void. They were his children, after all. Even if they were a bit rambunctious. The girl seemed to be somewhat enjoying speaking with the slave girl.

Another problem solved. She was eating.

Touching his comm, he said, "Givanis, send the scouts out along the outer ridge, and keep a few along the back hills. It's not like Jezerah to try something risky. Therefore, we must watch our rear, as well as our flanks. By all reports, his Quartermasters are running them straight towards our riverbanks, reinforced by his Knights, including the *Siday. But keep me advised.*"

"Yes, my lord. They are still two days out. But we will keep all options open."

Calling over his field captain, he said, "Watch those southern banks, Mizpan. It's the easiest access. If that fool Jezerah brings most of his force there, we'll buckle him like a calf's neck." The general just nodded. Emorion's generals had already covered the southern bank with extra charges and hidden troops. There was no way Jezerah was taking the western shore of the river.

No way.

CHAPTER 81

K'Thul watched the sky cruiser fly in a large circle around his troops. Jezerah had one. So did Emorion. K'Thul had never secured one after the Battle of Megiddo. Only a handful had survived the Elder Race war. As the cruiser hit the horizon and accelerated out of sight, he snorted. Whichever of those fools had seen him, he doubted it was going to matter. Even if they could suddenly end their own differences and combine forces, K'Thul would crush them.

Marshalling his forces had taken several weeks. But there had never been any doubt in his mind: to rule the universe was *his* destiny. None other. To master the galaxy, he needed to beat down his former Brethren on this world. The Void was clearly the source of power. The greatest gravity in the cosmos, enough to swallow entire solar systems, star clusters…even light itself.

Nothing could stop it.

K'Thul was the Void's biggest fan. And it's most devoted disciple. He had waited in silent patience. The Triumvirate that emerged from their victory over the Lost had always been utilitarian. K'Thul had no illusions that it could last forever. The moment they ever found a way off this Dark-cursed planet – that would herald the day that he declared war on his former allies.

The second and the third cavalry ranks marched by crisply mounted on their horses, saluting K'Thul as they passed. He nodded and waved his appreciation. He'd been brutally preparing these humans and his Dark Horde for centuries. No amount of sky cruisers, devotees to his cousins, nor any amount of humankind was going to keep him from the prize. Within weeks, he would be the ruler of this world. And then he was going to crack open the universe.

After all, the best war planner in the history of the Elder Race should end up the god-king of the cosmos. It made as much sense and was as inevitable as the light vanishing at the event horizon of a black hole, one of the Void's many manifestations in this universe. The pull of the Dark never stopped until it had consumed all.

And neither would he.

CHAPTER 82

Nathan watched as Brianna walked by him into the hatchway. He'd stopped and sat down in the back bay, waiting for Morgaine to come in. Just a minute of talking might be nice. After all, they'd had that unbelievable night and then…all back to business. The only legacy of that incredible time was the black medallion around his neck with the huge clear gemstone. If it was a diamond, it had to be worth $100,000.

Maybe add a digit.

Not that he was planning on pawning it once he got back to New York City. Probably. He might have to if he didn't have a job when he returned. For the first time in a long time, he thought of his friends. They probably thought he was dead. Idly, he wondered if Jenn was even at HDS anymore, or if she'd moved on from her internship and gotten a job somewhere else. Nathan remembered the intensity of his feelings for her. After all that had happened, it seemed like it was ten years ago. He just hoped they were ok and not thinking about him too much.

Morgaine walked in, looking thoughtful. In her hand was her green and gold ring. The one she'd used to get out of the city of Rondor. Curious. Why she had it now, or why she'd be holding it walking in like that didn't make a lot of sense.

But what the hell…? Neither did the fact that she was over a thousand years old, was the most stunning woman he'd ever met, or anything else. Not to mention this tiny woman was a genuine badass fighter in her own right. At least he'd been told so by everyone. He himself had not seen it, but that didn't lessen the fact that he believed it heart and soul.

Noticing him, Morgaine replaced the ring back in her trouser pocket. Crooking her finger at him, she continued her walk back into the inner cabins, opening her room and letting him in first. There was no one in that back hallway. No guards were required in the land cruiser in the middle of the wilderness. But it was immediately arousing just remembering the last time he'd been alone with this woman. She was, by just about every definition, a goddess.

As she shut the door, she asked, "How may I help you, Nathan?"

Her eyes turned towards his, and it just took his breath away. Instead of answering, he just had to break the tension. So, he lowered his head and chuckled.

"I didn't realize what I said was so funny."

Looking up at her, he saw annoyance on her face. But there was a spark in her eyes, as well.

What's that about?

"I'm sorry…It's just that…well…we were together. And then, the world crashed around us. I just wanted to talk."

Sitting down, he added, "Maybe see if there's something we can do other than 'sneak in, steal Ellie, get out'. Can we even do that much? What are our chances if there are thousands of those Dark Men all around us?"

Morgaine took a deep breath in, then let it out. She lowered her head and came to sit next to him on the one chair in the room. It was barely big enough for one person. Let alone two. Being this close again made Nathan's heart race. All the memories from a couple nights ago came flooding back.

Morgaine took his hand, "We don't have to do this. Not the way we talked about it. If we leave your Ellie as a secondary goal – if we make the goal something else – we might just be able to snap her up in the aftermath and do more than we ever imagined."

Nathan, trying to calm his breathing, looked at her. Her face was right next to his.

Damn! Those lips…. those amazing eyes…!

"What did you have in mind?" was all he said.

CHAPTER 83

Gary pulled out his phone, turning on the flashlight. Jenn did the same. They were crouching behind a huge fence that surrounded a very dark, very old warehouse.

"The tracking device says it's up a story or so in that building." Gary said, pointing to the GPS tag on his phone map.

"Couldn't the device be attached at the top? It's more likely they wouldn't find it up that high."

Jenn was no longer shivering. The adrenalin that was coursing through her veins was plenty to keep her heart pumping. The trash bins out in the alley behind the warehouse were smelly and old. But they provided cover well enough. Jenn just hoped the government didn't have a ton of surveillance cameras everywhere. She had to hope they had just put the monolith here because the warehouse was big enough, not something they usually used for highly secret things. Or to house spies or a kennel of big dogs.

They wouldn't just be arrested in that event. Nope. Then they'd be dead.

Gary pulled out a long wiry thing from his inside coat pocket. Unraveling it took some effort, especially from their crouched position.

"What's that?" Jennifer whispered in his ear.

The hoarse stage whisper came back, a bit too loudly for Jenn's taste, "It's a grounding mechanism. I'm going to try to cut into that fence.

But if it's an electrical fence, instead of shocking me with 10,000 volts, it should go to ground and mostly keep me from getting fried."

"Mostly?" Jenn said, looking at him with wide eyes.

"Yeah, theoretically." Gary didn't sound super certain.

The device was basically an old wire coat hanger, affixed with a copper plug on one end. The other end he wound around some very large bolt cutters. They should be able to make short work of that fence. Assuming it wasn't the electrical kind – or at least assuming the homemade ground worked.

Mostly.

Gary took a deep breath and scooted around the dumpster, keeping himself in the dark. Finding the fence nearest him, he made sure the copper nut was touching the ground and touched the fencing with it. Sparks flew, including several sparks flaring around the copper.

"Holy shit!" Gary half-shouted, but he kept crisply cutting a hole into the fence. About halfway around the circle, the ball flaring and sparks flying stopped. Either the fence had burnt something out, or it had simply shut itself off. Or…*someone* had shut it off.

Gary stopped for a minute, bracing to run. No one came. No alarms sounded. No flashing lights. No S.W.A.T. team raced from around the building with automatic weapons. Gary laughed, and Jenn joined him, nervously.

"I'm not a very good thief!" she whispered.

Gary just nodded.

Dropping the cutters with the wire attached, he took his still gloved hands and pushed the wire hole he'd cut out into the warehouse concrete yard. Again, no laser sights appeared, and no one came running. Crawling through, he motioned for Jennifer to follow him.

Still crouching, he ran towards the shadow of the great building with its massive windows largely still intact. A few gaping holes showed what the neighborhood kids did for fun on their off days.

Jennifer angled further towards the nearest shadow, then walked along the walk slowly to join him. There were no lights within the building, and none in that yard. It was almost pitch black.

"Damn!" Gary said, scuttling back towards the gate and retrieving his bolt cutters. He'd need those if there was an actual lock to cut. He had told himself how many times while planning this out to bring it along after the fence! He sighed even as he ran back.

Jennifer waited for him where he'd left her. Once he reached her again, together they made their way around towards the back side of the building. Hoping to find a doorway there that maybe had been used for loading docks or taking out trash, they found a raised truck gate and a broken five-step staircase to a metal door. The truck bay was locked down tight with metal sheeting placed over it. The door itself was bolted shut with a huge padlock affixed to it. There was a very rusty metal handrail hanging to one side. This place looked like it had been abandoned right after the war. World War I, not II.

Gary pulled up his bolt cutters and tried to get a good angle. Whoever had put this here had known what they were doing. It seemed easier to cut the metal strap holding the lock first, so he started working on it.

Minutes passed, and Jennifer finally said, "Gary, come on! We can't stay here all night! We either get in or we go. That was the plan."

Nodding without saying anything, he finally got the latch mechanism loose and took it off. The lock was much easier to access now. Putting the cutter to use once again, he made quick work of the lock, snapping it off neatly. It fell with a loud clang onto the pavement.

Jennifer looked around, but there was no one to be seen. Nothing moved.

Trying the door, it didn't budge. "Damn it!" Gary said, giving it a shove and throwing his whole weight into it. The door gave way – apparently it had simply been a tight fit or rusted to the doorframe. Either way, it gave with a shriek that Gary was sure could wake the dead. But again… no one came. No lights suddenly flashed on. No one yelled. Halfway into the warehouse already, he stepped in, grabbing his phone for light. Jenn followed with her hand on his back.

The room they were in was separated from the main hangar or whatever by another doorway. No door was in it, however, and in the other room, a dim light could be seen. And a rather loud humming sound. The monolith stood on a metal base, tied down in several places, but upright as they'd seen it before. It was on the back end of a very large truck, in fact. Several other pieces of metal were around it, along with a huge bale of plastic wrap.

It looked like they were planning on covering it with these other metal parts to hide it, then wrap it in plastic and haul it out on the flatbed. All that was missing was the truck driver. As they approached, the light from their phones made the crystals in the monolith glitter and sparkle.

The humming increased, and as they approached it grew far louder than it seemed it should. It echoed in the otherwise huge empty chamber. By the time they were next to it, the sparkles were everywhere, and Jenn could feel it pulsing. Like a heartbeat.

"What now?" she yelled over the noise, not caring if anyone could hear her. Clearly no one was here, or no one cared. She hoped it was the former.

Gary just shrugged. "This is as far I got! Frankly, I didn't think we were going to make it this far!"

Jenn just looked up at him in exasperation. "Well, what do we now? Nathan was wandering around ignoring the bloody thing, held up his phone and 'POOF' he was gone! From what we heard about Ellie – albeit much more conjecture – she wasn't near the thing either. She was also in the computer room, not near the unit. Why don't we back away and see if we can get the phones to work…?"

"You mean so we can die or be transported to another world and not be able to come home?" Gary yelled. "I'm not a fan of that idea!"

"Then why are we even here?" Jennifer asked him angrily. "I thought we wanted to try to get Nathan back! We can't just steal the monolith!"

Gary's head just whipped around to look at her, "Why the hell not?"

CHAPTER 84

Jezerah's forces were moving at a slow and steady pace. The idea was to have Emorion certain of what was coming, how much, and when. Curtaise was now leading an entire division of Dark Men out of the hill country north of Rondor and racing to get behind the hills of the Arc Gate. According to Curtaise's reports, that should be there by evening. This was the hammer.

The visible army would slowly advance the following day and fortify rear watch positions, so that they could strike them fast and hard when the real attack pushed around toward the west and southwest. Since at least 70% of these troops would also be needed for this, they would slowly filter off and merge in the forest that lay at the foot of the mountains to the west of the attack point. Since it was a trickle, it would look like normal circling motions, not supplementing the true assault.

Via light comms and signal words already set up, they were to advance in a pincer-like movement, strike the rear scouts, and then wash around and over the mountainous hills, striking Emorion's troops from behind. Omrion would lead the charge, as directed by Curtaise and Jezerah.

The actual reserve troops, which were to appear as the front until the attack, would keep their enemy penned in by their own bunkers, mine fields, and the riverbanks. They'd set up their long-range blaster cannons and start peppering them at will. Once the defensive cannons were removed, the front lines (turned into back lines) would be decimated.

Everything was going as planned. Imutaph, one of the Dark Quartermasters, strode up, saluting and bowing.

"What is it, Quartermaster?" Jezerah asked quietly.

"Master, the eastern scouts are reporting that Emorion is holding back a significant force in the rear of his perimeter. But advance scouts in the hills are virtually non-existent. It may be advantageous to pour more of our troops over those hills. But, of course, we are here to serve the Dark Lord and obey his words."

Jezerah looked at the man, again bowing after speaking as was customary. "Hmm…I shall think on it and discuss it with the commanders and General Curtaise. How many men are in the rear, and of what type?"

"It appears his Dark Knights and personal guard are in a tight cordon around the perimeter of the Arc Gate itself, towards the rear and butting up into the hills themselves. Scouts along the flanking positions are substantial. But in the mountains behind, there is nothing. Most of his forces are positioned as we expected in the forward zones, setting up boundaries along the riverbank."

Nodding thoughtfully, Jezerah considered. Each of the Quartermasters were to report to him directly, if possible. No comms, no discussion of side troops or flanking attacks except in person. Imutaph was ambitious. But that was to be expected. He may be more so than most, however. One always had to consider how far that ambition went.

"I shall discuss it with the General. Do not leave the area yet. I will get back to you shortly." The man bowed again and walked away.

Jezerah loved efficiency. And Imutaph had always been efficient. Even when he was coming up in the ranks of the Dark Men. He always stood out. Perhaps it was time to give him a new boost and put him in with the Dark Knights and see how he fared. Well, that was for another day.

Touching his direct comm link, Jezerah asked, "General Curtaise, I've been advised of more flanking troops than we anticipated, and in high caliber forces. The hills behind are almost bare. What is your assessment? Should we perhaps alter our forces somewhat?"

"With all due respect, Master, I would think that is more of a trap than an avenue. Emorion is no fool, and he must keep some forces on the flanking positions and to watch the rear by the Gate itself. If we all go over the hills, even with the speed of our forces, it will slow the brunt of the surprise. Should Emorion fear that, leaving that 'easy avenue' open would allow him to respond more adequately. I suggest no changes, Master. Let's continue to let the snake appear to see our plan, and play into his hands, as far as we can in the frontal forces."

"You are in command, Curtaise. I agree with your evaluation. Proceed as planned." Imutaph would have to prove himself in other ways – perhaps as a new Lieutenant in the Knights.

Should he survive the week, of course.

CHAPTER 85

Nathan walked down to the medical bay in the base of the land cruiser. Smyslin was still in a coma, but Maitan had assured him that he would recover. Reaching his cot attached to the wall, Nathan glanced at the lights and screen monitor. He'd learned to read some of them well enough to see that Smyslin's pulse and heart rate were stable.

Smyslin stirred as Nathan touched his arm. Groggily, Smyslin's eyes fluttered open. "M…Master…?"

"Smyslin! How are you feeling? You were shot…"

"I am aware, Master. Jezerah's trackers are uniquely bred for their work. Apparently, I have offended my former Master enough that he wanted me dead. Perhaps my influence and knowledge being in your service was an additional motivator. Thank you for saving me."

"I didn't do anything. It was Maitan and Morgaine's medical staff and equipment. I'm told they had to do some massive cell regeneration on your back. I'm pretty sure had you had those injuries on my world, you wouldn't have made it."

"Then it is good I am not there," Smyslin replied matter-of-factly. His eyes were still half-lidded, and he was clearly still medicated. Nathan just nodded, gripping his hand.

Smyslin returned the grasp by clasping his hand over Nathan's on his arm. "I will return to serving you as soon as I can, Master."

Nathan said, "Your orders are just to get better. We've got to go run a bit of an errand and try to do something about the Arc Gate. I'm not sure what yet. But Morgaine has a plan."

"I see she has loaned her medallion to you. It is right. You are the bearer of Light. Just remember me when you are fighting amongst the Dark Men. My being around you, even when I did not want to be, drained the Dark from me. I was horrified at first. Now, I see it as right. I was always taught that the Dark sucks even the light into it. The Dark rules and consumes all. What you have taught me, if nothing else, is that the Dark must bow to the Light."

Nathan nodded without quite understanding. Smyslin patted his arm and fell back asleep. Nathan turned and left, uplifted knowing that Smyslin would be all right. Once they reached the second facility, he was sure he would recover now.

Climbing the ladder stairs to the front hatchway, Nathan ran into Treyborne heading the other direction. Nathan asked him in passing, "Have you talked with Morgaine? She has made some…adjustments… to our plan."

Treyborne nodded, but kept going, apparently in a hurry, "I heard. Don't know how I feel about exposing her even more than the original plan. But she's lived centuries before I came here, and she likely will live many centuries after I'm gone. I'm preparing and gathering the team into the sky cruiser. Meet us there in an hour."

Then he was gone.

Nathan hurried to the twin bunk chamber quarters he'd been assigned, the one he was supposedly sharing with Smyslin, and gathered everything he might need. His shock-lance, a hand-held blaster weapon he had yet to use, and his pack with a bit of food and water bottles. He'd likely be leaving the last on the airship. It was also likely they'd have some supplies on board. But having your own was never a bad idea.

Checking the room for anything he was forgetting; he grabbed his phone off the nightstand. It seemed to feed off some ambient energy whenever it was on his person. So, he kept it with him, even though it wasn't much more than a glorified digital camera and flashlight at this point.

Then he made his way outside to the sky cruiser. Everyone but Morgaine had arrived, and Nathan took his seat next to Trey in the co-pilot seat. About fourteen of Trey's men and their gear were squeezed into the seats and back retainer wall. A seat behind them had been left for Morgaine.

As she climbed aboard, she had the strange sword strapped her to back, a uniquely beautiful black, green, and silver body armor on, and had two blasters on either side. A belt with some small chrome-like balls was strapped from her left shoulder down across her right hip. Nodding to her troops, she said, "Let's go make some noise."

With that, they were off.

The first part of their plan hadn't altered. They were to drop half the troops with Treyborne about four miles (roughly the same as what they called "clicks") out on the western side. Those troops were to make their way through the high passes and get into position on top of the hills behind the Arc Gate, awaiting notification to move in.

Nathan and Morgaine and the other half of the troops, two of which were to man the piloting and the dual blaster cannons, were to drop down on top of the hill behind the Gate itself. Nathan and Morgaine were to go first, cloaked with the now two cloaking devices they had in their possession. Morgaine's retelling of the one Bantor had stolen as a little child was both fabulous and timely. Now fully recharged, they both would have the ability to vanish from the vision of most, if not all, of their opponents. Therefore, there was now no Nathan approaching. This was about stealth.

100%.

The tricky part was going to be when they began attacking. Both teams were told to stay tight to each other. The sky cruiser was to be the backup escape, either by simply throwing drop lines down, or landing completely to pick them up. Both maneuvers involved high risk to the ship. Therefore, retreat and escape executed by each group would be best, if possible.

The rest was up to Morgaine, Nathan, and their inhuman abilities. Something Nathan was not entirely comfortable with. Shock-lances didn't scare him. But blasters and edged weapons did. And there were going to be a lot of them. A minor explosion east of the camp was to draw as many away from the Gate as possible. But that wasn't going to make the entrance or exit any easier. Further explosions from that side would help, and the sky cruiser was to do its part by firing cannon and drawing fire from afar.

Nathan just shook his head as they flew into the night. Noticing the action, Treyborne looked over. "It's not the first time I've gone into a fight with Morgaine and our team that I thought we weren't coming out. Trust in everyone's abilities. Especially your own."

"That's the problem." Trey looked over at him. "I'm not sure what my 'abilities' are. I've just been kind of winging it!"

"Then it's time to learn to fly," Trey said nonchalantly. "Because it's about to get heavy!"

Nathan wasn't sure what that meant, and he decided he really didn't want to know.

CHAPTER 86

The greater moon Alonna was shining alone in the evening sky this night. Stars were everywhere, but her little sister Sanshe was hiding. Completely dark for the first time in over a year. The peoples of most lands celebrated this as her "night of passion" with the Void. Those of the Dark Cult took it as a holy day, celebrating with Bonfires for Sanshe and eating roasted goat or pig.

This night, however, was not being celebrated by those around the Gate. The instigators of this pseudo-religion were all quite busy, not having noticed or even cared that their so-called 'holy day' had even arrived.

Bantor had noticed, however, as they were stopped for the night, cloistered under a canopy of trees which still could see a good portion of the night sky. The fires were low, trying to make sure no Dark Men scouts from the Eastern Empire would find them so close to their projected path.

In Rondor, feasts and celebrations on this night were forbidden. It was a pagan holiday, and the Creator frowned upon all such activities. Still, though, house parties and small get-togethers had been occasionally fun to attend. No pagan revelry, of course. But masquerades and several rather large dinners with dancing and singing.

Bantor had met his wife at one of those parties, almost forty years ago now. He hoped she was safe wherever she was — having died and gone to the Creator's bosom some twelve years past. The heavens were a wide expanse. Who knew where she might be at this very moment?

Sighing, Bantor stood up, about to head into the hatchway and get some rest. There were only a few stragglers out this late. A couple of the cooks, one of the janitors, and a few of the serving people were cleaning up the evening meal. All the horses had been taken in as well. The fires were low as everyone prepared to leave. Four of Morgaine's Elite Guards were on duty, but they were mostly just talking amongst themselves, not keeping a sharp watch as they were almost twelve miles from the path of the army.

A small noise made him turn around. As he did so, he saw one of the guards literally fall face forward. The other just pulling his weapon, did the same a moment later. Suddenly a blade was in his face, and Bantor had to dive out of the way.

Shouting, "Intruders!" he rolled several times, lunging to the side as another blade thrust came at him from above, seemingly out of nowhere. Reaching into the inner pocket of his outer coat, he flicked a switch and rolled one more time away from the blade. As it came whipping back, Bantor jumped up, cramming the small package into the man's trousers.

Then he leaped again, rolling as fast as he could. Yelling began all over the camp, as the few reserve guards and others came out with weapons. The explosion and resultant spraying blood and body parts of his attacker covered Bantor. It had the added effect of knocking several Dark Men down, as well.

Jumping up once again, and happy he was still spry despite being a fat, old man, Bantor picked up the blade still in the hand (and only the hand) of his former attacker and lunged to stab the two stunned Dark Men nearest him. One was killed, but the other managed to roll out of the way of Bantor's thrust, still getting slashed enough to jerk his arm back. The man kicked, then leaped to his feet, whirling his weapon menacingly.

Bantor slowly backed away. He was overmatched, and he knew it. But this Dark Man might not, having seen two of his friends die so quickly. Suddenly flood lights came on everywhere and blaster fire came from all sides. The reserve guards had come out armed. The few remaining Dark Men disappeared into the forest. Those first two guards didn't get up.

Bantor hadn't even known their names. Idly, he wondered if the Dark Men were simply ordered to attack anyone they saw, or if this was a targeted attack. They were somewhat close to the path the army was likely going to take, but not that close. And this was the course they'd had to take to get to where they needed to go. It had been a risk Morgaine knew she had to take.

It didn't matter now. They were in danger.

"Get everyone back in the ship!" he yelled, suddenly realizing he was taking charge. Old habits of leadership died hard, it appeared. "We need to move, now! No more stops until we get to the compound!"

Surprisingly, everyone did as he said. The two fallen guards' bodies were picked up and the rest of the food supplies and plates and bowls were simply left. One of the maids was bleeding from a leg wound. The other maid was helping her walk, having wrapped her wound with a towel.

The land cruiser was moving before Bantor was quite inside the hatchway. Looking back to make sure no one was left, he counted seven bodies of Dark Men. Hopping out, he quickly snatched up a comm from the nearest one, and another *Djune*. As a last second thought, he grabbed a mask, as well. Might come in handy someday. He rushed to get back onto the cruiser, and the hatch closed behind him.

No more stops.

Morgaine had left him in *de facto* charge at least, as he was the guide to the central base. He hadn't done anything she hadn't – allowing for meal stops instead of continuing to move. But two men had died under his watch. That was not going to be repeated. And if anyone found out who was missing, and where…they might come a looking. That just wouldn't do.

CHAPTER 87

Landing at the compound, Maitan, Brianna, Trey, and Morgaine all went separate ways. Maitan to the medical reserves, to put a whole crate into the sky cruiser just in case. Two of the Guard went with him to help and to protect, most likely. Brianna headed to her quarters, as she'd left several utilitarian clothes she'd bought "for later" while shopping in Bistern – along with her own set of guards, and Treyborne went straight to the charger coils. Morgaine began surveying the perimeter, pointing out areas for some guards to investigate. The rest of the Guard took up defensive positions in the main crossing area of trails between the buildings.

The sky cruiser was going to need full power for this. The original idea had been to recharge at the Nyx compound. Running low on time had pushed them back to the discovered base. Treyborne appeared behind it, and Nathan came down to help.

Dragging the coils out with an effort, they pulled and cajoled the heavy metal coils from the trough they usually rested in as far as they would go. The sky cruiser was landed just close enough to take advantage. Treyborne hadn't wanted to execute the "hangar fall", as taking off could prove problematic if the base had "more visitors". And this didn't slow the charging time down at all. The cruiser guns were also able to be used in the event of an attack outside now. In the hangar, they'd be almost useless, more likely to destroy something inside the hangar, or harm a friend, rather than a foe.

Connecting the coils to the Na- and Ca-cells took a few minutes. The hum of power soon was coming from the generators somewhere within and below the grounds.

Nathan looked up as they started to hum just as Morgaine disappeared into the compound; weapon drawn. "Don't you think we should follow her…?" Nathan asked, watching her go. None of the Guard were following, either. They obviously had other orders.

"She's a killer, Nathan. And she said she didn't need any backup. But not a bad idea, under the circumstances. You go. I've got to double-check that we're refilling the power cells on the cruiser and check for any anomalies. Can't be finding out we're out of power in the air!"

Nathan caught up to Morgaine just as she hit the first stairwell leading up to the main halls. Stopping to let him catch up the last few steps, she turned and said, "I wondered if that might be you." Brianna had already flicked on the lights, so they entered the middle dormitory area, the kitchens, the living areas, and then finally the stairway to the upper suites and her rooms. Turning on the lights in the upper area took a few extra moments.

"What are we coming back for?" Nathan asked.

Without an answer, Morgaine turned on the lights in her own quarters, heading back toward her bedchambers. Being in that room and watching her go in had all the effect he didn't need right now. The woman practically oozed sensuality. She couldn't help it. It was like the grace of a cat walking, or maybe a panther or a cheetah coupled with her unique beauty.

"Ah here they are!" came her voice from the other room. "I knew they would be here." Morgaine walked out, wearing what could only be called a thin eye mask, coupled with a circlet of black stones coiled into a crown-like mantle that touched her forehead. She truly looked like a bandit queen. She then handed him a small blue-black comm pin. She also kept one for herself, putting it in her ear.

Nathan just stood there speechless, staring at her new accessories. "So, you like it…?" she asked in a sultry tone, rotating in a full circle so he could get the full impact. Nathan found himself gulping, not for the first time around this woman.

He nodded, saying, "Who wouldn't...? But why the mask and the 'crown'? What's the angle?"

"Remember, our game is to direct their attention wherever and whenever we need it to go. There are too many of them, even for the caliber of fighters we have with us, including the two of us. It's going to be a 'show'. And when we're ready, we reveal the big finish! They will think what we want them to...or..."

"...or we likely just end up dead," Nathan finished for her.

She nodded gravely. Then her mouth twisted into a smirk. "Perhaps we should treat this like it may be the last day of our lives...what do you say?"

"What do I say...to..." he began. As he did, she just walked over to him, grabbed him by the hair and started kissing him. Not the soft caresses of the other night. But hard, passionate, deep tongue kissing. She started pulling at his clothing, and then her own.

Dragging him into her bedroom, she nearly tore off his shirt, and then her own. Somehow, the woman never stopped kissing him for more than a few seconds. Nathan was helpless to resist her. All that passion focused on him from this magnificent creature...was simply unreal.

They were finished in minutes. Morgaine was up and putting her clothing and armor on just as quickly. "Get dressed, Nathan. We have work to do!" Smiling back at him, "Much less fun work, I'm afraid. But I know we can pull this off. Just follow my lead. Before the next day is over, we will either have won a great victory – or died trying. I would prefer it to be the former. So, get your pretty ass up. We need to move!"

She was out the door before he'd properly gotten his pants back on.

CHAPTER 88

"What do you mean, 'Why the hell not?'" Jenn demanded. We're in a government warehouse, Gary! We've already broken at least a dozen laws! I'd rather not add motor vehicle theft and grand larceny to the charges if you don't mind! And how do we even drive that thing? I don't know how to drive a semi. Do you?"

"Jenn! We committed to doing something for Nathan. Let's face it: the government doesn't own this thing! It belongs to the Egyptian people, for crying out loud! We're just…stealing it back for them! And maybe borrowing it a for a day or two in the process. We'll drop it off at the museum or NYU or something in two days if we can't get it to do anything in the meantime. And…yeah, I can drive a semi. My dad was a truck driver. I grew up thinking I'd be one, too. Until I learned about computers and how easy it was to meet girls playing guitar. Deal?"

"Guitar…?!" was all she said to this. She paused, stamping her foot in exasperation.

Finally, he had to ask again, "Deal?! We're running out of time here, Jennifer! There has got to be at least a motion sensor or something in here. An alert that a door was opened. Even if they're all the way across the harbor in the city, we've don't have a lot of time. Let's roll, or let's run."

Jenn looked up to him, and a light from the nearby window ran across her face.

She is so damned pretty.

"Let's roll," she said.

Minutes and a few gear shifts later, the hangar door was jimmied open (after cutting yet another lock off), and the truck with the monolith bare ass naked to the world was being hauled out into the parking lot. Reaching the edge of the parking lot there was yet another gate with a load of chain and two locks on it.

Sighing, Gary began to cut. About halfway through, the sound of sirens reached their ears. "Hurry!" Jenn yelled; I see about a half dozen cop cars getting off the tollway. I think they're headed right for us!"

Another twenty seconds, and they were rolling out the gate and down the back road away from the oncoming police. Knowing they had little time, Gary stepped on it, running a couple red lights that fortunately had no one around to see or get clipped.

Two minutes later, they were on the tollway themselves, headed south down the Jersey turnpike. Hoping to make some time, Gary then got off, headed down one of the side roads and began to turn the other way, heading back to New York state.

"Where are you going?" Jennifer asked him after his third or fourth change of direction.

"I'm trying to confuse any cameras that pick us up going by them. If they see us going south, then west, then north, then east all in a short amount of time, they won't know where we're going."

"We also won't get anywhere!" Jenn pointed out.

"True, but my goal is to take the back highways until at least near dawn and head north into up-state New York. I have a place we can go where we won't be seen. We can just make it if I step on it."

With that, he got back onto a side highway and began speeding as fast as he dared back towards his old stomping grounds. His buddy Ben would know what to do. And he had a big enough barn to hide this truck in, for starters.

CHAPTER 89

"The Creator does as the Creator wills." [Rondorian Holy Scriptures]

Less than two hours later, the sky cruiser was back in flight, heading for the Arc Gate. Brianna and Maitan were already busy setting charges and laying plans for how to escape should more attackers come.

Trey was now heading straight for the hills that Nathan had first come from just a few short weeks ago. Morgaine sat next to Nathan, leaning on him in full view of her whole team. It seemed the rules weren't going to apply any more. After a moment, she took his hand in hers, as well.

Nathan looked down at the hair on her head, pulse racing once again.

The woman simply could just look at me and I'd be a puppy in her hands! I've never met anyone like her, ever. Then again, how could I have? Not too many women out there are from another race, or who have lived twenty or thirty of our lifetimes…

After a moment, he just leaned his head on hers and he dozed off. After all, the flight itself was going to be almost four hours. Waking with a start, Nathan realized that the sky cruiser had just been bumped by something. Morgaine was awake, also. Only a couple of the guards were awake, however.

"Is everything all right up there," Morgaine asked via comm.

"Fine, Morgaine!" Treyborne's voice answered. *"We've just hit some rough air. It appears there's a storm brewing to the northwest. We've just run into the front and it's getting bumpy."*

"All right. How far out are we?"

"About another forty minutes. We've got to fly lower as we get nearer, so it'll only make it rougher. Make sure you're all strapped in back there."

"Aye aye, Captain!" she said, turning to Nathan with those amazing, purple-tinted eyes. "It's almost time. Let's check our individual comm. No one else but we will be able to hear what we're saying and doing down there."

Nathan nodded and they tried out the tiny blue-black ear comms. They worked perfectly. Despite all the noise in the cabin, even a small whisper came through loud and clear.

Interesting. Higher tech than the regular ones for sure.

Another thirty-eight minutes, and the sky cruiser was skimming treetops, before finally coming to rest what they all hoped was just a few miles from the Arc Gate. They landed behind the mountainous hill that the Arc Gate touched, acting as an entrance to the large cave that sat in front of it on the other side.

Trey and his contingent of Morgaine's guards started loping off in the direction of the highest part of the hills as soon as they were all together. Morgaine and Nathan headed off in a similar, but lower trajectory direction. The remaining four men, including Messau, got back into the cruiser and shut the doors. They were to wait there until instructed to move. It would only take them minutes to get to their destination. Even though theirs would be the first move.

Nathan had been given some night vision goggles, and the trees showed up white against the darker background. Morgaine had no need of them at first, but soon she also was wearing a pair. It was, after all, a very dark night and they were in the woods.

Twice they came upon a pair of Dark Men hiding in the trees. Twice Morgaine had turned on her ring, walked right up to them and shot them at point blank range with blaster fire.

Within the hour, they were in sight of the Arc Gate, the huge encampment around it, and the massive amounts of fires, people, and equipment. They were readying for war.

Tapping her ear, Morgaine whispered, *"It seems Brianna's instincts were correct! Only another army of Dark Forces would dare to hit the Dark Men all the way out here. It also means they're going to be on high alert. It's time to activate our cloaking devices. Keep an eye on the time and go find your friend. Once you say you have her, we'll start the activities. Be wary! Dark Men will be everywhere. As will some of their more…potent leaders and perhaps some of the Darker creatures they employ."*

Reaching up, she kissed him again. Not the passionate kisses of hours earlier, and not quite the tender caresses of their first night together. It was…. just something different. Nathan returned the kiss but wasn't sure what it meant.

"Ten four, good buddy!" Nathan said quietly, picking up what she was receiving like he'd said it on a loudspeaker.

"What is a 'buddy'? And what does the number fourteen have to do with anything?" Morgaine asked, quizzically.

Nathan started to answer, then just shook his head, "I'll explain later. Let's go and get back before we get killed." He twisted his ring as she did, and they both vanished. Carefully, Nathan began to make his way towards the encampment. They'd be keeping Ellie in a cage, a bunker, a tent maybe…but wherever she was, she'd be somewhere well-guarded and likely somewhere in the middle of the camp. Close to the Gate, most likely.

Passing a bunker of Dark Men, even invisible, was more than a little uncomfortable. The men were not talking, or out walking around. They were actively listening and watching, unlike their cohorts in the hills a few miles back. Those men in the hills thought they were wasting their time. These men were expecting an attack. Possibly tonight.

Still, he managed it, as the noise from the camp was enough to hide the quiet footfalls of his boots. Nathan was also back into his jeans, having them recently washed and mended by Maitan before the attack on the compound. It just felt good to be in his own clothes. Some of them, at least. The shirt and the body armor were definitely not his own. Nor were the boots, for that matter. These had been purchased in Bistern. Adidas just weren't military-grade material.

Another bunker, and still another. Whatever they were preparing for, these Dark Men were ready. Skirting these holed out areas by a wider margin each time, Nathan finally made his way into the camp proper. People were milling about everywhere. Several huge bonfires were burning, likely as watchfires as much as for cooking or heat in the chilly night air of the upper hill country.

Nathan crouched down, even though he knew he was invisible, and began working his way around toward the Gate. It was standing like a sentinel, towering above the campsite, and glowing in the light of dozens of fires. There was a large cage near the Gate, but Nathan veered away once he saw it was open and empty. Someone or something had been in it, but no longer. Likely Ellie. But where was she now…?

"I'm in position, Nathan. How much longer?"

"I have no idea. I haven't even caught a glimpse of…wait! I think I see her! I'll let you know once I have her in hand."

Ellie appeared to be sitting and eating near a campfire with another woman. They were talking and laughing like old friends. That was weird. Running through the open area in between took only thirty seconds. There were two Dark Men standing guard over the area, but another two dozen were moving about within a fifty-foot radius. Everyone seemed to have a job to do.

Crouching down, Nathan whispered in the ear furthest from the other woman, "Ellie! Don't answer back! It's Nathan. Just nod if you can hear me!" Ellie jumped a foot when he'd first spoken and then touched his arm to calm her. It had had the opposite effect. While Ellie nodded quickly, the other girl asked, "What is it? Did you get bitten by something? The bugs here are unusually bad at night."

"Yes, yes…Exanna. It was a bug…or a nasty spider." She turned her head slightly, meaning that comment for Nathan. "Could you please get me another drink, Ex? I'm super thirsty tonight. Everyone is rushing around so much. It's making me nervous."

The other girl, a rather voluptuous dark-haired beauty with long legs responded, "Of course, Ellie! I understand. There's talk of a battle tomorrow and the men are jumpy. Another of these ales…?" Ellie nodded and smiled her practiced fake smile at her. Nathan hated that smile. The girl wandered off, taking her time to flirt with several Dark Men on her way to a long table filled with food and drink.

"Nathan!" she whispered, "Why can't I see you? What are you doing here? Are you insane? These people are killers! Go get some real help….. we…"

"Shut up, Ellie! You were always too bossy!"

"Bossy?! I was not…! I'll tell you something, Nathan…".

He cuffed her arm, at least causing her to finally be quiet. "I'm getting you out of here, Ellie. Just say you'll do exactly what I tell you and when, and we will get you out of here. PS: I did bring an army. It's just a small one to extract you. Got it?" She nodded, looking like she'd eaten a can of worms. "Good."

"Morgaine, I've got her. Do your thing."

"Check, Nathan. Hold on…!"

"Messau, are you in position?" this over the main comms.

"Aye, Lady M! Guns are hot and ready. Just like that little…"

"Enough, Messau! Fire when ready. I repeat, fire when…"

Explosions started ripping up the camp nearest the river, followed by blaster cannon fire. The air cruiser's guns weren't the biggest ones Nathan had seen. Those had been on the land cruiser and in the compound's main bunker. But these were big guns. Bigger than most of those in this camp, and clearly coming from the air above it.

Chaos erupted.

Multiple Dark Men started running towards the blasts, and several gunnery positions on the ground opened fire on where it appeared the blasts had come from. A moment later, another pair of blasts struck the camp on the southern banks of the river, coming from a completely different angle.

More chaos. One of the reserve units nearest the Gate bolted for the southern banks.

A final volley of shots came from the northern banks a minute later. At that moment, Morgaine appeared, standing on the very table that Ellie's 'friend' had been sent to get her to a drink. In fact, Morgaine was standing directly above the woman, sword in hand, and light flaring from her from somewhere. The mask and the black crownlike thing on her head only added to the mystique.

She looked like a rock star.

"Hear my words, Dark filth from the Void! I am none other than Morgaine, the White Falcon! And I have come for your *souls*!" With that, she leaped impossibly high into the air (anti-grav boots looked quite fun, although Nathan couldn't get the hang of them the one time he'd tried). Flinging some of the black stones from her hair in an arc around her, explosions ripped, and blasts flung tables, boxes, and people into the air all around where she'd thrown them. Bodies were landing burned, and some of the Dark Men – or their servants, perhaps – were screaming and wailing, running around in panic. Grabbing Ellie's hand, Nathan twisted his ring, becoming visible himself. Ellie was following and said, "Who the hell is that?! And…what are you wearing??"

Not bothering to answer her, Nathan made for the way he'd come. He knew there'd still be Dark Men in some of those bunkers, but hopefully less than before.

"*Trey and team coming in,*" came on the main comms. Then some laughter and whooping following each set of explosions down on the riverbank. "*Messau, stop your hollering! We need clean comms! And Messau…prepare for Option C.*"

"*Sorry, Cap'n,*" came the instant reply. "*Thought I'd switched off. And check that! Messau out!*"

Suddenly Treyborne and his group of men came storming over, firing in all directions. Morgaine had vanished again, but more explosions said she was still doing her work to distract and destroy. Nathan kept jerking Ellie's hand, then grabbed her wrist when she tried to pull back.

He stopped for a millisecond, looking back in anger, "Ellie…!" But the girl was not alone. The female who'd been with her had grabbed her other arm and was pulling her away from Nathan. Letting her go, he pulled out his blaster.

"Nathan, no!" Ellie cried, but he fired anyway. Ellie screamed, but the blaster bolt glanced harmlessly off some sort of body armor the girl had beneath her clothing. She drew a long, black curved blade and smiled wickedly.

"The Master said you'd come. He also said I can't kill you," she pouted at this for a moment. "But he didn't say anything about taking a limb or two…!" She glared and smiled like a caricature.

This girl is insane!

Trying two more shots, Nathan gave up and holstered his blaster, opting instead for the shock-lance. Two Dark Men who'd been running away from the blasts came into view, running onto the level area. Seeing Nathan with Ellie and engaging the girl, they too pulled out edged weapons and advanced, starting to flank him immediately.

"I have no time for this!" Nathan screamed. Instinctively, he grabbed for the amulet around his neck. It had been boiling with power since he'd gotten within half a mile of this place. Now it was positively on fire! As soon as he touched it, there was a wave of power and air that blasted out in all directions from his position. Ellie was only rocked by it, but the two Dark Men and the girl screeched as they were literally torn apart. Nothing was left. Not even their weapons.

Dark Men all over the area around the Arc Gate were knocked down, some at impossible angles that living bodies cannot achieve.

Ellie looked up at him in horror. Her eyes were as big as saucers. "*Nathan*…! What…did you…do?? She was my friend…! Is she…*dead*? Where did Exanna go?". Grabbing her and not waiting for more of the inane questions that were to follow, Nathan began working his way over to the base of the Arc Gate. He'd only have another two minutes or so to do what he had to do there before the sky cruiser came in for the lift out.

That was "Option C".

This was going to get tricky. As if it weren't already.

CHAPTER 90

Gary had pulled over into a truck stop. The last place one would look for a stolen truck would be a massive truck stop, he reasoned. Plus, he wanted to make sure the semi they'd stolen wasn't low-jacked. And he also wanted to find the tracer the scientist had put on the monolith in the event they needed to know where that was, as well.

The semi did indeed have a tracking device under the hood. Gary took the cutters to it and put it on the trailer of another truck that was just gearing up to leave.

Jennifer was looking for the Apple tracker on the monolith they'd used to locate it. "I can't see it!" she said. "It must be way up on top!"

"Well, ok!" Gary responded. "I found mine and I'd like to get some distance between it and us before someone gets the bright idea to track the semi, too!"

Jennifer nodded, climbing down from the truck bed and back into the cabin. Gary had filled up using all his available cash, as they'd already used up a quarter of a tank. And he wanted to be sure he had enough to get to Ben's place.

Pulling back onto the highway, they passed a patrol car just pulling in. A few breathless seconds later, however, no lights flashed and no sudden turnaround. Apparently, the word wasn't out this far yet. Or at all. Nobody liked to admit they'd lost a priceless alien artifact these days.

Cowards.

Gary laughed to himself, causing Jennifer to look over at him. "Sorry," he said, "Just thinking how crazy we are. I'm sorry I got you into this."

She reached over and touched his arm. "I came willingly. Nathan is *our* friend. Not just yours. This crazy thing is the only link we've got to him. And to his ex, not that I care. I will say, you've got some balls, Gary! I'll give you that!" she said laughing. Shaking her head, she added, "It's kind of hot," giving him a look.

That was good news.

Back on the road again, Gary checked his phone for the time before turning it off. No more pinging cell towers. And still almost five hours until dawn. Should be plenty of time.

CHAPTER 91

Jezerah's advance forces were camped only a click or so from the northern riverbank that surrounded the Arc Gate encampment. Curtaise was surveying the landscape with his distance goggles. Suddenly a series of explosions rocked the riverbank along its eastern edge.

What in the name of the Void…?

Apparently, something had accidentally exploded near the edge of the campsite.

How unfortunate…

Curtaise started to smile. Then another series of blasts. Was that blaster cannon fire coming from the air…? The southernmost shore was getting shot at repeatedly. The camp was beginning to return fire.

"General…we have an issue…" came over the comm.

"I'm aware. I'm looking at it now…". Another series of blasts. That was most definitely coming from above the ground. Someone had brought a sky cruiser to the party, and was throwing all in, to boot!

"Get me eyes on that cruiser! I want it down now! It isn't one of ours; so, we must assume it's coming from K'Thul…". Though wasn't that impossible? K'Thul had made quite a show of being angry about being the only one of the three without one! Curtaise was certain of it. He could have been lying of course…

Could anyone else…? Morgaine!

"Belay that! You'll never get there in time! Master Jezerah, we have a problem! I believe Morgaine is here and firing on the camp. What do you advise?"

"Morgaine…? What…? Get down there, Curtaise! Rally the troops! Execute your plan immediately. We're not waiting for morning. We're going in now! Omrion…get to your attack position immediately…"

So. The fight had begun without them. Curtaise slowly straightened his jacket and began barking orders. It may have started without them, but it was damn well going to end with them.

CHAPTER 92

K'Thul had been pushing his troops hard for weeks. The rest being given currently was the most he could afford. His generals and quartermasters had been urging him to give the men a break. As they would be unfit for fighting if they kept up this pace.

K'Thul wasn't tired. He didn't see why his men should be. Especially his Dark Men. But he had relented. They were still a good many clicks away from their target. But he'd sent men ahead to investigate the area, and to report anything unusual.

A team of his men had discovered a land cruiser not ten clicks from their advance position to the south. That was unusual. But the men had botched it, attacking it immediately seeing mostly women and children. They'd been almost completely wiped out. Twelve men went in, four had come out. One was missing entirely.

Sending a battalion of Dark Men to the area, they'd found the bodies. But no cruiser. It was long gone. No trace of it anywhere.

Keeping a portion of his army on the southern side, in the event that this land cruiser was an attempt to waylay a portion of his army had to be considered. Perhaps it and the spying sky cruiser had been related, but they were avoiding contact so far. And carrying non-military personnel…along with combatants didn't seem to fit either Jezerah or Emorion.

However, K'Thul wasn't going to waste all his time chasing one land cruiser full of women and children. What that meant, K'Thul could not fathom. But he had decided not to care. Choosing to press on and avoid whatever trap there might be, he commanded them to pull up their campsite and leave immediately.

This was not a popular decision.

K'Thul had to care a little, as he knew that obedience and morale were important for an army. But he also couldn't delay, and now he had this other issue to worry about. Great generals were never surprised. They planned for every contingency. Therefore, he left some explosives in some tents, a few of the wounded men from the attack on the land cruiser, and some campfires behind in a periphery to make it appear they were still there to the careless eye.

Perhaps that would be enough. If not, he would deal with that when he had to. K'thul would not be delayed by a gnat.

"General K'Thul. There is a disturbance at the Arc Gate." What was this about?

"What kind of disturbance…?"

"Explosions. Several of them. Blaster cannon fire. It looks like it's a battle, Master."

Jezerah apparently had arrived.

"Good. Let them destroy each other."

K'Thul would arrive just in time to clean up the mess and finish off the victor. Tomorrow would be a good day. Tired troops or no, they'd find a battered victor and a torn up enemy line.

Child's play.

CHAPTER 93

Morgaine was running. Cutting down Dark Men right and left, she made her way away from the table towards the Gate itself. Most of the Dark Men were running away from her by now. The White Witch had made her mark. It was easy to bow and scrape to your own god. To run into the evil goddess that was the villain in every child's tale – well – it had some advantages. The eerie wailing amongst the Dark Men was everywhere.

Smirking, Morgaine spun her ring again. It was time to vanish.

Morgaine suddenly spotted Emorion making his way from a large group of field-erected military buildings between the Gate and the riverbank. The blasting of the riverbank had ceased, per the plan. Emorion was looking upwards towards the Gate area and pointing.

Redoubling her speed, Morgaine made her way over to the Gate. Spinning her ring, she reappeared next to a woman cook hiding behind the larger pots. The Dark Woman, something Morgaine had only seen a few times in her life…fainted upon seeing her. Knocking her anti-grav boots into action again, she leaped up, carefully landing on the cave ledge just behind the Gate.

"Nathan…?"

"It's set, Morgaine. And I've attached the little thingy you added, too."

"Excellent! Get up the hill as far as you can. Meet me at the Cruiser."

"Check that…Mistress."

"Watch it."

Large groups of Dark Men were crossing the riverbanks on all sides, looking for attackers. But another very large group were also racing up the hillside, with Emorion right behind them.

"Messau? Now would be a good time." Morgaine said over comms.

Chuckling, Nathan grabbed Ellie and shouldered his shock-lance. The ruckus and blasts, coupled with his disappearances had been enough to escape any more direct confrontations. Another woman running away from the blasted areas wasn't going to be noticed. He and Ellie were together at the base of the monolith.

About to leave, he felt the monolith pulse and hum…in time with his necklace. Shaking his head, he bolted, half dragging Ellie with him. The trees were big here, but sparse. It was also a very steep climb. Ellie wasn't wearing the right type of shoes for this. She still had on sneakers. Not the worst thing she could have been wearing. But not the best. They were causing her to slide and reach to catch tree trunks, slowing them both down.

Nathan waited until she was parallel with him, then picked her up and started running uphill. The medallion necklace began to pulse harder, and Nathan could feel it pouring energy into him.

"Nathan, what…?" Ellie seemed to be lacking for words. That was a trait Nathan would have liked more of when they were together.

"Just accept we're here to help and please…just don't talk, Ellie. OK?" He felt rather than saw her nod. Within minutes, they were at the designated spot, a small bald spot on the back side of the hill. They'd be exposed, even vulnerable, for as long as it took to get on board and fly out.

It had to be enough time.

Looking back, Nathan saw their leader retreating down the hillside, but he was calling all the troops now. They were all turning back around. Morgaine was going to have quite an audience, that was for sure.

The medallion was pulsing wildly. But it didn't seem to be just the plethora of the Dark Men all about them. Nor the presence of the Gate. It was...*different*. It was like…. the Hymn of Mourning. That was odd. A weird sort of vibrational "wail" was going on….and the gem was burning bright white. So much so, that Ellie said, Turn off your neck light, Nathan! It's blinding me!"

"I can't," was all he said, setting her down next to those who'd already gathered. "Ellie, go with these men. I'll be right back. Trey, I'm sorry…I have to go back down. I'll be careful," then he added, "Probably."

Treyborne saw the gemstone burning brightly right through Nathan's shirt, and just looked into his eyes and nodded.

As the rest of the troops came up the hill, Morgaine stepped forward, letting the luminesence from her light stick catch her fully. Good. Emorion was right behind them.

Morgaine shouted, "I am taking back the Arc Gate in the Name of the Creator! You will never leave this planet, Hordes of the Dark!" With that, Messau opened fire on the entire area, spraying it with blaster cannon fire. Simultaneously, Morgaine pressed the activator switch on her wrist. And the Arc Gate seemed to fold in upon itself…and vanished! Other explosions all around the upper area seemed to come from nowhere.

The Dark Men reeled from the air raid blaster fire, running anywhere they could for cover. Emorion just stood there, watching in amazement. More blaster fire and he started to duck a little. He clearly had a massive shield in place. But it wouldn't hold forever. He turned and ran down the hill again, infuriated.

"I hope those phase shifter charges work like you said, Morgaine."

"As do I. If we're lucky, they should keep the Arc Gate invisible and mostly intangible for at least a day or two. I hate giving up those rings! But if we can get them to either leave the area, or at least continue to fight over what appears to be nothing — we've won a small victory. I do have a return drone that should activate when the charges fail. But only having one day to prepare this was not ideal. It may not work."

"That's why I'm going back down, Morgaine."

"You're…what? No, Nathan! Stay on the hilltop, the sky cruiser will be back in a moment! We've got to go…!"

"It's already there. But no can do. I've got a plan, too. And it just came to me. That Medallion of yours…well…it seems I can hear it a bit now. If this works, I'll see you in about three minutes. If not, well… Ellie is already up there with Trey. Get her out of here. If you ever get the Gate open, send her home before terminating it."

"As you command," came Morgaine's terse reply.

CHAPTER 94

Dark Men were flooding the upper tier of the area that had once been dominated by the monolith. Shock and horror were plain even on the very dark faces covered in scarves.

Emorion slowly walked up to where the Gate had been. Shaking his head in disbelief.

Then the blasts resumed, this time coming from both the riverbanks and around the sides of the hill. Emorion screamed, and several Dark Men nearby blew apart like confetti. Then he raced towards the riverbank, where blaster cannon fire was raining down on their forward positions.

* * *

Nathan skidded to a halt halfway down the slope. Dark Men were flooding all over the lower reaches about a quarter mile from his position.

"Nathan! Get back here! There are other forces attacking from around the hill, with blaster fire coming across the river…! Get out of there! It's too hot."

That was Treyborne. Suddenly, Nathan spotted Morgaine storming right towards him.

"Check that, Captain! I've got the White Queen blowing in, as well. Heading back. See you in a five."

Together, they raced back the way Nathan had come. Apparently, Morgaine wasn't planning on letting him go down back alone, so she'd cut him off instead of going over the hill, which would have been much faster. The anger pouring from her as they ran was palpable. She didn't speak, but her face was red, and she was so furious, her eyes were tearing as they ran.

Wow. I really know how to piss women off! He sighed even as he ran.

Blaster fire from the woods as they entered showed that some of the troops circling the large hill were also coming down it. And fast. As they approached, Morgaine hit something on her wrist and bolts began to go around them at odd angles.

"That's handy!" he yelled as they ran up into the cruiser. It took off before they could even reach their seats. Blaster fire rocking the under panels as they did so.

Then they were away.

Ellie had taken the couch seat with the medical equipment tied down at her feet. Morgaine sat next to Nathan, but there was no hand holding or leaning on him this time. Her face was still just as red; as red he'd ever seen anyone.

CHAPTER 95

Gary and Jenn pulled into Ben's farm around 4:32 am eastern time. Gary had had to call Ben four times to wake him up. It didn't help using Jenn's phone, as he wouldn't recognize the number. Then it was another four or five minutes of explaining they needed to park a semi-trailer in his barn…and they had some cargo that "perhaps" might have been stolen from the government. Who had themselves stolen it a week or so prior.

Gary even pulled out the old "Blues Brothers" line: "We're on a mission from *God!*" But Gary and Ben had been friends since grade school. Even after Gary's parents had moved to the city, they had hung out every chance they could. If there was anyone who would always have his back from those early days, it was Ben.

Ben had ultimately laughed and said, "The barn door is open, Gary! The back door will be too. Just shut the barn doors and come on in and get into bed. I've got the guest room open for you and your friend. I hope you're good friends, too, because the bed is kind of small for two. Just don't wake my wife up. She's a total bear if you disturb her nightly hibernation!"

So it was that by the time the dark gray of dawn started to brighten the horizon, Gary and Jennifer were in the tiny guest bathroom, brushing their teeth and then taking their turns with the toilet. Ben had been good enough to leave them toiletries and even towels for the morning.

The bed was indeed small. Barely enough for Gary alone. "I'll take the couch in the living room," he said, grabbing the quilt at the foot of the bed and a pillow.

"Don't be silly! There's room enough for both of us," Jenn replied. "And that living room doesn't even have any decent curtains! You'll never even get to sleep. And if you do, you'll be awake in an hour when their kids get up. I won't bite. Just get used to holding a little woman in your arms. Because I'm already chilly and you look like you can keep me warm tonight."

With that, she took off her pants, leaving her in her panties and a long shirt. She had a firm little body. Not that he'd noticed before. Not more than a thousand times, anyway. Gary continued to just stare at her. "Uhm…are you…sure?"

"Do you mean, am I sure I invited you to sleep in the same bed as me? Yes, I'm pretty sure! Get in! I won't ask again."

CHAPTER 96

Landing the sky cruiser in the olive grove receiving zone was surreal. The land just opened up and then seemed to swallow them whole as it closed above them. At some point the decision was made to go to the new base to pick up some supplies from the larger compound to bring back to the former base to repair the monitoring system. Maitan had made the request shortly after their departure from the Gate.

Ellie was asleep, as were most of the team that had come with them. For once, no one had sustained significant injuries, although there were several cuts and bruises. Nothing the medical kit hadn't been able to handle. They'd flown for many hours before finally landing. It was still dark out, but the sun would be rising soon enough in what Nathan always had to remind himself was not the east, as he'd assumed, but more like the north by northeast. The horizon was already brightening.

Morgaine had maintained her icy cold demeanor the entire flight, refusing to engage in conversation with him. Apparently, he'd struck a nerve. It was a gift, apparently, being able to cause extreme anger in any woman he cared about.

Finally, when they landed, and Treyborne and Messau came up from the pilot box, did Morgaine speak, as they were walking off the cruiser. "We've accomplished what we set out to do. We should be happy about that. If things go as planned, the Gate will remain out of sight and out of phase for at least 37 hours."

"I'm not sure if someone as clever as Emorion will even buy that it's gone. After all, I've had centuries to remove it. Of course," she added looking at Nathan for the first time since they'd gotten on board, "we have the wild card that could explain all our new stunts now."

Ouch.

Ellie spoke up from behind them, "Uh…hello? Can someone get me out of this harness? I can't get it." Turning and looking back, Nathan smirked and just shook his head. One of the guards turned and went back to help her.

Morgaine, ignoring her, turned, and kept walking, "We are going to need some reconnaissance and see what happened after the battle that was just beginning as we got out. Trey, get the sky cruiser on recharge before you hit the dorms. And get some fresh guards…"

Trey interrupted, "The others aren't here yet, Morgaine. Remember? They are going to be at least a day behind us."

Her eyes closed for a moment. "Yes. Well then, get Messau and yourself and get the sky cruiser on its charger pad. I want you up in six hours and heading back for a high flight check on that battle. I want to see if they've uncovered our little prank, as well. I'm praying I get at least one of my rings back! It was, I admit, a desperate play! But we cannot allow anyone from the Triumvirate in control of that area. The Gate is acting more and more like it's activating. Even I can feel it, and I'm no longer…" she looked behind her at Nathan's chest without looking into his eyes, "directly connected to them."

Ellie raced to catch up with them, "Nathan! Where are we? Who are these people? Thank you for getting me away from those horrific monsters. That was great. But … how do we get home? How did you get in with these…people, anyway?"

"Guys!?" Nathan said, stopping the group ahead of him in their tracks. "Ellie would like to be introduced. Ellie, this is the Lady Morgaine, Captain Treyborne, and his men. They all risked their lives to free you.

You're welcome." Without another word, he started walking away from her. The rest of them also turned and started walking.

"Where are you going?" Ellie barked, starting to follow.

"I'm going to bed once I can find one. I suggest you do the same. Although you slept almost the entire way. Trey," he said.

Treyborne turned from talking with Morgaine, "Yeah, Nathan?"

"I'm going with you on reconnaissance. I just feel like I've got unfinished business at the Gate. And it may not happen this trip either," he added pointedly, looking into Morgaine's eyes, who had also stopped to listen and who finally was looking at him directly. "But I want to see for myself what it looks like down there."

Finding beds was easy. They all had their own rooms, with plenty to spare. The caretakers and support staff already here had set up the rooms with blankets and pillows, even a few fans, as the air underground was still a bit…stale. No lights in the rooms, skylights only in the upper hallways. So even when the daylight did come, it would still be like midnight in those rooms.

Of course, finding the beds had been the easy part. Sleep turned out to be much harder to find, however.

Very hard to find, indeed.

CHAPTER 97

A soft knock came on the door, waking Gary up. Eyes bleary, he still felt exhausted. Cuddling still with him was the very beautiful, very asleep Jennifer. Even unconscious and drooling a bit on her pillow, she was lovely. Light gold hair covering her face. The curtains in the room were darkening types…but…

Another couple soft knocks. *Oh yeah. The door.*

Gingerly getting up, still in his underwear and overshirt, Gary popped the door and slipped out. Ben was standing there with a steaming cup of black coffee.

"I love you," Gary said, giving him a one-armed hug as he took the coffee and started for the kitchen. "Jenn's still asleep. I want to let her rest as much as possible."

Ben followed behind him chuckling. Gary could almost hear him shaking his head. "Hot girl in bed with you…making the morning news…you're *infamous*, bro!"

"Morning news?" Gary exclaimed, spilling a little coffee as he swiveled to look behind him. Ben was back there, sandy blond hair nodding. Ben was always the good-looking one. Girls flocked to him. His former wingman's marriage had signaled the end of Gary's fun. Until he'd met Nathan.

Reaching the kitchen, the morning news was on the small flatscreen TV hanging on the wall by the patio doors. There were some shadowy pictures of the flatbed truck on the Jersey Turnpike. They were apparently looking for them south of New York City. Perfect. Mentally patting himself on the back for his plan to make sure he was seen going all ways, especially the wrong direction on the turnpike…

I've still got it.

Years prior, he'd made quite a bit of money doing some dark web things and hacking places he'd rather not have known. Therefore, no one did. Except for Ben, of course. Ben knew all his dirt. Giving his near brother another hug, he asked, "So how hot am I?"

"Hot enough that I sent Terri off with the kids to visit the grandparents. I just told her, 'Gary,' and she nodded and started bundling the kids off into the car."

Gary just started laughing. Somehow that was the funniest thing he'd heard in a year…drinking his coffee became impossible. Ben just sat there, smiling, and sipping his own coffee.

As the laughing subsided, Ben just added, "So what's the big black thing from Egypt you had to steal, Gary? I mean…you've got the US State Department and federal investigators looking for you. Somehow, its 'disappearance' from the museum is now your fault, too. Just FYI." Another coffee sip with a smirk. "I love that you're involved in this, by the way. *Love* it! Just wondering what your play is."

Gary's eyes got a bit wider with each sentence. Into the break, he just said, "I don't have…a 'play' yet…Ben…" Ben did a double take. Then he started chuckling again, shaking his head, only stopping to sip his coffee, then shake it some more.

"Am I missing something…?" came Jennifer's voice from the back hallway. Wandering in, with her pants back on, but otherwise as unkempt as she had been while asleep on the pillow, she just had to look up at them both with those big, green eyes and both of them went silent.

"Sorry if we were too loud," Gary began, but Jenn waved him off.

"Where's the coffee? I need some 'go juice'! Oh wow…it's after 11! I wonder if we're going to be late for work…?" Laughing, Ben got up and got her a mug and poured her some coffee, pointing out the sugar and pulling some creamer from the frig.

"Hi! I'm Ben, I'll be your parole officer for the next few days…!"

Jennifer just shook his hand while sipping some coffee. "Nice to meet you. How bad is it?"

Ben just looked wide-eyed over at Gary, who shrugged. "Bad."

CHAPTER 98

A knock on the door for Nathan showed a distraught Ellie at his open doorway. At some point, he'd fallen asleep with the hallway lights still on. Or someone had left them on.

It was still dark. This according to the chronometer set into the wall reading 0150. Hours were broken into different segments on this planet. And a day had exactly 15 hours of 100 minutes. If Earth had 15 hours every day, we'd have 96 minutes per "hour". For whatever reason and by whatever similarity or difference, these hours were supposedly extremely precise at making 15 one hundred minute "segments" each day.

"What can I...do for you, Ellie?" Nathan asked, leaning up on his elbow, still lying in bed.

"I'm...afraid, Nathan. I'm alone here. You know everyone. You've been here a month or more! Two? How long as it been? I don't even know! I've only been here a week or so, and all I got was kept as a prisoner by.... whoever they were!"

"Uh...the 'bad guys', Ellie. Even your 'friend'. Morgaine would say they were people... 'consumed by the Dark'."

"What does that even mean, Nathan?! Who *are* you?! I was working double shifts trying to figure out what happened to you. And here you are, playing 'space hero' with some white-haired goddess, exhibiting wild powers! And by the way, what the *fuck*, Nathan?! She looks like she could be your sister...! Who..."

"I'm glad I'm always the subject of conversation," Morgaine said, walking in behind Ellie, who jumped at her entrance.

"I'm sorry…Morgaine…I'm just…". Ellie stammered an apology and stepped away instinctively. She was always like that.

"…completely out of your element? Wanting to know what's going on because you understand basically nothing?" Morgaine looked at her, touching her arm and nodding seriously. "I get it. No offense taken. I am not; however, I assure you…Nathan's *sister*."

"It's late, Morgaine," Nathan said, a bit startled at her abrupt entrance himself, "Besides, I thought you weren't talking to me."

Morgaine gave him a completely unreadable look.

Turning to Ellie, she said, "Ellie, I understand your confusion. But could we put off your education until tomorrow? I have some…*issues*… that I'd like to discuss with Nathan alone, please. I'm finding I'm not able to sleep, either. And as our issues involve life and death, I'd prefer not to stand in line. If you please…?"

Ellie just looked at them both, then nodded slowly. "Ok…sure. I'm actually better a bit already. Just speaking my mind and seeing things here are deeper than just me helps. Thanks. Good night."

She left as quickly as she'd come in.

Morgaine hit the button and closed the automatic door, watching it slide into the doorframe before sitting down in the small chair. She was about as far away from him as she could be and still be in the room. Nathan tried to sit up and pay attention. But he was still very much exhausted himself. His eyes kept half-closing. Morgaine looked wide awake. She even had her hair perfectly tied back and a beautiful tight blouse on over her nightshirt. Even as withdrawn as she was, she was alluring.

Nathan just waited for her to speak. Her eyes were round and wide and then she lowered them, speaking quietly. "You hurt me, Nathan. And you scared me. I didn't think I could feel either feeling again. *Ever*."

She looked up and tears were in her eyes. "I cannot explain it, and I don't want to. But when you said you were going back there, I freaked out. I got scared. For you. For me. You cannot do that again. We must stick to our fight plans. Doing your own thing…Nathan…it gets you killed! If you'd gone back a *minute* earlier…"

"I'd have been surrounded by opposing forces about to fight each other and caught in the middle. I know. I thought about it for at least an hour before finally passing out on the flight back. I just felt…the medallion…" he touched it and a faint light lit up on it.

She nodded knowingly. "I understand. It talks to you, almost. But you are its master, Nathan. Not the other way around. You must always measure the fact that you're not immortal. I've lived a long time…" she turned her head, then lowered it again, along with her voice. "I've lived…a *very* long time because I've been careful to have a path out, always. I have backup plans. I even have backup plans to backup plans."

Looking up she said, "You blew all that apart turning back around and running into what we knew was going to be an escalating bonfire. That was *before* those opposing forces, likely from my brother, were thrown in just for added sauce!" Her eyes were fire again.

Nathan sighed and got up. Walking over to her, he got on his knees and said, "I promise to stick to the plans from now on…ok?" She was *crying*. Actually…crying. The 'White Queen'…the 'White Witch'…Morgaine, the rock star and legend. *She* was crying. She just leaned into him, and he hugged her to him. Soon, her arms were on his and tears were coming from her for quite a while.

All Nathan could do was sit in wonder.

Brianna and Maitan finished laying the "spider mines" about everywhere they could, marking carefully on the map where they'd put them, about ten hours after starting the work. If there were any more to be found — they weren't at this compound.

Maitan carefully tucked the map away and had the display on his office wall scan it before he placed it in a small thin drawer in his desk. Brianna had never been in here before. Set next to Morgaine's quarters and with a wide-angle view of the compound below, it was impressive in its sheer size alone. Stark and utilitarian. But impressive. It was dark out again, and they were both bone tired.

"I will need to get back to the team as soon as we're able. As should you. We will be much safer at the other compound, as well. If all went according to plan, the sky cruiser should be here within the next 6-12 hours. Get some rest. You may sleep in the Mistress' quarters. I will be closer that way. Plus, she has the best beds in the facility."

Smiling gently, he helped Brianna to her feet, as she'd been slumping on his rather firm couch long enough to look to have conformed to it completely. Holding her by her elbow, he walked her into Morgaine's outer chamber. Noting the messy bedroom in the back, and realizing he'd not done anything to pick up since Morgaine had slept here over a day ago, he sniffed.

"Perhaps your rooms, after all." Turning around, he walked her down the hallway to her own chambers, making sure she was moving on her own before closing the door.

Maitan was tired, as well. He was, after all, over 100 years old. These types of days just didn't come any easier. Working that long and hard with that much worry and concern was not good for the internal organs. Retiring to his "office" again, he flicked a button and a small bed flopped down out of the wall. It was made perfectly, of course. Crisp lines, just how he liked it.

Walking over to the large bay window, he poured himself some of the best of his rare Amoxian wine. Sitting down on the couch Brianna had just vacated, Maitan slowly eased himself into a meditative state, sipping the wine and listening for anything in the compound that sounded like a threat. He hadn't told Brianna, but he wasn't going to sleep any more than was absolutely necessary until someone came who was proficient with blaster weapons.

Of course, it was against *Biaki Mor* Code to use anything but a bladed weapon or hands for fighting. He'd never touched one himself, even though, officially, the Code was dead. Sniffing again, he savored the wine. There were only seven bottles left of it in the world, to his knowledge. Made before he was born by a people that no longer existed.

Such a pity.

Some people were just made for making good wines. Nodding to himself, he leaned back, hoping the need to hit his bunk would not come soon.

Hitting another button, some quiet music came on to fill in just enough to keep him awake, but not interfere with his hearing. Plus, he didn't want Brianna to know that over half the outside monitors were no longer functioning. Maitan himself would have to do for now.

That sky cruiser couldn't come too soon.

CHAPTER 100

The sky cruiser was soaring at over eight miles in the air when it first flew over the Arc Gate battleground. Hordes of troops were amassed everywhere, and it seemed that someone had come out the victor. From all the damage to the eastern riverbank and the amount of horseback riders and sheer volume of Dark Men, it appeared that the Eastern Empire wave had hit sometime last night, or perhaps very early in the morning.

Who had run where, and who owned what was impossible to tell at their altitude. That made it not their issue for now. The Gate was still cloaked, and it appeared that there was an army of people around the area where it had phased out. Someone was even standing in one of its deep footprints at that very moment.

Nathan just had to hope their little David Copperfield ruse was going to hold. Morgaine had said with those solar batteries they should last for at least two and a half days. Up to four, if the sun kept shining.

And it was beating down on the area at the moment, so their luck was holding, at least for now.

Treyborne hadn't bothered to shave before getting out this morning. And he had to be tired. But he'd let Nathan sleep once he told him a brief version of the night's events and how little he'd gotten. He had only awakened him upon reaching the battlefield. Then he let him sleep again while they flew to the first compound.

Nathan really liked Treyborne. He just kept doing for everybody. Morgaine had chosen her Captain well. When he woke up again, they were a little over an hour out, according to Trey. His eyes were red, and he'd clearly been drinking some stimulant.

After a while he said, "Hey, take the controls for a minute, will you? I need to pee and get some food from the stores back there. Want anything?"

Nathan looked startled, "I don't know…".

Treyborne laughed and chucked his shoulder as he stood up. "It's on autopilot! But in case you see something big like a mountain and we're heading right for it, hit this button," he said, pointing to a large green lit switch, "Grab those handles like I do. Hold her steady!"

"Ok…" Nathan said, and Treyborne was off. It didn't take much to stay awake when you were in an alien sky cruiser, and at the controls with no idea how to fly it.

The five or so minutes Trey was gone seemed to last an eternity. Treyborne flipped a small wrapped package to Nathan as he sat down and handed him a sipping bottle which had some of that sweet and tart juice in it.

"You didn't answer, but I figured you must be hungry. Morgaine is a handful all by herself. She acts super tough, but she's got feelings in there. Somewhere. And it looks like that Ellie friend of yours is, too. A handful I mean. *Women!*"

He said it like he meant it.

Nathan just nodded. Morgaine had gone to her room after staying with him for a while. He hadn't seen her before he left, but it seemed to have cleared the air between them. He hoped so. The woman was simply incredible. It was impossible not to be drawn to her. Her charisma and leadership alone made her a force. Her beauty made her unstoppable. Then there was the whole 'Elder Race' thing and living nearly forever…

Trey was looking at him from the corner of his eye. "You want to talk about it?"

"Not really…" Nathan replied, then began to unload, "It's just that Ellie is … Ellie. She dumped me a few years ago, and…"

"Wait a minute. 'Dumped'? What does that mean? Did she leave you by a street somewhere unsavory like a pile of garbage? That's what comes to mind when…"

"Yeah. Just like that. Anyway, she dumped me while we were on a research team together. Left me for another guy who was supposedly my friend. So, I left. I went and hid in a corporate job in IT…uh… working with computers…and then they found the monolith and I got pulled into it…"

Trey didn't say anything, but he was looking straight at Nathan now. His eyes said he knew what that must have been like.

"Anyway, Ellie came into my room. Who knows why…? But she wanted me to tell her more about what was going on. I mean, we barely had time to talk after picking her up from that mess. She's been alone here the entire time with the Dark Men. Not exactly a talkative bunch, I know from experience!"

Trey nodded again.

"Then Morgaine comes in. I guess I pissed her off something fierce going back down. Or trying to before that other force swept in right below us! She said it 'hurt her' and I needed to stick to plans or I'd be killed. Implying she or someone else might be, as well, if I didn't stick with whatever was laid down. I get that…but she was so freaking upset. It was like…"

Trey turned back, holding the controls tightly. "Yeah…well…Nathan. You have one advantage that no one else will ever have with her: You're Elder Race, too. It's written all over you. The hair, the skin, the eyes… the way you can take the old shock-lance!"

He laughed.

"The way you wipe out Dark Men whenever you're near them…! I saw that blast you did, Nathan. No one else did but me, as I was looking for you and Morgaine when I saw you…what…? *Vaporized* three of them that were close to you, and blasted another several dozen all over the field? I've only seen Morgaine do that shit."

He turned back to Nathan, and his eyes were intense, "Seriously, she has powers that just sometimes manifest when she needs them the most. That's not human, Nathan. And for the *first time*…I guarantee you… because I know her, maybe better than anyone…she finally doesn't feel alone anymore. Think about that. She's been alone for *hundreds* of years, Nathan. And she's finally not alone…any…more…"

Nathan leaned back trying to take that in, nodding. Finally, he spoke. "But if I'm not human, and I am not just someone who happens to… look like she does…how did I get to New York?"

How did my parents adopt me from an adoption agency in Queens? Where… where do I come from? How will I ever know…?

"I don't know…. but we're here," was all Trey said, pulling up on the air brakes, and preparing to land the sky cruiser.

CHAPTER 101

Brianna woke to Trey gently shaking her. "Mmm…?" she said, reaching up and hugging his arm.

"Uh…Brianna?"

Snapping awake, she let his arm go like it was a snake. "I'm…so sorry!" she said. "It was a long day…and I…what time is it?"

"It's almost 1200. Sun will be going down shortly. You slept all day, huh?"

Brianna just nodded, yawning.

"Maitan said you were still asleep. He's doing some quick repairs on the monitors, but we need to go soon. Can you get yourself together? We should leave before dark." Nodding again, Brianna watched him go.

Mmm…that dream! She vaguely remembered kissing him…and other things…in her dreams.

That could have been embarrassing! Yikes!

Gathering herself, she got up, cleaned up and brushed her hair and teeth. She pulled some more clothes out and changed quickly, sacking up her used clothes to be washed once they reached 'Base 2', as Maitan called it. When she reached the courtyard between the buildings, the sky cruiser was being unhooked from its cabling. Trey clearly still didn't trust there wouldn't be another ambush here. With good reason, she had to admit. Once your enemy knew your position, you moved.

Permanently. You didn't go back and hang around.

Nathan nodded to her as she walked up, carrying her large bag full of clean clothing and her cloth sack with her dirty clothes in it. Maitan was already inside, adding to the medical and food supplies on board. One would think they were going for a weeklong cruise and not a six-hour flight back east.

Treyborne came last, carrying a large blaster rifle and wearing his body armor. Nope. Not a bit of trust in that man. Somehow that made him seem even more rugged. He was beautiful.

Sighing, Brianna quelled her hormones and emotions, buckling into her harness and tried to stay as far back from the pilot's area as possible. Maitan took the co-pilot seat at Nathan's behest, leaving him alone with her in the rear.

He looked as tired as she felt, however, and he proceeded to say, "I'm sorry, Brianna. But I'm not going to be much of a conversationalist. I'm locking in, and then going to sleep if I can."

He even spread himself over three seats and barely buckled in at all!

Brianna raised an eyebrow, but it was his life. She found she hated flying. It was unnatural and scary. But she was tough. She'd survived Dark Men, a flight from Rondor, and much worse. Closing her eyes, she just nodded and answered, "I'm tired, too. Long day and although I was still asleep when you arrived, I'm at least a day behind. Let's both get some sleep before we arrive at Base 2."

"Base 2…?" Nathan said, opening one eye.

"It's what Maitan called it. I don't know. Were we in Base 1 then, or Base 3? He said it came from a time when the barbarian lords ruled the north. That was over a hundred years ago. He's old." Yawning, her jaws cracked. Brianna then shut her eyes and was soon asleep. She barely remembered taking off.

CHAPTER 102

Morgaine awoke hours after Nathan and Trey had gone on reconnaissance and recovery of their strays. Someone had left a morning meal – and a mid-day meal – tray at her door. A cold pot of tea and some cream were lying beside her door, as well.

Her quarters at this compound were smaller, more military and utilitarian. Technically, the oldest base, and one she had shared with others during the last of the Elder Race War, her rooms were not anywhere near the 'Queen' level. They were, in fact, quite ordinary. An officer's quarters, to be sure. But plain, neat, organized, efficient.

As one of the toughest warriors and perhaps the most determined amongst her kind, she had slept with the military crew as corps commander. Others had led back then. Slowly, their numbers had dwindled. Mantles of leadership kept needing to be bestowed upon her. By the time this base was mothballed, Morgaine and her Elite Guard had been its only inhabitants for over a century.

Briefly reopened for business during the Barbarian Wars, she'd only used this base as a go-between and winter getaway for her team a handful of times since. It just held too many bad memories. A few good ones, to be sure. But far too much pain. Besides, the amount of charging bays, weapon stores, and even manufacturing that this underground base held was beyond the need of her group.

Walking its halls brought it all back. Here was the room where Chryanis breathed her last. Over there, the war council where they decided to attempt to 'unplug' the Dark Brethren and draw them into the Megiddo Fields. Four of the Dark Lords, and almost a hundred thousand of their 'disciples' died with them. But every single person in Morgaine's army, minus the ones who had fled into the forests and every single member of the Elder Race excepting Morgaine herself had died that day.

Well, it had been three days.

Having taken the cold bowl of porridge and adding extra cream from the tea tray, Morgaine ate while she walked. A few of her Guard were up, and two immediately had fallen in behind her. New base, same rules. Nowhere was trusted now. A couple of her other men were charging electronics and gear, reloading weapons, dragging cases of heavier ammo towards the cruiser bays.

As she turned a corner into the command bunker on the first floor, the land cruiser broke through on main comms, *"Bantor and company of the Land Cruiser requesting permission for bays to open. We are less than five minutes out!"*

"Check that, Land Cruiser. Where's Jairus? Wasn't he in charge there?"

"Jairus is deceased, and several others wounded. Dark Men attack two nights ago. Came at us at dusk right after dinner. We've been on radio silence awaiting either a call from you or drawing up to the bays. Clearly, it was the latter."

"Check, Bantor. I'll inform the Lady Morgaine of your arrival."

"No need, lieutenant. I'm right here," she said from ten feet behind him. Origen was a good man, but a little dense. Good fighter. Good soldier. Not much more to him. He'd been recruited from the southlands somewhere. She couldn't remember where.

"Yes M'Lady! Didn't know, and apologies. You heard, then?"

"I did. I will debrief Bantor and the surviving senior officer myself, seeing as how Messau is busy working, and Trey is off flying about."

"Check that, ma'am."

Ten minutes later, an exhausted Bantor and Mikell made it into the conference room closest to the docking bays. People were still streaming out, and loads were being moved into various areas and marked. The house staff was working like they had been waiting here all day just for this, as opposed to having ridden day and night for two days since she'd seen them. She could see them all from the meeting room windows. She hit a switch, dimming the windows to outside viewers. They could all see out perfectly, albeit with a bit less clarity.

"So, what happened Mikell?" Mikell was one of her most competent junior officers, and she could see him clench his jaw a moment before answering.

"I take full responsibility, Lady Morgaine. We were done eating and about to break camp. Cam and Jairus were keeping final guard. I was supposed to be standing in the bay doors as backup, but I'd gone for a break to relieve myself. Stanslin was on duty still. I was just walking back when we got hit. Cam went down, then Jairus. Both dead, ma'am. Stanslin grabbed his blaster and opened fire, I ran back, hit the floodlights, and then grabbed a heavier blaster cannon.

Soryin was injured, and a maid – I'm sorry I don't know her name, ma'am. They didn't do so well. The maid died en route. Blood loss from getting sliced up. Bantor, Kolvin, and I fought them off, however. Must have been a single cadre. Scouting group. Maybe a dozen of them. We got 7 or 8 of them, I think."

He shook his head, lowering it.

"Anything to add, Bantor?"

"Only that Mikell is being too hard on himself, Morgaine. You know the Dark Men. They came out of the blackness like shadows. Mikell and his men fought like wolves! I managed not to die, and I'm proud of that. It was only seconds, and then they were gone. Had those men not done their jobs, we'd all have died."

Morgaine shook her head, first negatively. "The forces of the Dark are at war. With themselves, and with anyone they can find. It was unfortunate. 'Bad luck.' Whatever you wish to call it. But it is not anyone's fault. Except maybe Jairus, as he was in command. And he has paid the ultimate price if that's the case. You both did well getting everyone else safely home."

Bantor, it seems you are becoming a 'member of the family' again. If you're ready for a more permanent position, I would ask you to recruit from the tenant family farmer above and see who might want to join us for maid and janitor positions. I'm hoping there won't need to be any more 'hazard pay' for them, but say it is included. Death benefits to all families involved. Catch up anyone else's family from the records with Maitan when he returns. I'll show you the gold stores."

It was barely a question, but Bantor was glad for it, regardless. "I'd be honored, Lady Morgaine. I'll see who wants to volunteer for this outfit. Not exactly a great track record, if I do say so myself. Sorry, but we've lost a lot recently."

Morgaine could only nod. She didn't even look at him. Instead, she focused on Mikell. "Mikell, you are now lieutenant commander. I need you to go into the city of Nyx and recruit me some high-grade mercenary fighters. Clean, at least to the naked eye. Get some more from this area, as I believe you're from here, yes?"

He nodded, looking down. "Is there a problem?"

Looking up, he said, "No M'Lady. It's just that…Nyx is kind of known for its thieves, assassins, and those of the lower class of that business. Talim is probably a better city for…"

"There are good men in every city, Mikell. I'm not giving you an easy job. I'm giving you a lieutenant commander's job! Get it done. At least five, preferably closer to ten men. I'll … I'll have to ask Nathan to check them for signs of the Dark when he gets back. That will be all."

Bantor and Mikell got up to leave, Bantor hesitating.

Morgaine looked up at him.

"I'm sorry, Morgaine. I should have had us moving faster. It was just such a nice night."

"When the enemy attacks you, it is never your fault, Bantor. Remember that. It's how you respond that matters. And you responded like a champion. A leader. People didn't die because of your inaction; people are alive because of your action. I'm done talking about it. Now, the gold stores are literally open for anyone to get what they need from in this base. It's always been that way. Good people have always lived here. The room they're in might be locked though," she suddenly remembered. "It's been a long time since we've stayed for more than a week or two."

Bantor spoke up, "I'll…help Mikell with recruiting. I've done far more hiring of such folk than he has. Once I get the people staffed here, of course."

Morgaine looked up at him, then nodded. With that, she got up and began walking him down to the stores area. A veritable warehouse of dry goods, Na-cells, Ca-cells, chargers, wiring, couplings, and a treasure house of metal. Once, it had all been necessary.

Once, this had been home.

CHAPTER 103

Ivory crested waves crashed into the coastline, roaring as they did so. Several figures stood talking in the Emperor's Summer Palace, west of Nelrae. Naked serving girls bringing in fine wine and fruit trays mixed with sweets and cheeses were everywhere. The three men hardly noticed, although each woman was exquisite. Multiple men in white garb and red sashes were stationed nearby, but simply as ornamentation. Their swords would not be necessary.

These three were family, as well as friends. Even though it had been nearly a decade since they had all been together, it was like no time had passed at all. The Emperor and his two cousins were all sitting on the rounded tile balcony, shaded partially from the sun even at this late hour.

Eating the food and drinking the wine, they were discussing the eventual reabsorption of the rebel kingdom of Rondor into the Empire's lands. The cousins had been the first to promote the idea in the Emperor's Court some time ago. They were younger than he by almost eight years, twins, the sons of his mother's sister.

All three had curly dark hair, wide brown eyes, and a propensity to laugh. Alecoren VII was much like his predecessors. Everyone in his line was of ruddy dark skin, high cheekbones, and very muscular. It was said Alecoren's namesake, Alecoren the Generous, had been able to lift ten stone weights in one hand. He also was said to have serviced ten women in one 15-hour period.

But legends grew over time. The current Emperor could barely handle six women in that amount of time. And that was in his prime. Now almost forty, he didn't have time for such idle hedonism. At least not that much. War kept a man alert. As did cousins who were both ambitious and proud. Yes, they were all friends. And they were all family. But Alecoren VII had no illusions about the reasons they had wanted this war. They were his two generals and had a large amount of their funds invested in the army. No war, no profits. Alecoren was Master of the Navy, as had been his father before him. Even today, they spent most of their time making him money, trading with the Near East at Talim and the Far East with their rival empire.

Less than sixty of his ships were hugging the coastline of western Rondor, attacking a few coastal towns, and making more of a commotion than a real impact. The others were still making him money.

There had been word of an army of Dark Men closing in on Rondor's northern border. Alecoren had assumed this was the Dark Cult's influence, as they had blessed the idea of an assault on Rondor, saying it would be "aided from the Void" if they did so. Nasty creatures, all of them. Not like these…serving girls, for example. Dark Cultists were hideous, often diseased, and hiding their faces behind masks and scarves.

On the other hand, this serving girl pouring his wine was exceptional. Perhaps he would try her out this evening. He must remember to ask his steward to prepare her for the event. Sighing, Alecoren turned his attention to his cousins. One or both had always been leading the armies this way or that. Securing this border. Bringing down that rebellious city.

The Empire had shrunk since his predecessors. But what remained was still well in hand. Now, with both generals here, he decided he should at least listen to their endless chatter about the war.

"…and it appears, cousin, that the southern border has caved in entirely! The King seems consumed with internal matters and has yet to even appear at the front. It seems to me…"

Blah blah blah. MMMM…yes, that one will do nicely. Maybe I'll add her to the evening, as well.

"Are we boring you cousin?" General Mateo asked suddenly.

"What…? Oh…no, no, of course not! I just knew that between your combined skills and the blessings of the Dark Cult, that our victory is assured. I do care about the details, but I'm assured both in my spirit and by your reports that things are going very well."

"Yes…" Mateo said, looking over at his brother Masin. "Of course. Well, as we were saying, the King might be vulnerable to a…helping hand out the window, if you get my meaning. Word has it that the Vizier and several other of the principal nobles are more than willing to negotiate for retaining their lands, perhaps with some additions, should the King's line…for whatever reason… cease to exist!" He smiled.

Masin added, "I've got men in place that could take their shot even now…!"

"All we await is your command. We would never act without you, of course," Mateo added.

No. You'll just slide the knife up to my throat, without me knowing, if I don't play along with your land grab.

"Fine, cousins! It's a fine plan! Make sure that it all comes under Empire again. One way or the other. Pays taxes, etc. What you do with the repossessed lands is, of course, up to you, and your officers. As is customary."

They nodded. Mateo flicked his hand and one of his retainers ran off to deliver the message.

Good. It was done then. Rondor would collapse without it's 'Holy King'. What a bunch of rubbish! Who believed in that whole Creator stuff, anyway?

Fools and weaklings. The Void consumes all. You either joined with it, or perished and joined with it, anyway.

That is what Alecoren had always believed. That had always been his experience.

CHAPTER 104

Morgaine spent several hours dealing with the fallout of the deceased. She never got used to it. It turned out that one of the fallen maid's children was Cam's, who had also died in the land cruiser attack. They'd been together for over a year. Her other child's father had died years prior. So, Morgaine now had two orphans in her camp. Fortunately, the maids were a clan, always helping each other care for the children. She would have Maitan work with whoever took them in.

But that didn't make this any easier. Brianna helped with dispensing small leather pouches filled mostly with gold and some silver. She was sending the women out both to get more supplies for the children and themselves. Morgaine promised them that she'd already sent Bantor out to find some replacements, and that they'd be staying in Base 2 for "the foreseeable future."

With the road to the Eastern Empire boiling with armies, her other base would be almost impossible to get to without skirmishes, anyway. And she simply did not want to put any more of her people at risk. Not one.

Once she was finished, Morgaine had a headache that simply would not go away. Even after she had the kitchen help fetch her some of the good wine that was still in the cellars. The wine was excellent. The headache simply was stronger than the wine. Brianna was very quiet, probably having never dealt with this much death before. Soon, she said she was heading to bed. Morgaine nodded her consent.

Walking slowly up the stairwell, Morgaine remembered too late this building had elevators. Shaking her head, she walked wearily towards her quarters. Ten feet behind her followed her Guards.

She'd almost forgotten them amidst dealing with all the grief and all the logistics their losses had caused. Turning, she realized these were the same guards who had gone down with her. They'd not left their posts for a second.

"What are you two still doing here?" she asked them. Go find your replacements and get some food, for heaven's sake! I'll be ok for ten minutes."

One of them, Gerantor, a tall, dark-skinned man from Talim answered, "No ma'am! I like my hide and Captain said if we left yours, we lost ours!"

Raising an eyebrow, Morgaine said, "Fine. Follow me. We're going right back to the kitchens and you're eating. I could use a bite myself."

Taking the elevator this time, she traveled down the three floors and ended up having quite a nice time getting to know Gerantor and Physian. Physian was from the Eastern Empire and had the characteristic smaller eyes and a very quick wit. Gerantor was also quite the entertainer, able to sing just about any tune from memory. Morgaine found herself feeling much better upon retreating again to her chambers.

It was too bad Brianna had missed it.

Gerantor and Physian were relieved from their duty, finally. The new guards had been busy unpacking stores, restoring air ducts, and doing other defensive setups – including getting comms online in all quadrants all day. Base 2 was set up like a hexagon, with tunnels in between and toward the central complex. Their replacements were tired but had rested some before going on duty again. They told Morgaine of all that had gotten done. Although less entertaining, the information was useful.

The complex had a war room, monitors all over the site with orbital ones set up centuries ago – some of which still actually worked – and an arsenal of anti-aircraft weaponry. Something that long since had lost its usefulness. Almost all air ships of any size or design were destroyed or lost during the war.

No one went into the war room. But the men had been told to get everything up and running. So Gerantor and Physian had had the simpler duty according to their replacements: stay with Morgaine no matter what. Pee in a corner if necessary.

Morgaine would never understand how she suddenly had become a fragile porcelain ornament. Not even the Hollow Men would dare attack her in here. Probably. And of the couple that had tried over a span of over hundreds of years, none had ever been left to even crawl away.

Of course, Morgaine no longer had her early warning system in the Corillion medallion. But she was quite certain her enemies would not know that, and likely did not want to "waste" such a precious commodity on her again. She had interrogated enough Dark Men to know the amount of death generated to spawn one Hollow Man.

What she had was the dark sword that she always kept with her. It would be enough.

As she emerged from the elevator, Nathan was just walking up the steps. With her guard behind her, she gave him a nod, walking to her rooms and shutting the door. His rooms were just down the hall, beyond Maitan's, Brianna's, and an empty suite that hadn't been used in centuries, for reasons Morgaine kept to herself.

Why does he make me always hold my breath when I first see him?

Irritated, she shook her head free of the hair restraint she'd put it in hours ago, rubbing her hands into her scalp. Undressing, she reviewed the scar developing on her side, the wound was still red around the edges, but healing nicely overall.

Slipping off all but her underpants, she saw that Brianna had gotten in here already, leaving her a glass bottle of water, turned her bed down, and had filled her decanter across the room with one of the wine bottles she must have left here ages ago.

The small light above the bed was also on, with a note that read, "Good to be back - B"

Even though this was somewhere she'd never been, the girl had found her rooms, and gotten them ready.

She just might be the best hire I've had in a century.

Sleep came quickly. Dreaming came afterwards. But her dreams were troubled. Her father was dying in almost all of them. Other times, he was telling her about the future. Her future. The future she had felt certain for centuries that he simply had been wrong about. Until a few weeks ago.

Waking up, she realized she hadn't been asleep for very long. After those dreams…she might not be able to sleep again for a while…

CHAPTER 105

Nathan saw Morgaine get off the elevator, but she barely gave him a nod of acknowledgement before turning into her chambers and quietly shutting the door behind her.

She was magnificent. A creature of sheer beauty. But she was as unreadable as any woman he'd ever known. And that was saying quite a lot.

Oh well, I'm tired. I need to sleep some more myself.

Turning on a small lamp above his rather large bed, Nathan realized these may be officer's quarters, but they weren't nearly as open or extravagant as the last compound had been.

The room had a sink, a bath with water lines, and another of their curious 'table toilets' where you sat on a hole set in a table-like plank like an outhouse. Washcloths instead of toilet paper. Soaps were gels. They'd used bars in the compound before. The place was much more advanced in technology, however, including room chargers for… something or other. Plastics and metal were everywhere. But it also seemed much, much older. Undressing, he ran the bath water and made it extra hot. A little soak before sleeping would do wonders.

Nathan was curious. But he was pretty sure Morgaine wasn't in the mood for company with the sour look she'd given him before turning in. No sense knocking on that door. And it was the middle of the night, by now. They'd flown straight here, and reached 'Base 2' by early, early morning. Now, it was past bedtime for all but the night staff.

Trey had gone straight to bed, having been up two straight days. Maitan had gone to the kitchens first, but his rooms were just down the hall, and he was fairly certain he'd heard a door shut down that way not a minute ago. If that was him, he hadn't been in the kitchens long enough to do more than grab a piece of fruit.

Finally getting out of the bath, and toweling off, he heard a light knock at the door.

Hesitating, he heard Morgaine's voice. "Nathan…? Are you awake?"

"Just a minute!" Finishing his drying, he put on some underpants. Going to the door with his shirt still off, he pressed the button and opened it, "Look, Morgaine…"

Placing her hand on his chest, she pushed him in, shutting the door behind her.

"Shh…! I don't want everyone to know any more than they already do. But I just…I just need to sleep with you tonight, all right? Not sexual… at least…not right *now*," she said, with a sly look and a smile. "I'm just… drained from today. The deaths on the land cruiser were hard on me. It's not many nights in my life I could just sleep with someone I trust. Is it all right? I don't want to be alone. Too much of my life, I've been alone."

Nathan realized he was just staring at her. Half dressed, with a see-through negligee night shirt, all he could think was that *"goddess"* did not quite capture it with her.

"Yes, yes, of course…!" he finally got out after she gave him yet another look.

"I'm sorry, she said," clearly with zero 'sorry' in her tone, "am I wearing something distracting…?"

What Nathan wanted to say was, *"Bitch, you could distract a dead man in that!"* What he did say was, "Only to the living."

She chuckled and took it off. "This should help then!"

Women.

CHAPTER 106

Emorion's men had been routed. There was no other description for it. Immediately after Morgaine's appearance, Jezerah's forces had swept in. Almost as if they had timed it.

Emorion paused… considering.

No…! After all these years…is it possible…? Have they been allies all along? It would explain much. Including her multiple "resurrections" and their painful failures to eliminate her all these years.

After such a setback, no possibility should be overlooked. An alliance between Jezerah and Morgaine even seemed likely, based on the events of today. One thing was clear: Jezerah and K'Thul were not working together. Even in full retreat, Emorion's men had reported that Jezerah's men had barely begun setting up a perimeter before being similarly overrun by K'Thul's Eastern Empire hordes.

Although incurring heavy losses, perhaps largely because of the mine fields his own men had set up on the far riverbank and beyond, K'Thul had taken the ground in less than two hours. Jezerah's men were also forced into full retreat, running back into the holes from which they'd come.

The Triumvirate was broken.

Well, they'd all known. Or should have. But losing over half his men put Emorion at an extreme disadvantage. He had two options, a new alliance with one or the other of his former "brothers" – either way coming in as the lesser partner – or pulling out all the stops on their own power.

Only this would allow him to regain supremacy.

And there was, of course, the matter of the lost Arc Gate. Somehow, after hiding for over one hundred years, and after no attempt to ever move the Gate itself, Morgaine had spirited it off just prior to Jezerah's assault. Or in tandem with it.

If the latter, then Jezerah and Morgaine had the Gate, and his position might already be lost. That didn't sit well with him. It meant he'd been taken for a fool. That didn't sit well with him, either. Because then he simply was a fool, letting events play out around him like a pawn or a slave. He was neither. He was *Emorion*. Born to rule with the full power and might of the Void itself.

But with shattered troops and a scattered army of Dark Men, now was the time to regroup. Realign, perhaps. Slide the knife into the support chain of his now open enemies. And perhaps, finally…to rid this world of the one being he hated more than Jezerah. His *sister*.

CHAPTER 107

Jezerah was in a similar mood as his cousin, it turned out. The stories of Morgaine's appearance and disappearance with the Arc Gate had barely reached him before reports of a surprise attack from a massive army appearing at full gallop from the east! His own forces had been so focused on Emorion, they'd not considered it possible an entire horde would appear out of the east. Or from anywhere else, for that matter.

It had taken all the skills of his newly assigned General Curtaise and himself to save what they could of their forces. It was far more than Emorion had been able to do, in his crushing defeat. But Jezerah himself had lost over twenty percent of his own army, along with quite a bit of their supplies, which he'd had to abandon on the grounds surrounding the former hill of the Arc Gate.

Morgaine! How had she known just when to strike? It must be that she's somehow turned one of the others. Probably that dullard, K'Thul. He was always so willing to just rule here on this backwater planet! She probably promised him a touch of her breast and he wilted immediately!

Scorn for his former comrade filled him until the Void Rage was almost out of control. Stilling his thoughts and calming his mind, he returned to the present.

Emorion had been surprised and crushed, so I know he was simply caught like a rat in a trap. K'Thul…he's making a show of acting surprised the Arc Gate is gone. But he's not moved yet, either. Almost like he's waiting for something. He did bring almost his entire army from the East though. That had to have cost him much. And the Empire, albeit not having had an internal war for centuries, might finally be vulnerable to some… outside influences.

But the one thing Jezerah had to do was find that damned Arc Gate! Wherever Morgaine had taken it, wherever she had run to – he would find her! And this time, he was going to squeeze the life out of her himself.

He entertained himself with various mental scenarios of wringing her pretty little neck.

All the while, his personal guard kept watch as they marched back towards Jezerah's compound.

K'Thul's men rested on either bank of the river. Its name had changed so many times over the centuries, he'd lost track. Looking over the battlefield and the bodies that were now being neatly bundled together and burned, he couldn't help reminding himself.

This is the result of winning the battle but losing the war.

The timing of Jezerah's attack with Morgaine's sudden stealing of the Arc Gate right out from underneath them was too perfect. Too well-timed.

It reeked of collusion.

Emorion was routed and his forces decimated. His scouts said he barely had left anyone back to even see what happened after he left. He must have lost over half of his pathetic troops. He'd never had much of a standing army to begin with. Just his Dark Men and his pets: Hollow Men and Lurkers.

But Jezerah. Now there was a mind he could admire. Always on top of the game, always powerful, playing his cards beautifully. K'Thul, even in defeat, had to admire it. Once he'd seen the entire thing play out, he realized that he'd still shoved a sharp stick into Jezerah's mid-section. He'd killed perhaps a quarter of his troops before they'd scattered.

Of course, Jezerah knew the land was meaningless now. K'Thul had to admit, he'd lost a third of his horse in the mine fields that Jezerah's men had somehow known to avoid. He'd lost more men than Jezerah had, almost as many as Emorion had.

He could afford it, though. They could not. The trick was to find the Gate. And eliminate the brother-sister alliance that somehow had arisen from the ashes.

Just like...*she* had. Shaking his head, K'Thul hit his own forehead, drawing a stare from his generals. "Of *course*!" he shouted. "Of course!" The woman had never been an 'agent of the Light'. She was Jezerah's secret weapon. The best lure to those who resisted the Dark was to present them a Dark alternative clothed in 'the Light'.

Jezerah had done just that.

It likely helped precipitate the Battle of Megiddo all those years ago. And the subsequent obliteration of all but Morgaine herself. What a perfect play. Brilliantly executed.

But now, K'Thul was aware of it. Jezerah's treachery had to be dealt with. And deal with it, K'Thul would.

CHAPTER 109

Before dawn, Morgaine slipped out of Nathan's room. He woke up and she gave him a soft kiss before pulling on her nightshirt and slipping away. It hadn't taken her long to fall asleep, but he'd taken quite a long time.

For one thing, they'd never "just slept" together, and she was, in fact, half naked. The most beautiful woman in the world had passed out in his bed half naked. So, it had been with great difficulty that he calmed down, tried to ignore the perfect ass tucked right in the wrong place for calming down, and fallen sleep.

Once she left, he went back asleep and didn't wake up until well after lunchtime. The place was abuzz with activity. Even some of the olive grove farmers…what did you call people who ran a huge orchard of olive trees? A bunch of them were down here, as well. Mostly women.

They seemed to be cleaning and organizing the rooms on the tier below this one for more occupancy. But he saw them everywhere. The kitchens when we went to get some food and some tea. They were in the common rooms, dusting and organizing. Mopping floors in the hallways. It seemed there was an army of them all over. Well, the place would be clean, at least.

Nathan headed back to the "officer's quarters" and went into what appeared to be the common room. It had a large view on monitors of the perimeter outside. It also had a large meeting table, comfortable chairs, a couch, a small bar area with wines and other fermented drink, glasses, and a small cooler or refrigerator.

Nothing was in either the cooler or refrigerator when he checked. But before he could even turn around, one of the many olive grove invaders came in with a large rolling tray of what appeared to be large sausages and bricks of cheese. Nathan couldn't get away from them! As he watched, the woman filled the cooler to the top.

Grabbing a knife he got from a drawer, Nathan cut himself some wedges of the meat and cheese, found a small plate in a cabinet, and poured himself some of the wine. He even found a small cloth that he assumed was some sort of napkin.

He was just finishing up when Maitan, Brianna, Morgaine, and Treyborne all converged on the meeting room. "There you are!" Morgaine said, closing the door. "One of the maids said you were up here. I thought you were still sleeping off your sojourn to the Gate and to our former base to pick these two up!"

Nathan eyed them skeptically from the couch. "What's up? Haven't we fought enough this month? When's the vacation time in this group?"

"I can only assume that is a joke," Morgaine said, pouring some of the wine into a glass and taking a seat at the head of the table. Treyborne took the seat opposite her on the far end. Brianna and Maitan both stood. A finger pointing to a chair between her and Treyborne, and a crooked eyebrow told him he was expected to join them.

Instead of sitting where she pointed, however, he sat on the other side, making a point of taking his time. Sitting down, he leaned back, sighing heavily.

"Ah good. Everyone is here," Morgaine began, ignoring Nathan's slight. "It appears the phase shift has worked a bit too well. If that were possible. They really do believe we just transported it out of there instantly. I'm sure that would be impossible. They can be moved, of course. When we built them back whenever that was, we had to. But they're immensely heavy and quite resistant to movement. Or so I was told. I was too young to be involved."

Morgaine continued, "They should know all this, but it seems their internal bickering and war has gotten them more emotional than contemplative. The result, however, is that we might want to actually try to move it. It would be a gigantic win to have it in our possession. I just never had the drive to when it was dormant. I had hoped it was locked forever."

"So, she asked, "What obstacles do we have to getting there and moving it?"

Treyborne chimed in almost immediately, "Well for one thing, we honestly have no way of ascertaining for sure who won the battle, although it seems likely it was K'Thul's forces that our land cruiser had the … unfortunate encounter with, and that we spotted in the sky cruiser. But the other two could bring forces to bear on that hill again at any time. Any time."

Morgaine asked, "But why would they? There's nothing left to fight for there. As far as they know."

Nathan spoke up, "I'm just curious what you might have to move it in the first place, and how fast can that vehicle go? It would take a railcar… or maybe a semi-trailer in my world. It would also take a usable road or railroad tracks." Realizing those words held no meaning for them, seeing only blank stares, Nathan went quiet again.

Treyborne turned towards him. "That's a reasonable question, Nathan. I *think*…emphasis on think…that we can use the sky cruiser. But we'd be loaded down and couldn't move very fast. We'd have to have some strong cables and we'd be easy targets for far too long. The lower bay of the land cruiser could be opened wide enough to accept it – lying down only. But…it's a gamble either way. The land cruiser doesn't move very fast through the forest, over hills, or over water. Any decent sized force of Dark Men there, and that doesn't work."

"What do we have to gain from moving it, Morgaine," Brianna asked. "Whether they guard it or not, it's still dormant, right?"

"I'm not so sure," Morgaine started, "We have evidence of two people coming through from Nathan's world now. Himself, of course, and his friend Ellie. Nathan is Elder Race, and I believe he somehow triggered it. The question is, how did his friend? She certainly doesn't know, as I've asked her about every way I can."

"And the next time, if someone is right there should someone port over from Nathan's world…again…" Trey began.

"…someone could just portal through from here at the same time," Morgaine finished. "There is a slim possibility it has already happened, and we just don't know about it. When Ellie came through, she said Emorion's Dark Men were all around it."

"It may be why they were fighting so hard for it. But if one of the Dark Lords or even one of their higher underlings got through," Maitan began, "then the plague that is the Cult of the Dark went with him."

"I just cannot risk it staying in their hands," Morgaine said. "Nothing has changed. We simply went in and did as much as we could do with our small team and the forces arrayed against us at the time. Now…*now* the door may be wide open. If K'Thul leaves the area and no one really stays, we might be able to take out any skeleton crew remaining behind and fly right out with it. Once it's secured in a base – as in here – their access to it would be forever limited."

Trey was nodding thoughtfully but was looking at Nathan for some reason. "Hey, don't look at me!" he said, "I'm just the interloper from Planet Nathan!"

Morgaine kept her head down, but the way she went all tight showed this irritated her for some reason.

Sighing, he added, "Look, I'll help, of course. Without the Arc Gate, neither I nor Ellie can go home." Did Morgaine's eyes cut to the side for a second at that....? "And you all helped me rescue her. You didn't have to do that."

"Yes," Morgaine said, looking up at him, "it should allow you access to your home world, should you figure out how to trigger it from here," was all she said, though.

"So…how do we pull off this *next* miracle?" Nathan asked.

CHAPTER 110

K'Thul was still steaming.

He had led his entire army out here from the Empire…pushing them hard for weeks…just to be tricked by Jezerah and Morgaine working together! Looking back one last time at the empty hill, he thought for a moment he saw the Arc standing there.

But…no. It must have been a trick of the setting sun behind the hill. A few of his men would remain behind, salvaging what was left to salvage. They'd done the bulk of that already. They were resupplied, and then some.

His options were: head directly back to the Eastern Empire and sulk… looking weak to his generals and his entire army. Or he could continue forward and crush the insipid Western Empire – who called themselves "The Empire of Nelrae" these days. It was time to take away Jezerah's base once and for all. Then the Eastern Empire would simply become "the Empire".

It had a nice ring to it. Plus, Jezerah's schemes had to come to an end.

And if that little rebel kingdom in the north got in their way, they'd be swept away along with the tide. K'Thul was going to seize his revenge. And Jezerah was going to come begging to share his Arc Gate with him. With no army to lead through that Gate, K'Thul would at worst be needed again. At best, Jezerah would come with his little bitch, and beg at his feet to join him. Either way, this move was clearly the only move to regain his rightful position.

Shaking his head as he rode away, he realized that once again Jezerah had outmaneuvered both himself and Emorion. Well, K'Thul had to admit…Jezerah been top dog for a long while. His understanding of the vastness and power of the Void was incredible. But he still wasn't the deep strategist that K'Thul was. He ignored glaring weaknesses while exploiting key strengths. It kept him on top, but barely. He was very unbalanced. K'Thul would rectify that.

The Triumvirate had survived for over 500 years because it took from each of their core strengths. Now that it was dissolved, if only one would be able to stand, in the end K'Thul was determined it was going to be him.

Keeping Morgaine in his back pocket all these centuries as "the enemy" and waiting to play that card when he absolutely needed it had been sheer brilliance. There was no denying it. He had shown amazing restraint. It also helped explain the number of deaths the Dark Brethren had experienced during the war. With Jezerah's secret aid, the others would be unsuspecting victims. But now that the card had finally been played, K'Thul knew just the right thing to set things right.

Nelrae would bow.

And with it, Jezerah and his bitch. Killing her could wait…. *hmm…* maybe he'd even allow her to service him. She had always been the crown jewel of the Elder Race. A beautiful goddess with a hot temper to match. Perhaps, she could be the jewel in *his* crown. It was a better use for her than acting on emotion and killing her simply because she deserved it a thousand times over. K'Thul would save that for Jezerah. Or Emorion. Utilizing resources was something he was best at. And Morgaine could be a resource now that she had shown her allegiance to the Dark. A beautiful one. Morgaine…would look *nice* on his arm, as ruler of the galaxy's inhabited planets.

Quite nice indeed.

Smiling now, he began leading his army back into the wilderness and towards the forests to the west. His army would slip through those and emerge on the eastern banks of the Empire of Nelrae completely by surprise. With their armies focused on the war in the north, the capital would be laid bare to him.

The Emperor would be dead within a week of their invasion. And then all the power in the world would be in the hands of K'Thul.

CHAPTER III

Maitan spoke up, going to get more wine for those seated as he spoke.

"I'm afraid we have little time to plan, My Lady. The solar chargers on the cloaking devices, coupled with the phase shifters, are surely running out of power. I've overseen those devices and their power cycles for…a very long time. Trust me. We have little time left before the Arc Gate is back in phase and visible. Also, according to the satellite uplinks that are still operational, there is a big storm coming through the area within the next 15-30 hours. You will not want to be hauling a heavy package through the air in that."

"This time, no fireworks. No blaster fire," Trey said. "This time, I suggest we bring in five or six people, keeping the sky cruiser as light as possible. We bring the power cables, and we'll use them as tow ropes. They're made of copper and gold wire, and they're as thick as my thighs. They won't break." He looked up. "I think."

Morgaine nodded at him. "It's the best we can get, I'm afraid. Nathan, you and I should take point again. The phase shifters, assuming they're still powered, must be decoupled first. I'll go over that with you – but it's essentially the reverse of what we did to attach them in the first place, minus adding the power supply. Then we can attach the cable, remove the cloaking devices, and get out. Trey, we'll need at least four others to watch our flanks. I'm afraid we'll need you, Messau, and four others on the ground with us. I think we can hook ourselves to the cable and use the secondary lift hoist to haul us up into the sky cruiser after we're in the air."

Nathan was just watching and listening up to this point. "So, we're just hoping there won't be another ten thousand Dark Men to deal with? We're *assuming* they're going to abandon the hill by the time we arrive?"

Morgaine looked at him for a moment, then nodded. "Indeed. We should plan for some distraction. But they think I 'stole' it two days ago. Why stay? The hill has no value by itself. They won't be expecting it to suddenly just pop up again, or for me to return it. Some residual troops might be there, dealing with bodies, weapons…etc. But if, as we suspect, K'Thul took that hill…his army might be gone entirely. He is nothing short of efficient. I should know…"

Trey looked up under his brows at her at that but said nothing. Brianna spoke up, "May I ask why I'm here? No offense, but this is a war room or a battle plan. I'm a… farm girl dressed up as a maid. What do I add here, Morgaine? Maybe I should go oversee the cleaning of the compound, or…"

Morgaine gave her a level stare. "You are far more than a 'maid', Brianna. You are here because you provide wisdom and insight from a perspective none of the rest of us share. Your title now officially is my 'Assistant'. I believe I informed you that everyone on my team wears many hats. What are your thoughts? What is the weak link in all this, in your opinion?"

"All of it?" Brianna said without hesitation. "The weather is turning awful. So, you're *hoping* it stays good. You could still be facing an army of Dark Men led by one of the Triumvirate trying to get the horrible thing out for real, this time. You're *hoping* they haven't figured out your trick. You're *hoping* they're gone – or mostly gone. You've got a makeshift tow rope that you're *hoping* is going to hold…?" She paused. "Do I need to go on? Like I said, I'm a farm girl. Maybe not stupid, but a farm girl just the same. Practical. And if I were getting sold this bill of goods, I'd demand a refund!"

Morgaine's eyebrows just kept rising throughout. By the time she was done, Morgaine was almost laughing, with a big smile on her face. Shaking her head and looking at her team, she asked, "Ok…our plan has been gutted by our 'farm girl'! Give me other options."

Nathan sighed. "Well crap. She's right. But maybe if we just take a slightly bigger gamble, we can remove some of these other risks, and perhaps add to our hopes of success."

"Go on," Morgaine said, her eyes laughing still.

"Maybe we need to hope that storm *does* come in. What if we wait another 7-10 hours and fly in close and wait for it?"

"What does that accomplish…?" Trey asked. Then we're just making our job ten times more difficult."

"Not necessarily…! If your storms are anything like ours – and I have reason to believe they are, because I had to hide from a couple while making my way to Rondor – it'll be dark. If it's nighttime, it'll be pitch black. Not that that matters to Dark Men, but they'd have to be standing right there for it to matter. If our phase shifters or even just our cloaking devices can't hold for an extra eight hours, it reemerges on its own…in the middle of the night during a storm. No one's going to see it returning anyway! Certainly, no one is going to be next to it singing songs and dancing around it. It'll be returning completely by itself in the dark at night. We sneak in, getting soaked in the process, but with zero interference. The storm should guarantee that if they haven't just completely withdrawn already. Even if we can't fly out with it, we can escape as a unit the same way we came in two days ago. The sky cruiser gets up in the air and, hopefully avoiding any lightning, carries it out in the dark of night, and we catch up down the road."

Morgaine sat back sipping her wine for a few moments. Trey's head was cocked, thinking about it. Brianna spoke up first, "You're still hoping for a lot of perfect conditions, perfect tow cable working…"

"Agreed," Nathan said. "But it does reduce our 'hoping' factors by several notches. The biggest obstacle to making this work isn't the tow cables or anything else, but the high chance we're going to be facing a horde of enemies while trying to tow our car out of the 'hood!"

Blank looks again.

Nathan sighed, leaning forward, and clasping his hands. "Look! Let's assume the worst happens: the Arc Gate returns early. Some, or all, of K'Thul's thugs are still hanging around. Others return. OK. Once that storm comes, they won't be expecting us to just show up and steal it! If the storm is as bad as Maitan indicated…"

Maitan nodded at this.

"Then we have the perfect cover to steal it back. They'll be in their tents, or maybe in the cave to avoid the storm. That's the worst case. The best case is, they have almost no one there, or the area has been completely abandoned. We still just need to get it hooked up and go. Not in broad daylight, where one blaster cannon shot, and we're splattered all over the hillside."

Morgaine's expression was unreadable. She took another drink of wine. "Does anyone else have a better plan…?" Trey sat back shaking his head. Brianna remained silent.

"Then it's settled. We gear up in two hours. Trey, bring your best men. Your best! Messau at the controls, as I want you handling the lift, and if we need rescuing, Trey you're on point. Nathan, Brianna, you're with me."

She got up abruptly, setting her wine glass down half full.

The White Queen had returned.

Once they were out in the hallway, Morgaine turned to Brianna, "You are never to denigrate yourself in my presence again! You are not only now my personal assistant, officially, you have great insight. Now, if you wish to play the servant again for a moment – go and get meals for Nathan and me. We will dine in the conference room once the others leave, as my quarters are not set up yet for that. I'd also like to review the satellite views, plus get some points of our attack wrapped up with Nathan. Get some for yourself, as well. You may need to stay up with Maitan in the event we don't come back all in one piece."

Brianna rushed off to get their food. Morgaine, glancing back at her two shadows – the guards in the hallway – looked up at Nathan and purposefully took his hand, walking down the hallway for a moment to talk privately.

Maitan and Treyborne left the conference room going in opposite directions just as they stopped, so Morgaine just sighed and turned and walked back into the room, with Nathan in tow.

Shutting the door, she pushed herself a bit closer to him, eyes wide. "Your plan is a good one, but it still is hoping for surprise. Pulling the same trick sometimes is the perfect shocker. But with someone like K'Thul…if he even suspects we have reason to come back…he will be ready. Therefore, we must be also. Turning away and moving to sit down, Nathan realized his heart was beating faster and he'd been holding his breath.

The woman was completely mesmerizing.

When she pressed so close…shaking his head, he went to go and sit down next to her in the seat Brianna had vacated a few minutes prior. Grabbing their wine glasses and the carafe off the side table, Nathan refilled them.

"You might want to slow down on the wine," Morgaine said, "we're going to have a long night."

"That's why I'm drinking now. I'll be stone cold sober by the time we even reach our waiting point – wherever that is. Then we'll have to walk through the storm to get to the Arc Gate. There won't be any wine in me by then. Or you. Drink."

She gave him another of those looks. Then she picked up her glass and raised it, "To Brianna's hope."

Nathan saluted, then he took a long drink to drown out the next madness they were about to embark upon.

CHAPTER 113

Emorion lay in his home base bedchambers, boiling. He'd accidentally killed the last two or three slave girls he'd had brought in to distract him. He'd lost track of how many, exactly. Oh well, there were more where those came from.

Jezerah and that little white slut must pay! How long had she truly been on Jezerah's side?

Emorion made his decision.

He would go through the process of making a Hollow Man one more time. It would cost him another thousand or two of his Dark Men to cull the most loyal to the Dark from amongst them. A cost he did not want to pay after losing so many already. But it would work. It always did. He would need one more in reserve to save for Jezerah.

While he was doing his…*experiments*…he would send out every single Hollow Man left on one mission: Slay the Bitch. Together, perhaps they could succeed where the single Hollow Man had always failed. They hated each other almost as much as they hated life itself. It would not be easy for them to work together, by any means.

But for this goal, Emorion was certain he would be able to garner their cooperation. Shrugging, he had to admit, one or more might kill one of the others before or after succeeding in their mission. But that was a price he was more than willing to pay. Killing Morgaine, finally and for good, would accomplish two things: revenge at being tricked, and weakening Jezerah's position.

Morgaine must have been the one to reactivate the portal. The reports of it being reopened by another Elder Race male, appearing after over 500 years were seeming more and more ludicrous by the day. Even if true, and the human girl weren't just a programmed decoy, Morgaine had to be the trigger that created the fallacy. The most believable lie is always the most outrageous. Anything to point away from her. Perhaps when he said he'd killed her, Jezerah had finally turned her to the Dark.

Another nod to Jezerah's treachery.

He truly was the master. Throw in a completely impossible story to cover the opening of the Gate. Something that could not be hidden. Perhaps he didn't know she was doing it until later. But he was the first on site and his people were all working eagerly to supposedly reopen it when Emorion's troops had arrived.

Far more engineers than should have been necessary. Far too few Dark Men regulars.

In retrospect, however, it all seemed very simple. Distract and act like you didn't know. Emorion had done well to take the land, knowing what he knew now. But perhaps that was why Jezerah had left it so poorly defended in the first place.

If they were planning to move it and have the White Bitch steal it, all along, then why defend it? Jezerah could act just as shocked and revolted, all the while having the Gate all to himself. They'd all be "searching" for Morgaine's whereabouts to find the Arc Gate, while Jezerah himself would be funneling all his power and armies through the Gate to set up his kingdom in any number of new worlds.

Emorion had underestimated Jezerah.

Again.

This time, Emorion was going to go for his throat. Never again would he be played like a fluted windpipe. Never again would he be so thoroughly beaten. All Emorion's power must be played. All his guile put to the ultimate test.

Emorion admittedly may have lost this most recent battle – but he was determined to win the war. After the little white slut was dead, he'd turn the Hollow Men left on Jezerah. Assuming there were enough of them left to do the job. Hence the need for the experiments.

It was time to begin.

CHAPTER 114

"I'm getting a little tired of sitting in this airship!" Nathan said to Morgaine as they sat next to each other *en route* to the landing zone.

"I'm sure," she said drily.

The satellites all showed the same picture: the storm was going to hit the Gate hill around 0050, approximately 3 hours before dawn. It had come faster than expected. Nathan was still getting used to their way of timekeeping. It was still odd to him. But it made more sense, really. 100-minute hours and all. But it was just simply not what he was used to.

Nonetheless, they were going to be landing in the middle of the night, in a torrential downpour with tons of lightning. *Super*. If you liked being buffeted by high winds, soaked in seconds, and risking being struck by 300 million volts of lightning. At about 30,000 Amps.

Morgaine was acting more and more…*different*. She was openly holding his hand in front of the guards. She was even leaning on his shoulder like she had awhile back. Nathan had to admit, it felt good. Morgaine was just the most captivating woman he'd ever met.

But it still felt odd. She was just so…. *alien* sometimes. Alien even for a female, which from his perspective, was like saying "alien squared". Of course…she was, in fact, an alien. Can't blame her for that. The miles flew by, and the night grew dark. Nathan fell asleep leaning on Morgaine's head.

Nathan awoke to the air brakes, once again…now a familiar sound. It had already started to rain as they landed. The hatch opened, and everyone got out, except Messau and Trey in the pilot box. Shouldering their packs, including clamps to help attach the cabling, emergency power packs, blasters, and Nathan's shock-lance, they headed out. Both teams were going to go the same route but take different sides of the Arc Gate once they got to it. They were all wearing black and had only directional lights to point at the ground, so they didn't fall off a cliff or into a hole as they ran. Pulling hoods up over their heads, they began to make their way to the Gate.

There was no resistance. No rear guard. No ambush points…each time they slowed down to circle a potential hot spot, nothing came of it. Nathan couldn't see Morgaine's face, but he could sense her tension. But the medallion was dark also. No Dark Men were nearby.

The rain was torrential and coming down in sheets.

Morgaine was clearly concerned that K'Thul suspected they were coming. If he had, according to her, he'd leave the trap wide open. It would have been better had they found the occasional Dark Man duo waiting somewhere. This was spooky. But after making it almost three miles in, nothing had changed. Except that the rain was coming harder and harder, lightning flickering over the entire sky.

Morgaine had given Nathan their one-on-one comms again. *"Maybe we didn't need to do this during the storm…!"*

"And maybe it's a trap. I know. Either way, it's unlikely they'll be looking for us in the hot mess this is turning into. Let's just stay on script. If they're really all gone, this should be relatively fast and painless."

"Agreed."

Nathan saw her draw her sword out, though. It glinted enough in their walking lights, crystals sparkling for a moment before it went out of sight.

"How much further? I can't read the metrics on these wristbands…?"

"Only about three or four more minutes." On the general comm, she added, *"Trey and Messau, get that bird in the air! We will need you soon enough, either way."*

They traveled in silence the rest of the way, even cutting their lights once they got within a mile or so of the hill. Goggles with IR went back on, but with the rain, it wasn't easy to pick out the way. They'd been soaked within minutes and the rain hadn't slowed down. If anything, it was getting worse.

Lightning was now striking all around, and that only added to the confusion of the goggles. But eventually, the team made its way to the side of the hill. Just above them and to the right was the clearing with the Arc Gate. Morgaine had led the way this entire time, so when she held up her hand, a lightning strike revealed the Arc Gate, clearly no longer cloaked nor being phased.

How long that had been the case, was anybody's guess. But the need to move became readily apparent. Going around the hill and a bit downhill until this point, they now had to try going uphill a bit onto the plateau holding the Gate.

But the torrential rain and water flow had turned the entire area into one huge mudslide. Attempts to go straight up, as they had during the fight, was impossible. They were forced to take the long way around, where the hill sloped down towards the riverbank.

Days ago, this had been where the heart of Emorion's camp had been. Now, it was a jumble of mud, trampled grass, and puddles. But they were able to walk here, albeit slowly. No one was here. Not a soul appeared.

Another series of lightning blasts across the river and heat lightning showed the area completely clear, except for the Gate itself. The Gate seemed to be pulsing in the storm. Clearly, the dark crystals within it were getting charged or something from all the electricity in the air.

The entire face of it was glowing in little flecks and pieces. Like a piece of the cosmos had appeared, and the stars were glistening everywhere in various strength.

On the general comm, Morgaine said, *"Three to each side! Recover the cloaking devices and phase packs. Assuming this isn't still some sort of elaborate trap. If anyone appears, shout it out and defend your team."*

With that, she and her two guards sprinted across the muddy field, heading for the far side of the Gate. Nathan and his team went to their side. Not that they were incredibly distant. Maybe a total of thirty-five or forty feet apart. But it was enough in this to barely see them.

Within seconds, they got to work. Nathan tried to remove the apparatus just as Morgaine had instructed him. The equipment was still there. Nothing had been touched from where he'd left it. Shaking his head, he couldn't believe their good fortune.

"Sky bird is in position, Morgaine! Dropping cables. We've already given the shackle hooks enough length that you should be able to wrap and grab! As we lift it, the cables will travel up a bit as the tension hits and due to the slighter size, slide towards the top. But they should hold."

"Equipment off, waiting on the cables," came her response.

Within a few more minutes, they had the cables looped and the massive shackles they'd adapted to fit over the cables to turn them into cinches were in place.

"Ready to lift, Captain. Take her up slowly…"

"Check that, Mistress! Here we go…!"

The cables cinched tight and moved up the Arc towards the top. The Arc Gate began to lift off the ground. The cables strained but held.

Nathan was looking up watching, when his necklace suddenly flared as bright as a flash of lightning, nearly burning his chest with the heat.

"Morgaine…! My medallion is suddenly on fire! What does…"

An inhuman shriek came back over the comms. Whipping his head around, Nathan could make out nothing, despite the lights from the sky cruiser shining down in a tight beam on the cables.

Racing over there, Nathan pulled out his blaster, not knowing what a shock-lance might attract in a thunderstorm. He also threw off his goggles and flicked on his light. What he found was both guards face down in the mud, and Morgaine, lying face up, eyes staring, wheezing, and covered in blood. Her sword lay by her hand. It was only then that he saw what appeared to be where another man had fallen right where her sword lay, clearly having made an impact on the ground in the mud. There was no blood, however, nor any tracks coming or going. It seemed as if she'd stabbed someone who then had fallen, perhaps even died. But whoever or whatever it was, it had shed no blood and the body was no longer there. If the man had gotten up, he'd had to have flown away.

Nathan had no time for any more thought, however, as with every breath Morgaine was bleeding out from three massive wounds in her abdomen.

Her eyes were wide in fear, and she was clearly going into shock. The two men behind him suddenly were in a fight, yelling and firing their blasters.

"Hang on! I'll get you out of here!" Nathan screamed above the noise of the fight and the storm.

His medallion went white hot again and Nathan suddenly felt the need to duck and roll. Pulling up his shock-lance as the roll had dislodged his blaster, Nathan saw a man enveloped in the shadows, holding a long *Djune* like those used by Morgaine's men. The blade seemed to be held by a shadow itself. His light had almost no effect in aiding him seeing the man.

He held out his hand and a white flare shot out from the gemstone, blinding him for a moment.

When he could see again, the man was gone. Nathan looked around wildly. The guards with him had stopped firing, as well. One of them, holding his side.

"What's going on down there?" Trey demanded. *"I thought I heard blaster fire. Does anyone have a read? What's your status?"*

"Two men down, Trey." Nathan responded, *"Two wounded. And Morgaine is hurt bad, Trey. Really bad. She's bleeding from multiple wounds. I'm not sure who hit her team, or how many. I only saw one and he's gone. We've got to get her out of here. And I mean now!"*

In seconds, Trey was down, blaster rifle in hand via his anti-gravity boots. Morgaine had passed out. Nathan hoped she wasn't already dead. Trey had brought medical supplies and was wrapping her abdomen as best he could in the rain. The monolith had stopped being pulled up, hanging about twenty feet off the ground.

Morgaine's two guards were dead, gutted as she had been. Nathan hadn't even known their names, although he recognized them. The guard that had been with him was indeed also bleeding from a huge gash in his side that had cut him right through his armor. It all seemed surreal. A half dozen thin cables came down.

Nathan and the healthy guard wrapped the wounded guard up and tugged. They then wrapped up the men who were already dead, tugging again. Trey had finished wrapping Morgaine's wounds, checked for life signs, and then another line was pulling them up seconds later, Trey holding her body tight to his own.

"I should have been with her! I should have been down here!" he shouted as they were lifted up together.

Nathan was feeling just as helpless. Tugging his own cable, he began to rise steadily. The last guard standing from his team did the same.

It was going so well. What did we miss? What happened…? What went wrong? And why weren't there more of them, if they were waiting for us to return to the Gate?

Then it occurred to him.

They weren't here to stop the Arc Gate from being taken, they probably didn't even know we were here or what we were doing…or that could easily have been stopped, as well. Whoever it was, they were here for Morgaine. They'd come here for Morgaine. And her alone.

Just then several lightning blasts struck all around them. Another white hot flash enveloped him, and Nathan screamed in pain.

The world flashed in reverse.

CHAPTER 115

Ellie was sipping some tea and trying to focus on eating her breakfast. She had just been informed this morning that Nathan, the crazy white-haired lady (that woman was too pretty), and her team had gone on yet another foray to the Gate. Her maid was tight-lipped about it. But it seemed they had unfinished business there. Nathan had turned into some sort of Airborne Ranger, apparently.

Oh well. His life.

Ellie was grateful Nathan and his team of otherworld troops had come for her. But the how and why was beyond her. Still utilizing the translator clip, she was able to not only understand what was being said but hear better than she could with her normal hearing.

Everyone was talking about the sudden trip. Apparently, it was going to be even more risky than the mission to go rescue her. That didn't sound good. The cooks and all the staff, who were all around her as she ate, could talk of little else. Even the guards in the corner that were apparently assigned to her were yapping about it. They followed her everywhere, but never talked to her directly.

She hated them.

They made her still feel like a prisoner again. She understood they were likely just to keep her safe and make sure nothing else happened to her in this unfamiliar underground bunker in an unfamiliar world.

But come on! Give a girl a break!

It was worrisome, though. Nathan could die out there. She wanted to talk with him – tell him she was truly sorry. All of that. Closure. Of course, there was the small matter of getting home. Finding out Nathan wasn't instantly vaporized by the monolith was one thing. But having to live the rest of her life because she kept looking for him was another. He was, after all, her ex.

Scrubbing her hands in her hair, Ellie realized she hadn't gotten a proper shower since getting to this base. She'd slept, washed her face, ate, slept some more…slept a bit more after that. Ate some more…and here she was. Usually, she kept herself clean. Immaculately so. Being a prisoner had shoved that into a deep hole. Getting up, surreptitiously sniffing her armpits, she decided she definitely needed to clean up. Stopping one of the wait staff, she asked, "How and where do I shower or…?"

"Oh, I show you!" said the woman. Diminutive and stout, she moved fast despite that. Up the elevator and to her rooms, she showed Ellie where the showers were on her floor, and even showed her how to use them. There were also baths, she said, down in the lower quarters.

"A shower will do, thanks," she said. "Uh…. where's the soap…?" After showing Ellie where the soaps, washcloths, spray nozzles, towels, and 'optional air dryers' were, she left.

Ellie shut and locked the door, even though this shower room had four bays. The guards were out there, of course. But she didn't want just anyone wandering in, either. Having grabbed some fresh, clean clothes they'd given her from her room, Ellie hopped into the shower.

It felt heavenly. The water was just a bit too hot, the soap was divine, and Ellie got dirt out of spaces she didn't even know it had gotten into. A very long time and much steam in the room later, she stepped out, deciding to try the 'optional air dryers' and found it quite lovely. It even helped dry her hair, although she hadn't brushed it yet, it was short and straight enough she'd be able to fix it with the brush in her room later.

Sighing in satisfaction, she dressed in the clothing she'd been given. The 'panties' were a bit grandmotherly. The loose-fitting pants didn't fit quite right – but had a nice tie inside the belt – and the blouse was downright huge. Oh well, nightshirt.

Feeling tired again, she opened the shower door and saw her guards dutifully standing on either side of the shower room, waiting for her. Nodding to them, she realized her hair was still fairly wet when some droplets struck one of the guard's pants.

"Sorry!" she said, hurrying to her room. Shutting the door behind her, she grabbed the huge brush she'd been given, and worked to get the knots out of her hair.

Realizing she'd left her dirty clothes in the shower room; she opened the door just as the far door of the hallway burst open.

Racing down the hallway was that burly commander pushing a gurney at full speed with another man on the other side. The other man was holding a fluid bag up, while the commander was yelling, "Hang on!"

Fear gripped Ellie's gut. *Nathan!?*

But no, as the gurney raced by and the other hallway door blasted open, she saw it was the crazy lady…Morgaine. Ellie felt guilty feeling relief at it not being Nathan. The white-haired woman looked to be in bad shape. For the first time, Ellie realized the room at the end of this hall led straight into a major medical room with all sorts of equipment, another bed and what appeared to be a surgery table.

As the dual doors closed, Ellie shouted, "Where's Nathan?"

No one answered her. The fear was back.

What if he's dead? What if he never comes back? What if I can never go home…??

CHAPTER 116

Gary and Jenn had been staying at Ben's farmhouse for two days, and both were getting a little restless. Jenn had called in sick, as she was not "wanted for questioning," like Gary was. But she had called from a burner phone she'd picked up in town yesterday, just in case. Apologizing for not calling the day before due to "…excessive vomiting…".

Their boss Andy hadn't even bothered to ask when she'd be in. He just said, "No worries, we're slow today anyway. And…we've got other things going on right now." He didn't go into details, and Jennifer didn't want to ask and get caught in a lie. So, she'd just hung up and dumped the thing in the nearest trash receptacle.

Borrowing Ben's car and using cash, she'd also bought herself some extra panties, a shirt, and some toiletries. Ben's wife was a much larger woman, apparently, and regardless she wasn't going to wear any other woman's panties. Ever.

Eww.

She also had worn a hat just in case there was some facial recognition stuff going on, and that she was secretly also being hunted. Gary just stayed low, hanging out in the house most of the time.

Ben was great. He was not only Gary's childhood friend, but a cool guy. Funny, bright, hard-working. They'd all gone out the next night and just stared at the monstrous monolith in the huge barn.

"We could just leave it in your barn awhile…" Gary suggested. But Ben would have none of it. "I wouldn't mind, you know that. But Terri…she'd have a fit. We'd be "aiding and abetting". Not that this is new for me," he chuckled. "But it's new to her. And I've got the kids to think about."

"I understand," Gary said. And he clearly did. They'd cooked out on Ben's huge deck. There were zero neighbors for miles, and a creek with some beautiful trees butted up to his property line. It was idyllic. Except for Gary wearing a hat down low the entire time, and Jenn getting mild chills from the very late autumn wind.

Doesn't December really mean 'winter', anyway?

By the next morning, though, Ben was getting a little anxious. "Terri wants to know when you might be…able to leave. She said they're just missing pre-school stuff now, but they usually only stay with the grandparents two or three days. So, if they stay too much longer, there might be questions she would be unprepared to answer. Like, 'is everything ok at home', or 'what's up that you can't go home'?"

"I get it," Gary answered. "Jenn, you should just take a bus and get back to the city. You can go back to work and claim you and I aren't that close. Maybe add in that I went a little bonkers once my roommate and best friend – sorry, Ben – went missing."

Ben just put a hand up and smiled.

Cool dude.

Jennifer considered. "I really do need that job. And even though I texted my roommates that I'm out of town visiting my mom…it would be weird if I didn't go back soon." Her face looked pained. "I don't want to leave you, though…! I feel some of this is my fault. Like, I should've said, 'No way should we take that huge black monolith, Gary!'"

Gary chuckled. "This was all me, Jennifer. Plus, I'd feel sick if you really got tied up in it. I've done my fair share of duplicitous things…it serves me right if I get caught for something now. I'm not intending to get caught," he added quickly, when she took in a big breath.

"You'd better not!" she said.

"I'm not…but…just sayin'. Now, Ben, is there some warehouse storage or deserted farmland somewhere that I could throw this thing for now? I mean…it was outside for ages supposedly at some point, before getting buried in a tomb for another bundle of them."

Ben started to shake his head slowly, then, "Wait! You know, the old Benson farm hasn't had tenants or anything for almost three years! Their fields are worked in the summertime, but their barn isn't being used and is all locked up. Nothing two former juvenile delinquents couldn't handle!" he said, smiling broadly. "Let's move it over there tonight. Then, at least, you can try to get some help with the 'wanted for questioning' part of the story…"

"Yeah, and you could have your life back," Gary added. "I also would have the negotiating chip of having the knowledge of where the thing is in case I need it. And I might need it."

Jennifer looked worried. Gary could be facing federal charges. Something in her felt very sick about that. It hurt. She knew she cared for Gary, but she'd always had…*feelings* for Nathan. Now…now she was just confused. She wanted Nathan to come back. But Gary…there was something about Gary. He was just so cute, and cuddly. It had taken her awhile to get to sleep with him so close last night. He'd fallen asleep almost immediately.

Men!

But she had had to will herself to think of him as a big, warm blanket.

The memory was still fresh in her mind.

"Jenn?"

Startled her out of her reverie, she just said, "Hmm…? Sorry, got lost in thought. What did you say?"

"Uh…. never mind!"

Ben was laughing out loud this time. "You guys are hilarious. Hey, what was that?"

A bang suddenly rang outside. Followed by several more. Gary looked up at him, "That sounded like it came from…"

"The barn!" they all said in unison.

CHAPTER 117

Nathan awoke...slowly. His body ached all over. Looking down, he saw that much of his clothing under his body armor had been shredded. The shock-lance looked like it had snapped in half, with a big black burn hole in the middle.

What...happened...? Still very groggy, Nathan, turned over and slowly crawled to his hands and knees...

Is that...hay?

Looking around from his position on the ground, he couldn't see much from where he had been lying. "Is this...a barn?!" he said out loud, as he slowly got to his feet.

Finally able to stand, Nathan leaned on a nearby hay bale. Dizzily turning his head, he saw the Arc Gate, sitting on a riser or something in the back of the building he was in. But...did the compound have a barn like... this? It looked more like a barn one would find in upstate New York. Some brick base with wood structure built onto it. Some, of course, were just all bright red painted wood. This one would fit right in.

I suppose the olive grove farmers have horses and a barn...but why did they leave the Arc Gate and me... in a barn? I mean, we were hit by lightning. I'm pretty sure. Judging from that shock-lance, I'd have to say, 'very sure'. Did they think I was dead...? Was it because...

"Morgaine!" Nathan yelled, running to the nearest door. It was locked from the outside.

What the hell?!

Banging on the barn doors brought no one. Something was odd. This… barn…looking around again – really looking – he saw a tractor wheel. It had a *John Deere* imprint. The shovels and all the tools looked like they were from home. Running over and leaping up on the tarp-covered pile that hid the "riser" the Arc Gate was sitting on…

"Holy shit!" Nathan said, stumbling as he jumped down on the other side. "That's not a riser. It's a fucking semi!" Looking around some more, he saw the guard who'd been getting pulled up with him. *Stanslin.* He wasn't moving. Or breathing. His face and hair looked burnt; eyes open.

"Holy shit…" Nathan said, flopping down on a hay bale. "I'm home. And if I got struck by lightning, so did they! It must have triggered the Gate, sending whoever was in front of it here."

God knows how I even survived. Stanslin sure as hell didn't. Maybe…that crazy electricity absorption I acquired while there, but…who knows?

Standing up; Nathan's mind fuzziness began receding. "Why is the monolith stuck in a barn…? How did it get here from the museum?" Fear that he might have traveled to yet a different world got quelled a bit remembering the semi (it was a Peterbilt) and the tractor tire (John Deere). All this meant 'Earth'. Nathan's heart hurt at the thought of Morgaine possibly dead.

And Ellie! She's still stuck back there…!

It was just too much to handle. *'Portaling'*, or whatever it was called, did seem to leave one in a bit of a brain fog. Or maybe that was just from the lightning bolt. Nathan realized his ears still were ringing a bit. And he was severely dizzy, to boot.

Going over to the barn doors, he found them just as locked as the other door – from the outside. Heading to a nearby tool rack, Nathan grabbed a shovel and started hitting the door as hard as he could. Either his accidental captors were going to come let him out, or he was going to break the barn doors down. Either way, he was going to get out. After all, he did still have his blaster.

I hope that works, at least.

CHAPTER 118

"It is done, Master…" came the voice from the shadows. *"The White Witch is dead."*

Emorion was sitting in the darkness of his office. A vast, complex web of monitors, communications, and displays of his trophies from past wars…mummified heads of former kings and nobles.

"You are certain? The woman died in front of you…?" Emorion asked quietly.

There was…interference after we jumped her and her men, but yes. I am certain of it. She killed O'Lesh immediately. The woman moved like lightning. Her reputation was deserved. But the rest of us…we all landed home. She managed to avoid getting stabbed directly in the heart, even from me – and I was directly behind her – but she was skewered through her belly by all of us."

"And…the 'interference'?" Emorion asked calmly.

"There was another…Elder Race man. I did not recognize him. He wore the Corillion medallion, Master. He avoided our blows with ease. He also managed to…eliminate…the others. I alone escaped. We left the woman bleeding on the ground. I felt her heart stop as I left."

"So…at least that much of the fable is true. What can you tell me of him?" Emorion sat forward, engaged for the first time.

Morgaine is dead! Let the Dark rejoice!

"He is tall, muscular, a bit thin…I was not around for the wars, Master. As you well know. But from your descriptions, I would say he was most definitely of the Elder Race. Lost, of course. But not a hybrid. He had the eyes. I saw them flash when he struck Kraan."

"How…unfortunate your brothers didn't survive. Perhaps they could have told me more of him."

"Yes…unfortunate…" his glee was clear.

Ah well, the price of victory. Soon enough, he would have another.

"To the death of the White Witch" he said, raising a toast to himself. The Hollow Men did not drink. Or eat, for that matter. Sustained by the Void itself.

They were the perfect assassins.

"Leave me! I have my next phase of planning to do." Emorion felt, rather than saw, the Hollow Man leave. Nodding to himself, he allowed a moment of reflection. How many centuries had that woman tortured him?

Far too many…

A weight had been removed from his shoulders. If he were the type, he would have started humming to himself. But of course…he was not.

He was *Emorion*.

CHAPTER 119

Morgaine died not once that night. But three times.

Each time, Trey – and then Maitan – got her heart pumping again. Critical blood loss had been supplemented by stores of her own blood. Maitan had blessedly packed a blood pint for each of them in the med cooler before they'd left. Everyone but Nathan, of course. He'd not been there long enough. So, Maitan had packed two for Morgaine.

Trey had to wonder if that was an accident. Divine Providence? Or premonition? The *Biaki Mor* were said to have prophetic insights. It had helped them fight in the wars, long before Treyborne or even his grandfather's grandfather had been born. Until they were all gone. Maitan was descended from those warriors. Either way, it was the Creator's own Grace that she had had that extra blood.

As soon as he got her on board, he'd started working on her. The reserve had barely started pumping when the lightning struck. Then all hell had broken loose. Morgaine was alive again, to be sure. Aided perhaps in part by that very stroke of lightning.

Could that have been the Creator's doing, too?

Yinsen had just gotten pulled up, bleeding from a nasty wound himself. After the strike, Yinsen didn't move again.

And then Messau had just tried to keep them in the air. Comms went down, and the sky cruiser was reeling. They managed to get out of the area a few clicks before Trey even realized the cables holding Nathan and Stanslin had been severed. Apparently by the strike.

They had held onto the Arc Gate as long as they could. Finally, "setting it down" a few miles away in the forest. More like half-dropping it into the mud. It had just been way too heavy – at least after the lightning strike had scrambled half their scopes and equipment.

Morgaine hadn't died again until they'd reached the landing bay. Trey had sutured her up as best he could, but she was still bleeding internally. Another cardiac arrest – and Maitan was there.

The man performs miracles.

They'd communicated with the individual comm taken from Yinsen's corpse. His was completely undamaged somehow. The sky cruiser comms had been completely blown, along with all other individual ones. So Maitan being there with more blood and all that equipment was another near miracle.

She was revived a third time after they reached the surgery room on Floor 3. It was the best one, with the most equipment. Maitan had just finished cleaning it that morning. Another fortuitous event.

Currently, Morgaine was breathing (with aid), had enough blood, and hadn't gone into cardiac arrest for over 10 hours. Maitan literally stood by her side, talking with her, praying over her…even smoothing her hair and brewing her some tea "just so she could smell it". Not only did he not sleep for all those hours, he hadn't even sat down. Brianna was sitting in the corner of the hall, just watching everyone.

She hadn't even looked up at him when he'd gone by her.

Trey was sitting down himself now. His body armor had blood all over it. Mostly Morgaine's. A little of Yinsen's from when he'd ripped the comm out of his ear.

Even Messau hadn't escaped injury. He'd held onto the controls right through the strike and had severe burns on his hands and up his arms.

Maitan didn't even look at them for hours. Messau hadn't either. He'd just wrapped them with cloths and started drinking. He hadn't stopped until he passed out on the hallway floor outside the surgery center. Maitan got to him right before he was completely gone. Then he'd run right back in to be with Morgaine.

No one left the hallway that night. Even the alien girl, Ellie, once she found out Morgaine had died repeatedly, had stayed with the rest of them in the hall all night. Maybe she just didn't want to seem callous. Every one of the remaining guards had come and sat down. Some of them even drank with Messau. But none of the others passed out. Technically, they were still on duty.

They would have been forgiven for doing so. Messau most assuredly was. Trey had been burned like that once. It was agony. As was the thought of losing Morgaine.

About 0500, Maitan came out and said, "She is awake. But she is very weak. She is asking for you, Captain." He stopped him with his hand, in complete command, "Be brief. She could still die from her wounds. If she does, I fear I won't be able to revive her a fourth time."

Treyborne just nodded, walking in.

Morgaine's eyes were slits. Her voice came out cracked and thin, "Don't you look dapper!" she said, coughing at the effort of making the simple joke.

"Easy, easy, Morgaine!" he said, laying his hand on her arm. "You gave us quite a scare. I'm shocked you're even awake."

"I have always been…resilient. You know that." she answered.

He just nodded. "What of the Arc Gate? And what happened to Nathan and the others…?" she asked quietly. Trey looked at her. Her eyes were sharp, even though barely open. He didn't want to lie to her. But he didn't want to shock her into dying again, either.

He hesitated.

"Captain…I'm giving you an order to answer me."

"Honest answer is I don't know, Morgaine. How much do you remember?"

"Enough. We were about to haul the Arc Gate out, then I was suddenly surrounded by…Hollow Men!"

This was news to Trey, "What? I never knew they worked as a team! How is that possible? I thought you said they were … 'so full of hate they hated even themselves'. In the multiple attacks on you, was there ever more than one?"

"Never. Not until today."

Trey whistled. "Wow…you really pissed someone off this time, Morgaine."

"Not 'someone' – Emorion. They are his creations, and his alone. He's given them as gifts for things he's wanted. The Dark Men used to speak in awe of them. And him. It's also probably why the others didn't ever use them much. It's hard to trust in their world."

"Ok…so you pissed *Emorion* off. Why now? He was going to lose the Arc Gate to someone that day, anyway. Jezerah and ultimately K'Thul were pouncing on him, right?

"True…but you're avoiding the question. Where are Nathan and the Gate? Not being sure is not having any idea…"

Damn the woman! Even drugged and half dead, she was too sharp for her own good.

Clenching his jaws, he said, "We were struck by lightning, Morgaine. Nathan and Stanslin weren't in the sky cruiser yet. I think they fell. I don't know how far, or if they survived. The place was receiving multiple lightning strikes, and we were hauling around a giant lightning rod with us!"

"Messau, despite burning his hands to cinders, managed to keep us in the air. But we were reeling. We got the ship stabilized but had to set the Arc Gate down again. Maybe three or four clicks from the original spot – deep in the woods."

Morgaine's lidded eyes were like stone.

"By the time I even realized Nathan and Stanslin were missing, we were already two minutes from the site. I was kind of busy, don't you know? Someone was in the process of bleeding out and going into cardiac arrest. I won't mention who…"

She nodded slowly, closing her eyes for a moment. "So, Nathan and Stanslin are likely casualties, as well. We three are the only survivors. And the Gate is not in our possession."

Treyborne could only nod. He almost choked on it. So many had died. And he had failed. "I think I should…"

"Shut up, Trey. You're not resigning," she said, reading his mind. "Get my remaining men battle ready. Take as many of the new hires as you dare. Fix that sky cruiser and make her safe again, then go get me that Gate! If it's all I have left from this disaster, it will have to be enough."

CHAPTER 120

His back fully healed, Smyslin trudged slowly through the lower chambers of the complex. They'd shown him how to get outside, but he didn't want to see the sunlight. He just wanted to see the Master. They had a connection, the Master and him. And now that connection was gone. It felt like the Master had died.

The big Captain of the Lost One…*Morgaine's*…forces even said it was likely he had died. Smyslin believed it. The Hymn of Mourning was ever escaping from his throat. Apparently, it annoyed others, so Smyslin walked the darkened walkways beneath the others.

He was utterly alone.

A strange hum was coming from one of the doorways as he passed it. Had that been there before? He'd passed this way several times, wandering. Or had he? All these passages and doors looked alike.

Pushing the doorway open, he found several panels and monitors lit up. A few of them had fuzzy pictures. One was blank. It appeared to be monitors of all the personnel rooms and hallways on the upper floors.

Suddenly, Smyslin stopped dead still. A Creeper! It was showing up on one of the surveillance cameras. It was in the upper hallways. Someone had to be watching! There were two guards there outside the Lady Morgaine's chambers…!

But Smyslin could tell. These men were blind to it. It had veiled their sight with its power. The Dark could always cover the light. At least they all believed that. Smyslin was not so sure anymore.

The Creepers were strange things. But they only had one mission: kill all they could find. Smyslin started to run, yelling long before anyone could hear him. Dark Men could run as fast as a horse could run – when powered by the Dark. Smyslin no longer was, and he found this running on his own power difficult. Even tedious.

He was nearly exhausted when he burst upon the first floor with any guards, "Guar…..guards!! The Mistress! She…she is in danger! Run…! Go….!" He was gasping for air, but he was gesturing wildly. The two guards in the hallway looked at each other – then they began to run.

Hands on his knees, Smyslin finally leaned back against the wall, drinking in air. After a few moments, a woman from the kitchens came up meekly, offering him a glass of water. He gulped it down completely before thanking her. She left and brought him some more. The woman smiled at him warmly. He smiled back. Then he gulped down that water, as well.

If only the Dark had left him the ability to run. Couldn't an old man be left with something?

CHAPTER 121

The banging was coming from inside the barn. And the banging on the barn door didn't stop. Ben and Gary ran out, just staring at each other. Jennifer right behind them.

"I thought you locked…"

"I did!" shouted Ben over the banging.

"Hello! Stop hitting the doors!"

The banging suddenly stopped. "Let me out!" came a muffled voice.

"Who are you? Why should we?" asked Gary.

"Open the doors, or I'll blast them open. Your call," came the voice.

Ben said, "Give me a minute," and ran into the house.

The voice responded, "You've got one minute."

Jennifer whispered, "How did someone get into the barn but can't get out?"

Gary just shrugged. He knew Ben. Sure enough, he came out loading his shotgun, then cocked it. Throwing Gary the keys to the padlock on the chain, he pulled up the gun, holding it ready. He nodded.

Gary began to unlock the lock, then pulled the chain off.

"Come out slowly!" Ben yelled. "I'm armed."

"So am I. You want to see who wins? Just back off and let me out and no one gets hurt…!"

Ben shot an alarmed glance at Gary, who just shrugged and whispered, "I'm getting the hell away. Just tell whoever it is that it's your property and you're just being cautious."

Ben nodded, "Look. You're on my property! I don't want to shoot anybody, and I'm sure you don't, either. Just don't point at me, and I won't point at you…come out and let's talk. Slowly, if you would."

"Fine…" came the response. Gary looked at Jennifer, whose face was bemused.

Could that be…?

"Nathan!!!!" Jennifer yelled, running into his arms as he emerged from the barn. He did indeed have a pistol of some type, which he quickly put into a holster at his side…a *holster*…?

Jennifer was still hugging Nathan, who was half laughing, half trying to peel her off him. Gary came up and hugged them both, rather than waiting for his turn.

When they finally pulled back, Ben said, "You must be Nathan…"

Nathan looked over at him, nodding. "Good guess. Thank you for not shooting me. And from the pictures on Gary's desk, you must be Ben…" Setting his gun down and leaning it against the tires stacked there, Ben nodded and went to shake his hand.

Gary stepped back, looking perplexed. "Nathan…if you don't mind me asking…what the fuck are you wearing??" Jennifer chuckled, then really looked at him.

Nathan's head went back, and he let out a huge sigh. "I'm home," he began…

"You're home!!" Jennifer half-screamed, leaping on him and wrapping her legs around him again.

"Jennifer, Gary, it's great to see you, truly. And you're a sight for sore eyes. And…I'm sure you've got questions. But I have some, too. And, frankly, I'm exhausted."

Looking at Ben, he asked, "Can we go inside? It's cold out here… and we'd better lock this back up again. Just in case the next person to come out isn't as friendly."

Ben gave him an odd look, then quickly picked up the chain, shutting the barn doors and locking the lock again with the chain once again in place, pocketing his keyes. Then they all went inside. Beers were passed around, and Nathan sat down in the nearest chair.

Jennifer was overjoyed, and not hiding it at all. She didn't even care. Her beautiful green eyes tearing up as she looked at him.

He looks so…tired and worn down! Well, of course he is! He just spent a month or more in … well…somewhere else!

Gary and Ben sat down on the couch, Nathan in the chair opposite them across the coffee table, and Jennifer sat in the only other vacant chair in between.

After a few sips, Gary asked again, "So…what's with the outfit, Nathan? You look like you just popped out of a Halo game! And your clothes look shredded! That gun isn't standard issue Glock either. Where did the monolith take you?"

Nathan smiled a grim smile, looking at his friend. "You are good with words, Gary. I wish I could do that! OK…first things, first. I think where I went is called 'Arth', not 'Earth'. Not sure if that's a coincidence, or what. Yes, this is body armor. It's light and takes a beating. The people I was with…we were in a fight…we'd already gotten Ellie back…"

"Ellie? She was with you?" Gary asked.

Nathan nodded. "She was. For a minute. She was being held captive and the…people I was with, they helped me get her back. We got her to safety, but we'd left something…actually…a big something. That world's monolith – they call it an 'Arc Gate' – in the hands of Ellie's captors. Mor… uh, their leader wasn't going to stand for that. Plus, Ellie and I needed it to return. So, we went back in. They'd helped me get Ellie, so I went to help them."

Nathan shook his head.

Gary chimed in, "It went badly?" he asked gently.

Nathan nodded, head down. "It went badly. It had taken me weeks to find these people. I won't go into details right now," he said, looking up. "But there was a horrific storm. Their leader – someone I care about – got hurt really bad. Then when we were getting airlifted out, we got struck by lightning."

"You got struck by lightning?!" Jennifer said, her voice quavering. *'Someone I care about'…? Why did that have to sound like…no! Stop it! Listen. It's nothing. Their leader is obviously a great man.*

Nathan nodded. "Yep. Full on boomer. It fried my other weapon…oh… and…" he sighed again. "One of the other fighters. He's lying in your barn. He's dead. A good man. His name was Stanslin."

Gary said, "I'm sorry." Jennifer and Ben both nodded.

"Thanks. I didn't know him well. But these men. They're brave. And great fighters."

Gary finished his beer, then smirked, "So…that leads me to my next question. How and when did you become an Airborne Ranger?"

Nathan tried to stop himself, but his smile grew, then he started chuckling. Sipping again from his beer, he said, "So before I explain being an 'Airborne Ranger from Planet Arth'…can you tell me how the Arc Gate got onto the back of a semi…? Or why it's hidden in your friend's barn? It is hidden, isn't it? Not just there by 'accident'?"

It was Gary's turn to smirk and then smile. He looked over at Jennifer.

She was looking back fondly.

Hmmm…

"Yeah, we…. kind of stole it," Gary finished. Jennifer giggled.

"Why does that not surprise me…? May I ask why?"

"Because, after Ellie vanished, the government stole it first, Nathan!" Jennifer piped in. "We just…stole it… back…" she finished hesitantly.

Nathan just shook his head. "That has to be an interesting story!" To which Ben just nodded emphatically. "So, what's your exit strategy? I'm assuming they know you took it. Or suspect."

"Strongly suspect, I'm afraid," Gary said. "They have footage of someone driving that semi on the Jersey Turnpike that looks a helluva lot like me.

Nathan nodded. Looking over at Jennifer, he asked, "How did you get mixed up in this? You're such a good girl! Don't tell me he didn't tell you what…"

"I was there all the way!" Jennifer said, somewhat angrily. "Fortunately, no one seems to know I was involved, though. I was about to take a bus back to the city before you arrived. And I am not a 'good girl'. If you'd bothered to get to know me better, you'd know that already!"

Her face flushed after saying that.

Nathan said, "Ok, ok! You're a badass, Jennifer! My apologies," he laughed, hands in the air.

Ben chimed in, "How about I go get us some pizza? Can't have anyone accidentally seeing the FBI's Most Wanted in my kitchen, but I can't have you all starving, either."

Gary said, "Thanks, Ben. You're the best."

Nathan added, "Thanks, I could eat." Jennifer just nodded, still trying to calm down after her outburst.

Ben grabbed some keys and took off in his truck.

Nathan just sat back, drinking his beer. They didn't talk for a bit, until Gary asked, "Need another…?" Nathan nodded affirmatively.

Jennifer just held hers up and said, "I'm slow."

Gary grabbed two more bottles from the refrigerator and popped off the lids. Handing one to Nathan, he asked, "So what now, Nathan? Can you help me get out of this somehow? Did your alien world happen to have a 'Get out of Jail Free' card?"

"Sorry, no. I appreciate you making sure I didn't end up in a government facility in New Mexico strapped to machines for the rest of my life. But I'll have to think on that one for a bit. I hope you're not in a rush."

"No. Not…yet, anyway. We were working out plans on how to hide that thing and then I was going to turn myself in, keeping that black sucker as my ace-in-the-hole."

Nathan nodded, distracted.

Jennifer just sat watching them. Nathan was…different. Somehow. He was both more tired and stronger than she'd ever seen him.

"I need a shower," he said finally. And if there are some clothes that aren't shredded, caked in blood, and the like, that would be great."

Gary got up to get him a towel. He then went into the back rooms and came out with a pack of underwear. "New in package! Found them in Ben's underwear drawer! 99% certain not to have been used yet. I'll call Ben and have him get you some clothes. Jeans…shirts…?" Nathan chuckled, catching the package mid-air. He nodded. "Size 32 and large for the shirts. Maybe two of each? I'll pay him back. Or…pay *you* back when I can…"

Gary laughed. "No need, brother."

"I can wash those for you, Nathan, if there's anything left to salvage" Jenn said, "I'll clean up the 'body armor', too. It looks important."

"Thank you, Jenn," he said, stripping off right there down to his ripped T-shirt and underwear, then leaned over to give her a kiss on the cheek. "Thank you both for being such good friends. And I'm going to need that armor again soon. Because I have to go back."

"Go back!!" Jennifer cried. "Why???"

"Unfinished business, Jenn. It's…hard to explain."

"Is it … Ellie?" Jennifer asked quietly, looking down.

"Some…yes…" Nathan admitted. "I can't just leave her there. "But it's more than that, Jennifer," he said, looking her in the eye for the first time since he'd gotten back.

"There's a war going on over there. A war they've been fighting for over five hundred years! I've got to go back and see if their…*leader*… has died. If she's gone, well…" he sighed quietly. "If so, then I'll grab Ellie and we'll come back. If not, then I'll send Ellie back. But I may not return for a while longer. At the very least, I need to return this," he said violently, grabbing a black medallion necklace on his chest, before heading for the bathroom.

She? Jennifer hung her head.

Their leader…is a 'she'. And Nathan is going back. Not for Ellie.

He's going back for her.

CHAPTER 122

The war was going badly. Even after the Dark Men suddenly disappeared into the north, allowing Rondor to move virtually all his forces to the south. Nothing was having a positive impact. The Empire was winning. Slowly, inexorably, the front was moving northward.

The battle could now be seen from the city walls. His generals, fighting with one third the men the Empire had, were sustaining heavy losses even though they killed more men at every turn. Rondor III's face twisted in anger.

"Get me Duke Iranias! Now!" he barked.

His mistress, the Lady Chantagne, had withdrawn from him in the morning. She had detected his foul mood and had slipped away to her own chambers. Best, probably. He didn't want to snap at her, as he had the Queen the other day. It made for rumors. And rumors were best left in bedrooms. Sniffing, he tapped his foot impatiently.

His steward returned, bowing deeply, "I regret to inform the King that Duke Iranias has left for his estates. Sometime last night, apparently."

"What?! He's left his own troops to run away to his keep?"

"I'm afraid not, sir. The Count Eschelon has informed me that Duke Iranias and his cousin have taken their troops and withdrawn, as well. This has left the General and his men even more short-handed. I'm told morale is…very low, sir."

Rondor ground his teeth but nodded. "Get out! Wait! Call the General in here immediately."

The steward ran off.

Rondor fumed. Gripping the stone balcony, he watched as the battle raged on. "Everything has fallen apart since that…*witch*…got away from justice! 'The Law must be supreme!'"

He recited it like a mantra.

Of course, the Law shouldn't apply the same to all people. Himself at the front of that line. The Law was for the masses. They must be kept in line! Waiting was not Rondor's strong suit, but he distracted himself by taking a walk in the gardens before returning to his study. Almost as soon as he'd returned, the General arrived.

He looked harried. "Your Majesty," he said, saluting.

"I'm told my cousin has withdrawn his men," Rondor began evenly.

"Yes, Your Majesty! About 10 hours ago, in the middle of the night."

"Why was I not informed of this immediately?"

The General stopped from staring straight ahead to look into the King's eyes, shock showing in his own, before returning to stare at the wall behind him. "But…Your Majesty! I sent two runners! They should have reached you last night and this morning. I only sent the second when I didn't hear back the first time."

"More treachery?" he asked, again evenly.

"Perhaps, my King! But…they also could have died. Since Iranias' withdrawal, we've been under heavy attack on the southern flanks of the army. We just reestablished order there an hour ago. It was why I could even come myself! It is quite possible the boys simply did not make it."

Nodding, the King deliberately sat down as if they were discussing the weather. Not an imminent threat to their very walls. Not as if they were in danger of losing the war itself.

"What are our options, General?"

The General looked at him directly again, and asked, "May I sit in your presence, my King?"

"Of course, uncle. Sit!" he gestured.

Duke Mantessa, the General of all Rondor's armies, sat down with a tremendous sigh. "Your Majesty, the troops were hard-pressed before the withdrawal of Duke Iranias! I have used every trick in the book and written a whole new chapter this morning! The Empire's armies are overwhelming us. Our men are good men who worship the Creator and revere his Name! They are opposed to the Dark and to every corner from which it crawls. But we're tired, sir. And we're now outnumbered at least five to one. I suggest you sue for terms of peace. Before they come for my head…and yours."

Rondor bowed his head. *What would my father think of me now…?* Then he nodded. "Do it. Send up the white and green. See if they will allow us to be…" he ground his teeth on the word, "…subjugated."

The General nodded sadly. "I will do so. On the break from fighting as evening approaches, so no one is 'accidentally' killed on the way. I will bring you news myself upon the report I receive."

"Thank you, uncle. You have done a fine job in a hopeless situation."

"Had Iranias just…stayed…!"

King Rondor III…could only nod. There would be no 'Rondor the IV'.

CHAPTER 123

Jezerah's Creeper was dispatched hours before the news arrived that K'Thul's armies were not heading back east as he had supposed. They were marching straight west!

What is that old fool up to?

Jezerah had Blage summon Curtaise and his other generals. At least three times since he'd promoted Curtaise, he'd called Blage by Curtaise's name. It was irritating. Blage, of course, did not flinch and simply did his job.

As he should.

But Jezerah had to stop doing it. It was embarrassing. One could hardly blame him, however. Change was coming from all sides. A perfectly planned and executed attack on Emorion had dissolved into a rout at the hands of K'Thul and a collective loss of the Arc Gate!

Somehow, his bitch sister had figured out how to teleport short distances, and clearly had swooped in to stop any or all of them from reactivating the Gate. He had to admire her for the sheer panache, the steel balls it must have taken to even attempt what she'd done amidst all their armies!

But admiration for one's enemy – even for his sister – had to be tempered with reprisals. The Creeper would hopefully do that. If it didn't reach Morgaine, which was unlikely in the extreme, at the very least it should chew through about half of her people. Wherever they were.

The Dark had its limits.

But once her status amongst the living was known again, she had to know such attacks were going to occur until that little detail about her 'breathing' was rectified. Even more so after that stunt she'd pulled with the Arc Gate.

The generals all filed in, Curtaise last. He'd been mortified upon returning, thinking Jezerah would be furious with him. Instead, he had clapped him on the shoulder, congratulating him on getting as many of their men out as he had.

But even now, he walked cautiously. He felt he'd failed. But it wasn't he who had failed. It had been Jezerah himself who had failed. The Void would be the final judge between himself and his rivals. And that is what they were now. Rivals. He had underestimated Emorion. Then, while moving to rectify that mistake, he had underestimated K'Thul!

But Curtaise had kept the forces together, organizing a chaotic retreat into some semblance of order. Men died. But not nearly as many as should have. It had been brilliant. So much so, that he'd watched the satellite footage of it again, even more impressed the second time, seeing the onslaught coming out of nowhere!

Jezerah sat down, nodding to the group of the darkest of the Dark Men. The best of the best.

They saluted, bowed, and sat down.

"I've called you," Jezerah began, "to warn you that K'Thul has not stopped at the Gate. Now that my ... *sister* has stolen it, he is still marching west!"

This drew worried glances amongst them.

"Fear not, however. General Curtaise is going to review their march, come up with a plan, and we are going to trap them before they reach whatever goal it is they're trying to attain. General Curtaise, take every resource, use every man, send any and every Knight, but get me those answers! I know you can do it," he added, looking right at the man.

"You've proven more than capable," to which the others nodded firmly. Even Omrion, who had lost half his Knights in the retreat. Even he had admitted to Jezerah in private conversation that Curtaise's use of his Knights in the retreat had fundamentally saved the army.

"Master," Curtaise replied calmly, "I've already ascertained K'Thul's goal. When news reached you, it had to pass through my ears first. Looking at the map, the size of his army, and after the last several days' events – it can only mean one thing."

Jezerah had to clench the table not to get angry. It cracked, but just a bit. "And…?" he asked quietly.

"And…Master, he's going for your throat. You are so solid in who you are and what you are, you forget that those lesser than you – and I include all beings in that, Master – they think you are like them! K'Thul, as you have yourself said, is rather dull-witted. The…unfortunate timing of our attack coinciding with Morgaine's theft of the Arc Gate…well…."

Suddenly it dawned on him. "He thinks I'm working with *her*! With… *Morgaine*!" The idea brought a raspy dark laugh from his throat. Then another. He almost lost it and had to get up to get himself a drink. Blage was faster, handing him a stiff Nelraen whiskey. Throwing it back, he slammed it down, starting to laugh again.

Curtaise was still nodding, "Indeed. I believe he thinks…as likely does Emorion, that you have been on the same side for some time now. Perhaps always on the same side. This backstabbing end to the nearly 500-year-old Triumvirate has coincided with what can only be perceived by your rivals as a revelation of betrayal. "

"And so now, K'Thul means to pull the rug out from underneath my feet…"

"By subjugating or possibly even destroying the Empire of Nelrae. Yes. I'm afraid so. You should, perhaps…warn the Emperor? Or perhaps not. His cousins are made of stronger metal. Perhaps it is time for a change… Let the armies know their leader is a true general. It cannot hurt our chances."

Curtaise was proving himself yet again.

Jezerah nodded. "Do it. And give me a realistic summary of our forces versus theirs. I want a war plan as soon as possible. The only way we beat that bastard, with as many forces as he's brought, is with ultimate preparedness!"

"As you command, my Master."

CHAPTER 124

Treyborne woke to shouting and screams in the outer hallway. Out the door, blaster rifle in hand – he was taking no chances with Morgaine ever again – he reached the hallway just in time to see a nightmare.

Several of his guards were firing weapons, but most of the blaster fire was ricocheting off the armor plating of a giant blue bulbous centipede-like creature crawling on the side wall. It had huge teeth in its mouth, bulbous eyes, and tentacle like corona around its gaping mouth. As he watched, three of the seven men in the hall were each in turn grabbed by the beast's tentacles, pulled into the air, and flung carelessly behind it.

Two of the three didn't even get up. The third did, but slumped back down to the floor, dazed. "Aim for the eyes!" Trey shouted immediately. Eyes were always more vulnerable. And it couldn't be worse than the uselessness of hitting that body armor.

As the men redirected their fire, sure enough some of the tentacles around the face curled up to defend the eyes, which had caused the beast to at least flinch and draw back.

It didn't seem to harm it much, either. But it was at least on the defensive. Suddenly, streaking out of nowhere, Smyslin of all people came running out from the back stairwell door, right at the creature from behind. He carried a shock-lance he must have had or found somewhere and… jammed it right up its ass!

The creature screamed and whirled, turning around, and rearing up on its back…however many legs flailing in the air.

"Fire at its belly! Now!" Smyslin managed, before the creature hurtled towards him. Blaster fire erupted at the creature's underbelly. Treyborne ran to flank the creature immediately, peppering its undercarriage with blaster fire.

Just as the tentacles lashed out at Smyslin, the underbelly of the creature erupted in purple ooze and goo! It collapsed, tentacles falling and knocking Smyslin to the ground. The creature was dead. Smyslin started to remove the gooey barbed tentacles from his body, receiving several gashes, leaving bright red marks.

Treyborne ran up to him, "Are you all right?"

Smyslin nodded. "Go help your men, Captain, I will live."

Treyborne ran to the men who had fallen. Several more had been run through on the lower staircases and hallways. After tallying everything up and finding the pathway the creature had gotten in – it had come through the sewer system that bled into the river – Treyborne returned to the hallway amid the cleanup. Seven injured amongst the staff, two dead. Five more soldiers would serve no more. Six more were injured enough to require treatment, including two who would need at least one full week or more to recover.

Even with the new recruits being brought in by Bantor, they were now at half strength. Recruiting was by no means easy either. One did not waltz into a sailor-filled thieving town like Nyx and just wave a banner and say, "The White Queen is hiring mercenaries!"

Treyborne watched as his men began cutting up the massive centipede-like thing into chunks they could haul out. "Keep some of those tentacles, one eye, and a piece of that body armor for research! I want whoever has a brain looking at these and find something that can pierce that hide or make those tentacles less dangerous! If there's one, there's more than one. Move!"

Smyslin had some burn marks where the tentacles had hit him. As did many of the men. It appeared they were coated in stomach acid as a bonus. Smyslin rose as Treyborne approached and put his arm on his shoulder.

"It is called a 'Creeper', Captain. One of my former master's own inventions. A well-placed *Djune* will cut it, but it takes many cuts to kill. Hitting the eye, if possible, is best. It is hard to get to the eyes. We did not have that kind of time."

"You are one brave son of a bitch," Treyborne noted. "Tell me, why were you an engineer rather than a warrior?"

"I have a son…or I did," Smyslin said. "And a wife. Both died many years ago. My son was a warrior. Highly respected. I wanted to live for my family. They are gone now. But back then…sometimes being brave is making the wise choice for one's family, rather than the one that favors oneself the most."

Treyborne nodded. "I don't disagree. That is often the braver choice. Could you possibly help our staff in dissecting this thing and finding more weaknesses? I'd like to be more prepared for next time. And there will be a next time."

"I will gladly help them. But you should know this: the Dark Men – we are merely a people raised in proximity to the Masters. We live to serve and are blessed…or perhaps cursed…with the power of the Dark. I am no longer one of them. But I was. And I know them. These creatures… like the Creeper, or the Hollow Men that attacked poor Morgaine… they are warped from the sacrifice of hundreds, sometimes thousands of good men, women, and children who their whole lives have only lived to serve the Masters."

Smyslin leaned back against the wall, bleeding where he stood. "Their blood, their bodies, their very souls…are crushed into making these hideous things. The Dark Lords do not make many of the Wildlings, not because they care about their people, but because they fear us. Slaughter too many and we might revolt. Or deny their sovereignty. I would never have thought of such a thing. But now, looking from the outside – I see it. My Master Nathan…should he still be alive… is quite the opposite. As are you and your Mistress. You live to fight against the Dark and to help those in need. Considering the small people as you go about your work. When I realized this in my heart, I could no longer be devoted to my old Master or his Void. The good news, if there is any, is that like Hollow Men, these creatures are sent to one person. I'm sure it was focused on your Mistress. But these things kill anything in their way. It was a message. I'm sure my former Master knew it would not reach her."

Trey nodded. "Good to know. And I'm sorry about your family. Get those cuts and acid burns dealt with. You're a mess!" Treyborne turned to go, then looked back. "Like I said before, you're needed here Smyslin. I have no idea where Nathan is now. Or even if he's alive. But you can stay here as long as you want. And…if you don't mind…I could use your help trying to get the sky cruiser up and running again. Today, if you can make it happen. It's a mess, too."

"I will be happy to," Smyslin said, heading towards the lower medical room. The one upstairs was taking the more severely wounded from the fight. "I'll meet you downstairs in the hangar in half an hour."

Treyborne nodded. Smyslin was a good man. Only later, after Smyslin had worked with him tirelessly through the day and into the night, did he hear that it was Smyslin who had originally sent the warning up about the creature. Had he not, it might have made its way into Morgaine's room after all, only a short distance away around the corner. Treyborne made sure to thank him personally for it as they worked.

"I only did what anyone on the base would have done, Captain," he said humbly. "Everyone here is out for the others. It is why I like it here so much."

Not able to finish their work, they both slept in the sky cruiser's main cabin, lying on the seats. Leaving instructions to wake him should Morgaine regain consciousness again, Treyborne fell asleep.

CHAPTER 125

"Morgaine…!?"

Turning to look, Morgaine saw her father waving to her. They were on Home World…at a villa overlooking a massive, picturesque beach.

"Yes, father?" she said as she stood. Only an adolescent, Morgaine was still stick-like, rather than curvy. Very self-conscious in bathing suits, she wrapped her arms around herself.

"Now, now…" her father said, coming up and hugging her. "Don't be like that! It won't be long, and men will be drooling just to get a good look at you!" He laughed when Morgaine gave him a skeptical look.

"Someday…someday…not too soon, mind you! You will have a family of your own. I have seen my grandchildren in a vision. Pure, white hair…! Beautiful. One boy, one girl. I'm never in the picture, though…" he said that very softly, but Morgaine heard him.

Alarmed, she asked, "Why not? You'll live forever!"

Laughing at her, he hugged her again, "None of us live forever, dear. We all must go to the Creator eventually. He is the Judge and the Maker of us all. He's good, though. Very good. Forgiving, loving…I look forward to that day when I'm home again. It is just not…a happy thought…that in this life I may not get to hug my grandchildren."

"I am never going to marry, father! Never!" Morgaine hated boys. They were always so mean to her. Especially her brother.

Her father sat down, and together they watched the ocean waves rolling in over and over. "Someday, Morgaine…this world will be no more. It's oceans and its tides…forever silenced. Only then will you be the woman I've seen in those visions. I wish I could spare you the loneliness…" he said this, looking over very sadly at her.

Then he laughed and scrubbed her hair, "Never mind me! Morose old fool that I am! Just know that someday that loneliness will be over. I may be gone, as will your mother. But my spirit will live on with you. Just as the Creator will be with you and watch over you. Things will happen…by chance it will seem. But there is no 'chance'. Only the course of conviction."

Snapping awake, Morgaine stared, looking around at her surroundings. Her eyes wouldn't focus.

Drugs.

Moving her head slowly, so as not to make the walls whirl, she saw Maitan sitting upright in a chair next to her, reading from a viewscreen on his lap. Without looking up, he asked, "And how is my Mistress this morning?"

Laying her head back on the pillow, she answered, "I'm…awful, Maitan. How many days?"

"Four, I'm afraid. Five since we hauled you in here dying on the table. Treyborne has completed his work on the sky cruiser – with help from Smyslin, I might add. But they needed to manufacture parts in the shop downstairs and go into town to get a certain rare…something or other."

"Anyway, they just completed it a few hours ago," he hesitated a moment looking up, "There was…another attack while you rested," he said, turning towards her. She just looked at him, staring through her drug-induced haze. "Smyslin called it a 'Creeper'…nasty thing, like a giant bug…"

"I've seen them," Morgaine said sleepily. "I've fought them. I thought we'd killed them all centuries ago." She sighed deeply, "How many more?"

"We lost seven, five of which were soldiers. Including the missing, that makes thirteen dead soldiers and five staff members since the attacks on you began. This doesn't include the wounded, either. We've lost multiple staff members in these attacks, Mistress. Some of the others have asked to be let go and go get jobs within the city. I can hardly blame them."

Morgaine nodded, "Let them go, of course. If they must go, they must be sworn to secrecy. Perhaps even…taken to other areas of the world, so they cannot lead anyone here. I leave that to you. Has Bantor been able to…?"

Bantor and Mikell have recruited a half dozen worthy men of action, my Lady. But without your…medallion…we cannot ascertain for sure who amongst them might secretly be of the Dark. Therefore, none of them are allowed to guard anything but the upper perimeter. They don't know about the lower compound at all, nor what they are truly guarding. They've been told that threats have been made on the olive grove, and it must be defended. That is all for now."

Morgaine remembered. The attack on her at the Gate. The lightning strike. Nathan missing, presumed dead. Feeling her torso with her hands, she gingerly checked the entire area. Wincing in pain, even through all that medication, told her all she needed to know.

Nathan cannot be dead! But as much as I wish that to be true…I need the Corillion near me, as well. Not having it is like being blind!

"So, nothing has been done to try to retrieve the Arc Gate?"

Maitan shook his head matter-of-factly. "As I already said, Mistress. The sky cruiser repairs were just completed. Frankly, it's a miracle it was even possible. The ship was struck by lightning while hauling a very heavy weight wrapped in conduit designed for charging the ship. Not carrying loads. It's a miracle any of you survived…". He sniffed. "Treyborne and Smyslin are both asleep at my orders. When they awake, you may order them to do whatever you wish."

Morgaine said, "I need…"

"I know, M'Lady. You need some tea. I am off to get it. Anything else?"

"Get me a comm. And wake up the captain. I need to talk to Trey *right now.*"

It was morning. Gary and Jennifer had convinced Nathan that he needed rest, rather than an immediate return to … wherever. After eating some pizza and making small talk, he had gone to sleep on the couch while watching TV with them before 8 PM.

Covering him with a blanket, Jennifer kissed his forehead. Gary and Ben had gone outside to dig a big hole behind the barn for the dead soldier. Nathan had asked them to salvage his gear, and anything that seemed worthy of recovering before burying him.

Those articles were placed by Nathan as he slept, at almost midnight.

They sat down on the other couch, with Nathan snoring away, drinking beers and talking quietly. Jennifer had gone to bed hours ago. Her plan was to catch the early bus into town and go to work late, saying she was "finally healthy", and do some recon on Gary's situation from there.

"I'll leave in the morning, too," Gary said. "You need your life back."

Ben stared into his bottle without looking up, "Where will you go, Gary?"

"Like I said, I am going to turn myself in. Let's get that semi-trailer moved out to that abandoned farmhouse if we can though. I'd like to keep my ace in the hole…in the hole."

Ben nodded, "Thanks. I mean…Terri will be happy, and I'd rather not have to explain anything to her. The less she knows, the better. What about Nathan? He's been missing for over a month. He can't just … go back to work, can he?"

"I thought you were here for that! We had to talk him into staying the night. He was ready to go back once he'd showered and Jenn had washed his … Halo gear."

They looked over at him, and the pile of gear from the dead soldier he'd come with. Ben spoke up first, "Can he just… 'port over' like that? I thought he said he'd been struck by lightning last time. And you all were trying to recreate whatever took him in the first place back here. Is there some button he can press or…?"

"I have no idea," Gary said slowly, "Nathan could know, or it could just be wishful thinking. If it were so easy, we'd have gone in after him weeks ago. And Ellie wouldn't have accidentally winked out, either. It seems like it's random. At least on this side. Weird we're talking about space portals like they're a regular, everyday occurrence. Or a household appliance or something."

Ben nodded, finishing his beer. Setting the bottle down gently on the coffee table, he said, "Well, it's late, and I've got to get stuff done around here in the morning before anyone comes back. So, let's move your 'ace' and get it hidden again. Then we can get Jennifer to the buses, and Nathan to his 'space portal'. Which reminds me…he will need a ride to where we're moving it. Maybe we should wait until morning. It's all back roads and only three miles to the farm."

"Shit! That's right," Gary sighed. "OK, I'm going to head to bed then. Let's make sure that Nathan doesn't find the key to the padlocks and get up and go without talking with us first."

Ben patted his chest, "Got 'em right here! No one gets in there without taking these off me!"

Gary gave Ben a hug and headed into the bedroom. As he got undressed, Jennifer spoke, clearly wide awake, "Do you think he's all right, Gary?

He's only been gone a month, but he seems so…*different*. Like a stranger who used to be our friend."

Gary stopped cold, then removed his outer shirt. "It still ok for me to sleep here?" he asked.

"I would have locked the door, silly," she said, pulling the covers back on his side of the tiny bed. "I've been waiting for you."

Getting in, she spooned with him, keeping her head turned away. When he tried to keep his distance, she grabbed his arm and wrapped it around her, pulling the covers up. Gary's mouth went dry. He couldn't help feeling her breasts. She was jamming his hand down on one of them.

Shaking his head, he said, "I don't know…he's still Nathan. But he's distracted. Different. Like he was when I first saw him after college. Ellie had just left him, and he'd just left the University. The soldier gear is a bit weird. But he's always been athletic, and I've seen him in a fight. He can handle himself…"

Jennifer turned over. Her face was right next to his. "I've been helping you look for a man we both held as a close friend who was lost. But he came back *more* lost. He's our friend still, yes. But it doesn't seem like he has missed us nearly as much as we missed him. At least…not *me*. I've been waiting for *that* Nathan to come back. Today…tonight…I've thought about it, and I don't think that Nathan is ever coming back."

With that, she reached up and grabbed his neck and pulled him towards her. Gary couldn't help himself. He knew Nathan – at least the one who had vanished – had been kind of crazy about this girl. Now…he had barely noticed her or talked with her. Even when she'd jumped on him!

Damn it, it's my turn to take a shot at her!

Returning her kisses with emphasis got her breathing harder. Kissing her neck, she started biting his ear, then she pushed back suddenly.

"What…? Did I do something wrong?" he asked, scared he'd somehow upset her, or turned her off.

In the small amount of light, he saw her smirk. Leaning far away from him, she pulled her shirt off. "I have to be honest, Gary. I liked Nathan… and I'm not sure if this is a rebound or just a continuation from awhile back before I even knew him. But I need you. Tonight. *Now.*"

Looking at her for a moment, he smiled back, "I have no problem with that…"

CHAPTER 126

Ellie was again sitting in the kitchens, eating alone. No one talked with her, except the cooks.

I've been here a week, for *fuck's* sake! *This world is a nightmare. Pure and simple.*

She'd gone from a relatively serene stint in captivity, to a harrowing 'rescue' (where people died), learned second-hand about their return visit (where nearly everyone including Nathan had died), and now an attack from a giant bug within the confines of their "super safe" underground compound (where, yes, additional people had died).

Fuck this place!

Throwing her spoon down, she stood up, grabbed her water bottle, and stormed out of the kitchens. Heading back towards her chambers, she blew right past her own rooms, making straight for the upper-level stairs. The level where all the "important people" stayed.

As she got to that floor, she was met with two guards immediately standing in her way. Her own had been removed after the latest attack. Apparently, she wasn't that important. And with the body count continually rising, they probably couldn't afford to keep her under watch all the time any longer.

Trying to push past, the guards didn't budge. "Let me through, asses!" She grunted, trying to make them move, "I need to talk to…"

"Let her through," came Treyborne's voice. He was trudging down the hall in full military gear, rifle in hand. Or whatever it was. It looked like a rifle. Standing aside, the men let her pass and she stormed up to him.

Shit, this guy is big! Cute too, especially with that super-annoying smirk on his face!

"Look!" Ellie began… "I've been doing nothing since I got here! All I see is people dying all over the place! No one can tell me if Nathan's even *alive* – just that I'd better count on him being dead! No one can tell me if I can even go home! All I know is that the one fucking thing that might get me home, you apparently dropped off in the middle of a forest somewhere?! I want to *fucking* go home! Do you *fucking* understand me???"

"You seem to need to interject 'intercourse' into every other word or thought. Do people just 'fuck' all the time where you come from? Or is that translator just not working right?"

That damned smirk! I'm going to wipe that right off his … fucking face…!
"You will never know, asshat! I asked you a question. Answer me!"

"I couldn't find the question amidst all the people having intercourse…" Still smirking.

"Ahhhhhhhh!" she screamed in his face. "I want to go home! Can anyone just take me … *fucking*…home?"

"Ah…now it makes sense! You want to go home so you can have intercourse with someone!" Looking behind her at the other two soldiers guarding Morgaine's floor, he said, "I'm sure someone here could service you."

His face turned suddenly serious, "But if you want to know if you can go home, we have no 'fucking' idea. You are welcome to come along with me. I'm about to go looking for Nathan. Or at least what's left of him. Oh…and retrieve the one 'fucking' thing that could possibly get you home. You want to come along? Come along! I could use the extra bodies. Even *yours…*".

That look. *That had better not mean what I think it means…*

"I'm in," was all Ellie said, her face still furious.

Walking past her and the guards at the stairwell, he nodded and waved; and the two guards who'd prevented her entrance to the floor fell in line behind Treyborne like…well like soldiers. "Get her some gear," he said, looking back at her. "Smalls," he turned around again, walking ahead of her.

What an infuriating man!

"We're about to head into enemy territory. Again." He didn't sound happy about it.

Now that Ellie thought about it, neither was she.

CHAPTER 127

The city of Nyx was a bustling place. Especially if one preferred the "seedier" parts of town. The portside and the docks never stopped. Ships came in, goods came and went, sailors were everywhere…as were drugs, thieves, prostitutes, and the inevitable city watch.

The upper westside, which received neither the blessings of the harbor odors, nor the cacophony that reverberated down by the docks, was a much gentler part of town. It was still bustling, to be sure. Jewelry stores, women's boutiques, hair shops, makeup artists, and musicians favored this quarter. It held the beautiful "Well Market" district. A huge circle of shops, aspiring artists, younger nobles and noblewomen, plus the area was kept clean of beggars and cutpurses. The Watch kept guards at every street coming into the market and they were merciless to interlopers.

It was at an inn called the "Stone and Satin Lodge" that Bantor found himself these days. He'd had his invitations to interview for mercenary positions with "high pay and high excitement" posted all over the city for weeks now. It had been six days since the last applicant had even bothered to try.

Apparently, news had gotten around town that Bantor actually had standards. His mercenaries couldn't also be thieves, mistreat women — even in brothels! — and other such "nonsense". At least that was what the last would-be employee had called it.

Bantor sat just outside the doorway, covered in the shade of an umbrella set up for that purpose, sipping a glass of tea and watching the goings and comings on "Aspen Road". Since it held zero trees, it wasn't exactly a fitting name. But the street was paved in beautiful white and gray stones and had not a single crack in the seams. Horses and carriages were everywhere. Everyone was dressed in finery. It was, perhaps, nicer than any street even in Rondor.

Merchant cities had their place. And from it came a new wealthy class of nobles. And those within it worked to gain said titles through greed and avarice alone.

A brunette young lady walked by, smiling kindly. Smiling back and tipping his cap, Bantor looked back towards the well. A sundial had been placed above it, sheltering the well from direct sunlight, with the bonus of allowing one to view the time. It was half past seven. Exactly midday.

Bother!

There would likely be no more applicants again, today. Mercenaries were notoriously late risers. But by now, anyone who was going to come would have…

"I hear you're hiring," said a gruff voice from directly in front of him.

Whipping his head back from the well, which was behind him on the right, Bantor saw a man sitting in the chair across from him. He jumped a bit. "I…ah…Yes! I am!"

Grabbing the empty cup of tea and pouring from the pot, the man asked, "What's the job…?" The man was…big! Dark curly hair, with dark skin and a large mustache and beard. He looked like a pirate. Those did exist in this part of the world. But Bantor tried not to judge on appearance alone.

"It's a…military group. You would be extremely well-compensated. But it's quite possibly a lifetime commitment. If you like us and we like you…you become part of the team! All food, lodging, gear, weapons – and we have a lot of them you'd like – everything is paid for by us. Every silver you earn…is yours."

Sitting back and taking a sip, the man eyed him over his cup, "That…" he said slowly, "…doesn't answer my question."

"Ah…! No, it doesn't!" We pay one gold per week. That's…50 per year! For people who show promise, it's doubled! I…"

"I'll take 200 gold a year, Rondorian. That's…four per week, if you're not good at math. No less."

Bantor looked shocked. "Our…*commander* himself barely makes that much money!"

"That's not my problem. And he's probably not as good me!" the man said.

"That's…easy to say, sir. Even our lowest of rank…". The man pulled out a blaster…and pointed it directly at Bantor, who squealed.

"Duck!" the man said.

Bantor ducked. The blaster went off, whistling by his left ear. The sound of a plop and clank right behind him startled him out of his chair. Looking back, he saw a man lying on the ground, with a long dark knife in his hand, not ten feet away. "Sit down!" the man commanded. Bantor did, looking back at him wide-eyed.

"That skank has been watching you for hours. I had heard someone was hiring, but when I saw you…" he shrugged, "I immediately wasn't interested. I didn't think it was what I was looking for. No offense! That is, until I saw *him*."

He pointed with his cup. "I noticed him sitting just over by the bakery. But he wasn't eating. He wasn't drinking, either. I never trust a man who doesn't drink! So, I came over to talk. He must've thought you'd be distracted enough to…uh…". He finished his tea and mimed getting shot in the head and reeling backwards from it. "Boom!"

Pouring some more tea, he added, "Anybody that attracts that level of assassin has my interest. I don't know who you are, and frankly, I don't care. But pay me right, and I'll be your best friend. I like a challenge!"

Bantor swallowed. "Two…. two hundred, you say?" The City Guard were rushing over.

"It just doubled," turning his head, he yelled, "Clyffin, get this scum out of here! I thought you boys kept watch over this place! Don't make me tell Innis! He will be butt hurt if he knew you'd let a Guilder up here to attack the constituency. I'll pay the fine, as usual. Have him send me the bill. I'm staying…or was staying…upstairs."

The guard surprisingly didn't even question the man. They just nodded and three of them dragged the body into the alley, apparently just leaving it there.

"Four…hundred…?" Bantor swallowed.

"Yes, and I'm worth every flaming copper!" Looking into the Stone & Satin, he called, "Marcia! Get me some ale! I'm thirsty for something cold!"

"Coming right up, dearie!" came the barkeep's voice from within.

"But…I don't even know your name!" Bantor stammered. "I…I…who *are* you? And where did you get that weapon?"

"What's a name?" the man said. "But you can call me 'Jasper'. That's what they call me around these parts. You want references? I can get them for you…but it'll cost you *extra*." He leaned forward eagerly.

Looking at the guards returning from the alley, Bantor said, "No… that…that won't be necessary!"

CHAPTER 128

Nathan awoke to the smell of coffee and bacon. Ben was in the kitchen, coffee pot full and steaming, bacon getting fried up on the stove. When Ben saw he was up, he pointed towards the hall bathroom, where he'd left a toothbrush, toothpaste, and a towel. There was a comb in the cabinet, as well. Brushing his teeth, he looked in the mirror. His eyes were dark hollows. Even after sleeping. His hair…hadn't been brushed before falling asleep. Bending to rewet his hair and then brush it, he looked again.

Better. Not great, but better.

"Gary took my truck to take Jennifer to the bus station," Ben said as he walked back into the kitchen. "She said to say, 'Sorry' and 'Goodbye'! She had to catch the early bus so she could get into the city before it got crazy, she said."

Nathan nodded, sipping the coffee from the mug he'd been handed.

"What's with you two, anyway? She was rabid to see you, then you came and…" he shrugged turning back to the bacon. "None of my business, of course. But it seemed to cool down awful fast once you zapped your way back in. I mean…as much as she was trying to save you, and all."

"I guess…I don't really know, Ben," Nathan said. "We're all friends. At work. Jennifer is…well…you've seen her! And both Gary and I developed 'more than friend' feelings for her. I suppose I was just trying to stay alive so much where I was…that I didn't have time to think much about how they were doing. Or what they might be feeling." He sighed. "I'm human, I guess. And…there was a lot going on. Back there."

He jerked his head toward the barn.

Ben stopped to look at him squarely, "Yeah…I think that was clear. Hand me a plate. No. Back behind you." Nathan turned and handed him the plate, and Ben put all the cooked bacon on it. He began cracking eggs. "How do you like your eggs?"

Nathan said, "Cooked. Go for it." Ben just nodded.

A few minutes later, as Nathan was reclining at the table watching Ben finish up their breakfast, the car pulled up and Gary came in, sporting a big hat and sunglasses.

"Nice look, Don Gary!" Nathan joked.

"Very funny!" Gary responded, taking off the oversized hat and the sunglasses, plopping into a chair just as eggs (scrambled) and the salt and pepper hit the table.

They all ate in silence for several minutes. Nathan looked up at Gary and did a double take. "What…is *that* look?"

Gary sighed, "That…my friend…is the 'guilty' look. I know we've had some gamesmanship with Jennifer, and all. And she was…extremely bummed you weren't as excited to see her as she was to see you. She risked her neck to help me, Nathan. Just for a shot at … *somehow*… pulling you out of that space portal monolith *nightmare*! We were afraid we'd lost your forever…!"

"I know. I got that from Ben already," Nathan said, laying his fork down and grabbing the last of the bacon.

"So…long and short…she jumped me last night. She said it might be a rebound, too. So, if anything and everything changes…in the future…I'm sorry," he said putting his hands up, "But…"

"I understand," Nathan said. "Truly. Congrats. It's probably for the best. I'm happy for you. And her. Gary…I…I may not be coming back," he said, looking down, "I could easily die, too. I might not even get back there, I realize that. But if I do, there's no guarantee I can come back again."

And I haven't even considered if I will want to.

Gary dropped his head and nodded.

Ben said, "Well…we didn't want to move your time continuum thing, or whatever, Nathan. But we have got to move it soon. What say we all get in that truck and head over to the Benson farm…? I went by yesterday on my way home. It's still deserted. The barn is still…the barn."

He shrugged.

Nathan said, "Sure! Let me gear up and we'll go. Ben…?" he said, and Ben stopped on his way out the door, "how attached to that shotgun are you?"

Minutes later, taking all the battle gear, putting his own on, and trying to make it all work was a bit harder than he expected. The ruined shock-lance was even there. Nathan strapped it back to his side, just so he didn't leave it. No sense leaving alien tech around. Gary helped him by grabbing Stanslin's armor.

No one mentioned where the body was buried.

Soon, Nathan and Gary were in the semi following Ben in his truck to the neighbor's deserted farm. None of the three plus miles were paved. But no one came down them, either.

Pulling into the weedy, broken-down farmhouse setting, Nathan whistled. "What a dump! Perfect…!" Fall leaves were everywhere… snow piles in small areas. It truly looked as deserted as it was. Gary laughed, then parked while Ben went to open the semi-shut barn doors.

As expected, nothing and no one was inside. The Arc Gate barely could get in under the barn doors. It scraped the upper frame a bit going in. But it made it. Turning the wheel so the whole thing could fit in the barn easily, Ben shut the door to the possibility of eyes coming from the road. Going to the back doors, he pulled one of them open, letting in some sunlight.

"Ok!" Gary said, still sitting in the cab with him, "Now what?"

Nathan looked at him and said, "Honestly, I don't have a clue. I'm going to try something, Gary. It may not work. If it doesn't work…well…. I do know what I *will* do! As soon as you turn yourself in, I'm going to appear as well, and tell them after I'm stuffed and bagged that I have all sorts of alien info. I'll also imply heavily I know how to activate the portal. And that your release and the dropping of all charges is part of the deal to let them have a shot at using it, too. Whoever 'they' are! Ellie's parents will fight for me, too. They have connections. And they always liked me. Plus, if I'm the only hope of them ever seeing their daughter again…"

Gary nodded and looked at Nathan, "Thanks, bro. But, for your sake, I hope you can go back there. It sounds like you kind of need to. I've still got the monolith itself. That's quite a bargaining chip. And from what I've read on Ben's computer and from Jennifer's phone…the Egyptian government is *hot* right now! I've kept my phone off and even pulled the card on it since leaving the city. But…" he shrugged. "I'll make sure to let everyone know that I 'stole' it from an unmarked government warehouse. At least the conspiracy theorists will be on my side. I'll probably get a very good, very free attorney."

Nathan gave him a hug.

Then they got out. Ben was waiting, holding the back barn door open. Finally, he found a big rock and placed it where it could work as a doorstop. "All right!" he said excitedly, "Let's do this! I want to see some alien tech magic!" Reaching into the back of his covered truck, he pulled out the Remington model 870 and a box of 12 gauge shells, handing them to Nathan.

Nathan laughed and said, "Me, too!" nodding his thanks for the shotgun. He put the gun between the straps of his backpack after putting the shell box inside it. He had Gary lay Stanslin's armor at his feet. He had both blasters on his person, with Stanslin's pack still strapped to the armor.

Walking up to the Arc Gate, he could feel it pulse and thrum. Moreover, he could feel the power within himself, through the medallion. The gem stirred, coming to light. The crystals within seemed to answer it, winking on with light from nowhere.

"Whoa!" was all Ben could say. Gary was silent, watching him.

Closing his eyes, he reached up and grasped the necklace. *OK, Morgaine's Creator…! Show me you're real! I want…I need to get back to her! I have to find out if she's all right!*

The humming and the throbbing became a steady pulse. Then it was like a wind, or a force of some kind pushing him back away from the Gate. Nathan fought to hold his ground, tripping and nearly stumbling over the armor at his feet.

The gemstone was a white fire in his hand.

CHAPTER 129

Treyborne and his skeleton crew of six plus Ellie reached the monolith site in just over four hours. It had taken most of the last hour sweeping the area to search for the thing. Fortunately, or unfortunately, it had fallen on its side, smashing through several trees. It hadn't quite reached the ground, as the trees around it held it up slightly, rather than lying completely flat. As they approached it, Trey could feel the pull of its magnetism.

"That's new," he said to Messau, who just nodded. Messau's hands were completely wrapped. Maitan had done some cell regeneration on them. But it wasn't complete. And most of the machine's time was spent trying to repair Morgaine's stomach, intestines, and other internal anatomy. From what Trey had been told after four full days of doing it, Maitan was uncertain of her ever fully recovering. The fact that she was alive was a miracle.

But the *Biaki Mor* could work miracles with those machines. And not only were Messau's hands nearly fixed – near enough to steer with wraps, anyway – Morgaine had regained consciousness. Permanently, apparently. She was almost her old smug-ass self again.

Almost.

Trey had noticed the haunted look in her eyes. Whether that was from nearly dying, from losing Nathan, or from leaving the monolith 'somewhere in the forest' in the wilderness, he did not know. Possibly all three.

"We're going to have to set this down and get the cables on it first!" Trey said loudly. "If we aren't ready, I think it may cause us problems. I don't want to have to do any more repairs on this sky cruiser. Ever."

Ellie looked over at the only other non-combatant type in the ship: Nathan's…*friend?* The weird-looking old man who called himself "Smyslin". He seemed to care deeply what had happened to him. Maybe more so than Ellie herself did. Ellie was told he'd fixed the ship. Not a bad guy to have around in case things went sideways.

It seemed to do that a lot around these people.

Landing several hundred yards away in the nearest clearing, Ellie and the rest of them got out, minus Smyslin and the other pilot. Ellie didn't know his name. She did know he'd been on the original strike force to save her – and the one where Nathan went missing and everybody died.

His hands had been burnt badly in the second.

Ellie brushed her short, brown hair back and looked up at the sun. It was the middle of the day, roughly. And there were only few clouds in the sky. The ground wasn't even very wet, despite the slew of rain it had received earlier in the week. But it was getting hot out here. And muggy.

Just like summer in New York. Yay.

Walking the short distance with the rest of them, she watched as they attached very thick heavy-looking cables around the top of the thing. Going up to examine it, she realized it was significantly different than the one she'd been studying on earth. It was…more oval, had less black crystals, and skewed a bit to one side. It had different symbols on it, too. And it seemed to have some sort of metal panel or box built into one side near the base. Since she had been a prisoner the entire time around this one, she had never had the chance to really see it up close.

Fascinating.

"Hey breeder lady," the big one yelled, "come over here and take a look at this!"

Turning, Ellie tried not to show her anger as she walked…not stomped, she was sure of it…over to the commander. Treyborne was pointing at some broken cable laying off to the side. Two of them.

"Those are pieces from the hoist cables we were using. And those look like they've been cut in half. Like by a laser or very sharp knife or something. They didn't tear. No bodies…" he pointed around them. "No imprints or body armor. Short version: Nathan didn't die here. Looks like Stanslin didn't, either. Whatever happened, it cut through the cabling like a hot knife through butter, though. But whatever it was," he shrugged. "I'll bet my life that he's around here somewhere walking in circles trying to find us."

For days? Ellie doubted that.

Ellie looked at the razor-sharp cuts in the almost 1" metal cabling. Looking around, she also saw no signs of egress or exit. No tracks. Maybe they washed away with the rain. Maybe…but…then why didn't they ever come back? This would be here waiting for rescue. Right? Not wander off like lost deer. Holding onto the cable, Ellie just shook her head.

What cuts through metal like that? If they're alive…and not cut through like this cable…where the hell are they? Where the hell are you, Nathan?!

CHAPTER 130

Morgaine still could barely walk, but she knew she had to get up or she'd be trapped in that bed forever. With Maitan's help, and after several stern admonishments, they gingerly went back and forth across the floor. Three times.

Her insides were in agony. Slipping back into bed, she looked up at Maitan in true pain. He had rarely seen her cry, in over one hundred years; but she was nearly to tears in that moment.

"It's bad, Maitan. It still hurts!"

Nodding, he helped her get comfortable in bed again, propping her up with pillows and blankets behind her head and back.

"When will I get better? I can't lead like this!"

Looking at her, his eyes unreadable, he simply replied, "Mistress, you died. Not 'nearly *died*'. You were *dead*. Three times, total. We revived you. I revived you myself twice! Mistress, your internal organs looked like you'd been eaten out from the inside by *merashi* fish. The surgery alone took over thirteen hours! I had to give you four measures of your own blood and… two more of my own."

Her head whipped up to stare wide-eyed at him. To *Biaki Mor*, blood was sacred. Blood was for family. Only. Ever. "I…am honored," she managed, stunned.

He nodded as if he had not just said a monumental thing. "All of which is to the point: You need much rest. If you can walk down the hallway by yourself in three weeks, I will be thrilled."

Morgaine just closed her eyes slowly and sighed. "How is the rest of me?"

"The rest of you? Fine! Your mind, your…. legs and arms. Of course, you lost the baby." He sniffed.

Her eyes snapped open, then moved…very…slowly…over to his own. "The…*what?*" she said quietly, tilting her head.

He sighed and did what he rarely did unless she was unconscious, or not in the room. He sat down. "The baby, Lady Morgaine. I gave you my blood in hopes of saving it, as well. Not just you. But it was no use. Your… uterus was all cut up and blood was everywhere. I…tried my best," he said. "I'm sorry. So…very sorry."

She could only nod…wide-eyed.

Was this a dream? Nope. Not a dream. She'd pinched herself, just to be sure.

Shaking her head in confusion…she asked, "How…?" But she knew the answer to this one, already.

Stiffening her resolve, she continued, "Never mind. Get me an update on Trey and what they've found. I can run command from here. I can think, damn it! If I can't move, I'll run point from this hospital bed. I want updates on our new hires, who's leaving and where they're going. Everything. *Move!*"

He nodded, heading for the door.

"Maitan…?" He turned, not quite looking at her.

"Thank you again. You are a true friend."

He nodded again and then left, closing the door behind him.

CHAPTER 131

"What do you mean… 'they aren't there'!?" Rondor demanded. "Their generals agreed to meet us two hours ago!"

His uncle, the general, was sitting across from him on the royal couches. He held a brandy in his hand, and he was smiling. General Mantessa nodded, "Yes, Your Majesty. They did. And then, this morning before light, they withdrew. Completely. Of course, we'd heard noises in the night. We always hear noises. But nothing out of the ordinary while camping across a valley from your enemies." He just shook his head.

"So, they…withdrew…?" Rondor III couldn't believe the good news. "What could possibly have…made them do that?"

"Again, I have no idea, Your Majesty," he sighed. "Shall I engage the military and pursue?"

"Oh Creator, no! Let's refortify…resupply. Tell the people the Creator has forced them to run! But … once the day's celebration is over, send for Duke Iranias…I will have a word with him. If he doesn't come, *then* you'll have something to do with your army!"

His uncle nodded, stood, bowed, and then left. But he quaffed the brandy first.

King Rondor III couldn't believe his good fortune! He'd prayed for help, of course. He'd even given walking papers to his mistress and asked his wife to pardon his indiscretions. She had graciously done so. But … this!?

Clasping his hands together, he suddenly realized this could be some sort of elaborate trap. But why bother with that? They were … *winning*! We were capitulating. They knew that. It must be something else. What would …or even *could* cause an army of that size to suddenly wheel…?

Rondor III decided he didn't care. "Steward! Get me the scribes. We're going to have a celebration!"

CHAPTER 132

K'Thul's armies finished sweeping across the eastern banks of Nelrae about five in the morning that very day. Still numbering well over 60,000 men combined, the eastern trade city of Connlan had surrendered immediately. K'Thul himself set up his base in the fortified city, overlooking the Alisandre River that his armies had just pushed across hours before.

Word today from his scouts said that Nelrae's armies had turned around that very morning, as well. It would take them days to get here, as slow as they marched.

K'Thul would be at the capital if they detoured here. If they didn't… well…he'd have himself a nice base of operations.

Emorion had sent word to him that very morning, as well. It was an… *interesting* offer. He also had concluded that the White Witch had been Jezerah's pawn all along. Working in tandem, the two had kept the entire Dark Brethren on their heels. For centuries. All of the others had 'somehow' died. Emorion was as convinced as himself how far back that alliance truly went.

Blood runs deep, apparently. And the 'White Queen', as the Dark Men called her, wasn't as white as they had all thought. K'Thul's admiration for the long play was still with him. But with it came the iron resolution to gut Jezerah's power at its heart. Hence this very encampment and campaign, that had begun so admirably.

Emorion had included another bit of news, however. That news might make this next part easier. Or harder. It said that the White Witch was, in fact, dead…killed by four Hollow Men he'd sent for her after the Battle at the Gate. Being Hollow Men, they'd tracked her through shadow. Three had died, in fact. Emorion still had no idea where her new base of operations was. He'd apparently found the old one and given that information to Jezerah some time ago. According to him, they'd fled soon thereafter.

Nodding to himself, K'Thul had to admire the attack Emorion had sent to rid the world of Morgaine. He knew the sacrifices he had to go through to create even a single Hollow Man. K'Thul had only ever had one. But the idea of them working together…brilliant.

Brilliant and toxic.

K'Thul's knowledge of the nature of those creatures ran deep. He felt akin to them in more ways than one. If the Triumvirate had worked together from the beginning, not all walking away, things could have been different. At least he and Emorion could have. Emorion had paid a very high price to end the life of that little tart. It was a pity, of course, but K'Thul would find someone else to place on his arm when the time was right.

Surveying the fields around the city of Connlan, K'Thul nodded to himself. It was time to eliminate Jezerah. There was no question. Emorion agreeing and aiding in that had made him at least a circumspect ally again. *Perhaps*…perhaps they could reforge an alliance. With K'Thul at the head, of course.

The Gate must be found. Jezerah's head placed next to Morgaine's.

But Emorion was showing he still had his usefulness. Plus, if there was an alliance, the chance that he'd send four of those things after K'Thul himself became increasingly unlikely. The chance that creatures of the Dark, especially Wildlings, surprising anyone of their ilk was beyond low to begin with. Now that he knew what Emorion was capable of… he would have his own watchdogs around himself, though. Just in case.

No sense giving even the slightest chance to that sniveling little coward. But coward though he was, he was an inventive one. And he'd always been so very clever. He deserved to live, if only for the honorific of being the 'Witch Slayer'. Yes, that was a good title. K'Thul would rule the empire…and 'Witch Slayer' could be his loyal right hand. He would send word once he got around to it. Nelrae was the focus now.

Perhaps if Emorion lent even a little aid from within, the Empire of Nelrae would crumble even faster. Efficiency. That was the key. Emorion hadn't left word how to reach him though. Problems for another day.

CHAPTER 133

Nathan had been standing by the Arc Gate for an indeterminate amount of time…every other time he'd been 'ported', it had happened instantly. This time, it was like…the Arc Gate was *resisting* him.

Not that he'd ever 'forced it' before, trying to use the Corillion. Before, it had just been "Boom, done"! For what seemed like hours, Nathan had held the fire of the gemstone in his hand. But when he'd decided to stop and take a break, Gary had informed him it had only been five or so minutes. Ben agreed.

Two more times, he'd tried. They snacked on sandwiches Ben had gone into town to buy. Ben had eventually driven home, saying he'd be back to pick up Gary after making sure his wife had gotten home ok. The plan was, he'd come back and take Gary – or both of them – to the bus station and drop them off. He'd been gone quite a while and was just pulling up when Nathan was readying for his fourth and final attempt.

Ben pulled up and said, "No luck yet, eh?" Gary just shook his head.

Nathan looked back at Ben, "Thanks again for putting up with me. I thought…I don't know. I thought this would work. Morgaine… Morgaine said the gemstone is 'attuned to the Void'. The power *behind* the power of the Arc Gates. Not part of it, but like a 'leash', she said. I don't know…"

Gary came up next to him. "Man, you got this. You're clearly doing something! It's doing things it was never doing for Ellie or her scientists. And you're the guy who got it to work in the first place. So you…and the thingy around your neck …you know. Use the Force. Whatever. You can do it!" He backed down off the semi-trailer bed.

Nathan took a deep breath, this time sitting down. He tried to talk to the gemstone in his head. *OK, you … whatever! 'Leash on the Void!'… let's get this done!* One more prayer couldn't hurt, either. *And…Creator… friend of Morgaine's dad…I guess I never knew his name…come on. I have to know … if she's ok. I just…have to. Please?*

The Arc Gate came alive…lights swirled within its center.

"Nathan, it's doing something…it's doing something different!" came Gary's voice. Opening his eyes, Nathan saw the swirling lights. No push back this time. No resistance like the previous times.

What changed? I guess I don't care.

Waving to his friend, he picked up the gear and walked through the portal.

CHAPTER 134

Flying in at nighttime, the hydraulic doors opened skyward to the hidden hangar, as usual. This time, however, the lights on the edges lit up the night sky like a stage show was about to begin. Instead of landing first, the sky cruiser slowly set down its prize, gingerly and slowly descending, despite the massive weight.

Trey looked at his chronometer. It had taken over nine hours to fly back. They had had to fly low and far more slowly. Even at that pace, the energy it had taken had almost run them completely out of power. Looking back, he saw Ellie was awake again. She's complained at least three times about the length of the flight. She had eaten twice her weight and slept half the time on top of it all. He'd be glad to be rid of her.

Once they'd set the Arc Gate down on a moving riser, a large group of people rolled it away to another portion of the hangar so the sky cruiser itself could land. The hangar was deep, going down multiple stories to the main floor hallways down below.

Once they docked, the auto-charger cables came out and plugged in. The hatchway doors dropped and out popped Ellie, Smyslin, Treyborne, Messau, and the others. The first thing they saw was Morgaine, sitting in a rolling chair and covered in a blanket. As late as it was, she had stayed up to see them in. A few of the staff with them, along with her two guards.

Maitan was behind her and apparently the one who'd pushed her in. Treyborne advanced, with the others behind him.

"Captain..." she said, eyes up at him. Those eyes were sharp.

"Lady Morgaine," he said formally, "Your Arc Gate," he said, gesturing toward it with his arm, but keeping his eyes on her. Noticing Brianna behind Maitan stopped him for a second. Then he looked over at it. In the intervening moments, something had happened. Upon touching ground, the Gate had started to create a light vortex. The dark crystal gems embedded in the Gate metal itself were sparkling and swirling.

Morgaine's gasped. "It…it's opening. Right now!"

Ellie, hearing this, ran over to the metal riser they'd set it on, followed by Smyslin and the other guards. Trey looked at Morgaine and then ran after them.

"Don't get too close!" Morgaine tried to yell, but it came out as no more than a hoarse whisper. Maitan heard her, though, and ran after them, "Wait!" he cried. Brianna tried yelling as well. The portal was thrumming far too loudly for anyone to hear them.

Morgaine looked from her to the portal.

No one has witnessed a live portal transport in over five hundred years. This will not go well.

Get me over there!" she snapped. One of her guards hesitated, then started pushing her towards the light. Brianna followed. The Arc Gate, meanwhile, was gyrating light. It looked like a vortex of stars swirling faster and faster.

"Move!" Morgaine said, but the man barely increased the speed. Apparently, he either didn't care to keep his job, or he hadn't heard her. Or…Morgaine supposed, he was trying to be cautious with the nearly dead woman. Tamping down her fury, she looked back and shouted, "I said '*Move*'!"

Looking down at her, he began to run. But it was too late. Light inverted to darkness and the Portal went dark. The lights of the hangar bay lit back up just in time to catch Treyborne racing up to the top of the riser, Maitan at his heels.

Standing alone stood none other than Nathan Arvad. The gemstone in his hand was fading…and Morgaine, her wheelchair having stopped when the lights went dark, just sat there, and nodded approvingly. Something…also went light in her heart. Some weight that she hadn't even realized was there, lifted. Gingerly, she stood up. As she did so, she realized that none of the others who'd raced to the Portal were there. Two of her Elite Guard…Smyslin…and Ellie, the girl from Nathan's world, were gone.

All of them.

But Nathan was there. Dropping his gear, he started to run over to where she was standing down below, but Trey grabbed his shoulder, "She's still hurt. Slow down…you might injure her!"

Nodding, Nathan turned again, and Trey released him. He walked over to where she was standing. She'd been in a wheelchair. She was in loose, light cloth and he could see where she was still heavily bandaged. This was way worse than before. But he had known that when he'd seen her lying in the mud. Bleeding – to death, he thought.

She was steady, though. Maitan came and stood behind her, watchful like a nervous mother. Her eyes were bright. "You came back," she said. "Of course, we didn't know you'd gone in the first place. But it appears you have figured out the stone."

Nodding he gently hugged her. She hugged him back much harder.

"I'm glad you're alive!" Nathan said, "When I last saw you…right before the lightning hit…"

Stepping back, she nodded, and sat down. Clearly even that little bit had exhausted her. She looked dizzy. "I…have had some issues from my wounds."

Maitan cleared his throat, causing Nathan to look back at him. "She *died*, Master Nathan. *Three times.*" Nathan just stared from him to her, open mouthed. "She lost an incredible amount of blood. A human being would have most assuredly stayed dead. As it was, she is very…*blessed*… to still be breathing. She just woke up yesterday, in fact."

"You say that like it's been a while. I've only been gone two days!" Nathan said, confused. "At least, in my world, it was only one night. Unless I was passed out there longer than I realized."

"This is the sixth day since the attack, Nathan," Treyborne said, strolling up. "It took us this long to fix the sky cruiser – what you call the 'airship'," he said smiling. "We just got this thing into the hangar."

"Time has a way of…moving differently in different parts of the galaxy," Morgaine said. "I experienced some of that myself…back in the day. The further your world is from here, the more it can skew. And," she added looking him in the eyes, "you may have been out longer on your home world than you thought, as well."

Those freaking eyes! So beautiful, even as beaten down as she is!

"Well," he said again, "I'm just glad you're alive. Whoever stabbed you …they ran. At least the ones you didn't kill."

Morgaine took his hand, "I'm glad you're alive, too. Don't worry about them. They won't be back. Maitan, take me back to my prison cell of a hospital room. I'm feeling tired. Nathan, if you could come see me in the morning, I would appreciate it."

With that, Maitan and her guard departed. Brianna lingered, staring at Treyborne for some reason, then turned and followed them.

Treyborne watched her leave but said nothing. Then, he chucked Nathan on the shoulder, "I knew you were alive!" he said, grinning. "Sounds like you have a free night! Let's get a drink!" Stopping to look at what Nathan was pulling from behind his shoulder, he asked, "What's that?!"

"It's called a 'shotgun'! I have a limited supply of ammo, but I thought it might come in handy. So, I brought one with me."

Eyeing it appreciatively, Trey grabbed some of the other gear and they walked off. Trey stopped suddenly, "Wait. Where's Stanslin…?" Looking back, he saw the armor where Nathan had left it up by the Arc Gate.

Looking back himself, Nathan said, "He didn't make it, Trey. He came through with me. But when I awoke, he was already gone."

Trey nodded slowly…then sighed, turning back to walk again. "Ok. Let's drink to him, then. Him and all the other men who've recently given their lives to the cause. It's been a hard road these last few weeks."

Nathan nodded, heading down the stairs and out of the hangar with him.

It had indeed.

CHAPTER 135

Nathan had gone. The monolith or "Arc Gate" as Nathan had called it had gone dark. Sighing, Gary turned and headed towards Ben's car. This was not going to be fun. Suddenly, the monolith burst forth with light again, and the swirling pattern returned.

What, did Nathan forget his toothbrush…?

Suddenly, out fell four figures! Four! Racing into the barn and back up to the back of the semi, they all began to stand up. Two were dressed in armor just like Nathan and the dead dude had been wearing. When they saw Gary, they quickly raised what looked like rifles at him. Gary's hands went up. Behind them stood…a very weird looking old man… and Ellie!

"Ellie! What the fuck, girl? Can you tell your big, black-armored friends that we're … well, *friends*?"

Ellie turned to them and said something completely unintelligible. They lowered their weapons and gave a timid wave.

Gary waved back. "Ellie! What's going on?! Did you see Nathan…? Did he send you back…?"

Ellie was looking around like she'd never seen a barn before. She came first, and the others followed her. Hands still on weapons. The old man was fidgeting nervously.

Ellie said, "Hey, Gary…! What the *fuck*, man! Why's the monolith on the back of a semi inside an old barn?" She reminded him in that very moment why he hated her.

"Well, now Ellie…that's a long story," he began.

So, like the little bitch she was, she sat down and spread her arms. "I've got all day!"

"Well, welcome home you little…" Gary started, but Ben was there holding his arm. Breathing slowly, he said, "Why don't we all sit down?" and he proceeded to sit. Gary sat down on a higher hay bale than she was on, just for tactical advantage. The others said nothing. He pointed at them, "Can they understand me?" Ellie looked back and shook that short, dark brown hair of hers. Everything she did annoyed him. "Nope. They're aliens, Gary."

Then she said something in that weird language. They laughed. That annoyed him, too.

"I'm listening," she said impatiently over their laughter.

"And I'm waiting for them to shut up! Look, Ellie…you know you don't look so pinched without your glasses." She turned and gave him a hard look, but he just kept on talking, "After you disappeared, well… the government decided this little wormhole was too hot for little old brainiacs like your friends to have. So, they took it. They also, I might add, created a conspiracy rumor that you and Nathan – being former… you know – had concocted this whole 'vanishing' thing up and it was just one big stunt. But one of your co-workers planted a GPS on the thing, and he gave me the tracking info. I guess he figured once the government had it, that was that. I had other ideas! So, I stole if from their warehouse and brought it here."

"What?! Why did you do that? You couldn't do anything…?" Ellie asked incredulously.

"I don't know!" Gary shouted. "But I wasn't going to let them put Nathan's one chance at returning into a recycling bin or ship it off to

Mars or something! It was our only connection to him. And to you, too, I might add!"

Ellie turned and started talking in that language to the others, and they nodded, after a minute.

"And how did you learn that language of theirs so fast?"

Ellie tapped her brain. *What an arrogant little…*

Then she turned her head and he saw a small metal clasp stuck next to her temple above her ear. "Oh wow," was all Gary said.

She turned back to him, "So what's your plan now…? And…did you see Nathan, or were you just asking about him? Because he's been missing for almost a week back…"

"He was just here!" Ben said. "He just left to go back."

"Really?" Ellie said in low tone, "I wasn't there with him very long. He and these armed thugs got me away from some of their…." She turned and clearly asked a question of the others with her, "Dark Men."

"'Dark Men', huh," Gary said. "Sounds ominous. Hey…since you're back…and you don't seem so keen to go back, either. Maybe you can help a brother out…? The government has kind of put a big target on my back!"

Ben pointed at the others, "Why did they come…? Did they want to visit or something…?"

Ellie nodded her head in the negative. "No…I'm afraid we all came through by accident. Maybe Nathan's return is what triggered the portal taking us. We were all pretty close to it. I guess…we all got sucked in…? I certainly don't mind! But them…? They're just waiting on me to give them an idea of what's going on and what the plan is. I just told them to wait until we were done talking. So, they're doing that."

"What obedient little soldiers!" Gary exclaimed. The look Ellie gave him quelled his humor.

"They're now as lost and screwed as I was, Gary! And this one," she pointed at the old man, "for some reason worships the ground Nathan walks on. These others were just guards that got too close. You know…" she looked back and spoke in that language again for quite some time.

After a while, Gary started tapping his foot. Ben whispered, "I kind of have to go. My wife is texting me like crazy. You're supposed to be at the bus stop by now…and I'm supposed to be eating lunch with her."

Gary nodded.

Attempting to break up their ongoing conversation without being a complete jerk was impossible. Fortunately, Gary had majored in "Jerkism" in college. "Hey! Uh…Einstein Girl! What's the sit rep here? Ben has to go, and I may be missing my bus. We need a plan. Or I need to go, too!"

Turning that look of hers on him was almost enough for him to…. clenching his fist behind his back, he smiled his nastiest smile back at her.

"We've decided to help you," she said. "They're going to come with me, and I'm going to present them to the University…or the government, more likely…as what they are: aliens. I've promised them they won't be harmed – I hope I'm right, Gary – and that they will eventually get home. But since the only person who for sure can open that Gate is not here right now, we're not going to sit around here for weeks and wait on him, either! They'll let people poke and prod them, with me as translator until I can get them out and get them home. I gave them my word."

She got up and walked towards Gary, pointing her finger. "You're going to tell them that you knew I was coming back with aliens, and I had instructed you to steal the thing if it ever got taken away. Got it? Simple: you were my bitch. Any questions?"

Gary kept that fake smile on and nodded. "Sure, Ellie. Sure. I was your *bitch*. 'Take me to your leader' for them. Got it. But what if Nathan never comes back?"

Ellie looked directly up at him but she had no answer.

Morgaine got back to her "hospital bed" and Maitan became immediately concerned. "Your heart rate is quite elevated!" Maitan said. "You need to relax. Too much excitement, Mistress! I'm going to give you a sedative so you can sleep…" He first hooked up her liquid drip and then put her fingertips from both middle fingers into the testers to gauge her blood levels.

"You'll do no such thing!" she ordered. "I'm fine!"

In fact, she was more than fine. Nathan was alive…and he had returned from his home world! On top of that, she had the Arc Gate. Yes, it was apparently fully functional. Something would have to be done about that. But for the time being, there was little danger of it being hijacked or used. And…Nathan was *alive*! He was…*here*! Morgaine felt like a little girl…for the first time since…when? When she was a little girl? She giggled out loud and Maitan looked over at her sternly.

"Are you all right," he asked in his most clinical voice. "Perhaps I've given you too much medication…"

Morgaine almost laughed at him. The smile simply would not leave her face. Feeling her head and neck, he said, "You have a fever, as well, apparently."

Brianna walked in as he was checking her temperature. "Mistress, once he's done with you, I'd like a word alone, please."

Morgaine sobered up a bit, then smiled and said, "Of course, Brianna!"

Everything was good today, suddenly. Maitan pressed a button on the screen and clucked his tongue. "It's as I thought! You got too much piritosin." Pressing another button, Morgaine started to feel quite a bit woozier, and simultaneously less happy.

She frowned.

"That should do for now," he said, nodding to Brianna. He then left, shutting the door behind himself.

Morgaine looked over at Brianna, blinking and trying to remember. "Did you…have something you wanted to say to me, Brianna?"

Brianna came over, sitting next to her. She sighed, putting her hands into her lap, and looking down. "I have something…I want to ask you. And…it's hard for me. I know you and Trey…"

Morgaine tried to focus on her. Why was it so hard…? "What…iss it?"

Did I just slur a bit?

Brianna looked up at her, gave her a critical stare, and said, "I'm not certain this is the time, actually," and stood up.

Morgaine grabbed her arm, forcing herself to be as sober as possible. "If it's about Treyborne, the answer is, 'Yes'! You may recall, I was trying to get him to hire a prostitute, for goodness' sake! Those orders, I'm quite certain, he did not carry out, by the way! You are a beautiful woman, Brianna! And he has shown interest in you. If you want to explore that a little more, you have my blessing. You always have. You'd be good for each other. Believe me!"

Brianna smiled, and a tear ran down her cheek. "Not so 'out of it' as I thought. As usual, you read the room immediately." Squeezing Morgaine's arm, she added, "Get better soon! We need you out there!" Then she left.

Morgaine stared at the wall, listening to her monitors beep for a time. For a little more, she let herself dwell on a baby she would never meet. In all her years, Morgaine had never…*ever*…been pregnant. Until that moment, she had never known it was even possible for her. Had it been a boy, or a girl? Certainly, whichever it was, it was not the grandchildren her father had seen. Morgaine's mind wandered back to Nathan. And that heart lift was there all over again. She had really feared he was dead. Her soul could now truly rest.

Soon afterwards, she did just that.

CHAPTER 137

Bantor and Jasper rode up the hill, taking their time as the sun was setting slowly, with a beautiful cloud cover at the horizon to capture various shades of red, orange, yellow, and even some purple.

Jasper's horse was enormous, an equal of Morgaine's "Steel" – a purebred, magnificent creature with a temper to match. The obvious difference was that Jasper's stallion was mostly light brown with a white slash on his forehead – Razor – and had black fetlocks, tail, and mane. Bantor rode a docile brown mare that has zero interest in Razor, despite his multiple attempts to engage her.

Other than having to keep them apart, the ride had been very pleasant. Bantor loved to ride, but this mare was not one he'd have chosen for himself. But she was good enough for short travel. As they climbed the last hill and approached the perimeter of Morgaine's land covered in olive trees, the sky cruiser was just lowering itself into the hangar doors…and the land slid shut.

Jasper turned and just stared at Bantor. "I won't raise my price on you again," he said with mirth, "but I might after I get an explanation of… whatever that was!"

Bantor just nodded. "All in good time, my friend! You are certainly worth the coin; from what I can see. But all that must be explained by my Master – or rather, Mistress." He said that last while looking back and up at Jasper.

"You may well be assigned to guard me. But the real job is guarding her. Honestly, we usually reveal things in stages to our new personnel, as we deem it safe to do so. Unfortunately, what you just saw may cause us to accelerate things a bit. I will say this once and only once," he added, stopping his horse, and looking pointedly at Jasper. "If you have one shred of the Dark in you…we will root it out. You will not live to see the daylight again. I will not chase you, nor send anyone after you, should you decide to turn around at this point. If you continue on from here, however, your blood is on your own head."

Then he just sat and waited.

Jasper looked at him for a good, long minute. He fiddled with his mustaches for a moment, then pointed forward. "Lead on, my good man! I think it is time for me to meet your Mistress, who flies around in metal birds!" He sniffed. "Perhaps she can find me a second weapon for my other hand like this one," he tapped his side where the blaster was.

Bantor just nodded, turning his horse back towards the compound, "I have no doubt she can, Jasper. I think you will find she is quite… resourceful. Oh, and I doubt that was her in the sky cruiser. It is usually her men. Eventually, you'll be expected to know how to fly it!"

CHAPTER 138

Nathan and Treyborne stayed up quite late, toasting the fallen…and generally getting to know each other better. Trey was, in truth, a very cool dude, and Nathan found he liked him quite a bit. And whatever or wherever that brandy was from – it was the bomb.

Nathan found himself laughing and drinking, toasting and drinking, listening to stories…and drinking some more. Having gotten back and finding Morgaine alive had pulled some huge relief strings inside. He hadn't known the woman for long…but…there was just something about her. The most unique woman he'd ever met or ever could meet.

Seeing her on that muddy ground with those huge gashes in her, blood going everywhere had been the single most horrific moment of his life. Knowing she was ok and being able to see her in recovery had been all he had ever hoped for. He couldn't quite get over how "stranded" he had felt for those two brief days he'd been back on earth.

His home. Amongst his friends, who had risked so much trying to rescue him.

More than anything, he'd been burning to come back here. And that was all because of Morgaine. So, it had seemed a great idea, once all that stress had been relieved, to spend a night drinking with the man he'd come to regard as a friend. Oh…! Trey had said something he was supposed to be responding to…hadn't he?

"Umm…say again Trey, I'm sorry. The brandy has taken hold of my brain."

Trey just laughed and toasted again, drinking more himself. "That's what this stuff does. The best brandy in the world!"

"What is it called again?" Nathan asked.

"Orakin Brandy," Trey answered, showing him the bottle. Nathan couldn't read the bottle from that distance. Not for the first time, he had to stop and remember he wasn't speaking his native language. But he spoke it fluently…after being shocked nearly to death all those weeks or months ago. And the few times he'd had to read anything, he'd been able to do that, too.

"Trey…" Nathan began, "Morgaine is convinced I'm Elder Race. And all signs point towards her being correct. That raises…a lot of questions I don't have answers for. Like: what happened to my real parents? How did I end up in a New York City orphanage? Why do I remember so little of my childhood? Not to mention stuff like: How did I suddenly know how to speak this language we're using right now, when I'm from earth? How old am I…really?"

Treyborne had gotten quiet as he listened. "You've suddenly gotten serious," he said, adding a wry smile. "But obviously I do not have those answers. And I doubt anyone here does. Including Morgaine. But if you really want to find out – ask her. She will tell you the truth. If she knows any of your back story, she won't hold back. Trust me!"

He paused, then added, "All I know is, if you asked me if you were Elder Race, I'd say, 'Hell yeah!'. It's obvious. But…do I really know? Of course not. Maitan should be able to run a blood test, though. Maybe even do some DNA screening. Maybe you don't want to know…it would be ugly if you and Morgaine turned out related."

His eyes turned sharp, watching him.

Nathan nodded, "That would be…interesting," he said. "But I guess since we've finally gotten the Arc Gate secured and Morgaine is…well…

breathing… I suddenly realized sitting here that I've got some questions and issues of my own I might need to figure out. They're not pressing, *per se*, but it might be important at some point. The biggest question to me is: If all the Elder Race came here and fought their way into total extinction, how did I end up being born in the 1990's in upstate New York back on earth?"

Treyborne, as expected, had no answers for that, either.

He did, however, have more brandy.

CHAPTER 139

Brianna left a note at Treyborne's door. Then ran back and slid it into the crack as best she could when it fell from where she'd put it. The sliding doors at this base didn't have enough room underneath them even for a slip of paper. But jamming it into the crevice where it opened at least kept it out of plain sight.

Hopefully, only Trey would see it. Racing back down the hall and into her quarters, she felt like a child on her first fertility dance. Blushing in her room alone to literally no one, she couldn't stop her heart from racing.

Heading to her mirror, she spent some time preparing for…what was she preparing for? Shrugging to herself, she continued. Lip paint, eye paint…washing and drying her hair. Then putting on the most provocative summer dress she had bought. How long ago was that…? When Treyborne had simply been her guard as she traipsed from store to store in Bistern.

Pouring herself a full glass of wine, Brianna turned down the heat and snuggled up under a white blanket. The blanket was simply divine… Brianna had never felt such a soft fabric in her entire life! Curling up, she almost fell asleep before she realized the time was far later than she had thought.

Did I fall asleep?

Getting up and looking up and down the hallway, there were still the same two guards at the stairs, hands on rifles, talking in low tones and chuckling occasionally. Sticking her head out as far as she could, she tried to see to where Treyborne's doorway was. Was the note still in it…?

She couldn't tell.

Tiptoeing in her socks, she slipped out a few more steps and got a better angle. Yes. It was. Where was he…? Could he possibly still be drinking with Nathan…? It was well past midnight!

Hmph. Well, I can stay up as long as he can! Captain Squarejaw!

The guards had seen her by now and waved. She waved back, mortified. Rushing back into her room, she heard the automatic door hiss shut behind her and she pressed the "hold" button.

Heading back to her wine carafe – the one she'd filled down at the kitchens for this very purpose earlier that evening – she poured another full glass and went back to sit down on her couch and wait for Treyborne to knock at her door.

Turning the lights down a bit more, she sat and sipped her wine and became lost in her own thoughts. Setting the empty wine glass down on the center table, she curled up and decided she could wait him out just as well with her eyes closed.

Within minutes, she was fast asleep.

Tap tap tap.

Hmm…?

Tap tap tap.

"Uhmmmm….oh!" Brianna sat straight up. *What time is it?!*

The daylight simulators the building utilized had not shown daylight, nor had any of the actual atmosphere indicators shown it was morning. Of course, skylights in the upper hallways let light in, but she wasn't on one of those levels. Hastily standing up and straightening her dress… she saw that it was 0140.

Unbelievable! If he thought he was going to get any consideration by coming here this late, she would give him an earful!

Heading to the door, she pushed the "Release" button and began saying, "Trey…! It is simply unconscionable of you to…*Maitan*!? What are you doing here? And at this time of night?"

Maitan just stood there a moment, one eyebrow raised for a moment, "It is all right for Captain Treyborne to visit in the middle of the night… but not myself?" he asked. "How interesting. May I come in, despite that fact?"

Nodding guiltily, she stepped aside, and he walked in and sat down on one of the seats opposite the couch on which she had fallen asleep. She saw him notice the mostly empty carafe, the second wine glass on the tray and her own with a little residual at the bottom.

"How may I help you, Maitan?"

He spoke in clipped words, obviously a bit uncomfortable for some reason. Brianna hoped it wasn't her dress and all the makeup. "It has come to my attention that our Mistress has…acquired some feelings for our semi-permanent guest."

"You mean…Nathan?" she asked, realizing instantly how stupid that sounded.

Damn being so tired!

If it seemed stupid to Maitan, he failed to react, merely nodding as he continued, "It is also of note – and I want you to keep this in the strictest of confidences – that until she was nearly cut in half by her assailants in the second attempt to retrieve the Arc Gate, our Lady was pregnant! I have told her of the loss of the baby, which she had had no clue about – totally reasonable based on the short length of time she must have been in said state – but I am concerned regarding several things about which I have zero control and can provide even less help. Being a woman, as she is, perhaps you can address some of these issues with her…"

Brianna had stopped cold for a moment upon hearing that not only had Morgaine gotten pregnant – but that she also had lost the baby. "What issues…?" she asked, coming to sit down. "And how awful that she lost her baby!"

Maitan looked at her and nodded curtly. "Yes. And now you see the reason for my unusual level of discretion. I could not risk anyone overhearing such a conversation between us. Nor could I wait until a good time to talk with you about it. I was under the impression, while she was unconscious, that it was possible – however improbable – that she had actually tried to get pregnant with…Nathan. He does appear to be a true Elder Race being, and having a child with him is…at least *fundamentally*…logical."

Brianna leaned back and asked, "Maybe I'm too tired for logic right now, Maitan. But what is it exactly that you are saying here? I'm not getting it."

Maitan was sitting very stiffly on the chair, she saw. He was extremely uncomfortable speaking as he was, clearly. Seeing this, Brianna stood up and reached over, grabbing the carafe from the far side of the table. "Let me get you a glass of wine." The fact that he just nodded and waited for it spoke volumes.

Handing him the other glass with the remainder of the wine, she sat down again. Maitan took it and literally drank the entire glass in one long drink!

Setting the glass down, he finally spoke again, "Morgaine has been having sex for centuries without fear of getting impregnated. I had always assumed – as I assume she has – that it was not something she had to worry about. That it was, in fact, impossible. When I discovered the now deceased baby – still a small fetus – in what was left of her womb, I again thought it had been a deliberate act to resurrect her race. After speaking with her, however, I realized she had had no clue. Now…it would be…*extremely* inappropriate for me to speak to her about contraceptive methods…"

Brianna burst out laughing.

Startled, Maitan whipped his attention directly to study her face, "Did I say something amusing?" he asked, apparently offended.

"Nooooo!" Brianna said, still laughing uncontrollably.

Maitan's neck pulled back even more if that were possible. "Clearly, you think the subject a joke of some kind. I assure you; this is quite serious…"

"Nooo…..nooooo…..noooo! I don't! Really!!!" Brianna was covering her mouth and still the laughter just would not stop. Maitan sat back, dispassionate at best. Completely offended, more likely. Finally, Brianna was able to spit out a full sentence, still holding back more laughter. *Barely.*

"It's…just that…you want me…to…tell Morgaine…to have…safe sex?" Maitan actually nodded at that, which made her laugh again so hard, she had to hold her stomach. While she was still doing so, he got up and started walking towards the door.

Holding her hand up, she said, "Wait…! Wait!" and he stopped, still facing the doorway. Getting up, she got up and gently touched his arm. "Maitan, I know you love Morgaine. We all do! But she…she's not only a grown woman, but she's also lived fifty of my lifetimes! I'm sure she knows how to avoid getting pregnant. I'm sure she also probably wasn't doing so…when that happened. But she doesn't need me to remind her of that. And yes, it would be inappropriate for you to bring it up! I just envisioned me talking to her about sex…like she was my little girl or something…! And…it struck me as funny. I'm sorry! But it would be like lecturing my great grandmother's great grandmother's grandmother about sex. The woman doesn't need *me* to tell *her* anything! If anything, I should be going to her for advice. And believe me! If she doesn't want to get pregnant, it won't happen again." Suddenly sober, she quietly added, "I just hope…for her sake…she still can."

With that her laughter died completely, she pecked him on the cheek, and he turned to her, and nodded. Once. Mollified, clearly, but not completely unmortified. As he left, she belatedly followed him out and tip-toed over to see if that damnable Trey had gotten…

No note.

Doorway closed. That bastard! He probably hadn't even read it! Maitan saw that she had followed him out. She was leaning around him to see Treyborne's doorway, as it had been directly behind him. So, as he turned back to her, she straightened up faster than a schoolgirl caught with her hands on someone else's candy.

"Is there…something else, Lady Brianna?" he asked formally.

"Oh no…she said. "No, no! Just making sure you made it out ok. I'll see what I can do. Maybe I can bring it up in a sideways fashion that won't make it seem like I know all about…you know." She nodded towards the guards.

Looking behind him, Maitan then turned back to her and winked. "Ah…yes! I do know. Good night, Miss Brianna!" With that, he headed straight for Morgaine's room where he would again spend the entire night in vigil.

Brianna watched him go. Sparing a short, but hard glare for Treyborne's doorway, she stalked back to her room and let the door close behind her. She hit both the "Hold" and "Do not disturb" buttons.

Men are just filthy, stinking, selfish bastards! And that Treyborne will not be getting any of this sweet candy for quite some time! If ever!

CHAPTER 140

Nathan stumbled into his room…well, he really didn't know what time he got there. But as he was undressing, he suddenly realized something.

Where is Smyslin? He should be fully recovered by now…

Feeling woozy, he stumbled back out into the hallway just in time to see Treyborne's door slide shut. Looking at the guards for a moment, he walked as carefully as he could, acting as sober as he could until he got to Smyslin's room. It was just down the hall from his own, but the walk seemed to take a bit longer than it should have.

Knocking, he received no reply. Frowning, he tried to remember if he'd seen him at all after he'd gotten back. He was pretty sure he had not.

Let's face it, Nathan. You're a bit tipsy. It is possible our memory of today isn't that great. We'd better just look for him in the morning.

With that, Nathan made his way back to his rooms, only to realize he had not actually put his shirt back on after he'd taken it off.

Oh yeah. I'm sure the guards think I'm totally sober.

Laughing a bit at himself, he went into his bedroom area and threw himself onto the bed. He was snoring before the lights had even dimmed.

In the morning, or perhaps a bit closer to afternoon, Nathan awoke with a splitting headache. He was seeing double, and it took a moment for him to recalibrate and focus properly. Sitting up, he realized his mouth was bone dry. And tasted awful. Getting up and brushing his teeth was cathartic…and only after he'd sat down in the outer room, did he remember.

Smyslin!

Jumping up; this time remembering to put on his shirt, he hurried down to Smyslin's room and knocked. No answer. Turning to the guards, who were different than the ones last night, he asked, "Where is Smyslin? Have you seen him recently?"

The two guards looked at him dumbfounded. Then they both looked at each other. One finally spoke up, "But…sir…he was with…your friend. The loud girl."

"Ellie? So…what?" *Wait, I haven't seen her, either!* "What happened?"

Again with the looks! "I said, 'What the hell happened?'!"

The same guard who spoke before said, "Sir! They ran to the portal as you arrived. Everyone knows. It's all anyone could talk about all night and this morning. They left when you arrived!"

"Who did?!"

"Your friend…Smyslin… Rost and Agino…! They all got sucked into the portal. When you arrived, they vanished!"

CHAPTER 141

Morgaine spent the morning trying to stay awake. She was sure she had asked Nathan to come by for a *morning* meeting. She was also sure he had heard her. Checking the chronometer showed her it was well past the eighth hour. Mid-day had come and gone.

Sighing, she laid her head back on her pillows. Sitting for more than an hour was pure torture. But to have to lay in this bed doing nothing for weeks…it made her want to scream!

Trying not to feel disappointment at Nathan's apparent snub, Morgaine pressed a button that would bring in whoever was in charge of being her mother hen for that particular time of day.

Brianna stuck her head in a moment later. Apparently, it was her task for the afternoon. "What do you need, Mistress?" She appeared both tired and annoyed. Probably at having to do nothing for hours but wait to be called.

Morgaine waved her hand so she would come in. Brianna hesitated a moment, then slipped in. Morgaine suddenly noticed that she had on full makeup, but her lipstick had worn off. Like she'd forgotten it was on and had simply let the lipstick go when she ate…

Morgaine frowned.

"What's wrong, Morgaine? Did I do something wrong…?" Brianna looked confused now. No sense in telling her. It would only embarrass her.

"No, dear. I simply wanted another person to talk with me. Sit." She gestured to the chair nearest her. Brianna promptly sat down, looking at her curiously. "I feel absolutely useless and bored! There has got to be a way for me to function without having to move much. I don't have to be jumping around and firing a blaster or waving my sword... but I need you to get creative. Find Maitan. I don't care if you have to wake him! Get me a room where I can sit, dressed and looking alive. I will conduct as much business as I can from whatever desk-like thing you can rig up for me. At least I'll be doing more than lying here and getting bed sores!"

Brianna looked at her doubtfully. "Morgaine...you...were *dead* a week ago! Perhaps you can just take it slow for a *few* more days?"

Morgaine gave her an icy stare. "I'm not dead now! Get it figured out! Tell that old bird that I'm not taking 'no' for an answer! I am going to be doing something, or I will die of boredom!"

Brianna looked at her more than a little skeptically. "OK...but..."

"No 'buts', Brianna! Last time I checked, it was my gold that paid the bills here. It's my compound, my equipment, my people. Just do it!"

Brianna looked at her blankly, then saluted. Like the Guards.

Whatever. "Get it done." Brianna left. Even that outburst had cost her a great amount of energy. Maybe a little nap...

A knock came at the door. Opening her eyes, she saw Nathan looking inside the door crack.

Ugh! Of course he comes now! Beckoning with her hand, she said, "Come in, Nathan...". She sounded weary even to herself.

Closing the door behind him, he said, "I'm sorry I didn't get here earlier, Morgaine. I just...I was up drinking a bit too late. Then when I got up, I was told Smyslin had been sucked into the portal with Ellie...and two of your guards."

Morgaine just nodded at him. Her expression was completely unreadable.

"Well," he continued, "I honestly didn't know! I was just…so…. glad to see you. Alive and all. I just wasn't aware completely of everything that had happened, I guess."

She nodded again. She wanted to say more, but she was afraid of her own words. It hurt, just sitting here watching him and knowing that, somehow, he hadn't awakened and been here right at dawn.

Irrational child! She chastised herself. "I'm glad you came, at least. It's fine."

"I'd…like to make it up to you."

"And how would you like to do that?" That eyebrow arch itself was erotic on her.

Just wow.

Minutes later, he was wheeling her down the hall to the conference room. A small luncheon had been set up, with meats, cheeses, fruit, a very light looking wine, and some tea in a pot. Apparently, he'd at least planned his recovery.

She smiled at him approvingly. Helping her get up and then sit in one of the lounge chairs, he got her a tray of food, poured her some of the wine that he said had been 'forcibly watered down' by Maitan before he would let them bring it, and a bowl of fruit.

He then grabbed the same for himself and sat down across from her. "So…" he said, "tell me… what is dying like?" Seeing her reaction, he added, "Unless you don't want to talk about it, of course! I was just… trying to…" he shrugged.

Laughing, she said, "I am so happy you got me out of my prison cell! For that, alone, you are forgiven for your tardiness. As for dying…it felt a lot like… sleep. I don't remember it, really. Just…". She paused, looking down. "Nathan, I have to tell you something."

She looked up, and for the second time Nathan saw a truly vulnerable Morgaine. This person though…maybe he had never seen before. Nathan could only nod. His eyes were wide. She seemed so frail.

"I don't remember what it feels like to die, Nathan. But before meeting you, I had not known how to live, either. I have always kept myself so… guarded. I can't even remember a time that I wasn't the 'White Queen' anymore. Maybe I should say, 'White Witch'."

She looked down again. Then she sat back purposefully, chin raised. The Morgaine he knew had returned. Somewhat.

"I think you're too hard on yourself, Morgaine. Everyone leans on you. Everyone counts on you. It must be…very disconcerting to find out you're not immortal. I know it sure rocked everyone else. Including me," he added quietly.

Looking at him, she made a decision. "I am not used to being open, Nathan. It makes me feel naked. And not naked…" she smiled for the first time, "in a good way. I mean 'naked' as in 'exposed', vulnerable, weak. I hate being weak, Nathan."

"I get it," he said, "I've been there! And I swore it wouldn't happen again."

She nodded emphatically. "Yes! Exactly! So, now I'm going to go against everything in me screaming to not say anything. I'm going to tell you something that I did not want anyone else to know. And I'm going to do it…" she paused to look into his eyes, her own wide.

My Lord, those eyes…!

"…because I need you to know." She paused, eyeing him.

"Ok…I think I'm ready."

"I doubt it. I wasn't." She sniffed, suddenly the proud warrior princess he'd first met. "I was pregnant, Nathan. And when I was wounded. When I…*died*, so did the baby. I didn't know until Maitan told me a couple days ago. I just didn't *know*…. Nathan…I can't get *pregnant*! At least…that's what I thought." She swallowed, clearly trying not to cry. Nathan got up, but she put up her hand, "No! Just let me finish. Please," she said more gently.

He sat back down, leaning back, trying not to quell the knots that had suddenly appeared in his own stomach.

"I know we just met, Nathan…and I'm not putting any pressure on you. Please understand that" she raised her eyes, and they were moist and clear. Simply the most beautiful eyes in the most beautiful face on any world. He shook his head without realizing it.

"Why are you shaking your head…?" she asked softly. She was clearly afraid of his answer. She…the woman who was maybe a thousand years old…who'd lived more lifetimes than Nathan could imagine.

"No, I'm shaking my head because…you're still hurt. And you're still the most beautiful woman I have ever seen. Or ever will see."

Her head went down. Morgaine wept. Trying not to sob, she sat back and put her finger under her nose, "I'm sorry," she got out. "I'm still… not well. I'm still drugged, too. Don't think I am like this normally!" she snapped her head up, defiant. Tears were running down both cheeks.

"I know…believe me, I know!" Nathan said, starting to laugh a bit.

"Now you're *laughing* at me!" she said, starting to laugh herself.

"Well, you are pretty pathetic!" he said, smiling. "Seriously, though. You are the strongest woman I've ever met. I'm….so sorry…*we* (he said, emphasizing the word 'we') had to lose our baby. So…*very* sorry. And I can tell you one thing and one thing only."

"What is that?" she asked, half smiling, half crying, tears still streaming down her face.

"I'm not leaving this world until we make those bastards pay."

CHAPTER 142

Jasper sat at a wooden table on a wooden bench in the most drab, under-decorated room he had ever seen. Bantor had assured him repeatedly that today would be the day that he would get to meet "her". It had already been two days. He was beginning to wonder.

Nodding to himself, he toyed with his blaster. He remembered the day he'd won the thing in a game of 'stripper'. A lewd game, to be sure. But a profitable one. Casinos everywhere allowed the game, because the skimming they made was often more than the games already skewed to their monetary gain in the first place.

Running his hand over the fine metal workings and the intricate markings, he still marveled at the excellence with which it had been made. The fact that he happened to have acquired several other artifacts of the so-called 'Elder Race' had been his motivation. He was quite certain the weapon would no longer work when he'd gotten it.

And it didn't. Until he'd found that it fit quite perfectly into another artifact, one he had acquired almost ten years earlier. Something that he found absorbed sunlight and glowed at night. He'd used it as a nightlight. For years. It turned out it was far more than that. It was what the archivists called a 'solar battery'.

Jasper was not an educated man beyond what was necessary for doing the business of … well… his business could be quite unsavory. Nonetheless, he was not stupid, nor uneducated by any means. He simply had not dedicated his life to doddering around in musty old libraries seeking knowledge. He was a man of action! And, as such, he liked his toys.

This toy had saved his life more than once. But the day he'd figured out that the formerly useless weapon fit like a glove in his nightlight. Well…that had been a good day!

Since then, he'd become one of the highest paid bounty hunters, well…ever. At least he liked to think so. But this place, this place was intriguing. Not the simple table, nor the stupid front of olive grove sharecroppers. No, that was disgusting.

But a group that had artifacts…from those ancient times…not held by the Triumvirate…that worked! Artifacts that flew…! This was revelatory! Even knowing what he'd known coming here.

Tapping his hand and then his foot, Jasper again became impatient. How long was this going to take? Sighing and lighting a pipe bowl of tobacco, he sat back on his uncomfortable seat and took another sip of wine. At least the wine was excellent.

Someone, somewhere had good taste…

A door opened from what he could only presume to be the kitchens. Out walked Bantor, followed by two armed guards – and by armed, they were wearing artifact armor, holding artifact weapons that made his own look like a slingshot, an obvious commander that appeared – quite capable – and behind him…

Oh my…Creator! Standing, he immediately bowed at his waist until they arrived.

The military man in charge, a man perhaps thirty years old and tough as nails spoke first, "Please lay your weapons on the table."

He did so. First the blaster, which raised an eyebrow from the guards. Not the commander. Apparently, he had been informed, at least. Then an impressive array of knives, throwing stars, and a thin cord that had only one possible use.

The woman behind them all raised an eyebrow looking at that, then looked at him. He shrugged, putting up his hands. "It has its uses."

Nodding, she sat down on a soft chair that a serving girl had brought in right behind them. The girl scurried away as soon as she had set it down. The man held their guns like they meant to use them. Jasper nodded appreciatively.

"I hear," the woman said regally, "that you saved my recruiter, Sir Bantor from a would-be assassin," the woman said.

He nodded.

"I was also told you possessed a weapon that most men outside our little group and the Dark itself do not possess. I see that is, indeed, the case." He nodded again. "Finally, I was told you are going to cost me both an arm *and* a leg to pay you. Tell me why you're worth it. Beyond saving my man and holding a blaster."

Jasper poured himself some more wine, raising the bottle, "Excellent vintage. My thanks." Sitting back, he eyed them as if he had to kill them all. Which, he realized, he might.

He cleared his throat. "I think it's quite simple. And, keep in mind, I'm telling you this completely without a weapon on my person. And with no malice at all. I was hired to kill you." He said this plainly, looking directly at Morgaine. His guards all bristled at this, and she had to put her hand on the arm of one.

"No, I wasn't sure this was where you lived, or ran to after leaving Rondor. But I knew you must have lost men in the process and suddenly someone was hiring a great many men in Nyx. It sounded too coincidental to be anyone but you. So..." he said, taking another drink of wine, "I took the first ship to Nyx, and I waited. I've been around this city many times before, and I knew if I waited long enough, the half-decent mercenaries would all run themselves out. Someone of your…quality…would only accept the best."

"So why are you telling me this? Why shouldn't I kill you now and remove the threat?" Morgaine said coldly. She meant it.

Jasper was impressed. She didn't even flinch at the idea.

"Because I can now be your greatest ally. Rondor put a bounty on your head. 'Dead or Alive', surely you knew that…?" Morgaine looked at her commander, who shrugged. "Or…not. Maybe it's something someone like you is used to. After all, you've supposedly been alive since before the Elurrian Empire. Not that one should believe everything one hears…"

"I was two hundred years old before the Elurrians first learned how to build a boat," Morgaine said calmly. "And I expect to live another two hundred after the Empire of Nelrae, which conquered them, falls into the sea! You still have not answered my question, Jasper…or whatever your real name is. Why should I not have you killed right now? I'll bag a new blaster as a bonus for the effort!"

"Indeed. But as I said, you would then not have me as an ally. Not only do I know every bounty hunter worth his salt enough to even try to find you, but I also can defend you better than perhaps anyone currently in your employ. Minus this one, perhaps," he said, nodding at Treyborne. "And a man of my connections and skill is not to be taken lightly. Nor discarded quickly."

Jasper sat back, taking another sip, rolling the wine around in the glass. Raising his eyes, he continued, "Hire me and it's a clear win for me. Rondor is falling apart at the seams. Even should I be able to return to Rondor to collect the bounty, they're not likely to pay it! They're under siege as we speak. Or were the last time I received any report of any credibility. But…if I am allowed to join your side…a legendary figure with amazing technology and weaponry; frankly I gain far more than coin. Which, I might add, I will recoup over time in your employ, regardless. I then can finally be amongst my peers! I can work with technology only dreamed about by most of the people toiling to live in a hut with a dirt floor on this Creator-forsaken planet! And…" he leaned forward to emphasize his point, "I hate the Dark as much as you do. The Dark Men took everything from me. You may be only a mark to other bounty hunters. *Lesser*…bounty hunters, I might add. But, to me, you represent the one hope I have of avenging my family. I took this job because I knew I could find you. Up until recently, everyone thought you were dead! So, instead of fulfilling some pathetic contract on your head for mere money, I stand to gain far, far more. I would get a handsome sum if I brought them your head – and hear me – I'm not failing to try because I don't think I can. Clearly, I would have had my shot today, had I wanted it. No, I am 'switching sides' if you will, because I want to. And that was always my intended goal."

Jasper sat back, drinking his wine, and carefully watching their reactions.

Bantor was stunned and clearly nervous he had even brought him in. To be expected. Jasper had told the simple truth. He could have taken his shot a few minutes prior. The two guards were standing there, doing their duty – looking for him to move an inch the wrong way. The commander…he was looking like he had caught a fox in the hen house and then realized he had just quite possibly caught the most valuable animal he could ever own.

Morgaine…she seemed…smaller than he thought she would be. Yet she was every bit as regal as someone nicknamed 'the White Queen' could ever be. Besides that, she was stunningly beautiful. Her eyes flicked behind him, making Jasper naturally turn his head. Far across the room, a man was standing there. A man…with white hair. He also was wearing armor. One of her men. But…that was impossible, wasn't it?

The man was nodding at her. He then walked away, as if Jasper were no more a concern than a common beggar.

Morgaine seemed to take some meaning from that nod.

She looked back at Jasper, nodding her own head. "Fine. *Commander* Jasper. You will report to Treyborne," she nodded to the tough one, "and to me alone. We will pay you 500 gold instead of the 400 you requested. But hear me," she said, also leaning forward as he had, "double-cross me, as you did that weak little progeny of Rondor…and you'll not live to tell of it. You will also get zero chances to be alone with me for the foreseeable future. That may last until you die of old age. And if you ever try anything, or get caught doing anything I do not like, justice will be swift!" She stood up.

Did she wobble a bit? No, it must have been the uneven flooring. Jasper stood, as well. "I thank you, madam. And I will not be expecting dinners alone with you for some time then," and he smiled, bowing again.

She smiled a smile that had no mirth in it. "My good Commander Jasper, I think you will fit in perfectly here. Just remember. You are a self-admitted bounty hunter, thief, and liar. I have reason to believe you, for now. That is all I will say on that subject. But I will expect you to fully brief Captain Treyborne regarding your personal reasons for revenge against the Dark Lords. And your story had better be a good one."

CHAPTER 143

Smyslin looked around at the metal walls that made up his new living quarters. The previous 15…no 24 hours on this world…had been very upsetting. Or at best unsettling.

The woman, Ellie – Nathan's previous lover – which was news to Smyslin, had made a single comm conversation on her handheld unit. And less than an hour later, the quiet little old farm they'd been sitting at was crawling with men holding blaster-like weapons, full gear, and many, many men with visors on their eyes to shield them from the sunlight.

Smyslin hoped their dislike for the sunlight was not a sign that they were in league with the Dark. Ellie assured him they were not. And that there was no such thing as a Cult of the Dark here. No hidden agenda in her 'democratic government'.

Watching how these people operated had put many doubts into Smyslin's heart. They acted and even spoke (their tone, as he could not understand their words) much like his former Master's Dark Men. His son had died trying to be like these men.

He did not like them.

Now, he was alone. Or at least he wasn't in the room with anyone. The far wall appeared to be some sort of one-way glass. They had similar type observation rooms in the laboratories at Command Central. His former master Jezerah's home base on the western shores of Nelrae. Smyslin shuddered at the similarities.

"Rea oiu dloc?" came a metallic voice from nowhere.

Not understanding, he shook his head. The door opened a moment later, and a girl with dark hair, dressed in military gear, brought in a thin, white blanket and a small pillow. The room he was in had a cot, a strange looking relief zone, and a sink. Going over to the sink, he turned a knob and leaned under it to get a drink while she watched.

Taking the blanket, Smyslin covered himself with it and huddled on the small bed. It was cold here, too. The girl nodded and left the room.

After a time, he laid down, staring at the ceiling. The girl Ellie had said she would protect them. Now Smyslin was alone. On his master's home world without his Master. Shaking his head at his foolishness, he finally fell asleep.

When he awoke, the room was dark. There was a strange thing hanging on the wall with red characters that appeared to be a chronometer. It didn't mean anything to him. It changed frequently. All Smyslin knew was someone had turned out the lights to let him sleep. So, there was some mercy in these people.

Hours before, they had stuck pins into his arms several times – very uncivilized versus the way medications were administered at even the Dark Men's complex. He'd seen how Morgaine had been dealt with, which was more similar, but at least even at her base, they'd used injection methods that didn't hurt. They'd even taken some of his blood and put it into little vials.

His blood had looked strange to him. It was dark and looked a little blue. Scratching the sticky bandage they'd put on his forearm, he stood up. He was hungry now. Knocking on the window, he pointed to his stomach. He hoped that made sense to them.

Another voice came through the walls and then was silent.

A short time later, a tray full of food came, which included some steaming liquid that looked like dark tea. Sipping it, he found it tasted like bad tea. But he drank it anyway. There was also some sort of weird-colored liquid in a glass that seemed like juice of some kind. Then there were recognizable items like meat, eggs that were half-cooked, and something in a box. He ignored that part. The rest of the items were good, though. And the fruity juice was delicious. He drank the last drop of that. The bitter liquid seemed to be their version of tea. It made him more awake, and he had to pee.

So…yes. Bad tea.

After an interminable amount of time, Ellie came into the room, escorted by two more of their military men, carrying those strange blaster rifles and another man dressed in strange shiny clothes and wearing the light blockers. Smyslin did not like him very much. Smyslin didn't think he looked that threatening that they needed those weapons in here.

Ellie sat down and took his hand. "Smyslin, they want to analyze your bones and do some body scans. It's not personal, they say they just want a better picture of the variances between your anatomy and ours. It seems eerily similar, like we came from the same DNA stock. But they don't have those results back yet. In the meantime, I'll be with you and let you know what they're doing."

Ellie's eyes were nice.

"They've already scanned the two others. They're back in their rooms already. If you're ready to go, they are ready for you." Smyslin just looked at the man in the glasses and nodded. He hoped he didn't look too frightened. Walking down the hallways, no one else was there. The lights were too bright out there, and he winced, putting his hands up. The one in the glasses spoke into a comm on his chest and the lights suddenly dimmed.

Well, we know who is in charge for sure now, don't we?

Ellie looked over at Smyslin and she whispered, "It's going to be all right. They haven't violated anything in our agreement, and…they haven't mistreated you, have they?" Smyslin shook his head.

"No, Nathan-friend Ellie. But I wish to go home. This is not where I live. It is not where I am from. I am an engineer, not a lab specimen! I simply want to go and serve my Master. Please. Get this over with so we can go home."

She nodded, but she didn't seem too confident. She looked back at the men following them with the same fear in her eyes that he himself felt.

That did not make him feel any better.

CHAPTER 144

Treyborne got back to his quarters, scuffing his hands through his hair and yawning as he entered. Having been roused far too early after his night of drinking to go "meet the mercenary", his head and his neck ached. His back did, too. He wasn't as young as he used to be.

Stretching, he started pulling on his arms and shoulders. What was that on the floor? Reaching down, he pulled a muscle in his back and yelled. Picking up the folded paper, he opened it.

"Trey, when you get done male-bonding with Nathan, why not come to my room for a nightcap -Bri"

By all the hordes of the Dark! When was this note written??

It apparently had been slipped under his door or stuck in it so that when he entered it came in with him. He'd been so drunk, he hadn't noticed. Looking in the direction of Brianna's room from his, as if he could see through walls, he shook his head.

This will not be good. She's going to assume I ignored her. And if I apologize, I just look weak. No win there. Oh well. This is a problem for another day.

Not having to deal with any training or team responsibilities for another two hours, he set an alarm on the chronometer, laid down on the bed, and fell asleep. He awoke to the comm near his ear buzzing. He'd set it on "Quiet" mode as soon as he'd left the meeting with that Jasper character. That way, unless someone specifically called for him, the comm would remain silent.

"Trey here. What do you need?"

"Captain, this is…Jasper. Uh…Commander Jasper, my pardon. I was wondering if you could meet me in the training zone below quarters. I've found something…interesting."

"Sure. Give me twenty. Oh, and Jasper…?"

"Yes, Captain?"

"Never mind. See you in twenty minutes."

As he left his quarters, Brianna was leaving her rooms. Their eyes met, and she turned away, walking towards Morgaine's hospital rooms. He blew out his breath and walked the other way towards the stairwell, shaking his head.

Maybe I'll get lucky, and this Jasper character will just shoot me. And on second thought, I'm taking the elevator.

Three levels down, where Jasper had indicated he was, Treyborne exited the elevators to lights on everywhere. Several staff members were there with cleaning supplies, mops, and a handful of some powerful disinfection liquid.

He also noticed a rather foul odor wafting about the room.

Spotting Jasper at the cluster of people furthest from him, he strolled over and tapped his new subordinate on the shoulder. "What's all the fuss about?"

Jasper turned and nodded at Treyborne. Instead of answering, however, he just pointed at the floor a few squares away. On the polished dark tiles of the workout and practice area was what could only be the remains of some sort of animal. It was a large animal, but because it was so torn apart and had been rotting for at least a couple of days, not to mention missing its head, it was impossible to tell what. Perhaps a large deer.

Treyborne turned to Jasper and asked, "Who found this? And how in the world did that get in here?"

Jasper said, "OK, you can start to clean it up," to the staff, then walked away with Treyborne, "I just wanted you to see it first. I'm the first who found it. Apparently, with all the…losses you've experienced on your team recently, no one had come down here in the last two days or so. Understandable with all the assigned guards, of course. I simply wanted to see the practice area, and perhaps work out a bit. Instead, I find a huge rotting carcass…"

"Ok…so what else did you find?"

Jasper put a smile on his face and pointed his finger in the air. "Just this," he said walking Treyborne over to another area of the room. He just pointed to the floor, where there were three deep gouges ripped into the tile. Then, another three more about four feet away in the stone tiling.

"What could cause this?" Jasper asked him. "It appears the tracks go off down those corridors. From asking the staff, they indicated that no one is currently residing in the back half of those chambers. They're not even sure what's in them."

"Storage and old equipment mostly," Trey answered offhandedly. "So, it appears we have some sort of apex predator killing things topside and somehow dragging or chasing their prey down here to eat them…?"

"It would appear so," Jasper answered, amused. "I think we'd better find that breach, don't you? And perhaps rid ourselves of potential further loss of staff…" His eyebrows went up at that part.

"Is there any chance it's not another creature of the Dark that hasn't made its way upstairs yet, like the thing that attacked my team prior to your arrival?" Trey asked. "I'm assuming you've heard about that by now."

Jasper nodded, looking at him. "The cleaning crew told me quite a bit about it. That is certainly their greatest fear. But if that were the case, it would not stop to eat dinner and then go hide in the corridors which are, as yet, still uninhabited. With your permission, I'd like to take a couple of your team – our team – and hunt it down and try to get rid of it. Plus seal whatever breach allowed its prey to get away and have it chased all the way down here in the first place. Or…perhaps it just dragged it down here to eat it in private. Either way…"

Trey looked at Jasper for a minute. On the surface, he was just doing his job. But it was rather convenient he'd been the one to find it and now he had a great excuse to search every nook and crevice of the deepest parts of the old Elder Race command center.

Very convenient. "Of course, get two men. But I'm coming with you."

The smile on Jasper's face slid a little, but he bowed immediately and went to gather the other men.

CHAPTER 145

Nathan awoke with Morgaine's head on his chest. She had asked him to sleep in the room with her, which turned into trying to share the hospital bed, which became Maitan bringing in another bed with its back up and tethering them together.

How long he'd been asleep, he had no idea. But it was still dark in the room. There were areas that allowed sunlight in through skylights. But these hallways and rooms only followed day / night simulation if you allowed it. Morgaine's recovery room was not attuned. It could be the middle of the day and he'd never know it.

Gingerly, taking her head off his chest and placing it on a pillow he grabbed, he went to put on his shirt and slip out the door. Morgaine did not awaken, even when he almost fell trying to open the door with his hands full and having it suddenly open automatically when he tried pushing it like a regular door.

Shaking his head at his own stupidity, Nathan walked into the corridor to see Brianna and Maitan in some sort of heated discussion. Seeing him emerge, they stopped mid-argument. Maitan asked, "Is the Mistress still asleep?"

"She is," he managed, trying not to look guilty. "She wanted me to stay. She said it would help her sleep."

"Indeed," was the only reply.

Brianna raised an eyebrow at him, then stalked off towards the room he'd just left. Presumably to check on her, but Nathan had a sneaking suspicion she just wanted to get away from him.

What did I do to her?

Shrugging, he said, "I'm going to my own bed to get some real rest. Don't call me, I'll call you," he said and made his way to his rooms.

But Nathan couldn't sleep.

Sleeping with Morgaine had not been particularly restful. For one thing, sleeping with the most beautiful woman you've ever seen was difficult enough. Throw in the fact that other things had happened before she had become an Elder Race pincushion for the Dark Men, and then add a dash of her groaning in her sleep, and it became just a tad impossible to sleep well. Just the memory of cuddling with her was…distracting.

Groaning and throwing himself out of bed, he got up and brushed his teeth, slipped into his bath converted shower and just focused on their issues. First, they had several people on the wrong planet – again. That did not include himself. If he was being honest with himself, Nathan wasn't sure which planet he really belonged on. There was also the little factor of massive revenge for whoever sent the attackers at Morgaine. Maitan had said Morgaine was certain it had been the Dark Lord named 'Emorion'. But the only one Morgaine had ever spoken of by name before was her brother, Jezerah, going after her.

How certain was she?

Then, of course, they had the problem that Morgaine herself wasn't going to be doing any real revenge work for quite some time. Possibly months. Meanwhile, there was apparently a world war in progress in the Empire of Nelrae. The whole world appeared to be crumbling. Even the alliance amongst the Dark Lords had dissolved. All because Nathan had accidentally triggered the Arc Gate. Oh yes. And the King of Rondor had taken it very poorly when Morgaine had escaped. So, he had placed a bounty on Morgaine's head – and the former councilman Bantor, as well. Nice.

Laughing at the ridiculousness of it all, Nathan finished cleaning up and got out of the shower.

I remember when I thought a bad day was when I had to debug three infected PCs and rewrite some code for an old security profile or two.

CHAPTER 146

Morgaine awoke to catch Brianna peeking in to observe her. Looking over at the empty bed next to her, she turned back to her and asked, "What time is it?"

"Almost 0800, Morgaine. You've been asleep since last night." Seeing Morgaine's head turn to the other bed again, she added, "Nathan awoke and went into his chambers about an hour ago. He didn't want to wake you."

Morgaine nodded.

"Shall I get you some food? Or Maitan?"

Morgaine shook her head, "No…I need to be alone and try to find the energy to clean up. It took everything out of me to meet Bantor's bounty hunter and hold myself together. I cannot be seen as weak. But more importantly, I cannot be weak."

Something she said triggered Morgaine's visceral, internal mind. "Brianna, I've changed my mind. Get me Maitan. And when you see Nathan again, tell him to meet me in the conference room."

"Morgaine…"

Morgaine's head whipped to her, "I'm not asking, Brianna! That is an order. I am still the Mistress of this team and this compound. And I will be obeyed. Is that clear?"

"As clear as the night sky, Mistress," Brianna said, her eyes ablaze. "I will inform Maitan and Nathan, as you command." She even bowed before turning and walking out, back stiff.

As she left, Morgaine felt a tinge of regret.

Perhaps I was too hard on her. But no, I've been sliced and bled literally to death. Everyone thinks that I am frail now. Everyone is trying to coddle me. But without a strong leader, what's left of our little tribe will be wiped off the face of the planet. There is no time for weakness! We are at a time of opportunity. One might even say "crisis". There must be a way to take advantage now! While there's still time.

Maitan came into the room, "Mistress Morgaine…"

"Shut it, Maitan! Listen to me! We've got maybe *three months*. Three months before what's left of the Triumvirate wins this war and emerges with the world under one hand. Perhaps less. Three months before the timer on this window to finally destroy the Void-corrupted Dark Lords and eradicate their menace to the galaxy for all time goes away."

"Yes, Mistress, but…"

"I do not have time to be a convalescing invalid, Maitan! There are certain chemical mixtures in storage. Mixtures you are well aware of…"

"Of course, M'Lady, but…the *cost*…"

"There are no 'but's', Maitan! If I spend our window of opportunity lying in bed and sleeping through each day, fighting to stand still long enough to hide my weakness from a single new recruit…we are lost! Tell me I'm *wrong*! You are the lone descendant of the greatest fighters and strategists of all time. Tell me, if you can, that we will still have this opportunity to conquer our enemies in three months. Go ahead. I'm listening…"

Maitan's eyes met her own. His gaze never wavered. The seconds stretched into a minute. Another…Morgaine also never wavered. She merely crossed her arms and cocked her head, eventually raising her left eyebrow.

Maitan finally nodded. Whatever deep calculus he had done in his mind was over with. "You are correct, Morgaine. The chaos that the Triumvirate's disintegration has caused will be over with far too soon for you to recover in any natural way. But I have more bad news for you."

"What…bad news?" Morgaine asked, suddenly afraid to hear what he might say.

"We do not have three months. We have three, perhaps four…*weeks* before it's all over, Morgaine. But that's not all," Maitan said, dropping his gaze and then raising it, with eyes harder than she'd ever seen on him. "Should we not intervene in some meaningful way…it is nearly ninety percent likely that you yourself will become a concubine to the victor. Currently that would be K'Thul. Eighty-six percent, to be exact."

CHAPTER 147

Gary was sitting in a steel room with no windows and one incredibly obvious one-way window/mirror on the opposite wall. He was at a table with a huge ring that was clearly for chaining or handcuffing whoever might require it. Gary's hands and feet were currently free. But he was beginning to wonder how long that was going to last.

It had been a week already.

Two federal agents walked in. At least, that was what Gary assumed. No one had presented him with credentials. These wackos had simply swooped in with the military and piled them off to… somewhere. Gary wasn't certain where exactly. His head had been in a big, smelly green bag.

One of the men, slightly thin, middle-aged, and with a tight face and sharp features, removed his shades and set them on the table very carefully. He had a yellow legal pad with notes on it. He set that down in front of himself. The other man was much younger, with reddish brown hair. He produced a thin, black laptop from a satchel and appeared to be about to take notes. Gary rolled his eyes and tried to lean back and get comfortable.

Here we go again…..!

"Mister Rossi…" the man who wasn't taking notes began.

"Please, call me Gary," Gary interrupted, smiling. "We're friends by now, aren't we?"

The man stopped, looked up at Gary, completely expressionless, and looked back down at his legal pad. "Mister Rossi, please go over with me again the exact sequence of events as you recall them."

Oh, for crying out loud! Good thing I'm used to covering my own tracks. What, am I in third grade? I'm a practiced liar here! Give me some credit.

"Ok, sure. Just for you, pal. Look, it's like I said the other three thousand times…Nathan and his ex-girlfriend ran into each other at the museum…"

Always start with a truth point that they can verify.

"Nathan had come to see the monolith with me and went back because he thought he'd figured something out about how to use the thing, but Ellie – because they're exes – told him to go fuck himself. But later, she sent him a coded note saying to come back and try it. She didn't think it would work, but she wanted to know."

Gary stopped on purpose.

The men looked up from their note taking – one on paper, the other on computer. "I'm thirsty," Gary said, "and hungry. Before I go into this whole thing again, I want a sandwich. Not that crap you've been feeding me for days!"

The men looked at each other. The older one nodded and the other man left. "Please continue. He's not only taking notes, but this is also being recorded. I'm just 'old school' and like written notes to look back on. Watching recordings is exhausting."

Gary said, "Fine. But if I'm reaching the end before Jimmy there comes back with my John…we're gonna have a problem."

"Of course. Please proceed," the man said.

"So, anyways…Nathan goes on his own. He didn't want to tell me on account o' I'd tell him he was fucked in the head, and likely only bad shit was gonna happen as a result, either way." Gary wanted these men to get the full New York City 'fuck you' attitude. Therefore, he purposefully leaned into the swearing that comes second nature to people from the city.

The man nodded and kept his head down, taking notes.

Gary sighed looking at him. "Nathan must have gotten his procedure mixed up or something. To this day, I'm not sure because I don't know it. What I do know – and what you know – is it worked. He went bye-bye to Planet Smyslin. The problem is no one was there to record it properly. The security cameras got some of it, I'm told. But not enough."

"And this is when…"

"Hey, who's telling this story? Me, or you?" Gary asked.

"Go on, my apologies…" the man said, again without looking up.

"So, this is when Ellie tried to recreate his procedure from what he'd spoken to her and the security footage. Only, she couldn't. Until, according to how she tells it – I may be wrong here a bit – she figured something out on her own and had to try it that very night. Boom! She's gone!"

The man appeared with a glass of water and said, "Your sandwich is on its way."

"Thank you!" Gary said and drank down half the water. As he did so, he eyed them both. It seemed they were still believing the tale he and Ellie had whipped up in the hour they had had to do so before getting arrested. Of course, they called it 'being detained'.

"Ah…!" Gary said, "that's good water! Now…where was I? Oh yeah. Before she left, Ellie had sent me a note. She didn't want to give it to her boyfriend, because he was already salty about her trying to 'get Nathan back', which is how he saw it all. He didn't know they'd talked as much as they had, either. Now, to be clear – I think Ellie is a selfish little c…"

he looked up as they both did when he started saying this part. "…she's a selfish bitch. I still don't like her. But I guess there's a modicum of respect in there somewhere."

Yep. Still buying it…

"I mean…she's smart, and all. And she must feel that I'm trustworthy, at least. Or cared enough about Nathan to do what she said, at the very least. Anyway…I think she never figured she'd get the portal thing to work, either. The both of them are too smart for their own good, if ya ask me! But as you know…she did. And she'd sent me a note prior to trying to recreate what Nathan did before – and the note was simple. It read: 'If I vanish too, make sure that monolith doesn't vanish with me! If it does, find it and take it somewhere safe. It's the only way Nathan and I are assured of being able to come back. We'll bring back people with us, too, if we can. If some government (ours or Egypt or whoever) puts it back in a hole 50 feet down again – or destroys it – we're never coming back."

A female in military gear and a handgun came in and tossed a wrapped sandwich on the table. The younger man came in right behind her. Gary went to grab it, but the older man put his hand on it. "You're almost done. Sandwich can wait."

Gary sat back and said, "Ok…ok! Uhmm…yeah so then you yahoos – or someone you know – decided the monolith thing was suddenly government property and took off with it a couple weeks later. Me, being worried about Nathan mostly, just wanted to stay close to where he vanished. But when you all took the thing, I went into beast mode. I found out from one of the other researchers had put an Apple tracker on it where no one could find it. He was afraid of losing it, also. Smart dude. So, I talked him into giving me the codes and I tracked it right to your stupid abandoned warehouse. I think you know the rest."

"Tell us anyway, Mister Rossi. Please," the younger man added, sitting down again. "It all matters. Or it could."

"How it could be is beyond me," Gary muttered. "But sure, ok. I stole the truck; I went to my friend's farm – who you guys better leave alone – and stuffed it there for a few days. Nathan, who'd gotten Ellie out of some sort of trouble back there in that other world, helped her return. He said he had to go back for some reason – someone got hurt he wanted to check on – and he's coming back when he's ready. I guess Ellie is the one you really should be talking to. I know she said she knows how to use the thing but won't share how to use it for fear it'll get misused. But I sure don't. And I don't want to! The end."

Gary reached over, grabbed the sandwich, and unwrapped it. Taking a huge bite, he smiled as he chewed. Talking through the food in his mouth, he asked, not for the first time, "Can I go home now?"

To his surprise, the man set his pen down onto his legal pad and said, "Yes. You're not under arrest, Mister Rossi. But…don't go too far. No more trips upstate or vacations without letting us know. If we have further questions for you – we will be calling. In person." He pulled out a business card from his jacket pocket and slid it across the table at him. "In case you remember anything else that might be useful to us."

Gary looked at it. It had nothing on it but the man's name and a phone number. Not even any color, let alone an email address. "Brad Johnson, huh? You guys need to be more original than that."

He put it into his shirt pocket.

Taking another bite, he asked, "Can I go right now?"

"Not this minute, no. But we'll escort you back to your sleeping quarters and you can gather your things. There will be a guard who will take you out the way you came in. I hope you didn't mind the bag too much. We will be in touch."

CHAPTER 148

Several hours of searching tunnels later, Treyborne noticed another set of claw-like rents on some tiles in Hex 5. The guards armed their blasters, and Jasper pulled his own sidearm out. Trey kept his hands ready, and they followed the hallway toward a series of doorways. It was a pod of some sort. At one time, someone had lived or worked down here regularly.

Of course, that was centuries ago. Now, it was just a bunch of abandoned rooms and corridors. Treyborne noticed a pile of excrement the size of a large anthill near one of the doors. Using his fingers, he pointed and then jerked towards the opposite-most doorway. Most animals didn't defile their living areas, and avoided it in areas they frequently walked, as well. Lights had been turned on in all zones for this search, and the doors slid open, each in turn, as Treyborne approached them.

Suddenly, when the fourth of six doors opened, something huge and black leaped out, claws extended straight at Treyborne. Instinctively rolling and raising his arms, blaster fire erupted from behind him, and the beast tackled him, sinking its claws into his armor as he fell. The sheer weight knocked the wind out of him, and he saw stars for a few moments. Blaster fire had stopped. Suddenly, he realized the beast wasn't moving, so he pushed it off with some effort, as the other men rushed up to aid him. Standing up, Treyborne shook off the shock and looked at the thing.

It was a black panther. Huge, though, with claws more like a bear and fangs to match. Trey had never seen one before and had always thought they were smaller creatures than this. He surveyed the beast and saw two blaster marks had hit its right flank and one had hit it directly in one eye, killing it instantly. He looked over at Jasper, who shrugged as he holstered his weapon.

The man was good. Maybe he would be worth it, after all.

Searching the room behind the doorway, they found that the back wall had indeed been dug out – probably by something other than the huge cat. It seemed there had been a doorway there at some point, as well. Either way, the cat and whatever creature it had caught had found their way in here. Cats like to catch and recatch their pray. So, likely it had dragged the thing back into this lair and it had bolted the wrong way.

Strange, but not out of the question.

Trey wandered into the cave and found it, too, was man-made. Or… Elder Race made, rather. There was a large leveled out area that was completely unnatural but bled into a natural cave gradually going up, and an entrance thirty feet ahead with daylight pouring in. It appeared they'd kept large equipment in here at one time, by the marks that remained in the half dirt, half rocky ground. This was a back door where inside met outside. Trey had never known this was here before. It was a potential escape tunnel. Or a potentially dangerous entrance that enemies could exploit. Morgaine would have to decide what to do with it. And whatever had been stored here was long gone. Nothing had been left behind.

"Trey to base," he said on comms, "Get me Morgaine."

"Check that, Captain." A pause. *"Turns out she's looking for you, too, Captain. Just got word from her assistant. You want to come in, or should I go get her? No comms in her chambers per Maitan's orders."*

"No, I'll come in," Treyborne answered, "I need a break and some food, too. Trey out." Turning to Jasper, he said, "You're with me. Let's go see what she needs. Men, guard this area until I get back. We've either got to seal this, guard it, or both. We may have to fill it in, though I have no idea how to do that right now. But if wild animals can run in there, so can other things."

CHAPTER 149

The meeting room was crowded. Morgaine was there, of course, sitting in her black and silver leather traveling clothes, as if she were about to embark on a mission. Nathan knew it was more likely to cover her bandaging and hide her wounds from Jasper if no one else.

No weakness would that woman show here, or anywhere else, if possible.

Assembled and eating at the table were Nathan himself on one end, Morgaine at the other, with Brianna at her left side. There were plates set for Messau, who had just entered, and two more for Treyborne and their new Commander, Jasper. Messau was only his equal in rank, despite being here for seven years.

Maitan was making sure the serving girls got everything set out while still hovering near Morgaine while trying to make it look like he wasn't hovering. Nathan shook his head and took a bite of the food. Someone had slaughtered a cow upstairs and they'd been grinding beef into all sorts of meals for days. Nathan wasn't going to complain. It was grilled steak today. It tasted fantastic.

Morgaine eyed him for a moment while chewing. Brianna was speaking to her, but her eyes were all for him. He raised his fork and took another bite, "Excellent food from the kitchens, as usual Morgaine." She nodded and turned her attention back to Brianna. The woman reeked of grace. It just made her even more erotic.

Treyborne and Jasper entered, both still wearing battle armor. Trey's armor was…ripped near the chest and neck.

"Is that blood?" Nathan asked, pointing.

Treyborne looked down and a gasp came from Brianna, of all people. "Huh, I guess it is," and he looked up grinning. Brianna ran from the room and came back with antiseptics, bandages, and some sticky tape. Maitan snatched them from her as she tried to walk by him, giving her a glare. As Treyborne sat down to eat, Maitan wheeled his chair away from the table just as he picked up his utensils. "Hey!"

"A minute, Captain. Bleeding before feeding," Maitan intoned.

Treyborne rolled his eyes.

"Those gashes do look…intense, Captain," Morgaine said above the general noise. "Would you mind telling us what happened?"

He looked over at Jasper, who had just begun to eat, and he just pointed with his two-tined fork right back at him. Maitan was having Treyborne stand so he could lift the top piece of the light armor off his head.

"Mmmph!

The gashes were in his left pectoral muscle area and there was a bleeding rent on his lower neck on the side. Whatever had ripped into him had ripped his gray shirt badly, as well. But the cuts did not appear overly deep once the shirt was removed. The blood inside was extensive, however.

Trey glared at Maitan as he began to clean and fix the wounds, but he began to speak, "We tracked what turned out to be a huge black panther back to Hex 5 in the furthermost pod. There, it jumped us…well…me. And Jasper and the men shot it. Jasper's shot killed it instantly. I think the claws hit just as it died. I really didn't feel much pain. Though I do now! Ow!" he said and slapped away Maitan's hand, which went right back to where it had been.

Morgaine looked over and gave a thankful nod to Jasper who returned it. Maitan began to work on the smaller cut on Trey's neck.

Nathan looked over at Morgaine and noticed that the only person who had stopped eating was Brianna. She looked sick. "You ok, Brianna?" Shocked out of some reverie, she whipped her gaze to Nathan, gave him a strange look, and then just nodded and returned to her eating, head down.

Morgaine spared her a brief glance, "I'm afraid she's still not used to all the blood and violence that follows us everywhere, it appears." Brianna shot her a sideways look and then went back to her eating. "Messau, what is the state of the Arc Gate? You've had your men on it for the last two days. Any changes?"

Messau swallowed a large bite, "None, Mistress. It's all dark and humming all soft and quiet-like again. We don't get too close, though. Just keep a perimeter around it."

"Good. Maitan, you're done. Leave the man alone! Get the servants to bring up the desserts and a couple bottles of wine, along with some hot tea, and then get them to stay out until we open the doors again. We've got to plan."

Treyborne nodded his thanks and Maitan scowled over at her before ending his ministrations with a final piece of tape. Half of Trey's upper chest was now bandaged with another small one on his neck. He rolled himself back to the table and dug in. "What are we planning?" he asked around his first mouthful.

Morgaine sighed as she leaned back, "Another war, I'm afraid."

CHAPTER 150

Jezerah's forces were rallied in the northwest sector of Nelrae in a forested area overlooking the Western Ocean. The view was magnificent from their height.

Jezerah, of course, barely noticed.

Before him was his entire army of Dark Men, minus the few that remained at his headquarters, or those on specific missions he'd already sent them on. They numbered almost twenty thousand, not including the supplemental medical, engineering, and human servants working on supply lines. Jezerah had not had this many Dark men gathered in one place since the first war over five hundred years ago.

The human forces loyal to him and his 'sect' of the Dark Cult were already at war, fighting a losing battle trying to hold back K'Thul's superior forces – and superior tactics – over 120 clicks to the south. Jezerah knew that K'Thul was forcing his hand and making him fortify their positions. Because to not do so would be to cede the western empire and all its lands to him.

That would leave Jezerah with only his Dark Men and his compound, while K'Thul himself would rule both the east and the west. Emorion's scattered kingdoms and lesser forces of the Dark would be a distant second. Jezerah would become a hunted dog. Therefore, Jezerah was going to play right into K'Thul's hand – but only to a point. He would make sure that conniving bastard didn't take possession of the Empire of Nelrae, even for a single day.

But he would not simply walk right into K'Thul's open maw, either.

Emorion was rumored to have tried to ingratiate himself back into K'Thul's favor. But so far, no sign of Emorion's troops appearing on their side had emerged. Jezerah could only hope it stayed that way. He tried to think back on what had happened only two months ago that had so swiftly upended his superior position.

It all came back to the Arc Gate.

And now, the Gate had surged for a third time. He had felt it. He knew they all must have felt it. The Dark Power that fueled those gates was within his very soul. It was like it was a part of him. Such a vast surge of the Void's power could mean only one thing: the Arc Gate had either brought them more visitors, or one or both of those who had come had now returned. Either way, it meant little right now. The possessor of that Gate would rule the cosmos. Everyone else would be ground into dust.

Damn Morgaine and her trickery! He cursed, not for the first time today. *I had it in my hands! I barely had begun the research of how it had reawakened before it was snatched away from me!*

Looking at his troops, he smiled though. Curtaise had come up with a brilliant plan. It risked much. But his troops were by far the best trained of any of the Triumvirate and his former brothers' armies. This had always been so, and it still was. Facing more than their numbers would simply make it more of a challenge. Far from impossible.

Nodding and saluting, the men roared, and the two divisions split and began running. Half to the coast to follow the shoreline south, the others southeast to directly angle towards the current site of the conflict.

Curtaise cleared his throat.

"Yes, General?" Jezerah said, rasping as he always did when had to speak softly.

"I am going with the straight-line troops, as we discussed. But you said you yourself would decide where the Dark Knights were to go, and where."

"I already did, General. They're heading to the Petty Kingdoms."

Curtaise looked startled. "May I ask why, Master? We will need them in the battlefield. Not over four hundred clicks to the east." Curtaise looked concerned.

Jezerah laughed. "Because dear Curtaise…if we are to win this war, we must cut all supply lines. Not just those from the Eastern Empire itself! Emorion teeters on the brink. Should we suddenly strike K'thul in the throat, his help might then be acceptable. Even necessary. And then we'd be fighting two Dark Lords and all their combined force. If they really believe that Morgaine is my ally, it will most assuredly happen. Then, no matter what we do – we will fail. I mean to keep communication between them non-existent."

Curtaise nodded. "I agree, Master. And of course, your wisdom prevails."

"As it should be. The destiny of the Void is to consume all. It has simply become time to consume my former brethren. And consume them, it will!"

CHAPTER 151

Ellie had been allowed to leave and consult with her colleagues only because she held all the cards. If the United States government wanted her 'space portal' and the 'know-how' to use it – they needed her to show them how to use it.

She had made it clear: there's one person currently on the planet who knows how to use the thing – and that person is me. The people in power need to prove to me that they're worthy and reliable enough to use it. Otherwise, I'm never showing anyone how to use it.

Of course, this was all one monumental bluff. But, as usual – the bigger the lie -the easier it is to swallow. Ellie also knew that pressure would inevitably come. It might come in a week. It might come in one month. Or two. But sometime…they'd demand she show that she knew how to activate the monolith. Or "Arc Gate" as Nathan and his little band had called it.

Nathan.

It seemed he had figured out how to use the thing for real. Maybe that first time had been an accident. Probably, even. But at some point, in that world where she herself had only been able to become a captive and a victim – Nathan had managed to join a small militia of bad ass fighters and figure out warp hole technology on the side.

He has always been smarter than me! Everybody else – I kick their asses. But Nathan…

Ellie shook her head in frustration. For about the thousandth time, she told herself that had had nothing to do with why she had left him for Grant. A middling graduate student with a sweet smile and no aspirations beyond getting his Ph.D. and then tenure.

Back at the university, the news was starting to leak out and she had become somewhat of a celebrity. Inside and outside the academic community, people were talking to her differently. She also had been invited to two New York City based talk shows with national airplay.

She had declined, per her agreement with NASA, NEA, CIA, and all the other acronyms that were in on her little "secret". None of the scientists who had worked on the project were still even in New York, except Dr. Raines, her former advisor, and Ilya Nokrymovich from Bulgaria. Ilya was on the cutting edge of physics and mathematics, having already won a Nobel Prize regarding anti-matter and its role in the universe's gravitational fields.

Ilya was currently sitting across from her at a New York coffee shop named "the Bean Stops Here". Ellie hadn't been to this place in years. It was still great, though. Even had someone playing some guitar on the small stage area.

"So, you've been 'there and back again', it appears," Ilya said, not for the first time.

Ellie nodded again, not for the first time, either. "It's crazy, Doctor Nokrymovich! I mean…it's literally another world. Similar to our own, but with aa strange mixture of higher technology and much lower, depending upon where you are in the world…"

"That is not unlike our own world, dear," Ilya said, "and please call me 'Ilya'! I hate that 'Doctor this' and 'Doctor that' nonsense. South Africa and up the eastern coast of Africa still has millions of people without internal plumbing, living on dirt floors, and fighting for pennies or food."

Ellie nodded, "That's true. I guess I just hadn't thought of it that way. I guess there is more of it in terms of percentages than here, though.

Nonetheless, there's also the remnants of something they call 'the Elder Race'. A group of creatures that predate us as humans…I'm not sure how it's related. But it's fascinating!"

"Indeed!" Ilya said, obviously very interested. "And these monoliths… they are on every inhabited world…? These Elder Race beings…they made them, yes?"

Ellie nodded, taking a drink of her iced mocha.

"And you, of all people, can activate them now…?" Ilya said carefully, eyeing her.

Ellie nodded. "Oh, I'm not as practiced as Nathan is now, somehow. You know…he went back again already. Did I tell you that?" Ellie said, trying to change the subject. Or at least steer it away from her obvious lie.

Ilya nodded, watching her.

"When he comes back, we've agreed to discuss how to train others…and if we should. Until then, these vultures will just have to wait."

"I had thought you and Nathan no longer were talking awhile back. Did the appearance of the monolith spur that on…or had you already begun correspondence…or…. other things?" She asked with a twinkle in her eye. "Maybe you were already getting together prior to its arrival…!"

She laughed, not unkindly, but Ellie just kept her face stony. The idea of getting back with Nathan had been something in the back of her mind since the day she'd left him. But she had always been the type to never look back. Always look forward. But seeing him with that… *goddess*. It might…*maybe*…just a little…have made her feel just a bit… jealous. But just a bit. Maybe.

Turning her attention back to Ilya, she moved the conversation into the idea that dark matter and other gravitational factors – along with some elemental variances in the monolith itself – must be some of the forces at work here. She reminded Ilya that just because she may have figured out how to turn the light switch on – it didn't make her an electrician. Ellie wanted it all. Until she could build an Arc Gate – it wasn't enough. Of course, nothing was ever enough for her.

Ilya could relate. She was the same. Ellie knew she wanted in. And she would use that and every other bit of leverage she had to keep the circus going until Nathan came back.

That bastard had better come back!

CHAPTER 152

At that very moment, "that bastard" was sitting back and sipping some red wine. Morgaine had retired from their meeting almost an hour ago. The new guy Jasper, Trey, and Messau and he were all sitting around the table discussing the afterburn from the meeting.

"The real question is," Treyborne said, sipping his bourbon and then swirling it in the glass like it held some great mystery, "how do we attack the Dark Brethren – or whatever they are calling themselves now – and not help one of the others just do the same thing? Take over the world?"

Jasper had pointed out over an hour ago that picking the wrong one might be akin to suicide.

"…If we eliminate Emorion simply because you believe he assaulted you at the Arc Gate as some sort of act of revenge, what does that do to the balance of power? If you target your brother, simply because he's the one who's held all the cards in the past…doesn't that simply hand victory to K'Thul? And as for K'Thul…just because he seems to be winning on the battlefields in Nelrae right now, what happens if we suddenly and decidedly eliminate him? Do his armies continue without him? Doesn't that suddenly create a vacuum that either Emorion or Jezerah just swoops in and fills…? We need a plan to somehow eliminate all three. The order and timing must be impeccable!"

It was at this point that Morgaine had taken Brianna with her, then left with Maitan in her wake.

"You make excellent points, Commander. I shall have to think on them and answer on the morrow. We shall all reconvene here at 0500 hours. In the meantime, I suggest you warriors come up with a plan as to how to find and attack all three remaining Dark Lords."

Nathan watched her leave. As did Trey, whose gaze had lingered almost as long as Nathan's had.

Morgaine was suddenly and frighteningly pushing herself way too hard. Just last night, she was so weak, she'd fallen asleep on his shoulder and eventually ended up sleeping on his chest. He'd been so afraid to awaken her, he'd stayed there all night.

Now, she was Queen Morgaine again…?

He was concerned about her. But he also knew that if she didn't want him to intervene, he'd be slapped down, hard. His eyes kept wandering towards the door, though. He longed to go to her.

"Are we boring you with all this world war stuff, Nathan?" Trey asked, ribbing him.

"What….no, I'm sorry, Trey. I'm just worried about…you know." Trey nodded, pointedly not looking at Jasper.

Jasper poured himself more wine and said plainly, "Well, I certainly don't know, Nathan. I'm new here. Fill me in!" He sat back and just stared at Nathan, who sighed and glanced over at Treyborne, who shrugged.

"Ok, Jasper," Nathan said, "I think you've proven your worth. And I know for a fact that you're not in league with the Dark. So here it is: Morgaine almost died. Like…a week ago or so. I think you know she was stabbed by Emorion's Hollow Men. But it was *all* of them. She killed one – maybe two – but had Treyborne not gotten her home, she'd have died. It's probably worse than that – and she didn't want you to know, as she's really been weakened by it. But that's the hard facts."

Jasper nodded, "Ah…that explains…quite a bit. I had noticed a few oddities but had chalked them up to other things. There were also things said by the maids and staff that I could not understand. Now I do…" Setting his glass down, he looked at them both, craning his neck over to Messau, who rarely said anything, then added, "I think perhaps it is time for me to tell my story."

Looking at Treyborne, he said, "I believe you were to pull this from me anyway, Captain. Allow me to catch you all up."

Treyborne said, "If you just want it to be me, that's totally…"

"No, no!" Jasper said, "I want all the senior members of this team to know me and, preferably to trust I am not here to stab them in the back!"

Messau's head bobbed, and it was only then that Nathan realized that Messau had drunk most of the bottle of whiskey on the table by himself. Jasper had his own wine bottle, and Trey had only had about three glasses from his. Nathan had also worked his own wine bottle down. But wine and whiskey were two different cats.

"Well, "Jasper said, seeing Messau's condition, "I suppose it will just have to be you two. You see, I was born in the western trader lands of the Empire of Nelrae. My father was a merchant, and he had several mercenary types in his employ. At an early age, I despised my father's soft life and easy living – not understanding how hard he had worked to get there at the time – and idolized the guards and mercenaries for the adventurous lives they lived!"

Taking a sip of wine again, he continued, "My early years were spent learning swordplay from my father's men, riding horses, and chasing women. I found that the chase was often better than the 'kill', but not always." He smiled at this, remembering something or other.

"Regardless, I eventually defied my father's orders to become a merchant like him, and I enlisted in the military. Being from a family of note and wealth, if not nobility, I was admitted into officer's school and trained in both higher battle techniques and battle tactics. My younger brother took up the family business instead, and my father was mollified. Since I excelled in the Emperor's army, my father could brag about his older son and younger son with equal vigor."

"Did you father come to accept your army role, then? Or did he still resent it a little?" Nathan asked.

Jasper looked at him slyly, "He inwardly hated it, I think. But it was a social status he'd not attained before by himself. Having a son moving up the ranks in the military was of value in that realm, at the very least. When I reached the age of 25, my younger brother was just 20 years old. He was betrothed to a girl from a noble house, which would have again elevated our family's status, when he suddenly contracted the black lung disease during the plague and died. My father and I were devastated. My mother had died only two years after giving birth to Joshi – that was my brother – and we had been a tight group ever since. Even though we often fought, we never lost our love for each other. Once it became just me and my father…."

"Let me guess," Trey interjected, "it didn't go well."

"No, it did not," Jasper said gravely. Somehow, I was to blame for my brother dying and it was now my responsibility to leave the military, do my duty and both marry his betrothed (as I was his best man) and take over the family business."

"And you refused, I take it?" Nathan asked.

"No…I accepted. I resigned my commission, began to take over the business, and married Theresa. Theresa, although she had held true feelings for my brother…. I believe she developed real feelings for me, as well. By the time I was thirty…we had two children, and I was running father's business. Things were going well. So well, in fact, that we were suddenly offered a very lucrative deal to begin working directly with the Trader King of Talim."

"My father, as was customary for the head of the family, went to the city of Talim to finalize the deal. My wife and children accompanied him, as she'd never been, and it is one of the most beautiful cities in the world. She also wanted our son and daughter to see it. I agreed, and planned to meet them there after my deal with the trader ships heading to Rondor was complete."

He sighed deeply and bowed his head. His next words were very soft. "I made it to Talim on time, only two days behind them. But…you see…" his eyes looked up and Nathan saw that they were red and swollen with tears, "they never made it. A rare raid on trade ships near the southern border of Nelrae had hit their vessel. Dark Men from the central states – Dark Raiders were blamed." He sat back and finished the remaining wine in his glass.

"All aboard were lost. My four-year-old son and two-year-old daughter, along with my wife and father…were all killed. The Trader King, knowing nothing of this, only knew we'd missed our appointed time to meet. By the time I even thought to reach out and contact him, he refused to see me. On top of all that, we'd lost enough of our best goods – intended for trade in Talim – to the Dark Raiders that we were put in financial straits. Most men don't even know that Dark Men also control much of the high seas. I, myself didn't until that fateful day. But I found out in one day when my family, my … entire family … and our business were all lost. There was no one else to blame – but the Dark Raiders of the Seas. And the Dark Lord's name who controls them …is *Emorion*."

CHAPTER 153

Brianna went into her room, locking the door with the proper button sequence. Morgaine had fallen asleep hours ago, but Brianna had stayed in the outer room talking with Maitan about everything afterwards for an hour or more.

She had just come back to her rooms after Maitan had chastised her for the third time for yawning. "Get some sleep, Brianna! The days will be long again for a while now, I assure you."

Sighing, Brianna stood at her changing table – something she'd found and had hauled up from the lower levels – and began to undress. She'd taken to wearing more of the military type clothing common here. Pants instead of skirts and dresses, shirts instead of blouses, and had simplified her hair like she was back on the farm. It wasn't like she wasn't used to wearing men's work clothes. Once Sirles had died, she'd taken over most of the farming duties, including plowing. She had even built up muscles from all that work. Muscles she still mostly retained. Farming was simply the hardest job on the planet.

Brushing her long, curly dark hair, she stared at herself in the mirror. She'd always been told she was a pretty girl, then a pretty young woman, then a beautiful woman. Sirles had been handsome, but no 'prize' in terms of his looks alone. But he had been loyal, steadfast, and strong. Holding her arms about herself, she allowed herself to miss him again for just a little bit. He'd always been so … what was the word? Loving. He'd loved her for who she was, and she had known it. He had been a treasure.

Brianna had been alone for years now. She'd grown used to it. Becoming attracted to another man had surprised, perhaps even shocked her.

Taking a deep breath and shaking her head, she stood up and went to wash her face and clean and brush her teeth. Another mirror, and another Brianna stared wide-eyed back at her.

"He's a soldier, Brianna! Do you want to lose two men before you turn thirty?" she chastised herself in the mirror. "Yes, he's a handsome man. Some might even say he is more than that. But one Dark Man blade in the back, or if enough blaster shots hit that stupid sky cruiser he flies in all the time – and he's gone! Yes, you're lonely. He clearly is lonely, too. But does that make you a good match? Or just a lonely girl who misses being held in bed by a man?"

The Brianna in the mirror had no answers for her. So, she left her where she was and made her way to her bedroom. Pulling her hair back again and tying it off, she went to turn her light out.

A knock came at the door.

No one presses the buzzer around here. I think everyone is afraid to actually disturb someone's sleep! Like knocking is any different!

Too irritated to have time to think about who it might be, she jumped a bit when she saw it was Trey. Leaning on the doorframe, he looked up at her.

Suddenly self-conscious and realizing she was in her underclothes, she took the "I meant to do this" approach and raised her head, tilting her chin back.

"To what do I owe the pleasure, Captain? As you can see, I'm about to…"

"I wanted to give you an apology. For the other night."

Brianna turned stiffly and walked back into the room. "No apologies necessary," she turned. He hadn't moved. "Well come in, idiot! Unless you want the whole world to see me half-dressed!"

He came in, a bit uncertainly. The door slid shut behind him. Whether that was from too much to drink or hesitancy due to her state of dress, she did not know. About to put her overshirt on, she stopped herself.

No! He can just see what he missed! "Like I was saying, *Captain…*" she said, emphasizing the title to show she was not calling him by name.

He sat down right across from her. He smiled.

Damn it! He's too damn handsome! Why can't he be missing an eye or have some savage scar somewhere? He's too perfect. Muscles…and…ugh!

"Fine. Get it over with. I'm listening."

Looking to the side at nothing he began. "I'm sorry…after Nathan got back and after all that had happened…and keeps happening. I just needed a night with the boys."

She started to interject something, and he stopped her with a look.

"But I would have been here in a heartbeat had I seen the note any time before the middle of the next day…". He held up the note, folded, in his hand. "Somebody thought it was a good idea just to leave it lying around and hope it got read in time. But…I've read it over and over since I found it…"

"Was it so hard to understand?" Brianna pouted. Just a *little*.

"Not at all. I'm so sorry I didn't see it hours earlier. My mistake. Truly, I would have been here in a heartbeat." He looked up at her. "Brianna, you're an amazing woman! Beautiful, tough, sharp…what in the world would you want with me…?"

"Apparently, I'm not attracted to brains, it appears!" Brianna snapped. "You're selling yourself far too short! You're physically attractive, admittedly," she dropped her eyes a moment to control the flooding emotion, "But you're also the leader of this exceptional group of fighters for a *reason*. You run the ship as well or better than Morgaine herself! I've seen it. You're the first with a good idea in every meeting I've attended. And..." she paused, looking up again, "I think we'd be good for each other. I can't say for how long. Creator knows, neither of us might live..."

He stood and came to sit next to her. Her heart started racing and she became suddenly aware of how revealing her clothing had been. She'd decided to stand firm in wearing it to prove a point. Now, her heart was in her throat. She looked sideways at him.

He's right there...!

His face was an inch from hers. His eyes and hers locked. Suddenly, he was kissing her...and Brianna's brain exploded. At some point someone turned the lights out. She never could remember who.

CHAPTER 154

Nathan watched Treyborne leave the room and looked over at Messau, his last and only companion. The time on the chronometer read 0247. 0500 would be here far too soon. Leaving the room, he went to his own and retrieved one of the extra blankets stored in one of the cubby holes near the floor in his bedroom.

He brought it back, along with a small pillow and covered Messau with the blanket and put the pillow down so it would hold his head up a bit better. Messau had slid into almost a sleeping position as it was. Trey took off his boots, swung his massively heavy body around and laid him flatter on the couch, fixing the blanket again. Hitting the "all" light button, the room went dark, minus the waiting display screen on the far wall, which was black but clearly still on. Nathan decided to leave it alone and left, the door shutting behind him.

Two guards were in the hallway, standing and talking quietly. They saluted Nathan. He did the hand to chest salute himself. Had they ever done that before...?

Considering, Nathan decided to head down the hallway and rest a couple hours with Morgaine in case she needed him. Real sleep would have to come later. But a nap would at least clear some of the fog out of his head. Maitan was awake, sitting on a chair and checking something on the monitors. He nodded to Nathan and pointed to the door, which was cracked. He'd kept it open on purpose for him, apparently.

Nathan nodded his own thanks and went inside. Slipping out of his least comfortable clothing – which amounted to the jeans that he cherished and an overshirt, he slipped into the bed next to her. Maitan had made the bed so that the sheets covered both separate beds – making it one. That was thoughtful.

As he slipped into the sheets, Morgaine's voice said, "I've been waiting for you," and she moved to again rest her head upon his chest. "More foolishness ahead, it appears," she said after a time.

Nathan nodded, knowing she could feel the movement. Her hand rested on his chest, as well, and she rubbed it slowly, tracing patterns idly.

"You've been awake for a while now, it appears. Any bright ideas?"

"I've been running all the scenarios round and round in my head. Jasper's point is unfortunately filled with many smaller sharper ones. My predilection would be to cut off the head – attack my brother while he's down and finish him. He's the reason this entire mess – these last almost six hundred years – ever happened."

Morgaine looked up at him, and he looked down into her eyes. "But let's say we do that," she said, moving to sit up, pulling away from him. Somehow that didn't feel right, but Nathan said nothing. "That action literally hands K'Thul control of over two-thirds of the world with its two strongest lands. Emorion would become his pawn or be destroyed. K'Thul would be virtually untouchable again almost instantly."

"So why not hit one of the others first…?" Nathan suggested, knowing that was coming anyway.

Morgaine nodded, taking his hand as she talked, "Hitting Emorion would possibly weaken whomever he had reattached himself to – assuming he did so. But by how much? The war is going badly by all reports for the Empire. K'Thul has a vice grip and is moving closer and closer to the capital. Rondor will be spoils of war to whoever is the victor already…"

"Can't we use Rondor as a knife? Maybe stabbing someone's hand before cutting someone else's throat with it?" Morgaine looked at him. He could feel rather than see her eyes from where she sat.

"Perhaps, at one point we could have," she answered. "But Rondor III is hardly our friend any longer. If he ever was. I'd say he cut any ties to me the moment he put a bounty on my head."

"Agreed, but what does he have to do with it? You're the real champion of that realm, by everyone's account, including your own. They exist because you stepped in to help them however many years ago. This grandson of your friend is a fool. He's a worthless ruler. And, in my world, worthless rulers don't last very long…"

"Are you suggesting…?"

"I'm not only suggesting; I'm *encouraging*. I think our first move is to get a weapon that will be useful in this fight. Your enemies all have legions at their disposal, having worked centuries to cultivate them. Now, they're all in play and we're a force of maybe…eighteen? Twenty…?"

"Twenty-three again, thanks to Bantor's recruiting."

"Yea! Almost two dozen!" Nathan said, mockingly. "Even as crack a team as we had before getting beaten up, that's nothing compared to their numbers. Even with you and me fighting together," he added.

"But an army – motivated and mobilized because Nelrae already attacked them…? They're a spear in our hand, not just a knife. And we can aim them at whatever or whomever we choose, in the name of saving their realm and their way of life. My country uses that ploy all the time. Use someone else's army under the guise of protecting 'our way of life' and storm in guns ablaze!"

Morgaine nodded and pulled him close. Distracting, but motivating. She kissed him briefly. "I like it," she said. "But that doesn't solve which way we aim the blade, assuming we're even successful in taking over their kingdom and their armies."

"Well, the first target I can't help you with. You know the Dark Asshats better than I….by centuries! But what everyone from the Roman Catholic church to present day United States of America has done is find someone within their court that's willing to do as we say if we make that person king (or queen) instead of the current one. Simple. We handle the political coup; they take over the army and say it's in the best interest of the realm."

"And if this person betrays us…?"

Nathan laughed, "Then we execute that one, too and point out the fallacy of power to the next one. Always have a backup. CIA for the win!" he half shouted.

Maitan opened the door a bit – letting it slide open just enough that he could be heard, "Nathan, please. Our Mistress has been lying awake for hours, admittedly. But your shouting will not help her rest, let alone sleep!"

"Sorry, mom!" he said, laughingly.

Morgaine chuckled as well, and Maitan closed the door in a huff.

"Fine. I think that's a reasonable plan," Morgaine answered. "To start with, at the very least. In the meantime, we send a scout team to see what's happening with the other forces in play. From Emorion's ships in the Petty Kingdoms, to the vast armies in play in the battle between the empires. We can't rely on old news or secondhand information. From there, we decide where to strike first!"

Nathan was nodding, thinking about it. Suddenly he heard Morgaine's quiet snore. Apparently, finding a solution had been the only thing keeping her awake. He slipped out of bed and asked Maitan to send a note out to all the rooms – including the conference room for Messau – that the morning meeting would be delayed until 0700.

Maitan said, "I've already done that," and said, "Get some rest Nathan. I'll keep watch over her."

Nathan stopped and looked at Maitan for a moment, then said, "She's lucky to have you."

"Oh no!" Maitan responded, "We are all lucky to have her. This world would be lost – perhaps the galaxy – without that lone woman. She is the miracle the Creator decided to send."

Nathan could only nod, thoughtfully. Then he changed his mind and headed back into the room to curl up next to the frail, injured woman who was also the strongest woman in the world.

A miracle indeed.

CHAPTER 155

Gary walked into his workplace for the first time in two weeks to applause. Jennifer was there, clapping with them. "What's all this for…?" he asked.

His boss Andy came up and said, "Well, Jennifer told us you'd done something brave, but couldn't tell us what. But then the people with the suits and sunglasses that were here before looking for you like you were a criminal came back and said they'd found you and that they'd not only cleared you, but that you were to be allowed to return to work as soon as you wanted. They said they were almost done 'debriefing' you, but that the long and the short of it was you were a hero who was aiding the government in some classified, high-level computer espionage. They'd only become aware of the full scope of your mission recently because your mission was so 'Top Secret'; only a few people on a 'need to know' basis had been involved. They also said you were being retained as a consultant for possible future endeavors. But they in no way were pursuing you or seeking you for questioning any longer. Anyway, it all sounded super important! Welcome back, Mr. Bond! Your desk awaits."

Clapping some himself, he turned and walked away.

With that, everyone returned to their work. Gary did notice a lot more looks focused his way than was typical. Most of the people were smiling, as well. Apparently, word had gotten around.

Like it always did. Shaking his head, Gary sauntered over to the office he and Nathan had once shared. Of course, there was Jennifer, standing in the doorway as he approached. She ran to hug him and looked up at him. "Let's not get all weird, ok? One day at a time. Welcome back," she said and kissed him quickly on his bearded cheek.

Yeah, let's not make it weird.

"Let's talk later, ok Jenn? Too many ears in here. And frankly, I'd like to see the mess of crap that has piled up while I was away. Maybe lunch… or dinner?" he asked cautiously. Jennifer was still watching him with those beautiful green eyes. His memory of those eyes staring down at him that night was hard to set aside.

"How about both?" was all she said, and she fairly skipped over to her desk. Nathan and Gary had always had desks facing each other. Monitors to the side so they could type and work while maintaining some level of conversation. Jennifer and he adopted a similar approach.

Gary was afraid the conversation might be stilted, or even awkward. But somehow it was quite the opposite. It was as if the night at Ben's house had not occurred. Or at least, that it wasn't interfering with their friendship.

Jennifer talked about her roommates, and how they'd asked about the "renegade Gary" who was her friend. And how involved was she, really? Jennifer giggled like it was all some sort of soap opera.

Well, maybe it was.

The day moved quickly. Lunch turned out to be ordering deli sandwiches and continuing their work. It was amazing how much needed fixing that the other programmers had not been able to do or hadn't gotten to with their own work. Only the emergencies and things needing immediate attention had been done. Gary had an entire inbox full of things that needed rewritten and code correction that needed done.

Catching a cab together, Jennifer and he ate dinner, discussing Ellie's return and how they'd come through right as Nathan had left.

Wondering where Nathan was, and what he was up to brought on the only awkward silence of the evening.

As they got closer to Jennifer's apartment, she said as they parted, "I'm going to just walk home. It's only about ten blocks."

"Oh, hell no!" Gary said, "I'll walk you home, then catch a cab." Jennifer smiled at him and took his hand as they walked slowly towards her place. Despite the cold, Gary didn't mind one bit.

She looked up at him, nearly ten inches down from level and smiled again. "I like you, Gary. Don't worry so much! I just…need it to go slowly, ok? I know that's almost impossible with…what happened. But don't take my going slowly now as anything other than adjustment, ok? I'm glad you're back, too. It felt awful while you were away. You really didn't see Ellie while you were in there…?"

"Well, I saw her once or twice, but that was it. We didn't have any long, open chats or anything." He pointed to his ear and just shook his head.

Jennifer's smile waned, "Ah…I see. Well, I hope she and the…*others* are ok. It's weird how the media just keeps reframing it the way the government tells them to. It's kind of spooky. What else do that do that with…?"

Gary just looked at her and said, "Pretty much everything, I think. Never trust the mouthpieces, Jenn. If you learn nothing else from all this. Just know that everything we hear is controlled. Nathan will come back if he can. I know it. In the meantime, that little…. I mean 'Ellie' will keep a handle on them. She's got all the cards, like she told me. And I know she knows how to play when she holds all the cards."

Jennifer stopped, as they had reached her building. "I'd ask you up, but…" she looked up towards the windows.

"I know…four other roommates. Kind of awkward. Next time, my place. That is…," he added quickly, "…if you want. No pressure."

"Come here," she said and crooked her finger at him. He leaned over and she kissed him quite thoroughly. As she let him go, she said, "No pressure!" and stuck her tongue out at him. Then she was gone.

His heart racing, Gary hailed a cab. It was too late to hit the subway and get home without losing almost another hour. Maybe there would be time to play a game online before alarm hell and having to do it all again tomorrow.

Of course, this was better than a jail cell.

By quite a bit.

CHAPTER 156

Firewood was crackling in the beginning of this particular autumn evening. This far south, in the Empire of Nelrae, it was still usually hot, even at night this time of year. But it seemed the cooler season was coming early, which could be devastating to the troops out in the field attempting to defend the sudden and unprecedented attack from the Eastern Empire.

Everyone in the Empire now knew of the war. But to a man, almost none of them knew the why of it. But Major Winsell Day knew…he'd known about the Cult of the Dark and their influence on the world since he was a boy. His own family had been deeply divided over the subject as far back as he could remember.

Some of the less-liked members of his family – those in power and nobility in the Empire – they were either openly or secretly adherents to the Dark. They espoused its virtues, even defended their positions in family get-togethers. Those on the other side, those who worked for a living, toiled away on farms, or had to join the military and rise the old-fashioned way – these were the ones who hated the Dark and all it represented.

Long life – but at what price? The higher people and races who were so much more knowledgeable than the "masses". Trying to keep "the ignorant poor" from having as many children was a major point of emphasis – unless those children could be used as cheap or free labor, of course. These were the kinder points, from what Winsell had heard. He didn't even want to know the "deeper secrets" hinted at by his more "endarkened" relatives.

Looking out over the battlefield from his campfire next to his other officers, Winsell Day could see the price that was being paid – and fear for what worse may come.

The army of the Eastern Empire lay across the battlefield from his own forces, as a small part of a larger contingent of defensive troops fighting for the Empire of Nelrae. The Eastern Empire troops were openly led by a being in all black robes, wearing a golden crown like a ram's head – K'Thul – one of the Triumvirate Masters of the Dark. Within their ranks were over twenty thousand Dark Men alone. Not to mention thousands of horsed cavalries, and another several thousand foot soldiers. Their numbers were at least twice that of Nelrae's armies.

And now, for the first time since the surprise invasion across their eastern borders, the troops around him were singing. The wanted their enemies across the valley to hear them. And why were they singing so happily? Because the Empire had struck their own deal with a Dark Lord. The Emperor himself, who had suddenly and mysteriously passed away a few days back – would have never allowed such a thing. Winsell was sure. But his cousins…who now both ran the army as its two Major Generals…and the Empire as co-emperors, were all for it.

And now they were told Dark Men from the Hinterlands were apparently racing across the Brightshard Mountain range as the men sat here singing. Coming to their aid to do battle against the incredibly fast and dangerous Dark Men who had been decimating their lines since the beginning of this war. Even more so than the overwhelming amount of horsed cavalry. From the announcement, Major Winsell was supposed to tell their men that within three or four days these Dark Men would somehow miraculously arrive and, with them, would come K'Thul's nemesis: Jezerah the High Lord.

No one really knew about the politics of the Dark Lords. All anyone knew was that they simply didn't die. Of old age, at least. But one thing was clear: at one point in time, centuries ago, there had been far more than three of them. After those wars, in which it was rumored the so-called White Queen had killed all the others, three had emerged after her defeat. They had formed an alliance of the Dark to spread their evil religion called the "Triumvirate". Now, that Triumvirate was clearly broken.

Of course, since those early days, the Dark and its adherents had been advancing, as well. There was always resistance, to be sure. Wars were often fought due to good people trying to fight against the press of the Dark. But the inevitable tide went just as its ardent supporters kept saying, "the Light is consumed by the Dark".

Shaking his head, Winsell did not know what he could do about it. Soon, their "salvation" would be arriving. In the form of an even more evil Dark Lord than the one across the field from them. Jezerah was referred to as "the Damned" by his followers as if this were some sort of amazingly great thing! And now, Winsell was supposed to lead his troops alongside the Dark to battle the Dark to save their Empire from what…? Being consumed by the Dark? As far as he was concerned, it already was.

Dusting off his Captain's badges and polishing up the medals that hung from his coat, he finally stood up. He knew what he had to do. Writing a hasty note, he gave it to the runners, and had it sent straight to his own home on the western banks of their estates that lay upon the sea. It read very simply, "RUN".

Saddling his own stallion, he told his second-in-command, Captain Obekkan, that he was being sent on an urgent mission. He would return as soon as he could. Then he rode straight south, as if he were heading towards the capital. As soon as he was out of sight of the lines, however, he would curl northward.

He knew where he had to go. The Kingdom of Rondor.

Just ten short days ago, he had been leading the charge to defeat the High King of Rondor and their rebellious country. He had had his doubts about their supposed challenge to the Empire. But he had his orders.

They'd fought their way to within sight of their capital, incurring heavy losses in the process. Then word reached them about the invasion. Now, they were within fifteen clicks of their own capital, and had been fighting a losing battle just as Rondor once had.

Winsell just simply had to find a place where the Dark was not accepted as normal, or ok. His family had discussed this possibility behind closed doors for years. They knew what "RUN" meant. He just hoped they were able to escape before even more of the Dark Men came to "rescue" the Empire. Winsell was sure they wouldn't approve of his directional heading.

Therefore, he was determined to make it without getting caught.

CHAPTER 157

Morgaine awoke and found Nathan still fast asleep. The Vitalis stimulant concoctions that she'd sent Maitan to retrieve from the storage areas in the deepest reaches of the compound should have made her feel more exhausted after sleeping. Or at least a little strung out. Instead, she felt invigorated. Even her wounds didn't ache as much. Feeling them with her hand, she could tell the swelling had gone down, also.

Was that some sort of combination of elixirs she had accidentally taken? Or was it simply the administrations of Maitan and his antibiotics?

Raising her eyebrows and shrugging her shoulders, she began by finding the clothing Maitan had laid out for her. This was an outfit almost entirely made of blue cloth. Dark blue leathers coupled with silver and black clasps for decoration. She had not worn this particular outfit in decades. Maitan was a master of preserving old things. He also had mastered remaking and refitting.

As she finished putting the top on, Nathan awoke and whistled appreciatively. Instead of becoming irritated, as she likely would have on low energy, she smiled and spun around for him to observe her more fully.

There was just something…different…about being with Nathan. It wasn't all sexual. In fact, they'd only had sex twice. Well…two nights, anyway. But every moment they spent together, to her anyway, felt like intimacy. It was magical and she hated that she could not avoid feeling that dread that someday it would be over.

Possibly soon.

But time was for the present. That was what her father had taught her. Her mother having died when she was so little meant her father was both parents to Morgaine. And she relished every moment she'd had with him, despite him being so busy. Even back then, even fully grown into early adulthood, she had never understood the research he had done. It involved the Gates; she was sure of that. But it seemed to involve trying to warp time *and* space.

That he had "only" managed to warp one and not the other was hardly a failure.

"Where did you dig up that outfit? I don't think I've ever seen you wear any color before…let alone multiple hues of blue."

"I last wore this…Oh my…for Rondor I's coronation after the peace treaties were signed. I believe there is a picture somewhere inside the castle – not for public viewing – that includes me in it crowning the King."

Nathan raised an eyebrow.

"Oh yes, I crowned Rondor myself. His public coronation, held a day later, was done by the High Priest of the Almighty. But that day, with his friends, family, and the generals…he had me do it as a testimony to our 'eternal friendship'." Morgaine laughed at the irony. "And now, I will use it to seek another of his line – or elsewhere – and dispossess his own. Likely for all time."

"Hey, this is not your fault!"

"I realize that. And yet," the White Queen said regally from her modeling stance, "the duty of it weighs like a lodestone around my neck."

Nathan got up, grabbing his clothing, putting them on hastily. He hugged her gingerly, and she hugged him back, giving him a quick kiss. "I'm going to clean up. Since we have time before the meeting,

I'm going to grab some breakfast, too. Let me know if I should bring you anything…!"

Morgaine looked at him for a long moment.

A steady stare that was completely unreadable. Pausing to wait for the punchline, he finally said, "What?! Did I say something wrong?"

"No…of course not," her eyes averted. *Was she lying?* "You have such a good heart. My first inclination was to remind you that I have literally two full time servants dedicated almost entirely to me alone." She sighed and looked up at him. "I suppose I just don't want a third."

"I guess that makes sense. I just haven't had…*centuries* of being served, as you have," he said, shrugging. "I'm used to doing things myself!"

"If you must serve me…" a smile wrinkled its way into being on her face, "I…*may*…be returning to my chambers instead of this little piece of hell tonight. I could use some company…". An eyebrow…just raised on the most exquisite face in human history. Coupled with that evil little smile, Nathan just dropped his head and laughed, leaving the obvious unsaid.

Loping to his quarters, he saw Treyborne, wearing the same clothes he had the night before, doing the same. "Trey! I thought I saw you head to your quarters last night. Did you go back to check on Messau in the middle of the night or something and just…stay there for some reason? Was he sick?"

Trey's head jerked around, and he stopped cold. Laughing, he just shook his head. "No, I checked on him, though. Just never quite made it back as I intended."

"Oh…?" Nathan said. Then, "Oh! You didn't uh…happen to spend the night with a certain assistant of Morgaine's, did you? The one who keeps staring at you without speaking for days at a time."

"Does she do that? Well, I suppose she does. Usually after I piss her off or something."

"Is this like…a regular thing, or…?"

Treyborne shrugged, and turned into his room, "Who knows? I'd like it to be, though!" The door slid shut.

Laughing, himself, Nathan headed to his own designated quarters to shower and clean up. About 0689 he arrived at the meeting room to see that everyone else was already there. Morgaine in her blue and silver outfit, Jasper, who looked as crisp as if he'd slept an entire day, Treyborne, far less so and looking a bit rumpled, Messau – still in the same clothing with very red eyes, and himself. Maitan and Brianna were also there, immaculate, and well-dressed as usual.

The meeting door closed, and Morgaine sat down. She did seem to be feeling much better.

"Commander, you asked a very good question yesterday. After considering, I believe that Nathan has come up with the best answer: we target none of them first."

"But Mistress Morgaine…" Jasper intoned, readying his rebuttal. Morgaine held up her hand. Beautiful blue silk gloves with lace behind them. She was showing her 'White Queen' in full force today. "I have been advised," deigning to give Nathan a look and a nod while saying it, "that we need a knife. Or perhaps even a spear, to fight in this game. The Kingdom of Rondor was near collapse until K'Thul inadvertently saved it by attacking the flanks of the Empire, causing their armies to withdraw in defense of the capital. Rondor III himself has proven to be a weak leader, selfish and vile. Easily manipulated by adherents to the Dark Cult. And so," she said, leaning back and watching all their faces, "we are going to depose him."

Messau's eyes popped up at this, as did Treyborne's – who looked at Morgaine with amazement. Jasper just slowly tapped his lips, finally saying, "Yes," quietly. Almost to himself. Brianna and Maitan stood still, seemingly knowing this already. Or not caring enough to let it cause a reaction.

Treyborne finally said, "But Morgaine…they just sent Jasper, amongst many other *lesser*," this with a nod to Jasper, "bounty hunters, to kill you!" Jasper graciously accepted the compliment with a nod. "They're not going to just hand you the kingdom. Even if you do 'depose', kill, or otherwise incapacitate their king!"

"Oh, we don't want the bother of actual rulership, Trey! We are simply going to appoint someone more…inclined to look upon our ideas with favor. In exchange for our undying support, we get…how did you put it, Nathan?"

"We get a weapon that will work in this fight," Nathan put in.

Morgaine nodded, "Yes. And with that weapon, we then must deftly strike at all three, as Jasper indicated last night. Who we strike first, and just how deeply we must also determine. The blade must be swift and sure; however we decide to use it. If we do it right, we will topple all three of the remaining Dark Lords. At worst, we keep the world from falling completely under the spell of the Dark. Preferably with one or two less Dark Lords in it."

"How do you propose to do this?" Jasper asked, leaning forward, genuinely intrigued.

"The first part, you mean…? Because the rest is still quite out of reach of my mind, yet. With Rondor, it's quite simple, really. No one in that kingdom truly remembers what I did for them. It's in some private artwork in the castle, and in the official histories – assuming they've not already been rewritten – but no one cares about history anyway, sadly. No, we will set the kingdom ablaze the old-fashioned way. We're going to slip in, talk with particularly amenable candidates. Those who do not play along will be…sequestered until the deed is done. I haven't decided yet if we will kill King Rondor himself. I feel truly badly about that. But it may need to be done. After all, he and his heirs will remain a thorn if they live. And he *did* place a bounty on my head. Jasper, I forgot to ask: how much was the bounty?"

"Five thousand Rondorian gold, my Queen," Jasper said smoothly. Hardly a price worthy of one such as you, to be honest. I personally would be offended."

"I am offended! I'm worth ten times that amount. Five thousand gold isn't even a year's wages for the second-in-command of my own Elite Guard," she said, smiling.

Then she went all White Queen serious in a flash.

"We will need to move quickly and deftly. As difficult as it was to sneak out of the castle, sneaking back in and taking Rondor will be more so. I will want two or even three plans by the time we are in the sky cruiser. And I want us in the cruiser by 1100! It will take us the rest of the evening just to fly there. We will stay at an inn I know will have some discretion – with the proper amount of coin applied – and then sneak into the castle in the early hours of the morning."

With that, Morgaine stood and walked out, trailed by Brianna and Maitan, as usual. Blue leathers, blue silk, and silver accents awhirl. Shaking his head, Nathan turned to Trey and asked, "Did she just say we're leaving in less than four hours?!"

Treyborne nodded. "That she did! And now I've got to go and ask her now if it's just us going, or if we're taking some or all of the guards." With that, he got up and left.

Jasper was just sitting there idly, playing with one of his knives. He looked up as Messau got up to head to his rooms. Presumably to get ready. Although he looked like he was going to throw up first. Jasper looked over at Nathan, the only person left in the room with him. "Is it always like this?" Jasper asked.

"Not always," Nathan said. "Sometimes we just start shooting."

CHAPTER 158

Maitan couldn't help himself. Five or ten minutes after the sky cruiser had lifted off – with its full complement of fourteen in it – he descended to the old Command Center and turned on all its old tactical displays. Satellite feeds came in from all over the globe. Reorienting them, as he had been taught to do so long ago…within minutes he was watching the ongoing fight in Nelrae, had a bird's eye view on the City of Rondor, and was keeping a vigilant eye on both the Petty Kingdoms in the central bay zone and on the Eastern Empire's more militant quadrants. Just in case.

He then began to perform the far more detailed summary calculations of odds and variance. Tactical mathematics was intuitive to his race. Fighting was literally in their bloodlines. Bred for fighting by the Elder Race themselves – not the corrupted Dark kind – the *Biaki Mor* had been the front runners of the first War of the Elder Race. And the second. And the third.

Over time, their numbers had dwindled. Bred to fight and with the desire to be brave, there was less and less time for procreation and other such frivolous activities. By the time Maitan had been born, there were less than one hundred and fifty Biaki Mor left. More than three quarters of those were over one hundred years old. When Maitan reached the age of ascension, he was one of three remaining on the planet. All males. Swearing he would never take up weapons as his forebears had, he dedicated his life to aiding the last living member from the Elder Race: Morgaine herself. That was well over one hundred years ago. Now, at the age of 137, and feeling his years, he had to admit that calculation of the odds for Morgaine's "window of opportunity" had sparked something in him.

Now, he had to know it all. Maitan spent most of the next fourteen hours viewing all areas, taking notes on the various key positions and armies. He considered navies, tactical strength of generals and admirals, and the relative morale of the troops in each quadrant of the globe – focusing ninety percent of his mental gyrations on the western sub-continent in which all the current conflict was happening.

Plugging his DNA-instilled battle tactics into simulation programs in the Command Center led to multiple variants that he had considered, but not held as tactical solutions to various scenarios.

Once completed, he sat back and sighed deeply. Out of the over 170,000 battle simulations and scenarios, his calculations had led to one slim alley of success. If he was being honest with himself – and he always was – it was one more than he thought he would find. He was trying to make sure Morgaine and her team were not flying into a hopeless fight. He had planned on sending her a message telling her it was impossible and that returning to base and waiting out the current storm would be no worse for her. That perhaps in a few decades or centuries another opportunity to destroy the remaining Dark Lords would appear.

Maitan rubbed his semi-bald head and saw a dark hair fall. Another one. Taking it between two fingers, he carefully placed it in a trash receptacle.

If Morgaine followed the exact recipe he saw before him and hit every window…Something his odds calculations put at a dismal 1 in 11,434, she and her team would defeat all the Dark Lords and rid the galaxy of the threat of the Dark Cult and its mysterious Void for all time.

Flipping a few more buttons and making another set of calculations, he put her odds of defeating two of the three Dark Brethren at an almost believable 1 in 157. That third one, whichever was left for last…Maitan shook his head.

There was one variable he had not plugged into the computer. He stared at the blurred image on the one screen he had not engaged. It showed a tired, old *Biaki Mor*…balding. Bleary-eyed from nearly an entire day's worth of battle tactics calculations. Pressing a button, he added in the latent variable.

And everything changed.

CHAPTER 159

Brianna watched the sky cruiser go, and the sickening feeling in her stomach deepened. Maitan and she were the only ones not on that sky cruiser who had any inkling of their mission. And Brianna was quite certain she didn't want to know.

Treyborne and she had finally – *finally* – come together. Their night together had been wonderful, and sleep had been infrequent. But the very next day, her worst fears about the longevity of the relationship was being put to the acid test. Treyborne, along with their Mistress Morgaine, Nathan, and the best of their other Guard – were going to try to take over a country, attack a Dark Lord with its army, turn and try to assassinate another Dark Lord mid-stream, then go for the third before he suspected he was on the target list.

They were literally trying to defeat the three Dark Lords who had beaten Morgaine not once, not twice, but many times before. And they were in a hurry.

As the airship raced towards the horizon westward, Brianna went down below and started packing the things she would take with her if she had to leave. If they didn't come back in two weeks, she would give her notice. If they weren't back within a month, she would put on black and be in mourning for yet another lover.

Then she would find somewhere far away to live in solitude for the rest of her life. It wasn't that she felt their quest was hopeless.

It was because she knew it was.

CHAPTER 160

Jasper watched with open interest the interaction of the off-worlder Nathan with Morgaine. It was clear the woman was falling hopelessly in love with him. And he seemed to take it in stride. Like the White Queen was no more than a holiday romance or a fling with a barmaid. Not that he was acting like he was going to mistreat her.

But he just…took it so *casually!*

Of course, he hadn't grown up with stories meant to frighten children into behaving based around this woman. Stories of her battles – even in defeat – were glorious and the legends were epic. Jasper supposed that being hired to *kill* a legend, even though he hadn't really intended to fulfill the job, was somewhat along the same lines.

She was mortal, after all. Although – like the Dark Lords themselves – nearly immortal. Jasper wondered what it was like to live a thousand years or so. He would never find out. He would sooner gouge out his own eyes and cut off his own manhood than take any of the "secret elixir" given to the "Chosen Ones" within the Dark Cult.

The idea sickened him.

Watching the two of them was like watching two young lovers walking through a park. One could hardly tell they were both likely about to die. It was refreshing, the unbridled optimism of it all. Jasper had his own plan, of course. He'd stay the course. At least until it was completely pointless and their cause hopeless. He just hoped he didn't have to kill anyone to get away.

Treyborne called back from the pilot's crib, "We're going to fly very high to avoid detection, put on your air masks and close your eyes. If you feel like you're going to get sick, there are plastic bags under your seats for you to do so. Once you're done vomiting, put your air mask back on. Please put your thumb up if you understand me."

Twelve thumbs went up, including Jasper's own.

This Nathan was the most intriguing of all, of course. From what little intel he could get from the staff and guards, he had stated that he had been raised by humans and didn't remember any special past at all.

The girl Brianna had mentioned something about him not even realizing he was of the Elder Race until Morgaine proved it to him some way or other.

Rubbing his mustache, Jasper put his mask on when it came down on a little metal strip. It was getting cold, so he pulled his cloak over his arms and leaned back to rest. Keeping one eye open wasn't going to work, as the air was cold, and it was causing his eyes to tear up.

Sighing, he leaned back and made himself fall asleep.

There was a song he learned while in the Army of Nelrae: "Back in the Army again". It was a light-hearted song with an ironic twist about a man who kept re-enlisting and the world just kept on going without him. Each time he did so, massive change happened at home. Very little of it good.

That caught the mood of this day perfectly.

He hummed it to himself as he drifted off to sleep.

CHAPTER 161

Nathan held onto Morgaine's hand for a long time after she'd fallen asleep. The air masks were a bit uncomfortable, and he simply could not sleep with it on his face. It seemed he was the only one with this problem, however. One of the Elite Guard – fortunately only one – had gotten sick. But he'd followed procedure, and no massive issues came of it.

Nathan laid Ben's loaded shotgun across his lap. He had only one box of shells, and he meant to use them wisely. As good as blasters were, there was something truly satisfying about a shotgun. At close range, they'd do a hell of a lot more damage to whomever or whatever was coming at you. Nathan meant to fire it judiciously, but often, if things got sticky.

Morgaine had spent almost an hour speaking to Maitan privately before they headed out. Then he had gone off and gotten them enough medical supplies to fix up ten times the men they could load into the sky cruiser. Of course, they were hoping to scoop up an army soon. Not literally. But if they were going to support those troops in any effective way, high tech medical supplies were a huge advantage.

Morgaine's face was just there, leaning against his shoulder. Mask and all, she was just plain lovely. So much for making love tonight. That might be a bit awkward aboard the sky cruiser with everybody watching. Laughing at his own inane mental picture of that, Nathan again tried to get comfortable. Idly, he wondered again at what elixir had suddenly and so rapidly put Morgaine on the warpath again.

He noticed Maitan had given her three or four vials of something that she had stuffed into her shoulder pocket. She was in full military gear and armor, just as they were. Her black armor was stowed somewhere in the under carriage. Her black sword was nestled next to his shotgun like they, too, were lovers. It was fitting.

Nathan still wore her medallion around his neck. For some reason, right after takeoff, it had lit up for a moment. Morgaine had noticed but said nothing. The darkness of night descended, even in the high skies. Around 1350, Nathan finally fell asleep, too.

Waking up to a jolt, Trey called back, "Sorry! We're hitting some rough air as we're coming down. There's a storm brewing to the southeast and it's coming right for us. We will be on the ground before it hits though. But these winds are going to make it bumpy. Oh…! And you can take your masks off now. We're below the five clicks mark."

Nathan removed his mask, then moved to take Morgaine's off. Her hand touched his as he did so, and she looked up at him. He slowly began removing her mask, and her eyes never left his. It was a strange moment, then she just took the mask from him and let it slide back up the metal pole as they all ascended once everyone had their own air mask off.

Sitting up, Nathan saw that not only was everyone awake, but they were also in the process of getting up to use the single toilet, grabbing water bottles and moving about. Treyborne wasn't that close to landing apparently. About twenty or so minutes later, however, the entire crew was in their harnesses, and the sky cruiser was descending upon an estate outside the city.

Bantor had suggested that they head towards his southern estates. He was worried about his extended family, anyway. But assuming they were there, they would welcome Morgaine with the note he himself had written. The estates were quiet, however, and no light came from any of the buildings or windows. The stables and barn were also empty, and it appeared the place had been cleared out some time ago. Nothing was destroyed of burned down, at least.

And this carried with it the added bonus of giving them a night that might be a good one with restful sleep somewhere relatively safe. Morgaine contemplated trying to sneak into the city at night versus going in in small groups by day. She opted for the latter. As safe as the inn may be, giving no one the opportunity to misstep was better. Assigning guard duties for the watch and where to put them she left for Trey and Messau.

It was well past midnight, and the only light was from the crescents of the two moons.

Taking Nathan by one hand, Morgaine pulled her sword into the ready position and proceeded to head towards the main house. There were two guest houses on the grounds, a large garden, and some stables. The servant's quarters were on the back side of the main house, according to Bantor. But they couldn't see those from where they were. Nathan pulled his blaster out, not wanting to waste shotgun shells, if he didn't need to. Four of the Elite Guard, two in front and two in back, readied weapons as well. As a unit, they proceeded to check the entire perimeter of the house. But even the servant's quarters showed no signs of life.

Entering the house, using lights attached to their blaster rifles, the guards proceeded into the building. But it was, in fact, completely deserted. One of the guards reported this to Treyborne.

"Captain, no signs of life anywhere in the house."

"Same for the grounds. We've hit the entire perimeter and even checked the nearby stream bed and the forested area beyond. It's like they cleared this place out and even the stray servants that might have been off that day were scooped up. Or sent home."

Morgaine spoke into her comm, "Then Captain, I'm going to bed. Keep the perimeter guards sharp! Set laser trip alarms and whatever else we brought to alert us in case the situation changes. I'm quite confident we can get to the cruiser and take off if need be. They'd have to send the entire Rondorian army here to stop us. Wake me at 0300." Turning her comm off, she said, "Nathan, come with me!"

Two of the guards had already cleared the upstairs, two had hit the cellars, while Morgaine and Nathan had swept through the main floor. The stores were still here. It was eerie. Morgaine had given Nathan a few strange looks as they found literally no one and nothing.

Heading upstairs to the master bedroom, Nathan closed the doors behind them. He leaned the shotgun against a nightstand and whistled. "Bantor knew how to party! Look at that four-poster bed! It's like it's right out of the Versailles Palace!" he said as he surveyed the massive suite.

"I can only assume that is an impressive thing!" Morgaine said, drolly. Looking over at her, he gulped. She was completely naked. Like… completely.

"How…?"

"I'm a practiced veteran at getting disrobed. I'm rather disappointed at your lack of motivation!" she said, as she strolled over. The moonlight of one of the moons – he thought it was Allana – was spilling in through the huge upper window. Nathan's throat went dry.

"Uh…aren't we going to take over a rather large country tomorrow? I was assuming we'd actually be…uh…*sleeping* tonight!?"

"Well, after having told you earlier today what to expect – I simply cannot help you. Let's just say you assumed wrong. Now get undressed."

CHAPTER 162

Emorion was sailing on board the *Dark Horse*. One of the finest vessels in the Black Fleet. The secret of his naval superiority and the ongoing piracy of nearly all the southern seas as far east as the Eastern Isles had kept most of his power hidden from his two brothers for some time. Developing that power had taken great patience. He even had many of his Dark Knights turned into sea captains. The result was a magical amount of income, slaves, and goods. What Emorion lacked in ground troops, he made up for in guile and gold.

Losing the Arc Gate battle and having taken so many casualties had nearly crushed his land power. But it hadn't touched the sea forces. And it was time to use them. Sailing straight west with over 240 vessels, his navy full of almost 2000 Dark Men were going to hit the Eastern Empire's shores within two days.

Then let the havoc begin! It might take days, or even weeks, for word to reach K'Thul on the battlefields of Nelrae. But he was going to feel Emorion's knife sooner or later. He had thought K'Thul might be amenable to a deal, due to the obvious implications of Morgaine's involvement in Jezerah's dealings.

But since no reply had come, Emorion had been more than willing to overlook the obvious, and at least form a tacit alliance to pick apart K'Thul's burgeoning strength. A little balance of power could only benefit Emorion. The more time he gained from the unmitigated disaster at the Gate, the better it was for him.

Jezerah's punishment would have to wait is all. A small price to pay to avoid annihilation.

Ah, the breeze and the smell of victory returning were both sweet. The captain, a Dark Knight by the name of My'Rel, was the sharpest in all the fleet. The *Dark Horse* was the flagship of these raiders turned naval fleet. And the crushing of the ports across the Eastern Empire's southern borders would throw the entire region into complete chaos. Not to mention disrupt K'Thul's supply lines.

Emorion closed his eyes and watched the picture show in his mind of K'Thul getting word that the entire southern province of Santis-Echunn, along with Scim's Warding, were burning. Emorion loved the smell of flesh burning. It was the most beautiful scent in the world, especially as it blew right up K'Thul's nostrils.

CHAPTER 163

Winsell Day hadn't slept in nearly two days. His horse, a fine steed used to hard labor and even war, was completely spent. The walls of Rondor were shining in the distance as he dismounted and led his horse to the nearby stream to get some water. The trees here were full, and there was a very nice estate sitting atop the hill to the north.

They shouldn't mind if he and his horse got a little water and maybe some rest under these trees. It was early morning, maybe just past the third hour, and the sun had just risen awhile back. Taking off his hat, the former Major had made sure to change his clothes into non-military clothing. All his medals, uniform, and even his Commander's hat had all been buried at the bottom of his rather voluminous saddle bags. The rest of his personal belongings, including his diary, Winsell had buried near a large tree at the border. He hoped he'd see that tree again and perhaps someday recover the summary of his entire adult life that he'd buried there in a soft oilskin bag.

After tying his horse nearby where it could graze, but not get away, Winsell Day decided that two days riding without sleep was a bit more than his middle-aged body should be asked to endure. Lying down in the short grass by the stream, the bugs were everywhere. Swatting some and then lying down again, he was snoring within minutes.

A kick to his riding boots awoke him an indeterminable amount of time later. Sitting up, two strangely armored men with stranger weaponry stood over him. They had half-helms of the same strange material that their armor was made of. Looking a bit bewildered, he stood up slowly – as much due to being stiff and sore as to be safe, hands raised.

"How may I help you, gentlemen?" he asked in his most pleasant voice.

"Who are you?" one of them asked in a curiously strange accent. "Where did you come from…?"

The expression on his face must have shown he was as confused as he felt, because the one who spoke looked at the other. The other one spoke up, "Captain, he's wearing Nelrae-styled riding clothes. He's got Nelrae-styled boots and he's riding a Nelrae-bred horse," he said pointing at his far larger than average war horse.

Curious who knew horses that well out in the country of Rondor, Winsell nodded appreciatively, "I am indeed from Nelrae. But I am not a part of their military. At least…not any longer. I have come to Rondor to seek a country that is not being overthrown by the Dark. At least not today. Do you or your Master serve the King? Do you come from the estate upon the hill?"

The one who'd been addressed as "Captain" looked at him strangely, then answered slowly, "Yes, we're coming from that estate. Its owner asked us to check on it, as he's out of the country and may be gone for quite some time. What is your business in Rondor, then? Your statement about a country not being overrun by the Dark has me curious…"

Winsell cleared his throat. It was time to gamble. "I am…or rather, I *was* Major Winsell Day of the armies of the Empire of Nelrae. I am seeking asylum, and willing to lend my aid to any cause that still fights against the Dark. I deserted the army a mere two nights ago upon word that Dark Men, along with their Dark Lord, were coming to aid us in our battle against the Eastern Empire, which is also overrun with Dark Men and a Dark Lord of its own. I will have nothing to do with such people – who prey upon the weak and murder children. Since my country has decided to make an alliance with such, I am no longer wishing to be a part of said country."

Winsell leaned back on his heels; arms crossed. If these men were in league with the Dark, he was going to die soon, if not immediately. If not, and they were followers of the Creator – as it was rumored most were in this Kingdom – then they should at least take him to their lord, who could possibly take him to the King.

After a moment, the 'Captain' just said, "Come with me." And he turned and began walking towards the mansion on the hill. Grabbing the reins of his horse, the man turned and said, "My man will bring your horse, sir. Just come along and we'll go see the Mistress." He then handed them off and began walking.

CHAPTER 164

Breakfast was some sweetened oatmeal cooked over a fire in the fireplace. Treyborne had said he thought a smoke curl at this distance would be relatively safe. So warm breakfast was on. But he also said they should leave no later than lunchtime. The idea to slip into the city in twos and threes was still the plan. In fact, a group of two had left already, with orders to regroup at The Cat's Tale. Each was to get their own room. Morgaine and Nathan, with one solar charger between them, were going to slip into the city with their rings.

But they were going to quickly seek a deserted alley and become visible to save charge. Morgaine had a cloak to cover her hair and face. Nathan had a black cap to keep as much of his white hair hidden himself. Just in case.

But Nathan and Morgaine were currently eating breakfast, awaiting Treyborne, Jasper, and Messau to return from their morning perimeter check. They weren't waiting to eat, however. Tea with honey and a bit of honey in the oatmeal as well. Nathan had come downstairs starving. Probably due to the workout Morgaine had put him through. Her wounds were still wrapped in hard bandages and gauze. But the rest of her seemed to be working quite well. Shaking his head, he glanced over at Morgaine, who was discussing the infiltration schedule with her two guards on duty. They were to be relieved in an hour and leave immediately.

Morgaine's eyes flitted over to him as she finished talking and smiled. "How did you sleep, Nathan?" she asked, eyes bright.

"Poorly, if you must know, Mistress," he said, sitting down and sipping some of the tea. He added another dollop of honey, then added more tea back into his cup.

Morgaine nodded as if this were some problem to be solved. "A pity," she said. "Perhaps you should try a quieter room…?"

Her smile was positively evil.

Giving her a grimace, he opened his mouth to reply when Treyborne came in, followed by a strangely dressed, middle-aged man with a goatee and clothing that screamed wealth. The man carried himself like Jasper and Treyborne did, too. It bespoke of authority, someone used to giving orders, not taking them. Who was *he*…? And what was he doing here…?

Treyborne laid his hand out and said, "Sir…have a seat. Eat some breakfast. Morgaine, I give you…" he turned and said, "I'm sorry, I don't remember your name."

The man's busy grey eyebrows raised, but he simply said, "Winsell Day. Formerly Major Winsell Day of the Army of Nelrae. At your service," he bowed. His eyes were fixed firmly on Morgaine. No one suddenly stepped in for breakfast with this woman and mistook her for anyone other than who she was.

Morgaine stood and nodded. "Major…? I'm assuming Captain Treyborne has a reason for bringing you before me. Captain, will you be joining us…?"

"Mistress, I'm going to be right here. I'll eat after I get the guards movements sorted. But I'll be listening," he added, looking directly at the man, who nodded his understanding.

"May I sit?" Winsell asked. Morgaine nodded, and she returned to her seat. The man sat down, and a bowl of oatmeal and a spoon came with a cup for the tea. One of the guards left and Treyborne took his place.

Nathan finished his last bite of oatmeal and leaned back, deciding to keep his hand near his blaster. Although the man seemed to not be an immediate threat, he wasn't taking any chances. Nor was Trey, based on where he and the other guard were standing.

The man added honey to his tea, but not his oats, adding a bit of nuts from the table instead. Taking a bite, he looked up and asked, "May I ask, Mistress, if these are your estates? Was I under the mistaken impression that you lived outside any of the human kingdoms?"

"You may ask…" Morgaine said, donning the White Queen mantle as easily as Nathan put on a ballcap to go to a Yankees game. Morgaine paused. "But I'm going to ask my questions first. Then I will answer whatever you wish to ask, within my power. Captain Treyborne informed me of your discovery as soon as he found you. I hope their search for weapons and the long walk up the hill wasn't too difficult."

"No, Milady. Military men go through far worse far too often. I've been waiting for your Captain to bring me in for a while now, but I have no complaints."

"Good. So, tell me – may I call you Winsell?" when he nodded, she continued, "…tell me, Winsell: you've admitted to deserting. Can you explain to me why, as you did for the captain?"

"I'm sure you've heard the details by now, Mistress. But the long and the short of it is this: the Great Army of Nelrae, which I have given the better part of my life to, has made a deal with a Dark Lord. By now, the Dark Lord Jezerah has likely arrived with his Dark Men to 'aid' in the war effort against the Eastern Empire and their Dark Lord, K'Thul. I refuse to fight alongside evil simply to fight against evil. I left the hour I heard of it, feeling that perhaps the Kingdom of Rondor would offer me sanctuary – and perhaps I could lend some of my military knowledge in exchange. Are you on good terms with the King? Could you, perhaps speak to him for me?"

Morgaine's eyes, beautiful as always, glistened in the morning light. Nathan didn't see how this Winsell, or anyone wasn't distracted just looking at her. She answered him, "I was on good terms with him, until he himself became influenced by the Dark Cult and ordered me executed." She said this as if she'd offered him more tea.

Winsell's eyes showed shock, but to his credit, he didn't seem rattled. "I…see. So, there is truly nowhere to run to that will be safe. My family will be…" he sighed, "homeless." Nodding, he made to stand up. "My apologies…"

"Please sit down, Major," Morgaine said, showing a little impatience. "Our conversation is far from done." Looking at her a moment, he sat from his half-risen position.

"I have told you only part of the story. In answer to your previous question, these are not my estates. They belong to a friend of mine, however. A friend who also had a bounty put on his head simply for being associated with me. If you know of me, then you know I've battled the Dark for centuries. I'm not going to bow to it now. I've come here – just last night in fact – to right this wrong. I intend to not only restore my friend's estates to him and give him back his life. I intend to unseat Rondor's current king and help install someone who will not bend a knee to the Dark nor to its representatives on this planet!"

Winsell Day leaned back; eyebrows raised. At that moment, Jasper and Messau entered, stopping when they saw the new arrival. They didn't act surprised, just stopped a moment to take his measure before proceeding. The comms outside were likely alive with the news. Nathan had switched his off last night and had clearly missed it. Jasper and Messau took off their hats and moved to sit at the rather large table.

Jasper went and sat right next to their guest.

"I believe the Creator sends what and who we need when we need them. For example," she nodded at Jasper, "allow me to introduce Commander Jasper, who recently joined our team after pursuing me for the King." Winsell looked uncomfortably at Jasper, who grinned at him and nodded. "And this is Commander Messau – lead fighting trainer. Sitting next to me is Nathan Arvad – formerly of the planet earth." Nathan didn't like the 'formerly' part of that, but he nodded.

Messau waved and sat down, grabbing some oatmeal out of the pot on the table with a spoon. He then grabbed the honey jar and just upended it, waiting for the slow movement of the sweetener to flow out. It just kept going as Messau stared at the Major. When he set it down, there was far more honey in his oatmeal than there was left in the jar.

"Pleasure."

Morgaine took up the conversation, carefully finishing her oatmeal bite as she spoke, apparently looking for more in her bowl than there was, "Winsell…you'll be free to go whenever you wish. After we are gone from here. I'll let you go when my last two guards leave for the city. As long as you don't go to the city yourself. You may go anywhere else you wish. But I cannot have you warning the King or his Court."

Or…" she stopped with her spoon, looking at him intently, "…or you can join us and perhaps aid us in reestablishing this kingdom in the Light. A man of your station could very easily have come with a handful of guards. Doors will open for you to be listened to. Should you wish to aid us in the short term – or join our own fight against the Dark for the long-term, I shall pay you handsomely. I assure you of this: King Rondor III's reign has come to an end. Your aid could be useful and therefore rewarded proportionately. Perhaps that help can aid your family's flight or settlement in some way. If staying in Rondor afterwards is your choice, I will wish you well after our work here is done. But…if you wish to become a permanent part of this team…"

She leaned back, stroking the black sword that rested next to her chair, "I can promise you that the Dark will not oppress your empire – or your enemies' empire – for much longer should we succeed. Would you like that, 'former' Major Winsell Day? Would you rather be a refugee with little money and less power? Or would you prefer to take up arms and strike down the plague that has now, for whatever reason, fully infested your homeland? Wouldn't it be better to return to your home with your family someday, rather than run for the rest of your life?"

CHAPTER 165

Maitan had his saddlebags packed to the point of bursting. The mare he had chosen to ride he knew well; a sturdy, long-running pale white horse with strong flanks and stout legs. Somehow, riding her – a mare named 'Light – seemed appropriate. The letter he'd left in Morgaine's chambers explaining why he was leaving he hoped she would receive and read someday.

The staff remaining at the base was more than sufficient and efficient enough to keep things running smoothly with him gone.

Mounting up, checking his water bottles, feed bags, supplies and clothing one more time, it crystalized for him once again that he would not be returning. He'd had to dig to find all he had been looking for. Some of the gear with him hadn't been pulled out since long before Morgaine's blue coronation outfit. Patting the bundle behind him on top of the saddle blanket, he kicked, and Light shot out of the barn, heading away from the olive groves.

The sharecropper family watched him ride off without slowing in their work. The sun was already high in the sky, and it had become hot. Maitan placed a wide hat upon his head and began riding straight south towards Nyx.

He had a hefty bag of gold and silver with him. It should be plenty. Maitan nodded to himself. Plenty enough to take him where he needed to be. His window was just barely wide enough. If the winds on the seas were favorable. Praying a quick prayer for blessing and speed, he kicked into Light's flanks once again. All she had to do was get him to Nyx as fast as possible. He'd take her with when he boarded a ship. Just in case. But she likely wouldn't be needed much after that.

Brianna reached the stables just moments after Maitan had left. It was the kitchen crew that had alerted her to the fact that that Maitan had been packing saddlebags.

Curious, she had gone looking for him.

Watching him ride off towards the city of Nyx, she wondered why he'd needed to carry so much with him for such a short trip. Perhaps he was going there to buy or trade for things they might need.

But then why …

Something was wrong. Brianna ran inside. She had to get to some comms.

Right now.

CHAPTER 166

King Rondor III was celebrating. After the sudden withdrawal of Nelrae's troops from his border, he had ordered a festival in honor of the Creator and His miracles. He had then wined and dined the Court and their closest friends, stolen a night or two with his mistress – whom he had apologized to profusely for discarding – and even spent a night with the Queen, in hopes of making an heir. Albeit somewhat accidentally.

The court halls in the castle were bustling. Merchants were hustling in with goods for the feasts. Families of nobility were coming in from all around, taking their share of the castle that had been offered them to stay during the weeklong festival.

Some of the lesser lordlings were rakishly devouring what they could of the food, wine, and other goodies spread out in the main hallways. They were taking their shots at the other young nobility's choicest women, as well. When those ladies weren't amenable, he saw more than a few find one of the courtesans roaming the hallways.

What a grand week! Rondor sat sipping his ale, taking it slowly today, as he still had quite the hangover from the night before. Of course, had he not been so drunk, he might have had the sense to find his mistress' quarters, instead of his wife's.

Nonetheless, good work had been done!

"Your Majesty, there is a supplicant from the Empire of Nelrae. He says he is a Major who deserted their evil forces and wishes to beg the king's mercy."

"Send him in!" Rondor announced grandiosely. "Let us see this one with the wisdom and sense to come before the Rondorian Court and seek forgiveness for attacking our realm!" He said this so that every single person in the room, and plenty more in the outer hallways, could hear. All doors in the lower level were open. The people milling about obviously heard and whispering and murmurs increased dramatically.

Within minutes, an older man, clearly military, came striding in. He wore the full military gear of a higher-ranking officer – though not a colonel or general. He had medals enough for either, however. So…a highly decorated officer!

This should serve us well in the court of public opinion! I shall show great leniency, understanding, and mercy on him. I may even offer him an analyst role in the military itself!

Taking a deep breath, Rondor stood to greet the man. As the man bowed, Rondor came down off the throne mount and ran down the steps, hugging him. He took him by the shoulders as if he were an old friend and smiled his warmest smile.

"Friend! Anyone who begs forgiveness for misdeeds ordered at the hands of others, who shows your level of wisdom is welcome in the Kingdom of Rondor! Come! Sit at my feet and tell me your story." Turning he strode back up the steps, sat down on his throne, and took his royal scepter in hand, as if he were about to rule in judgment.

Hesitating, the man moved to obey, sitting several steps below the king, keeping his head properly bowed. Two of his guard moved in behind him as he came up the stairs, standing just one step below him on either side. No sense being foolhardy.

"Proceed," Rondor said.

"Tales of the deeds of the Kings of Rondor and their piety and grace are obviously quite true, it appears! Greetings, great king! It is more honor than I deserve, to be so close to one as magnificent as yourself! Please allow me to explain myself."

He awaited the nod before speaking further.

Then the King said, "Oh! And please speak just a bit louder, so everyone in the court may hear you!" He smiled at all his guests, waving to them. They all bowed and waved. As they did each time he bothered to acknowledge them.

The man sniffed and said, "Of course." Speaking much louder, he went on, "I was here during the attack on your kingdom. An action I regret with my whole being, King. Please forgive me."

Again, Winsell waited for the nod. It came with a smile.

"Thank you, King Rondor! Grace of the Creator be upon your kingdom! My name is Major Winsell Day. I have served in the military since my youth, almost thirty-five years in total. I have always been loyal to my emperor. I have striven to do my duty to the best of my ability. As you can see, I have been decorated for bravery, battles and sorties won, and leading my men in the face of incredible odds."

A bit of applause came after that. More people were filing in from the outer courts to hear him. He continued, "But recently, I have come to realize the error of our ways. As you well know, good King Rondor, the Eastern Empire has invaded our…that is…Nelrae's eastern shores across the river Alisandre. They are led by the Dark Lord K'Thul himself, with many armies of the Dark alongside him. Our armies were losing, great king. But we were not allied with the Dark. As we were fighting them, we ended up losing tens of thousands of lives!"

Turning and standing, never quite turning his back on the King, he continued, "Great King," he said, turning and acknowledging Rondor once again, what you may not have heard is that the Emperor had suddenly taken ill and died not seven days hence. Two days later, an alliance was announced between the Dark Lord Jezerah and the co-emperor's Mateo and Matin. The twins likely have been serving the Dark for quite some time, my lord. It is my belief that they were the ones who spurred the unjust and evil attack upon your land. Their hand in the Emperor's death is as likely as the sun rising in the morning, as well."

Shock had begun whispering its way around the room at the announcement of the death of the emperor. At the last, gasps broke out loudly everywhere. Winsell continued, "Furthermore, Jezerah and his Dark Men were to be fighting alongside me and my men. They likely are doing so at this very moment."

More shock and dismay floated all about the room.

"I could not, in good conscience, serve any longer under the banners of the Emperor and his generals, knowing they were in league with, and likely part of, the Cult of the Dark. I abandoned my post and rode for two straight days to get here, to beg asylum and your forgiveness. The latter of which, you have already graciously granted. I will await your response. Thank you, good king!" Winsell bowed and stayed low, as Morgaine had told him. They'd practiced this for hours at the inn before sending him to the castle. Winsell Day had to hope it had been enough. He had wanted to say far more.

The King rose, walked down the necessary three steps, and touched him with his scepter on his shoulder. "Rise, my child. You are both forgiven and granted sanctuary! I hereby name you Major Winsell Day of the Rondorian Army," shock rippled through the crowd, followed by loud applause for the grace of their king, and likely as much or more for the man willing to risk all to get away from the forces of the Dark.

The King continued, "It was not your fault, not knowing, as I'm sure most did not – of the true nature of their attack upon our realm. Of course, the Creator – His Name be praised – saved us from such an evil end! Which is why we celebrate even to this day. Please, with my thanks and to honor you – you may have the suites formerly reserved for ambassadors from the Empire of Nelrae. We will not be receiving such from them for a very long time. Once you have been properly fitted with a Rondorian Major's uniform, please come join us at the evening's feast!"

Pointing to the two guards closest to him, he said, "Show him his rooms, then get the tailors up into his chambers as soon as they are able. Spare no expense! And Major…" he said, causing Winsell to turn back and bow once again. "You may wear your medals from Nelrae. Everything you did of valor should be upon your breast. It is only fitting."

With that, Winsell bowed again and withdrew. His heart had been beating like a bird's. Then he turned and allowed the guards to lead him from the court to more applause. He nodded graciously to both sides of the corridor as the people made room for him to exit.

Taking him up two flights of stairs right outside the Hall, and down a long hallway, they opened into a beautiful suite with a huge veranda open to the air. Maids were already in there dusting, having somehow gotten there ahead of his escort. One of the maids was a fine young woman who filled out the maid's outfit…quite well. She was short, with short dark hair and gave him a beautiful smile when he nodded to her.

The guards bowed and shut the doors. "Whew!" he said, plopping down right on the couch the short woman had just finished dusting. She said to him, in a sweet, but high little voice, "Shall I get you some water, sir? Or some wine? You look parched."

"Er…please!" he said, then asked them if he could open the chamber doors to the hallway to let the air flow. The maids both nodded. One went to get him a glass of water from the pitcher that had already been brought in. It was in a carafe surrounded by ice and had condensation all over it. The water she poured looked delicious.

As he opened the doors, a voice came from near his ear, "Thank you.... Major." Morgaine had followed him right up the stairs, it appeared. As soon as the maids left, the doors seemed to shut on their own. And Nathan and Morgaine appeared. Nathan by the doors, Morgaine seated in the chair opposite him.

Nathan went to get them both a drink. Morgaine eyed Winsell appreciatively. "Thank you, Major. I will understand if you wish to go no further with us. The King, for all his pomp and self-righteousness, granted you far more than I would have – or even could have – imagined. Perhaps that is enough for you, and I would understand. But I very much appreciate you sticking to our arrangement." Nathan sat down and handed a drink to Morgaine from his seat, which she took and drank from, as did he.

Winsell Day took a deep breath. His heart rate had receded. "I've never enjoyed court antics. And frankly, I cannot believe I'm saying this, but this King of Rondor is more arrogant and more full of himself than the Emperor was, Creator rest his soul. What he did and said wasn't for me. It was for the crowd. Your idea to set up camp within the palace is perfect. However..."

There came a knock at the door. Winsell looked anxiously at Morgaine, who seemed to fold in upon herself and winked out. A second later, so did Nathan.

"Just a moment!" Winsell shouted, then under his voice he said, "This may take a while. They're fitting me, as you no doubt heard."

Morgaine's voice came right next to his ear, "I will be in the service quarters." A few moments later, the door to that room shut. Going to the doors, Major Winsell Day opened to three tailors coming in at once.

They spent less than ten minutes measuring him, checking this and that, and making notes on sheets of paper. Then they were gone. Sighing, he went to get up and tell them, but the door was already opening.

This time, Morgaine came out alone.

Sitting down, she kept her eye on the door. "Tell me, Winsell. Honestly, what do you want to do? I have somewhat coerced your aid. Although you gave it, my appearance has altered your destiny significantly. I need your own thoughts on the matter once again. You are a man who has seen much. But I don't feel I'm beyond myself to presume you weren't looking for me. You were looking for a safe place for your family. Which you now have. I have told you I can provide that, should they make it here to Rondor. Or should we, by some chance, find them ourselves. But…"

Winsell broke in, "Morgaine," he paused, "I cannot believe I'm sitting and talking with you as if you and I are old friends. Please forgive me." She nodded, but kept her mouth closed, frequently checking the door with her eyes. There was no window in it, like the veranda doors, but apparently her proximity to it was making her nervous. Winsell stood up and said, "Allow me to latch the doors. That way, not even a careless maid can blunder in and ruin the knowledge of your presence here."

Morgaine waited, watching him get up and lock the doors with the key set in the keyhole on this side of the doors. He came back and sat down, setting the key on the tea table.

Nodding, he began again, "Morgaine…may I call you 'My Lady? I believe until or unless I know you better, being more formal seems to suit the situation." She nodded again, leaning back, and sipping her water. The woman was amazingly beautiful. It was distracting. Winsell tried to keep his eyes focused on hers.

"Thank you," he sighed, finally beginning to relax. "My Lady, I also believe there are no coincidences. The Creator has made us all for whatever purposes He decided ahead of time. And mine, apparently, was and is to aid you in unseating that hypocrite they call their king! I have held my tongue in many a court appearance in Nelrae. Today was no different. And that, I believe, is all I need say about that. You may use my quarters for your headquarters. You may utilize me in any way you see fit. If, after that you see fit to employ me further, let's discuss that at that time. I will not be staying here unless it is the only option that allows me to recover my family, who should be on their way here even now." He stopped, then asked, "Where did Master Nathan go…?"

Morgaine sipped her water again, saying nothing. Then she leaned forward, "He has taken my Light Shield and his own to bring up our team, one by one. He waited in this room and then left when the tailors entered." Pausing, she added, "Winsell, I'm going to be bold here. It is in my nature, you understand. But here it is. We're going to need someone who can help direct the Rondorian army from within. This may be why the Creator has spun you our way. Whereas you are not a general, you may be able to apprise us of whether they're doing as we need them to, or not. Perhaps, should I gain enough leverage with whomever we can find as an ally – you will be quietly running a portion of the army, or all of it, through their generals from behind the scenes. That is what I truly need! If this army cannot be bent to my will, one or more of the Dark Lords will rule over all of Arth within a few weeks. Or so…I have been told…"

CHAPTER 167

Smyslin was outside walking with the two guards who had been sucked into the Arc Gate with him and the girl. This was their 'exercise time' and the only time they were allowed outside at all. The air was quite a bit colder here, perhaps this was simply seasonal, based on where on the globe they were, according to Ellie. But the sun also seemed smaller and more distant. Whiter and brighter, too.

Smyslin had not seen their moon – singular – but he had heard how perfectly it orbited the planet. Unlike his own planet, where the sisters were constantly fighting and tugging at each other, sometimes throwing the other far out and then causing one to slide back too close for a time.

Their tides here must be quite slow and boring.

Looking up again at the sky, he tried to make out whatever it was that was flying in a straight line. Some sort of sky cruiser, but it was spitting fog out of its tail, or something. And it was moving very fast. Their escort stayed back but did not comment on Smyslin's constant craning of his neck towards the sky.

Rost and Agino would look around as well, just not as much. Agino spoke up, "Hey Smyslin! What are you looking at?"

"Their sky is strange here. Similar but not the same. Their sun is too small. They also have only one moon, from what I'm told. But it is supposedly very big. I'd like to see it."

"Well, isn't that it over there?"

Smyslin followed where Agino pointed, and there was a massive ball, just as he'd been told, hanging low in the sky. It apparently had not set yet, even as late in the morning as it was. Smyslin was overjoyed and hugged Agino.

"Yes! Yes! I think it is!!" He kept squinting up at it, wishing he could make his mind remember. It was very large and was mostly lit up by the morning sun shining on it. Nodding in satisfaction, he said, "I must talk with the Ellie person about this! Maybe she can get a picture of it for my wall while we await Master Nathan's return to earth."

The guards looked at each other behind Smyslin's back. Not seeing them, he was about to go on, when Rost said, "Smyslin, what have you heard? Ellie has told us she's not sure when, or even if Nathan is ever coming back here. He and our...*employer*...have apparently become an item and are in some sort of relationship. We've only worked for the Mistress a few years. Me three, and Agino four..."

Smyslin had stopped his walk around the perimeter of the fenced-in yard to look back at them. His face was so sorrowful, Rost tried to ease his tone a bit, "Look in our experience, Morgaine has had her share of men. But it's one night and out the door. Kind of like we like our women!" he said and slapped Agino's arm, who smiled.

Smyslin's face hadn't changed, so Agino spoke up, "Look, Smyslin – it's like this: we have to get out of here ourselves! We're not sure how or where we'd even go. But if we stay here, they're going to pull blood from us until we dry up and blow away. And if we wait for Nathan to come back and save us...well...from what Ellie has said, he may not have much more clout than she does. In that event, even his return won't help us. So, every day from now on, we plan while we walk. Got it? We're busting out of this place! Even if we don't know where we'll go from there. Are you with us?"

Smyslin turned and began walking again.

Master Nathan might never return…? Didn't he know that poor Smyslin was trapped here and had become a lab animal? He must not know, or he would have come already. Surely…he must have heard. Maybe Master Nathan doesn't care. Or maybe he just can't come back. That might be it, too.

This thought made Smyslin feel a little bit better, except that he was still trapped here. The result was the same.

He nodded his head, "I will help you. We will work together. We will figure something out."

CHAPTER 168

"Brianna to anyone on expedition team, hello?"

Silence.

Oh! I forgot to let go of the "send" button.

Releasing it, then pressing it again, she said again, "This is Brianna from Base 2. Does anyone hear me?"

Static.

Damn it!

"Brianna from Base 2 to…"

"Brianna, this is Dax on the perimeter. If you want to reach the expedition team, you're going to need to use the long-range transmission uplink. When I get off watch, I'll come find you. Unless it's urgent…?"

"Of course it's urgent, Dax! Get down here or send someone right away! I'm on senior officer's level 4. I'm calling from my personal comms."

"Check that. Coming down. Give me five or so minutes."

It was almost seven before Dax came down, blaster rifle still in hand. Dax was one of the newer guys, but not one of the new recruits. He'd been with Morgaine's team for over a year, which made him more knowledgeable than Brianna by a stretch.

Setting down the blaster rifle, he said, "Follow me. I just got showed this the other day. I'd never been here before, either. Taking her down the elevator, they walked back past the training and practice areas and "lower level" guard dormitory to the central hub deep beneath the station. A couple of the off-duty guards were working out, but they paid them no mind.

Walking past them into the Central Command hub, they found several monitors lit up inside.

"Huh," Dax said, looking around. "I was only in here a few days ago, and this place was dark. But this is where, if you want to send a long-range message, it can be sent and received. It goes to the satellite uplink and from there broadcasts as far as the satellite can go. Which I guess is far, on account of how high it is in the sky…"

Brianna was skeptical. Dax seemed to know barely more than she did. But he showed her the built-in comm unit and turned it on for her. Then he sat down in a chair that was already pulled out from the command board, found a piece of dried meat in his pocket, and began to chew it, staring at the screens.

Brianna hit the button, "Brianna to expedition force, come in please! Emergency!"

Treyborne responded almost instantly, *"Brianna! What's up? Is something wrong? Are you under attack?"*

"No, Trey! No attack. It's just…"

"You missed me, didn't you?" This brought a sharp look from Dax, so Brianna whirled so he couldn't see her face redden.

"No! You bastard!" she responded in a hoarse whisper, "Listen! Less than thirty minutes ago, I saw Maitan ride off toward Nyx. Like full speed."

"So? He's probably going into town to buy something…"

"That's what I thought, at first. But the reason I even knew he was leaving was that the kitchen girls told me he'd come in and was packing saddlebags full of food. Why would he do that if it's just a few hours trip to Nyx? Even if he stayed overnight, why not just bring some coin, stay at an inn, and eat their food?"

"Ok, I see your point. But how does this constitute an emergency?"

"I don't know…!" Brianna half-wailed. "It just seems off. I mean when does Maitan ever go anywhere without Morgaine? He couldn't come on your trip. He understood that I'm sure. But if we needed supplies, why not send anyone else? That's what he normally does. He's technically in charge here! And if he's not…where could he be going and why the hurry? Why didn't he tell anyone what he was doing, or where he was going?"

"I have no idea. I'll consult with Morgaine when I get with her tonight, and we will get back to you if we figure anything out. Trey out!"

The line went dead. He must have had to go somewhere urgent. Perhaps getting to Morgaine required radio silence. Likely it did.

"I don't know where he's going," Dax said from his chair, still chewing the jerky. "But I think I know why! B, this is some messed up shit right here! I mean, I can barely read his notes, let alone figure out where all these numbers came from, or what they mean. But this right here – I think this tells us what he's doin'. If not where he's going exactly, or who he's going to do it to."

He handed her a digital notepad.

On it, in Maitan's unmistakable crisp hand, she read, *"Chances go up 170x with one single action. One person. One variable eliminated. Single assassin striking one Dark Lord. Any one of them. However, with timing being a key factor, eliminating the third in power tips the scales and the timeline in our favor."*

Looking up, she saw mathematics that made her head spin. All over the place. Maps…and dots…coordinates. Satellite pictures of armies and cities. What in the world…? Dax was still just shaking his head.

Running to the comm, she began to call again, "Brianna to expedition team, please respond!"

Static.

"Brianna to expedition team, please respond!"

More static. Panic grew like a knot in Brianna's stomach. She now knew what Maitan had set out to do. And it was impossible.

In more ways than one.

CHAPTER 169

Ellie stared at the white-hot lights, sitting in her chair. This was a "meeting" with senior officials, but she wasn't supposed to be able to see them at all, clearly. And their voices were being run through some sort of digital dampener to conceal their identities that way also.

Nice. Love the trust. Really makes me want to help you. Assholes.

Smyslin clearly had a bad feeling about these people and this place. He still did. The few times she was allowed to see him – she was the interpreter after all – his obvious fear and apprehension was as palpable as the glasses on Ellie's face.

It was nice to have her vision restored, at least. Seeing in a blurry world every day all day had not been fun. Not being able to recognize most people sitting across a table from you was embarrassing. Adjusting her glasses, so the glare didn't blind her, she asked, "How much longer do I have to sit here? I understand you're upset. But I told you time flows differently there – and I wasn't sure to begin with how long Nathan was planning on being gone. The transfer didn't allow us to speak. So, like me, you are all just going to have to wait!"

She sat back, trying not to feel like she was in her mother's kitchen again, sitting at the table with her back to the room in time out.

"What can you give us then?" came a female's muffled voice. *"We've been more than patient and given you everything you've asked for. Give us something to bring back to our superiors."*

"I'm sorry, but I was very plain about this from the outset. Nathan and I aren't 'together', we simply agreed that access to the monolith – Arc

Gate – whatever you want to call it, should be restricted to good people with good intentions. You know better than I do how something like this in the wrong hands could be devastating. For people here as well as over there! Until he and I talk, nothing happens. Besides: Nathan cracked the code. He's the one who can do it every time. I told you I can't. I got lucky once. I'm working on it. You see me working on it… but I can't. Nathan will be back. It's only been a week or so, also! Give him some time. Give *me* more time! I told you it'd likely be a month. At *least*! Do your superiors not have calendars? I can give you a calendar to take back for them!"

"I'm afraid that's not funny, Doctor," said a male voice. *"But we do understand you're limited in your knowledge still. We just can't keep telling our superiors to wait."*

"Then stop answering their calls! I don't know! You've got three fucking aliens in here! What more could you want?"

"A female, for starters." This was the female voice again.

"What?!"

"A female. We have three males. All we can ascertain is that we have two distinct races here, and both have been highly genetically modified. Or rather, their ancestry indicates that. There has been some random recombination going on for some time afterwards."

"And you want me to bring you a female. Test subject."

"Two or three would be ideal, actually."

"Well, fuck off! I'm not taking anyone else in here, you bastards! I'm…"

"Give us something Ellie! We're going to bat for you daily. And you've done nothing for us in over a week. Our patience won't last forever."

Shuttling people up via ring sharing took quite a while. Hours, in fact, due to charging issues. It took so long that Winsell received his tailored new army dress uniform for his new commission in the Rondorian army before they were even done. Considering that the guards outside the room had had to be circumvented, as well… all that took a lot of time.

By the time Nathan got up there with the last of them, Winsell Day had gone down to dinner over an hour ago. At least the guards had gone with him. He'd had some fruit and wine sent up to his room, as well – "for celebrating with the courtesans" he'd told the room steward before leaving, who had seemed delighted at the idea, according to Morgaine. They had all been hiding in the back rooms as he did so, but the man's tone had been unmistakable. The 'courtesans' weren't going to find much left, however. Nor did Nathan. The grapes and strawberries were all but gone. And the wine was completely wiped out. All five bottles of them.

Getting himself a glass of water, which was also almost empty, Nathan went and sat down next to Morgaine. Messau, Jasper, and Trey all sat around the tea table. Nathan with Morgaine on the couch, the others in separate chairs.

"Now comes the hard part," Trey said, shaking his head. "We've got hours, maybe one single day, to find someone suitable to put in as the King – or Queen – of this little monarchy. It's got to make sense, or the people will revolt.

"And who are our candidates? Bantor suggested a couple. I need more. You were all supposed to be hunting for suitable people amongst the crowd downstairs and outside the palace," Morgaine reminded them.

Jasper spoke up, "Duke Mantessa is both uncle to the current king and was brother to King Rondor II. He would be ideal, in my mind. He cannot be happy about how the Kingdom had reached the point of despair before K'Thul's armies bailed them out. Incidentally, and not directly, I might add. He was also general under Rondor II. Stability would be outstanding."

Morgaine nodded, but said, "We've already discussed him, however. I want new ideas. Yes, Messau…?"

"I say always go with the opposition. The enemy of your enemy is your friend. Duke Iranias withdrew his forces before the fighting was over. He's under virtual house arrest in the palace as we speak. Everyone in court is saying nice things. But the rumor I heard is that after the celebrations, he is going to be court-martialed and then executed. He's perfect. He's cousin to both the current king and the general is his uncle, as well. Plus, he's clearly not impressed with Rondor III."

Morgaine sighed, "I know you were asleep for most of this discussion, but again…we've talked about him. Are there any others?" Her eyes looking to Nathan were begging for a suggestion. He hadn't been listening much to the crowds. He had been too busy finding people and turning invisible with them and sneaking upstairs. "The King has several cousins and two sisters. But neither of the girls are old enough, being thirteen and sixteen. Nor would an army be likely to follow the apparent whims of a teenage girl." He shrugged. Those are the only two close relatives I heard of besides those other two.

Treyborne sat forward, folding his hands together, looking at Morgaine, "You know we looked. But Bantor suggested those two and they are the two best candidates. The only other options are the Queen, or to go with a conglomerate of nobles and the wealthy and truly create some political quorum. We could install Bantor as Prime Minister. The people will have to feel they have real power, though, when in fact it's still held by the nobles and the rich. Nathan, you said your government is like that. Any thoughts?"

"Yeah. First, it sucks and second, it's a joke. It won't work here. Next idea?"

Trey's eyebrows shot up, but he just laughed and said, "The definitive answer has been given!"

Nathan stood up, "Why do we need more than two candidates? I think we approach those two and see what gives. If they don't want it, or it doesn't work, then we seek alternatives. We also have a problem when one or even two of the most visible nobles don't show up after the dinner tonight! We have to move fast."

Everyone nodded at that.

"Morgaine," Nathan said walking back and forth in front of the veranda doors (closed for this meeting), "we know we must get rid of the king. It's really the first order of business. Why don't you and I go take care of him and send Trey and Jasper to go find and talk to the other two. We offer them separately and jointly to take power. If they both agree, they'll be implicated in the king's death and will have to play along. But whatever other leverage we can get we will need. It feels dirty, no doubt about it. But Rondor's become a pawn of the Dark Cult...and..."

"And..." Morgaine said, staring at him coldly, "we don't know where that influence is actually coming from! Yes, the Contessa was primary. But she was hardly acting alone! If we put an adherent to the Dark in power by mistake..."

"I do have this, Morgaine..." he said, holding up the Corillion medallion. "Don't forget...*we* have this!"

"I hadn't forgotten, Nathan. I'm just concerned if might be someone in one of their respective camps, and not the men themselves who might be corrupted. We can't capture every single member of each family, and all their senior staff, you know. And if we choose wrong, we hand this kingdom over to the Dark!"

CHAPTER 170

Maitan's ship was a Talim runner by the name of the *Fast Lass*. Talim runners were the fastest and finest ships on the seas, at least according to her captain. He'd paid a high price – doubled to allow his mare on board– just to get on a ship that could, according to its captain, "… outrun any other ship on the sea!"

Maitan was hopeful. But it was the reason he had paid over twenty gold Nelrae to take ship as a merchant trader. They had a stall for his horse below decks and a cabin for him midship next to the first mate and captain.

They had had smooth sailing the first day, but it had turned very stormy the second, and they had to harbor around the coast along the desert wall on the southern coastline. The next day, they sailed due east, and got a very good tailwind.

"We should be at Scim's Warding by nightfall, if this holds up!" he declared. Maitan was always amazed at sailors. Flying around the masts and rigging, lying around in the nets and crow's nest high above the deck of the ship. The *Fast Lass* was a very nimble craft, to be sure. It made better time over water than the land cruiser did over land. And that was saying quite a lot.

Maitan looked at his handheld chronometer, then put it back. They had two hours before daylight was lost. If his calculations were correct, Scim's Warding would receive the first of several attacks by Dark Raider vessels sometime in the middle of the night. Once those attacks started hitting the coast, trader ships would steer clear for weeks. Maybe longer.

No one would take him anywhere near those waters. He had to be on that island beforehand.

He had to be.

Looking at some of the hasty notes he'd tossed into his saddlebags, he realized he'd left his digital notepad. Muttering to himself, he tried to remember which notes that held. Well, no matter. The conclusions were the same. If someone or something didn't remove one of the Kyess pieces from the board, the chances of Morgaine toppling the Dark Lords by herself before one of them emerged victorious were slim and none.

The first mate approached him, sauntering as all of them did. He had a huge gold earring in his left ear lobe and was missing a front tooth – apparently from a brawl with another vessel's crew only a few weeks prior. His hair was brown, but sun-bleached. His eyes were dark brown. And sharp as knives.

"What yer in such a rush fer?" he asked, in the lazy sailor talk of the southern seas. "You coulda paid half, or less and gotten there in two more days! The weather this time o' year is near perfect! We even lost ya a day with that rare early autumn storm…!"

"I told you…I have business on the island. Scim's Warding must be underneath my heels by tonight, or your bonus doesn't happen, I'm afraid! That…*would* be a pity! And, assuming you all can make this incredible run after having lost half a day to that storm, well…! I for one will surely spout the virtues of the Talim Runner ships for the rest of my natural born days…indeed, I will!"

The first mate nodded, suddenly happy with the answer he'd already heard three times before.

Maitan had little doubt he'd hear it once or twice more before he was safely off the vessel. Going down to his saddlebags, he checked his gear.

Tucked into one of them, with the rest on top of the saddle bag, was his father's armor.

Pulling it out in the dim light, he could feel the supple support metal within, yet the material itself was amazingly light and soft, despite that. Feeling for his father's weapon, he pulled it out, pressing the button that brought out both the bright blade and the curved knife on the back side.

Spinning it easily in his hand, he threw it up, catching it over his head without looking. All those years of training. He'd been too young to fight back then. But his father had insisted he learn as soon as he could hold the *Myshar*. It was such an elegant weapon.

It was the weapon every *Biaki Mor* fought with. It was the one every *Biaki Mor* died holding. Pressing the button, it withdrew the blades, making it fit into the saddlebags with ease. Nodding to himself, Maitan went back up on top and watched the sun race for the horizon behind and to the south of them, as they themselves raced towards a growing dark island in front of them.

It seemed they would, indeed, make the westernmost port of Scim's Warding by evening.

The lone remaining *Biaki Mor* in the universe, let out a deep, heartfelt sigh and thanked the Creator in a silent prayer.

CHAPTER 171

It was getting late, and Winsell had not yet returned from dinner and the post-dinner festivities. Perhaps he was being 'forced' into carrying out his boast about the courtesans before being allowed to leave, or some other such nonsense.

As one of the 'honored guests' of the evening, it would have been in poor taste to try to withdraw early. Or so he had told them quietly over comms more than an hour ago.

Trey suddenly remembered the message Brianna had sent earlier in the day. *"Damn!* Morgaine!"

Morgaine was sitting quietly talking with Jasper and Nathan at the far end of the room. There were so many people in the Major's quarters, they had had to keep extra quiet and move as little as possible in the hopes of not alarming anyone passing by outside in the halls.

Getting up so that he wouldn't have to yell, Treyborne trotted over to Morgaine, who had heard him…or at least had seen he was coming, as her attention had turned towards him.

At that moment, Winsell's voice came over the comms, *"Ambush! Repeat, ambush! Get out of there now…!"* Then a sharp crack was heard, and his comm went dark.

Everyone in the room heard it. Leaping to their feet and grabbing weapons, suddenly the doors burst open and crossbows bolts and arrows started flying into the room. Everyone was leaping, rolling, diving, or running to take cover behind whatever furniture was closest. Others were moving slowly, some having already been hit by the barrage.

Return fire from blaster rifles and hand blasters also began quickly, dampening and slowly pushing back the initial impact of the attack.

Charging into the room came at least ten men armed with long blades and spears, bearing shields. Behind them came a dozen more and then the King himself came in behind, clearly drunk. Rondor was laughing like a man gone mad, "Never trust Nelrae!" he screamed. Seeing Morgaine crouching behind a sofa, he yelled, "Of course! It's Morgaine, the Witch with her Dark pawns! See them wielding their magic wands against us!"

The 'magical' blaster fire from Morgaine's men, however, never slowed. And the efficiency with which they were cutting down men caused Rondor's eyes to widen in panic and start backing away, sword still in his hand. Already nearly half the two dozen men in front of him were down.

Some of Morgaine's men had been taking arrow and quarrel hits, themselves, however. And despite the toughness of their armor, it wasn't impenetrable. The constant blaster fire quickly began pushing the King's men backwards, causing them to put up their shields while flailing uselessly with their swords and spears.

Morgaine and Nathan looked at each other. She held up her hand with the green and gold ring. Nathan nodded, and they twisted them together.

"You see!" the King yelled at his men, even as he was falling back. "The Witch just vanished into shadow! The power of the Dark has always been hers!" Treyborne and Messau started cutting down men right in the middle in front of the King, aiming for their armored legs, as some of the blasts were hitting true. Others began to follow suit. As his men continued falling, the King turned and ran out of the room, followed quickly by the remainder of his men who had charged in just moments before.

As some of Morgaine's men near the back of Winsell's room got better angles at the men shooting from the hallway, cries of pain and "Retreat!"

began to occur. Nathan suddenly saw three of the remaining four rear guard of the King's men gutted by a black blade appearing out of nowhere through their chests. In seconds, the hallway was clear of anyone living except Morgaine and her men. While they had forced their way forward, the King and more than a dozen of his men still in the hallway had escaped down the stairwell.

Morgaine's voice came from nowhere, "So much for the advantage of surprise!" She was furious.

Nathan reappeared as he said, "What now, Morgaine? Do we run…?"

She also appeared, clearly wanting to conserve what little shielding she had remaining. "No. We search the palace for that little bastard and either make him kneel or execute him! Trey, you and Messau go take the rest of the men who can fight and find me one of those Dukes! If we don't have a local puppet to install by morning, we're going to have to come up with a new plan. Nathan, go dark and follow me. Grab my hand!"

Taking Morgaine's hand in his own, they again twisted the rings and vanished from sight.

Walking down the stairwell as quietly as they could, they saw several men in key places on the next level ready to fire on whatever they saw. Watching nervously, the men were looking at each other as much as at the stairs. It seemed the news of the 'White Witch' suddenly appearing and disappearing in the castle was spreading fast. Separating, and whispering in their comms, they cut them all down with several bursts of blaster fire, without even a shot being fired in return.

Since no one else was on that floor, they went down to the main level, which was filled with even more of the same: men with crossbows everywhere, plus a contingent of armed guards with shields and in metallic chainmail. But they were far from the stairs to avoid getting hit with weapons they had heretofore never seen before. The sound of blaster fire was not something that could be masked. These men were petrified, knowing the enemy had weapons they could not stand against. Invisible enemies to boot. One fired a quarrel randomly from his crossbow that almost hit Nathan, as he walked stealthily down the side of the stairs.

The King himself was nowhere to be seen, but the main floor Assembly Hall doors had been shut – and hurriedly – based on how many tables of food had been thrown onto the floor in the massive halls. There was also a large cluster of armed men with spears and halberds standing in front of the double doors leading to the chamber. There were at least forty men in total, not including men further down the hallway. They were not planning on letting anyone in.

"There are a lot of men here, Nathan. What do you suggest?"

Nathan said one word, "Shotgun."

Walking at an angle to a large group of them, he cocked the weapon, causing some to whirl, then he fired it at the lot of them. Several went down, others staggered, hit by the buckshot. Cocking it again, he turned as others moved to stab or fire into the area where they perceived the shot had come from. Ducking to avoid getting hit by the others already firing arrows and bolts, he shot again. Rolling down the hallway and putting himself almost completely on the floor on his back, he reloaded, rolled, and cocked the gun again. Another blast. Another.

Men were falling everywhere, bleeding horribly. Others began to run.… "Demons! They've summoned demons!" The entire hallway seemed to panic and run, save for a few brave – perhaps foolhardy – men.

Reloading took a few more seconds. As he did so, Nathan called out, "I've got plenty more where this came from! Either get the hell out or go to hell! Your choice!"

The remaining four men bolted down opposite hallways. Some running mere feet from Nathan's position. Morgaine said over their personal comms, *"Well done."*

Reloading and cocking his shotgun once again, Nathan pounded on the closed doors. "Knock knock, you son of a bitch!" Nathan yelled. "We're coming for you! That wasn't nice, invading our little meeting without even knocking first. So, I'm giving you the courtesy you didn't give us. Open these doors, and we'll let you live. Don't and you end up like those out here. Bleeding out of their faces."

Morgaine became visible, walked towards him, obviously orienting on his voice, "Nathan…?"

Nathan twisted his ring so she could see him, rising as he did so. "Morgaine…this jackass accused you of being a murderess simply because you exposed his aunt's affiliation with the Dark. He was holding you against your will for a trial that appeared to be readying itself to be just as much a sham as the charges were. Then he sent men to kill you because you were cunning enough to get away. Minutes ago, he just tried to kill you again. He didn't come in and ask who was there, or why. He came in firing. I'm done with his idiot. *Done.*"

"I see…." Morgaine said, "I suppose that's more than valid. And we must find a way in…but…."

A muffled voice came from behind the door.

"What?" Nathan yelled? "We can't hear you!"

"I know the White Witch is out there! I hear you, too, whoever you are! But there's no possible way you can get through these doors! We have them bolted and barred. Another entire contingent of men awaits anyone who tries! So, you can just stay out there until the Duke has rallied the troops from the barracks! He'll be bringing a few thousand men, I'm sure. Let's see how you fare then!"

"If that were true," Morgaine whispered, "they would be here by now. Hundreds of men are in the barracks just down behind the castle. It's minutes away. He must be lying. Besides, he had no idea who was in that room, clearly. Nor that we had that level of sophisticated weaponry. He was expecting to surprise and slaughter everyone in that room. When he failed, he ran. The Duke is likely in there with him right now."

Nathan nodded. Seeing a man peek his steel capped head into the hallway, Nathan took aim. The head vanished. "Well, let's see how the door holds up after a few shotgun blasts!"

"No, Nathan. Don't waste your firepower," Morgaine said, and she slid her sword free of its sheath. "The doors aren't so tight that Manticore cannot fit through them. Can you…hand me the *Corillion* a moment, Nathan? This might just work…"

Taking off the gemstone pendant, he handed it to her. The gemstone shone brightly once it touched her palm. Suddenly little lights appeared all along her blade, making it appear that tiny little stars were coming into existence up and down the weapon. Then she slid the blade in between the crack of the massive doors.

There was a sudden 'CLANG!' and doors exploded open towards them.

Morgaine pushed Nathan to the side hard, almost tackling him to the ground away from the doorway. Twisting her ring, she vanished again. Nathan did the same a moment later. Crossbow bolts began flying through the open doorway, but all of them flew over their heads straight through the center of the opening. Some of the men with weapons and shields started advancing into the hallway, but many were crying out in fear.

"Do you see anyone…?" someone from the back shouted.

One of the men in the front, wild-eyed with fear, yelled, "The Witch! The White Witch has come for our souls…!" Others began to repeat it, causing gasps of dismay, shouting, and screaming within.

"You see…?" Morgaine whispered over comms to him, *"It helps to have a reputation."*

Nathan heard a small click. A moment later an explosion rocked the inside of the room, causing men to fly into the hallway.

"Come on!" she said again over comms. *"Stay low."*

The bolts had completely stopped by now, and the only people they could see were scattering and screaming in terror. The room was in total chaos. Many men and some women were lying about the middle of the room, clutching bloody limbs and even some bloodied stumps for arms and legs. Some weren't moving at all. Others were running towards the rear of the court, even though there was nowhere to run. The King was seated on his throne, but he also had a piece of something stuck in his leg and was holding it with his hand, blood pouring down his leggings. Two men were rushing to tend to his wound, even though he was clearly not as badly injured as many were near the doors.

"Stay near the doors, Nathan. Retain either of the Dukes if you see either of them try to escape."

"Yes, Mistress!" Nathan said, then chuckled.

Morgaine *'tsked'* in the comms.

Another few seconds and Morgaine appeared with a blaster pointed at the King's head. The men at his feet didn't know what it was she was holding, but they got the idea. Raising their hands, they backed away when she motioned with her other hand.

The King didn't move, but he shouted at her, "Witch! How dare you! Guards! Kill her!"

Morgaine looked up, regally. She said calmly, "Your men cannot kill me, King Rondor. At least not before I kill you. Have your guards drop their weapons. Then kneel to me, and abdicate, and I will spare your life. I am going to crown another king in Rondor today."

"Never! You're a witch and in league with the Dark Lords! I will never yield to you!" Pressing her blaster into his skull a bit more, she said, "Have your guards disarm themselves…!"

Rondor nodded and said, "Guards…yield. For now." Weapons clanged to the floor all across the vast room.

Morgaine looked down at him. "King Rondor, this is your court, but I am going to play the judge for a moment. You tried to frame me for murder simply because you found out your aunt was an adherent to the Dark, and you didn't like how you found out. Next, you put me under house arrest for a murder I didn't commit. Had the woman been innocent, she would be alive to this day. It was her ties to the Void that killed her. Not me. I didn't even touch the woman. You were there, and you know it. Yet you dared accuse me of murder! Me, the very woman, who crowned your grandfather 55 years ago in this very hall! Then, when I decided to leave your little charade behind and slip away quietly, you couldn't leave well enough alone…so you sent assassins to kill me!"

This brought more than a few gasps and mutters from the crowd.

"She's lying!" Rondor shouted, "I never…"

"Oh, but you did, your Grace!" Jasper announced, as he, Treyborne and another dozen men entered the room with blaster weapons raised. In his hand was a large parchment scroll. He threw it into the room. "I'm one of the men you hired. Or don't you recognize me, Your Highness?"

The King snarled but said nothing further.

Nodding, Morgaine turned fully, facing the court, keeping an eye on Rondor's head, aiming the blaster a little lower towards his neck and back. Nathan then appeared beside her; shotgun pointed at the King's head.

"As the person who crowned King Rondor I in these very halls, I claim the Divine Right granted me by the Creator himself as the one who crowned this line. I hereby revoke Rondor III's title as king….!"

"You can't do that…and you were not the one who crowned my grandfather!" Rondor shouted. "It was the High Priest himself who did it! I played along when I arrested you. But that is the truth!"

"No," Morgaine said looking down at him. She spoke softly, but loud enough that everyone could still hear her, "Go, people of Rondor…go into your archives and read the histories for yourselves! Go find the painting that was commissioned by King Rondor I from the famed Lady Alistaire only a few weeks afterwards. On it, you will see a woman with long, white hair dressed all in blue and silver, the exact outfit I now wear – placing the crown on Rondor's head. The official archives mention me by name, as it was King Rondor's way of honoring the work I did in the background to aid in your successful revolution."

Murmurs floated about the room at this.

"Your grandfather was crowned by the High Priest, to be sure. But that was outside for the masses the following day. But I did it first in this very court – as Alistaire herself painted it. King Rondor had it put into his library, so he could 'contemplate our alliance'. Or so he said. Send someone to go and see if I'm lying or telling the truth. I'll wait."

One of the court stewards stepped forward, saying, "I'll go find it. And I'll report whether the painting is there or not. If there's any painting of the coronation in the library, I'll fetch it and bring it." Then he ran out of the room.

"I doubt it," Morgaine murmured, "it's almost four spans wide and two high. It covers an entire wall." Nathan nodded, pushing the King's head down when he tried to stand.

The people in the room didn't speak. They barely moved. They were horrified at the scene before them. Morgaine motioned to the men who had come to aid the king, "You two, go help those who are bleeding and in pain. No more people need die today." The men slowly moved away to aid the injured. A few mutters were still coming from small pockets, but no one said anything that could be heard, nor did anyone do anything to attack them.

The young man came running back and said, "It's true! There's a painting of the White…a woman with white hair, dressed as she is today, placing the crown on the King's head!"

As the gasps and muttering died down, Morgaine raised her blaster and put it away. She then drew her sword, putting it to Rondor III's neck. "I think you know you'll find me in the Archives, as well. Rondor III… do you abdicate?" she asked. Cold steel in her voice.

"I do not." Nathan's eyes rolled. The guy had balls. That was for sure.

Morgaine nodded. "You have all heard him. He has made his choice. Therefore, by the power vested in me, I, Morgaine the White Queen, revoke the kingship from Rondor the First's grandson. A more worthy man shall be put in his stead. A man who will not lead the country to disaster. A man who will not succor the Dark by his actions or inaction. A man who will not take out contracts on innocent women – or City Council members, as he did for Councilman Bantor."

More gasps.

"These are the acts of the Dark." Morgaine said and lifted the blade high. Rondor made not a move. Then the blade fell, and his head rolled, bouncing down the stairs. Women shrieked and fainted, and men cried out in horror.

"Bring me Duke Iranias and Duke Mantessa. I do not wish to rule here in Rondor's stead this day. Let the line of Rondor, if not his direct heir, lead your country into the future!"

CHAPTER 172

It was late in the day when Gary got a call. It was Thursday and nearly quitting time. Jennifer was out. She had sent him a text saying she was sick with the flu and not to worry. No aliens had abducted her. Or federal agents.

So, when his desk phone rang at 4:17 PM, the last person he expected to hear from was "Jenn?" Gary asked quietly, seeing the caller ID on the little digital feed at the bottom.

"Yes, Gary…! It's me. I'm with Ellie. She came by a couple hours ago. I really am sick," she coughed apparently to emphasize the point, "But she said it was urgent. We've been talking, and I thought we should bring you in on this…."

"Bring me in on what?" he whispered. "I just got my life back here a few days ago. What's going on…?"

Gary heard an exasperated sigh and a moment later, he heard, "Gary? This is Ellie! Jenn's half dead and it took me all afternoon just to find her number and get to her apartment. I don't want to talk over the phone. How quickly can you get here…? What…?" A pause. "Oh, no. Not here. The Chai House. She says you know where it is, and that her roommates will start coming back in less than an hour. See ya there!"

"Yeah, but…." Beep.

"Shit," Gary said, looking around. His boss had been more than gracious about the massive time he'd simply been gone and most of that time being on TV as "wanted for questioning". Despite all he'd said the other day, he didn't trust Andy would just let all that go if he kept acting strange. Leave early now, and things might get dicey. Watching to see when Andy left, he was thrilled to see him grab his door pass and head for the elevators not ten minutes after he'd hung up the phone with Ellie.

Grabbing his jacket, and his own pass and hat, he headed for the elevators himself not sixty seconds later. By quarter after five, he was walking into the Chai House in midtown right by Jenn's apartment. Spotting the two of them was easy, as they were at a table right by the window. It was crowded for three, especially adding in a guy of his size, but he sat down. Jenn had ordered him his favorite awhile back, and it was still hot.

He smiled at her as she coughed into her arm and air hugged him. He did the same and took a drink. Ellie just waited for him to turn his attention to her.

"Hey Ellie," he said, leaning back, which allowed him to lean closer to Jennifer. He'd risk getting sick just to get close to her again. The memory of her and that night was still vivid.

Ellie looked upset. She almost looked human. "Gary, I'm worried. Admittedly, it's only been a little over a week. But they're pushing me, Gary. I mean…*pushing!*"

"Who's pushing you, El?" Gary asked, "The government people?"

She nodded. "They're getting impatient. I had to admit that I got lucky the first time – if you want to call it that – and activated the portal somehow. And they know that Nathan has gone back again, and apparently can do it on command. They've interviewed your buddy Ben if you didn't know…"

Gary nodded, "I knew. He called and told me after the fact two days ago."

Ellie continued, "Ok…so…after that came out… I had to tell them something. They've kept the others under 'quarantine' and they're treating them like lab rats! I'm helpless and I feel we've got to do something. But I don't know what! I did this partially to help you, Gary. Just a reminder here. Plus, I wanted to keep working on the monolith. But I've only had two full days with it this whole time! I'm barely getting in to try to figure out what's changed. And it has changed, Gary! It's all lit up like a Christmas tree and the magnetic field strength has tripled!"

She sighed and rubbed her eyes, "Because of that stupid translator thing – which I refuse to give them – I have to be there to interpret whenever anyone questions any of them about anything! They haven't just taken the translator – yet. They haven't just started dissecting one of our resident aliens – yet. But it seems that crap might be on the horizon. I just don't trust them. And the weaker my position gets, the situation itself just gets worse and worse. It's all just spiraling out of control!"

Gary sipped his coffee and blew out a long breath. "What makes you think you're not bugged now? Or not being followed? Where do they think you are?"

"I did research this morning and told them to get their language specialists in to try to learn their language. I told them if we were going to communicate with that other world on a regular basis, they'd need to learn it, anyway. Shockingly, they did what I suggested. I have a sneaking suspicion they were already doing it, in fact. Either way, I've got to head back to the monolith tonight and hopefully I'll get to study it alone for a while. That's where they think I am now. They've brought in their own team of scientists, too. Only a couple of them I know. And then there's me…"

Gary said, "Get back to the monolith. Learn all you can. See if there's any data from when Nathan and you went through that is different than the rest. I'm sure you've done that. But Nathan had some sort of… gemstone necklace. It seemed like a key or something. Maybe we – and

I mean like 'us' – can make one of our own. If you can figure out what that gemstone is made of…"

"Yes! Gary, I hate to say this, but you're a genius! Why didn't I think of that! You'd mentioned the stone and I completely missed making the connection. I was just so mad Nathan could…you know." Ellie got quiet.

Jennifer was looking at her strangely. Wide-eyed. Pitying.

She reached over and laid her left hand on Ellie's arm. Strangely, Ellie grabbed her hand and squeezed it. She looked up, eyes glistening. "Thanks, Jenn. Thanks, Gary," she said turning to him. She even got up and hugged him.

This is messed up.

"I'll head back and see what I can find. Maybe…" she sighed, "…maybe there's some geological switch or something that focuses it. I'll give them that and at least regain some control!"

Then she was out the door and walking up the street to hail a taxi.

Gary went over to sit in Ellie's seat across from Jenn. She coughed into her arm again. *Even ill, that girl is too damned cute!*

"What do you think, Gary?" Jenn asked quietly, sipping her chai. He leaned back and looked out the window at the gray, rainy street and the bustle of people making their way back to their apartments all over the city.

"I think I'm about to do something stupid again."

CHAPTER 173

Standing on the pier with his mare, Maitan paid the bonus gold happily to the First Mate and turned to step off towards the shoreline.

"Come back to the *Lass* whenever you wish, Merchant Maitan! Whenever you're done, if we're around, we'll be happy to rip you around the high seas for these kinds of wages!"

Maitan waved and nodded but didn't look back. He'd not be seeing them again. Or anyone, most likely. The Dark Raiders, according to virtually every one of his scenarios, would be hitting ships and harbors up and down the southern coast of the Empire by nightfall.

It was beyond hopeful to consider that of the hundreds of vessels to attack the area, that Maitan would be 'fortunate' enough to be hit by the one single ship that Emorion himself was sailing on. No, that chance was exactly as it should be – less than 0.3%. However, if his plan was successful, he'd be taken right to him.

As soon as they could.

This was his hope. And perhaps Morgaine's only hope. He hurt inside, wishing he could have hugged his Mistress and told her goodbye. That the over one hundred ten years working as her assistant and closest advisor had been a joy. Her strength, even in the midst of all the sadness and loss, was simply incredible.

Maitan wept. He rubbed his eyes and finally allowed himself to feel true pity. Not for himself. Well. Perhaps a little. But for the hopelessness this world had come to. The Creator had his reasons. The Dark's influence had been contained on this planet since before he was born. But that just meant all that evil was focused right here and right now. Maitan had to hope that at least some of it would be extinguished in part due to his own sacrifice. His eyes scanned the seas, even as the sky was turning to twilight.

Stars were coming out.

There were no black sails yet on the…wait! Was that…? Several massive ships had just emerged over the edge of the horizon. The distant last glimmers of day outlining them perfectly. It was as if they'd timed it so that they would be seen emerging from the twilight. To increase the panic. Nodding to himself, Maitan realized that was exactly what the plan had been.

Looking back at the *Fast Lass*, she was already free of the harbor and was raising her sails and catching the wind. They had surely seen the ships themselves and were making for the high seas as fast as they could. If they kept sailing east, they'd be safe. For a time.

Maitan stopped the mare and began to undo her saddlebags. She whinnied at him, and he patted her nose. "There, there, dear. I'll be setting you free in a moment. No sense in enslaving you to these blasted Dark Men! Unsaddling her, he then pulled off her bit and bridle along with it.

"Go!" he said, shooing her off. "Go!" Light was hurt. She pranced back a few steps and whinnied again, shaking her mane. She didn't want to. "Persistent shrew! Get out of here! I don't need you anymore!" She danced back a bit more and just stood there. Maitan made to chase her away, but she stood her ground.

Sighing, he just shook his head. "I'm hoping you change your mind. Because soon this shore will be crawling with Dark Raiders and I… I will be captured."

CHAPTER 174

The scene in the Court of Rondor had not gotten much better. Treyborne and Jasper were keeping their men stationed all about the room, blaster rifles in hand. Morgaine was purposefully sitting on the Queen's throne. The Queen herself had been brought in by some of the more rabid people who had become angry after they'd heard about the King's duplicitous dealings. Some apparently felt his bride should be punished for his crimes, since the King no longer could be.

Morgaine had let things progress as they must outside the hall. But when they had brought in the Queen, already bruised from getting beaten, she had to intervene. Messau, who had returned with two of her Elite Guard escorting a young man in extreme finery into the court a few minutes prior, had begun to personally attend to the Queen's injuries. The man, it turned out, was none other than Duke Iranias himself.

Messau and his men had gotten a maid in the castle to tell them where he was being held under "house arrest" by the King. Everyone knew it was simply one step away from court martial and execution for desertion. Proof of that was where he'd been laid up: the darkest cell in the dungeons. His clothes were fine. But they were also dirty. As was the rest of him. He stood proudly to one side, though. Nathan watched him. His eyes were sharp, and he was taking in the entire scene.

He appeared to be gloating.

Morgaine leaned forward and said to her men, "Clear the room! I wish to hear this man speak. The Queen may stay, as well." She leaned back as her orders were carried out. "Trey, take a half dozen of your men and stay in the hallways. Make sure they don't try to break in here and lynch us. Or anyone else."

Treyborne saluted and pointed to a few men. They left the room, shutting the doors behind them. The wounded had been treated and left upstairs. Bodies had been taken away, with the notable exception of the king. Several of Morgaine's men had been shot in the leg or the arm and had needed bandages or splints. One of her guards had died with an arrow to the throat. Several others were upstairs with their weapons. Winsell was with them, per instructions.

Morgaine didn't want him seen by the populace as her ally.

Morgaine turned to the Queen, "My apologies on the loss of your husband." Morgaine expected the woman to be angry, or even defiant. She was a beautiful young woman, barely twenty. She raised her chin, the bruising over her eye making her look both extremely awkward and brave, simultaneously. She began ascending the stairs toward the thrones.

Nathan moved out of the way as the woman approached Morgaine. She slapped her face, and Morgaine simply let her, looking back after she'd done it. Morgaine's eyes were hot. Nathan was amazed how beautiful Morgaine looked when she was angry. It was sexy. Not to mention mesmerizingly arousing.

Or is that sexy, too?

"Get out of my seat! I wish to sit on my throne one last time!" Morgaine slowly rose and went to sit in Rondor's throne for the first time.

Queen Peniella sat down, turning her head to Morgaine angrily. "The man was a pig! I hated him! But you had no right to execute him. That should have come at the will of the people, or at least his inner court. Now, you have made me a widow and a beggar! The Kingdom of Daystrom will reel from this. My family!"

Her head snapped towards Iranias. "But I wish to deal with you later. Woman to woman. Right now, I want to hear the coward speak! Come forward, coward! Speak your peace! The coronator of the first King of Rondor and executioner of the last wants to hear it!"

Morgaine quietly started laughing. Nathan had to hide his own face a bit. The girl was entertaining in her fury. And not for one second did she lose her poise. As Morgaine turned to face Iranias, who was approaching the steps up to the throne, she whispered, "Your mother trained you well…"

Nodding to Iranias – as did Peniella virtually simultaneously – Morgaine commanded, "Speak! I wish to know if you are a worthy replacement as King in Rondor. You are…were…cousin to him, yes?"

Duke Iranias bowed to the girl and nodded to Morgaine. "Indeed I am. First cousin. My mother was the Contessa…the woman you *executed* a few weeks ago…? Of course, I personally had no idea she'd succumbed to the Dark Cult. None of us did, I assure you. Such things are forbidden here. Frowned upon heavily in the Empire, as well, I might add. But it is an executable offense here." He stopped for a moment. "Or at least…it was."

Taking a breath, he asked, "May I sit? I've been standing in stocks for days. I'm exhausted." Morgaine moved her hand and one of her guards raced to grab him a chair. As he sat down, he sighed, "Ah! Such bliss! So, the Queen…excuse me, *former* Queen Peniella wants to hear me out, does she?"

He looked at her, and she nodded to him. Her face red, with one eye swollen shut did little to mute the effect. She hated this man.

"Very well. For years…" he looked directly into her one good eye as he said this, "*YEARS*…I had been warning the King of the temperament in the Empire. Remember, I grew up there with my mother until I became steward of the family estates here in Rondor, and my military training began under Duke Mantessa at age fourteen. The Duke himself will certify this is true."

He stopped. "May I have a drink, please? I've been drinking dirty water and not much of it, for days." Morgaine again motioned and this time another guard brought him a large cup of red wine. "Bless you!" he said. And it seemed he meant it.

Morgaine and Nathan exchanged glances.

He took a very long drink, then continued, "I have connections in the Empire, and I know the people. Something – or someone – has been stirring up hostility towards Rondor there for almost a decade. I told him to build forts, fortify the southern borders and begin preparing for war. That was over five years ago! Every year, I warned him of what I had been hearing from my friends. He ignored me. He laughed at me. He said I was 'a fool 'and that I had become soft in the Empire. Even though I was the older cousin and more worldly…I was the fool!" He spat and looked directly at the Queen for a second time, "I'm glad he's dead! He was a poor ruler! And he got what he deserved!"

She stood and pointed, "You are a coward and a traitor! It was your fault we almost lost the war! If you had stayed in the battle, the King and the General would never have gotten into such bad straits!"

Morgaine at some point had picked up Rondor's scepter. She tapped it softly, but repeatedly until they stopped and looked at her. "Please, Your Highness. I'd like to hear his story. You are welcome to cross him at your leisure upon its completion. And you," she said, looking at Iranias, "are to not make inflammatory remarks just to cause her pain. The Queen has just lost her husband. Give the woman some compassion!"

Queen Peniella stared at Morgaine, then nodded stiffly. The first sign of respect she'd given Morgaine.

Iranias nodded his agreement, "Very well," and continued. "Yes, it is true. I took my fourteen thousand men and withdrew seven clicks to my southern estates. I hadn't truly decided to utterly withdraw and simply run my men home, however. I was set to take a flanking position and attack their sides or their rear. Duke Mantessa himself is an excellent general, and he had approved that very plan two days prior. But Rondor kept putting his foot into it, and wouldn't allow it, making a mess of everything! We were imposing stiff losses on the Empire, no doubt. But it should have been more – much more than enough to halt their push – if he'd simply stayed out of it!" He took another drink and leaned back in his chair.

"The man…" he looked from Morgaine to the Queen and back, "was *not*…a warrior and he was far from an accomplished or trained field general. Mantessa, however, was….and I learned from him for ten years. Rondor learned nothing except how to sit in that chair and…" he looked to the Queen, "forgive me, Your Highness…sleep with prostitutes."

Queen Peniella made a noise, and Morgaine turned to her. The woman dropped her head. "It is true," she said, "I barely saw the man. I knew this to be the fate of many King's wives. Bed him at his leisure. Produce an heir. Repeat as necessary. But he had a penchant for both his mistresses and his whores. I felt unclean after every…" she looked over at Morgaine, her one eye showing real pain, "…*every* occurrence. As I said, he was a pig."

She nodded to Iranias, "I hold you no ill will to you for speaking the simple truth. Continue."

Duke Iranias was charismatic, Nathan had to give him that. The Duke took another drink of wine and set the cup down next to his chair. "As our forces continually got pushed…"

The doors opened and Treyborne came in with an older man who had a grey beard and piercing blue eyes. He was short and rather overweight, but this in no way seemed to diminish his presence. Here clearly was the other Duke, the Duke of Mantessa. Uncle to the former king and General of the Armies of Rondor. Treyborne nodded to Morgaine, then left, shutting the massive doors behind himself.

Morgaine said, "Guards get the Duke another chair. And bring us some more wine. Nodding to Peniella, Morgaine rose and said, bring me one, as well. Your Highness…?" Morgaine stopped and held out her hand to the young woman. After a moment, she took it. Morgaine retained the scepter. Nathan stayed standing up on the throne dais, leaning on his shotgun.

More chairs were brought, and they all sat in a circle on the floor at the bottom of the stairs. Morgaine leaned back, "Welcome Duke Mantessa," she said formally.

He nodded, but Nathan could see from the redness of his face that he was boiling. "We've met," was all he said in reply.

Taking his reply as a courtesy, Morgaine continued, "Duke Iranias here was filling us in on his feelings towards the former leadership of your lands. He also said he didn't retreat, but rather withdrew per your original plans before King Rondor changed them. Would you say his description is accurate?"

Mantessa turned his red face to Iranias, "That's not the whole story!" he blurted. Then a bit more calmly he said, "But…that is essentially correct."

Morgaine nodded, "Please continue, Duke Iranias…"

Iranias looked over at his former mentor and said, "I'm sorry, uncle. But the facts are the facts. King Rondor kept our forces tight and our losses low, yes. But we were doing little in terms of countermeasures or offensives. We were fighting a losing war. This is from your own mouth, General."

General Mantessa nodded curtly, "It is."

"We were at the point of breaking either way, so it was either appear to retreat and draw them in…then come around and hit them on their flanks, or simply roll over and die. I was afraid, for reasons I have made clear to the General, that if anyone knew my plans, the Empire would as well. I…*we*…could not afford that. Once my 'retreat' was fully known, and Nelrae pressed its advantage, however, Rondor decided to sue for terms of peace!"

Mantessa blurted, "That's because we didn't know you were doing it! We both thought you'd just left us to die!"

Iranias answered, "The King had killed the one plan we had conceived to save us. You wouldn't stand up to him. So, I did. I figured you would know!"

Duke Mantessa blustered a bit, then grew red-faced and remained quiet.

Iranias turned back to Morgaine, "Just as my offensive maneuver was in place, suddenly the Army of Nelrae began retreating. Rapidly. I watched from our outlook on a high hill to the southwest of the battlefield in wonder. But had I been able to execute it, I might have been too late. Because that simp of a bastard king had already agreed to surrender! Didn't he?" he said turning a steely-eyed gaze towards the General.

Sighing, and with redness almost completely gone from his face, he nodded. "He did, indeed. Had we gotten to the actual terms meeting in the morning. Had they not run back in terror at the sudden incursion of the Eastern Empire into their borders, Rondor would this very day be under the auspices of the Emperor once again. Likely, the king…your husband, my dear…" he said looking to the Queen, "…would have been dead a week sooner. Either I, or likely Iranias would have been set up as Regent and we would be at war again with the Eastern Empire even now." Shaking his head, the General added, "I couldn't help thinking…

what would father have thought of all this…? What would my brother have done to ensure it never would…? I felt like a failure."

"But it wasn't your fault!" yelled Iranias, jumping to his feet. "The King shackled you! You barely were able to call out sorties, even for defensive purposes. He entire idea was to use the superior hand-to-hand fighting of our men as a 'meat grinder', as he put it. Make them lose so many men they withdrew. It was asinine! They were willing to spend the lives to subjugate us once again! And he never saw that! We have a superior general, and superior fighters with superior horse! And he used none of it!" Iranias sat back down in disgust, folding his arms. "As for me, put me back in the stockade, or send me home! I'm through fighting."

The Duke of Mantessa, General of the Armies of Rondor looked over as his former protégé, "I shouldn't have doubted you. I should have known the course you were taking. Perhaps I could have convinced Rondor to wait a day or two. We both knew how long it takes to track around the southern hills with that many lance. Your horsemen could have made it in a day. But we needed everything." He sighed. "Either way, my hat is off to you. You were willing to do what I was not: fight for the kingdom when all seemed lost."

Morgaine interjected. "But you both realize that King Rondor III was ruining you by now, I hope…?" It was barely a question. Both men nodded. "Good. Because I need you both to renew your strength. Pray…seek the Father of all and consider carefully what I'm offering: One of you must be crowned king tomorrow. I'd like you to stay in the castle tonight. Not as my prisoners, but as my guests. I have no wish to rule. But I did help forge this country, and I will always defend it, as I promised your father," she said, looking at the General. "That is what I feel we did here today. But we have another enemy to deal with. The Dark threatens to sweep across all lands, taking over the entire world! And I will need you both to help me stop it."

The General started to say something, but Morgaine interjected, left hand up, "Tomorrow! I will explain tomorrow. The hour is very late, and the city will be in upheaval with the news of the King's execution by morning. I would ask that you send out your retainers to get the word out to the Council and the people that one of you will be taking the crown tomorrow. Rondor will still be ruled by the House and line of Rondor. We cannot have rioting in the streets. We have work to do yet. You two need to come together and make your decision. If you cannot make one, I will do it for you. On the morrow!"

Morgaine rose, and they rose with her. Nathan watched as the two candidates for the kingship of this rather vast kingdom both bowed to Morgaine and took their leave. Holding the scepter as she was, Nathan thought she was every bit as royal as they were. Maybe more so. As the Dukes left the hall, Morgaine stood as Queen over them all.

Peniella nodded to her, as well, standing there expectantly, "And what of me, Lady Morgaine? As I've already said, my future has become quite bleak. My country was planning on the open borders and tax advantages we were to receive with my marriage to…to the King. Now that that covenant is broken, Daystrom will be worse off by far than our rival Petty States. My father, who is already on the outs with the others for not supporting the Dark Cult and for making this alliance, will now stand alone without aid against the others!"

Morgaine considered her for a moment, "Why does the deal need to end? Iranias is not married. And he seemed to despise your former husband's practice of mistresses and whores. Let's face it: he cannot be a worse husband. And as a marriage of state, it would qualify. Whether he is crowned tomorrow or not, he stands as owner of half the kingdom with his Duchy. Not to mention his estates in Nelrae, assuming he's allowed to retain them. His prowess and tactics on the battlefield seem more than ordinary. His armies would be your father's shield."

Peniella glanced towards the doorway where the Duke had gone. The doors were standing open from their exit, and Treyborne and the other guards were looking in at them. Looking back at her, she answered, "It is a fair offer. I shall consider it. Can you arrange that and make it happen?"

Morgaine smirked at her with a look in her eyes Nathan couldn't pinpoint, "I am quite sure I can."

CHAPTER 175

Jezerah and his forces swept in from the northwest and, although he was sure K'Thul knew he was coming, they still made quite an impact on the battlefield. No one was more tactical than K'Thul. So even he would have to respond to over 10,000 Dark Men sweeping in from the north. Jezerah was going to pull out all the stops soon enough. Also, Curtaise's forces biting on the southern hills near the gates of the city should be driving them back within the hour.

For the time being, Jezerah's Dark Men and smattering of troops from the Northlands were pushing back the Eastern Empire lines. For the first time since this war had begun, the Empire of Nelrae was winning. At least in places.

This was extremely important for morale. Jezerah really didn't care how many in the Empire had to die, as long as he gained the time he needed to bring his other "forces" into play. K'Thul, if he had one weakness, it was his lack of creativity utilizing his power from the Void. Emorion had always delved into the heart of the Dark, Jezerah himself had tried many things. Many deaths had occurred, to be sure. But many victories. Like the Creepers, for instance. Beautiful destruction wherever they went! Not to mention the Lurkers and the Shadow Beasts. Expensive, time consuming…but Jezerah was sure K'Thul had little or none of the Dark's 'special creations' that Emorion and he employed. And because they'd all been one happy Triumvirate until recently, he'd never experienced the onslaught of the same.

He was about to.

Smiling, Jezerah went to speak with the generals of Nelrae's Army. They bowed deeply to him. As was right. Co-emperors, to be sure. But his own personal puppets, as well. They knew the true power and who held it.

"My dear friends…I am about to unleash pure hell on the humans of the Eastern Empire first. K'Thul will not be able to hold his ranks. By morning, their horse and most of their…mortal men…will have been scattered. The Empire will still have its superior numbers of Dark Men. But they have nothing like the creatures I'm going to unleash upon them. You need not fear backlash! And if they do come, my Dark Men will be in every one of your teams. I will send twenty to one hundred with each of your divisions. Should K'Thul attempt to surprise me… again…we will be ready."

"Afterwards, we will then mount a counter-offensive. With my Dark Men supplementing your own, we will push as one and surround their southernmost troops. By the time the other two move to engage our flank, we will withdraw. Should K'Thul be preparing for his own offensive – which I doubt – but will plan for – he will still have no horse left to use. His rear guard will be decimated. After this, I expect his army to be in a state of chaos. His Dark Men will not be rattled. But we will largely only have to face them. Do you understand the plan?"

Both men nodded, then looked at each other.

"Good!" Jezerah said, "Once you see the horrors I'm sending at them… always remember…" he stopped and let them stare into his coal black eyes, "I can do the same to you."

CHAPTER 176

Maitan was wearing his father's armor. Grey and white, he stood out like a sore thumb even at night. It took longer than he had expected, but eventually a small group of Dark Men ran up to him. Holding up his *Myshar,* he shouted, "I have come from Morgaine to deliver a message to your Master! She is not dead, as he doubtless thought! Take me to him and do me no harm until I give him the message!"

The Dark Raider group of four men stopped for a moment, then two of them engaged. Maitan spun, bright blade out cutting them both in half in seconds. The other two Dark Raiders stood, stunned, then started to attack, as well.

Maitan resumed his position, weapon held high, bright blade shining in the night, "I have come from Morgaine to deliver a message to your Master! Take me to him and do me no harm until I give him the message!"

The men stopped, staring at each other. Coming up slowly, one of them held out his hand for the weapon. After he had it in hand, he suddenly swung with his blade behind Maitan.

But Maitan was ready. Ducking perfectly, he swept the Dark Man's legs, which caused him to release the Myshar. It fell perfectly into Maitan's own hand, and he severed the Dark Man's head before he'd even reached the ground.

There was one left, but several others were rushing up. Holding his weapon up high once again, Maitan shouted for a third time, "I have come from Morgaine to deliver a message to your Master! Take me to him and do me no harm until I give him the message!"

The last of the four Dark Raiders who had initially rushed up to him, walked forward slowly. This one also held out his hand for the *Myshar*. Maitan handed it to him, looking him right in his dark eyes. The man simply nodded and held up his hand as the others rushed in.

"No! He has proven himself and his bravery! By custom and law, we must bring him. Did you not read when you were boys? Have you never studied? He wears the armor of our great foes: The *Biaki Mor!* They are not dead, as we supposed, just like the White Witch herself is not! For that alone, we must honor him. Come," he said, looking to Maitan again, "I will take you to the Master's ship. There, he will decide what to do with you."

Maitan nodded. Everywhere, up and down the beach, people were screaming. Houses were burning. Emorion's war had begun.

CHAPTER 177

Jennifer had gone home shortly after Ellie left, but Gary sat at the Chai House for another hour or more. The problem was simple: Gary was a good programmer and an accomplished hacker. He was also quite good at figuring out systems and finding weaknesses. But Nathan's friends were being held in a federal facility with maximum protection. It wasn't an abandoned warehouse where someone casually assumed their security measures were in place. This was the federal ass government at full alert with actual alien beings from another planet housed in that facility.

What could Gary really do here…? Shaking his head, he tried to drink from his empty coffee for at least the third time. Refilling it, he left to head home. There was nothing more he could do until he or Ellie came up with a viable plan. At least Ellie had left with some real ammo to hopefully help her. Gary was certain he would never like the woman. But he did respect her. And, for now, they were on the same side.

I wish Nathan would just get his ass back here!

He also hoped Nathan was still alive. No one wanted to talk about that possibility. But Ellie and Nathan himself had made it clear that the other world…where the aliens were from… was at war. And Nathan was in the middle of it. His friend, the one who'd gotten hurt…she was at the center of it, from what little Nathan had said before he left.

None of that sounded good. Maybe if she and Nathan both came back, they'd have some real leverage, and they could get Nathan's friends set free. Or whatever they were to him.

At least Ellie still had access to the monolith. Without it, everything was moot. Suddenly, Gary had an idea.

What time is it? 7:45…. How'd it get so freaking late?

Dialing Ellie's number, she picked up. "Yeah, Gary!? I'm doing my research, like I said. I'm kind of busy."

"Yeah, I know…! Just listen. Tell me where you are!"

"Why…? I *can't*! This is a secret facility, Gary. Like I told you, most of the people working on this thing aren't from the circle of physicists I know. They're all feds! Or tied in with them, at the very least."

"Yeah, but you also said they're not usually there at night. Which is why you're there now. Is anyone there with you right now?"

"No! But that doesn't change… What is it you want, Gary? Just to see the thing again?"

"Oh, hell no! I want you to send me through! I'll go get Nathan, assuming he's still alive. Sorry, just being real. Then, if he is, I'll bring him back and he can help you out, help your friends out…we all win! We even get Nathan back. At least for a while…."

"Hold it, hold it, hold it! Aren't you forgetting something? I don't know how I got through the first time! It's never worked for me again!"

"Yeah well…let's try it with me. What's the worst that can happen? We fail and I go home…?"

"No Gary, the *worst* thing that can happen is we both get arrested because I brought you into a Top Secret facility, and let you play around with an alien artifact. That's the worst thing that can happen!"

Gary paused. "You make a great point, Ellie. So…where are you at again?"

As they left the Assembly Hall, Morgaine's entire guard fell in all around her. They were leaving nothing to chance. Treyborne and Jasper were already on the next floor, and Messau had gone to treat the injured. Two more were strapping on weapons and coming to meet them.

There was lots of noise coming from the streets. It appeared that Morgaine's prediction of rioting was happening. However, the sounds were sporadic, and it seemed they were already quieting. Perhaps the news was getting out. Or maybe the City Watch was simply quelling the worst of it.

Either way, it was beyond anything they could do. Nathan walked a half step behind Morgaine, watching her. She was almost in another place, staring straight ahead, as they walked up towards the upper chambers.

Treyborne met them at the next floor's landing, "The King's chambers are clear, Morgaine. It's the most secure room in the entire castle. I think you should take it."

Looking back at Nathan for a moment, she said, "No Captain. That is not my place. Take me to my former chambers. Where we stayed here last. Keep at least two men on the veranda and at least two more in the main chamber. You may stay outside in the room next door or stay up all night. That is your prerogative as leader. Nathan and I will sleep in the main bedroom of my suite. If anything occurs, you know what to do. Our comms will be charging but they will be on. Recharge all your blasters. I'm saying this not because you don't know. But because it is very late, and we are all tired. In less than three hours, we must rise and do it all again. Lead on!"

She looked back then, stretching her hand out to Nathan. He came up the few stairs he had fallen behind, and she took his hand firmly, looking down at him. Nathan couldn't help himself. He shook his head. The woman still looked stunning, even clearly exhausted as she must be. She walked with grace and there was just something surreal about her.

"What?" she asked, as they walked in the circle of her small army.

"You're just…*stunning*. Beautiful…regal…I struggle for the words. You handled all that as well as anyone could have."

She smiled then, and said, "I am beyond myself right now. Even the elixirs I've been taking have worn off. I'm hurting, Nathan. But I don't want to sleep alone. I am sorry, but you are needed." She smiled a bit, looked over at him and said, "There was a time not long ago that I felt I needed nothing and no one. I am glad that time is not now."

Nathan felt something he hadn't felt in a very long time. Just holding her hand was taking his breath away. Looking over at her, Nathan nodded. "Me too, Morgaine. Me…too."

CHAPTER 179

"Hello, Expedition Team! Hello!" Brianna was downstairs at the satellite uplink again. It had been a full day since she'd last spoken with Treyborne. Three whole days since Maitan had ridden off. Since then, multiple storms had swept through the Petty Kingdoms. The orchard tending family farmers said it was the "seasonal autumn rains", but the storms had been fierce.

Surely, they had told Morgaine by now! Surely, they had said something, right?

"This is Brianna to Expedition Team! Can you hear me?"

"Creator above! Brianna! I…I'm sorry. It's been crazy here. I forgot all about what you told me with all that's happened. I'm going in to wake up Morgaine now. I'll tell her right away! Trey out!"

Forgotten all about … Maitan taking off? How was that even possible? How bad was it in Rondor? Or wherever they were now…

Brianna sighed and felt relief, though. The lack of communication had led to dreadful thoughts… *'Had Treyborne been injured…or killed?' 'Were they all dead?'* Brianna hadn't slept much. At least Treyborne and the team were all still together. Hopefully they were all alive, as well. That probably wasn't the case, based on recent history. Hopefully *most of them* were still alive, then.

The satellite comm crackled on again. *"Treyborne to Base 2."*

"I'm here, Trey! What did she say?"

"All she said was, 'That can't be good.' She told me to tell you to track his comm. I should have had you do that immediately! I can't do it with our local comms, but you can do it from there!"

"How?" Brianna asked. "I have no idea how any of this stuff works!"

"Get Mikell! He's been around awhile. He was wounded, but he should be healthy enough to help you out down there. His leg probably is still bad, but…wait! Did Maitan also leave everyone who was injured without any more treatment…?"

"Yes! He just took off! That's what I was saying. Three *days* ago!"

"Shit! Check that! My bad, but…like I said: it has been a little crazy here, Brianna. I don't have time for a lot of extraneous details. But let's just say there's going to be a new king in Rondor today. Anyway, let me know what you find out. I promise not to delay getting back to you this long again. If I don't answer, it's because we're in the middle of something. Keep trying! Got it?"

"Yes sir, Captain! But I'm not taking any more orders from you for a while. I'll find Mikell. Brianna out."

She felt some satisfaction at being the one who had ended the conversation first. But now was no time for basking in small victories. Maitan could be in danger, or worse. Racing upstairs past the training area, she suddenly realized she could just use comms. Stopping by the elevators, she pressed the comm button and said, "Brianna to Mikell, do you hear me?"

"Yes, M'Lady! Are you taking over for our Mistress in her absence?"

Smartass.

"Yes, in fact, I am. I have orders from Treyborne for you to come down to the Command Center and show me how to track a comm. We're missing…well, we're missing Maitan. I'm sure you've noticed more than most he's not been here for the last few days."

"Check that. And yes, I sure have! My leg is sore as the Void, and I have no idea what meds he was giving me. I'll grab something and head down there. Might take me a bit. I can barely walk."

"Can you talk me through it?"

"I doubt it, Brianna. It's got lots of steps. Just give me a few, ok? He's been gone this long; another quarter hour won't kill him."

Unless it does…Brianna hoped she was wrong. But if her guess was right, Maitan was probably already dead.

CHAPTER 180

At that very moment, a bound Maitan, still in his *Biaki Mor* armor, was being led onto a ship named *the Dark Horse.*

How appropriate.

Maitan smiled as he was led up the gangplank onto the docked ship. They were in the port of Normisa Bay. A large coastal city was set into the hills surrounding it. The wharf and many of the houses in this beautiful bay were engulfed in flames now, however. People could still be heard screaming from all over. Little dark dots of Dark Men were running through the streets, chasing men, women, and children. All were being cut down. Smoke rose from near and far. All up and down the coast. The air was so full of it, it seemed like it should rain.

But there wasn't an actual cloud in the entire sky.

Two of the Dark Raiders, one on each arm, were walking up with him. Looking across the deck, he saw, and then felt the enormous gulf of Darkness that was the Dark Lord Emorion. He was speaking with two of his captains, apparently. Both men were cowering in fear.

Apparently, they'd done something wrong. Suddenly, both men screamed, and their forms turned into black dust, drifting in the breeze. Emorion turned towards Maitan, and sheer malevolence poured over him. Standing in the face of the intensity of that emotional wave, something beyond understanding, Maitan staggered and almost fell. Had the men not still been holding his arms, he would have.

The … power these men had! No wonder men revered them as gods. Even though they were mortal, it was said this Dark power could keep them alive forever. And this one…the Dark flowed from him like a river. It was horrific and incredible all at once.

Maitan raised his jaw and set his face. This was his time.

The Dark Lord Emorion strolled over to him, so close he could smell the death on his breath. It was like death itself had taken on mortal form and was standing before him. The pull of the Dark on his very being…Maitan again mentally had to set his resolve.

I am the Creator's child! I will not yield to this Darkness! Help me now, Greatest one. These who call themselves gods deserve to be punished. Let me be the knife today!

Emorion stepped back a bit, cocking his head. *"Impressive."*

His voice was like rasping rock on sandpaper. Or the other way around. Maitan wasn't quite sure. Walking completely around Maitan in a circle, he came back and faced him again, crossing his arms. He even shook his head.

"And here I'd thought we'd eradicated your kind over a century ago! The handful that had made it that long with Morgaine…well…I thought they were all killed in the Barbarian Uprising! Who…are you? Where did you come from? Oh yes…Morgaine! You say that bitch is somehow still alive? How is that even possible? Can you prove it? Or is this just empty words? Perhaps your trek took you so long – being as you're from the distant past and all – you just didn't know she died!"

Maitan shook his head. "No Dark Lord, Morgaine lives. I am *Biaki Mor*. As my fathers were before me! My name is of no consequence, as I am soon to die. We have always fought your kind. But I bear a message from my Mistress…. you see, it was I who rescued her from death's door. To be sure, she did die. Three times. Once for each of the Dark Lords. Her message is this: 'It is now your turn to die! All of you!' She is readying to rid the world of your kind. And she allowed me…. the last of my kind…to precede you in death and send you this message."

Emorion stood silent for a long moment. "Why should I believe you?"

"You see Dark Lord; she has finally granted my wish. I am the last of my kind, and I wish to finally die and rejoin my people. She believes you fear her and will not kill me. My opinion differs. So, I volunteered to send her message to you. You sent your Hollow Men, and they did their worst. Now, she says…she is going to do hers." Maitan turned slightly, then kneeled. "I am ready to die now, Dark One! My time is past. As soon yours will be, also."

Maitan lowered his head. Emorion said, *"Show me his weapon. I haven't seen a* Myshar *in well…over a hundred years!"*

Maitan felt, rather than saw the bright blade surge out from the handle, then he heard the metal *"ching"* of the back blade emerge, as well. Then both the feeling of the bright blade's power, and the other blade's sound of retreat reached him, as well.

Maitan opened his eyes, looking up.

Emorion's breath was in his nostrils, and Emorion's face was literally touching Maitan's cheek. *"Let me tell you a few things, Biaki Mor! First, there is no afterlife! The Void swallows your soul and you are obliterated. You won't be joining anyone. Second, your former Mistress may be alive — somehow — still. But I will remedy that soon enough! And finally…"* he said, pressing even harder into his cheek. The rotting and horrific feeling from the cold of the Void was overwhelming. *"…she was wrong about much. The Dark Lords aren't going to die. At least, I won't be! But she was right about one thing, however…"*

Maitan found his voice enough to speak, although it came out in a whisper, "And…what was that…?"

"I will be killing you…"

Wait for it…wait for it…NOW!

As Emorion pressed the button to bring the bright blade to life, Maitan suddenly wasn't there. He'd rolled and spun his legs, sweeping the legs of his former captors, who had released their vice grips with Emorion so close. The blade came out right into one of their faces, and the other stumbled too…right down onto the blade, as well.

Emorion shouted, *"Whaaaaat???"* and staggered back himself. The *Myshar* fell to the deck. Maitan threw his bonds onto it, and they shattered like ice shards.

But Emorion was no mere Dark Man…or even a Dark Knight. He was a Dark Lord. Even as Maitan leaped up, *Myshar* blade in front of him, snapping the back blade into action, Emorion stood fully upright again, curling his hand, and snapping it into a fist. Suddenly Maitan could no longer move…he was being drawn right back to where Emorion stood… floating…it was like the air itself was bending to his will. With his other hand he stopped the counterattack that the other Dark Raiders on board were about to engage in. They all halted mid-step, bowing deeply.

Laughter came from Emorion then.

"Do you think me so easily killed, Biaki Mor?" Emorion said disdainfully. *"Do you think I've lived all these centuries to fall for so pathetic a trick…?"* He laughed then, a full laugh. An insane laugh. Maitan stood there, unable to move.

"I've killed dozens, no hundreds of your people myself! Your people threw an entire legion of their best warriors at me during the first war. Yet here I am. And here you are…one…lone…old…man! And you thought to somehow best me?"

The laughter started again. This time it seemed to have no end.

Maitan was floating three feet from Emorion. Unable to push his arm forward. Touching the button, he withdrew the bright blade and its rear guard. Holding the handle, he lowered it to his side. He was free again, at least that much.

Emorion said, *"I do admire your brazenness, however! Pledge to the Dark, right now! And you'll not only live forever…you can live at my side. My second-in-command! I have need of solid warriors such as yourself. I can find…better uses for you than Morgaine ever could."*

Maitan looked back into those black eyes…into the very heart of that black soul.

And he chuckled.

"You laugh…? I offer you eternal life…and you laugh…?" There was no more laughter coming from Emorion any longer.

"I will not yield, but you know that," Maitan said plainly, his voice back fully. His fear gone. Whatever power the Dark had over him, it was gone now. "Just do me one small favor. Kill me with my own blade, as you were about to do. To be killed by you, I can at least die as all the others you killed before me. Truly, you are the only one worthy of killing me. None of your Dark Knights can beat me. Not even all of those on this boat. You know this, as well."

Emorion snatched the *Myshar* from his hand. *"As you wish…"*. Taking the front of it and pointing it right at Maitan's face, he asked, "Here…? Or…here?" pointing the weapon at his heart.

"There, Dark Lord. Right…there. Please." Maitan closed his eyes. He raised his head, readying himself.

Emorion pressed the button to release the bright blade. Then he screamed, crumpling to the ground.

Pandemonium broke out.

CHAPTER 181

To say there had been no unrest overnight would be incorrect. But whatever issues were going on outside the palace did not penetrate the building itself. Whatever messages the Dukes had sent out to the people, if any, had been enough to quell whatever dismay and discomfort the people were feeling over the news of their King's execution in his own Hall of Justice.

Morgaine looked over at Nathan. He had his instructions, and Morgaine had to hope he was attuned enough to the Corillion medallion to listen if it had any insight into today's meeting. Morgaine had sent word to Peniella, as well, asking her to join the coronation and to meet with Duke Iranias, whichever way things went.

Now it was time. Dressed in her black and silver armor, Morgaine said as she left the chambers, "Creator be with us!" Morgaine wanted this coronation to be different. She wanted the people to see it. She wanted the people to remember.

The escort she had to the Assembly Hall was as big as the one she had left it with the previous night. Now that the breakfast hour was past, it was high time to crown a new king in Rondor. Someone who hopefully would help lead them to a position of prominence once again. Up until recently, the Empire had feared another war with Rondor. Rondor's army was virtually half their entire male population.

But since Rondor II had died three years ago, apparently the idea of taking it back went right back on the table. That had been no coincidence, Morgaine was sure. She had her favorite to be King. But she was going to let the two Dukes decide the fate of their own country.

She would abide with either one. As long as they went along with her idea on how to defend not only Rondor, but the world at large.

As discussed, the palace doors had been opened an hour beforehand, and the hall was packed with people. There was an alley to walk through ten feet wide, thanks to the Palace Guard who had been ordered by one of the two Dukes, probably Mantessa, to create a safe pathway for everyone to get into the hall. As Morgaine and her guard came down to the main floor, the noisy crowd became quiet. A few people yelled this or that. Some seemed to support her being there and the removal of Rondor III as king. Others were far less friendly. She ignored them, making her way into the Hall.

Duke Mantessa, Duke Iranias, and Queen Peniella were all there already. The Queen had retaken her seat on the throne dais. The Dukes were standing at either side of her throne, but as Morgaine entered, they made their way down the stairs to stand at the bottom. Morgaine nodded to them as she passed, still walking with Rondor's scepter.

As she ascended, Nathan walked behind her, holding the medallion, and focusing his energy and thoughts on the two men. As he sought to feel any presence of the Dark, he was relieved to find none in either man. Or the Queen, for that matter. He did feel its presence all about the room. That smallish man with the grey hat and scarf near the front. The petite woman in the corner filing her nails, clearly a lesser noble of some kind, in the back. Even several of the palace staff. Making a note of them all, he turned his gaze back up to the podium where he had stopped just short of the last step and shook his head to Morgaine. She nodded and he, as planned, returned to stand next to Treyborne and the rest of her Elite Guard in a circle around the stairway.

Treyborne reached behind his back, and said, "I found you one of these in the armory," and handed him a shock-lance. Trey smiled as Nathan hefted it and said, "Thanks! I've been missing mine." Looking back, they prepared to watch the spectacle.

Morgaine stood before the throne and addressed the crowded room. They'd let in commoners, lesser and greater nobility, and as many of each man's guard as seemed reasonable. The doors to the hall were still open so everyone outside could at least watch and perhaps catch a glimpse of everything.

The king's body and head had been removed during the night. The stain of his blood down the steps and on the flooring had also been removed. The crown that had been upon his head was now sitting on the throne, awaiting its new owner.

Morgaine went to retrieve it, sat down on the throne, and put it in her lap. Turning to the two Dukes below, she asked formally, "Heirs of King Rondor I, have you come to an agreement? Will either of you support the other as the next King?"

Nodding, the elder of the two, Duke Mantessa stepped forward. "We have, White Queen. We acknowledge the help you have given us, both in the distant past when the kingdom was forged and during our recent troubled times. It is our collective decision that I shall ascend the throne, with Duke Iranias' full support."

Cheers broke out immediately followed by loud clapping. The applause continued, and Morgaine let it go on for quite some time. After the noise had died down somewhat, she raised the scepter and the crowd quieted completely. Then she nodded, "I think that is a wise decision. I accept it and am ready to crown you as king whenever you wish it done."

The High Priest of the temple was standing at the bottom of the stairs near both men. When she said this, he spoke up from below, "Morgaine, friend of the Creator and King Rondor I, I wish to be the one to crown the new king. If you will allow it…?"

Morgaine looked down at the older man with the white beard and priestly robes. His headpiece marked him as high priest. He wore a purple shawl as well. The highest of the color rankings in the church. She called down to him, "High Priest of the Creator, I would never deny you anything. But I fear that if I am not a part of this, should another fifty years pass…my aid will again be forgotten. Should the kingdom again fall under shadow, my aid would be dismissed as interference. As it originally was by Rondor III."

"Then may we crown him together then? A symbol of our unity. You with this Kingdom and the Kingdom of the Creator, as well?"

Morgaine nodded. "That is an excellent idea! Come up, please, and join us."

The elderly man had a tall walking staff, but it took him some time to reach the dais. When he did, he bowed to Morgaine, who nodded her head at him. Nathan stood in awe of her. The woman truly was a Queen. Not just in name, but in reality.

"Step forward, Duke Iranias," Morgaine said, and he did so, clearly a bit confused.

"Do you accede to this? Are you in agreement that the crown should pass first to King Rondor II's brother instead of you?"

"I do, Morgaine. My uncle, Duke Mantessa and I have known each other a long time. We both thought it best for him to take the throne. And in yet another way, I can be mentored in how to do something important for the kingdom. Before it was how to run my troops and fight in a battlefield. Now, it will be in how to run a kingdom. I will support him in all ways, acceding to his authority fully. I swear it."

Morgaine nodded, "Good. Then I have one more burden I must place upon you. The King's sudden demise has put his widow and her kingdom in peril. The Duke of Mantessa is already married, plus he is too old to successfully aid her in bearing heirs to the throne. I place it upon you to betroth yourself to Queen Peniella today. And to marry her within a year with whatever pomp and circumstance is required. Then you are to bear this kingdom an heir to carry it forward into the future. Do you accept this responsibility?"

Duke Iranias' eyes had grown wider and wider at all this, and his eyebrows were up so high, they were almost lost in his hairline. Then he slowly looked up at the Queen, still sitting regally, and looking straight ahead. He stepped forward and she nodded a greeting to him. Looking over at Morgaine, he answered, "I…I do! Will the Queen have me, though? Are you in agreement with this, Peniella?" he asked, looking up at her.

She nodded, and looked over at Morgaine, "I am, and I do agree. Thank you, Lady Morgaine. This, I promise you, *will* be remembered."

Morgaine nodded. "So be it. You are now betrothed. Let both countries rejoice! Duke Mantessa, if you would…?" She pointed to the area below the throne, and she rose. She was magnificent in her black and silver. The most beautiful woman in any room, and in complete control.

Mantessa came and knelt on the first step. The High Priest, who had waited at Morgaine's side for this all to conclude, placed his left hand on the crown, and Morgaine took her left hand off it as they walked down the stairs together. Placing it on the kneeling Duke's head, she said, "By the power vested in me by the Almighty Himself…" and the High Priest said the same, "…we crown you King Rondor IV. Rise and take your scepter and your throne."

Morgaine stepped aside as Mantessa rose…now as King Rondor IV. He slowly took the scepter from her and ascended the stairs. He then turned to the crowd, who began to cheer again.

"Long live King Rondor! Long live King Rondor!" came from all around.

As they continued their acclaim, the newly crowned King took his seat. Everyone was clapping. Except Morgaine's guards and Nathan. Nathan finally chimed in. The press of the crowd was getting stronger, but no one was being too unruly.

The High Priest, and then Morgaine came back up the stairway, then bowed formally to Rondor IV, who touched his scepter upon her shoulder as she did so.

"I absolve Queen Morgaine in the presence of all here. What she did in executing King Rondor III was by the guidance of the Creator! She has been, and continues to be, a true friend of the Kingdom of Rondor. Let no one say otherwise!"

Looking up at this, she bowed again. Morgaine saw that Iranias and Queen Peniella were clapping also. Iranias had come up and bowed himself, then went over to stand behind Peniella. After they stopped… did they just take each other's hand?

Interesting. Well. It is time for my last card to be played.

"Thank you, King Rondor IV!" Morgaine shouted above the din. They quieted some, to hear what she would say, "Long may your reign be, and may your heir Iranias not have to take the throne until he has more grey in his beard than you do today!"

He nodded to her.

"There is one more issue that needs addressed. As we speak and celebrate today, we must acknowledge how narrowly the Kingdom recently avoided the fate of subjugation to the evil Empire of Nelrae to our south."

There were plenty of boos at this…so Morgaine waited until they quieted down.

"We must also acknowledge that if the Creator had not intervened, this day would never have happened. There is a war being fought as we speak. Two of the three Dark Lords wage war not one hundred twenty clicks from here in Nelrae. The truth of the matter is simple. Had the Dark Lord K'Thul not invaded Nelrae just when he did, the Kingdom of Rondor would be no more. Had his nemesis Jezerah not met him in battle a few days ago, the war in Nelrae would already be over, and K'Thul would likely be marching north to finish the job Nelrae started! What will you do about it, King Rondor? What will you do to defend the Kingdom that we both have fought so hard for?"

Nathan watched intently, as the room grew very quiet.

During the stillness, Nathan pointed out the three members of the Dark Cult to Treyborne. "Don't let any of those people leave!" he whispered. Trey, then began muttering into his comm and the remaining members of their group – those who had been injured but were still able to perform normal duties – slid into position behind each of them. The news might get out, but it wouldn't get out through any of those people. Trey's men had already captured the staff members out in the hallway, per Nathan's instructions.

The new king stood and addressed the crowd, "Although we would never give thanks to any Dark Lord for anything, their squabble has bought us time to reflect. Our ally Morgaine has pointed out a weakness in their current situations. As the two Dark Lords fight, a well-timed attack on both sides could well turn the tide forever in Rondor's favor. The Empire of Nelrae's armies, already dwindled from weeks of battle against the East and our own kingdom, will be vulnerable. And the Eastern Empire's army, already fatigued from long travel and weeks of battle themselves, will likewise be exposed."

He paused, sitting back down, as if reflecting, rather than immediately saying what they'd planned, "Should we hit their flanks, one army led by my heir, Duke Iranias – and the other led by me – both of these evil armies, with their Dark Men and allies amongst men, will be crippled for many years. The Lady Morgaine and her team will join us in our offensive. As we attack, their team will split also, led by the two members of the Elder Race: Morgaine herself, and Nathan Arvad. These two can then engage the Dark Lords in personal combat. The goal will be to do what no one has done in centuries – eliminate one or more of the true enemies of mankind: the Dark Lords themselves!"

The room erupted in cheers, but someone yelled, "But that's impossible! The Dark Lords have lived for thousands of years!"

Tamping down the crowd with his scepter, King Rondor IV continued. "Is it *impossible*? You yourselves know the stories – Lady Morgaine herself – this woman before you, killed four of the Dark Brethren over five hundred years ago. The price to her race was high. Too high to count. But it was done. Do not say 'impossible'. Of course, we need the support of the people, as well as the army itself. Anyone who wishes to enlist, do so at once! Those in the military, arm yourselves and make ready! My first act as King of Rondor will be to silence those who would have silenced us. And we will aid the Lady Morgaine in her quest to rid us once and for all of these menacing terrors."

There was much applause and quite a lot of cheering.

Nathan watched the lesser noblewoman. She'd long ago stopped filing her nails and looking bored. Her eyes were fire. She turned and picked up her skirts to leave, and one of the guard members in plain clothes acted like he stumbled into her. Then, he picked her up and started carrying her out, "The poor lady has fainted! Please step aside!" and he began carrying her body out. As this was happening, the other two he'd pointed out were silently executed, as well. They were dragged out in similar fashion. It was harsh. But if they wanted any element of surprise, this was the only way.

The coronation was over. Morgaine was kissing the High Priest's hand, then the King's. She went over and gave Queen Peniella a hug, and then had one for Iranias. She truly seemed pleased with herself on that particular point.

Nathan watched as she turned and strolled down the staircase. She came right up to Treyborne and him saying, "Well! Now all we have left to do is kill the Dark Lords!" Then she laughed as if that were the funniest thing in the world.

"Well…we also might have another problem…" Treyborne said, leaning in and speaking in her ear. Morgaine jerked her head back, looking shocked. When her eyes returned to their normal size, she nodded, saying, "You'd told me he'd gone, but no one had said why. It seems he is fulfilling his destiny, after all. Whatever happens, it is too late to stop it. Keep me advised, Captain," and she turned to walk away.

Shaking his head, Treyborne turned and made a new circle around Morgaine with his men. The plan was to set up the army movements by lunchtime, and head out with the two armies the next morning. It was about as fast as anything could be done. But Nathan could already sense the stress that waiting was placing on Morgaine. Every second between the announcement and the attack brought more possibility that even the distracted Dark Lords would get word of the move.

And Nathan had one additional worry: At her best and in the peak fighting form all that time ago, Morgaine hadn't been able to stop Jezerah. Now, she was heading for a direct confrontation with him still very much injured, exhausted, and clearly not fully herself.

How does she even stand a chance against Jezerah…or either of them, by herself? Will she even listen if I tell her it's suicide?

CHAPTER 182

K'Thul felt a sudden jerk within the Void. It was as if something had suddenly put the universe on a coin and flipped it. Reaching for his saddle horn, K'Thul closed his eyes until the dizziness passed. There was a horrible sickening feeling in his stomach…shaking his head…he tried to force the cobwebs out.

Where have I felt this before…? Whatever it was, it had been ages ago.

It was night, and the battle that day had not gone as the others previous. Jezerah and his Dark Men had rushed in from nowhere and bolstered key positions on the battlefronts. It wasn't that he hadn't expected counterattack. But he'd managed to wedge his forces in between K'Thul's front and the city gate. Another few days, and the Empire's army would have been crushed. Now, they would have to start over. He knew Jezerah would be coming. But he'd brought more men and hit harder than expected in two key areas, taking larger risks.

Shaking his head…the fog began to clear.

Jezerah! The bastard…!

Of course, he'd found his sense and realized K'Thul was aiming for the jugular. Erase his power base and K'Thul would stand alone as the master of the planet. Not that he could truly stop it. Then K'Thul could begin to dismantle the rest of Jezerah's forces – and secure the Arc Gate from him now that his 'White' sister was dead…

Wait! That feeling…Whenever that bitch slew our brethren centuries ago. Each time one died, the vortex from the Void tilted and pitched. The sudden loss of so powerful a receptacle…always caused it to whirl out of control for a few moments…but…if I just felt that again…

Then Emorion himself is no more. Impossible! Jezerah is here on the battlefield – how could he have managed it? Unless…Yes…that too, can mean only one thing: Emorion had been wrong. Morgaine is still alive! Only she could have killed him – a response to his attempt on her own life.

K'Thul had to admit…his plan had included eradicating his brothers. But between Jezerah's attack and Morgaine's sudden erasure of Emorion, they were clearly not hiding their alliance any longer. Not that they could have, K'Thul admitted. But the continuation of the ruse might at least have given him pause. Now, there was simply no way Jezerah could live. Or the White Witch.

Suddenly, screams erupted all over the campsite. Looking around in the darkness, he saw huge creatures boiling out from the ground in the horsemen's camp, attacking anything and anyone in their way. The entire area where the horsemen and their mounts were encamped was bubbling over with them. Even from this distance, K'Thul could easily see what they were: *Creepers*. Dozens of them.

Jezerah must have sent the entire nest. All in one concerted attack on the largest contingent of humans in the Eastern Empire's armies. More shouts from their rear brought a sharp turn of K'Thul's head. Shadow Beasts were running amok amongst the lance, slaying them as easily as gutting fish.

Brilliant.

Snapping his fingers, K'Thul pointed and screamed, "Send the Dark Men to kill those things! The humans will be powerless against them!"

They ran to obey.

Obedience was obviously expected in K'Thul's army. But these Dark Knights moved with a speed that even amidst the chaos made him proud. Dark Men poured from their tents all about the encircling campgrounds. Racing to engage the Wildlings, moving with the superior haste and zero fear that only the Dark itself could provide, within minutes the Creepers and Shadow Beasts were dispatched.

K'Thul sent the Dark Knight M'Sitan to go investigate and report on how bad the damage was. So…Jezerah hits from all angles, and in the meantime clearly aided Morgaine in finding and executing Emorion. Emorion had always been sloppy. He'd also become careless. He deserved to die.

But not at the White Witch's hand! It should have been my own!

K'Thul's Dark fury began to boil again…so much so that his generals cowered in fear. Minutes afterward, K'Thul saw that M'Sitan had returned. He had been standing and bowing patiently to be called upon.

"Report."

"Of the 7500 horsemen that began the day with us, 1300 were killed or wounded….and 960 of the horse also died."

"I know this already, M'Sitan! Tell me what damage the Creepers did!"

"Yes, my Master. In the time it took for us to end the threat, 4200 more of the horses and 1530 men were killed or injured. They…targeted the horses, Master. Without horse, horsemen are simply…men." He stopped speaking, waiting for the backlash. The report was similar amongst the lancers.

K'Thul was nodding now. He was acknowledging Jezerah's strategy. He had started out weak, or at least had appeared to. He secured the Arc Gate – but 'lost it' to Emorion. Then as soon as he could, he not only recovered the Gate with that bitch's help…but he also had dragged

K'Thul far afield from his power base in the east, decimating Emorion's own power, while his own had been weakened fighting them both.

Then Jezerah and the bitch launched phase two of their operation… appear to remain focused on Rondor in the North, while hidden in the weeds, Morgaine goes off and hunts Emorion down. Once located, Jezerah launches a counteroffensive – throwing all in while suddenly K'Thul is left without any possible allies. Now his cavalry suddenly and severely crippled. K'Thul found himself tapping his lips…

Have I been thus far so outplayed? It wouldn't be the first time Jezerah has suddenly slapped a collar on us. He has always managed to stand above us! It appears he's been pulling the strings since the beginning…

K'Thul had to reassess everything. The Empire, via Jezerah's new proxies in the twin generals, was even more firmly under his sway. K'Thul was far beyond his normal supply lines, and what he had brought – and he'd brought a lot – was dwindling.

What would I do next…if I were Jezerah…? By all that is Dark! The supply lines…!

Bolting for his command center, not even wanting to leave this to his men, K'Thul ran inside once he reached it. He had to warn the coastal cities. As he did so, the two Dark Men on duty stood up in shock.

"M….M…Master! We were about to call for you! How did you know?"

"How did I know *what?*" he answered.

"Sir…" the one who had spoken fell before him to his knees. "Our entire southern coastline is on fire! The island harbors are completely destroyed. Every one of our coastal cities has been hit by Dark Raiders as well, and hundreds of our ships have burned! Master…! Most of our resupply ships have been lost!"

K'Thul just stood there... the Dark boiling out from his pores. He had suddenly been pushed into a corner. If he didn't topple the Empire of Nelrae and capture the capital with its stores and supply houses soon...K'Thul's army would starve itself to death in the field within weeks. There was no way they could get home with what they had left. And now, no ships would reach them for many weeks. The man before him and the one behind him snapped in two, blackish blood oozing out of their midsections. The Dark must have sacrifice for such failure.

K'Thul had no choice now. He had less than two weeks to win this war before things got desperate. If he failed now...Jezerah and Morgaine would be the rulers of Arth by this time next year. And if they managed to reopen the Arc Gate again or had already – the galaxy was next.

K'Thul would either be destroyed in the aftermath or become their slave. And that, he could not abide. There would be no rest for the troops now. One way or another, this war was going to end.

Yesterday, I appeared to stand triumphant over my brothers. Today, I hang on the precipice. As incredible as it sounds, I must reach solid ground again before morning.

CHAPTER 183

Jezerah had expected retribution, to be sure. But he had half-expected K'Thul to throw mere feints and then withdraw to the southern shores waiting for ships to come. Either to resupply the army or to take them home. Instead, K'Thul's Dark Knights and a massive number of Dark Men, along with what remained of their cavalry had attacked every flank and encampment mere minutes after the Creepers and Shadow Beasts had been killed. Every one of them heading straight south towards the city.

Jezerah wondered if it had more to do with the disturbance in the Void than with the Creeper attack on his horsemen. Emorion had been a fool, to be sure. His armies had fared extremely badly under K'Thul's heavy assaults. Where Curtaise had invented deft maneuvers and quick release and run tactics on the fly, Emorion and his army had been fed heavy blaster fire with nowhere to run at the battle of the Arc Gate, losing several thousand troops.

It was concerning though, that, after all these years, Emorion had *died*. But there were only a few options there that Jezerah could think of: First, K'Thul himself had had a hand in it, and was now pressing the attack to push Jezerah to the brink, as well. The second option was that Morgaine had done the deed herself. But she'd supposedly been killed from an attack of Hollow Men…according to Emorion's own message bragging about it – along with again accusing him of conspiring with her all these centuries.

Even if she had lived, she should be in no shape to engage Emorion, let alone win. There was also the slight problem of finding him. So even had his sister known where to look, how could she have battled through his remaining Dark Men and Knights to kill him?

That seemed highly unlikely to downright impossible.

The last possibility was the most likely: his own generals and Dark Knights had finally had enough of his failures. The same ruthlessness that all the Dark Lords carried out amongst their men, especially their leaders…had likely just been applied to Emorion.

The result, however, would be that – in either of the two events that K'Thul wasn't behind it – he most certainly would suspect Jezerah of holding the knife. And, if he didn't know, or didn't believe that Morgaine was dead…

Jezerah looked up at the mauling waves of attackers of Dark Men from the Eastern Empire…like they were seeking death himself, but willing to share with all comers before going to meet him…

Jezerah's black eyes widened.

He would think I and Morgaine did it together.

CHAPTER 184

At that moment, Nathan and Morgaine were riding side by side at the head of a long column of Rondorian knight and lance. They were riding behind the King and Duke Iranias only. The crossbowmen were behind, followed by another whole army, led by some of the lesser captains.

When they were within a five hours or less of the battlefields, they would split the armies. Duke Mantessa would lead the attack to strike at the backside of the Eastern Empire's army with Morgaine as the "knife" to hit K'Thul himself. Duke Iranias would lead the secondary attack on Jezerah's weakened northern flanks with Nathan as the "knife" at Jezerah's throat.

Much arguing over who went where had occurred in the middle of their rush to pack and get ready to leave. Three of Morgaine's Elite Guard were too injured to travel, so they'd been tasked with standing watch over Queen Peniella, who was ruling as Regent until the Duke and the new King returned.

But Morgaine was bitterly angry that Nathan and Treyborne both thought it best to have Morgaine hit the Dark Lord who wasn't her brother, with Nathan going after Jezerah instead. That also gave Morgaine the better tactician in Mantessa, in the event things went badly. As they seemed to do so often.

In the end, the logic of their arguments won out. But Morgaine hadn't talked much with Nathan since that late evening "discussion". She seemed to still be irritated about it this morning. Although Nathan could not imagine why. If Nathan had an evil sister trying to rule the world, he still wouldn't want to be the one to knock her off. Morgaine, however, seemed to feel it was her birthright.

"Beware my brother, Nathan," Morgaine said, breaking the icy silence of over an hour. She turned to look at him, magnificent as always, her eyes dancing fire. "He is and has always been the most crafty, cunning, and ruthless amongst the Dark Lords. And knowing them as only I do, that is saying quite a lot." She turned back to ride face forward, as before. Their pace was such that talking was easy. It might even have been pleasant had it not been for the fighting earlier and the topic of discussion.

"I will be on my best behavior when I meet him, Morgaine…" he began.

"This is no joke, Nathan!" she said, whirling on him. "My brother has caused the death of literally millions of people! He killed our father in cold blood! He is the one who discovered the Dark…if you can call that a 'discovery'! He is pure evil, Nathan. And you had better be more than ready. Or he will destroy you, as he has destroyed so many of our people before!"

This outburst caused Iranias to look back and give Nathan a wide stare and a warning look. Shaking his head and laughing a bit, he turned back.

Nathan turned to her and added in a whisper, "I'm aware of who he is, Morgaine. But this is the plan, isn't it? Fight our way towards the real problem of this world and cut them off…? Then go and hunt down Emorion…?"

Morgaine's eyes grew distant for a moment, then she said softly, "We may not have to worry about him in the end, after all."

"What?" Nathan asked, bewildered, "What does *that* mean? Is he just going to just up and quit once we eradicate his rivals…?

Morgaine's eyes were veiled, and they looked distant – as if she were seeing something far away for a moment, but then she reached out her hand and touched his leg. "No Nathan…just a feeling. I'll tell you – if we live. If we both live," she added quietly. Her eyes grew distant again and she faced forward. "There is much more I wish to discuss with you. But it will all be meaningless if we fail." She turned back and grimaced a smile. "Please don't fail."

"Right back at you," Nathan said.

Treyborne rode up at that moment, as the Elite Guard were riding behind them and off on the edges of the trail to stay away from the Rondorian ranks. "It appears from our advance scouts that there's heavy fighting along the two valleys and on the rim towards the interior road to Nelrae City. We may need to separate sooner if the fighting expands at all."

Mantessa, the newest King in Rondor, had heard that last and said, "We won't need to divide any earlier. They cannot expand much more without leaving holes in their defenses. My worry is that one side will have defeated the other before we arrive. But even in that unlikely event, we should be able to push the spear in deeply. Iranias and I have a contingency plan for that, as well. Should one side be defeated, the other shall simply engage the backside of the victor. The effect should be the same. I just hope – if one is defeated, he is not still in the presence of the other Dark Lord. Two together might unify if they see we've come for them. Our scouts have given similar reports. Just hold steady and by tomorrow afternoon, we should be in the thick of it." He turned back towards the front and pulled his general's cap down against the sun.

It was cooler than it had been for many weeks, and the change was welcome. Nathan looked at the sky and saw a storm boiling in from the southeast. Winds and jet streams were certainly different here. "It appears before we get there, we're going to get wet," he said, pointing.

King Rondor IV looked up. Seeing it, he said, "Indeed."

CHAPTER 185

Maitan raised up his head and rammed forward right into the *Myshar* hilt, making sure the bright blade buried deeply into wherever it had penetrated Emorion's body. The impact between his skull and the handle knocked Maitan to the deck, stunned.

Within moments, he recovered, although he was quite certain he should have been set upon by the Dark Raiders by now. Lying there, he could still hear the echoes of the chaos all around the harbor still going on.

Perhaps they think I'm already dead…

Raising his head, he saw Emorion's black form. The *Myshar's* bright blade sticking out of what remained of Emorion's skull. Lifting his head completely, Maitan saw the entire crew of Dark Raiders on the *Dark Horse*…standing at attention. When he rose, they saluted in the fashion of the Dark Men. Fist to chest, then bowed, staying low.

Reaching for his *Myshar*, he withdrew it from Emorion's skull. The body began to fade away into black dust even as he did so. It was as if the bright blade itself had somehow anchored the body until he'd withdrawn it.

Slowly rotating, Maitan turned to look at the crew. None of them had moved. "Rise," he said loudly, as even deckhands far across the ship were bowing. "And someone tell me the meaning of this!"

A man in swarthy black clothing, with a scythe-like bladed weapon at his waist came up. His scarf completely covered his face, minus his eyes. He saluted again, "Master. We have been taught since birth that the strongest will lead us. Our former Master Emorion would raise those of us worthy to higher ranks. Those who were found unfit were either demoted or executed. This is our way. We have also been taught that should anyone emerge among us that somehow took the place of the Master…" he looked where Emorion's body used to lay, "…then that one was the Master. It is taught in every school in the Desert." He bowed again. "Master, my blade is yours," he said, pulling it out and holding it in his hands.

When he'd yanked it from its sheath, Maitan had leaped back and hit the bright blade button. By pure instinct. "Of course," the man said calmly, "my life is in your hands. I did fail my former Master. I could be held accountable, as his First Mate and acting captain of the *Dark Horse.*"

Maitan sheathed the bright blade. Taking the Dark Raider's weapon, he held it in his hand for a moment. He then held it high above his head, speaking at the top of his voice, "All Dark Raiders on this ship are under my authority now. I have found your First Mate not to be at fault in the death of your former master, the Dark Lord Emorion. Stand up," and the man did so, folding his arms, waiting. "But if anyone should choose not to want to serve under me, or wishes me ill will, I will let that person leave now. Otherwise, you are to a man – my Dark Men now!"

He and his new captain (or would he be First Mate still?) looked about them. To a man, none of them moved.

"Very well then," Maitan said, handing the blade back to the man, "we set sail for Nelrae within the hour. Get whatever provisions you need. We will burn no more docks or ships today." They all saluted. Turning to the captain, as he'd decided he himself knew nothing of ships and simply could be their 'master' for now. "What is your name, *captain?*" he said, emphasizing the title.

The man sheathed his blade, then bowed low. Apparently, he realized he'd just been promoted. "My name is My'Rel. I have served aboard this vessel, which is the flagship…or was the flagship…of Master Emorion's fleet, for seventeen years."

Nodding, Maitan said, "So I would assume this is the finest of the finest of the Dark Raiders…?" Proudly, the man nodded. "It has always been so. I served for over fifty years to even be brought aboard. All here did."

Maitan had to remember, that these Dark Men, fueled by the power of the Dark, living almost as long – perhaps longer – than the *Biaki Mor*. "Fine. I leave the day-to-day operations and sailing to you and your men, Captain. You may address me as 'Master' or 'Master Maitan'. Get these men ready. Know this: I serve Morgaine herself. So now, you and your men serve her as well. If any still wish to leave, they may do so here and now on this shoreline. After that, they will be serving their former enemy. I leave it to you."

My'Rel nodded. If there had been any shock in his eyes, Maitan had not seen it.

Realistically, who else has ever killed a Dark Lord…? My Mistress Morgaine…and now…myself! Well, in all actuality…

Maitan chuckled and had to hold it in, as one of the crewmen was passing by, grabbing some ropes to remove the moorings.

In all actuality…Emorion killed himself!

Maitan started laughing, something he simply did not do…but he just couldn't help himself. He was laughing loudly enough that he started receiving odd looks from some of the lesser crewmen. But he didn't care. Somehow, he had survived! And having a ship full of Dark Men as his own was somehow even funnier. He kept laughing, even as the *Dark Horse* left the harbor and raised sails, heading west.

CHAPTER 186

Brianna finally had gotten Mikell down below. It had taken far too long, but she then had to find the designation codes for each individual comm unit. It seemed to Brianna that, over time, certain comm links had been swapped for others, without it being documented in the database here on Base 2.

Of course, that made sense, if they hadn't been here much in the past decade or so. Perhaps there was another log at their original compound that was more accurate. Knowing Maitan, that one was perfect. But they weren't at Base 1 compound. They were at Base 2. And this was the only list she had.

Running through all the coded images on her screen, she finally found one that wasn't with the others. Blowing up the image, she saw that the satellite said Maitan was…

"He's on an island in the Eastern Empire…?" *That can't be right!*

Brianna was glad no one was down here with her at that moment. She didn't want anyone to see her fumbling around the instruments like an idiot. Of course, all this technology had been completely foreign to her until she'd met Morgaine. But as time had gone on, she'd grown used to comms, blasters, land cruisers, and even the sky cruiser.

It seemed that such instrumentation should be easier than this. Hitting the satellite uplink, Brianna said, "Brianna to expedition crew, can you hear me?" She knew she wasn't saying it quite right, but she didn't care. She was not a military person.

"This is Treyborne, Brianna. What's your status? Everything ok?"

"No Trey! Everything is *not* ok! Maitan is still missing. Did you ever get the message to Morgaine?"

"Yes, I did. She just said something cryptic. She seemed surprised for maybe a split second regarding your conclusions, and then she said something about his 'destiny'. I have no clue what she meant."

"Well, his 'destiny' is apparently to become a sailor. Or a pirate! His comm shows him near an island in the Eastern Empire called, 'Scim's Warding'. Whatever that is! Any idea what he's doing so far away to the east? If I call him, will he answer?"

"You mean you haven't tried? Keep in mind…if he's dead, his comm would still work."

"Of course I tried…!" *Didn't I?* "I don't know…maybe not since I learned how to call long distance. Well…what about the team, Trey? Is everyone ok?"

"We lost Ramus. But we're on plan if you get my meaning. Omar, Uther, and Jarmind are still in Rondor…they got wounded when the King…uh… former King attacked us."

"Still in Rondor? Then you're not…?"

"Check that, B. We're headed into the Empire as we speak. Morgaine and Nathan are gearing up to try to knock off certain individuals down there. The big ones – Jezerah and K'Thul. We're along for the ride and going to try to keep them both breathing. I think you know how much I like all this. But I'm not in charge. Let me know if you get ahold of Maitan. Trey out. Oh…wish you were here. Sort of. Out."

"Trey….!" The comm went dead. "Men!"

Pushing the button again and reorienting towards the zone on her map, Brianna called, "Base 2 to Maitan. Maitan…are you there?"

For a moment, there was nothing. Then Brianna thought she heard an odd sound. Like a little click or something opening or closing.

"This is Brianna at Base 2. Maitan are you out there?"

"This is Maitan. Good to hear your voice, Brianna."

"Maitan! It's good to hear your voice too, I've been so worried about you! What are you doing out there? Are you ok? I have your position as somewhere in…are you moving? It shows you offshore from the island I had you on a few minutes ago…"

"Yes, we just left Scim's Warding. I'm heading on a ship back towards the east. I'm going to sail with my crew right to Nelrae. Sorry, no time to stop and catch up in Nyx first. Get the word to Morgaine. This ship moves very quickly, and we have favorable winds. I should be there within two or three days, I should think."

"Your…crew? You own a boat now? Did you buy a boat?"

"No! I won it!"

Was he laughing?? "Maitan, are you drunk? I've never heard you like this before! What's *wrong* with you…?"

"Nothing is wrong with me, Lady Brianna. For the first time perhaps, absolutely nothing is wrong with me! Make sure to get word to Mistress Morgaine. I'm coming with help. Tell her! Maitan is coming! Out!"

"Wait!!! What?" The comms were dead again.

Men! They are all insane. Simply. Insane. Even the old ones, apparently.

CHAPTER 187

Winsell Day was riding along with the contingent of men he'd been given. Watching all the comings and goings of the scouts, he finally rode up beside Morgaine. She'd been riding along peacefully for a while by herself. Even her companion Nathan had ridden over and was discussing something with her Captain…Treyborne.

Noticing him riding next to her, Morgaine nodded to him, "Major. It is good to see you again this morning. What may I do for you?"

"If you please, Lady Morgaine, remember I am from the army of the Empire. Perhaps I can lend some assistance to the planning of our assault? But no one has asked me since I was given my commission…"

"Duke Iranias!" Morgaine yelled. The two generals had ridden further ahead and some of their captains and other men were walking or riding alongside them, discussing pre-attack details. Iranias turned and stopped, waiting for Morgaine and Major Day to catch up.

"Lady Morgaine," he said, flicking his reins so that his horse would start moving alongside hers as he spoke, "How may I assist you?"

"Major Day just reminded me of his former affiliation and wondered if he might be of assistance in planning the attack on the forces of his former army…. He might be useful," she said encouragingly.

Duke Iranias eyed Winsell Day skeptically. "To be frank, I do not have room to judge. My actions have been misinterpreted by others. Recently. But it is hard to trust someone fully from another country's army. No matter how good the reasons he left. My apologies if I am offending you, Major."

"I'm not offended, Duke Iranias. I'd be baffled if you didn't feel otherwise. But you should at least pick my brain as to who is strong and who is less strong amongst the leadership of the forces you yourself will be attacking. I know my team is part of the King's contingent to attack the forces of the Eastern Empire. I assume this is no coincidence, and that again does not offend me. I simply wanted to make my desire to help known. If you do not need it, I will not be offended. I simply wish to help us win the upcoming battles. As…much more is at stake here than the borders of my former country. Or yours."

Iranias eyed him again, then nodded. "Please," he said, "come up and join my captains and generals. You outrank half of them anyway. We could use your input." Together, they rode forward, and Morgaine was alone once again.

She glanced over to where Treyborne and Nathan were talking, riding side-by-side. They didn't seem to be talking about anything important. Both were smiling and laughing occasionally. Morgaine touched the Corillion at her neck as she watched them. Nathan had insisted she wear it until the battle was over. Her "weakened condition" was worrisome to all.

It was true, her body was weary. And the elixir's she'd been drinking every day since forcing her way out of her hospital bed were taking a toll. The price she paid later would be… expensive.

I just have to make it through this fight. Then I can rest. Either way.

Then why did she feel so…hopeless. Perhaps because the last time she'd faced K'Thul he'd beaten her down and knocked her back down a long hill. Quite easily. She thought she would never get another chance at him again. Jezerah had similarly beaten her. Then he'd stabbed her and thrown her into the sea. Nathan was right to be worried. She was worried herself.

Creator, help me, I'm more than worried. I'm scared. And I'm scared of more than losing my life. I'm scared by losing it… I won't have any more time… with Nathan.

Looking over at him again, she felt the pinch in her heart. How had she gotten this bad so fast? It was like…fate…the Creator himself… had waited to put Nathan into her life until right at the end. What was worse was that she wanted desperately to give the stone and the pendant back to him. It would work for either of them, but it was still attuned to him. Without it, he might die. With it, he was assured of living. And she wanted him to live even more than she wanted to live herself.

Stunned, she realized in an instant what that meant. Her eyes filled with tears. They were riding towards the deadliest fight they'd been in so far together. Worse, they wouldn't be together. Each one had to be with a different group for this plan to work. And she couldn't lose him. She looked over again and he was looking back. He waved. She waved back.

When she did so, the tears rolled down her face. She just hoped the distance was too great for him to see them.

CHAPTER 188

Ellie hoped this worked. Pushing the "Confirm" button on the security board, just as Gary swiped the card Ellie had left outside for him. He walked right in through the front doors. The security guard had gone to make Ellie a new card, as she told him she'd lost hers "somewhere outside".

She had had to knock on the doors for a minute before he noticed her. But she was easily recognizable – being the only cute, young woman on the entire list of scientists and other personnel who were being allowed into this facility. She had also just gone outside to get her gloves… supposedly. Gary flipped her card to her, per plan, and raced towards the elevators. They dinged and he slipped in, waiting for her to join him.

A minute later, the overweight young man running security for the building came sauntering back with a new pass card for her. Ellie held hers up and looked guilty – which wasn't hard. "Silly me! It was here in my purse! I don't know how I could have missed it. But thank you so much for the new card…! Will my old card work, or should I just take the new one…?"

"No," the guard said, clearly irritated. "It won't work now. Use the new one. I'll take the old one."

She handed the old card to him, and said, "I'm sorry again, thanks!"

He nodded and dropped his head. She started walking towards the elevators, then looked back and said, "You know…you've got a nice face." Looking at his nametag, she said, "Adam, is it…? Hold it up and smile some more, and pretty girls will take notice. Just a word of advice."

He blushed and waved at her as she walked away, "Thanks…uh…I will!"

There. Hopefully, he will feel a bit better about his life.

He really was kind of cute. Just needed to not sit at a desk all day and stare at his phone. Hitting the button, the elevator Gary had gone into opened immediately. She stepped in, turned towards the front saying, "If I get executed in a military prison, I will haunt you the rest of your days!"

"That might be hard," he said as she pressed the button for the top floor, swiping her card as she did so.

"Why is that?" she asked, not looking back.

"Because I'll be dead, too."

She turned and said, straight-faced, "Good point. Let's just not get caught then, shall we?"

Having no firm plan for him to exit was only one of the many huge holes in this ridiculous plan. If he didn't get through the Arc Gate and into Nathan's new playground, he'd have to hide in a bathroom or dress as a janitor to get out. Not super in either case. Another great non-plan was that Gary had found a bunch of white and clear gemstones and rocks. He'd supposedly found a nice clear glass piece that resembled the gemstone on the medallion Nathan had shown him.

Ellie was certain some costume jewelry gemstones were not going to help focus the magnetic fields of the monolith. Nor did any of the rest of it seem anything other than ridiculous. Of course, telling Gary that had zero impact. Rolling her eyes, not for the first time, she got off the elevator on the 12th floor and swiped her card again at the entrance.

The gamble was that no one had returned this late after they got started. It was nearly 10:30 already. It was also a time that Ellie often did come to do her research alone. She didn't like most of the other members of her "team", so she was sure to not share critical information, nor to collaborate on solving this puzzle with any of them. Oh, she pretended. Just like she pretended to like Gary.

But she wasn't going to give those butt-sucking feds a thing if she could help it. The gemstone idea had bought her some time, to be sure. And an array of actual gems had been brought into the room within hours. Since Ellie hadn't been specific. Gems of every size, shape, color, and quality were all about the room. On tables, chairs, desks, and in front of the monolith itself.

The thing was humming and vibrating loudly tonight. It didn't help that the floor it was set upon was metal flooring. The field was so powerful tonight, that Ellie could almost reach out and touch it. Forgetting everything for the moment, she switched on her computer and studied the log data. Yep. For sure. It was putting out an enormous amount of energy. The magnetic fields were so powerful, that the perpendicular electrical power being generated was both visible and audible.

There was a crack and a little boom at that very moment, making Ellie jump.

Gary said, "What the hell….? What was that, Ellie?"

"I can tell you what it was, Gary, but I can't tell you why it was. The portal is putting out so much more magnetic energy now that Nathan has gone through it again, that the fields are generating strong electrical current on their own. When those currents collide as the fields move, it's generating small bursts of electrical energy, and that's what you're hearing."

"Great," he said.

Looking back at him, she said, "No backing out now, Gary. You want to go get Nathan, go for it. I'm game. If I manage to send you through, I'm not sure how I'm going to hide it. The video cameras all over this room are likely recording you in here right now."

"I told you; I've got that covered." Gary proceeded to unpack his backpack, which was filled with a Glock 9 mm handgun, boxes of ammo, a box of Pop-Tarts, and some water bottles on the side. Oh, and his laptop.

Shaking her head, Ellie said, "Pop-Tarts…? Really, Gary? You have all the choices in the world to bring as your 'emergency snack' in Nathan's world…and you bring Pop-Tarts?!"

He grimaced at her, opening his laptop as he sat down on a nearby chair.

"What's the code for the building, Ellie?"

"What?"

"The WIFI code! I can hack it, but it'll be faster if I don't have to…"

Telling him the code, she said, "Can that get me into trouble?"

"Not the way I'm doing it. It'll appear I hacked into it and got the code myself. I'll put in a false login web address from Siberia. That'll make them happy. This just saves me a heckuva lot of time. Hold on! Just…. do your thing for a while. I'll let you know when I'm done." He got to typing super-fast on his keyboard while hunching over it like he was watching a porn video.

Maybe he was. Ellie wouldn't put it past him. Going to her own desk again and sitting down, she started watching the variance logs and charting the fields that were being generated. At times, it appeared the fields…

Suddenly, Ellie got excited. Hitting the video logs, she greatly increased the replay speed, flipping through the video at a super high velocity. The had short blips in them, where the electrical current snapped, for a few milliseconds afterwards…it appeared that the portal was open, just for that moment. Behind the fogginess of it all, it appeared to be viewing a large, mostly empty room. But there were clear areas that looked like equipment boxes and even a large hose or coil lying on the floor.

Ellie recognized it. It was the hangar bay in Morgaine's base. "I…I think Nathan has activated it or something, Gary!"

"What?"

"I think Nathan…has activated the portal! I don't know how the others missed this! The portal is briefly blipping and showing a room beyond it. It appears to be some sort of enclosed room with equipment and stuff on the floor. It's Morgaine's facility!"

"Well…is that good?"

"No, it's not good, Gary!! It means that soon the United States fucking military will be visiting Nathan's new Halo world real soon!"

"Uh…shit?"

"Yes! 'Shit', Gary! Now, I suddenly need you to get through this Gate. And I think I know how…"

"How is that…?" he asked, holding up one of his stupid little white stones.

She groaned and stood up. "No! Not your roadside gravel, Gary! Power!"

"Power?" Gary asked quizzically.

"Yes, Gary – a lot of fucking power! It seems that the fields are designed to generate a huge flux of current. Since Nathan's last portal jump, we've been tracking the harmonics, the frequency, the amplitude of the electrical bursts, along with the magnetic fields and their increases. It really looks pretty simple, actually. I just need about 0.4 Gigawatts or so of power!"

"Uh…that sounds like a lot, Ellie…"

"Oh, it is, Gary. But this is no ordinary building. It's built on top of a local adjunct to the power grid. Somebody somewhere thought having a bunch of juice might be helpful. I think they might have been right. The only thing is, I cannot let them figure out what I did or how I did it. And that much power is going to get noticed."

"There, I'm done!" Gary said, looking up again. "The video camera feed is looped from before you came in, and I've done a long loop of you sitting there looking smart. That was the hard part."

"You are an ass, Gary," she retorted, sticking her tongue out at him.

"This is well-documented, Ellie. Well-documented. I also erased all camera footage of me walking in from outside, inside this room, and in the elevator. You were right. They've got them there, too. Finally, I've got it ready to reset and remove the loop when I hit this button…" he pointed. "Or when you do." That will return the sequencer off and erase my invasion of the system, too. Like I said, I'm a professional."

"A professional ass?"

"That too," he gave her a big 'thumbs up' with both hands.

Sighing and shaking her head, Ellie got to work. It took her significantly longer. The capacitors and transformers downstairs somewhere could only hold so much juice without blowing. Ellie put a chair with a cup on it where the cameras could easily see it. The cup was to be her alleged "experimental target". Gary was to stand as far out of the way of the view, behind the monolith's leg, as possible. If the Gate activated, he was to run around once the lights got bright and run in. Of course, if that didn't work, or he was electrocuted first, Ellie was going to be arrested.

For manslaughter on top of treason. Fun times.

Hitting the final button, she began loading the charge that she thought was required. There was one more button to press, and then there was no turning back.

"Remember," she said, getting up, "…if you get through, you find Nathan and you get him to bring you back here with you. Smyslin is lost without him. And those other two military types will just get him into trouble. They've already started talking about trying to break out. Like, where would they go…?"

Gary was nodding as she turned towards him. "I get it. What do we do about you opening the portal…?"

"Well…" she said, looking down for a moment, "…in the short term, it will give me a lot of clout. But in the long term, they'll eventually figure out how I did it whether I tell them or not. That kind of power is going to leave a trail…"

Ellie stopped and looked up. "There's a worse danger, though," she added quietly, her eyes wide.

Gary swallowed. "Worse than dying by electrocution?"

Ellie just nodded; eyes still as wide as he'd ever seen them. "If I pour this much juice into the field and this thing opens up …I might not be able to close it. Then…"

"…then we just gave the government everything they wanted," Gary finished for her.

"Not just them…" Ellie said standing up, looking Gary in the eyes. "I didn't tell you what happened to me. Not really."

"Sure you did! You got captured by some people who knew you were an alien, and Nathan and his friends rescued you."

She nodded. "That's the gist of it, yes. And that's the story I gave the feds. But the real truth is…Gary, as scary as our government is on this side…they're way scarier on that one. The group that captured me…" she swallowed.

Actual tears started to flow.

"Holy shit! What happened, Ellie? Did they…" he shrugged.

She shook her head and dropped it, tears splashing on the metal floor. "No…" she said, looking up again and wiping her nose. "but they wanted this gate opened too. Gary, they're…they worship some kind of evil. They call it 'the Dark'. It apparently has something to do with these Gates. Either way…their Arc Gate, as they call it, hadn't worked for centuries until Nathan came through. Just like ours, I suppose. But they've been trying. Gary, they have…weird powers. And…their followers are like a military cult of bad asses."

Gary whistled, "Holy shit! I seem to be saying that a lot. Maybe we shouldn't be doing this."

Ellie looked up, furious, even with tears still streaming down her face, "I told you it was a bad idea! But you wouldn't listen! I know Nathan's friends need rescuing. And yes, I agreed to help. But I didn't think we'd actually have a chance to *do* it! And now that I think I see how…like I said, I…we…could be giving those 'Dark Lords' – there are three, by the way, not just the asshole who captured me – we could be giving those Dark Lords everything *they* ever wanted. Access to another world. It's what Nathan's friends have been fighting to prevent all those centuries Gary. That Morgaine…she's somehow related to the Dark Lords. She personally is over five hundred years old. And from what Nathan said, she's the one who shut them down in the first place."

Ellie shook her head. "I'm just afraid we're playing right into their hands…"

Gary leaned back on his heels, looked out and let out a big breath. "Well…what do we do now? I can try the janitor trick."

"No Gary, I've got the juice already stored up now. Whether this works or not – and I think it will – there are going to be questions. We might as well try to send you through. Once that light goes white…"

"I know. I know. I slip around the leg of that thing and run through."

Ellie nodded. She wiped her eyes with the back of her hand and went to her desk, grabbing a Kleenex. She blew her nose and said, "Just get Nathan! And tell Morgaine what we did. If she's still alive, that is. Tell her…we might need her help here soon enough, too. If she can shut these things down, maybe she can do it here, too."

Gary went over and hugged her. He didn't like her. But…*fuck!* She was risking everything for this. And the girl needed a hug. She turned and hugged him back.

She isn't so terrible. Maybe.

"Ok," she said pushing him away. "Go stand where we talked about. I'm going to hit this when you say you're ready."

Gary went over and grabbed his solar charger, his laptop and stuffed everything back into this backpack. Zipping it up, he placed it on his back. Checking his pockets, he showed her a lighter, a rain poncho, and a knife.

"You're a regular Green Beret, Gary. Get over there, please."

Chuckling, Gary went and stood behind and beneath the left leg of the thing. The magnetic force was strong enough that he had to push his way through the fields. He must have something in his pocket...oh! The knife! The knife was being pushed back with unbelievable force.

Hugging the leg like it was a tree in a hurricane, he yelled, "Ready! The looping video is stopping right about now."

"Ok...! Here we go!"

There was a click, and then a hum....and then an electric shock and minor report. The hum just kept getting louder and louder. The electrical shocks got bigger, longer, and louder. They started coming faster, too. Faster and faster...

The knife in Gary's pocket jerked out of his pants pocket and flew away. Gary kept holding on. It was becoming way too much like being in a hurricane. He closed his eyes.

Then he heard something. "Gary! Go now!!! Gary! Go now!!!"

It was Ellie, of course. He could barely hear her standing over by her computer, hands to her face, yelling.

Letting go, Gary felt himself slide towards the opening even before he came around the leg. He had to walk with his eyes almost closed, the light was so bright. The electrical field made his hair stand up...Stiff legged, he forced his way forward. Then the resistance suddenly dissipated.

And he was gone. Ellie hit the kill switch, breathing a sigh of relief.

Nothing.

Heart in her throat, she ran over and cut the power with the Emergency Manual Shutoff. Nothing again. The portal was open. Ellie couldn't close it.

CHAPTER 189

It was late evening, and the two armies were getting last minute instruction from their commanders. Everything had to be as coordinated as possible. The armies were going to utilize the "long distance signaling" capabilities of Morgaine's team and strike as close as possible to identically the same time on both sides of the battle.

Any sign of major losses or countermeasures, and the army was to retreat. The idea was to weaken both opponents, not Rondor. Plus, allow the "knives" to get onto the battlefield. Morgaine and Nathan had not shared about their ability to go completely invisible, just saying that the attack should occur at dawn, so the Dark men did not have any distinct advantage – beyond their Dark-given speed and agility. Morgaine had assured the King and Duke Iranias that she and Nathan were not worried about reaching their respective targets, regardless.

Treyborne and Messau were each leading a team. Treyborne and his team were going with Morgaine and the assault on K'Thul. Messau and his team were with Nathan for the strike at Jezerah. Jasper and two others were hanging back to coordinate both sides using comms, and aid whichever side needed it most.

When the final instructions were done, Morgaine took Nathan aside for a moment. They had many hours to wait, as they were within two hours ride of their target points, and the sun had just set an hour earlier. But they were separating and riding halfway tonight, keeping in communication via comms. In the twilight, Morgaine stood before Nathan, majestic in her armor, hair tied back. She held her head high but leaned forward to take Nathan's hands. "You have the hardest job, Nathan. And you know how I feel about it."

Nathan nodded, rubbing her fingers with his own. "I know. But you also understand why Trey and I are not wanting you to go after Jezerah. Someone new needs to try. Nothing personal, but you suck at killing at him."

She laughed then, a full, musical, almost carefree laugh. Just a little note of anxiety remained within it. "True enough, jackal! Just remember what I told you."

Nathan nodded. In the dim light of the few campfires, Nathan wasn't even certain she'd seen it. "I remember," he said finally. "And you also know that we aren't that far apart. If you need help, you call for it. Yes?"

She looked over at Treyborne and his half of their team and nodded. "Yes. But I won't call for them. I'll be calling for you," she said looking back at him. "If I call them, it's to their death. It is you and you alone, besides me, who have a fighting chance against them. The Dark has further empowered them. But each of those men were born to the Elder Race. Even Jezerah, a half-breed, was unbelievably fast and an accomplished fighter long before the Void drew him in."

"Ok. Well…let's get this over with," Nathan said, and pulled her close. She reached up and he kissed her. The soft caressing kisses from that first night. The kiss was far too short, however, and then she dropped down from her toes and hugged him, head hard on his chest.

Drawing back, putting both her hands in his again, she smiled and said, "I will see you tomorrow. Ride well, and sleep if you can. Dawn will come far too soon."

Then she was gone.

Shaking his head in disbelief. Just the magical feeling of being with her for those few moments. Nathan turned and walked towards Messau and their team. One of the guards was holding his horse. Mounting up, Duke Iranias looked over at him and nodded.

"I wondered who you were, Nathan Arvad. Brother or lover. You have answered the question favorably." He turned and said, "Now, let's go kill this spawn of evil! They will write songs of this night for all time!" And he rode off like he was heading straight into battle.

Chuckling to himself, Nathan kicked his heels into the flanks of his horse and took off after him. Nathan heard rather than saw Messau and the rest of the men begin to follow them. Rondorian knights and their lance began to make noise in the background, as well. One more hour of riding, then sleep.

Or perhaps not. Only Sanshe was in the night sky so far. Alonna was probably not far off, however. Then he'd have plenty of light to stare at while he didn't sleep, worrying that the woman that he could no longer imagine being without went to battle someone she'd never been able to defeat. A person, so he had heard, that even the other Dark Lords could never defeat in combat, either. Pushing that thought out of his mind, he caught up to Iranias, whose horse had slowed to a fast trot.

Iranias smiled as he did so. "It is an honor to meet the man who is the love of the White Queen!" he said with a hearty laugh. "Who would have thought? It is like finding out that the Scarecrow in the field has a wife! And children!"

Nathan laughed. "I don't think 'love of the White Queen' is quite right, either. I mean…we just met five or six weeks ago!"

Iranias turned, shock plain on his face, even in the dim light remaining. "I think…" he said, turning and facing forward again. "I think…you should reconsider your position."

CHAPTER 190

Brianna was heading for the elevators. She'd had another quick conversation with Maitan, who was only a half day away from the coast or Nelrae. It seemed he and his new crew might be there in time to help Morgaine after all. He was very mysterious about how he'd found them, though.

She'd called Treyborne right afterwards, and it seemed they were marching towards the battlefield and about to camp for the night. He was with Morgaine, of course, but they'd parted company with Nathan and his segment of their team hours ago. Trey sounded as worried as she'd ever heard him. They'd had a lot of horrific fights in the short time she'd been here. And nothing had seemed to faze him much.

Until now.

It was understandable. They were about to engage an enormous number of Dark Men – who had been conveniently knocking each other off for well over a week now. On top of that, Morgaine herself was going to try to kill K'Thul. *Kill….* a Dark Lord. Yes, she'd heard that 'back in the day' that was what she had done. But she had also never been able to kill any of the remaining, despite multiple attempts. And Morgaine was still nowhere near full strength.

And, of course, Messau and the other team were wading in just as deep against Jezerah's Dark Horde…with Nathan going in for the kill on him!

Just thinking about it seemed so surreal, she had to stop and wonder if she was dreaming. A very bad nightmare. She hoped Trey was going to be ok. It sounded beyond dangerous. Really, it sounded like suicide. And Treyborne's anxiety lent itself to that assessment far too well. Clearly, he was thinking the same thing. When she'd told him Maitan was 'coming', he'd just said, "What can he do?" Brianna sadly had to agree.

Creator, protect them!

Suddenly, the Arc Gate, which she'd just walked by a moment ago, burst into life. "What the…?" Spinning around, she saw what she'd only seen once before.

"Dax, this is Brianna, do you read me?" Dax was the lead guard on duty tonight.

"Check that, Princess Brianna. What's your sit rep?" He'd come to calling her that since she'd announced she was taking over while Morgaine was gone. That man was irritating in the extreme.

"Get down here now, Dax…the Arc Gate is opening up again!"

"Bright balls of…are you serious?"

"Yes! Do you think I would joke about that in the middle of the night? Or any other time, for that matter?!"

"How many of us do you need?"

"How many do you have?"

Smyslin, Rost, and Agino were no longer allowed to walk together outside. Somehow, their captors – as this was how Smyslin viewed them now – had figured out their plan.

He honestly wasn't sure how. They'd been speaking in their own language, talking, and pointing like they were just enjoying their time together. But one day, the walks just stopped.

Now Smyslin had to walk alone with four guards. Before, all three of them had only warranted two guards, total. Shaking his head, Smyslin simply could not figure out…

"Of course!" He turned and looked at the guards. "You've translated our language!" One of them gave him a sudden sharp look.

Oh yes. They know. How did they learn it so fast…?

Ellie hadn't been here in several days. She wouldn't have told them… would she? Smyslin hated thinking of her like that. He liked Ellie. She'd always been so nice to him. She truly seemed to care. Turning to the one who'd understood him, Smyslin asked, "Where is Ellie? I need to speak with her."

The woman (she was the only woman amongst his guard) looked directly at him and said, brokenly, "Ellie no here. She work black door."

Smyslin nodded. *Yes…she is a scientist.*

Nathan's former lover was the keeper of the Arc Gate on this world. That is why he liked her so much. She was like him. A person of science.

"I … understand…" he said slowly. "But…. I …. need….to…see…. her…"

The woman looked sharply at him again and nodded. "I try."

So, they'd put linguists amongst them and just listened to them talk. These people were as sneaky as his own people. That was not a good sign, either. He had to find a way to let Agino and Rost know.

"Can…I … see…. my…. friends?" The woman shook her head.

Oh well. They will have to figure it out on their own.

Smyslin needed to warn Ellie. If she ever opened the Gate, these people were not trustworthy. They would misuse it. Hopefully, he wasn't too late.

Maitan and his Dark Raider crew sailed into the bay east of the capital of Nelrae as dawn was approaching. There was a long running coastline that formed a nice crescent along the southern shores just east of the city itself.

Not wanting to alarm the capital, nor draw attention to their ship, Maitan had the crew drop anchor several leagues outside the city harbor. Some merchant ships were already sailing, but they were out into the deep waters, mostly heading east. Maitan had the crew lower the rowboats, and he climbed down into one of them. He was still wearing his father's grey-white armor, with the hood pulled back from his face.

Maitan had wanted My'Rel and a skeleton crew to stay aboard, in the event someone came along and caused any problems for the boat while the rest of them were away. My'Rel had been offended at the idea of fighting going on without him, however. So, he allowed My'Rel to choose a new First Mate – the lone woman on the vessel with a topknot of hair and a curvaceous, muscular body. Her name was 'Asharra'. Apparently, it was exceedingly rare for a woman to rise so far amongst the warrior class. But she had done so, and then some.

My'Rel said if her reach had been a finger knuckle longer, he'd have lost his challenge match with her not too long ago, and *she* would have been *his* captain. He had great respect for her, as did the other members of the crew. When Asharra was awarded the title, they all bowed very low to her. Out of respect, My'Rel had said.

Now, My'Rel and all but six members of the crew, about thirty men in all, were coming with Maitan and rowing for shore. Beaching the craft, they pulled them high onto the shore to avoid losing them to the tides. Strangely, they'd all taken to wearing white scarves instead of their customary black ones. Where they'd gotten them, Maitan had no idea.

When they were out of the craft and on the shore, Maitan said simply, "I go to my Mistress. The 'Lost One' you know as your former enemy, Morgaine. We are going there to aid in her attempt to defeat the Dark Lord K'Thul. I do not wish you to engage him yourselves unless my life or my Mistress' life are clearly in jeopardy. And do not engage alone! Come at him all at once. But remember who he is. The Dark is his weapon. As soon as whichever one of us is in peril is no longer at risk, withdraw immediately. Understood?"

They all saluted. *Hmm…I feel I'm liking this more than I should.*

"One more thing," he said, turning as he started running up the slopes to the hills surrounding the city. "We are a team. We leave no one behind. No matter what, we stick together. We are going to be battling our way through the back ranks of K'Thul's Dark Men. Kill all who stand in our way but let anyone pass who is running by or not engaging us. We will have plenty of men to fight without chasing down stragglers."

They all then saluted again as they ran. It felt good to push so fast through the grasses and not have to wait for them. The Dark Men flowed through the ground like water running downhill. Even as the hills rose and the run became difficult, no one slowed. So much like the *Biaki Mor*. Only…a Darker version. Maitan began to wonder about the origins of these Dark Men. If he lived past today, he was going to study them. Perhaps Smyslin or some of his own men could provide some answers.

Within the hour, they reached the top of a large plateau. They'd run into a few scouts, but they'd been ignored, although a few stared at the leader of a pack of white-scarved Dark Men wearing light grey armor. But with his face covered by a black mask (this had been My'Rel's idea), no one tried stopping them. On the overlook, they saw several areas of intense fighting all up and down the Alisandre River valley. The fighting had come within sight of the walls of Nelrae, and it seemed the fiercest fighting was in the southern quadrants leading to the gates of the city.

There were over seventy thousand humans and Dark Men fighting, in combined numbers from both sides. It was complete chaos, and bodies were lying dead all over the field. It appeared from the looks of it that the fighting had been going on for days. And it just might not stop when the sun set in the southwest, either.

Maitan looked back at his crew. "Down we go! Stay tight – and remember, no one is left behind!"

Then he leaped and began the rapid descent into the rear guard of the Eastern Empire's armies.

CHAPTER 192

King Rondor IV, formerly known as the Duke of Mantessa and General of the Rondorian Army, reigned in his horse on the northwest side of the Alisandre river. It wasn't even quite dawn yet, but the sounds of battle had been raging since they'd started their final approach.

Looking down on the fields, the fighting spread from below their position all the way towards the city into the distance. He couldn't quite see the city, or the shores to the east and south. But knowing they were there meant that this fight was stretching across many clicks of ground.

It seemed that the entire Eastern Empire forces had bunched together, then slowly disassembled as they pushed for the capital. Shaking his head in disbelief, he turned to Morgaine, who was eye level with him aboard her massive black stallion. She was looking directly into his eyes, reading his thoughts.

"Your Highness, you and your men do not have to engage in this madness. It appears that these armies are fully prepared to utterly destroy one another…"

"Lady Morgaine, we made a bargain. I help you defeat the Dark Lords if you help me stabilize my kingdom. You've held up your end. It is my turn now. If things go poorly for us, or if both armies suddenly turn on us as interlopers…well…then we will withdraw. Our lance is specifically set behind us to stand their ground here in the hills to allow for that contingency. You and your men do what you must do. Leaving two with me in the attack, and one in the rear with the lance to communicate as you do…" he said, stopping to look at the field again, "…will be enough. May the Creator shelter you, Lady. What you attempt to do, I have no idea how to say this. So, a simple 'thank you' and good fortune to you will have to be enough."

Morgaine nodded and looked over the field again herself. "I will ride with you for as long as I can. Once you see me slip off my horse, please make sure Steel has a good rider and have that person take him back to Jasper in the rear guard. If I am successful, I will meet you back there. It should all be done in an hour."

King Rondor looked at her for a moment, shaking his head. "I've never seen bravery like yours, Lady Morgaine. I am honored to ride with you!"

Morgaine nodded slightly at the compliment. "Need is more like it, Your Majesty. This world ever has need. And I, unfortunately, have often been the only one left to know how to fill it."

Not waiting for the King to give his command, Morgaine kicked Steel's flanks and started slowly riding down the long hills toward the sprawling battlefield below.

Nodding softly to himself a moment, Rondor IV turned to his army. "Remember your orders! Keep your tactical teams and sortie groups together! Do not leave the greater area that our army takes and holds! If you go out into that morass, your life is on your own head! Our job is to decimate the flanks of the Eastern Army. But any Dark Men or warrior from either side that opposes you – cut him down! We are not to leave anyone alive who challenges the Rondorian army. If we do, he may bring his friends and come to our gates next!"

The army raised their weapons and yelled, "Chief!" An old custom, but a good one.

He tipped his general's hat to them. "All right! Let's go to war! For Rondor!" With a loud cry, they kicked their horses into motion and raced down the slope. Their contingent of Morgaine's Elite guard had already begun following Morgaine herself down the hill, but Rondor and his horse quickly caught up with them.

Then together, they charged.

Ellie was right. Her popularity with the government types skyrocketed. She also didn't dare leave the facility once the portal had opened and remained so. Her story, both believable and mostly true…was that she had gotten an idea and gone in to try it out. Once it worked, she waited to verify the opening was stable. Then she called in.

Of course, she'd covered her tracks on Gary going through, although no one was going to be checking video logs for idiosyncrasies or looking for anomalies in the new hero of the federal tech group. Of which she was a most unwilling member.

Military types with big guns and every scientist she'd ever seen were in the room now, plus a dozen more, all scurrying about the place. Ellie hadn't gone to sleep yet, and she was frankly afraid to. Her cautions to the group were listened to, but likely wouldn't be heeded for long.

Supplies for an "exploratory mission" were already being assembled on the floor near the glowing portal. A team of five marines, including two techs, were planning to go through the portal's opening, take some readings, then return as soon as possible.

Ellie just shook her head. A massive headache was coming on, exacerbated by her lack of sleep. Throw in a big stress ball and there she was.

Dr. Eleanor May Cooper – government pawn.

An officer with more metal on his chest than there was chest to pin it on came over to her. "I hear you're the one to thank for figuring out this ancient monolith! I'm Brigadier General Davis, Ellie. Great work! You've opened a literal warp tunnel to another habitable planet! I cannot express enough how grateful we in the military – and the President – are for your work here."

Ellie stared up at the man. He was older, and certainly seemed friendly and enthusiastic. He also had one of those 'perfect old man' type mustaches. Her eyes must look black as hell. She tried to be personable. "Anything I can do for my country, general!" she said, trying to hide the tongue-in-cheek she really wished to convey. She gave him her best 'next door girl' smile.

If he caught the attitude, he didn't show it. "Glad to hear it. Glad to hear it. Well, I can tell you, you've got a bright future. Bright future!" He walked away. The image would have been perfect if he'd just have been puffing on a big fat cigar as he said it.

Ellie went back to her data screen. There was a residual pattern behind the magnetic field spin. It had been there before, but now it was more pronounced. If it meant what she thought it meant…

"General!"

The general was halfway across the floor, near where the supply pallets were being collected. Turning, he started walking back towards her. She got up and ran to him.

"Yes, Miss Ellie?" he asked, genuinely concerned.

"General, I think I see a flexing deterioration pattern in the magnetic fields. If I'm right…" she looked up at him and added, "…and I've been right a lot recently, the power we put in will eventually be spent. We can't add any more in, either. If we do, and we're not on exactly the same frequencies and amplitudes. The field harmonics, coupled with the electrical current infusion, could push the magnetic fields too far… overpowering them… I'm not sure that is the correct term…"

"Pretend I'm not a physicist and cut to the chase for me, if you would, please," the general said in a patently patient tone. He wasn't even being mean. Maybe he wasn't such a bad guy after all.

"Of course! Sorry. General, the field is collapsing. It should hold for several more hours. Maybe even a day or more. But it won't hold forever. And…General…?"

"Yes…?"

"I'm not sure what I did can be repeated. The monolith seems to have some sort of latent artificial intelligence. It doesn't like being… provoked? Each time the field has acted differently when the portal opened. Every time. It's like it's resisting and trying to shut itself down. If that makes sense."

"I think I get it, thank you," he said. Turning without another word, the general began barking orders. "All safety protocols are hereby concluded! I want my men on this platform within the hour! We need to figure out if there is a safe landing zone on the other side, then return ASAP. I mean now, men! Move! Whoever isn't here on time isn't going. Get on it!"

There were a lot of "Yes, General" and "Yes, sir" responses simultaneously and then people began scurrying in all directions.

The general turned back and saw Ellie standing there, "Doctor Cooper, thank you. I won't forget this. I promise you. The safety of my men is paramount to me. But I've got orders from the President himself to determine both whatever threat this gateway represents, and what opportunities, as well."

Ellie just stared at him. She had thought her saying the portal was becoming unstable might stop them from going through at all.

Strike three for me! 'Safety first', except 'we're going through no matter what'! Makes perfect sense, General. Perfect sense.

CHAPTER 193

Jezerah felt the pull of the Void from within the Arc Gate. But this time…the Arc Gate wasn't closing. Looking off to the distant east, as if he could somehow see it if he just willed himself to do so.

Morgaine! What are you up to?

Unfortunately, he didn't have time to deal with her right now. He had more pressing matters. Extremely pressing. K'Thul had not taken the attack on his horsemen and lance very well. That was putting it mildly. He had expected a response. To be sure.

How could he not respond? But this?

Every single bit of his military was pressing forward in a wedge straight for Nelrae. It was as if Jezerah had kicked a giant hornet's nest of Dark Men and they had spewed out in total rage. Jezerah's tactics had almost evened the odds in terms of troop numbers. Even sending in the Shadow Beasts that remained had only slowed them down now, though. Eventually, he'd had to recall even those monsters.

K'Thul's Fist had literally blasted halfway to Nelrae. Other fantastic tactics and unbelievable aggression had pushed the numbers and the position on the field severely in favor of the Eastern Army – what was left of them – and the Dark Knights that were leading them.

Jezerah surveyed the battlefield shaking his head. First Emorion gets eradicated, then the Arc Gate suddenly opens and remains open. And in the middle was this carrion sandwich of a war.

K'Thul was winning. *Again.* If nothing else from the never-ending fury of their onslaught. Since that attack two hours before dawn a day ago, K'Thul's counter measures had not ceased. Over a day of blistering tactics tossed in, and Nelrae's gates were within sight. Jezerah needed a break. He had prepared for just about anything, including a personal attack. In fact, he expected one. The Void had warned him of the inevitability of personal danger. He had taken some necessary precautionary measures, as a result. But he also had to be on the field. There was no way to get the responses required to keep his army intact without it.

Curtaise approached and saluted, bowing low.

"Approach, General. What do you need? The *Siday* are all in place, Master. They have returned and await your command."

Jezerah looked up at Curtaise. "What is your advice?"

"Master, I have given it. K'Thul is the heart. Rip the heart out, and the beast dies. These Dark Men, as rabid as they are fighting to this very hour, will cut and withdraw immediately, should their Master suddenly be severely injured. Or killed."

Jezerah nodded. "Is this not why I am defended as I am? Certainly, K'Thul has thought we might try this. He himself would be a fool not to be ready for something himself."

"Yes Master, but you now have the luxury of waiting him out. Our network informed me not five minutes ago that the Eastern Empire's resupply ships were sacked and burned by pirate ships along the coastline. My spies say they were linked to Emorion and full of Dark Men. Therefore, if we even weaken him some, he will be forced to withdraw."

Jezerah's head snapped up at the news. "Yes. Of course. If Emorion struck at his supply lines, K'Thul must have thought I was involved. That we were working together again. And therefore…"

"Yes, Master! Therefore, it is more likely that Emorion was killed by K'Thul's elite forces. Perhaps he anticipated this, as he has anticipated our defenses so well these last few hours…"

"So how do we find him, Curtaise? If you were K'Thul, where would you be?"

Curtaise surveyed the field for a long minute, then pointed. Right towards a spot between the dual-pincer attack closing in on the city, with a tight group of Dark Men that struck in all directions as necessary. "I would be right there."

Gary walked through. In truth, he scuttled through, carrying his backpack full of ammo, emergency Pop-Tarts and handgun. It was good he'd packed it in there instead of in his belt like the knife. The light inverted and the entire world seemed to turn upside down.

Staggering, the world seemed to right itself. But his eyes were totally blinded by the white light all around him.

He thought he heard a voice. A woman's voice.

The hum was still ringing in his ears. "Ellie…? Is that you? Did it not work…?"

Suddenly, Gary couldn't move. It wasn't that he was paralyzed; he could still feel everything. Trying to squint through the bright lights…he realized he was floating in the air. His feet weren't touching the ground.

Then he fell.

Crashing and falling as he hit, he grunted, and barely averted hitting his face onto the grated floor…wait! Wasn't the flooring solid metal? Trying to raise his head and push himself up, suddenly hands grabbed him on either side and hauled him to his feet.

As his eyes adjusted to the brilliant light now to his rear, Gary saw one of the most beautiful women he'd ever seen. She had dark hair, was dressed in a strange blue dress, and was pointing right at him. "Eid esu amoxian parshi?"

He'd gone through. Was this Nathan's girlfriend?

I thought he said she was white-haired like he was. Did I hear him wrong?

She certainly was beautiful. And she was obviously in charge. Maybe she dyed her hair. She wouldn't be the first woman to change her hair color on a consistent basis. "Uh…Nathan? Where's Nathan? Are you his friend…?"

The woman snapped her head up at Nathan's name. "Mycraya insen Nat'an?"

"Nathan! Yes, Nathan!" Trying to get himself free, the two men holding him held him even harder, until he grimaced. "Ok, ok!"

The woman put her chin up a bit, then said something to the men. They let him go, but immediately drew strange looking guns…just like the one Nathan had brought with him, but bigger. What had he called it? A… "blaster"?

Gary put his hands up. "I'm looking for Nathan. We need him. Smyslin needs him. He's been captured."

At Smyslin's name, the woman looked at him sharply again. She said something else to the men. One of them took his pack from him and then four other men showed up from the rather large room he'd appeared in.

Looking back, he saw the portal wasn't closing. That couldn't be good. Gary hoped Ellie was ok. The men started leading him out of the large room where they kept their monolith. Walking down a long hallway filled with strange equipment and other people watching him, they ended up taking him into some sort of meeting or monitoring room. It looked like a security room, with loads of camera screens and equipment.

The woman, turning to one of the men nearest her, went to a small cabinet and took out a small round metal object. It looked similar to the one he'd seen next to Ellie's ear. Handing it to him, the woman indicated he was to put it into his ear.

Doing so, she pointed to a chair. He sat down and looked up at her. *My Lord, she is pretty. She must be … Morgana? Whatever. It must be her.*

The woman spoke and kept speaking, and suddenly Gary could understand her perfectly. "My name is Brianna. Once you can understand me, start speaking your language."

She then pointed to him…and he started talking. "Hi…I'm Gary? I'm Nathan's friend. I came here to figure out how to get him home because your man…Smyslin? He needs…".

She suddenly held up her hand. "I understood only the last few words. Please start over."

"OK…again. My name is 'Gary'. I'm Nathan's best friend. Ellie sent me through the portal because she can't help Smyslin anymore. He and his two friends…they're being held by the feds…uh…our government. And, if that portal doesn't close…you'd better put some guards on it, because they'll for sure be sending somebody through. Soon."

The woman – Brianna – looked alarmed and pointed to someone outside the room, who was listening in. "Dax! Get four or five of the men and put a round the dial watch on that portal. As long as it's open, I want guards all around it. And get that stasis field juiced up! I want it to work not just on one or two people – but a dozen. Go!"

Whoever she was, she was in charge. And she was sure pretty enough to make someone be able to forget even Jennifer. Except maybe himself. "Are you uh…Nathan's girlfriend? He came back because someone – a female he cared about – had gotten severely injured and he wanted to make sure she lived. I thought her name was…Morgan…something though?"

The brunette woman, Brianna, turned her attention back to him. "No, Gary," she said his name strangely. "I am not Morgaine. She is my Mistress. She is the Mistress of all of us," she said waving her arm. And the men around her with the weapons all nodded.

"She is the owner of this place. Your friend Nathan is not here. He and our Mistress have gone on a mission to destroy the Dark Lords. We cannot reach them until they've either won or lost at this point. But you say that Smyslin and the two guards that went with him – Agino and Rost – are captives?"

Gary nodded. "Yes, I'm afraid so. Ellie was protecting them as best she could. At least she said so, and I believe her."

"Then we must help them. What is their situation?"

"Honestly, I'm not sure. They're being held at a secret government facility. Ellie knows where it is, but I sure don't."

"Then why did Ellie not return? Why are you here?"

Gary shrugged, "I guess because I was stupid enough to volunteer. Plus, I came up with the idea to try. Ellie was pretty sure she couldn't open the Gate. But…she did. Maybe a little too well. I know she was hoping it would close immediately once I got through. So far, it hasn't. She's probably busy trying to figure out how to close it right now."

The woman named Brianna sat down herself, leaned back, and sighed. "I do not have the personnel to handle this. We may indeed need to wait until Nathan and Lady Morgaine return. We at least need Trey and a full team of the Guard. Mikell, search his person and that bag. Take any weapons from him and escort him to the kitchens. Get him some food. He is Nathan's friend – or so he says – but until we can confirm it, keep a guard on him. Gary, I'm sorry, but I've got zero trust in me right now. I hope you understand. But whether you do or you don't, I'm not doing anything differently. Follow Mikell. Get some food and some rest. When I'm ready to talk with you and can come up with a plan, I will call for you."

The man she'd indicated searched his bag and found the gun right on top. It was similar enough to their blasters; he correctly identified it as trouble. He handed it to Brianna.

She held it up in her hands. "Is this a weapon, Gary?"

"Yes."

"If you thought you were coming to Nathan's friends, why did you bring this…?"

"Because I'm not a fool! Ellie was captured by 'the Dark Men'. She's still horrified by what happened. I can tell. I almost feel badly for her, and I don't even like her."

One of the men chuckled at this. More than one.

Brianna even smirked and looked at one of the men. Looking back at Gary she said, "We may have something in common, Nathan-friend Gary! Mikell!" She jerked her head.

And the man who'd found the gun half-helped, half jerked him to his feet. "Come on," he said, and he held his gun-blaster and directed Gary towards the door.

Brianna grabbed his arm as he passed her and she said, "One more thing, Gary. Tell me Nathan's last name."

"Arvad. I used to make fun of it, since I'd never heard a name like that before." Nodding, she let him go. Gary wondered what would have happened if he'd forgotten or didn't know Nathan's last name. As tough as that woman's eyes looked – despite her pretty face – it couldn't have been good.

CHAPTER 195

K'Thul drew more power from the Void.

He knew he was drawing so much that the light around him was getting sucked in around him, warping how others perceived him. It was also protective, of course. If anyone but a Dark Lord attacked, they'd have trouble seeing him, let alone hitting him.

Everything warped, including gravity and light, when one held this much of the Dark.

Each of his three generals was leading a faction of the army now. They'd splintered into three assault teams to overwhelm the last two large groups they were fighting. As he looked, it seemed there was now some sort of disturbance at the back side of the lower pincer near the southern shores.

Pointing to the three runners waiting for orders nearby, he waved his hand and said, *"GO!"* His voice was also cloaked and difficult to hear. His yell had come out as, at best, a hoarse whisper. Even K'Thul had limits. And he was reaching them. The good news was that Nelrae was within his grasp. Jezerah's best efforts at counter-offensives and defense both were getting crushed as the sun rose high into the sky on the second full day of unceasing battle.

The runner began to glide down the hillside towards the disturbance. A sudden crash to the north, followed by shouting and the sound of battle caused K'Thul to turn his attention that direction. Everything moved slower within the Void. He could afford to draw no more power without risking his connection to this life.

What he saw caused his eyes to widen.

Rondor? What are they doing here? Our attacks had the ripple effect of saving their country from extinction…! Why would they engage us even as we are about to crush our mutual enemy?

A sudden knot of fear hit K'Thul in the pit of his stomach. Something he had not accounted for was occurring before his eyes. He'd pushed all his pieces onto the board. Every reserve force was no longer being held back. Watching his northern battalion buckle caused the embattled Nelrae forces to begin rallying on the far side of the city's defense.

"NO!!"

There seemed to be more going on further into the belly of Nelrae's forces, however, as well. Reaching for his vision-scope, he looked out towards the Western Empire's reserves. More Rondorian forces were hitting Nelrae, as well!

What madness is this?

Snapping his scope down and placing it away carefully, he turned and sat down on a nearby rock. He had to think. What was Rondor up to…? K'Thul had been considered the best tactician of his age before he'd ever joined Jezerah and the Dark Lords. The power and the increased mental capacity that the Void afforded him made him – in friend and foe alike – the most feared general in the history of this or any other world. But tactics on the field was not strategy if there was a bigger game involved. K'Thul had been too focused on crushing Jezerah's stronghold. There was something bigger at play here…

The Void flowed around and through him as he pondered. Emorion had been suddenly removed, but not before he'd decimated the coastline and supply ships K'Thul had needed to sustain the war effort. Jezerah and Morgaine had been working together, likely since the beginning of the Dark Brethren…now the Arc Gate had opened and wasn't closing….

What…or…who….?

It all snapped together for him like a puzzle piece. A massively complex, three-dimensional puzzle. Morgaine had worked together with Jezerah to secure the Gate and open it, while Jezerah simultaneously had worked to weaken K'Thul's obviously superior military position with Emorion after the battle at the Gate. Emorion attacked the ships, then Jezerah sent Morgaine to eliminate him.

Simple. Elegant. Effective. Clearly some of the forces they'd traveled east with had just swept into the southern shores and were disrupting his forces nearing Nelrae's gates. Probably being led by Morgaine herself…

But something had gone wrong with Jezerah's plan…*someone* had rallied the Rondorian forces against both sides, to remove the threat to their lands. Was it someone internally…? Who amongst the humans would dare send their forces against not one, but two armies of the Dark?

Morgaine again.

She might not be as much on Jezerah's side as he thinks…but to keep him off guard, she will be coming…for *me*!

Now!

K'Thul leaped to his feet, drew his *Djune* and whirled, swinging it in a circle around himself. His blade struck home on something – or someone – and he quickly put his guard up and pressed the button on his wrist, activating his force shield. Pushing the Dark force outward, he felt it meet something…in the disturbance.

Swinging his blade back and forth, he completed a circle around himself. He hadn't imagined it. Someone had been there. He started kicking the ground…as he looked down, he saw blood smeared near his feet.

Ah! So, I did strike her!

"Morgaine, you might as well show yourself. I admit…you almost had me. Had your forces near the gates not struck before the others, I might not have had time to figure out the game. I admire your ability to manipulate the board…truly remarkable!"

Morgaine appeared before him, hair falling about her face, a nasty gash on her upper thigh, bleeding profusely from the wound. She was limping, but her guard was up.

"K'Thul…" she said, "I don't know what forces you're referring to. But our Rondorian allies are pummeling both sides on the northern front of this battlefield as we speak. Regardless of who wins our fight here, you're overextended. Surely the brilliant commander you are, you know this by now. And it appears to me that what's left of you is getting consumed by the Dark. You are drawing too much power, General. You cannot continue as you are. I don't need to fight you. I just need to stand here and wait."

Lowering his weapon and placing it before him, point down on the ground, K'Thul nodded slowly. "The 'secret alliance' with your brother has served you well, Morgaine. I admit I have greatly underestimated you. And Jezerah once again, it seems. I had always thought myself the greatest tactician in the field, but there is always more going on outside the battlefield…things I am not as adept at. I think perhaps someone forgot to check your aptitude as a strategist. You have my respect."

Raising his *Djune*, he flowed into his fighting stance. "But I think it's time we draw your interference in our affairs to an end, Witch." He lowered his defensive shield. Hand-to-hand combat being impossible with it on. And with her medallion, the Dark power would avail him nothing against her.

The power of the Dark flowed through him…swirled about him…even though she stood ready, his assault came at such speed and ferocity, he immediately began pushing her defenses to the limit. The Dark of the Void reached for her soul. Leaping back, she vanished again… forcing him to draw just a bit more of the Dark. Her outline appeared immediately, still blurred by the Light Shield.

K'Thul's feet barely touched the ground, while Morgaine was limping from her wound. Suddenly, the disturbance in light that was Morgaine flew into the air backwards – clearly wearing anti-gravity boots. As he advanced once again, sudden explosions erupted all about his feet, blasting him into the air. The Dark force rippled, absorbing the brunt of the impact.

K'Thul floated up into the air himself, several feet above the ground he'd stood upon. He began to laugh. "Is this your best, woman?"

The outline of her form flew towards him, and their battle re-engaged in the air. Morgaine struck with incredible speed. What power could she have, if she'd merged with the Void, as he had? And despite his earlier conclusions, he detected none within her. But as ferocious as she was, K'Thul was better. He was stronger. He was faster. He was also fueled by the Dark. And he was not wounded. Slowly, inexorably, he beat her attack back.

Floating away, she disengaged the light shield, knowing he could sense her regardless. Sweat beaded her brow, and several other nicks had appeared where he'd almost gotten through. Both forearms and another on her cheek. She was breathing heavily. K'Thul…utilizing the Dark, was barely winded.

The Dark Men that were his guard nearby had come to watch their Master in battle. They knew not to interfere. A small crowd that were not engaged in the defense to the north had gathered as well, just watching them.

He pointed with his *Djune* towards the Dark Men. "Morgaine, you have won the day. I admit it. But even should you defeat me, they will be happy to finish the job. And you won't defeat me…now or ever. You cannot win. I cannot lose."

He leaped at her, when suddenly a huge crash came from just behind him. Pushing her attack back, he finally had time to turn in the air for a moment to look. Jezerah's Dark Knights were ripping through the small amount of forces who'd drawn around him, decimating his guard and the few remaining runners along with them. Whirling to face her in the air again, he shouted, "I knew it! You have been Jezerah's ally from the beginning!! How are you hiding your alliance with the Dark?"

His fury turned into a whirlwind attack, pushing her back and back, higher into the air. Finally, she also disengaged with a sudden flip and landed on a large rock nearby, still above the fighting below.

Morgaine shouted, "I have never been allied with my brother, K'Thul! I see his forces crashing through, yes. And I hope they find your back as we fight! But I didn't invade his country first, K'Thul. You did! *You* made him your enemy. I am merely taking advantage and attempting to rid the world of the both of you!"

K'Thul was about to reply when another group crashed into his circle on the right. This time a group of Dark Raiders, dressed in sea garb, and wearing *white* scarves…At their head…was that…?

"What blasphemy is this? Dark Men led by a *Biaki Mor*!? How is that even possible? They're all dead!" he exclaimed. He also saw that his defensive circle had completely crumbled. Morgaine looked over at the group and did a double take herself, eyes wide.

K'Thul would have charged at that moment. But he was now surrounded by enemies. Had he had the time, he knew he would see that his army's offensive had been blunted as well. Likely, they were retreating even now.

Morgaine leaped back into the air right at him. Behind him, the last of his defenders fell.

Reaching for the Void, he grasped for more of the power of the Dark. There was nothing more he could draw. As he floated in the air, he made his decision. He turned and began to fly away towards the south.

Morgaine's hand grabbed the medallion around her neck, stopping and floating mid-air. The gemstone within flashed into pure white light. Pulling it off her neck, she held it towards him. "Hear me, Dark Lord! You have always claimed that the Dark swallows the Light. I am here to refute the lies you've been taught!" A beam of pure white light burst from the gemstone and struck K'Thul, blasting him backwards.

Gasping, K'Thul felt the Dark being sucked out of him liked he was simply a balloon struck by a dart. Before he fell to his death, he utilized the last of the power within him to land on the ground just outside the area he'd been standing in earlier. Sheathing his *Djune*, he reactivated his force shield. Both fighting groups, ignoring those next to them – the blasphemous white-scarved ones led by the *Biaki Mor*, and the Dark Knights of Jezerah – raced towards him. Folding his arms together, he reached back into the Void, and a huge blast blew both groups away from him, sending them flying into the air, blood and body parts spraying everywhere.

Behind them all, Morgaine, too, had fallen to the ground, and laid there, not moving. K'Thul drew his *Djune* once again, stalking towards her.

CHAPTER 196

Nathan moved through and around people with difficulty. Yes, he was invisible. But that just meant he had to give wide berth to anyone – friend or foe – who was wielding a weapon. He had never had time to get used to anti-gravity boots, like the ones Morgaine had taken with her. Therefore, Nathan had to do it the old-fashioned way: go around. And around again. And more going around.

Finally, he reached the area near the top of a hill where the Dark Lord Jezerah, surrounded by several of his attendants, was standing. The being was impressive. He'd heard of the Dark Lords. Even seen some Dark Knights in their attack on the Dark Gate. He thought he'd even caught a glimpse of Emorion then.

Walking right up to and in the presence of Jezerah…he could *feel* the oppressive Darkness. It was overwhelming. The overall sickening feeling of "wrongness" was palpable. Perhaps Morgaine and her team were just used to it. Or the lesser feeling that came off the Dark Men themselves was less horrific. Smyslin had even felt a little "wrong" to begin with when they'd first met.

Nothing like this. Breakers of it flowed out from Jezerah like waves on the seashore. Hefting his shock-lance and holding his shotgun in his other hand, Nathan prepared himself. There were at least a dozen Dark Men and Dark Knights in a circle all about the area. To get to Jezerah, he'd need to eliminate the other combatants. And quickly. He had two blast charges he'd been given by Morgaine. He assumed Jezerah always had protections against weaponry up.

But he could get lucky.

Clicking the button on one of the pods and throwing it into their midst, he went to hide behind a huge rock nearby. The blast sent bodies flying. Peeking around the rock, Nathan realized they still couldn't see him. Several of the Dark Knights and all the Dark Men that had been standing there were scattered over the hilltop. Many were not getting up. Those who were, were doing so slowly, some with massive wounds and broken limbs.

Jezerah was nowhere to be seen. "Damn!" he said out loud before realizing his mistake.

A blast shot right towards him from nowhere. Rolling to the ground to his right, he stayed low. There was nothing there.

Shit! Of course Morgaine's brother and his kind have the same tech! The question is, what do I do now?

"*Morgaine…!*" Came a voice from nowhere. "*Or is it K'Thul? Your blast may have harmed by men, but all you did to me was blow up my hologram! You see, he's still standing over there waving at you…*"

Chuckling echoed over the entire area. An image of Jezerah was waving, standing in the middle of the air.

Just then, Nathan heard the Rondorian army crash into the Dark Men below them on the hills to the north. Wherever he really was, Jezerah was silent for a time. Nathan wondered if he'd lost him completely. Then…

"I see you brought friends to the party, Morgaine. They won't be able to help you. With the reports of attrition to the supply chain, K'Thul needs simply to be waited out at this point. Rondor…it is them, isn't it? I will deal with them later."

Nathan quietly as he could, cocked the shotgun. The battle covered most sounds, but he wanted nothing to give away his position.

"I suppose we should show ourselves. It will be easier to finish each other off that way…". Jezerah's hologram vanished and Jezerah himself appeared not four feet away to Nathan's left.

At least apparently. Wheeling, Nathan fired his shotgun. Buckshot sprayed everywhere, some even ricocheting back at him.

Fuck!

Clearly, Jezerah had some sort of force shield. That had hurt. Nothing severe, but some spots on his leg were bleeding.

"Naughty, naughty…!" Jezerah laughed again. "I said let's show ourselves, and you…blast little rocks at me? What was that…? It was quite…. loud!" He was looking around, clearly enjoying himself.

Nathan had had enough. Spinning the ring on his finger, he appeared and simultaneously snapped the shock-lance to full power. He cocked the shotgun with one hand.

"And…who is *this*…? Is this our mysterious Gate traveler?" Jezerah eyed him for a few seconds. "Of course you are…! What did you do…with Morgaine…?" He started looking around and behind himself. "Surely, she is also here. I'm supposed to believe that you came alone?"

He scoffed.

Looking back at the battlefield, he stopped and his eyes – what Nathan could see of them through the utter blackness – were troubled. He sighed and looked back at Nathan. "I'm not going to bother with you, boy! It seems Nelrae's salvation with the attack on the Eastern Army will be short-lived.

He stood there, not caring – clearly utterly defended against personal attack – and spoke into a comm, "Get the men off the field, General

Curtaise. Find a way. Withdraw those you can to the city, the others across the valley and up the hillside. Now."

Then he vanished. Spinning around, Nathan vanished again, also. He rolled, he crawled, he stood right where Jezerah had been. But he was gone.

Reaching for the medallion…but no. Morgaine had it!

How do I find him if he doesn't want to be found?

Running down the hillside towards where Morgaine was likely engaged with K'Thul, he spoke into his comm, *"Morgaine, Jezerah bailed. He had a hologram, a Light Shield, and a force shield. He didn't fight. He ran. Over."*

Nothing.

Panic hit his stomach as he ran. Why did it have to be so far? Wading across the shallow river, he shook his head. *Why didn't I learn how to use those damned anti-gravity boots?*

Tomorrow, he was going to learn. No matter what. He hoped there was a tomorrow.

An explosion rocked the hilltop he was racing towards. Looking up, he saw Dark Men flying every which way. "Good," he muttered racing up the hill. "She's clearly doing better than I did. Maybe I can help her finish K'Thul."

CHAPTER 197

Jezerah raced away from the stranger. He would never have shown it but seeing another being from the Elder Race for the first time in over five hundred years…it changed everything. And now…the Arc Gate was open. *Remaining* open.

Why hadn't I thought of this before?

Clearly this was the one who had come through that first time, the one his men could not keep captive. A being that shouldn't exist. But how many more were there? How many more did Morgaine have pouring through at this very moment? Nelrae would survive this day. Even K'Thul and his decimated army would survive the day.

But for how long if the Elder Race has returned in force?

How many of the Elder Race survived? What new or additional weaponry was coming this very moment? Jezerah had to retreat. Morgaine had restacked the deck. Dozens or even hundreds of Elder Race beings could be pouring through right now. The risk of staying out in the open was too great.

Calling to Curtaise, he called for a full retreat to their compound. Not just away from the battlefield. The steady withdrawal needed to accelerate. Nelrae again was going to be fine. His new emperors were filled with the Dark. There was no more to do here. But there was a Void full to do back at the base.

Hearing Curtaise bark orders to the other generals, he called one more time. "Get me a head count on Dark Men and Knights, Curtaise. I want it within the hour."

"As you command, Master. May I ask why we are withdrawing in such haste? What if K'Thul regroups…?"

"He will not. Within the hour, General. Make is so." Jezerah could almost hear the snap salute over the comms.

It would have to be enough.

CHAPTER 198

Nathan reached the summit just as K'Thul reached the prone figure of Morgaine. He raised his weapon…he was saying something to her, but Nathan could hear none of it. He also could not care less.

"Oh, *hell* no!" he said. K'Thul jerked forward and the blade followed. Nathan fired his shotgun's last shell, dropped it, and grabbed his blaster.

K'Thul, struck by buckshot in the back, whirled. Blaster bolt after blaster bolt came from his weapon. Enraged, Nathan leaped and swung his shock-lance.

It was only much later that Nathan realized he'd been invisible the whole time. Because K'Thul seemed not to even have noticed. After the initial blast from the shotgun, K'Thul tracked Nathan coming right at him. Blaster bolt after blaster bolt missed. It was like K'Thul could move faster than any human possibly should be able to. The Dark seemed to ripple around him. This guy was clearly more powerful than Jezerah. No matter what Morgaine said.

Once Nathan was close, K'Thul's blade whirled and stuck, struck, struck at Nathan…who could barely parry and was suddenly and relentlessly thrown back. K'Thul's weapon was like a viper. And Nathan was barely holding on.

He'd saved Morgaine, but he was suddenly in need of some saving himself. Another blow knocked Nathan on his back. K'Thul never slowed, and Nathan was stabbed twice, barely avoiding a critical hit to his heart by a millisecond. Kicking with his feet, he managed to cause K'Thul to stumble backwards a half step.

Even with that, K'Thul was so fast, he was on Nathan before he could quite get back up. Nathan was in pain, and it was getting worse. Seeing his shotgun lying a few feet behind him, Nathan kept parrying with the shock-lance, which was taking a beating. Nathan wasn't sure it could even keep the electricity going as much as it was getting hit. K'Thul lifted his other hand, and Nathan's throat grew suddenly tight.

I can't breathe!

Panic widened Nathan's eyes. K'Thul knocked Nathan down onto his back again with a powerful shove. Rising up, a blade suddenly struck through K'Thul's chest. It was Morgaine.

Seizing the blade, impossibly still alive, K'Thul leaped off the black sword and whirled swinging for her head. Morgaine parried it easily, however, and K'Thul stumbled backwards, almost knocking into Nathan as he scrambled to get back up, gasping for air.

"Get away from my man, Dark Lord! If anyone gets to stab him, it's *me*!" Morgaine's anger was palpable. Nathan stumbled over to pick up his shotgun, holding his side as it bled through his fingers.

K'Thul…*shimmered*. A dark halo over his entire being billowed and pulsed. It blocked him from even seeing Morgaine behind the man. But he could see they were still engaged in battle.

Grabbing a shell from his pocket, he slid it in, cocked the gun, and walked forward. Sidestepping right by K'Thul to his left, away from Morgaine's blade, Nathan aimed and fired, point blank. Right at K'Thul's skull. His head exploded like a watermelon.

Staggering, his body stumbled forward, and with only half of a head remaining….

Again…impossibly…the head seemed to try to look at what had shot the other half off. Morgaine swung her blade, burying it into his chest…

then he was down. And K'Thul moved no more…. a few seconds later, K'Thul's body…and the shattered pieces of his head and brain… began turning to black dust and blew away.

Looking over at Morgaine, he saw she was on one knee, breathing heavily. Looking up, she said, "You took long enough." She held a hand up to him.

"I guess I could say the same." Walking over to her, he helped her to her feet. She was bleeding badly from wounds all over her body. Even her face on the left cheek was gashed badly and had blood pouring from it.

Holding her close with their hands still clasped, he asked, "What did you mean by '…if anyone gets to stab him, it's me…?'"

Leaning back a bit, she looked up, "Let's not find out, shall we?" She smiled then…the most beautiful smile in the world.

CHAPTER 199

Treyborne had noticed the explosion on the hill where Morgaine had gone. Looking over at his men, he said, "We're going to that hill! Now!" His men, seven in all, nodded and they all began running. Dark Men were pouring over the battlefield, engaging the Rondorian attackers. The field was scattered with men fighting, lunging, stabbing, screaming, and dying.

Treyborne and his men formed a tight wedge and blasters began firing holes through the Dark Men. Whenever they came in behind a Rondorian knight in trouble, they quickly fired and blew several holes into the Dark Horde's lines.

Suddenly, as one, all the Dark Men broke away and simply ran the other direction as fast as they could. The Rondorian commander looked back, waiting for the King to point. But he did not. He blew a horn, and rather than give chase, they began to retreat themselves.

Treyborne and his team, once the Dark Men broke cared nothing for that. They all as one marched towards the hill, shooting stray Dark Men as necessary.

Finally, reaching the hill, he saw Morgaine clasping hands with Nathan. They were talking. Both looked to be badly injured. Blood was all over them both. If he hadn't known better, he would have guessed they'd fought each other, as no one was left on the hilltop at all.

Rushing up and saluting, Treyborne shouted, "Are you hurt, Mistress? We are here to assist!"

Looking around Nathan's shoulder, Morgaine answered, "What do you think, Captain? I don't think I look nearly as good in red as I do in black." Limping around Nathan, she held onto his shoulder, so Nathan put his arm around her waist, until he realized he could barely walk himself.

"I might need a little help." Two of her guards got on either side of him. "I didn't get Jezerah, Morgaine. He ran."

Her head whipped towards his from between Treyborne and the other guard helping her to the ground so they could address her wounds. "Where did he go?"

"I have no idea. He refused to fight me. He kept looking for you. Then he vanished and never returned. So, I ran to you." Looking over at the ground, he said, "Someone get me that shock-lance."

"Damn!" Morgaine looked over at him, even as she was lowered herself to the ground. Her leg looked bad, her thigh and lower leg were gashed badly, and blood still was pumping out from the thigh. Grimacing as Trey started to clean it and wrap it with gauze, she looked up at Nathan, eyes unreadable.

Trey said, "You're going to need stitches…like all over, Mistress." She only nodded without even looking at him. Firing up his shock-lance, Nathan handed it to her. "You do it. I prefer it to more stabbing and stitches."

Raising her eyebrow, she shocked him. "Bad Nathan! Letting my brother go. Bad!" He laughed as the pain flowed through him. Within seconds his wounds were gone, leaving only gashes in his armor and clothing. "I still don't understand how that works. Why doesn't it work for you?" he asked her. It did make him feel drained, though.

Like he needed sleep. For about a week.

Shutting it off, she said, "I have no idea. But I can assure you, it does not. I've been hit with them plenty and nothing like that has ever happened to me." Looking down at Treyborne stitching her wounds she looked up and said, "But I sure do wish it would."

Another smile. They hadn't done everything they'd set out to do. But they had done a lot. A moment or two later, Morgaine's smile faded, and she started looking around. "Where is Maitan?"

CHAPTER 200

Maitan himself was lying on the far side of the hill. Many of his men were lying nearby, groaning, or patching themselves as best they could. Looking back further up the hill, he saw the other contingent of Dark Men that had attacked K'Thul, all dead. They'd taken the brunt of the blast, as they'd been much closer.

Looking about him, Maitan saw several of his Dark Raiders had severe lacerations and broken bones, and many of them could not even stand. Maitan looked down at himself, and his chest armor was nearly torn off his torso completely.

Father would not have been pleased. Still stunned a bit from the blast, Maitan groggily tried to make the pieces that were torn meet.

My'Rel walked up, lowering his white mask for the first time that Maitan could remember. His face had no noticeable injuries. Curious. "Master, the Lost One…the White Queen. She has won. She and the other one – I saw them slay the Dark Lord K'Thul. They are not far, Master. Shall I go get them?"

"No!" Maitan said, then, "No…." more quietly. "It is dangerous for you. I must lead. Help me up." My'Rel did so, handing him his *My'Shar* as he did so. Taking it, Maitan nodded. "You did well. Help your men now. I am going to find her before she gets too far." Limping slowly, he shuffled rather than walked towards the hilltop again. Looking back, Maitan stopped and asked, "How many did we lose today, Captain?"

"Seven, Master. But all are wounded."

Maitan nodded and turned again towards the hilltop. "Get them back to the ship, Captain. Await my return. I won't be long." Captain My'Rel saluted fist to chest and bowed quickly. Maitan saw none of it. My'Rel must do as he must do. Barking orders, he looked up to survey if any threats were nearby. Looking down, Maitan saw the oozing wound he had in his own stomach. He hoped he could make it back to the ship. Helping another man up, he placed his hand over it to slow the bleeding.

It would be a long walk back. A minute later, Maitan finally crested over the lip of the ridge, just as Treyborne and two other guards were racing towards him. Almost colliding, Treyborne stopped, amazed. "Maitan?!"

Maitan bowed as best he could. It wasn't very good.

"What happened to you? What are you wearing?! How did you get here?"

"That…is far too much to tell right now, Captain. I could use some medical assistance. I may need them for a few of my men…". He looked back behind him and not a trace of his men could he see. Of course, men were running everywhere, some still fighting. They'd picked up their dead and left. No man left behind, as he had commanded.

Nodding, he turned back. "Perhaps not." Reaching for Treyborne's shoulder, he began limping over to where Morgaine was sitting, leaning against a rock. She turned her head towards him and began to get up.

"No, Mistress! No…you're badly injured yourself, as I can plainly see. K'Thul was both tricky and deeply aided by the Dark. We are fortunate this day to have anyone able to limp away, let alone walk. That," he added, reaching her, and bowing – again badly – "would include me, I'm afraid."

Treyborne helped him to the ground, reaching for his comm, "Trey to Group 2. Trey to Group 2. We have Nathan. Find us on the battlefield.

High hill on the eastern banks. We have injured." Treyborne looked back at them all, "Lots of them."

"Check that, Captain," Messau responded, "We're on our way. No one injured on this side, sir. Iranias beat their asses. We just sort of watched and shot a few strays. Five to ten minutes, sir. We've got you in our sights now. Jasper is bringing up the reserves, as well."

The battlefield was mostly quiet by the time they were all able to move again. No Dark Men were to be found anywhere. The Rondorian lance had advanced all the way to the rear of the cavalry's flanks. Nelrae's armies had scattered, mostly into the city. By the time they reached King Rondor, Duke Iranias and he had already combined their forces again. The sun was tilting towards the horizon, well past noon. A breeze had begun to blow the stench of death and blood away from their nostrils.

King Rondor got off his horse as they approached. Morgaine's steed was brought to her, and she and the rest of them mounted. Maitan had followed her, being half-carried himself by two of the guard. Rondor eyed her quizzically and looked over at Maitan with a squinted stare. "You bring strange new friends to us, Lady Morgaine."

Morgaine looked over at the King and bowed slightly from her saddle, garnering his full attention. "Your Majesty, I regret to report that only one Dark Lord died today. But that is one less fount of evil for the world. My brother escaped Nathan's attack. But together – and I will say, *only* because we were together – did K'Thul perish. It was also with the aid of my personal assistant," she pointed to Maitan, "the last of the *Biaki Mor*. Had he not arrived, I surely would have died before Nathan ever got to me."

For the first time, the King looked startled. "The *Biaki Mor*...? I thought they no longer existed, or perhaps were even a myth."

Morgaine looked over at Maitan, who had replaced his hood after bowing to the King. "Surely no one has seen one in over a hundred years, Your Majesty. But I would like to hear how he got to the battlefield in such a timely fashion."

Maitan bowed, "I am afraid that will have to wait, My Lady Morgaine. King Rondor," he said again bowing.

Looking up at Morgaine, he said, "I did not think to see you again, Mistress. But how I got here and what transpired, I cannot go into detail at this time. All I can tell you is these two things: First, I am happy to report a second Dark Lord has died, several days ago. The Dark Lord Emorion will trouble this world no more, as well. And second…I have a ship full of Dark Raiders awaiting my orders, as I am now their Master – having slain their former one. I will sail with them to Nyx and meet you there. If you wish to join me, you may. It will surely not be much slower than if you travel back the way you came…."

No one spoke a word for several seconds. "I…. knew you must be going to engage the Dark Men and perhaps stop some portion of one of the Dark Lord's plans. Brianna told me what she thought…but…I had… no idea…she was actually right." Getting down from her horse took several seconds. And it was clearly very painful.

Trey raced over to her, as did Nathan, but she was down before they could help her. Getting down on one knee before Maitan she said to him, "In the presence of these witnesses, I release you from your oaths of service. Be as your father wished you to be – a *Biaki Mor* in truth and forever!"

Maitan looked down at her and then almost forced her to her feet. "Mistress…where would I go? You are the one battling the Dark. That is the true calling of the *Biaki Mor*. Whether I battle them with *My'Shar* or scalpel, I will battle them at your side. But I must go now.

Captain Treyborne, thank you for aiding me. If I could borrow a horse, however…?" He started looking around.

The King also got down, signaling behind himself, and a horse was brought to him from the Rondorian ranks. He walked the horse over, leading it by its bridle. He bowed low himself, and said, "Maitan, *Biaki Mor* warrior, you will ever be welcome in the city of Rondor!" He took a medal off his own vest and pinned it on Maitan. "You have done what no mere man has ever done before. I am honored to be in your presence."

And the knights within the circle that could hear all applauded. Maitan looked around bewildered, clearly shocked at the attention he was getting. By this time everyone had joined in, including Morgaine.

"I…suppose it was…a *bit* of an upset," Maitan said humbly. Treyborne burst out laughing and chucked his shoulder so hard, Maitan almost fell. Trey quickly grabbed him and helped him stabilize himself, and then mount his horse.

"Sorry, old friend! I'm just not used to you being battle wounded! That's usually my role."

"Indeed," was all Maitan said. Looking at Morgaine, he said, "I shall see you back at the base, Mistress. It appears we still have some work to do."

As he rode away towards the southern shoreline, Trey's comm suddenly crackled to life.

"Brianna to expedition team. Brianna to expedition team! Is anyone out there? Can you hear me?"

Morgaine held her hand up to Treyborne, who was about to respond, and turned her comm back on. Nathan wasn't sure when she'd turned it off. "Brianna, this is Morgaine. What's happening?"

"Morgaine! Is Nathan with you?"

Morgaine turned to look at Nathan with a blank stare, "Yes, he is… Why do you ask? Isn't he supposed to be?"

"No, Mistress! It's just that…he has a friend here again. A 'Gary' this time. He came through the portal this morning."

Nathan's jaw dropped, "Gary's here?! Ask her why…. what happened….?"

Morgaine kept staring at Nathan and responded. "I can feel the Arc Gate is still open, Brianna. Has anyone else come through?"

"Not yet, Mistress, but it's been open for hours! I guess you know that, though, don't you? We've got guards around it every second. And…we've got the stasis field ready, as well."

"Yes, Brianna. I knew already. And excellent on the guards and stasis field. Why is Nathan's friend here?"

"He said Smyslin and the others are in danger. They're being held captive and… their leaders won't let them go! He says if Nathan comes back, he thinks they will."

Morgaine responded, "Or they might just make him a prisoner as well. Tell his friend we are on our way. As is Maitan in his own … way. Look for us in two days. Morgaine out."

CHAPTER 201

Ellie walked with Smyslin, and due to her sudden clout with the general, she actually got some time alone with him. No guards, no others following them. She had zero illusions that they couldn't be heard. But she wanted to make sure Smyslin and the others made no moves to escape.

"Smyslin, I just came to see you, so you'd know things aren't as dire as you think. We've gotten the gate open again, and so far, it's holding. Nathan should be coming back. I…managed to send a message through tied to a chair. And by now, the General likely will have sent his team, as well. He didn't want anyone in the room when they used the portal due to Top Secret clearance being required. Which I currently don't have…"

She looked around at all the cameras and other equipment lining the barbed-wire fencing as they walked. "…but the General assures me he will have my background check concluded and get me that clearance by end of day today. I should be back in the monolith room, and I'll bring Nathan to you as soon as he arrives. Maybe faster if these guys get their wish."

Smyslin looked up at her with a miserable look on his face. "Master Nathan won't be coming back, Mistress. He has gone to fight the Dark Lords. I don't know how I know. But I know. Perhaps someday these people will let us return home. I thought our deal was to let them do their testing and their picture-taking until the Arc Gate opened. Shouldn't I be able to leave now…? Shouldn't Agino and Rost be able to, as well?"

Ellie said, "Good point. I'll see if I can get the General to agree. After all, he'll have all the specimens he wants now that his team has gone through. They can even take more 'volunteers' back with them if they desire. As soon as I get my Top Secret clearance, I'm going to push for all your releases. They practically worship the ground I walk on now that I've opened the Gate for them. And as long as it remains open, I need to cash in some chips. Because," and she lowered her voice as low as she could when she said this, "I don't think the opening is stable, Smyslin. We need to get you all through before it closes again. I sort of…forced it open? And I'm not sure what damage that may have done. They know it's unstable. But I don't think the General grasps *how* unstable."

Smyslin looked over at her. Suddenly neither miserable, nor sad. He looked wise…and very old. His eyes were sharp, and he nodded. "Yes, you should 'cash in your gold chips' before the price of its value lowers with the portal closing. If you could spend some of those on little old Smyslin and Morgaine's guards, I would be forever grateful."

Ellie grabbed his hand and walked in silence with him for several minutes. The sky was clear, although the air was cold. It was a beautiful day, really. If you ignored all the military personnel, guard towers, men with guns, and fences with barbed wire.

She'd calculated as best she could. The portal had more time than she had initially thought when she saw how unstable the power flow was. It seemed to create some of its own power with the magnetic fields spinning so fast. So, the decay was significantly slower once she sat down with the math. Two days. It should last from the time she hit it with all that voltage for almost two days. It'd been most of one day already, though. If she got her clearance today, she'd need to immediately request the General's release of his prisoners and let them go home. Because that's what Smyslin and the others were.

Prisoners.

And it was up to her to set them free if she could.

CHAPTER 202

Maitan reached his ship as the sun began setting over the waters. The men rowed back in the second vessel. They'd taken their dead and the severely wounded in the other rowboats already. Finally getting on board with the last of his men, My'Rel stood before him and saluted, Asharra at his side. All the Dark Raiders bowed. "How many men did we lose total, Captain?"

"Fourteen, Master. I am counting those who cannot work for many days or weeks. In terms of lives, seven, as previously mentioned. None on the ship were lost, or even threatened." He pointed behind him and said, "But we are ready, master. We now wear the White Mask of the *Biaki Mor.* You are our Master. We are your loyal subjects."

Noticing a few other ships at anchor not far beyond them, Maitan asked, "Are those merchant vessels or navy vessels of the Empire? How is it that they're not fighting with us?"

"Oh no, Master. Those are your ships. They also await your commands."

Maitan's eyebrows raised. "*My* ships? How are those my ships? Who are they?"

"They are now *Biaki Mor*, as well, Master. When word spread of your defeat of the Lord Emorion, our former mentor and master, some decided to follow the way of the White Mask. They said, 'It must be a better way, since it has defeated the Dark and the Dark Lord.' Others said that was blasphemy and have gone another way. Those were the ones who responded in this way, 'Our last orders were to plunder the Purple Coast of the Eastern Empire. Until Emorion or another Dark Lord return to give us new orders, this is what we will do."

Maitan looked and counted. At least a half dozen other ships were anchored all the way out into the ocean, towards the setting sun. Perhaps there were even more. "What am I going to do with a navy full of Dark Raiders?"

Asharra stepped forward, bowing. She was very dark tan, almost black-skinned, but he noticed her eyes were no longer pure black. Perhaps her native skin color was simply that dark. In fact, Maitan realized that none of those on his ship had the 'all dark' eyes of the Dark Men any longer. "Master," she said, waiting to be answered.

"Rise, Asharra. What do you wish to say?" Maitan felt like Morgaine suddenly. It was an odd feeling.

"I wish to point out that we are no longer 'Dark Raiders', Master. And to say so would offend us should you continue doing so. The Dark Raiders are those who have rejected your way. We have all accepted the Way of the *Biaki Mor* as the better path. You defeated the Dark Lord. And although the power that sustained us is leaving our bodies, another one is filling us. We follow the Light of the Lost Ones now. It is, we believe the light from the Creator. Or so some of our clerics are telling us."

"I'm not so sure about all that," Maitan said. "But if you wish to become *Biaki Mor*, I have much teaching to do. That much I do know. There are many things my father taught me that will have to be resurrected. How did your people separate themselves; may I ask? Did they simply follow whatever each captain decided? Some went towards us, while others stayed as raiders along the coast?"

My'Rel answered, "Our way amongst our own kind is to respect and honor those with different callings. Some are warriors. Some are engineers, some are breeders, some are fishermen. Others bake or perform medical duties upon the injured or sick. Those who wished to follow were gathered onto ships with captains who agreed to this change. Those who did not on their ships were exchanged to go with the Raiders. There was no killing or fighting. No one threw themselves from a ship to try to swim here."

He chuckled at the thought.

"There is much to the Dark Men…and yourselves as the new *Biaki Mor*," he corrected hastily, "that I must learn. We will teach each other. Send word to the other ships. We sail for Nyx City and its port. Tell them they will need to create a new flag and bleach their black sails. We don't want to start riots in the city before we even arrive. And Talim's merchant vessels need not run from us any longer. Let everyone do this on the second night while we anchor somewhere along the coast. But tonight, we sail."

Everyone saluted. Maitan suddenly felt the weight of the day upon him. His wounds, although treated, were aching and sore. He was still bleeding from one and several were itching. Half walking, half limping, he made it to the captain's cabin – as everyone went down a notch while he was on board, just as they had for Emorion – and began removing what remained of his father's light grey armor.

Shaking his head, he sighed. K'Thul had made a mess of it. Besides the rent in the chest, there were several other tears on the arms and leggings. But it could be repaired. He placed it in the sea chest at the foot of his bed and began to remove the clothing beneath. It was soaked in sweat and dried blood. Removing those and tossing them to the floor, he then unhooked the *My'Shar* and placed it on top of his father's armor reverently. He still couldn't think of any of this as his own. This was his father's, and always would be to him. Maitan was simply a servant. He'd worn the armor in a time of great need. But he would forever be Morgaine's servant.

Laying on top of the surprisingly comfortable but small bed, a knock came at his door. Leaning upon his elbows, he said, "Come!"

The door opened, and Asharra appeared. Suddenly realizing he was half-naked, Maitan threw the blanket from the bed over his midsection. Asharra turned until he did so, closing the door behind her.

She waited until he said, "You may turn around now, First Mate. What do you need?"

She turned and bowed low, and he saw she was carrying medical supplies and ointments. She also had brought a small bottle of whiskey or rum. "I've come to help with your injuries, Master. The others are being tended to or have been."

She kept her eyes low, not looking into his own.

"Asharra, look at me," Maitan commanded, and she did so, still looking at him under her brows. "I accept your help. Please do what you can. I am in pain and my wounds were tended only partially by my Mistress' guard before I returned. I could use the aid."

She nodded and proceeded, coming to the foot of his bed. Maitan removed the blanket and closed his eyes. Being a physician of sorts himself, he was impressed with her knowledge and acumen. She repaired several cuts, pulled, and reworked stitches expertly, and poured the alcohol (rum) upon the wounds to remove infection. She rebandaged all his wounds and put salve on the smaller cuts and bruises. He had far more than he'd realized.

"Turn over, Master," she said, and he did so.

She began working on his back, pulling out shards of metal from the blast, pouring in rum, and closing them up one at a time. It took over an hour. After she got everything patched up, she began kneading his muscles and rubbing his neck, making sure to avoid the multiple areas where he'd been wounded.

Within minutes, he was asleep.

When he awoke, she was gone, but the medical supplies were sitting in his chest next to the armor, so they wouldn't move around or break. The ship was moving, and it was night. Returning his head to the pillows, Maitan decided he liked traveling by ship. The moving and tossing of the waves was, for him, as peaceful as being rocked in a crib by his mother.

The port window was open and the waves crashing into the side of the hull were like waves crashing on a shore.

Maitan fell asleep again. He dreamt of the mornings when he had been a child, his father training him from the earliest of his days. Those times had been the happiest of his life. In the dimness of his thoughts, as he floated through those times again in his dreams, he sleepily wondered why they had come upon him so suddenly again now.

After all this time.

CHAPTER 203

Dawn was approaching the following day…and Morgaine, riding next to Nathan, was in a great deal of pain. She tried not to wince as she rode, but her discomfort was clearly intolerable.

Nathan, riding beside her, finally ordered their column to stop.

They'd decided to head back immediately and try to get back to the open Arc Gate portal as soon as possible. Whereas the King and the Rondorian army had set up camp near the battlefield and would leave in the morning for their homeland. King Rondor IV and the Duke had given their goodbyes and Morgaine had promised to visit sooner than ten or twelve years to celebrate their victory before they had departed.

Nelrae had been cowed. The Eastern Empire was routed. Rondor was restored and the Dark influence had been cut out from amongst them. For now, at least. Nathan, seeing Morgaine, cared for none of that at this moment.

The woman was in agony. Dismounting and going over to her, he placed his hand on her saddle. She looked down at him, pain clear on her face.

"Maybe we should send Treyborne ahead to get the sky cruiser and have him come back to get us? We can camp here for a day or so and you can rest. The fact that she simply nodded to this and began to slowly dismount was evidence enough of her suffering to Nathan.

Treyborne, who'd already heard it, nodded, and said, "Messau, Jasper, Gerantor…you're with me! The rest set up a tight perimeter along that tree line," he pointed to a hill a quarter of a click away. "Then come retrieve our Lady after camp has been set up and a safety perimeter has been established. Not before!" Turning to Morgaine, he said, "I'll be back in less than a day if I push. And I intend to. Messau is as tough as old rock. And no one else coming has any injuries. We'll be back before you know it!"

She nodded, grimacing as she did so. Holding her head, she looked up through her fingers, "Do that, Captain. I will be awaiting you. Leave me any alcohol you have. I need to assuage this headache."

Captain Treyborne pointed and miraculously two bottles of wine appeared from someone's saddlebags. Apparently, this wasn't the first time she'd asked for alcohol in the middle of nowhere. Popping the corks, he turned to Nathan and said, "Enjoy!" Then he whispered, "Her headaches – especially after fighting – can be horrendous. Keep an eye on her. She's always pushed herself. But…" he looked back at her, "… she was injured coming into this. You know how bad she was. I'm afraid this one is going to be far worse than normal. Plus, her physical injuries are again not without some danger."

Nathan just nodded, taking the bottles. The other guards had already ridden off and were amongst the trees, searching for whatever squirrels and birds presented some sort of danger. There was simply no one around. Nathan couldn't imagine there were any. But he also understood that if there were, Trey's precautions would be saving their lives. And he also was exhausted. He couldn't even imagine how Morgaine must feel.

Morgaine came and leaned on his back, wrapping her arms around his waist until Treyborne and his team rode off. "I need that wine," she said, almost mumbling. "but I'll hold on to you until I get some."

Laughing, he turned, and she was right there. Bruised, bloodied, eyes drooping and back bent in pain. But she was still the most magnificent woman he'd ever seen. Beautiful enough to dry any man's mouth and get his heart racing. She looked up at him.

Those…eyes…

"What am I going to have to do to get some of that wine…?" she asked, looking at his hands.

"I can think of something…"

"Well, whatever you propose, I'm going to have to save it for a future day and time." She fell, rather than sat down, and Nathan handed her a bottle, as they had no cups. She tilted her head back and drank a long, multiple swallow drink.

He took a sip of his own, saying, "You might want to go a little slower…"

She looked over at him, her hair falling amongst her eyes, almost hiding them. "I have no intention of doing so. And you will take no advantage of me whilst I linger in your tent drunk, I might add! I will have my revenge if you do!" She then pulled another long drink from her bottle, eyeing him suspiciously. She cracked a smile.

"Does wine help you that much that quickly?" he asked, incredulous.

"No…! But thinking of you taking advantage of me does!" She winked, then took another drink. "Perhaps I will let you live, should you dare to violate me. I will entertain the idea…".

Shaking his head, Nathan took another drink. One of the riders was heading their way.

Standing Nathan said, "They're coming back. Come on, I'll ride with you on Steel, and you can just hold on. We'll get over there and you can rest in the shade."

Taking another drink, she tried to get up, but winced in pain. Nathan came over and gently helped her up. The guard, whose name Nathan did not know, saluted.

"Mistress, the tents are set up, and the perimeter is secure. We will have guards watch all four corners and patrol the area until Captain Treyborne returns."

"You'll do no such thing, Tramm! You'll all sleep in rotations and keep watch. Patrolling is ludicrous. We're not a click or two from the battlefield any longer. Yes, there will be stragglers. But none are going to attack a group of our size. And if they do, we have blasters. Keep an eye out, but we'll make camp, eat food, and sleep. A maximum of three guards on duty at any given time. Is that clear?"

"M'Lady! Captain Treyborne gave us specific instructions…"

"Who is in command here, Tramm?" She glared at him. Clearly the wine was kicking in a little.

"You are, M'Lady!" he said miserably. He sighed as he turned and waited for them to mount up. Nathan knew Trey would ask and then Tramm would get into trouble. He shared a commiserating glance with him. The man just nodded.

He seemed to read Nathan's mind.

Helping Morgaine up took a considerable amount of effort, despite her petite size and weight. Another sign of her level of energy and the pain levels she must be experiencing.

After she was up, Nathan handed her both bottles he'd placed on the ground and climbed up behind her. Wrapping one arm around her and taking his bottle from her other hand, they rode off slowly, following Tramm to the campsite.

One of the men had started a fire, even though it was just morning, and had a pot already sitting over it. He was throwing something into it, possibly some meat and vegetables for a stew. Nathan couldn't tell what they were, but he hardly cared. He suddenly realized he was hungry.

Morgaine was sipping from her bottle, as long drinks while riding a horse was difficult.

Once they got to the tree line, the shade coupled with the breeze became quite pleasant. There were three tents up as well. Morgaine started towards the furthest one on the left, and Tramm spoke up, "Lady Morgaine…the central tent…"

"Is not going to be mine," she said, "Nathan and I need rest. Especially me. We will be on the edge of camp. If you wish to sit quietly in a circle around us, you are welcome. But I'm going to sleep. As soon as I've finished…" she took another swig, "….my wine."

As she shook it, it appeared to Nathan that she wasn't far from accomplishing that goal.

Nathan just gave Tramm another look and got down before helping Morgaine. One of the men handed him two bedrolls and a couple small pillows they had packed behind their horses. Nodding, Nathan took them and laid them in the grass inside the tent. Morgaine finished her bottle, throwing it into the trees. She then laid down on one of the rolls, grabbed both pillows and closed her eyes. She was asleep before Nathan could even close the flaps. Keeping them open instead, he went outside to see what was cooking.

It was indeed a stew, and packets of spices and salt were just being added. Apparently, one of the men was a pretty good cook, and the others always gave him their meats and things they found for him to make stews with. The man's name was Rostinow. And he was from somewhere back east. Sitting down with the men, they talked about the battle.

They were all amazed at Maitan, who had always been like an older man secretary and part time medic for the team. It seemed to Nathan that they'd all heard he was a descendant of these *Biaki Mor* – an ancient people bred for war by the Elder Race – but no one knew what that really meant. And no one alive had ever seen one. Except Morgaine and Maitan himself, of course.

The stew was excellent, and Nathan ate two bowls. Finally, along about midday, he went to lie down in the tent himself. Morgaine hadn't moved. So much so that Nathan panicked for a moment and checked to see if she was still breathing. She was…and he breathed easier himself. Her side still oozed, and her leg gash – bandaged and stitched yesterday, needed a change. But she was so peaceful lying there. He hoped the wine did her some good and didn't just make her headache worse tomorrow. Lying down next to her, he laid his arm on her and just looked at her. Her hair had fallen over her face again. Somehow this just made her more beautiful.

She was such an amazing woman. Having lived so long, fought against the Dark so long…and to be such an incredible beauty. Nathan couldn't imagine what it must be like to be her. He still didn't quite get her infatuation with him. Would it even last…? Was it just because she thought – and she had more than half-convinced him – that he was from her 'Elder Race'?

That was still a mystery he meant to get at. But to do that, he had to go home. Perhaps going back home for a time was going to be necessary. It would if he were ever to figure that part of his own history out.

Thinking about these things, Nathan fell asleep.

He awoke to the moons shining overhead. It had to be past midnight. First, he checked on Morgaine. At some point, she had risen, because her bandages had been replaced. And she had changed her clothes.

Wow. I must've been out of it!

But she was sleeping again. Nathan noticed the remainder of his wine was gone, also. She had apparently helped herself to it while he slept.

He could almost imagine her gloating over him while he slept, drinking the remainder right in front of him.

The guards were out patrolling. Apparently, their fear of Treyborne was stronger than it was of Morgaine. Nathan got up and started for the single remaining fire. There was a rustling in the trees, and Nathan pulled his shock-lance out, snapping the electricity on the end to life.

A few moments later, a buck deer bounded out and down the hill. Followed by his doe. The guards, who'd also heard it, re-holstered their blasters. Looking up, Nathan asked one of them, "Any idea what time it is?"

The man hit a button on his wrist and said, "0175, sir!" Almost two hours past midnight. "Sun will be up in a couple hours. Get some rest. We've got these deer handled!"

Nathan laughed. He headed back to his tent, closed the flap, and Morgaine's voice drifted over to him, soft like a river, "I thought you'd never wake up."

"I woke up a while ago, you were asleep again."

She sighed in the dark. "Yes, I figured that happened when I looked for you, and you were gone. I drank the rest of your wine. You shouldn't just leave things like that lying around!" She laughed, a sweet, musical laugh.

Her hand touched his face. "I don't want you to go back. But it seems you have things to do there. I cannot leave here, lest my brother breach the portal. Plus, it seems when you go over there, you may have much more to deal with. I wish I could help you…"

"You've done plenty, Morgaine! Including dying a few times just to prove your point. I think *we've* done a lot here. And you and your team have wiped two of the Dark Lords from existence. That's quite an accomplishment!"

"You have no idea…" she said softly. "But as long as one remains, especially with it being my brother…"

"I realize how that must eat at you," he said. "But yes, I should go back. Not just for Smyslin and your men. But I've also got some questions regarding my own parentage, and how I came to be on Earth and living in the 21st century. It seems you should know what happened, also. How the timing of my coming was so…"

"Perfect…?" she finished for him. "The Creator is the answer. Whether you believe in Him or not, He exists. Not only that, but He controls all things, including time. All things work to the good of those who love and serve Him. How you came to that time, or why I was left to believe I was the last of my race, when clearly that is not the case, I have no idea. My father knew, though."

"Oh? How so…?"

"He…told me things. Things that didn't make sense once I became the lone survivor of our race. Now, they do."

"What things?" She was silent. "Morgaine?"

"I'm here. I don't think I'm ready to tell you yet. I'm sorry. But tonight…"

Suddenly, her body was next to him. She pulled him close, and he found she was anything but clothed. Looking up, Nathan saw that the tent flap was open just a bit still, although it was very dark outside. The only light under these trees and this tent was leaking in from the campfire. No one could see anything in here. Least of all, them.

Morgaine was kissing him, while fumbling with his pants and trying to pull his shirt off simultaneously. How many hands did this woman have?

Feeling her press against him, he helped her unclothe himself. Then he lost himself in making love to the most beautiful, sensual woman he'd ever met.

General Davis nodded as Ellie entered the room. His squad of 'missionaries', as he called them had been ready for hours. Apparently, he didn't want to send them through until she returned.

The President had demanded it, in fact. The President and his Chief of Staff wanted to ascertain the portal's stability one more time before sending their men through. They had expedited her paperwork, and she was inside the room within the hour.

Ellie walked over and stopped before him. "General…"

"Miss Ellie. How quickly can you verify for me that the portal is still stable? I cannot be sending my men through without knowing for sure they can come back. We'll give them a timeline based on your recommendations, and then can move forward. Finally. I want this done and them gone within the next thirty minutes, if possible."

"Well, General…that depends."

"Depends on what, Doctor?"

"On how fast you can release the prisoners you have from this other world and send them home. They can go with your team, or separately. I don't care. But the deal I made with the feds was that once I got this gate open, they could go home. It's open. They're not home. I won't give you a timeline until you agree to let them go and they leave in front of my own two eyes."

"Now, Miss Ellie…"

"Don't 'Miss Ellie' me, General! I mean now! I've done more than you've asked. More than you could have possibly dreamed. I'm simply asking – no, I'm *demanding* – that the government honor their word and let those men go home!"

The General stepped back half a step and looked at her. Then he laughed, shaking his head. Turning his head, he yelled, "Get me the President! I need to talk to him." He looked over at his staff. "Now, gentlemen!"

About ninety minutes later, Smyslin, Agino, and Rost were all shuffled into the top floor of the building. They were wide-eyed at the Arc Gate, humming loudly and the lights within the ring circling. The electricity crackling.

Ellie noticed they had neither the weapons they'd come with, nor their clothing. Everything they'd brought in, except their very bodies alone was staying, apparently. Well…technically, that *was* the deal. Ellie had little doubt their 'blasters' were being reverse engineered as she was thinking about it. Or already had been.

Rost nodded to Ellie. Agino waved. Smyslin came up and hugged her. "They say they're letting us go, Ellie! They said you were 'obstinate' and that you refused to help them unless we were released."

She nodded, smiling. "It was the least I could do, Smyslin! Boys, when you go back, be careful. We really don't know what's happened over there since you left!" They all nodded but were clearly overjoyed at their pending return.

The General came up. "We had a deal, Miss Ellie. What's the stability look like?"

She turned to him, letting Smyslin go for the moment. "It's got at least 24 hours left, sir. I'd say 30 tops, before the power cycle collapses in on itself. That should give your men more than enough time to get whatever samples they want and collect whatever data they choose...."

"Ellie!" Smyslin said, "No! The Gate is in the underground Base Morgaine and her people built centuries ago! She wouldn't want them coming through and..."

"I'm afraid that's not up to us, Smyslin. You're just going to have to trust that the General here..."

"No!" he said and began racing for the portal.

"Stop him!" the General ordered. "No guns!" Several marines standing nearby tackled and subdued Smyslin. Rost and Agino looked at them, then at Ellie.

"General! What do you think he was going to do...?"

"I have no idea, Miss Ellie. But that's why I stopped him. He and his friends can come through. But only after my team has been there a good hour. Are we clear? *One hour.* Then you can send them through – or I will – after they've had a chance to get in there and set up camp a bit."

Ellie just nodded. Shrugging, she turned to Agino and Rost. "Go sit in those chairs over there, boys. It'll be a bit before you are able to return home yet." Then, looking over at poor Smyslin, laid out on the ground with three marines holding him, she yelled, "Let him go! For goodness' sake, he's a hundred-year-old man!" Or so she thought, anyway.

The general nodded, but added, "Keep him away from that portal." He turned, "Major, post a guard around it! Strike team, suit up! You're on the clock. You have 24 hours to get in and get out with whatever you find suitable. Get going! Now!"

The four men and one woman, already suited up, grabbed their gear, and walked towards the portal. And, for the first time in several days… the portal pulsed. Light flashed as the group approached.

And they were gone.

CHAPTER 205

Brianna had now gone through several sleepless nights. Worrying about the open Gate. Worrying about Trey. Worrying about Morgaine. It just didn't lend itself to good rest. Even when she managed to get to sleep, the first time she awoke, her worries came crashing down on her.

Bleary-eyed, she was visiting the Gate again. She came by at least three or four times each day to check directly on its status. She just didn't trust that whoever or whatever might come through from the other side might not be some horrific monster, or a large military force. Or something worse.

The guards on site were good men. The area was set up with the stasis field that could be activated at the touch of a button. But still…it was all so new to her.

She had to remind herself that only a few months ago, her biggest worries were milking her cows and getting into town for some seed or honey.

Shaking her head, she walked by the Arc Gate, waving at the men. They waved back. The Gate was pulsing as usual. And the humming seemed louder than ever. It was like a swarm of bees or locusts had mated until they'd turned into light. And they all just swirled around each other in a circle inside the portal area itself.

Noise and light seemed to be its primary function. It was so bright. Brighter than the sun.

Heading upstairs in the lift, she came to the kitchens. They'd been massively resupplied since arriving, with new supplies coming every day.

They now had enough to feed their little army for at least two years. That was just in dry goods.

One of the kitchen staff sat her down and made her eat some porridge. With some honey and butter. It was delicious…but once she got up again, she felt again how just horribly tired she was.

Hitting her comm, she spoke into it, "Mikell, Dax, Ethan…this is Brianna. I'm going to take a two-hour break and sleep some more. I've not gotten enough, and nothing had changed. Awaken me if anything does. Or if the expedition team gets home."

"Check that, Princess Bri," Dax responded, *"All's quiet on the portal front. Plus, I saw you walk by not ten minutes ago. Outside is fine, too. Looks like a good olive crop this year."*

"I'm thrilled. Truly," she said, "Brianna out."

Getting to her room, she felt how cool it was. The lights were all out, as well, so the dark fit her mood. Disrobing to her underclothes, she luxuriated in the bed for a long moment. She even took off her undershirt to get a little cooler. Her worrying tried to hit her, but this time she either didn't care enough, they were too old, or she simply was too tired.

She fell asleep.

A jarring sound hit her ear, shocking her awake in an instant. *"Dax to Bri! Dax to Bri! We have visitors. Repeat! We have visitors!"* There was a lot of yelling.

Brianna hit her comm as she leaped to her feet, "Hit the stasis button, Dax! Hit the stasis button!" Racing to put her clothes on, she flew out of her office, still throwing a shirt over her chest. The guards in the hallway might just have gotten a free look. Brianna hardly cared.

Running down the stairs to avoid waiting for the stupid elevators, she got down to the main central cargo bay where the Arc Gate still pulsed crazily. Dax had indeed hit the 'Stasis' button. And what Brianna saw did not please her.

In fact, it was frightening.

Dax turned to her, along with another guard. He said, "Five of them Mistress. They've got weapons and all sorts of tech we've never seen before. What do we do with them?"

"How long can we keep them like this?" she asked.

"Indefinitely. But if forty or fifty more of their friends decide to come, we won't have room for them all in the Stasis Field. It'll crack." He looked to her for answers.

How did I, as a small town farmgirl, get to be in charge of all these people?

"Can we take away their weapons and gear without injuring them? Are they awake in there?"

"Yes and…" looking at one of the more experienced guards, who nodded, Dax answered, "…yes. They can see and hear us, assuming their hearing is good. And they speak our language."

"Then disarm them, but don't assume they're powerless simply because we took their guns. Dark Men aren't. After you have all their stuff, release them on my command."

Saluting as if Brianna were Morgaine herself, Dax went up to the elder guard and whispered something. The man went over to the Stasis Field Generator and hit a couple buttons. All the blaster weapons they carried, and all the extra things made of metal zipped straight to the floor, sticking there. He then turned and looked at Brianna, holding his finger over another button.

The yellow one.

"Guards!" she yelled, "Aim your blasters right at them. Make sure they know we mean business." They did so, all eight of them, as more had been called before Brianna had arrived.

She nodded.

The field dropped and the people, to a man (and woman) fell to the ground, then leaped back onto their feet and put their hands up as if they were going to fight. Not in acts of surrendering. Brianna called out to them above the still loud thrum of the Arc Gate. "Who are you? Why are you here?"

The woman stepped forward. She'd have been pretty with longer hair and some makeup. As it was, she was dressed like the men and just looked like a shorter version of one of them. "Us come in peaceful. Want talking with leader."

Rolling her eyes, Brianna said, "Get me another vocal translator. I saw one more in that cabinet area where we found the one for Gary. And get him down here! Maybe he can be of some use to us!" One man ran one way, the other another.

Brianna spoke loudly again, "If you came in peace, why all the guns?"

The woman spoke again, seemingly prepared for this question. "Just for we walked in peaceful, no mean see we peaceful here. Might could wild animals chewing, or no smart animals."

Brianna grimaced. *Fair enough.* "Do you know Ellie? Or Nathan?"

"Ellie swallowed portal we. No knowing Nathan. Him name heard, maybe?"

Brianna elected to wait for the translator before any further questioning could occur. Gary arrived before the translator piece, oddly enough. He came in and said, "Oh shit."

"'Oh shit,' Gary? What does that mean?" Brianna demanded.

"It means a big pile of stinking poop, Brianna. But that's not important right now. What it means is that the US fucking Marines have landed in your home world. And no matter what they say, I wouldn't trust them as far as I could throw them…"

"Who big rat speak such stinky?" the woman yelled. "Me demanding big person speak now."

Brianna rolled her eyes again. She still needed more sleep, and irritation was a constant threat to cause an explosion. "Shut it, woman! I'm getting you a translator piece, now…hold on!"

The guard finally came back, holding the clip. Brianna nodded to the woman. "Give it to her. She seems like she's most likely to get the best use out of it. Take them all down to the lower floor dorms. We can keep them there until we figure out what to do with them."

Turning, Brianna asked the woman just as she got the clip put in, "How did you learn our language so fast? Did Smyslin and the others teach you?"

The woman shrugged. "They speak, I listen…Hey! This is like awesome! I wish I had one of these!" That last half was with the translator in her ear.

"You do now," Brianna said to her, waving as she turned away. "Come on and follow me. All your people. Let's see how 'peaceful' you are while we get you some food and talk about whether we're going to let you go." Turning to Dax, she added, "Get their weapons and equipment and put it somewhere safe."

Nodding and saluting, he ran to comply with her orders.

CHAPTER 206

Jezerah brooded in his compound. Dark Men were bustling here and there. Curtaise was silent, standing at attention. How long had he been there? Hours, surely.

Well, he could wait.

Omrion had come and stood beside him at some point, as well. No matter. Jezerah had to think. There had to be a way to take advantage of all this. He'd done it once before. Back when he'd been the first the Void had reached out to. The Dark had instructed him who amongst the travelers should be contacted. Each one indicated had joined their cause. Even when they'd numbered less than a dozen and just begun, they had been beyond powerful.

Acting as a team, they'd destroyed the orbital platform that had held the last of their people within their mother system. At least half of the Elder Race had died that very day. The stragglers, across the cosmos, they'd hunted down while they were performing their 'consultative roles' with various species. Always in groups of ones or twos. None amongst the Elder Race had had children – purebred children at least – for a hundred years even back then.

Emorion, Markam, K'Thul, Mordron, Pallatriax, Fenix, Pirimo…they had all been together then. A team. A team of the Dark. Scouring the galaxy, they sought out and killed nearly all they could find. Then they began to be attacked. Half of the Dark Brethren were killed. Gathering together, they retreated to the planet Arth that they had set aside for the purpose of creating their armies. The remainder of the Elder Race would eventually form into the strike team that came after them here all those centuries ago.

Arth, being the furthest out on one of the arms on the edge of the galaxy, had seemed the safest place to consolidate their power. Especially after Mordron had successfully erased its terraforming records from the Platform's databases. It was here on this planet that they'd warped its peoples, where they'd begun experimenting with the genetic codes and creating creatures more suitable to their unique purposes.

None of them had even considered they'd be attacked here. Not as a group. Until their forward scout teams off world had warned them of it. Morgaine, with their brother Tabor and a host of others, had poured through the Arc Gate. It had seemed to Jezerah at the time that it must have been every single Elder Race being left in the entire galaxy. It was not only his belief, however. They'd all thought it. Even Morgaine.

How wrong they must have been!

All this time, a few must have survived, somehow even having children again. It was the only explanation for the young man he'd seen on the fields of Nelrae. And all the while, Jezerah and his former Dark Brethren had been left on this rotting twig of a world to wither and die! Morgaine had played her part to perfection. Perhaps she'd even been led to believe it herself on purpose. Maybe they all had.

Fools!

He wasn't sure if he should include himself in that or not.

Snorting in derision, he stood up suddenly. His quick action had led to salutes from both Omrion and Curtaise. He acknowledged them finally. Perhaps if he spoke with them, they'd leave him alone long enough to come up with a plan. One had not emerged thus far. He was losing faith that one would come to him. The Void had been unusually silent for quite some time.

"What is it, generals? Have we not lost enough battles?"

Omrion spoke first. "Master. The Dark Knights are down to fourteen members, sir. I wish to promote some of our best from the ranks of the Quartermasters…".

"Fine. Do it. Leave! Next…? Wait!" Omrion turned from departing and bowed again. "Make sure to promote Imutaph. Assuming he survived." Omrion bowed and withdrew.

Curtaise saluted, "Sir, we have done our head count. A full two thirds of our forces are gone. Many are also injured, but we are applying our medical treatments and the Dark elixirs to them. They will recover. But we did at least get away from both the Eastern Empire forces and the Rondorian Army incursion as you commanded. Had we not left when we did, we'd have lost even more."

He stepped back, then lowered his head. He again seemed to expect execution.

Jezerah made a sound of frustration. Curtaise didn't move. Jezerah almost obliterated him for his quiescence at the idea of being destroyed. Again, this failure wasn't any more his fault than it was Omrion's. It was his own.

"Stand up, Curtaise…" he said finally, irritation clear in his voice. "You are not going to die today. Or any time soon. Again, you've done what you could with what you were dealt. K'Thul's attacks were ferocious and never ending. Then we were hit by both Rondorian forces and Morgaine herself. I still want to know where these other Elder Race beings have come from. And how many there are. What weapons they bring…all things I must know to proceed. I admit – Curtaise – only to you, that I thought the stories of another purebred Elder Race being were at best wild exaggerations. If not outright lies or mistakes from the field. Even a half-breed would have been believable. But this…?"

Curtaise nodded grimly.

"The one thing I'm certain of now: the only Dark Lord remaining is standing before you. I felt K'Thul die even as I fled the battle. Whoever was with Morgaine on that side of the attack finished him. Or she did."

"Yes, Master," was all Curtaise said.

What could he say? 'You were all fools?'

"Find me that information, Curtaise! That is your new mission. Emorion has died…I want to know how and by whom. K'Thul is also dead. Details. Information! Get your spies on it. Find out all you can about the new influx of Elder Race beings. Are there more than one, to start. This is our new war now. Get on it."

Curtaise saluted, bowed, and left.

Sighing, Jezerah announced over his comm, "Bring me some of the slave women! I need a distraction! And if anyone comes to speak with me or disturbs me for the next five hours, I will execute everyone responsible!"

One of the staff had the audacity to respond. *"As you command, Great One."* Jezerah decided to promote the man in the morning. Or execute him. He would decide tomorrow.

Jezerah stormed off to his personal chambers. But it wasn't sleep that was on his mind. He needed something else this evening. He could almost feel pity for those women.

CHAPTER 207

The following morning Treyborne and company landed the sky cruiser in the field where they'd left Morgaine the day before. Morgaine, Nathan, and the guards had already broken camp as he'd let them know by comms that they were incoming over an hour ago.

Loading up took mere minutes. The horses were a bit of a burden. They didn't want to get into the cramped thing. Finally, two of the men were left to take all the horses the slow route. Which would take over a week.

Treyborne said he'd send the land cruiser for them if he could. Once the humans were all aboard, Trey lifted off and said back into the comms, *"Not sure you heard, as it was over the satellite uplink, but we have some new visitors back home, Morgaine."*

Her head swiveled. Speaking into the comm herself, she answered, "No. I hadn't. What are the details?"

"Military types — five of them. Nathan's home world. They came heavily armed. Brianna's debriefing them after stasis field stripped them of any harmful…articles."

"I'm not sure Brianna is equipped to deal with alien military and their intelligence squads. I've not even dealt with such before. And they won't just be sending simple militia. If these don't come back, more will come. Get us there as fast as you can, Trey. Get me on the uplink, as well. I'm assuming Briann left it open. I want to check in with her and see where they are at this very moment."

"Aye, Mistress!" Trey said, saluting to the air in front of him. *"Uplink coming in three minutes."*

True to his word, the satellite uplink was operational on their end in minutes. Brianna reported that the squad of four men and one woman were separated and abiding by the rules that were laid down by her and the guards. She said she was considering letting them go topside and then retrieving them in an hour. They apparently wanted soil samples, wanted to take pictures of the landscape, and other minor things like that.

"They also said that Smyslin and the others should be returning any time." Brianna said. *"Let me know what you think we should do, Morgaine. I'll follow your lead, of course."*

Morgaine looked at Nathan. "What are your thoughts?"

"Me…? Well, I'm not one to trust the government or the military overmuch. But if you just let them topside to gather some dirt and plants, I don't see any long-term pain in that. If they're letting Smyslin go, that should be able to delay any of my traipsing back through the portal for a while, as well. I mean…I really need to find what happened to my parents and all that. But other than that, I'm here for now. We should get Gary back, though," he added.

Nodding, she said into the comm, "Let them gather their samples. Set a time limit and make sure they understand your timing. Call me if anything goes sideways or if anything seems strange. Clear?"

"Yes, Morgaine. And thanks. I'm glad you're all right."

"Much appreciated, Brianna. I couldn't agree more. Morgaine out!"

"I'd like to see Gary before he goes back. But I'd also like to know why the Arc Gate is still open," Nathan said to her over the sky cruiser propulsion systems. He didn't want everyone hearing all this.

Morgaine nodded, looking at him strangely again.

"What?" he asked. She reached into her blouse, and he was wondering where this was going, when she pulled her hand out and the medallion was there. She unclasped it and gently reached over, putting it back around his own neck.

"This belongs to you now. And you do have to go back. The Corillion told me so when I first gave it to you."

"But…I did go back after that. The medallion is how I returned."

Morgaine looked away, eyes distant. "Yes, you did. But that was just the first time. You must go back three times. And the third time…you aren't coming back." She looked over at him, eyes glistening. "I'm hoping you only go twice. But Nathan…if there is a third time, we will never see each other again."

CHAPTER 208

Bantor was sitting in the same marketplace where he'd met Jasper. Several other lesser candidates had come since then. And Bantor had learned. He had placed several of the men in regular local clothing about the market circle, to keep an eye on him.

Although the King had changed in Rondor – and he was expecting his estates and land to be formally returned to him by the new one soon – he still had a job to do. Recruiting for Morgaine was a full-time job these days. Men were dropping right and left (he wasn't bringing this up, but it was the reason for the outrageous sums of money these men received), and mercenaries that were both reasonably good men, and good at what they did, did not grow on trees.

He also helped recruit staff members and workers for the fields when he wasn't sitting in the market circle watching the people barter, sell, and trade. The bakery nearby did have amazing muffins, as well. So, he often enjoyed a warm muffin with his tea. Sandwiches with fresh beer would be his fare by lunchtime. And then he would make his way back to the farm.

A certain girl had caught his eye. He hoped it wasn't just because she was rather comely. A beautiful form with long blond hair tied behind her. She worked at one of the farmer's stands, clearly a farm girl. But she also apparently had a bright mind and he often saw her bartering with the other farmers and even going into the shops, trading goods, and appearing to come out handsomely.

Her parents ran a vegetable stand, and she couldn't be more than eighteen or nineteen years of age. Often in the farming communities, girls like her were married once they reached sixteen or higher. Apparently, her parents had some education or followed more of the civic codes that required a young woman to be at least eighteen to marry.

Many farmers came every weekend to sell their cash crops. But this weekend the only farmers who came was the young woman's family and one other. They set up shop across from each other, so this time the girl and her family were right in front of Bantor's favored "watching post".

The girl kept carrying rather heavy loads of beans, baskets of corn, tomatoes, and onions. Each time, she glanced his way with a sly eye. Finally, on what was apparently her last trip, she stopped and stared at him rather plainly, carrying a large bucket of potatoes.

Bantor raised his cup of tea and toasted her.

She responded in the sassy country accent of the Petty Kingdoms, "Why aren't ya workin'? I think I've a seen ya every weekend I've come for near two months! Don't ya have a job? Or is it just sittin' and drinkin'?"

Laughing at her boldness, Bantor stood and bowed formally. "My apologies if my dalliance with the fair weather of your city annoys you, my child. I am Councilman Bantor of the City of Rondor. I am, however, currently employed by a local…conglomerate…to hire various people of differing skills before I return to my native lands."

The girl set the potatoes down by her father, who was categorically ignoring her. Clearly, she had blasted other people for not working in the market before today. Bantor saw her father glance at her sideways, similarly to how the girl had done to him – he saw where she got it from. Walking over, she sat right down in the chair in front of him.

"Ok," she said sharply. "Interview me."

Bantor was taken aback. "I'm…not sure what job you'd qualify for, let alone want…" Sitting down, he saw she was indeed a handsome girl, with strong features and beautiful blue eyes.

He shrugged. "All right then…". Looking over at her father, the man literally shrugged and turned away. Her mother made a sound mothers make when exasperated to the point of giving up. "…what are your qualifications?"

"I work my ass off!" she retorted. "As you can see, I've barely got one left!" she lifted her butt off the chair and turned around. She seemed to still have one to Bantor, but he wisely made no comment, merely nodding.

"I see…and…?" he kept his eyes looking straight into hers. The farm girl's clothing did little to hide some of her other qualities, which included ample bosom and strong, tan skin.

"I'm smart. My pa says I've 'got the mind', and he lets me do all the 'horse trading' with the locals in town. He said they used to take him to the cleaners, him not knowing the worth a things in da city! Well, I got me a list in my 'ead, and there's no arguin' wit' me. The shopkeepers know ta stick to the rules and not try to cheat us when I come in!"

Bantor said, "I've noticed you going from shop-to-shop selling and trading before. You do seem to do well, by my poor estimation at least."

"By any, I tell ya!" she yelled. "Are ya dense or somethin'?" She gave him a stern look and seemed to scrutinize his face to see if he did, in fact, have a brain underneath.

Sitting back, he answered, "Perhaps you…could use a little work on your manners, however."

The girl made a sound but lowered her head a bit. "Dat's prolly true… my ma…" she looked over, "would agree wit' ya. But I can be trained on that! What's the job? I need a one, as my pa's selling the farm and they're retirin' this year. Movin' to da city. I don't know nothin' but farmin'. But I'm good at it. That and horse tradin'!"

Bantor sat back and took off his hat. Taking a sip of tea, he looked at the girl, who was sitting there, starting to squirm.

Good. At least she has some idea of how brash she is. But brash is better than timid. By a fathom or two.

"What's your name, farm girl? Mine is Bantor."

"Shireen. Most folks just call me 'Reena'. It's my grandmother's name," she said, looking back towards her parents. "My ma's ma."

Clearly listening, her mother just nodded, keeping her back to them, finishing setting up their booth. It seemed nearly ready to Bantor.

"Well, we do have a rather large olive grove. As well as a field or two of wheat. We could use a good steward of the grain and olives. Someone to keep the books. It seems no one topside…er…on the field team has a good accounting mind. How does five silver a week to start sound?"

Her eyes bulged, "It sounds like I'm quittin' today. Ma! I'm gonna count money and sell olives and wheat!"

Her mother said, "That's nice, dear. Make sure you get back here and do your tradin' first. You can quit later." Her mother looked over at her fondly. The girl looked back, clearly excited. She was a cutie.

Bantor watched and just felt the simple desire to help the girl out, plus smart people with practical sense were in a bit of a shortage these days. He stood up, putting his hand into his coat, "I'm done here today," and he bent down and wrote on a small piece of paper he pulled from his coat pocket, *"Please accept this young woman – named Shireen – into the farmer's group. NDA – Bantor."* He handed it to the girl. "There is a small map to the farm on the back."

The designation 'NDA' meant "No Downstairs Access". Only those who had "need to know" needed to know. Oftentimes, these days, with all the people downstairs coming and going, the farmers, sharecroppers, and their assistants would see things. The olive grove was so enormous that even a sky cruiser landing would be difficult to spot off the landing area. But it was sure easy to see within the confines of it. Not to mention the military-types coming and going. Up until Morgaine's arrival here, these people hadn't seen anything out of the ordinary in over a decade. Now, it was nearly a daily event.

Nonetheless, NDA meant "NDA". If questions were asked, stupid looks were the answers. The sharecropper family that knew all about Morgaine and the military complex below their feet were masters at it. Those folk could make you feel stupid saying the sun was yellow.

Shireen stood, still holding the note, and said, "Thanks! You won't regret it!" with a slight bow. He nodded and smiled.

"I certainly hope not. The owner of the property is very strict and expects a high level of performance. Nice meeting you." The girl practically bounced over to help her parents continue setting up their booth.

Bantor felt good about today. The girl really was special. And soon, Brianna may need help, as she was taking over more and more of the daily responsibilities of running all that went on "downstairs". At that point, the 'NDA' could come off, if deemed appropriate. Bantor hoped he was back home at his estates by then. Either way, it likely wouldn't be his concern. Bantor and the men that were his shadows all left via different paths from the market area. Another man left a few minutes later.

No one saw that last one leave.

CHAPTER 209

Maitan's ship, the *Dark Horse* pulled into Nyx harbor that very afternoon. Unloading some of the admittedly pirated goods and waiting for the harbormaster to assess any taxes and sign papers Maitan was leaving to Asharra. My'Rel and company were causing a bit of a stir on the docks. They were clearly Dark Men, wearing almost all black, but sporting white masks.

They were flying a flag that designated it as Rondorian. And their First Mate was a woman. A black woman also wearing a mask like the Dark Men did, but with the anomalous white. They were neither raiding, nor attacking. They were unloading. They were paying taxes.

They were also ignoring those around them. A circle of sailors, mostly from the trader city of Talim were gathering, weapons not out, but certainly in plain sight. Talim, sitting on an island oasis on the southern side at the mouth of the Yellow River and on the edge of the Great Desert was a trader city full of merchants…and thieves, if reports were correct.

But if anyone did any stealing around Talim, it was the people of Talim. They didn't take to others upping their game. And the Dark Raiders were notorious pirates and brought fear into the hearts of many a sailor.

So as Maitan watched from the deck, more and more sailors from around the harbor were gathering, just staring in open hostility at his crew and officers. As Maitan had instructed, they ignored anyone around them, and went about the business of setting up the goods for sale. If the City of Nyx wished to purchase them, they had first choice, as long as they paid ninety percent of fair market value. Then the merchants and traders down on the wharf were allowed to begin bartering and buying what remained.

Asharra finished paying the taxes assessed on the goods, and someone yelled, "That's the first they had to pay for those, I reckon!" Several others chimed in, "For sure!" and "You said it!"

Asharra looked that way a moment, displaying the wax seal of the harbormaster on her paperwork. She then pointed to her goods and said, "The city seems to have no need for any of this. Goods come from Eastern Empire and the islands. But I'm sure you won't be needin' any of that!"

Maitan raised an eyebrow, aware that her cockiness might get her in a handful of trouble. A dozen or more of the Dark Raiders on board were paying close attention. As was My'Rel, coming up on Maitan's left. The gangplank was down. And the over thirty men of Dark Raider caliber fighters were plainly seen walking around. Some sported shock-lances, while others had their *Djune* out and were sharpening their blades.

The tension was building. Enough that Maitan started walking forward, but My'Rel touched his arm and said, "Hold a minute, Master. Please. I think she's got this."

Then someone came forward, a merchant woman from Talim. She was dressed in the finery of the merchant class and had two very dark-skinned guards with her. Walking up, she began perusing the goods, especially those that had clearly come from the cedar trees of Scim's Warding. She also was ignoring the crowd, and asked, "How much for all these chests?"

A man yelled out, "You can't have 'em all! They're worth over ten gold apiece!" Several others yelled out, and more came forward, eager to get after some of the more valuable goods displayed on the dock. So, when the rest of the crowd surged forward, it was mostly the merchants, not the armed sailors, who sullenly and slowly began to disperse.

Once the trading had begun, and offers were coming in from all sides, coin and goods began changing hands. My'Rel gave Maitan a knowing glance and went back to the pilot's deck. Maitan nodded and strolled down the gangplank, not with the intention of interfering, but rather with the goal of going to find a horse to ride up to Base 2 with all speed. His armor, torn as it was, was packed into his saddlebags. His body was noticeably better after only two days under Asharra's direct medical ministrations, and he nodded cordially to her as he passed. The woman, despite being in the middle of a trade, bowed low to him and said, "Master."

This brought no small consternation amongst the people, as he was dressed in his normal clothing and appeared to be what he really was: a middle-aged man. At least for a *Biaki Mor*. But he nodded again to her and said, "First Mate. Please continue. I will return on the morrow."

Rising, she returned to her work. It seemed they'd be resupplying several ships with just this amount of goods. It also seemed he owned almost forty ships now. Seven of which were somewhere within the rather large confines of this bay, but far from shore. Anchored there and awaiting his further instructions. Maitan needed Morgaine's wisdom and insight here. These events had been completely unexpected. How could his calculations have accounted for this?

He had simply gone out to do what needed to be done.

His own life was irrelevant. Expendable. He had assumed he wouldn't be breathing by this time. His own calculations said that survival for him had been far less than one percent. Now, instead of being at the bottom of the sea, he was in control of nearly a fourth of the former Dark Raider navy. Or at least a very healthy chunk. No one on board seemed to know exactly how many there had been in total. The one person who might have known was dead.

Blessedly.

Finding a stable, he bought a horse instead of renting one. He owed Morgaine the price of her mare. Buying new saddle, blanket, bit, and bridle was another chunk. But he had plenty of coin. He made sure to use some of the money found in the captain's chest, however.

Morgaine shouldn't be forced to buy a new horse with her own coin. Attaching the saddlebags, Maitan mounted up on the small quarter-horse sized mare and began his ride by leaving the city through the North gates about twenty minutes later.

The city guardsmen of this city were about as corrupt as they came. But it was late afternoon, and these were simply lounging around. One was even snoring. Shaking his head, Maitan kicked the horse into faster speeds, and he began the journey up the hills to the olive grove.

He had to hope Morgaine was back by now. It simply depended on how far away they'd parked the sky cruiser from the battle itself. Either way, he needed her. What does one do with a navy full of former enemies, known as pirates and harbor raiders? It was a conundrum that neither his battle training, nor his deep understanding of battle tactics had prepared him for. Nor had his decades as Morgaine's servant and "team physician".

This mare was younger and more spirited than Maitan's last one, Light, had been. So, he started murmuring to her and talking so she would get used to his voice. Calming down a bit, she stopped her prancing step and the ride moved forward more smoothly. He decided to name her "Prancer."

As he rode, he caught up with Bantor, who was riding, but going slowly as three of the guards were walking back with him. Maitan waved and Bantor did a double take. "Maitan?! Where have you been?"

Maitan raised an eyebrow at him. "My good man, I've been out slaying Dark Lords and securing a navy for the Mistress. What have *you* been doing?"

Bantor's puffy eyebrows drew together, then went towards his forehead in surprise. Then he started laughing. "I should know better! You're as good a straight man as they come!" Then he got back to laughing, as did the guards.

Of course, they had no idea. Maitan tried not to be annoyed. He was largely unsuccessful. He could hardly blame them, however.

He was Morgaine's attendant. A waiter, a butler. A sometimes doctor. More often the latter recently, of course. But hardly a warrior or such similar nonsense. He could hardly believe it himself.

And he'd been there.

CHAPTER 210

The sky cruiser landed in the open bay that evening. Everyone was there to greet them. Maitan, Brianna, Bantor, Gary, and the ever-present resident guard team, currently headed by Mikell.

The military group of five had been released with non-weaponry equipment only to gather samples topside for two hours before returning. Brianna had restricted them to the olive grove grounds to avoid contact with anyone outside their circle.

She was sure they'd seen the sky cruiser come in, though, as they were surely still very close. She was glad about that for some reason. As the team disembarked, Brianna tried not to be nervous. It would be the first time she'd seen Treyborne in many days. And she didn't know how he would respond.

Or how she would. Calming her nerves, she came up and hugged Morgaine, who gingerly hugged her back. "Oh, I'm sorry!" Brianna exclaimed. "I forgot for a moment there…"

"It's all right, Brianna. I'm not a porcelain statuette. I've been handled worse," she said, looking to Nathan at her side, "But yes, I'm still very much in pain." Moving gingerly, Morgaine stepped down the small stairwell from the landing bay. Deeper down, as the bay was multi-level, Morgaine could see the Arc Gate rippling with power. Guards still encircled it, vigilant. Some turned and waved at her, however.

She waved back.

Even as they landed, Smyslin, Agino, and Rost all came through. The portal quivered for a moment. Treyborne and Messau ran down towards it almost immediately, followed by several of the other guards. Morgaine felt, rather than saw the power fluctuations. The portal was not going to remain open much longer. Apparently, the visiting team from Nathan's world was aware of this and had strict instructions to go back through within 24 of their hours. Only 12 of their hours remained, according to Brianna. Half a day. That was good. They had maybe 7 Arth hours remaining in that case. Assuming time was running close to evenly. It usually had in the past when there was an open bridge between worlds.

Meanwhile, Nathan was giving Gary a big hug and talking with him avidly. His friend was a large, burly man with dark hair, a beard, and a warm smile. Morgaine liked him instantly. Nodding, she came up to them as they parted. Nathan turned and said, "Gary, this is…Morgaine. She runs all this. This is her team, her complex…everything."

Gary's eyebrows went up a bit, and his eyes widened also. Then he smiled again, and extended his right hand, "Nice to meet you. Gary Rossi. Italian American at your service." He bowed over her hand as she grasped it.

"I see Nathan isn't the only gentleman from your world," she said laughing.

"Nathan's hardly a gentleman. Clearly you don't know him that well." Gary said, straightening. Nathan was looking at him strangely. "How… ah! The earpiece. And yes," he said, turning to Morgaine, "He's right. I'm no gentleman."

Morgaine nodded knowingly, then winked at him.

Gary tapped his head. "You should have seen me when I first saw one of these. Ellie was still wearing hers when they came through right after you went back. When I asked her how she could speak the language so well, she looked like she was pointing to her brain. In the irritating way only she can manage. Man, I was hot. I thought, 'What a little…'" then he looked at Morgaine, "…well you know."

Nathan laughed, "I can imagine!" Noticing someone else coming up to the sky cruiser, Nathan turned a bit and saw Smyslin. He was bowing and staying low. At the same time, Maitan had come up and touched Morgaine's arm.

"Smyslin…?" he said, and Smyslin rose.

"It is very good to see you, Master. It is…very good to be home!" He started to bow again, but Nathan grabbed him and hugged him. "I'm so glad you're ok and that you're back! I was about to go back to get you with Gary! You know he came through just to come get me so I could, didn't you?"

Smyslin looked over at Gary with an unreadable look. "Yes, I had heard. Thank you, Gary, Nathan-friend. Until Ellie pushed the military leader there, we were prisoners. I'm not sure what you could have done, Master," he said looking back. "There were many of them, and we were being held at a large facility with many defenses. I'm glad you didn't have to risk yourself coming for little Smyslin."

Nathan hugged him again, then said, "I'm sure we would have figured something out. But yeah, I'm glad, too. Welcome home."

Nathan looked up and saw Morgaine was still speaking with Maitan off to the side, away from the others. Brianna was standing nearby, and both women were looking perturbed. Maitan was also using his arms to speak – something Nathan had never seen him do. He was always so staid and…dry. Nathan tried to keep his attention on what Gary was saying, but there was something going on there. Seeing Maitan show up on the battlefield dressed in (admittedly tattered) armor, had been eye-opening. Oh well. No time for that now.

Grabbing Gary, he said, "Hey! Let's get some food and a drink. When do you go back?"

Gary turned to follow Nathan off the platform. "I'm not sure. The military types said Ellie told them less than 24 hours they needed to be back. That means I need to go with them. Since time doesn't go the same on both sides, according to you and her both…"

Nathan nodded. "Ok. Let's get some grub, have a beer or two and get you back. You've got to get back to Jenn, right?" Nathan gave him a chuck on the arm.

Gary's eyebrow rose, and he shrugged, "Maybe…? We're somewhere in between now. It's a little weird. She's at your desk now, and we talk like we used to. We laugh like we used to. It's just weird since…well…"

Nathan looked at him for a moment.

"Remember…she even admitted it might be a 'rebound' thing. I don't know…I'm just hoping it isn't, but you know. Can't pressure her either."

"Yeah, that never works. Well…you spotted her before I ever met her. You and she are a good fit. Just give it time. I have…" he looked over at Morgaine, "…someone else now. At least for a while."

"Yeah, I saw. Holy shit, Nathan. I mean, Jennifer is awesome…cute, sexy, even downright gorgeous at times. But that…?" He jerked his head towards where Morgaine was standing, still talking excitedly with Maitan. "That's simply inhuman, dude."

Nathan shook his head, "You have no idea, my friend. Come on…! Food, beer…well it's more like 'ale' here, but it's good! Then the portal."

The rest of the night went somewhat as expected. There was a big meal, and even the four marines and lady linguist joined them down in the main mess hall. The kitchens could hardly keep up, and the wine and beer kept flowing. One of the marines noted Gary's presence, clearly, though. He seemed to recognize him but said nothing. He scowled a lot, though.

Bantor, Jasper and a few of the others were having a discussion and playing a card game at the same time at another table. Jasper was clearly winning, causing no little amount of consternation on Bantor's part. Others joined in later and it became a bit of a rowdier part of the evening.

Around midnight, the military crew gathered up their gear, gave their thanks, got their weapons returned, and a watchful Treyborne and Morgaine saw them off. Nathan and Gary were there too, but they tried to stay as much in the background as he could, standing around where the other guards were positioned.

Morgaine watched the portal for a long time after they left, seemingly watching for something. Nathan's gemstone flickered a bit after they'd left also. That was odd.

Then it was Gary's turn.

Hugging each other goodbye, Nathan promised to come through soon. "I'm not ready," he said, looking straight at him. "But I'll let you know as soon as I do." He held up his phone, still mysteriously fully charged after all this time.

Gary nodded, "You'd better! You owe me bigtime. And I mean like rent, too!"

Nathan laughed, "I'll be sure to bring large piles of gold, as well." Gary laughed and nodded, said his goodbyes to the others he'd met, handed back the translator clip as the woman had, and grabbed his gear. Then he headed for the portal.

As he approached it, Nathan's gemstone suddenly lit up like a star, glowing and spinning light like he'd never seen it before, right through his shirt. Seeing it, Morgaine turned and yelled, "Gary! Wait!"

But it was too late. Waving, he stepped into the glowing portal entrance. Immediately it all winked out. The Arc Gate was no longer active.

Morgaine's hand was still held up high in the air. She turned to Nathan, lowering her hand slowly as she did so. The smile gone from her face.

"What's wrong?" Nathan asked, coming over to her. The gemstone had winked out as soon as the Arc Gate had.

Looking up at him, Morgaine said, "I'm not certain. But I suddenly felt the Dark…the Void. It was like it was right up here in this room! That's probably why the Corillion lit up so brightly. Didn't you feel anything?"

"I felt…something," Nathan responded. "I'm not sure what it was. Just a lot of power and tingling, then…nothing."

Morgaine nodded, looking back over towards the now dark Gate. "I'm just hoping he made it back all right. It was very close, Nathan. *Too close.* Perhaps it was just the feeling of the Void's power as it shut down. The gravitational forces of black holes and anti-matter is what fuels those things. That is the essence of the Void. I just wish I knew how they worked. But I wasn't even old enough to know how to put on my own clothes when they were invented. The technology on how to build them was lost with my father's generation."

She drew close to Nathan, looking up into his eyes. "I hate saying this… but you need to open the Portal again. You need to go back. Now. Or as soon as we can get you ready. I'll be fine here. I've got… many weeks to properly recover from the beatings my body has taken. The price those elixirs do in circumventing normal recovery must be paid."

Her hand was on his chest, looking up at him. "But maybe not tonight, all right? One more night before you go…"

Nathan nodded distractedly, looking at the darkened portal within the Arc Gate. That was how it normally was. He knew that. Why did it now appear so ominous? Worry for Gary gripped him. And until that worry was resolved, he wouldn't be able to sleep.

Looking down at Morgaine, leaning on his chest, he couldn't say no to her, though, either. "I'll go in the morning. Tell Trey and whoever else to get my stuff ready for me. But we'll have another night together first."

She hugged him tightly. She really was worried he would never return. Well, this wasn't the ominous 'third visit', anyway. Nathan was determined that visit never happened. Just in case this 'secret medallion prophecy' was real. Either way, it was real to her.

The Corillion medallion flickered again. *Go quickly.*

The inner voice was peaceful, even loving. But it had a sense of urgency. He tried to answer it in his head.

Like…now?

It flickered again. *Go quickly.*

Sighing deeply, he pulled Morgaine from him a bit and said, "I think the medallion is speaking to me now. It's saying I need to not delay. 'Go quickly,' It said."

Morgaine's eyes dropped to his chest where the Black medallion lay hidden beneath his shirt.

She nodded after a moment. "You must listen then. I will aid you. Do what you must, and I'll make sure the team has everything prepared."

She looked up then, and Nathan saw something in her eyes he'd hoped to not see again.

Hurt.

She hid it well, and her chin was high. Proud. Regal. The ultimate woman. But it was there. She smiled at him, but the hurt in her eyes never diminished. "I'll await your return."

Then she was off, giving orders like the old Morgaine. People started scurrying. Trey came up and asked, "You have to go now? We just got back! Give it a day. Or two. Rest up! You've just had a battle with the Dark Lords…for the Light's sake! You're beat up. What's so urgent?"

Nathan looked at his newest friend and said simply, "It's Gary. Morgaine thinks he might not have made it all the way through. I don't know what that means, or how I can find him. The medallion seems to be prodding me too. But if I do go, I can make sure in a New York minute whether he did or not. If he did, maybe I'll go and figure out my parentage while I'm home. But I shouldn't be long, either way. If he's not there…"

Nathan shrugged. I'll have to come back and figure out where he did go, I guess!" Suddenly, Nathan realized that *that* – right there – would be the third time he left.

Holy hell.

Treyborne was nodding. "Ok, I get it. Loyalty. I admire that. Gary came through to get you. You feel you have to go through to make sure he got back ok. Understood. I'll have you a freshly charged photon blaster, some emergency rations, and a fully charged shock-lance. Oh, and your shotgun is up in the sky cruiser still. Don't forget it! I might accidentally acquire it, in that event."

Nathan laughed and went off to take a shower, change his clothes, and gather his wits.

You'd better have made it, Gary! Shit! I hope you're already home, snuggling with Jennifer. Maybe tearing her clothes off this very second.

Running up to the sky cruiser, Trey turned and yelled, "Do you want one of the rings? I've got them charged up. I put it on charge with the blasters last night."

Nathan nodded and put his thumbs up. "It couldn't hurt, right?" Making his way to the upper levels where his quarters were, Nathan couldn't get the pit out of his stomach.

If he made it back, why is the medallion stressing urgency? What is so important?

CHAPTER 211

As Reena made her way up the road, following her little map, a strange man rode up behind her, hood covering his face. She moved aside to allow him to pass, but he just kept following her.

Feeling a little skittish, she looked back again. The man's face was completely obscured in shadow. And it was hot out today. The sun was shining and the shade that hood afforded could not be worth the stifling heat it would produce. Swallowing hard, she stopped.

The man's horse stopped, also.

"What do you want?" she asked in a quavering voice.

"I'm not here to harm you child…" came the quiet answer. Too quiet.

Real fear hit Shireen for the first time since she'd been a little girl. She was alone on this road. No one had been on it but her for over an hour. She looked around, desperate to see if anyone would even hear if she screamed. "I don't know who you are," she shrieked. "But leave me alone!" The being on the horse just sat there, not speaking. "I said leave me alone!" she screamed.

Then she heard a chuckle. It was like dry bones creaking together. It was horrific. *"I'm afraid I cannot do that,"* the voice said. *"I said I wouldn't harm you. I didn't say I didn't need you for something."*

CHAPTER 212

Ellie watched as the portal shut down. It was over two and half hours earlier than all her prediction models had said. Even the most conservative power loss model.

What happened?

Something had…sucked the power right out of it at the end there. She shook her head in confusion.

Well, Gary will have to come through with Nathan, I guess. Whenever or if ever he comes back.

General Davis was debriefing his team somewhere else in the building already. They'd come through not ten minutes ago. She knew nothing other than that they had come back, and that they were all safe. She didn't even know if they'd seen Nathan or Gary there.

Grimacing at her alleged "Top Secret" status, Ellie shut down her computer for the night. The monitoring system and gravitational meters would keep collecting data, of course. The new electrical pulse meters would, as well. Assuming there were any more to record. The video equipment was all on. There were even permanent guards in this room now.

Yea! I'm officially a federal slave. Just missing the shackles.

Packing up her things, she went to grab her coat and purse from the back of her chair. Grant had moved out the previous Thursday. She'd been so busy, she'd hardly noticed. She hadn't meant to be so distant, and there were a lot of things she simply hadn't been allowed to tell him.

It just wasn't meant to be. She'd kicked out the one man who had made her feel special. Largely over her own issues. She was very aware of that now. Seeing him with…*her*…it rankled a bit. But there was no one to blame but herself. She shrugged on her coat and adjusted the collar.

Best to be alone…

The monolith suddenly pulsed. She thought she heard something…it was like the faintest blip on the satellite radio she used on her computer when the signal failed. It had sounded like an eagle's cry.

Or a scream.

CHAPTER 213

Brianna sat and watched as the late-night preparations for Nathan's imminent departure were being completed. Trey had not even come over and hugged her yet. He had waved but had been running from job to job ever since he got back.

He'd said, "Hi," at least. Barely.

He's also sat with his men at dinner – which she understood. Brianna had been with Morgaine, as she had to be. But still…she watched as he directed men here and there to get things. Apparently, there was a lot more to this than just a quick trip home for Nathan.

Sitting on the ground off to the side, she had her arms wrapped around her knees. I guess I'm not in charge here anymore, either.

Well, if I'm not needed…

Getting up, she headed for the elevator. Trey could catch up with her tomorrow. If he wanted to. Brianna, despite being surrounded by so many people and activity, had never felt so alone. Even when she'd been home alone at the farm right after Sirles had died. Somehow, this felt worse. Holding her arms around herself, she stepped out of the elevator and headed to check in on Morgaine.

But no…she was still downstairs too, despite Maitan following her around like a hen telling her to rest. Which she should do. Morgaine looked like she had been whipped. But Brianna knew the woman wouldn't rest until Nathan was gone.

Probably not much after that, either.

Entering her chambers, she felt...*something*. It was cold in here! Going to the temperature controls, she saw a note on her table. Opening it, it said, "There's something wrong at the base. I can feel it. – Smyslin"

How did he get in here? And why did he leave me the note and not just tell me in person? What's going on?

Shivering, she grabbed the comm she'd just set down – just in case – and headed for her washroom. She needed to clean up and ignore the last few hours. She needed to sleep. But she thought her chances of sleeping were about as bad as Morgaine's right now.

Maybe worse.

EPILOGUE

Gary stepped through the portal, waving goodbye, and smiling. The next moment, he seemed to be floating…but it also felt like his feet were on something solid. This hadn't happened the last time. Had it?

It was the blackest place Gary had ever been in. so black that spots appeared to his eyes as they tried to adjust to nothingness.

He reached down but couldn't feel any floor. It was like he was in a room full of empty space, and he couldn't see a thing. He could stand, but not feel the ground that was obviously supporting his feet. Grabbing his phone to try to get some light, he hit the face of it repeatedly and tried to get a response. It was dead. How was that possible? He'd hardly used it for anything but a few pictures while he'd been there…

"Gary…."

What the hell? "Who is that?" he whirled around, trying to see anything.

"Gary…"

"Who the fuck are you? Where the fuck am I?" he yelled. His voice sounded odd. It didn't echo…it seemed rather to…dissipate.

"Gary…"

"Look, I'm not asking you again! I'm from New York, see? I'm not easily…"

"We're going to be good friends, Gary. You'll see. If you want to survive, you had better start listening to me."

END BOOK ONE